select
editions

Reader's
Digest

Reader's Digest

The condensations in this volume
are published with the consent of the authors
and the publishers © 2012 Reader's Digest, Inc.

www.readersdigest.co.uk

Published in the United Kingdom by Vivat Direct Limited
(t/a Reader's Digest), 157 Edgware Road,
London W2 2HR

Printed in Germany
ISBN 978 1 78020 105 4

**select
editions**

THE READER'S DIGEST ASSOCIATION, INC.

contents

before I go to sleep
s.j. watson

9

For eighteen years Christine has been living a nightmare—every morning when she wakes she has only fleeting memories of her past. How can she get her life back? Who can she trust? This intensely gripping, thriller slowly reveals the answers.

siege
simon kernick

163

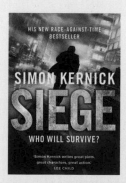

Panic reigns on the streets of London as bombs are detonated and terrorists hold guests and staff at the Stanhope Hotel hostage. As police try to negotiate, time is running out—for everyone. A first-class, action-packed thriller.

women and children first
gill paul
317

The sinking of the *Titanic* not only stole lives but also changed the futures of those lucky enough to survive. In this centenary year, Gill Paul's richly evocative tale follows four survivors as each learns to cope with the aftermath of that fateful night.

outwitting trolls
william g. tapply
453

When lawyer Brady Coyne learns that an old friend has been found dead in his hotel room, he offers his services to the widow who is accused of the murder. But as Coyne digs deeper into the case, he finds himself in grave danger.

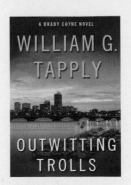

BEFORE
I GO TO
SLEEP

S.J.WATSON

Memories define us.

So what if you lost yours every time you went to sleep?

Your name, your identity, your past, even the people you love—all forgotten overnight.

And the one person you trust may be telling you only half the story.

Welcome to Christine's life.

PART ONE

Today

The bedroom is strange. Unfamiliar. I don't know where I am, how I came to be here. I don't know how I'm going to get home.

I have spent the night here. I was woken by a woman's voice, but realised she was reading the news and that I was hearing a radio alarm. When I opened my eyes I found myself here. In this room I don't recognise.

I look around. A dressing gown hangs off the back of the wardrobe door—suitable for a woman, but someone much older than I am—and some dark-coloured trousers are folded neatly over the back of a chair at the dressing table. I manage to silence the alarm clock.

Then I hear a juddering intake of breath behind me and realise I am not alone. I turn round. I see an expanse of skin and dark hair, flecked with white. A man. There is a gold ring on the third finger of the hand. I suppress a groan. I have screwed a married man in what I am guessing is his home, in the bed he must usually share with his wife. I ought to be ashamed.

I wonder where the wife is. I imagine her standing on the other side of the room, screaming, calling me a slut. I wonder how I will defend myself, if she does appear. The guy in the bed doesn't seem concerned, though. He has turned over and snores on.

Usually I can remember how I get into situations like this, but not today. There must have been a party, or a trip to a bar or a club. I must have been pretty wasted. Wasted enough that I don't remember anything at all.

I fold back the covers as gently as I can and sit on the edge of the bed. First, I need to use the bathroom. I creep barefoot onto the landing. I am aware of my nakedness, fearful of choosing the wrong door. Relieved, I see the bathroom door is ajar and go in, locking it behind me.

I use the toilet, then flush it and turn to wash my hands. I reach for the soap, but something is wrong. The hand gripping the soap does not look like mine. The skin is wrinkled, the nails are unpolished and bitten to the quick and, like the man in the bed, the third finger wears a wedding ring.

I look up at the mirror. The face I see is not my own. The hair is cut much shorter than I wear it, the skin under the chin sags, the lips are thin, the mouth turned down. I cry out, a wordless gasp, and then notice the eyes. The skin around them is lined, yes, but I can see that they are mine. The person in the mirror is me, but I am twenty years too old. More.

This isn't possible. I step away from the mirror and see photographs taped to the wall, to the mirror itself. Pictures interspersed with yellow pieces of gummed paper, felt-tip notes, damp and curling.

I choose one. *Christine*, it says, and an arrow points to a photograph of me—this new me—in which I am sitting on a bench next to a man. The name seems familiar, but only distantly so. In the photograph we are both smiling at the camera, holding hands. He is handsome and I can see that it is the man in the bed. *Ben* is written beneath it, *Your husband*.

No! I think. *It can't be . . .* I scan the rest of the pictures. They are all of me and him. In one I am wearing an ugly dress and unwrapping a present, in another both of us stand in front of a waterfall as a small dog sniffs at our feet. Next to it is a picture of me sitting beside him wearing the dressing gown I have seen in the bedroom next door.

It is then I get a glimmer that I associate with memory. As my mind tries to settle on it, it flutters away, like ashes caught in a breeze, and I realise that in my life there is a then, a before—though before what I cannot say—and there is a now, and there is nothing between the two but a long, silent emptiness that has led me here, to me and him, in this house.

I GO BACK into the bedroom. The man is sitting up in bed.

'What's going on?' I say, tears running down my face.

'I'm your husband.' His face is sleepy, without a trace of annoyance. He does not look at my naked body. 'We've been married for years.'

'What do you mean?' I say. I want to run, but there is nowhere to go.

He stands up. 'Here,' he says, and passes me the dressing gown. He is wearing pyjama trousers, a white vest. 'We got married in 1985,' he says. 'Twenty-two years ago.'

'What—?' I feel the blood drain from my face, the room begin to spin.

A clock ticks, somewhere in the house, and it sounds as loud as a hammer. 'But—' He takes a step towards me. 'How—?'

'Christine, you're forty-seven now,' he says. I look at him, this stranger who is smiling at me. I don't want to believe him, don't want even to hear what he's saying, but he carries on. 'You had a bad accident. You suffered head injuries. You have problems remembering things.'

'What things?' I say.

He approaches me as if I am a frightened animal. 'Everything,' he says.

My mind spins. 'When . . . when was my accident?'

His face is compassionate. 'When you were twenty-nine.'

I close my eyes. Even as my mind tries to reject this information I know, somewhere, that it is true. I hear myself start to cry and, as I do so, this man, this *Ben*, puts his arms around my waist and holds me. Together we rock gently, and I realise the motion feels familiar. It makes me feel better.

'I love you, Christine,' he says, and though I know I am supposed to say that I love him too, I say nothing. How can I love him? He is a stranger. Nothing makes sense. I want to know how I got here, how I manage to survive. But I don't know how to ask.

'I'm scared,' I say.

'I know,' he replies. 'But don't worry, Chris. I'll look after you. I'll always look after you. You'll be fine. Trust me.'

HE SAYS HE WILL show me around the house. I feel calmer. I have put on a pair of knickers, an old T-shirt, then put the robe over my shoulders. He opens the door next to the bathroom. 'This is the office.'

There is a glass desk with what I guess must be a computer, though it looks ridiculously small. Next to it is a filing cabinet, above it a wall planner. 'I work in there, now and then,' he says, closing the door. We cross the landing and he opens another door. A bed, a dressing table, more wardrobes. 'Sometimes you sleep in here,' he says, 'but usually you don't like waking up alone. You get panicked when you can't work out where you are.' I nod. I feel like a prospective tenant being shown around a new flat. 'Let's go downstairs.'

I follow him down. He shows me a living room, a dining room and kitchen. None of them is familiar. 'There's a garden out the back,' he says and I look through the glass door that leads off the kitchen. It is just beginning to get light, the night sky turning an inky blue. I can make out a shed sitting at the far end of the small garden, but little else. I realise I don't even know what part of the world we are in.

'Where are we?' I say.

'North London,' he replies. 'Crouch End.'

Panic begins to rise. 'Jesus, I don't even know where I bloody live.'

He takes my hand. 'Don't worry. You'll be fine.' I wait for him to tell me how I will be fine, but he does not. 'Coffee?'

For a moment I resent him, then say, 'Yes.' He fills a kettle. 'Black, please,' I say. 'No sugar.'

'I know,' he says, smiling at me. 'Want some toast?'

I say yes. He must know so much about me, yet still this feels like the morning after a one-night stand: breakfast with a stranger in his house, plotting how soon it would be acceptable to go back home.

But that's the difference. Apparently this *is* my home.

'I need to sit down,' I say.

'Go in the living room,' he says. 'I'll bring this through.'

I leave the kitchen.

A few moments later Ben follows me in. He gives me a book. 'This is a scrapbook,' he says. 'It might help.' I take it from him. It is bound in plastic and has a red ribbon tied around it in an untidy bow. 'I'll be back in a minute,' he says, and leaves the room.

I sit on the sofa for a while. The scrapbook weighs heavy in my lap. To look at it feels like snooping. I untie the bow and open it at random. A picture of me and Ben, looking much younger.

I slam it closed. I am certain there has been a terrible mistake, yet the evidence is there—in the mirror upstairs, in the creases on the hands that caress the book in front of me. I am not the person I thought I was when I woke this morning. But who was that? I feel as though I am floating. Untethered. I need to anchor myself. I close my eyes and try to focus on something solid. I find nothing. So many years of my life missing.

This book will tell me who I am, but I don't want to open it. Not yet. I want to sit here for a while, balanced between possibility and fact. I am frightened to discover my past.

Ben comes back in and sets a tray in front of me. Toast, coffee, a jug of milk. 'You OK?' he says. I nod.

He sits down beside me. He has shaved, and is dressed in trousers and a shirt and tie. He looks as though he might work in a bank, or in an office. Not bad, though, I think, then push the thought from my mind.

'Is every day like this?' I say.

'Pretty much,' he says. 'You seem to be able to retain information while you're awake but when you sleep, most of it goes.'

He takes the book and opens it. 'We had a fire a few years ago so we lost a lot of photos and things, but there are still a few bits and pieces in here.' He points to the first page. 'This is your degree certificate. And here's a photo of you on your graduation day.' I look at where he points; I am smiling, squinting into the sun, wearing a black gown. Just behind me stands a man in a suit, his head turned away.

'That's you?' I say.

He smiles. 'No. I was still studying then. Chemistry.'

I look up at him. 'When did we get married?' I say.

He turns to face me, taking my hand between his. 'The year after you got your Ph.D. We'd been dating for a few years but you—we—both wanted to wait until your studies were out of the way.'

That makes sense, I think, though it feels oddly practical of me. I wonder if I had been keen to marry him at all.

As if reading my mind he says, 'We were very much in love,' and then adds, 'we still are.'

I can think of nothing to say. He turns over some more pages.

'You studied English,' he says. 'You had a few jobs once you'd graduated. Just odd things. I'm not sure you knew what you wanted to do. I left with a B.Sc. and did teacher training. It was a struggle for a few years, but then I was promoted and, well, we ended up here.'

I look around the living room. It is blandly middle class. A framed picture of a woodland scene hangs above the fireplace, china figurines sit next to the clock on the mantelpiece. I wonder if I helped to choose the decor.

Ben goes on. 'I teach in a secondary school nearby. I'm head of department now.' He says it with no hint of pride.

'And me?' I say, though really I know the only possible answer.

'You had to give up work after your accident. You don't do anything. You don't need to. I earn enough. We get by.'

This all feels too much. There is only so much I can process.

He takes the tray out. When he comes back he is wearing an overcoat.

'I have to leave for work,' he says. I feel myself tense. 'Don't worry,' he says. 'You'll be fine. I'll ring you, I promise.'

In the kitchen he shows me which things are in which cupboard, points out a wipe-clean board screwed to the wall, next to a black marker pen tied to a piece of string. 'I sometimes leave messages here for you,' he says.

I see that he has written the word FRIDAY on it in neat capitals, and beneath it the words *Laundry? Walk? (Take phone!)* Finally he has written that he should be home by six. 'You also have a diary in your bag. It has important phone numbers in the back of it, and our address, in case you get lost. And there's a mobile phone—'

'A what?' I say.

'A cordless phone. You can use it anywhere. It'll be in your handbag. Take it with you if you go out.'

'I will,' I say.

'Right,' he says. We go into the hall and he picks up a battered leather satchel by the door. 'I'll be off, then.'

He kisses me on the cheek. I don't stop him, but neither do I kiss him back. He is about to open the front door when he stops.

'Oh, I almost forgot!' His voice sounds forced. It is obvious he has been building up to what he is about to say for some time. 'We're going away this evening for the weekend. It's our anniversary. Is that OK?'

It is not as bad as I feared. I nod. 'That sounds nice,' I say.

He looks relieved. 'A bit of sea air will do us good.' He opens the door. 'I'll call you later, see how you're getting on.'

'Yes,' I say. 'Do. Please.'

'I love you, Christine,' he says. 'Never forget that.'

He closes the door behind him.

LATER, MIDMORNING. The dishes are done and the laundry is in the machine. I have been keeping myself busy.

But now I feel empty. It's true, what Ben said. I have no memory. There is not a thing in this house that I remember seeing before. Not a single photograph, not a moment with Ben that I can recall, other than those since we met this morning. I try to focus on something. Anything. Yesterday. Last Christmas. Any Christmas. My wedding. There is nothing.

I move through the house, drifting like a wraith. I look at the carpets, the patterned rugs, the ornamental plates arranged on the display racks in the dining room. I try to tell myself that this is mine. My home, my husband, my life. But these things are not part of me. In the bedroom I open the wardrobe door and see a row of clothes I don't recognise. This morning I had selected my underwear guiltily, searching through pairs of knickers as if I was afraid of being caught. I chose a pale blue pair that had a matching bra and slipped them both on, before pulling a heavy pair of tights over the top, and then trousers and a blouse.

I had sat down at the dressing table to examine my face in the mirror, approaching my reflection cautiously. I traced the lines on my forehead, the folds of skin under my eyes. I noticed the blotches on my skin, a discoloration on my forehead that looked like a bruise that had not quite faded. I found some make-up, and put a little on. I pictured a woman—my mother, I realise now—doing the same, calling it her *war paint*, and this morning the word felt appropriate. I felt that I was going into some kind of battle, or that some battle was coming to me.

I tried to think of my mother doing something else. Anything. Nothing came. I saw only a void, between tiny islands of memory.

Now, in the kitchen, I open cupboards: packets of a rice labelled arborio, tins of kidney beans. I don't recognise this food. I remember eating cheese on toast, boil-in-the-bag fish, corned-beef sandwiches. I pull out a tin labelled 'chickpeas', a sachet of something called couscous. I don't know how to cook them. How then do I survive, as a wife?

I look up at the board that Ben had shown me. Words have been scrawled on it and wiped out, each leaving a faint residue. I wonder what I would find if I could go back and decipher the layers, if it were possible to delve into my past that way, but realise that it would be futile. All I would find are messages and lists, groceries to buy, tasks to perform.

Is that really my life? I think. I take the pen and add to the board: *Pack bag for tonight.* Not much of a reminder, but my own.

I hear a noise coming from my bag, in the living room. I go through and open it, emptying its contents onto the sofa. My purse, some tissues, pens, a lipstick. A diary a couple of inches square with a floral design on the front.

I find something that I guess must be the phone that Ben described. It is ringing, the screen flashing. I press what I hope is the right button.

'Hello?' I say.

The voice that replies is not Ben's. 'Is that Christine Lucas?' it says.

I don't want to answer. My surname seems as strange as my first name had. I feel as though solid ground has vanished, replaced by quicksand.

'Christine? It's me. Dr Nash. Please answer.'

The name means nothing to me, but still I say, 'Who is this?'

The voice takes on a new tone. Relief? 'Your doctor,' he says.

'My doctor?'

'Don't worry. Nothing's wrong. We've just been doing some work on your memory.'

'What kind of work?' I say.

'I've been trying to work out exactly what's caused your memory problems, and if there's anything we can do about them. We're making progress.'

Why had Ben not mentioned this doctor before he left this morning?

'How?' I say. 'What have we been doing?'

'We've been meeting a couple of times a week.'

But I've never met you before, I want to say. You could be anyone.

The same could be said of the man I woke up with this morning, and he turned out to be my husband.

'I don't remember,' I say instead.

His voice softens. 'Don't worry. I know.' He explains that our next appointment is today.

'But my husband hasn't mentioned anything to me.' It is the first time I have referred to the man I woke up with in this way.

Dr Nash says, 'I'm not sure Ben knows you're meeting me.'

I notice that he knows my husband's name. 'That's ridiculous! How can he not? He would have told me!'

There is a sigh. 'I can explain everything, when we meet.'

When we meet. How can we do that? The thought of going out, without Ben, without him even knowing where I am or who I am with, terrifies me.

'I'm sorry,' I say. 'I can't.'

'Christine, it's important. If you look in your diary you'll see what I'm saying is true. It should be in your bag.'

I pick up the floral book from the sofa and register the year. It's 2007. Twenty years later than it should be.

'Look at today's date,' he says. 'November the 30th.'

I skim through the leaves to today's date. Tucked between the pages is a piece of paper and, printed in handwriting I don't recognise, are the words *November 30th—seeing Dr Nash*. Beneath them are the words *Don't tell Ben*. I wonder if Ben has read them, whether he looks through my things.

Dr Nash explains that he will pick me up in an hour.

'But my husband—' I say.

'It's OK. We'll be back long before he gets in from work. Trust me.'

The clock on the mantelpiece chimes. It looks old enough to be an antique, and I wonder how we came to own such a clock.

I'll see him just this once, I think. And tonight I will tell Ben. I can't believe I'm keeping something like this from him. Not when I rely so utterly on him.

But there is an odd familiarity to Dr Nash's voice. Unlike Ben, he does not seem entirely alien to me. *We're making progress*, he'd said. I need to know what kind of progress he means.

'OK,' I say. 'Come.'

WHEN HE ARRIVES Dr Nash suggests we go for a cup of coffee. 'There's a park at the end of the street,' he says. 'It has a café.'

I nod and say yes. I was in the bedroom when he arrived and watched him park his car, saw him rearrange his hair, smooth his jacket, pick up his briefcase. He looked young—too young to be a doctor—and, though I don't know what I had been expecting him to be wearing, it was not the sports jacket and grey corduroy trousers that he has on.

The cold is biting and I pull my scarf tight around my neck. I am glad I have in my bag the mobile phone that Ben has given me. Glad, too, that Dr Nash has not insisted we drive somewhere. Some part of me trusts this man, but another, larger part, tells me he could be anyone. It would be easy for this man to take me somewhere, though I don't know what he would want to do. I am as vulnerable as a child.

We reach the main road and wait to cross. The silence between us feels oppressive. I find myself speaking. 'What sort of doctor are you?'

'I'm a neuropsychologist.' He is smiling. I wonder if I ask him the same question every time we meet. 'I specialise in patients with brain disorders. I've been particularly interested in researching memory process and function. I heard about you through the literature on the subject, and tracked you down. It wasn't too difficult.'

'The literature?'

'A couple of case studies have been written about you. I got in touch with the place where you were being treated before you came to live at home. I thought I could help you. I had a few ideas about how real improvements could be effected and wanted to try some of them out.' He pauses. 'Plus I've been writing a paper on your case. It's unusual. I believe we can discover a lot more about the way memory works than we already know.'

We cross the road. I feel myself get anxious. *Brain disorders. Researching. Tracked you down.* I try to relax but find I cannot. There are two of me now in the same body: one is a forty-seven-year-old woman, calm, polite, aware of what behaviour is appropriate—and the other is in her twenties, and screaming. I can't decide which is me, but the only noise I hear is that of children from the park and so I guess it must be the first.

On the other side of the road, I stop. 'Look, what's going on? I woke up this morning in a place I've never seen but that's apparently my home, lying next to a man I've never met who tells me I've been married to him for years. And you seem to know more about me than I know about myself.'

'You have amnesia,' he says, putting his hand on my arm. 'You can't retain new memories, so you've forgotten much of what's happened to you for your entire adult life. Every day you wake up as if you are a young woman. Some days you wake as if you are a child.'

Somehow it seems worse, coming from him. A doctor. 'So it's true?'

'I'm afraid so. The man at home is your husband, Ben. You've been married to him for years. Since long before your amnesia began.'

We walk into the park. There is a children's playground next to a hut from which I see people emerge carrying trays. We head there and I take a seat at a table while Dr Nash goes to order. When he returns he is carrying two plastic cups of coffee, mine black, his white. He adds sugar but offers none to me, and that, more than anything, convinces me that we have met before.

He asks how I hurt my forehead.

I remember the bruise I saw this morning. My make-up has clearly not covered it. 'I'm not sure,' I say. 'It's nothing, really. It doesn't hurt.'

He doesn't answer. He stirs his coffee.

'So my husband looks after me at home?' I say.

'Yes, though at first your condition was so severe you required round-the-clock care. It's only recently that Ben felt he could look after you alone.'

So the way I feel at the moment is an improvement, then. I am glad I can't remember the time when things were worse.

'He must love me very much,' I say, more to myself than to Nash.

He nods. 'Yes. I think he must.'

I look down at my hands holding the drink, at the wedding ring, at the short nails. I don't recognise my own body.

'Why doesn't my husband know that I'm seeing you?' I say.

He leans forward in his seat. 'I'll be honest, I asked you not to tell Ben that you were seeing me.'

A jolt of fear goes through me, yet I want to believe he can help me. 'Go on,' I say.

'He has made it very clear that you have had extensive treatment before, and in his opinion it has achieved nothing other than to upset you. Naturally he wanted to spare you—and himself—from any more upset.'

Of course; he doesn't want to raise my hopes. 'So you persuaded me to come and see you without him knowing?'

'I approached Ben first on the phone. I asked him to meet me so I could explain what I had to offer, but he refused. So I contacted you directly.'

Another jolt of fear, as if from nowhere. 'How?' I say.

'I waited until you came out of the house and then introduced myself.'

'And I agreed to see you? Just like that?'

'Not at first. I had to persuade you that you could trust me. I suggested that we should meet just for one session.'

'And I agreed . . .'

'Yes. I told you that after that it was up to you whether you chose to tell Ben or not, but if you decided not to I would ring you to make sure you remembered our appointments.'

'And I chose not to.'

'That's right. You've spoken about wanting to wait until we were making progress before telling him. You felt that was better.'

'And are we making progress?'

'I believe so, though progress is somewhat difficult to quantify exactly. But lots of memories seem to have come back to you over the past few weeks—many of them for the first time, as far as we know. And there are certain truths that you are aware of more often, where there were few before. For example, you occasionally wake up and remember that you're married. And you're gaining independence, I think.'

'Independence?'

'Yes. You don't rely on Ben as much as you did. Or me.'

So that is the progress he is talking about. Independence. Perhaps he means I can make it to the shops without a chaperone. But I have not yet made enough progress for me to wave it proudly in front of my husband. Not even enough for me always to wake up remembering I have one.

'That's it?'

'It's important,' he says. 'Don't underestimate it, Christine.'

I don't say anything. I look around the café. There are voices from a small kitchen at the back, the occasional rattle as the water in an urn reaches boiling point. It is difficult to believe that this place is so close to my home and yet I have no memory of ever being here before.

'I don't understand,' I say. 'I have no memory of yesterday, or the day before, or last year. Yet I can remember my childhood. My mother. I remember being at university, just. I don't understand how these old memories could have survived.'

He nods. I don't doubt he has heard it before. Possibly we have the same conversation every week.

'Memory is a complex thing,' he says. 'Human beings have a short-term memory that can store information for about a minute or so, but also a long-term memory. Here we can store huge quantities of information for a seemingly indefinite length of time. We now know that these two functions seem to be controlled by different parts of the brain, with some neural connections between them. There is also a part of the brain that seems to be responsible for taking short-term, transient memories and coding them as long-term memories for recall much later.'

He speaks easily, as if he is now in well-known territory.

'There are two main types of amnesia. Most commonly the affected person cannot recall past events, with recent events being most severely affected. If, for example, the sufferer has a motor accident, they may not remember the accident, or the days or weeks preceding it, but can remember everything up to, say, six months before the accident perfectly well.'

I nod. 'And the other?'

'The other is rarer. Sometimes there is an inability to transfer memories from short-term to long-term storage. People live in the moment, able only to recall the immediate past, and then only for a small amount of time.'

He stops talking, as if waiting for me to say something. It is as if we each have our lines, have rehearsed this conversation often.

'I have both?' I say. 'A loss of the memories I had, plus an inability to form new ones?'

'Yes, unfortunately. It's not common, but perfectly possible. What's unusual in your case, however, is the pattern. You seem to process new memories in a way I have never come across before. If I left this room and returned in two minutes most people with anterograde amnesia would not remember having met me at all. But you seem to remember whole chunks of time—up to twenty-four hours—which you then lose. That's not typical. To be honest, it doesn't make any sense. It suggests you are able to transfer things from short-term to long-term storage perfectly well. I don't understand why you can't retain them.'

'Why?' I say. 'What caused it?'

The room has gone quiet. When he speaks, his words seem to echo off the walls. 'Many things can cause an impairment of memory. Disease, trauma, drug use. The exact nature of the impairment seems to differ, depending on the part of the brain that has been affected.'

'Yes,' I say. 'But what has caused mine?'

He looks at me for a moment. 'What has Ben told you?'

I think back. 'He just said I'd had an accident.'

'Yes,' he says, reaching for his bag. 'Your amnesia was caused by trauma. That's true, at least partly.' He takes out a book and passes it across the table to me. 'I want you to have this. It will explain everything better than I can. About what has caused your condition, but other things as well.'

It is brown, bound in leather, its pages held closed by an elastic band. I take that off and open it at random. The paper is heavy and faintly lined, with a red margin, and the pages filled with dense handwriting.

'It's a journal you've been keeping over the past few weeks.'

I am shocked. 'A journal?' I wonder why he has it.

'I asked you to keep it. I thought it might be helpful for you to have a record of what we've been doing.'

I look at the book in front of me. 'So I've written this?'

'Yes. I told you to write whatever you like in it. Many amnesiacs have tried similar things, but usually it's not helpful as they have such a small window of memory. But as there are things that you can remember for the whole day, I thought you should jot down some notes every evening; it might help you to maintain a thread of memory from one day to the next. Memory might be like a muscle that can be strengthened through exercise.'

'And you've been reading it as we've been going along?'

'No,' he says. 'You've been writing it in private.'

'But how—?' I begin. Then say, 'Ben's been reminding me to write in it?'

'I suggested you keep it secret. You've been hiding it at home. I've been calling you to tell you where it's hidden.'

'Every day?'

'Yes. More or less.'

'Not Ben?'

He pauses, then says, 'No. Ben hasn't read it.'

I wonder what it might contain that I do not want my husband to see. 'But you've read it?'

'You said you wanted me to read it. That it was time.'

I look at the book. I am excited. A journal. A link to a lost past.

'Have you read it all?'

'Yes,' he says. 'Everything important, anyway.' He looks away from me. Embarrassed, I think. I wonder if he is telling me the truth. 'I didn't force you to let me see it. I want you to know that.'

I nod, flicking through the pages of the book. On the inside of the front cover is a list of dates. 'What are these?'

'They're the dates we've been meeting, as well as the ones we had planned. I've been calling to remind you to look in your journal.'

I think of the note tucked between the pages of my diary. 'But today?'

'Today I had your journal,' he says. 'So we wrote a note instead.'

The book is filled with a dense handwriting that I don't recognise. Days and days of work. I wonder how I found the time, but the answer is obvious; I have had nothing else to do.

WE WALK BACK the way we had come. The ground feels soggy underfoot.

'We don't normally meet here?' I say. 'In the café, I mean?'

'We normally meet in my office. We do tests and things.'

'So why here today?'

'To give you your book back,' he says. 'I was worried you didn't have it.'

'I've come to rely on it?' I say.

'In a way, yes.'

We walk back to the house I share with Ben. I still can't quite believe this is where I live.

'Do you want to come in?' I say.

He shakes his head. 'No, thanks. Julie and I have plans this evening.'

I notice his hair, cut short, neatly parted. I realise that he is only a few years older than I thought I was when I woke this morning. 'Julie is your wife?'

He smiles. 'My girlfriend. Actually, my fiancée. I keep forgetting.'

I smile back. Perhaps it is these trivialities I have been writing in my book, these small hooks on which a whole life is hung. I feel I ought to show more interest, but there is little point. Anything he tells me now I will have forgotten by the time I wake tomorrow. Today is all I have. 'We're going away this weekend,' I say. 'To the coast. I need to pack.'

He smiles, turns to leave, then looks back. 'Your journal has my numbers at the front. Call me if you'd like to carry on with your treatment. OK?'

'If?' I say. 'I thought we had more sessions booked?'

'You'll understand when you read your book,' he says. 'It will all make sense. I promise.'

'OK.' I realise I trust him, and I am glad. Glad that I don't have only my husband to rely on.

I MAKE A CUP of coffee and carry it into the living room. I take the journal out of my bag. I feel nervous. I do not know what this book will contain. What shocks and surprises. What mysteries. I see the scrapbook on the coffee table. In that book is a version of my past, but one chosen by Ben. Does the book I hold contain another? I open it.

I have written my name on the first page in black ink. *Christine Lucas*. Something has been added. Something unexpected, terrifying. More terrifying than anything else I have seen today. There, beneath my name, in blue ink and capital letters, are three words.

DON'T TRUST BEN.

There is nothing I can do but turn the page. I begin to read my history.

PART TWO

The Journal of Christine Lucas

Friday, November 9

My name is Christine Lucas. I am forty-seven. An amnesiac. I am sitting in an unfamiliar bed, writing my story dressed in a silk nightie that the man downstairs—who tells me he is my husband, Ben—apparently bought me for my forty-sixth birthday. I am writing this in secret. If my husband comes upstairs, I will put this book under the bed, or the pillow. I don't want him to see it. I don't want to have to tell him how I got it.

It is almost eleven; I imagine that soon I will hear the TV silenced, a creak of a floorboard as Ben crosses the room. Will he go into the kitchen and pour himself a glass of water? Or will he come straight to bed? I don't know his rituals. I don't know my own.

According to Ben, according to the doctor I met this afternoon, tonight, as I sleep, my mind will erase everything I know today. I will wake up tomorrow as I did this morning. Thinking I am still a child. Thinking I still have a whole lifetime of choice ahead of me. And then I will find out, again, that my choices have already been made. Half my life is behind me.

The doctor was called Nash. He called me this morning, collected me in his car, drove me to an office. I told him I had never met him before; he smiled and played me a video clip on his computer. It was of me and him, in different clothes but sitting in the same chairs, in the same office. In the film he asked me to draw shapes on a piece of paper, but by looking only in a mirror so that everything appeared backwards. When I had finished he seemed pleased. 'You're getting faster,' he said on the video, then added that somewhere, deep down, I must be remembering the effects of my weeks of practice even if I did not remember the practice itself. 'That means your long-term memory must be working on some level,' he said. The film ended.

Dr Nash said we have been meeting for the past few weeks, that I have a severe impairment of my episodic memory due to some kind of neurological problem. Structural or chemical, he said. Or a hormonal imbalance. It is very rare, and I seem to be affected particularly badly. He told me that some days I can't remember much beyond my early childhood.

'Some days?' I said. His silence told me he really meant *most days*.

There are treatments, he said—drugs, hypnosis—but most have already been tried. 'But your symptoms do not suggest that your memories are lost for ever, Christine. You can recall things for hours. Right up until you go to sleep. You can even doze and remember when you wake up, as long as you haven't been in a deep sleep. Most amnesiacs lose their new memories every few seconds.'

He slid a brown notebook across the desk. 'I think it might be worth you documenting your feelings or memories that come to you.'

I reached forward and took the book. Its pages were blank.

So this is my treatment? I thought. Keeping a journal? I want to remember things, not just record them.

He must have sensed my disappointment. 'I'm also hoping the act of writing your memories might trigger some more.'

What choice did I have? Keep a journal or stay as I am, for ever.

'OK,' I said. 'I'll do it.'

'Good,' he said. 'I've written my numbers in the front.'

I took the book and there was a long pause. He said, 'We've been doing some good work recently around your early childhood. We've been looking at pictures.' He took a photograph out of the file in front of him. 'Do you recognise it?'

The photograph was of a house. At first it seemed totally unfamiliar, then I suddenly knew it was the house in which I had grown up, the one that, this morning, I had thought I was waking up in. 'It's where I lived as a child.'

I told him that the front door opened directly into the living room, that there was a small dining room at the back.

'More?' he said.

'Two bedrooms,' I said. 'One at the front, one at the back. The bath and toilet were through the kitchen. They'd been in a separate building until it was joined to the rest of the house.'

He asked if I remembered any small details.

It came to me then. 'My mother kept a jar in the pantry with the word "Sugar" written on it. She used to keep money in there. She'd hide it on the top shelf with the jams she made. We would pick blackberries and my mother would boil them to make jam.'

He showed me a couple more pictures. One of a woman whom I recognised as my mother. One of me. I told him what I could. When I finished he smiled. 'That's good. You've remembered a lot more than usual.'

I wondered where he had got these photos, how much he knew of my life that I didn't know myself.

'Can I keep it?' I said. 'That picture of my old home?'

He passed it over and I slipped it between the pages of the notebook.

He drove me back. He'd already explained that Ben does not know we are meeting, but now he told me I ought to think about whether I wanted to tell him about the journal. 'You might feel reluctant to write about certain things. Plus Ben might not be happy to find that you've decided to attempt treatment again.' He paused. 'You might have to hide it.'

'But how will I know to write in it?' I said. 'Will you remind me?'

He told me he would. 'But you'll have to tell me where you're going to hide it.'

'I'll put it in the back of the wardrobe.' I thought back to what I'd seen this morning. 'I'll put it in a shoebox.'

'Good idea. You'll have to write in it before you go to sleep. Otherwise tomorrow it'll be just a blank notebook. You won't know what it is.'

I said that I understood.

Now I sit in bed. Waiting for my husband. I look at the photo of the home in which I grew up. It looks so mundane. And so familiar.

How did I get from there to here? I think. *What happened?*

I hear the clock in the living room chime. Midnight. Ben is coming up the stairs. I will hide this book in the shoebox where I have told Dr Nash it will be. Tomorrow, if he rings, I will write more.

Saturday, November 10

I am writing this at noon. Ben is downstairs, reading. He thinks I am resting but I am not. I have to write this down before I lose it. Ben has suggested we go for a walk this afternoon. I have a little over an hour.

This morning I woke not knowing who I am. I expected to hear my mother downstairs cooking, or my father in the garden, whistling as he trims the hedge. I expected the bed I was in to be single, to contain nothing except me and a stuffed rabbit.

I was wrong. I am in my parents' room, I thought at first, then realised I recognised nothing. The bedroom was completely foreign. I lay back in bed. Something is *wrong*, I thought. Terribly, terribly wrong.

By the time I went downstairs I had seen the photographs around the mirror, read their labels. I knew I was not a child and had worked out that the man I could hear cooking breakfast and whistling was not my father but my husband, Ben. I hesitated outside the kitchen, about to meet him, as if for the first time. What would he be like?

A vision came from nowhere. A woman—my mother?—telling me to be careful. *Marry in haste . . .*

I pushed the door open. Ben had his back to me. He turned round quickly. 'Christine? Are you OK?'

I did not know how to answer, and so I said, 'Yes. I think so.'

He smiled, a look of relief. He looked older than in the pictures upstairs but this had the effect of making him more, rather than less, attractive. I realised he resembled a slightly older version of my father. I could have done much worse, I thought.

'You've seen the pictures?' he said. I nodded. 'Why don't you go and sit down?' He gestured towards the hallway. 'The dining room's through there. I won't be a moment.'

A few minutes later he followed me with two plates. As I ate he explained how I survive my life.

Today is Saturday, he said. He works during the week; he is a teacher. He explained about the phone in my bag, the board in the kitchen. He showed me where we keep our emergency fund—behind the clock on the mantelpiece—and the scrapbook in which I can glimpse snatches of my life.

I helped him tidy away the breakfast things. 'We should go for a stroll later,' he said, 'if you like?' I said that I would. 'I'm just going to read the paper. OK?'

I came upstairs. Once I was alone, my head spun, full and empty at the same time. I felt unable to grasp anything. Nothing seemed real.

I sat on the edge of the bed in which I had slept. I should make it, I thought. I picked up the pillow and, as I did, something began to buzz. My bag was at my feet and the buzz seemed to come from there.

I stared at the phone for a long moment. Some part of me knew exactly what the call was about. I answered it.

'Hello?' A man's voice. 'Christine, are you there?'

I told him I was.

'It's your doctor. Are you OK? Is Ben around?'

'No,' I said. 'What's this about?'

He told me his name and that we have been working together for a few weeks. 'I want you to look in the wardrobe in your bedroom,' he said. 'There's a shoebox in there. I saw you yesterday. We decided you should keep a journal. That's where you told me you'd hide it.'

I went to the wardrobe. He was right. Inside was a shoebox and inside that was a book wrapped in tissue. I lifted it out. 'I have it.'

'Good. Have you written in it?'

I opened it to the first page. I saw that I had. *My name is Christine Lucas*, it began. I felt nervous, excited. It felt like snooping, but on myself.

'I have,' I said.

'Excellent!' He said he would phone me tomorrow and we ended the call.
I didn't move. There, crouching on the floor by the open wardrobe, the
bed still unmade, I began to read.

At first, I felt disappointed. I remembered nothing of what I had written.
Not Dr Nash, nor the offices I claim that he took me to, the puzzles I say
that we did. Despite having just heard his voice I couldn't picture him, or
myself with him. The book read like fiction. But then, tucked near the back
of the book, I found a photograph. The house in which I had grown up. It
was real; this was my evidence.

Yesterday I had described my old home, the sugar jar in the pantry, picking berries. Were those memories still there? Could I conjure more? Images
formed, silently. A dull orange carpet, an olive-green vase. A yellow romper
suit with a pink duck sewn on to the breast and press-studs up the middle. A
plastic car seat in navy blue and a faded pink potty.

Colours and shapes, but nothing that described a life. I want to see my
parents, I thought. Then I realised that I knew they are dead.

I sat on the edge of the bed. A pen was tucked between the pages of the
journal and I held it over the page and closed my eyes to concentrate.

It was then that it happened. Whether that realisation—that my parents are
gone—triggered the memory, I don't know, but I saw myself coming home.
I am thirteen or fourteen, eager to get on with a story I am writing, but I find a
note on the kitchen table. *We've had to go out*, it says. I get a sandwich and sit
down with my notebook. Mrs Royce has said that my stories are *strong* and
moving but I can't think what to write.

The image vanished, but straightaway there was another. My father is driving us home. I am sitting in the back of the car, staring at a fixed spot on
the windscreen. I speak. 'When were you going to tell me?'

Nobody answers.

'Dad? When were you going to tell me? Will you die?'

He glances over his shoulder and smiles at me. 'Of course not, angel. Not
until I'm an old, old man. With lots and lots of grandchildren!'

I know he's lying.

'We're going to fight this,' he says. 'I promise.'

I opened my eyes. The vision was gone. My heart raced in my chest. I had
remembered something. Something important. I started writing this.

When I try to will the image back, I can. It is still there. Even so, I am glad I have written it down. At least now it is not completely lost.

Ben has called upstairs, asked if I am ready to go out. I told him I was. I will write more later. If I remember.

That was written hours ago. We have been out all afternoon.

We parked the car by a low, squat building. 'The lido,' said Ben and we walked towards the top of the hill. There I could see life: a little boy flew a kite, a girl walked a small dog on a long lead. I thought of my father, of his death and the fact that I had remembered a little of it.

'This is Parliament Hill,' said Ben. 'We come here often.'

The city sprawled before us. I could see the thrust of the Telecom Tower, St Paul's dome, the power station at Battersea, shapes I recognised, though dimly. There were less familiar landmarks, too: a glass building shaped like a fat cigar, a giant wheel. The view seemed both alien and familiar.

'I feel I recognise this place,' I said.

'Yes,' said Ben. 'We've been coming here for a while, though the view changes all the time.' We sat down on a bench and he pointed out some of the landmarks. 'That's Canary Wharf,' he said, gesturing towards a building that looked immeasurably tall. 'It was built in the early nineties, I think.'

The nineties. It was odd to hear a decade that I could not remember summed up in two words. I must have missed so much. Disasters, tragedies, wars. Whole countries might have fallen to pieces as I wandered, oblivious, from one day to the next.

'Ben?' I said. 'Tell me about us. I don't even know how we met, or when we got married.'

He put his arm around my shoulder. I began to recoil, then remembered he is the man I married.

'We were both at university,' he said. 'You had just started your Ph.D.'

'What did I study?'

'You'd graduated in English,' he said, and I recalled vague ideas of a thesis concerning feminist theory and early twentieth-century literature, though really it was just something I could be doing while I worked on novels, something my mother might not understand but would at least see as legitimate.

'I would see you all the time,' he said. 'At the library, in the bar, whatever. I would be amazed at how beautiful you looked, but I could never bring myself to speak to you.'

I laughed. 'Really?' I couldn't imagine myself as intimidating.

'You always seemed so intense. You would sit for hours, surrounded by books. I never dreamed you would be interested in me. But then one day you accidentally knocked your cup over and your coffee went all over my books. You were so apologetic, we went for a coffee. And that was that.'

I tried to remember the two of us, young, in a library, surrounded by soggy papers, laughing. I could not, and felt the hot stab of sadness.

'What happened then?' I said.

'Well, we dated. The usual, you know? I finished my degree, and you finished your Ph.D., and then we got married.'

'Where? Tell me how it happened.'

'We were totally in love,' he said. He looked away, into the distance. 'You shared a house, but you were hardly there at all. It made sense for us to live together. One Valentine's Day, I bought you a bar of expensive soap, the kind you liked, and I took off the wrapper and pressed an engagement ring into the soap, and then I wrapped it back up and gave it to you. That evening you found it, and you said yes.'

I smiled to myself. It sounded messy, a ring caked in soap, but it was not an unromantic story.

'Who did I share a house with?' I said.

'A friend,' he said. 'I don't really remember. We got married in a church in Manchester, near where your mother lived. The sun shone, everyone was happy. And then we went to Italy for our honeymoon. It was wonderful.'

I tried to picture the church, my dress, the view from a hotel room. Nothing would come.

'There aren't any photos of our wedding in the scrapbook.'

'We had a fire,' he said. 'We lost a lot of things.'

I sighed. It didn't seem fair, to have lost both my memories and my souvenirs of the past.

'What happened after the marriage, the honeymoon?'

'We moved in together. We were very happy.'

That can't be it, I thought. A wedding, a honeymoon, a marriage. But what else was I expecting? The answer came suddenly. Children. I realised that that was what seemed to be missing from our home. There were no pictures of a son or daughter and none of grandchildren either. I had not had a baby.

'We never had children,' I said. It was not a question.

'No,' he said. 'No. We didn't.'

Sadness etched his face. For himself, or me? I could not tell. I let him hold my fingers between his. I realised that, despite the confusion, I felt safe with this man.

'How did it happen, Ben?' I said. 'How did I get to be like this?'

I felt him tense. 'You're sure you want to know?' he said.

I knew this couldn't be the first time I have asked him. Possibly I ask him every day. This time I will write down what he tells me.

He took a deep breath. 'It was December. Icy. You were on your way home, a short walk. We don't know if you were crossing the road or if the car that hit you mounted the pavement, but you were badly injured. Both legs were broken. An arm and your collarbone. There were no witnesses.' Ben squeezed my hand. 'They said your head must have hit the ground first, which is why you lost your memory.'

I could remember nothing of the accident, and so did not feel angry, or even upset. I was filled instead with a kind of quiet regret.

'What happened to the driver?'

'He didn't stop. It was a hit-and-run. We don't know who hit you.'

I didn't know what I had expected. I thought of what I had read of my meeting with Dr Nash. *A neurological problem*, he had told me. *Structural or chemical. A hormonal imbalance*. I assumed he had meant an illness. But this seemed worse: it was done to me by someone else; it had been avoidable.

'Where was I?' I said. 'What had I been doing?'

'You were on your way home from work,' he said. 'You had a temporary job as a secretary—well, personal assistant really—at some lawyers.'

'But why—' I began.

'You needed to work so that we could pay the mortgage,' he said.

That wasn't what I meant, though. What I wanted to say was, You told me I had a Ph.D. Why had I settled for that?

'But why was I working as a secretary?' I said.

'It was the only job you could get. Times were hard.'

I remembered the feeling I had earlier. 'Was I writing? Books?'

He shook his head. 'No.'

So it was a transitory ambition, then. Or maybe I had tried and failed. A moment later, there was a loud bang. I looked out—sparks in the distant sky.

'A firework,' said Ben. 'It looks like there'll be a display.'

The sky was dark for a moment, before exploding in orange brilliance with an echoing bang. It was beautiful. We sat in silence, watching the sky turn to colour and light. The night air turned smoky, shot through with a flinty smell, dry and metallic. I licked my lips, tasted sulphur and, as I did so, another memory struck.

I saw myself with a woman. She has red hair, and we are standing on a rooftop, watching fireworks. Even though I am wearing only a thin dress I feel warm, buzzing with beer and the joint that I am holding. I look across at the girl as she turns to face me and feel alive, dizzily happy.

'Chrissy,' she says, taking the joint. 'Fancy a trip? I'm pretty sure Nige has brought some acid.'

I take the joint back, inhaling a lungful as if to prove that I am not boring. We have promised ourselves that we will never be boring.

'I don't think so,' I say. 'I just want to stick to this. OK?'

'I suppose so,' she says. I can tell she is disappointed, though not angry with me, and wonder whether she will do it anyway. Without me. I doubt it. I have never had a friend like her before. One who knows everything about me, whom I trust sometimes even more than I trust myself.

We stand in silence for a few more minutes, passing the joint between us.

'We should go downstairs,' she says, eventually. 'There's someone I want you to meet.'

We go into the party and find a spot by a window. The room is full of people, mostly in black. Art students, I think, and finish my beer.

'Want another?' I say.

'Yeah,' says my friend. 'Then I'll introduce you to that bloke I mentioned.'

I laugh. 'OK. Whatever.' I wander off, into the kitchen.

A voice, then. Loud in my ear. 'Christine! Are you OK?' I opened my eyes. With a start I realised I was on Parliament Hill with Ben. 'You had your eyes closed,' he said. 'What's wrong?'

'Nothing,' I said. My head spun; I could hardly breathe.

'You're shivering,' he said. 'Are you cold? Do you want to go home?'

I realised I was. I did. I wanted to record what I had just seen.

'Yes,' I said. 'Do you mind?'

On the way home I thought back to the vision I had seen. It had sucked me into it as if I were living it again. I had felt everything, tasted everything. The cool air and the fizz of the beer. The burn of the weed at the back of my throat. It felt almost more real than the life I had opened my eyes to when it vanished.

I didn't know when it was from. University, I supposed, or just after. It did not have the feel of responsibility. It was carefree. And, though I could not remember her name, this woman was important to me. My best friend. For ever, I had thought, and even though I didn't know who she was I had felt a sense of security with her. I wondered if we might still be close.

For a moment I considered telling Ben about the vision, but instead I asked him who my friends were, when we met.

'You had lots of friends,' he said. 'You were very popular.'

'Did I have a best friend? Someone special?'

He glanced over at me then. 'No,' he said. 'I don't think so.'

'You're sure?' I said.

'Yes,' he said. 'I'm sure.'

As soon as I had finished writing, Ben called me down to dinner. I left most of my meal. Then I offered to wash up, running hot water into the sink, all the time hoping that later I would be able to come upstairs to read my journal and perhaps write some more. But to spend so much time alone in our room would arouse suspicion and so we spent the evening in front of the television. Finally, as the hands of the clock approached eleven, I realised I would have no more time tonight, and said, 'I'm going to turn in.'

'OK, darling,' he said. 'I'll be up in a moment.'

As I left the room I felt a creeping dread. This man is my husband, I told myself, yet still I felt as if going to bed with him was wrong. In the bathroom I used the toilet and brushed my teeth without looking at the photos. I went into the bedroom and began to get undressed. I wanted to be ready before he came in, to be under the covers. For a moment I had the idea that I could pretend to be asleep. I pulled my nightie on, slipped between the covers and, closing my eyes, turned onto my side.

I heard the clock downstairs chime, then Ben came into the room. I listened to him undress, then felt the sag of the bed as he sat on its edge. I felt his hand, heavy on my hip. I opened my eyes and turned onto my back.

'Christine?' he said, half whispering. 'What did you remember today?'

'A party,' I said. 'We were both students, I think.'

He stood up and I saw that he was naked. I could not remember ever seeing male genitals before, yet they were not unfamiliar to me. I wondered how much of them I knew, what experiences I might have had.

'You've remembered that party before,' he said as he pulled back the

bedclothes. 'You have certain memories that crop up regularly.' So it's nothing new, he seemed to be saying. Nothing to get excited about.

He lay beside me and pulled the covers over us both.

'Do I remember things often?' I said.

'Yes. A few things. Most days.'

'The same things?'

'Usually. Yes. It's rare there's a surprise.'

I looked away from his face. 'Do I ever remember you?'

'No,' he said. 'But that's OK.'

'I must be a dreadful burden to you.'

He began to stroke my arm. 'Not at all. I love you.' He kissed my lips.

Did he want to have sex? To me he was a stranger, though intellectually
I knew we got into bed together every night.

'I'm very tired, Ben,' I said.

'I know, my darling,' he said. His hand moved lower beneath the covers,
and I felt a wave of anxiety, almost panic.

'I'm sorry.' I grabbed his hand and stopped its descent. 'Not tonight. OK?'

He lay on his back. Disappointment came off him in waves. Some part of
me thought I should apologise, but some larger part told me I had done
nothing wrong. And so we lay in silence, not touching, and I wondered how
often this happens. How often he craves sex, whether I ever want it myself,
or even feel able to give it to him.

'Good night, darling,' he said, and the tension lifted. I waited until he was
snoring softly and slipped out of bed and here, in the spare room, sat down
to write this.

I would like so much to remember him. Just once.

Monday, November 12

The clock has just chimed four; it is beginning to get dark. Ben will not be
home just yet but, as I write, I listen for his car. If he comes in I will put my
book in the wardrobe and tell him I have been resting. It is dishonest, but
not terribly so. I must write down what I have learned. But that doesn't
mean I want anyone to read it.

I saw Dr Nash today. We were sitting opposite each other, on either side of
his desk. He asked me how I'd been getting on. It was a difficult question to
answer—the few hours since I had woken that morning were the only ones
I could clearly remember. I met my husband, as if for the first time, and was

called by my doctor, who told me about my journal. Then he picked me up.

'I wrote in my journal,' I said. I told him about the memories I'd had. The vision of the woman at the party, of learning of my father's illness.

'Do you still remember those things now?' he said.

The truth was I did not. Or only some of it. This morning I had read my entry for Saturday—of the trip to Parliament Hill. It had felt as unreal as fiction, and I found myself reading and rereading, trying to cement it in my mind. It took me more than an hour.

I read of the things Ben had told me of how we met and married, and I felt nothing. Yet other things stayed with me. The woman, for example. My friend. Her memory still existed within me and this morning more details had come. The vibrant red of her hair, the black clothes that she preferred, the studded belt, the scarlet lipstick. I could not remember her name, but recalled the night we met, in a room alive with the whistles of pinball machines and a tinny jukebox. She had given me a light when I asked her for one, then introduced herself and suggested I join her friends. We drank vodka and lager and, later, she held my hair out of the toilet bowl as I vomited most of it back up. 'I guess we're definitely friends now,' she said. 'I wouldn't do that for just anyone, you know.'

I thanked her and, for no reason I knew, as if it explained what I had just done, told her my father was dead. 'Fuck . . .' she said, and took me back to her room. We ate toast and drank black coffee, listening to records and talking, until it began to get light.

She had paintings propped up against the wall. 'You're an artist?' I said, and she nodded. I remembered her telling me she was studying fine art. 'I'll end up a teacher, of course, but one has to dream. What are you studying?'

I told her. English. 'Ah!' she said. 'So do you want to write novels or teach?' She laughed, not unkindly, but I didn't mention a story I had worked on in my room before coming down.

'Dunno,' I replied instead. 'I guess I'm the same as you.' We toasted each other with coffee.

I remembered all this. But my memories of my life with my husband? They had gone. It was as if not only had the trip to Parliament Hill not happened, but neither had the things he told me.

'I remember some things from when I was younger,' I said to Dr Nash. 'But I can't remember what we did yesterday at all.'

'Is there anything you remember from Saturday evening?'

I thought of what I had written about going to bed. I realised that I felt guilty that I had not been able to give myself to my husband. 'No,' I said, lying. 'Nothing.'

I wondered what Ben might have done differently for me to want to let him love me. I realised how closed the avenues of seduction are to him: he can't even play the first song we danced to at our wedding, because I don't remember what it was. And, in any case, I am his wife: he should not have to seduce me every time. But is there ever a time when I let him make love to me, or perhaps, even, want to make love to him?

'I had no idea who Ben was this morning,' I said.

'You'd like to?'

'Of course!' I said. 'I want to remember my past. I want to know who I am. Who I married. It's all part of the same thing.'

Dr Nash paused, as if thinking carefully. 'What you've told me is encouraging. It suggests that the memories aren't lost completely. The problem is not one of storage, but of access.'

'You mean my memories are there, I just can't get to them?'

He smiled. 'If you like. Yes.'

I felt frustrated. Eager. 'So how do I remember more?'

He looked in the file in front of him. 'Did you write that I showed you a picture of your childhood home?'

'Yes,' I said. 'I did.'

'You seemed to remember much more, having seen that photo. Which isn't surprising. I'd like to see what happens if I show you pictures from the period you definitely don't remember.'

'OK.'

'We'll look at just one picture today.' He took a photograph from the back of the file and then walked round the desk to sit next to me. 'Before we look, do you remember anything of your wedding?'

'No. Nothing.'

He put the photograph on the desk. 'You got married here.' It was of a small church with a low roof and a tiny spire. Totally unfamiliar.

'Anything?'

I tried to empty my mind. A vision of water. My friend. A tiled floor, black and white. Nothing else.

'No. I don't remember ever having seen it before.'

He looked disappointed. 'You're sure?'

I tried to think of my wedding day, tried to imagine Ben, me, in a suit and a wedding dress, standing on the grass in front of the church, but nothing came. Sadness rose in me.

'No,' I said. 'There's nothing.'

He put the photograph away. 'The church is called St Mark's. That was a recent photograph—the only one I could get—but I imagine it looks pretty much the same now as it did then.'

'There are no photographs of our wedding,' I said.

'No. They were lost in a fire apparently.'

Hearing him say it made it seem more real.

'When did I get married?' I said.

'It would have been in the mid-eighties.'

'Before my accident.'

Dr Nash looked uncomfortable. I wondered if I had ever spoken to him about the accident that left me with no memory.

'You know about what caused your amnesia?' he said.

'Ben told me everything. I wrote it in my journal.'

He nodded. 'How do you feel about it?'

'I'm not sure,' I said. I had no memory of the accident, and so it didn't seem real. 'I feel like I ought to hate the person who did this to me. Especially as they've never been punished for ruining my life. But the odd thing is I don't. I can't imagine them. It's like they don't even exist.'

'Is that what you think? That your life is ruined?'

'Yes.' I paused. 'Isn't it?'

I suppose part of me wanted him to tell me how wrong I am. But he didn't. He just looked straight at me. I noticed how striking his eyes are. Blue, flecked with grey.

'I'm sorry, Christine,' he said. 'But I'm doing everything I can, and I think I can help you. I really do. You have to believe that.'

He put his hand on top of mine, where it lay on the desk between us. He squeezed my fingers and for a second I felt embarrassed, but then I looked at the expression of sadness in his face, and realised that his action was that of a young man comforting an older woman. Nothing more.

'I'm sorry,' I said. 'I need to use the bathroom.'

When I returned he seemed reluctant to make eye contact, leafing through the papers on his desk. At first I thought he was embarrassed about squeezing my hand, but then he looked up. 'Christine. I wanted to ask you something. Two things, really.' I nodded. 'First, I've decided to write up your case. It's pretty unusual and it would be beneficial to get the details out there in the wider scientific community. Do you mind?'

I looked at the journals, stacked on the shelves around the office. Is this how he intended to further his career? Is that why I am here? For a moment I considered telling him I'd rather he didn't use my story, but in the end I simply said, 'It's fine.'

He smiled. 'Thank you. Now, I have something I'd like to try. According to your files, a year or so after you and Ben were married you moved to a house quite near to where you live now. You stayed there until you were hospitalised. I thought we could visit it on the way home. What do you think?'

It was an almost unanswerable question. I knew that it might help me but I was reluctant. It was as if my past suddenly felt dangerous. A place it might be unwise to visit.

'I'm not sure,' I said.

'We can just go and look at it. We don't have to go inside.'

'Go inside?'

'I've spoken to the couple who live there now. They said they'd be more than happy to let you look round.'

I was surprised by this. 'Really?'

'Yes,' he said, and then, 'I don't go to this much trouble for all my patients. I really think it might help, Christine.'

What else could I do?

The house was similar to the one I live in now, with its red brick and the same bay window and well-tended garden. I found it hard to understand why we'd left this place to move only a couple of miles away to an almost identical house. After a moment I realised: memories. Memories of a better time, before my accident. Ben would have had them, even if I did not.

'I want to go in,' I said.

A woman—Amanda—answered the door, greeting Dr Nash with a handshake and me with a look that hovered between pity and fascination. 'You must be Christine,' she said. 'Do come in!'

We stood in a bright, carpeted hallway, the sun streaming through the glass panels in the window, picking out a vase of red tulips on a side table. The silence was uncomfortable. 'It's a lovely house,' Amanda said, eventually. 'We bought it about ten years ago. We just adore it.'

We followed her into the lounge. The room was sparse, tasteful. I felt nothing; it could have been any room in any house in any city. I looked at the sanded floorboards and white walls, at the cream sofa, the modern-art prints that hung on the wall. I thought of the house I had left this morning; it could not have been more different.

'Do you remember how it looked when you moved in?' said Dr Nash.

Amanda sighed. 'Only vaguely. It was carpeted. A kind of biscuit colour. And there was striped wallpaper.'

'Christine?' said Dr Nash. 'Anything?' When I shook my head he said, 'Do you think we could look round the rest of the house?'

There were two bedrooms upstairs. 'Giles works from home a good deal. He's an architect,' she said, as we went in the one at the front dominated by a desk, filing cabinets and books. 'It's quite a coincidence, because the man we bought the house from was also an architect.'

An architect, I thought. Not a teacher, like Ben. These can't have been the people that he sold the house to.

Dr Nash turned to face me. 'Anything?'

I shook my head. 'No. Nothing. I don't remember anything.'

We looked into the other bedroom, the bathroom and then went downstairs, into the kitchen. The units were chrome and white, and the worktop looked like poured concrete. A bowl of limes provided the only colour.

'I think we ought to leave soon,' I said.

'Of course,' said Amanda. Her breezy efficiency seemed to have vanished, replaced by disappointment. I felt guilty.

'Could I have a glass of water?' I said.

She brightened immediately. 'Let me get you one!' She handed me a glass and, as I took it from her, I saw an uncooked fish, lying on an oval plate. Amanda and Dr Nash had both disappeared and I heard a man's voice. 'White wine,' it said, 'or red?' and I turned and saw Ben coming into a kitchen—the one I was standing in with Dr Nash and Amanda—but it had different-coloured paint on the walls. Ben was holding a bottle of wine in each hand, slimmer, with less grey in his hair, and he had a moustache. He was naked and his penis was semi-erect. His skin was smooth, taut over the muscles of his arms and chest, and I felt the sharp tug of lust.

He put both bottles down and his arms encircled me. Then I was closing my eyes, my mouth opened and I could feel his penis pressing into my crotch, my hand moving towards it. Even as I was kissing him, I was thinking, I must remember how this feels. I must put this in my book. His hands began to tear at my dress, groping for the zip. 'Stop it!' I said. But even though I was asking him to stop, I felt as though I wanted him more than I had ever wanted anyone before. 'Upstairs,' I said, 'quick.' And then we were heading up to the bedroom with the grey carpet and blue-patterned wallpaper, all the time thinking, This is what I ought to be writing about in my next novel.

The sound of breaking glass, and the image in front of me vanished. I was still in that kitchen, but now it was Dr Nash and Amanda standing in front of me, and they were both looking at me, concerned and anxious. I realised I had dropped the glass.

'Christine,' said Dr Nash. 'Christine, are you OK?'

'I remembered something,' I said. 'I remembered Ben!' I began to shake.

'Good,' said Dr Nash. 'Good! That's excellent!'

They led me through to the living room. I sat on the sofa. Amanda handed me a mug of tea. She doesn't understand, I thought. She can't. I have remembered Ben. Me, when I was young. The two of us, together. I know we were in love. I no longer have to take his word for it. It is important.

I felt excited, all the way home. Lit with nervous energy. I looked at the world outside and did not see threat, but possibility. Dr Nash seemed excited. *This is good*, he kept saying. He said he'd like to arrange a scan and, almost without thinking, I agreed. He gave me a mobile phone, too, telling me it used to belong to his girlfriend. It was smaller than the one Ben had given me, and the casing flipped open to reveal a keypad and screen inside. *A spare*, he said. *You can ring me any time. Keep it with you. I'll call you on it to remind you about your journal.* That was hours ago. Now I realise he gave it to me so that he could phone me without Ben knowing. He'd even said as much. I'd taken it without question.

I have remembered Ben. Remembered that I loved him. He will be home, soon. Perhaps later, when we go to bed, I will make amends for last night's neglect. I feel alive. Buzzing with potential.

Tuesday, November 13

Soon Ben will be home from another day at work. I sit with this journal in front of me. A man—Dr Nash—called me and told me where to find it. I hadn't believed him, but he had stayed on the line while I looked, and he was right. Once I had said goodbye to Dr Nash, I read every word.

I am writing this in the window of the bedroom, in the bay. It feels familiar here, somehow, as if this is a place where I sit often. I can see down the street, in one direction to a row of tall trees behind which a park can be glimpsed. It begins to rain. Large droplets spatter the window in front of my face, and begin their slow slide down the pane. I put my hand up to the cold glass.

So much separates me from the rest of the world.

I read of visiting the home I had shared with my husband. I read of the day I had remembered, too. Of kissing my husband—in the house we bought together, so long ago—and, when I close my eyes, I can see it again. The image shimmers and resolves, snapping to sharpness with an almost overwhelming intensity. Ben, holding me, his kisses becoming more urgent, deeper. I remember we neither ate the fish nor drank the wine; instead, when we had finished making love, we stayed in bed for as long as we could, our legs entwined, my head on his chest, his hand stroking my hair. Happiness surrounded us like a cloud.

'I love you,' he said. He was whispering, as if he had never said those words before, and, though he must have done so many times, they sounded new. Forbidden and dangerous.

'I love you, too,' I said, whispering into his chest as if the words were fragile. I felt as if here, against his body, was the only place in which I belonged. We lay in silence for a while, holding each other, our skin merging, our breathing synchronised.

Ben broke the spell. 'I have to leave,' he said.

'Already?' I said.

'Yes. It's later than you think. I'll miss my train.'

'Stay a bit longer?' I said. 'Get the next one?'

He laughed. 'I can't, Chris,' he said. 'You know that.'

I showered, after he left. Then I went downstairs, into the dining room. On the table in front of me was a typewriter, threaded with blank paper. I sat down and began to type. *Chapter Two*.

I could not think what to write next, how to begin. I rested my fingers on the keyboard. My fingers danced across the keys, almost without thought. I had typed a single sentence.

Lizzy did not know what she had done, or how it could be undone.

Rubbish, I thought. I knew I could do better. I had done so before, two summers previously when the words had flown out of me. I took a pencil and drew a line through the sentence. I felt a little better with it scored out, but now I had nowhere to start.

I stood and lit a cigarette from the packet that Ben had left. I drew the smoke deep into my lungs, held it, exhaled. For a moment I wished it was weed, wondered where I could get some from, for next time. I poured myself a drink—neat vodka—and took a mouthful. It would have to do. Writer's block, I thought. How did I become such a cliché?

How did I do it last time? I went over to the bookcase and took down a book from the top shelf. There must be clues here, surely? I rested my fingertips on the cover, as if the book were delicate, and brushed them gently over the title. *For the Morning Birds*, it said. *Christine Lucas*. I opened the cover and flicked through the pages.

The image vanished. My eyes opened. I dimly registered the surprise that I had once smoked, but it was replaced by something else. Had I written a novel? Was it published? If so, I had been someone with a life, with goals and ambitions and achievements. I ran down the stairs.

I scanned the book shelves in the living room. Nothing by me. Nothing to suggest I had had a novel published. It must be here, I thought. It must. Then another thought struck me. Perhaps my vision was not memory but invention. Perhaps, without a true history to hold, my mind had created one of its own. Perhaps my subconscious decided that I was a writer because that is what I always wanted to be.

I ran back upstairs. The shelves in the office were filled with box files and computer manuals. I stood for a moment, then saw the computer in front of me. I knew what to do, though I didn't know how I knew. I switched it on and it whirred into life, the screen lighting up. Then an image appeared. A photograph of Ben and me, both smiling. Across the middle of our faces there was a box. *Username*, it said, and beneath it, *Password*.

In my vision I was touch-typing. I positioned the cursor in the *Username* box and held my hands above the keyboard. Was it true? Had I learned to type? I let my fingers move effortlessly. When I had finished I looked at what was written in the box. I expected nonsense, but I saw: *The quick brown fox jumps over the lazy dog*.

It was true. I could touch-type. Maybe my vision was not invention but memory. Maybe I *had* written a novel.

I had the almost overwhelming feeling that I was going mad. The novel seemed to exist and not exist at the same time. I could remember nothing of its plot or characters, not even the reason I had given it its title, yet still it felt real, as if it beat within me like a heart.

And why had Ben not told me? Not kept a copy on display?

He had told me I had been working as a secretary. Perhaps that was why I could type: the only reason.

I dug one of the phones out of my bag, not caring which one. My husband or my doctor? I pressed the call button.

'Dr Nash?' I said when he answered. 'It's Christine.' He began to say something but I interrupted him. 'Listen. I just remembered I was writing something years ago. Did I ever write a novel?'

He didn't seem to understand what I meant. 'A novel?'

'Yes. Ben told me I worked as a secretary, but I was just thinking—'

'He hasn't told you?' he said. 'You were working on your second novel when you lost your memory. Your first was published. It was a success. I wouldn't say it was a best seller, but it was certainly a success.'

The words spun in on each other. *A novel. A success. Published.* It was true, my memory had been real.

I said goodbye, then came upstairs to write this.

The bedside clock reads ten thirty. I imagine Ben will come to bed soon, but still I sit here on the bed, writing. I spent the afternoon wondering why he would so thoroughly remove evidence of even this modest success. Was he ashamed? Embarrassed? Had I written about our life together? Or was the reason something darker I could not yet see?

At the dinner table, I spoke as casually as I could. 'Ben, what did I do for a living? Did I have a job?'

'Yes,' he said. 'You worked as a secretary for a while.'

'Really? I have a vague memory of wanting to be a writer.' He held out his hand across the dinner table and took mine. His eyes seemed sad. What a shame, they seemed to say. 'Are you sure—?' I began.

He interrupted me. 'Christine, please. You're imagining things.'

For the rest of the evening I was silent. Why would he pretend I had never written a word? Why had I not told him that I knew I had written a novel? Did I really trust him so little? I had remembered us lying in each other's arms. How had we gone from that to this?

But then I began to imagine what would happen if I did stumble upon a copy of my novel. What would it say to me, other than, Look how far you have fallen. Look what you could do, before a car on an icy road took it all from you, leaving you worse than useless.

No wonder Ben might want to hide it from me. I picture him now, removing all the copies, before deciding what to tell me. How best to reinvent my past to make it tolerable.

But that is over now. I know the truth. One I have remembered. And it is written now, etched in this journal rather than my memory, permanent. I know that the book I am writing may be dangerous. It is not fiction. It may reveal secrets best left undiscovered. But still my pen moves across the page.

Wednesday, November 14

This morning I asked Ben if he'd ever grown a moustache. I had woken early and, unlike previous days, I had felt adult. In the bathroom I looked at my reflection with horror, but the pictures around it seemed to resonate with truth. My age, my marriage, these facts seemed to be things I was being reminded of, not told about for the first time.

Dr Nash called me almost as soon as Ben left for work. He reminded me about my journal and then—once he had told me that he would be picking me up to take me for my scan—I read it. There were things in it I could remember writing, as if some residue of memory had survived the night.

Perhaps that was why I had to be sure the things contained within it were true. I rang Ben. 'Did you ever have a moustache?'

'That's an odd question!'

'I just—' I began. 'I had a memory, I think.'

Silence. 'A memory?'

My mind flashed on the things I had written about the other day and those I had remembered yesterday. The two of us in bed. 'I seem to remember you with a moustache.'

He laughed, and I felt solid ground begin to slip away. Maybe everything I had written was a lie. 'Did you?' I asked, desperate. 'It's important.'

'I suppose I might have done, once,' he said. 'Actually, yes. I think I probably did. For a week or so. A long time ago.'

'Thank you,' I said, relieved. The ground on which I stood felt a little more secure.

Dr Nash picked me up at midday. 'We're meeting a colleague of mine,' he said in the car. 'Dr Paxton. He's an expert in the field of functional imaging of patients with problems like yours.'

'OK,' I said. 'Did I call you yesterday?'

He said that I had. 'You read your journal?'

'Most of it. I skipped bits. It's already quite long.'

He seemed interested. 'What sections did you skip?'

'There are parts that seem familiar, as if they're just reminding me of things I already know.'

'That's good.' He glanced at me. 'Very good.'

I felt a glow of pleasure. 'So what did I call about yesterday?'

'You wanted to know if you'd really written a novel.'

'And had I? Have I?'

'Yes,' he said. 'Yes, you have.'

I felt relief. I relaxed into the journey.

Dr Paxton was older than I expected. He was wearing a tweed jacket and looked as though he ought to have retired.

'Welcome to the Vincent Hall Imaging Centre,' he said and winked. 'It's not as grand as it sounds. Let me show you around.'

We made our way into the building and walked through into an empty waiting room dotted with empty chairs. Dr Paxton paused at another door. 'Would you like to see the control room?'

'Yes,' I said. 'Please.'

'Functional MRI is a fairly new technique,' he said, once we'd gone through. 'Have you heard of MRI? Magnetic resonance imaging?'

We were standing in a small room, lit only by a bank of computer monitors. One wall was taken up by a window, beyond which was another room, dominated by a large cylindrical machine. I began to feel afraid.

'No,' I said.

'MRI is a fairly standard procedure, a little like taking an X-ray through the body. Here we're using some of the same techniques but actually looking at how the brain works. At function.'

Dr Nash spoke then. 'If someone has a brain tumour then we need to scan their head to find out where the tumour is. That's looking at structure. What functional MRI allows us to see is which part of the brain you use when you do certain tasks. We want to see how your brain processes memory.'

'Which parts light up, as it were,' said Paxton.

'That will help?' I asked.

Dr Nash paused. 'We hope so.'

I took off my wedding ring and my earrings and put them in a plastic tray.

Dr Paxton handed me some yellow ear-plugs. 'You'll need these. She's a bit of a noisy old beast.' He winked at me again. 'Ready?'

I hesitated. 'I don't know.' Through the glass the scanner loomed. I had the sense I had seen it before, or one just like it.

Dr Nash came over to me then. He placed his hand on my arm. 'It's completely painless,' he said. 'Just a little noisy. I'll be here, just on this side of the glass.'

Dr Paxton added, 'You're in safe hands, my dear. Nothing will go wrong. Think of your memories as being lost, somewhere in your mind. All we're doing with this machine is trying to find out where they are.'

It was cold, despite the blanket they had wrapped around me, and dark, except for a red light blinking in the room and a mirror, hung from a frame a couple of inches above my head, angled to reflect the image of a computer screen. As well as the ear-plugs, I was wearing a set of headphones through which they said they would talk to me, but for now they were silent.

In my right hand I clutched a plastic bulb filled with air. 'Squeeze it, if you need to tell us anything,' Dr Paxton had said. 'We won't be able to hear you if you speak.' I caressed its rubbery surface and waited. I wanted to close my eyes, but they had told me to keep them open, to look at the screen. Foam wedges kept my head perfectly still; I could not have moved even if I'd wanted to.

A moment of stillness and then a click so loud that I started, despite the ear-plugs, followed by another. Then a noise, like an alarm or a drill, over and over again. I closed my eyes.

A voice in my ear. 'Christine,' it said. 'Can you open your eyes, please?' They could see me then, somehow. 'Don't worry, it's all fine.'

A different voice. Dr Nash's. 'Can you look at the pictures? Think what they are, say it, but only to yourself.'

Above me, in the little mirror, were drawings, one after the other, white on black. A man. A ladder. A chair. I named each one as it came, and then the screen flashed the words *Thank you! Now relax!* and I wondered how anyone could relax in the belly of a machine like this.

More instructions flashed on the screen. *Recall a past event*, it said, and then beneath it flashed the words, *A party*.

I tried to think of the party I had remembered on the roof with my friend but nothing would come. My mind turned to childhood parties. Birthdays, with my mother. Twister. Pass-the-parcel. Musical Chairs. Trifle and jelly. I am sitting at a table in front of a cake, with candles. I take a deep breath, lean forward, blow. Smoke rises in the air.

Memories of another party crowded in then. I saw myself at home, looking out of my bedroom window. I am naked, about seventeen. There are trestle tables out in the street loaded with trays of sausage rolls and sandwiches, and bunting hangs from every window. I can see my mother on the other side of the street and, just below my window, my father sits in a deck chair.

'Come back to bed,' says a voice. I turn round. Dave Soper sits in my single bed. The white sheet is twisted around him, spattered with blood. I had not told him it was my first time.

'No,' I say. 'You have to get dressed before my parents come back!'

He laughs, though not unkindly. 'Come on!'

I pull on my jeans. 'Get up. Please?'

He looks disappointed. I didn't think this would happen—which doesn't mean I didn't want it to—and now I would like to be alone. My world has changed, I think. I have crossed a line, and I cannot go back.

A voice brought me back to the present. 'More pictures now,' said Dr Paxton. 'Just look at each one and tell yourself what, or who, it is.'

The first photograph was black and white. A girl of four or five in the arms of a woman. With a shock of recognition I realised that the little girl was me. *Me*, I said silently. *Mother*. The picture faded and was replaced by another, also of my mother, now older, her eyes sunk deep in her thin face. Other words came, unbidden: *In pain*.

The images came quickly then, and I recognised only a few. One was of the friend I had seen in my memory, in old blue jeans and a T-shirt, smoking, her red hair loose. It was followed by a photograph of my father reading a newspaper in our front room and then one of me and Ben, standing with a couple I didn't recognise.

Other photos were of strangers. A black woman in a nurse's uniform. A man with ginger hair and a round face, another with a beard. A boy, six or seven, eating an ice cream. A man, attractive, his hair black and slightly longish, with glasses, and a scar running down the side of his face. They went on and on, these photographs and, as I tried to place them, I began to panic. The whirr of the machine seemed to rise in pitch and volume and my stomach clenched. I could not breathe, and I closed my eyes and squeezed my right hand, but I had dropped the bulb. I called out, a wordless cry.

'Christine,' came a voice in my ear. 'Christine.'

I cried out again, and began kicking the blanket off my body.

Then the siren noise whirred to a halt, a door crashed open, and there were voices in the room, and hands on me. I opened my eyes.

'It's OK,' said Dr Nash in my ear. 'You're OK. I'm here.'

Once they'd calmed me down and given me back my handbag, my earrings and my wedding ring, Dr Nash and I went to a coffee bar along the corridor. I let him buy me a cup of coffee and a piece of carrot cake and then selected a seat by the window while he paid.

'What happened?' I said.

'You panicked. It's not that uncommon.'

'The photographs. Who were they? Where did you get them?'

'Some I got from your medical files. Ben had donated them, years ago. I asked you to bring a couple from home for the purposes of this exercise—you said they'd been around your mirror. Some I provided—people you've never met. What we call controls. Some were people you might remember. Family. Friends from school. The rest were from the era of your life that you definitely can't remember. Dr Paxton and I are trying to find out whether there's a difference in the way you attempt to access memories from these different periods. The strongest reaction was to your husband, of course, but you reacted to others. The patterns of neural excitation are definitely there.'

'Who was the woman with red hair? Do you know her name?' I said.

'I don't. The photos weren't labelled.'

'You said that I reacted to the pictures—is that good?'

'We'll need to look at the results in more detail before we know what conclusions we can draw. This work is very new.'

'I see.' The carrot cake was too sweet and I offered it to him. He declined, patting his stomach, though I could see no reason for him to worry, yet. He was young, and age had hardly touched him.

I thought of my own body. I wondered what will happen in the future. Perhaps I will grow fat. Or stay the same size as I am now, never getting used to it, watching as I turn into an old woman in the bathroom mirror.

'Oh,' Dr Nash said, with a cheeriness that sounded forced. 'I brought you a gift.' He retrieved his briefcase from the floor. 'You've probably already got a copy,' he said, taking out a package.

I knew what it was as I took it. What else could it be? He had wrapped it in a padded envelope, sealed it with tape. 'It's your novel,' he said.

Evidence, I thought. Proof that what I had written was true.

Inside the envelope was a paperback, not new: there was a coffee ring on the front and the edges of the pages were yellowed with age. As I held it, I saw myself again as I had the other day—much younger, reaching for this novel in an effort to find a way into the next. Somehow I knew the second novel had never been completed.

'Thank you,' I said. 'Thank you.'

I put it underneath my coat, where, all the way home, it beat like a heart.

As soon as I got back to the house I wrote as much as I could remember in my journal. Once I'd finished I hurried downstairs to look properly at what I had been given. My hands began to shake as I opened the book. Inside was a title page, a dedication: FOR MY FATHER, and then the words, I MISS YOU.

A fluttering of memory. I saw my father, lying in a bed under bright white lights, his skin translucent. My mother, sitting on the other side of his bed, trying not to cry.

The image disappeared. I turned to my novel. I had written about a woman called Lou, a man—her husband, I guessed—called George, and the novel seemed to be rooted in a war. I felt disappointed. It seemed any answers this novel could give me would be limited.

I turned it over to look at the back cover, where there was a short biography. *Christine Lucas was born in 1960, in the north of England. She read English at University College London, and has now settled in that city. This is her first novel.*

I felt a swell of happiness and pride. I did this. I wanted to unlock its secrets, but at the same time I did not. I was worried the reality might take my happiness away. Either I would like the novel and feel sad that I would never write another, or I would feel frustrated that I never developed my talent. I knew that one day I would make that discovery. But not today.

There was something else in the envelope. A note, folded into four. Dr Nash had written on it: *I thought this might interest you!*

I unfolded the paper. Across the top he'd written *Standard, 1986.* Beneath it was a review of my novel and a picture of me. I shook as I held the page. How was my work received, all those years ago? I scanned the article. Words jumped out at me. *Studied. Perceptive. Skilled. Humanity. Brutal.*

I looked at the picture. It showed me sitting at a desk, my body angled towards the camera, holding myself awkwardly. Despite this I am smiling. My hair is long and behind me there are patio doors. The caption read *Christine Lucas, at her north London home.* I realised it must be the house I had visited with Dr Nash.

In the picture I look uncomfortable, but also radiant in some way. It is as if I am keeping a secret. I looked closely. I could see the swell of my breasts in the loose dress, the way I am holding one arm across my stomach. A memory bubbles up from nowhere—the journalist with whom I have just discussed my work hovering in the kitchen. She has lit a cigarette and calls to ask whether we have an ashtray. I feel annoyed, but only slightly. The truth is I am yearning for a cigarette myself, but I have given up, ever since I found out that—

I looked at the picture again, and I knew. In it, I am pregnant.

My mind stopped for a moment, and then began to race. It caught on the sharp edges of the realisation that, not only had I been carrying a baby as I had my picture taken, but I had known it, was happy about it.

What had happened? The child ought to be—how old now? Nineteen? Twenty? But there is no child, I thought. Where is my son?

I felt my world tip again. That word: *son.* I had said it to myself with certainty. Somewhere deep within me I knew that the child I had been carrying was a boy. We called him Adam.

He was absent from the scrapbook in the living room. I knew that. I would have remembered seeing a picture of my own child as I leafed through it. I would have asked Ben who he was. I would have written about it in my journal. I crammed the cutting back into the envelope along with the book and ran upstairs. In the bathroom I stood in front of the mirror, looking at the pictures of the past.

Me and Ben. Me, alone, and Ben, alone. The two of us with an older couple I take to be his parents. Me, much younger, wearing a scarf, petting a dog, smiling happily. But there is no Adam. No baby, no toddler. No photos of his first day of school, or at sports day, or on holiday. Nothing.

Surely these are pictures that every parent takes and none discards?

Adam. The name spun in my head. More memories hit, each triggering the next. I saw Adam, his blond hair that I knew would one day turn brown, the Spider-Man T-shirt that he insisted on wearing until it was too small. I saw him in a pram, sleeping, and remember thinking that he was the most perfect thing I had ever seen. I saw him riding a blue tricycle in a park, grinning as he peddled towards me and, a second later, slamming to the ground as it twisted beneath him. I saw myself holding him as he cried, finding one of his teeth on the ground next to a still-spinning wheel.

I wanted to remember him at school, or as a teenager, or to picture him with me or his father. But I could not. When I tried to organise my memories they fluttered and vanished, like a feather caught on the wind that changes direction whenever a hand snatches at it. Instead I saw him holding a dripping ice cream, then with liquorice over his face, then sleeping in the back seat of a car.

No photographs on the mantelpiece. No teenage bedroom with posters of pop stars on the wall. No tattered trainers in the cupboard under the stairs. Even if he had left home there would still be some evidence of his existence, surely? But no, he isn't in this house. With a chill, I realised it was as if he didn't exist, and never had.

I don't know how long I stood there in the bathroom. At some point I heard a key in the front door, the swoosh as Ben wiped his feet on the mat. He called upstairs, asking if everything was all right. His voice had a nervous fluting to it that I had not heard this morning, but I only mumbled that, yes, I was OK. I heard him go into the living room.

I hid my novel in the wardrobe and went downstairs. I didn't know what to say to Ben: how I could tell him that I knew about Adam? He would ask me how, and what would I say then? It didn't matter, though. Nothing did. Nothing other than knowing about my son. When I felt as calm as I thought I would ever feel, I pushed the living-room door open.

Ben was watching television, a plate balanced on his lap. I felt a wave of anger. I wanted to grab him and shout until he told me why he had kept my novel from me, why he had hidden evidence of my son. I wanted to demand he give back to me everything that I had lost.

But I knew that would do no good. Instead, I coughed. A cough that said *I don't want to disturb you, but . . .*

He saw me and smiled. 'Darling!' he said. 'There you are!'

'Ben, I need to talk to you.' My voice sounded alien to me.

He stood up. 'What is it, love? Are you all right?'

'No,' I said. He stopped a metre or so from where I stood. He held out his arms for me to fall into, but I did not. He appeared to be in control, as if he was used to these moments.

'Where's Adam?' I said. The words came out in a gasp. 'Where is he?'
Ben's expression changed. Surprise? Or shock?

'Tell me!' I said.

He took me in his arms. I wanted to push him away, but did not.
'Christine,' he said. 'Please. Calm down. I can explain everything. OK?'

I began to shake. 'Tell me,' I said. 'Please, tell me now.'

We sat on the sofa. Me at one end, him at the other. It was as close
as I wanted us to be. We'd been talking. For minutes. Hours. I couldn't tell.
I didn't want him to say it again, but he did.

'Adam is dead.' His words, sharp as razor wire. 'I'm so sorry.'

I forced myself to speak. 'How?'

He sighed. 'Adam was in the Royal Marines. He was stationed in
Afghanistan. He was killed. Last year.'

I swallowed, my throat dry. 'Why?' I said, and then, 'How?'

He reached across to take my hand, and I let him, though I was relieved
when he moved no closer.

'You don't want to know everything, surely?'

My anger surged. I couldn't help it. Anger and panic. 'He was my son!'

He looked away, towards the window, and spoke in a whisper. 'He was
travelling in an armoured vehicle. There was a bomb on the roadside. One
soldier survived. Adam and one other didn't.'

I closed my eyes, and my voice dropped to a whisper, too. 'Did he die
straightaway? Did he suffer?'

Ben sighed. 'They think it would have been very quick.'

You're lying, I thought. My mind began to spin. Questions. Questions
that I dared not ask in case the answers killed me. What was he like as a boy,
a teenager, a man? Were we close? Was he happy? Was I a good mother?

'What was he doing in Afghanistan?' I said. 'Why there?'

Ben told me we were at war. A war against terror, he said, though I don't
know what that means. He said there was an awful attack, in America.
Thousands were killed.

'I don't understand,' I said.

'It's complicated,' he said. 'He always wanted to join the army. He
thought he was doing his duty.'

'Did you think he was doing his duty? Did I? Why didn't you persuade
him to do something else?'

'Christine, it was what he wanted.'

'To get himself killed? Is that what he wanted?'

Ben was silent. A single tear rolled down my face, and then another. I wiped them away. To start to cry would be never to stop.

I felt my mind begin to close down. 'I never even knew him,' I said.

Later, Ben brought in a grey metal box and put it on the coffee table. 'I keep these upstairs,' he said. 'For safety.'

From what? I thought. Whatever it contains must be dangerous. 'There are some things it wouldn't be good for you to stumble on by yourself, some things that it's better if I explain to you.'

He sat next to me and opened the box. 'This is Adam as a baby,' he said, taking out a handful of photographs and handing one to me.

It was a picture of me, walking towards the camera with a baby strapped to my chest in a pouch. His body is facing mine, but he is looking over his shoulder, the smile on his face a toothless approximation of my own.

'You took this?'

Ben nodded.

Me. A baby. It did not seem real. I tried to tell myself I was a mother.

'When?' I said.

'He would have been about six months old, so that must be about 1987.'

I would have been twenty-seven. A lifetime ago. My son's lifetime.

'When was he born?'

He passed me a slip of paper. A birth certificate. I read his name.

'Adam Wheeler,' I said, out loud.

'Wheeler is my last name,' he said. He handed me a few more photographs. 'We don't have that many. A lot were lost.'

'Yes,' I said. 'We had a fire.' I said it without thinking.

He looked at me oddly. 'You remember?'

Suddenly I wasn't sure. 'Well, you told me about it.'

'When?'

Had it been that morning, or days ago? I thought of my journal. He'd told me about the fire as we sat on Parliament Hill.

I could have told him about my journal then, but something held me back. 'Before you left for work,' I said. 'When we looked through the scrapbook.' He frowned. It felt terrible to be lying to him, but I didn't feel able to cope with more revelations. 'How would I know otherwise?'

I paused for a moment, looking at the handful of photographs. They were pitifully few. Were they really all I would ever have to describe my son's life?

'How did the fire start?' I said.

'It was years ago. In our old house.'

'But how did it start?'

'It was just an accident.'

I wondered what he was not telling me. I imagined myself in the kitchen I had stood in the day before yesterday. I saw myself standing over a sizzling fryer, shaking the wire basket that contained the sliced potatoes. I saw myself hear the phone ring, go into the hall.

What then? Had the oil burst into flames as I took the call, or had I forgotten ever having begun to cook dinner?

It was kind of Ben to tell me it had been an accident. Domesticity has many dangers for someone without a memory. I touched his arm, and he smiled.

I thumbed through the handful of photographs. There was one of Adam wearing a cowboy hat and in another he was a few years older, his face thinner, his hair beginning to darken. He was wearing a shirt buttoned to the neck, and a child's elasticated tie.

'That was taken at school,' said Ben. 'An official portrait.' He pointed to the photograph and laughed. 'It's such a shame. The picture's ruined!'

The elastic of the tie was visible, not tucked under the collar. It wasn't ruined, I thought. It was perfect.

I tried to remember my son, tried to see myself combing his hair, or wiping blood from a grazed knee. Nothing came. The boy in the photograph shared a fullness of mouth with me, and had eyes that resembled, vaguely, my mother's, but otherwise he could have been a stranger.

Ben took out another picture. 'Do you think he looks like me?'

Adam was holding a football. 'A little,' I said. 'Perhaps.'

Together we carried on looking at the photographs. They were mostly of me and Adam, the occasional one of him alone; Ben must have taken the majority. Among the pictures there was a letter addressed to Santa Claus written in blue crayon. He wants a bike, he says, or a puppy. It is signed and he has added his age. Four.

As I read it my world seemed to collapse. Grief exploded in my chest like a grenade. I had been feeling calm and that serenity vanished, as if vaporised. Beneath it I was raw.

Ben hugged me, told me I would be fine, reminded me that he would always be here for me. As he closed the box, I was sobbing. I could see that he was upset too, yet already his expression seemed tinged with something else. Resignation or acceptance, but not shock.

I realised that he has done all this before. It is only my grief that is fresh, every day.

I came upstairs, to the bedroom. Back to the wardrobe. I wrote on. It floods out of me, pages and pages. I cannot stop.

I wonder if this is what it was like when I wrote my novel.

After I went back downstairs, I made us both a cup of tea. 'Was I a good mother?' I said, handing one to Ben. 'I mean, how did I cope? He must have been very little when I—'

'—had your accident?' he interrupted. 'He was two. You were a wonderful mother, though. Until then. Afterwards, well—you were too ill for me to look after you at home. You couldn't be left alone. You would forget what you were doing. I was worried you might run yourself a bath and leave the water running, or try and cook yourself some food and forget you'd started it. So I stayed at home and looked after Adam. My mother helped.'

'How about my mother? Did she help?'

He nodded.

'She's dead, isn't she?' I said.

'She died a few years ago. I'm sorry.'

I felt my mind begin to close down, as if it couldn't process any more grief, but I knew I would wake up tomorrow and remember none of this. What could I write in my journal that would get me through tomorrow, the next day, the one after that?

An image floated in front of me. A woman with red hair. A name came, unbidden, and the thought, What will Claire think?

'And Claire?' I said. 'My friend Claire. Is she still alive?'

'Claire?' He looked puzzled. 'You remember Claire?'

I reminded myself that—according to my journal—it had been a few days since I had told him I had remembered her at the party.

'Yes,' I said. 'We were friends. What happened to her?'

'She moved away a few years after we got married. To New Zealand.'

'Are we in touch?'

'You were for a while, but not any more.'

It doesn't seem possible. *My best friend*, I had written, after remembering her on Parliament Hill, and I had felt the same sensation of closeness when

I had thought of her today. Otherwise, why would I care what she thought?

'We argued?'

He hesitated, and I sensed a calculation. I realised that of course Ben knows what will upset me. He has had years to learn what is dangerous ground for us to tread.

'No,' he said. 'I think you just drifted apart, and then Claire met someone. She married him and they moved away.'

An image came then. Claire and I joking that we would never marry. 'Marriage is for losers!' she was saying and I was agreeing, though at the same time I knew that one day I would be her bridesmaid, and she mine.

I felt a sudden flush of love. Though I have barely remembered any of our time together—and tomorrow even that will have gone—I sensed somehow that we are still connected.

'Did we go to the wedding?' I said.

'Yes,' he nodded, opening the box on his lap and digging through it. 'There are a couple of photos here.'

They were not formal shots; these were blurred and dark, taken by an amateur. By Ben, I guessed. She was as I had imagined her. Tall, thin. More beautiful, if anything. She was standing on a clifftop, her dress diaphanous, blowing in the breeze. I looked through the rest. In some she was with her husband—a man I didn't recognise—and in others I had joined them, dressed in pale blue silk. It was true; I had been a bridesmaid.

'Are there any of our wedding?' I said.

He shook his head. 'They were in a separate album. It was lost.'

Of course. The fire.

'I'm tired,' I said. 'I need to rest.'

'Of course,' he said, taking the photographs from me and putting them back in the box.

Midnight. I am in bed. Alone. Trying to make sense of all that has happened today. I don't know whether I can.

I decided to take a bath before dinner. I locked the bathroom door behind me and looked quickly at the pictures arranged around the mirror.

Most days I realise I don't remember Adam at all, yet today he had come to me after I saw just one picture. Are these photographs selected so they will anchor me in myself without reminding me of what I have lost?

The room began to fill with hot steam as the bath filled. I could hear my husband downstairs. The sound of jazz floated up to me, hazy and indistinct. I don't blame Ben for not telling me, every day, about Adam, my mother, Claire. In his position I would do the same.

I folded my clothes, placed them on the chair by the side of the bath. Naked, I stood in front of the mirror forcing myself to look at the wrinkles, my sagging breasts. I recognise neither my body nor my past.

I am lucky, I thought, to have Ben. I am not the only one suffering. He has been through what I have, today, but will go to bed knowing that tomorrow he might have to do it all again. Another husband might have felt unable to cope, might have left me. I stepped into the water. I fell asleep.

When I woke I was confused. I was in a different bathroom, the water still warm, a tapping on the door. I recognised nothing. The mirror was plain and unadorned, bolted to white tiles rather than blue. A shower curtain hung from a rail above me; two glasses were face down on a shelf above the sink.

I heard a voice. 'I'm coming,' it said, and I realised it was mine. I looked over to the bolted door. Two dressing gowns hung on the opposite wall, both white, monogrammed with the letters R.G.H. I stood up.

'Come on!' came a voice from outside the door. It sounded like Ben, but not Ben. It became singsong. 'Come on! Come on, come on, come on!'

'Who is it?' I said, but it did not stop. I stepped out of the bath. The floor was tiled, black and white, diagonals. It was wet; I felt myself slip and crashed to the floor, pulling the shower curtain down on top of me. My head hit the sink as I fell.

I woke for real then, with another, different voice calling me. 'Christine! Are you OK?' With relief I realised it was Ben and I had been dreaming. I was lying in the bath, my clothes still folded on the chair beside me.

'Yes,' I said. 'I'm fine. I just had a bad dream.'

I ate dinner, then went to bed. I wanted to write down all I had learned before it disappeared. I have to record these things, otherwise I will lose them for ever.

'I think I'll sleep in the spare room tonight,' I'd said to Ben. 'I'm upset. You understand?'

He'd said yes, told me that he will check on me in the morning, then kissed me good night. I hear him now, turning the key in the front door. Locking us in. It would do no good for me to wander, I suppose. Not in my condition.

I cannot believe that in a few moments, when I fall asleep, I will forget about my son all over again. The memories of him had seemed so vivid. And I had remembered him even after dozing in the bath. It does not seem possible that a longer sleep will erase everything, yet Ben, and Dr Nash, tell me that this is what will happen.

Do I dare hope that they are wrong? I am remembering more each day, waking knowing more of who I am. Perhaps writing in this journal is bringing my memories to the surface. Perhaps today is the day I will look back on and recognise as a breakthrough. It is possible.

I will stop writing soon and sleep. Pray that tomorrow I may remember my son.

Thursday, November 15
I was in the bathroom. I didn't know how long I'd been standing there. All those pictures of me and Ben. I stared at them, as if that might make Adam's image emerge. But he remained invisible.

I had woken with no memory of him. I still believed motherhood to be something that sat in the future. Even after I had seen my own middle-aged face, learned that I was a wife, old enough soon to be having grandchildren—even after those facts had sent me reeling—I was unprepared for the journal that Dr Nash told me I kept in the wardrobe when he called. I did not imagine that I would discover that I am a mother, too. As soon as I read it I knew it to be true. I had had a son. I felt it inside my pores.

Then I discovered that he is dead. My heart resisted the knowledge, tried to reject it even as I knew it was true. The journal slid from my lap and I stifled a scream of pain. I went into the bathroom, to look again at the pictures in which he ought to be. I did not know what I was going to do when Ben came home. I imagined him coming in, making dinner, and then we would watch television and all the time I would have to pretend that I didn't know I had lost a son.

It seemed more than I could bear. I began to claw at the pictures, ripping, pulling. It seemed to take no time at all, and then they were gone. Scattered on the bathroom floor. Floating in the toilet bowl.

I put this journal in my bag, took one of the twenty-pound notes that I had read were hidden behind the clock on the mantelpiece, and ran out of the house. I didn't know where I was going. I wanted to see Dr Nash but had no idea where he was. I felt helpless. And so I ran.

At the street I turned left, towards the park. It was a sunny afternoon, but it was cold. I pulled my coat tight and stepped off the kerb. The sound of brakes. A car crunched to a halt. A man's voice, muffled, from behind glass. *Get out of the way!* it said. *Stupid bitch!*

I was in the middle of the road, a stalled car in front of me, its driver screaming with fury. I had a vision: myself, metal on bone, crumpling to lie a tangled mess, the end of a ruined life. Would a second collision end what was started by the first, all those years ago? Who would miss me? My husband. A doctor, perhaps. But there is no one else. Did my friends abandon me? How quickly I would be forgotten, were I to die.

I looked at the man in the car. He, or someone like him, did this to me. Yet there he was, still living.

Not yet, I thought. However my life was to end, I didn't want it to be like this. I thought of the novel I had written, the child I had raised, even the firework party with my best friend. I still have memories to unearth. My own truth to find.

I mouthed the word *Sorry*, and ran on, through a gate and into the park.

There was a café in the middle of the grass. I bought myself coffee and sat on one of the benches. Opposite was a playground. A slide, swings, a roundabout. A small boy sat on a seat shaped like a ladybird that was fixed to the ground by a heavy spring.

My mind flashed on a vision of myself and another young girl in the park. I saw the two of us gliding to the ground on a metal slide. We would muddy our dresses and be told off by our mothers, and skip home, clutching bags of penny chews.

Was this memory? Or invention?

The boy was alone. 'Hey! Lady!' he shouted. 'You spin me!'

He got up and went over to the roundabout. 'You spin me!' he said. He tried to push the metal contraption but it barely moved. 'Please?' he said.

He looked so fragile. Helpless. I went over to him.

'You push me!' he said.

I put my coffee on the ground. 'Hold tight!' I said. I heaved my weight against the bar and walked round with it so that it gained speed. 'Here we go!' I sat on the edge of the platform.

He grinned excitedly, clutching the metal bar with his hands. His hands looked cold, almost blue. He was wearing a green coat that looked far too thin. I wondered who had sent him out without gloves, or a scarf or hat.

'Where's your mummy?' I said. He shrugged his shoulders. 'Your daddy?'

'Dunno,' he said. 'Mummy says Daddy's gone. She says he doesn't love us no more.'

He had said it with no sense of pain, or disappointment.

'I bet your mummy loves you, though?' I said.

He was silent for a few seconds. 'Sometimes,' he said.

I watched the bench I had been sitting on come towards us, then recede. We spun again, and again.

'What's your name?'

'Alfie,' he said. 'Mummy says sometimes she'd be better off if I lived somewhere else.'

My whole body tensed. I saw myself asking him if he would like to come with me. I would lift him up—he would be heavy and smell sweet, like chocolate—and together we would go into the café. I would buy him a drink, and some sweets too, and we would leave the park. He would be holding my hand as we walked back to the house I shared with my husband, and that night I would read him a story before tucking the covers under his sleeping body. And tomorrow—

Tomorrow? I have no tomorrow, I thought. Just as I had no yesterday.

'Mummy!' he called out. For a moment I thought he was talking to me, but he leaped off the roundabout and ran towards the café. I saw a woman walking towards us, clutching a plastic cup in each hand.

She crouched down as he reached her. 'Y'all right, Tiger?' she said as he ran into her arms, and she looked up at me. Her eyes were narrowed, her face set hard. *I've done nothing wrong!* I wanted to shout. *Leave me alone!*

Instead I looked the other way and then, once she had led Alfie away, I got off the roundabout. The sky was darkening now, turning to an inky blue. I didn't know what time it was, or how long I'd been out. I knew only that I couldn't go home yet. I couldn't face Ben. I couldn't face having to pretend I knew nothing about Adam. For a moment I wanted to tell him about my journal, Dr Nash. Everything. But I pushed the thought from my mind. I did not want to go home, but had nowhere else to go.

The house was in darkness. I didn't know what to expect when I pushed open the front door. Ben would be missing me; he had said he would be home by five. I realised I felt guilty and went into the house ready to make an apology.

'Ben?' I called out.

'Christine?' came a voice. He appeared above me, standing at the top of the stairs. He was wearing the clothes he'd put on that morning to go to work, but now his shirt was creased and hung loose from his trousers, and his hair stood out in all directions.

'I . . . I had to get some air,' I said.

'Thank God.' He came down the stairs and took my hand. His eyes were wide, glistening in the dim light as though he'd been crying. How much he loves me, I thought. My feeling of guilt intensified.

'I'm sorry,' I said. 'I didn't mean to—'

He interrupted me. 'Oh, let's not worry about that, shall we?' His expression changed to one of happiness. All traces of anxiety disappeared. 'You're back now. That's the main thing.'

He flicked on the light and tucked in his shirt. 'I thought we could go out? What do you think?'

'I don't think so,' I said.

'Oh, Christine. We should! You look like you need cheering up!'

'Ben, I don't feel like it.'

'Please?' he said. He took my hand again. 'It would mean a lot to me.' He took my other hand and brought them both together, between his. 'I don't know if I told you this morning. It's my birthday today.'

I told him I would freshen up and then see how I felt. I went upstairs. His mood had disturbed me. He had seemed so concerned, but, as soon as I appeared, that concern had evaporated.

I went into the bathroom. Perhaps he hadn't seen the photos scattered all over the floor, genuinely believed I had been out for a walk. There was still time for me to cover my tracks. To hide my anger, and my grief.

I locked the door and turned on the light. The floor had been swept clean. There, arranged around the mirror as if they had never been moved, were the photographs, every one perfectly restored.

I told Ben I would be ready in half an hour. I sat in the bedroom and, as quickly as I could, wrote this.

Friday, November 16

I don't know what happened after that. Maybe we went out, for a meal, to the cinema. I cannot say. I didn't write it down and do not remember, despite it being only a few hours ago. Unless I ask Ben it is lost completely. I feel like I am going mad.

This morning, in the early hours, I woke with him lying next to me. A stranger, again. The room was dark, silent. I lay, rigid with fear, not knowing who, or where, I was. Then words floated to the surface. Ben. Husband. Memory. Accident. Death. Son. Adam. I could not connect them. Then the dream came back to me, the dream that must have woken me up.

I was in a bed. In my arms was a man. He lay on top of me, heavy, his back broad. I felt peculiar, my head too light; the room rocked beneath me. I could not tell who the man was but I could feel everything, even the hairs on his chest, rough against my naked breasts. He was kissing me. He was too rough; I wanted him to stop, but said nothing. 'I love you,' he said, his words lost in my hair. I remembered how I had both wanted him and wanted him to stop, how I had told myself, as he began to kiss me, that we would not have sex, but his hand had moved down the curve of my back to my buttocks and I had let it. And, as he had moved his hand farther still, I thought, This. This is as far as I will let you go. I will not stop you now, not now, because my body is responding with tiny shudders of pleasure. But I will not have sex with you. The word *No* had even began to form in my mind, but it had turned into a moan of something I dimly recognised as pleasure.

'I love you,' he said, forcing my legs apart with one of his own. I did not want to let him, but at the same time knew that I had left it too late and now I had no choice. I had wanted it as he stepped clumsily out of his underwear, and so I must still want it now that I am beneath his body.

I tried to relax. He arched up and moaned and I saw his face. I didn't recognise it in my dream but now I knew it. Ben. 'I love you,' he said, and I knew that he was my husband, even though I felt I had met him for the first time just that morning.

I felt him tear into me. Pain or pleasure. I could not tell where one ended and the other began. I tried first to enjoy what was happening, and then, when I could not, tried to ignore it. I asked for this, I thought, at the same time as I never asked for this. Is it possible for desire to ride with fear?

I closed my eyes. I saw a face. A stranger, with dark hair, a beard. A scar down his cheek. He looked familiar. As I watched him his smile disappeared and I cried out, in my dream. That was the moment I woke up with Ben lying next to me and no idea where I was.

I got out of bed. If I had known of its existence I would have opened the wardrobe door and lifted out the shoebox that contained my journal, but

I did not. And so I went downstairs and sat on the bottom of the stairs. The sun rose, the hall turning blue through to burnt orange. Nothing made sense, the dream least of all. It felt too real, and I had woken in the same bedroom I had dreamed myself in, next to a man I was not expecting to see.

Now that I have read my journal after Dr Nash called me, a thought forms. Might it have been a memory I had retained from the previous night? If so, then it is a sign of progress, I suppose. But also it means Ben forced himself on me and, worse, as he did so, I saw an image of a bearded stranger.

But perhaps it means nothing. It was just a dream. Ben loves me and the bearded stranger does not exist.

But how can I ever know for sure?

Later, I saw Dr Nash. We were sitting at traffic lights, Dr Nash tapping his fingers on the steering wheel, not quite in time to the music from the stereo. I'd called him this morning, as soon as I had finished writing about the dream that might have been a memory. I had to speak to someone and he'd suggested we move our next meeting to today. He asked me to bring my journal. I hadn't told him what was wrong, intending to wait until we were in his offices.

The lights changed and we jerked into motion. 'Why doesn't Ben tell me about Adam?' I heard myself say.

Dr Nash coughed. 'Tell me what happened.'

It was true, then. Part of me was hoping he would ask me what I was talking about, but as soon as I said the word *Adam* I realised how futile that was. Adam feels real. He exists within me, in a way that no one else does.

I felt angry. He had known all along.

'And you,' I said. 'You gave me my novel. So why didn't *you* tell me about Adam?'

'Christine,' he said, 'tell me what happened.'

I stared out of the front window. 'After you'd given me my novel, I looked at the article that you'd put with it and, suddenly, I remembered the day it was taken. I remembered that I'd been pregnant.'

He said nothing.

'You knew about him?' I said. 'About Adam?'

He spoke slowly. 'Yes. It's in your file. He was a couple of years old when you lost your memory. Plus we've spoken about him before.'

I felt myself go cold. The bare truth—that I had gone through all this before and would therefore go through it all again—shook me.

Without warning I remembered what I had read this morning. 'When I had my scan! There were pictures of him!'

'Yes,' he said. 'From your file.'

'But you didn't mention him! Why? I don't understand.'

'Christine, I can't begin every session by telling you all the things I know but you don't. Plus, it wouldn't necessarily benefit you. It would be very upsetting for you to know that you had a child and have forgotten him.'

We were pulling into an underground car park. I wondered what else he might feel it unethical to tell me.

'There aren't any more—?' I said.

'No,' he interrupted. 'You had only Adam. He was your only child.'

The past tense. Then Dr Nash knew he was dead, too.

'You know he was killed?'

He stopped the car and turned off the engine. For a moment I thought there was still a chance. Maybe I was wrong. Adam was alive. My mind lit with the idea. Adam had felt real to me as soon as I read about him this morning, yet still his death did not. For a moment my happiness hung, balancing, but then Dr Nash spoke.

'Yes,' he said. 'I know.' He told me the same story as Ben. Adam, in the army. A roadside bomb. When he had finished he put his hand on mine.

'Christine,' he said softly. 'I'm so sorry.'

'Ben keeps the photographs of him locked away in a metal box. For my own protection. Why would he do that?'

'Let me ask you the same question. Why do you think he would do that?'

I thought of all the reasons. So he can control me. Have power over me. So he can deny me this one thing that might make me feel complete. I realised I didn't believe any of those were true. 'I suppose it's easier for him. It must be horrible to have to tell me every day that he has died.'

'Any other reasons, do you think?'

I was silent, and then realised. 'It must be hard for him, too. He was Adam's father.'

'You must try to remember that it is difficult for Ben, too. He loves you very much, I expect, and—'

'—and yet I don't even remember he exists.' I sighed. 'I must have loved him once. After all, I married him.' I thought of the stranger I had woken up with that morning, of the photos of our lives together. I thought of Adam.

A panic rose in me. I felt as though there was no way out. *Ben*, I thought to myself. I can cling to Ben. He is strong. 'What a mess,' I said. 'I just feel overwhelmed.'

'I wish I could do something to make this easier for you.' .

He looked as though he really meant it. There was a tenderness in his eyes, in the way he rested his hand on mine, and I found myself wondering what would happen if I put my hand on his, or moved my head slightly forward, opening my mouth as I did so. Would he try to kiss me? Would I let him, if he did?

Or would he think me ridiculous? I may have woken this morning thinking I am in my twenties, but I am almost fifty. Nearly old enough to be his mother. He sat perfectly still, looking at me. He seemed strong. Strong enough to get me through.

The muffled ringing of a telephone interrupted me and I realised the phone must be one of mine. I retrieved it from my bag. BEN, it said on the screen. When I saw his name I realised how unfair I was being. He was bereaved, too. And he had to live with it every day without being able to come to his wife for support. And he did all that for love.

I thought of the photos I had seen that morning, in the scrapbook. Me and Ben. Smiling. Happy. We had been in love; it was obvious.

'I'll ring him back later,' I said. I put the phone back in my bag. I will tell him tonight, I thought. About my journal. Dr Nash. Everything.

Dr Nash coughed. 'We should go up to the office. Make a start.'

'Of course,' I said. I did not look at him.

I began to write that in the car as Dr Nash drove me home. Much of it is barely legible, a hasty scrawl. Dr Nash said nothing as I wrote, but I saw him glancing at me as I searched for the right word or a better phrase.

Before we left his office he asked me to consent to him discussing my case at a conference he had been invited to attend. 'In Geneva,' he said, unable to disguise a flash of pride. I said yes, and I imagined he would soon ask me if he could take a photocopy of my journal. *For research*.

When we arrived back at the house he said, 'I'm surprised you wanted to write your book in the car. You seem very . . . determined. I suppose you don't want to miss anything out.'

He is right. I am determined. Desperate to get everything down.

Once I got in I finished the entry and put the journal back in its hiding place. Ben had left me a message: *Let's go out for dinner tonight.*

I had given Dr Nash my journal during our session—he'd asked if he could read it. This was before he'd mentioned his invite to Geneva, and I wonder now if that's why he asked. 'This is excellent!' he'd said when he finished. 'Lots of memories are coming back. You should feel very encouraged.'

But I did not feel encouraged. I felt confused. Had I flirted with him, or he with me? It was his hand on mine, but I had let him put it there. I felt guilty because I had enjoyed the attention. For a moment, there had been a tiny pinprick of joy. I had felt attractive. Desirable.

At the back of my underwear drawer I found a pair of black silk knickers and a matching bra. I put them on, all the time thinking of my journal hidden in the wardrobe. What would Ben think, if he found it? If he read all that I had written, all that I had felt? Would he understand?

I stood in front of the mirror. I examined my body with my eyes and my hands, as if it were something new, a gift. Something to be learned from scratch. Though I knew that Dr Nash had not been flirting with me, for that brief space in which I thought he was I had not felt old. I had felt alive.

I don't know how long I stood there. For me time is almost meaningless; years have slipped through me, leaving no trace. I looked at my body, at the weight in my buttocks and on my hips, the dark hairs on my legs. I found a razor in the bathroom and soaped my legs, then drew the cold blade across my skin. I must have done this before, I thought, countless times, yet still it seemed an odd thing to be doing, faintly ridiculous.

Back in the bedroom I put on stockings and a black dress, selected a gold necklace and a pair of matching earrings. I sprayed perfume on my wrists and behind my ears. A memory floated through me. I saw myself rolling on stockings, hooking up a bra, but it was a different me, in a different room. Music played softly. I felt happy. I turned to the mirror, examined my face in the glow of the candlelight.

I saw a bottle of champagne on a bedside table. Two glasses. A bouquet of flowers, a card. I saw that I was in a hotel room, alone, waiting for the man I love. I heard a knock, saw myself walk towards the door, but then it ended.

I looked up and saw myself, back in my own home. Even though the woman I saw in the mirror was a stranger, I felt ready. For what, I couldn't say. I went downstairs to wait for my husband, the man I married, the man I loved.

Love, I remind myself. The man I love.

I heard his key in the lock. 'Christine? Christine, are you all right?'

'Yes,' I said. 'I'm in here.'

For a moment I thought he was going upstairs, without coming in to see me first, and I felt ridiculous to be dressed as I was. I wished I could scrape away the make-up and transform myself back into the woman I am.

He came into the living room and stopped. His eyes travelled over my face, down my body, back up to meet mine.

'Wow,' he said. 'You look—' He shook his head.

'I found these clothes,' I said. 'I thought I would dress up a little. It's Friday night, after all.'

'Yes,' he said, still standing in the doorway. 'Yes. But . . .'

I went over to him. 'Kiss me,' I said, and put my arms around his neck. He smelled of soap, and sweat, and work.

'Kiss me,' I said, again. His hands circled my waist.

Our lips met. Brushing, at first. A kiss good night or goodbye, a kiss for being in public, a kiss for your mother.

'Kiss me, Ben,' I said. 'Properly.'

'Ben,' I said, later. 'Are we happy?' We were sitting in a restaurant, one we'd been to before, he said, though I had no idea, of course. 'I mean, we've been married . . . how long?'

'Twenty-two years,' he said.

I thought of the vision I'd had as I got ready this afternoon. Flowers in a hotel room. I can only have been waiting for him. 'Are we happy?'

A family arrived and took their seats at the table next to us. Elderly parents, a daughter in her twenties.

'We're in love, if that's what you mean. I certainly love you.'

And there was my cue to tell him I loved him too. Men always say I love you as a question. What could I say, though? He is a stranger. Love doesn't happen in the space of twenty-four hours.

'I know you don't love me,' he said. I looked at him, shocked for a moment. 'I understand the situation you're in. You don't remember, but we were in love, once. Totally, utterly. Romeo and Juliet, all that crap.' He tried to laugh, but instead looked awkward. 'We were happy, Christine.'

'Until my accident.'

He flinched at the word. Had I said too much? I'd read my journal but was it today he'd told me about the hit-and-run?

'Yes,' he said, sadly. 'Until then. Now I wish things could be different, but I'm not unhappy, Chris. I love you. I wouldn't want anyone else.'

How about me? I thought. Am I unhappy?

I looked across at the table next to us. The girl sat with her mouth slightly open, a thin string of saliva hanging from her chin. Her father noticed me watching and I looked away. They must be used to people looking away a moment too late.

'I wish I could remember what happened.'

'Why?' he said.

I thought of all the memories that had come to me. They were gone now but I had written them down; I knew they had existed—still did exist. They were just lost. I felt sure that there must be a key, a memory that would unlock all the others.

'I just think that if I could remember my accident, then maybe I could remember other things, too. Our wedding, for example, or our honeymoon. I can't even remember that.' I sipped my wine. I had nearly said our son's name before remembering that Ben didn't know I had read about him. 'Just to wake up and remember who I am would be something.'

'The doctors said that wouldn't happen.'

'But they don't *know*, do they? Surely they could be wrong?'

'I doubt it.'

He thought that my past had vanished completely. Maybe this was the time to tell him about the snatched moments I still had, about Dr Nash. My journal. Everything.

'But I am remembering things, occasionally,' I said.

'Really? What things?'

'It depends. Just odd feelings, sensations. A bit like dreams, but they seem too real for me to be making them up.'

I expected him to ask me more, to want me to tell him everything I had seen. But he continued looking at me sadly. I thought of him offering me wine in the kitchen of our first home. 'I had a vision of you,' I said.

'What was I doing?' he said.

'Not much,' I replied. 'Just standing in the kitchen.' My voice dropped to a whisper. 'Kissing me.' He smiled. 'I thought that if I am capable of having one memory, then maybe I am capable of having lots—'

He took my hand. 'But tomorrow you won't remember that memory. You have no foundation on which to build.'

What he was saying is true; I can't keep writing down everything that happens to me for the rest of my life, not if I have to read it every day.

I looked at the family next to us. The girl spooned minestrone clumsily into her mouth, soaking the bib that her mother had tucked around her neck. I could see their lives: broken, trapped by the role of care-giver.

We are the same, I thought. I need to be spoon-fed, too. Like them and their child, Ben loves me in a way that can never be reciprocated.

And yet, we were different. We still had hope.

'Maybe if there was someone I could see? A doctor?'

'We've tried before—'

'But maybe it's worth trying again? Maybe there's a new treatment?'

He squeezed my hand. 'Christine, believe me. We've tried everything.'

'What?' I said. 'What have we tried?'

'Chris, please. Don't—'

'What have we tried?' I said. 'What?'

'Everything,' he said. 'Everything. You don't know what it was like.' His eyes darted left and right as if he expected a blow and didn't know from what direction it might come. I could have let the question go then, but I didn't.

'What, Ben? I need to know. What was it like?'

He said nothing.

'Tell me!'

He lifted his head, and swallowed hard. He looked terrified, his face red, his eyes wide. 'You were in a coma,' he said. 'Everyone thought you were going to die. But not me. I knew you'd get better. One day, the hospital said you'd woken up. They thought it was a miracle, but I knew it was you coming back to me. You couldn't remember anything about the accident, but you recognised me, and your mother, though you didn't really know who we were. They said that memory loss was normal, that it would pass. But then—' He looked down to the napkin he held in his hands.

'Then what?'

'You seemed to get worse. I went in one day and you had no idea who I was. And then you forgot who you were, too. You couldn't remember your name, what year you were born. Anything. They realised that you had stopped forming new memories, too. They did tests, scans. Everything. They said your accident had damaged your memory permanently. That there was nothing they could do.'

'Nothing?'

'They said either your memory would come back or it wouldn't. They told me that all I could do was look after you. And that's what I've been trying to do.' He leaned forward, so that his head was only inches from mine. 'I love you,' he whispered, but I couldn't reply, and we ate the rest of our meal in near silence. I could feel anger growing within me. He seemed so determined that I could not be helped. Suddenly I didn't feel so inclined to tell him about my journal, or Dr Nash. I wanted to keep my secrets for a little longer. I felt they were the only thing I had that I could say was mine.

We came home. Ben made himself a coffee and I went to the bathroom. There I wrote as much as I could of the day, then took off my clothes and put on my dressing gown. Another day was ending. Soon I will sleep, and my brain will begin to delete everything.

I realised I do not have ambition. All I want is to live like everybody else, with experience building on experience, each day shaping the next. I thought of my old age, tried to imagine what it will be like. Will I wake up, in my seventies or eighties, thinking myself to be at the beginning of my life? How will I cope, when I discover that my life is behind me and I have nothing to show for it? What are we, if not an accumulation of our memories? How will I feel, when I look in a mirror and see the reflection of my grandmother? I can't allow myself to think of that now.

I heard Ben go into the bedroom and realised I would not be able to replace my journal in the wardrobe. I put it on the chair next to the bath, under my clothes. I will move it later.

Ben sat in bed, watching me. I climbed in next to him. I realised he was naked. 'I love you, Christine,' he said, and began to kiss me. His breath was hot and had the bite of garlic. I didn't push him away. I have asked for this, I thought. By wearing that stupid dress, by putting on the make-up and perfume, by asking him to kiss me before we went out.

Though I didn't want to, I kissed him back. I tried to imagine the two of us in the house we had just bought, tearing at my clothes on the way to the bedroom. I told myself that what I was doing was an expression of love, and when his hand moved to my breast I didn't stop him. Neither did I stop him when he slipped his hand between my legs and cupped me. I only knew later, much later, that when I began to moan softly, it wasn't from pleasure at all: it was fear, because of what I saw when I closed my eyes.

Me, in the hotel room I had seen earlier. I see the candles, the champagne, the flowers. I hear the knock at the door, feel excitement, anticipation; the air is heavy with promise. Sex and redemption. I take the handle of the door. I breathe deeply. Finally things will be all right.

A hole, then. A blank in my memory. The door swinging towards me but I cannot see who is behind it. There, in bed with my husband, panic slammed into me. 'Ben!' I cried out, but he didn't stop, didn't even seem to hear me. I clung to him and spiralled back into the past.

He is behind me. This man, how dare he! Pain, searing. A pressure on my throat. I cannot breathe. He is not my husband, not Ben, but still his hands are all over me, his flesh, covering me. I try to breathe, but cannot. My body, shuddering, pulped, turns to nothing. Water, in my lungs. I see nothing but crimson. I am going to die in this hotel room. Dear God, I think. I never asked for this. I have made a terrible mistake, yes, but I do not deserve this punishment. I do not deserve to die.

I feel myself disappear. I want to see Adam. I want to see my husband. But they are not here. No one is here but me and this man who has his hands around my throat. I am sliding, down, down. Towards blackness. I must not sleep. I. Must. Not. Sleep.

The memory ended suddenly. I was back in my own home, in bed, my husband inside me. With tiny, muffled grunts he ejaculated. I clung to him, holding him as tight as I could. After a moment, he kissed my neck and told me he loved me again, and then said, 'Chris, you're crying . . .'

The sobs came, uncontrollable. 'What's wrong? Did I hurt you?'

What could I say to him? I shook as my mind tried to process what it had seen. A hotel room full of flowers. Champagne and candles. A stranger with his hands around my neck.

All I could do was cry harder and push him away, and then wait until he slept and I could creep out of bed and write it all down.

Saturday, November 17—2.07 a.m.
I cannot sleep. Ben is in bed, and I am writing this in the kitchen. He thinks I am drinking a cup of cocoa that he has just made me. He thinks I will come back to bed soon. I will, but first I must write.

I had hidden my journal in the wardrobe and crept back into bed after writing about what I had seen as we made love. I felt restless. I could hear the ticking of the clock downstairs, its chimes as it marked the hours, Ben's gentle snores. You are lying to me, I thought. Lying about my novel, about Adam.

And now I feel certain he is lying about how I came to be like this.

I wanted to shake him awake. To scream, *Why?* Why are you telling me I was knocked over by a car? I wonder what he is protecting me from. How bad the truth might be. And what else is there I do not know?

My thoughts turned to the metal box in which Ben keeps the photos of Adam. Maybe there will be more answers in there.

I decided to get out of bed and crept onto the landing, pulling the bedroom door closed behind me. I had to see a photograph of Adam. But where would I look? *I keep these upstairs*, he had said. *For safety*. I knew that. I had written it down. But where, exactly?

I went into the office, closing that door behind me, too. Moonlight shone through the window, casting a greyish glow around the room. I didn't dare to switch on the light, couldn't risk Ben finding me. I had no reason for being in there. There would be too many questions to answer.

The box was metal, I had written, and grey. I looked on the desk first. A tiny computer with an impossibly flat screen, pens and pencils in a mug, papers arranged in tidy piles. Under the desk was a leather satchel and a wastepaper basket, and next to it a filing cabinet.

I pulled out the top drawer quietly. It was full of papers, in files labelled *Home, Work, Finance*. The second drawer was full of stationery and I closed it gently before crouching down to open the bottom drawer.

A blanket, or a towel; it was difficult to tell in the dim light. I raised one corner, felt beneath, touched cold metal. Underneath was the metal box, larger than I had imagined it, so big it almost filled the drawer. I almost dropped it as I lifted it out and set it on the floor.

For a moment I didn't know whether I wanted to open it. What new shocks might it contain? Like memory itself, it might hold truths that I couldn't conceive of. I was afraid. But, I realised, these truths are all I have. They are my past. They are what makes me human. Without them I am nothing.

I breathed deeply, closing my eyes as I did so, and began to lift the lid. It moved a little way but no further. Ben had locked it.

I tried to remain calm, but an anger came then, unbidden. Who was he to have locked this box of memories? To keep me from what was mine?

The key would be near, I was sure of it. I looked in the drawer. I tipped the pens and pencils out of the mug on the desk, and looked in there.

Nothing. Desperate, I searched the other drawers as well as I could in the half-light. I could find no key, and realised it might be anywhere. Anywhere at all. I sank to my knees.

A sound. A creak. Ben's voice. 'Christine?' Then, louder, 'Christine!'

A door opened, the landing light flicked on. He was coming.

I moved quickly. I put the box back and, sacrificing silence for speed, slammed the drawer closed. I shoved the pens and pencils back in the mug on the desk and then crouched on the floor again. The door began to open. 'Christine?'

I didn't know what I was about to do until I did it. I reacted instinctively, from a level lower than gut. 'Help me!' I said as he appeared at the open door. He was silhouetted against the light on the landing and, for a moment, I really did feel the terror that I was affecting. 'Please! Help me!'

'Christine! What's wrong?' He began to crouch down.

I skirted away from him until I was pressed against the wall. 'Who are you?' I said. I had begun to cry, to shake hysterically.

Ben held out his hand to me, as if I was dangerous, a wild animal. 'It's me,' he said. 'Your husband.'

'My what?' I said, and then, 'What's happening to me?'

'You have amnesia,' he said. 'We've been married for years.' And then, as he made the cup of cocoa that still sits in front of me, I let him tell me, from scratch, what I already knew.

Sunday, November 18

That happened in the early hours of Saturday morning. Today is Sunday. A whole day has gone unrecorded. Twenty-four hours lost. Twenty-four hours spent believing I have never written a novel, never had a son. Believing it was an accident that robbed me of my past.

Maybe, unlike today, Dr Nash didn't call, and I didn't find this journal. What would happen if one day he decides never to call again? I would never find it, never read it. I would not know my past.

It would be unthinkable. I know that now. My husband is telling me one version of how I came to have no memory, my feelings another. The only truth I have is what is written in this journal.

I think back to this morning. I woke suddenly. I had the sense of looking back on a wealth of history, not just a few short years. And I knew, dimly, that that history contained a child of my own.

I turned over, aware of another body in the bed. I didn't feel alarmed, but secure. Happy. The images and feelings began to coalesce into truth and memory. I saw my little boy, Adam, running towards me. And then I remembered my husband. His name. I felt deeply in love.

The feeling didn't last. I looked over at the man next to me and his face was not the one I expected to see. A moment later I realised that I didn't recognise the room in which I had slept. Finally, I understood that I could remember nothing clearly.

Ben explained it to me, and this journal explained the rest, once Dr Nash phoned me and I found it. The journal told me who I am, what I have, and what I have lost. It told me that all is not lost. That my memories are coming back, however slowly. And the journal told me that the hit-and-run was a lie, that somewhere, hidden deep, I can remember what happened to me on the night I lost my memory. That it doesn't involve a car and icy roads, but champagne and flowers and a knock on the door of a hotel room.

And now I have the name of the person I had expected to see when I opened my eyes this morning. I woke expecting to be lying next to some-one called Ed.

At the time I didn't know who he was, this *Ed*. I thought perhaps he was nobody, it was a name I invented, plucked from nowhere. But now I have read this journal. I have learned that I was assaulted in a hotel room. And so I know who this Ed is.

He is the man who was waiting on the other side of the door that night. The man who attacked me. The man who stole my life.

This evening I tested my husband. Is there only one version of the past that he tells me, or several?

We were eating lamb, a cheap joint, fatty and overcooked.

'How did I get to be like this?' I asked. 'I need you to tell me everything.'

He looked at me, his eyes narrow. 'You're sure?'

'I know I wasn't always like this. And now I am. So something bad must have happened. I have to know what it was. Don't lie to me, Ben. Please.'

He took my hand. 'Darling, I would never do that.'

And then he began. 'It was December,' he said. 'Icy roads . . .' and I lis-tened, with a mounting sense of dread, as he told me about the car accident.

When he had finished he carried on eating.

'You're sure it was an accident?'

'Why?'

I tried to calculate how much to say. I didn't want to reveal that I was keeping a journal but wanted to be as honest as I could.

'Earlier today I got an odd feeling,' I said. 'Almost like a memory. Somehow it felt like it had something to do with why I'm like this.'

'Did you remember specific things about what happened? The type of car that hit you? Even just the colour?'

I wanted to scream at him, *Why are you asking me to believe I was hit by a car?* Can it be that it is an easier story to believe?

An easier story to hear, I thought, or an easier one to tell?

I wondered what he would do if I was to say, Actually, I remember being in a hotel room, waiting for someone who wasn't you.

'It was more just a general impression,' I said.

'What do you mean, "a general impression"?' He sounded almost angry. I was no longer sure I wanted to continue.

'It was just an odd feeling, as if something bad were happening. But I don't remember any details.'

He seemed to relax. 'It's probably nothing,' he said. 'Just the mind playing tricks on you. Try to ignore it.'

Ignore it? I thought. How could he ask me to do that? Was he frightened of me remembering the truth?

It is possible. He cannot enjoy the thought of being exposed as a liar. Particularly if he is lying for my benefit. I can see how believing I was hit by a car would be easier for both of us. But how will I ever find out what really happened?

And who I had been waiting for, in that room.

'OK,' I said. 'You're probably right.' We went back to our lamb, now cold. Another thought came then. What if he *is* right? What if my mind had invented the hotel room? Was it possible that, unable to comprehend the simple fact of an accident on an icy road, I had made it all up?

If so, then my memory is not working. Things are not coming back to me. I am not getting better at all, but going mad.

I fished out the little diary from my bag and thought I was in luck when I saw Dr Nash's name. Then I saw the word *Office* next to the number. It was Sunday. He wouldn't be there. I wondered what had made me think that Dr Nash would have given me his personal number, when I remembered reading that he had written it in the front of my journal. *Ring me if you get confused*, he'd said. What am I now, if not confused? I dialled his number on the mobile phone he'd given me.

'Hello?' he said. He sounded sleepy, though it wasn't late.

'Dr Nash,' I said, whispering. 'It's Christine.'

'Oh. OK. How—' He didn't sound pleased to be hearing from me.

'I got your number from the front of my journal.'

'Of course,' he said. 'Is everything OK?'

'I'm sorry,' I said. The words fell out of me. 'I need to see you. I had a memory last night. I wrote it down. A hotel room. I couldn't breathe. But it doesn't make sense. Ben says I was hit by a car.'

I heard movement, as if he was adjusting his position, and a woman's voice. 'It's nothing,' he said, and muttered something I couldn't hear.

'Dr Nash?' I said. 'Was I hit by a car?'

'I can't really talk right now,' he said, and I heard the woman's voice again, complaining.

'Please!' I said. The word hissed out of me.

His voice again, now with authority. 'I'm sorry,' he said. 'I'm a little busy. Have you written it down?'

Busy. He spoke again. 'We'll talk tomorrow. I'll call you, on this number. I promise.'

Relief, mixed with something else. Something I don't know that I have ever felt before. Anticipation. But anticipation of what? That he will confirm that my memories are beginning to trickle back to me? Or is it more?

Perhaps the truth is more simple. I'm looking forward to talking to him.

'Yes, please,' I had said when he told me he would call. I thought of the woman's voice, realised they had been in bed.

I dismiss the thought from my mind.

Monday, November 19

The café was one of a chain. I drank my coffee out of a paper cup, dauntingly huge, as Dr Nash settled himself into the armchair opposite.

He had called not long after breakfast and then picked me up an hour or so later, after I had read most of my journal. This morning when I woke I knew that I was both an adult and a mother, although I had no inkling that I was middle-aged and my son was dead. My day so far had been one shock after another—the bathroom mirror, the scrapbook, and then this journal—culminating in the belief that I do not trust my husband. I felt disinclined to examine anything else too closely.

'How are you feeling today?' Dr Nash said.

'Confused. I woke up knowing I was an adult. I didn't realise I was married, but yesterday I wrote that I woke up and knew I had a husband . . .'

'You're still writing in your book, then?' he said, and I nodded. 'Did you bring it today?'

It was in my bag. But there were things in it now that I didn't want him to read. Personal things. Things I had written about him.

'I forgot,' I lied. I couldn't tell if he was disappointed.

'It doesn't matter. I can see it must be frustrating, that one day you remember something and the next it seems to have gone again. But it's still progress. Generally you're remembering more than you were.'

I wondered if what he'd said was still true. In the first few entries of this journal I had written of my childhood, my best friend, writing a novel. But lately I have been seeing only the son I have lost and the attack that left me like this. Things it might almost be better for me to forget.

'You said you were worried about Ben? What he's saying about the cause of your amnesia?'

What I had written yesterday seemed distant. A car accident. Violence in a hotel bedroom. Neither seemed like anything to do with me. Yet I had no choice but to believe that I had written the truth. That Ben had lied to me about how I ended up like this.

I told him what I'd written, starting with Ben's story about the accident and finishing with my recollection of the hotel room, though I mentioned neither the sex we'd been in the middle of when the memory came, nor the romance—the flowers, the candles and champagne—it had contained.

His expression was more thoughtful than surprised.

'You knew this, didn't you?' I said when I'd finished.

'Not exactly. I knew it wasn't a car accident, although since reading your journal the other day I now know that Ben has been telling you that it was. I knew you must have been staying in a hotel on the night you lost your memory. But the other details you mentioned are new. As far as I know this is the first time you've actually remembered anything yourself. This is good news, Christine.'

Good news? 'So it wasn't a car accident?'

He paused, then said, 'No, it wasn't.'

'But why didn't you tell me Ben was lying when you read my journal?'

'Because Ben must have his reasons,' he said.

'So you lied to me, too?'

'I've never lied to you. I never told you it was a car accident.'

I thought of what I had read this morning. 'But the other day,' I said. 'In your office. We talked about it . . .'

'You said that Ben had told you how it had happened, so I thought you knew the truth. I hadn't read your journal then, don't forget.'

I could see how it might happen. Both of us skirting around an issue we didn't want to mention by name.

'So what happened in that hotel room? What was I doing there?'

'I don't know everything,' he said.

'Then tell me what you do know.' The words emerged angrily, but it was too late to snatch them back.

'You're certain you want to know?' he said.

I felt like he was giving me one final chance. *You can still walk away. You can go on with your life without knowing what I am about to tell you.*

But I couldn't. Without the truth I am living less than half a life.

'Yes,' I said.

His voice was slow. He began sentences only to abort them. The story was a spiral, as if circling around something better left unsaid.

'You were attacked. It was . . .' He paused. 'Well, it was pretty bad. You were discovered wandering in the street. You weren't carrying identification and had no memory of who you were or what had happened. There were head injuries. The police initially thought you had been mugged.' Another pause. 'You were found wrapped in a blanket, covered in blood.'

I felt myself go cold. 'Who found me?' I said. 'Ben?'

'No. Not Ben. A stranger. Whoever it was called an ambulance. There was some internal bleeding and you needed an emergency operation.'

'But how did they know who I was?'

'It wasn't difficult. You'd checked into the hotel under your own name. And Ben had already contacted the police to report you as missing.'

I thought of the man who had knocked on the door of that room, the man I had been waiting for.

'Ben didn't know where I was?'

'No,' he said. 'Apparently he had no idea.'

'Or who I was with? Who did this to me?'

'No,' he said. 'Nobody was ever arrested. It was assumed that whoever attacked you removed everything from the hotel room and then fled. Apparently the hotel was busy that night—lots of people coming and going. You were probably unconscious for some time after the attack. It was the middle of the night when you left the hotel. No one saw you go.'

I realised the police would have closed the case, years ago. I will never know who did this to me, and why. Not unless I remember.

'What happened after I was taken to hospital?'

'There was difficulty in stabilising you after surgery. Your blood pressure in particular.' He paused. 'You lapsed into a coma and it was touch and go for a while, but you came round. Then it became apparent that your memory had gone. At first they thought it might be temporary. A combination of the head injury and anoxia.'

'I'm sorry,' I said. 'Anoxia?' I had stumbled over the word.

'Oxygen deprivation. You had symptoms of a severe lack of oxygen to the brain. Consistent with carbon dioxide poisoning—though there was no other evidence for this—or strangulation. There were marks on your neck. But the most likely explanation was thought to be near-drowning.' He paused as I absorbed what he was telling me. 'Did you remember anything about almost drowning?'

I closed my eyes. I saw nothing but a card on a pillow upon which I see the words *I love you*. I shook my head.

'Your memory didn't improve. When you were well enough to be moved, you were transported back to London.'

Back to London. Of course. I was found near a hotel; I must have been away from home. I asked where it was.

'In Brighton. Do you have any idea why you might have been there? There could be any number of reasons, of course.'

Yes, I thought. But only one that incorporated flickering candles and bunches of roses and didn't include my husband. I wondered if either of us was going to mention the word *affair*, and how Ben must have felt when he realised where I had been, and why.

It struck me then. The reason Ben had not given me the real explanation for my amnesia. Why would he want to remind me that once I had chosen another man over him? Look at the price I had paid.

'What happened then?' I said. 'Did I move back in with Ben?'

'No, you were still very ill. You had to stay in hospital.'

'For how long?'

'You were in the general ward for a few months. Then you were moved to a psychiatric ward.'

'But why? Why there?'

He spoke softly, but his tone betrayed annoyance. I felt suddenly that we had been through all this before, many times. 'It was more secure. You had made a reasonable recovery from your physical injuries but you didn't know who you were. You were exhibiting symptoms of paranoia, claiming the doctors were conspiring against you. You kept trying to escape.' He waited. 'You were moved for your own safety, as well as the safety of others.'

'Of others?'

'You occasionally lashed out.'

I pictured someone waking up every day, confused, not sure who they were. Asking for answers, and not getting them. Being surrounded by people who knew more about them than they did. It must have been hell.

'And then?'

'You stayed there for a while,' he said.

'How long?' He said nothing. I asked him again. 'How long?'

His face was a mixture of sadness and pain. 'Seven years.'

We left the coffee shop and Dr Nash turned to me. 'Christine, I have a suggestion,' he said, casually. A casualness that can only be affected.

'Go on,' I said. I felt numb.

'It might be helpful for you to visit the ward where you spent all that time.' My reaction was instant. 'No!' I said. 'Why?'

'Think of what happened when we went to visit your old house. You remembered something then. I'll be honest. I've already made the arrangements. They'd be happy to welcome you any time.'

'You think it might help me to get better?'

'I don't know. It might.'

'When do you want to go?'

'Today.' And then he said something odd. 'We don't have time to lose.'

The journey was not long and I took my journal out of my bag—not caring that I had told Dr Nash I didn't have it with me—and wrote that last entry. We didn't speak as he parked the car, nor as we walked through the antiseptic corridors. People were wheeled past us on trolleys. Overhead lights flickered and buzzed. I could think only of the seven years I had spent there. It felt like a lifetime ago, one I remembered nothing of.

We came to a stop outside a double door. Fisher Ward. Dr Nash pressed a button on an intercom mounted on the wall, then mumbled something into it. Another double door. A long corridor. There were doors off each side and, as we walked, I could see that they opened into glass-windowed rooms. In each was a bed, some made, some unmade, some occupied, most not.

'The patients here suffer from a variety of problems,' said Dr Nash. 'Many show schizoaffective symptoms, but there are those with bipolarity, acute anxiety, depression.'

I looked in one window. A girl was sitting on the bed, naked, staring at the television. In another a man sat on his haunches, rocking, his arms wrapped around his knees as if to shield himself from the cold.

'Why did they bring me here?'

'Before you were here, you were in the general ward. You would spend some weekends at home, with Ben. But you would wander off. Ben had to start locking the doors to the house. You became hysterical a couple of times, convinced that he had hurt you, that you were being locked in against your will. Then you went missing for something like four and a half hours. You were picked up by the police, down by the canal. Dressed only in pyjamas and a gown. They had no choice.'

He told me that Ben had campaigned to have me moved. 'He felt that a psychiatric ward was not the best place for you. He wrote to the doctors, the head of the hospital, your MP. Then a residential centre for people with chronic brain injuries opened. You were thought to be suitable, though funding was an issue. Ben had had to take a break from work to look after you and couldn't afford to fund it himself, but he wouldn't take no for an answer. There were meetings and appeals and so on, and eventually you were accepted as a patient, with the state agreeing to pay for your stay. You were moved there about ten years ago.'

I tried to imagine my husband writing letters, campaigning, threatening. It didn't seem possible. The man I had met that morning didn't seem like the kind of person to make waves. I am not the only one, I thought, whose personality has changed because of my injury.

'The home was fairly small,' said Dr Nash. 'There were lots of people to look after you. You had more independence there, and made improvements.'

'But I wasn't with Ben?'

'No. He lived at home. He needed to carry on working, and he couldn't do that and look after you. He decided—'

A memory flashed through me. I saw myself walking through these same corridors, being led back towards a room that I dimly understood as mine. I am wearing carpet slippers, a blue gown with ties up the back. The woman with me says, 'Look who's here to see you!'

A group of strangers are sitting around the bed. I see a man with dark hair and a woman wearing a beret. A child—four or five years old—comes towards me, running, and he says *Mummy* and I see that he is talking to me, and only then do I realise who he is. *Adam*. I crouch down and he runs into my arms, and I hold him and kiss the top of his head, and then I stand. 'Who are you?' I say to the group around the bed.

The man looks sad, the woman says, 'Chrissy, it's me. You know who I am, don't you?' and then comes towards me and I see that she is crying.

'No,' I say. 'Get out!' and I turn to leave and there is another woman there and I don't know who she is and I start to cry. The child is there, holding on to my knees, and I don't know who he is, but he keeps calling me *Mummy*, saying it over and over again, *Mummy, Mummy, Mummy* . . .

A hand touched my arm. I flinched as if stung. 'Christine? Are you OK? Dr Wilson is here.'

I looked up. A woman wearing a white coat stood in front of us.

'Christine? Pleased to meet you. I'm Hilary Wilson.' I took her hand. She was a little older than me, and a pair of half-moon glasses dangled on a gold chain round her neck. She nodded down the corridor. 'Shall we?'

Her office was large, lined with books. She sat behind a desk and took a file from the pile on her desk. 'Now, my dear,' she said. 'Let's have a look.'

Her image froze. 'I've met you before . . .' I said.

'Yes, you have. Though not that often.' She explained that she'd only just started working here when I moved out. That Dr Nash had said it might help me to see the room in which I'd lived. She squinted in the file, then after a minute said she didn't know which it was. 'Could we ask your husband? According to the file he and your son, Adam, visited you almost every day.'

I had read about Adam this morning and felt a flash of happiness at the mention of his name. 'No,' I said. 'I'd rather not ring Ben.'

Dr Wilson didn't argue. 'A friend of yours called Claire seemed to be something of a regular, too. How about her?'

I shook my head. 'We're not in touch.'

'What a pity. But never mind. I can tell you a little bit of what life was like here back then. Your treatment was mostly handled by a consultant psychiatrist. You underwent sessions of hypnosis, but I'm afraid any success was limited.' She read further. 'According to the notes, you were occasionally violent. Don't be alarmed: it's not unusual in people who have suffered severe head trauma, particularly when there has been damage to the part of the brain that allows self-restraint. Patients with amnesia such as yours often have a tendency to do something we call confabulation. Things don't seem to make sense and so they feel compelled to invent details. About themselves and other people around them, or about their history. It's thought to be due to the desire to fill gaps in the memory, but it can often lead to violent behaviour when the amnesiac's fantasy is contradicted. Life must have been very disorientating for you. Particularly when you had visitors.'

She paused, then continued. 'We have some pages from a sort of diary that you were keeping,' she said. 'Take a look at them. You might find it easier to understand your confusion.'

She pushed a sheet of blue paper over to me. I saw that it was covered in an unruly scrawl. At the top the letters were well formed, but towards the bottom they were large and messy, inches tall, just a few words across. *8.15 a.m.*, read the first entry. *I have woken up. Ben is here.* Directly underneath I had written, *8.17 a.m. Ignore that last entry. It was written by someone else*, and underneath that, *8.20 I am awake NOW. Before I was not. Ben is here.* My eyes flicked further down the page. *10.07 NOW I am definitely awake. All these entries are a lie. I am awake NOW.*

I looked up. 'This was really me?' I said.

'Yes. For a long time you were in a perpetual state of feeling that you had just woken up from a very deep sleep.' Dr Wilson pointed at the page in front of me. *I have been asleep for ever. It was like being DEAD. I have only just woken up.* 'They encouraged you to write down what you were feeling in an effort to get you to remember what had happened before. But I'm afraid you just became convinced that all the preceding entries had been written by someone else.'

'Was I really this bad?' I said.

'For a while, yes,' said Dr Nash. 'You retained memory for only a few seconds. That time has gradually lengthened over the years.'

It seemed to be the work of someone whose mind was completely fractured. I saw the words again. *It was like being DEAD.*

Panic hit me. I stood up, but the room began to spin. 'I want to leave,' I said. 'This isn't me. I—I would never hit people. I just—'

Dr Nash stood, too, and then Dr Wilson. She stepped forward, colliding with her desk, sending papers flying. A photograph spilled to the floor.

'Dear God—' I said, and she looked down, then crouched to cover it with another sheet. But I had seen enough. 'Was that me?' I said, my voice rising to a scream. 'Was that me?'

The photograph was of the head of a woman. At first it looked as though she was wearing a Halloween mask. One eye was open, the other closed by a huge, purple bruise. Her cheeks were distended, giving her face a grotesque appearance. I thought of pulped fruit. Of plums, rotten and bursting.

'Was that me?' I screamed again, even though, despite the swollen, distorted face, I could see that it was.

Part of me was calm. It watched as the other part of me thrashed and screamed and had to be restrained by Dr Nash and Dr Wilson. The other part was stronger. It had taken over, become the real me. I tore open the door and ran. An image of bolted doors. Alarms. A man, chasing me. My son, crying. I have done this before, I thought. I have done all this before.

My memory blanks.

The next thing I can remember is sitting next to Dr Nash as he drove. He was talking, but I couldn't concentrate. I wondered whether this search for truth was really what I wanted. It might help me to improve, but how much can I hope to gain? I don't expect that I will ever wake up as normal people do, knowing what I did the day before, what circuitous route has led me to the person I am. The best I can hope for is that one day looking in the mirror will not be a total shock, that I will remember I married a man called Ben and lost a son called Adam, that I will not have to see a copy of my novel to know that I had written one.

But even that much seems unattainable. I thought of what I had seen in Fisher Ward. Madness and pain. I am closer to that than I am to recovery. Perhaps it would be best if I learned to live with my condition. I could tell Dr Nash I don't want to see him again and I could burn my journal, burying the truths I have already learned. Then I could live simply. One day would follow another, unconnected. How easy that would be, I thought. So much easier than this.

I thought of the picture I'd seen. Who did that to me? *Why?* The memory

I'd had of the hotel room was still there, just out of reach. I had read this morning that I had reason to believe I had been having an affair, but now realised that I didn't know who it had been with. All I had was a single name, with no promise of ever remembering more.

Dr Nash was still talking. 'Am I getting better?' I said.

'Do you think you are?'

'I don't know. I suppose so. I can remember things from my past sometimes. I remember Claire. Adam. My mother. But they're like threads I can't keep hold of. I can't remember my wedding. I can't remember Adam's first steps, his first word. I can't remember him starting school, his graduation. Anything. I can't even remember learning he was dead. Or burying him. Sometimes I don't even think that he's dead. Sometimes I think that Ben's lying to me about that as well as everything else.'

'Everything else?'

'Yes. My novel. The attack. The reason I have no memory. Everything.'

'But why do you think he would do that?'

A thought came to me. 'Because I was unfaithful to him?'

'Christine,' he said. 'That's unlikely, don't you think?'

He was right, of course. Deep down, I didn't believe Ben's lies could really be a protracted revenge for something that had happened years ago. The explanation was likely to be much more mundane.

'You know,' said Dr Nash, 'these snatches of memory are definitely a sign of progress.'

I turned to him, sudden anger spilling out of me. 'You call this progress?' I was almost shouting. 'If that's what it is, I don't know if I want it.' I closed my eyes and abandoned myself to my grief. It felt better, somehow, to be helpless. I didn't feel ashamed.

Dr Nash stopped the car. Switched off the engine. I opened my eyes. We had left the main road and in front of me was a park. Through the blur of my tears I could see a group of teenagers playing football.

'Christine,' he said. 'I'm sorry. Perhaps today was a mistake. I thought we might trigger other memories. I was wrong. In any case, you shouldn't have seen that picture.'

'I don't even know if it was the picture,' I said. I had stopped sobbing now. 'It was everything. Seeing those people, imagining that I'd been like that once. And the diary. I can't believe I was that ill.'

He handed me a tissue. 'But you're not any more,' he said.

'Maybe it's worse. I'd written that it was like being dead but this is worse. This is like dying every day. I can't imagine going on like this for much longer. I know I'll go to sleep tonight and then tomorrow I will wake up and not know anything again, and the next day, and the day after that, for ever. It's not life, it's just an existence. It's how animals must be. The worst thing is that I don't even know what I don't know. There might be lots of things waiting to hurt me. Things I haven't even dreamed about yet.'

He put his hand on mine. I fell into him and he opened his arms and held me. 'It's OK,' he said. 'It's OK.' I could feel his chest under my cheek and I breathed, inhaling his scent, fresh laundry and, faintly, something else. Sweat and sex. His hand was on my back and I felt it move, felt it touch my hair, my head. 'It'll be all right,' he said.

'I just want to remember what happened on the night I was attacked. I feel that if I could only remember that, then I would remember everything.'

'There's no evidence that's the case.'

'But it's what I think,' I said. 'I know it, somehow.'

I felt his body, hard against mine, and breathed in deeply. As I did so, I thought of another time when I was being held. Another memory.

My body is being pressed up against that of another, though this is different. I do not want to be held by this man. He is hurting me. I am struggling, trying to get away, but he is strong. He speaks. *Bitch*, he says. *Slut*. And though I want to argue with him I do not. I am crying, screaming. I see the blue fabric of his shirt, a door, a dressing table with three mirrors and a picture—a painting of a bird—above it. I can see his arm, strong, muscled. *Let me go!* I say, and then I am falling, or the floor is rising to meet me. He grabs a handful of my hair and drags me towards the door. I twist my head to see his face.

It is there that memory fails me again. Though I remember looking at his face, it is featureless, a blank.

Please, I cry, please don't! But my attacker hits anyway, and I taste blood. He drags me along the floor, and then I am in the bathroom, on the cold tiles, black and white. The room smells of orange blossom, and I remember how I had been looking forward to bathing, thinking that maybe I would still be in the bath when he arrived, and then we would make love, making waves in the soapy water, soaking the floor. Because finally, after all these months of doubt, it has become clear to me. I love this man. I love him.

My head slams into the floor. Once, twice, a third time. My vision blurs.

He shouts something, but I can't hear what. It echoes, as if there are two of him, both holding me, both twisting my arm, both grabbing handfuls of my hair as they kneel on my back. I swallow. Blood. My head jerks back. I am on my knees. I see water, bubbles, already thinning. His hand is round my throat and I cannot breathe. I am pitched forward, down, down, and then my head is in the water. Orange blossom in my throat.

I heard a voice. 'Christine! Stop!' Somehow, I was out of the car. I was running across the park, and running after me was Dr Nash.

We sat on a bench. I felt the sun against the back of my neck, saw its long shadows on the ground. The boys were still playing football. Dr Nash had asked me what had happened.

'I remembered something,' I said.

'About the night you were attacked?'

'Yes,' I said. 'How did you know?'

'You were screaming. You kept saying, "Get off me," over and over. Do you want to tell me what you saw?'

I felt as if some ancient instinct was telling me that this was a memory best kept to myself. But I needed his help. I told him everything.

When I had finished he said, 'You don't remember what he looked like? The man who attacked you? Or his name?'

'No,' I said. 'Do you think it might help to know who did this to me? To see him? Remember him?'

He was silent, then said, 'It might help to go back to Brighton.'

'No,' I said.

'It might help. We can go together.'

'I can't go back there. I just can't.'

He smiled, but seemed disappointed. I felt eager to give him something, to have him not give up on me. 'Dr Nash?' I said. 'The other day I wrote that something had come to me. Perhaps it's relevant.'

He turned to face me. Our knees touched. Neither of us drew away.

'When I woke I knew I was in bed with a man. I remembered a name. But it wasn't Ben's name. I wondered if it was the person I'd been having the affair with. The one who attacked me.'

'It's possible,' he said. 'It might have been the beginning of the repressed memory emerging. What was the name?'

'Ed,' I whispered. 'I imagined waking up with someone called Ed.'

Silence. A heartbeat that seemed to last for ever.

'Christine,' he said. 'That's my name. I'm Ed. Ed Nash.'

My mind raced for a moment. My first thought was that he had attacked me. 'What?' I said, panicking.

'That's my name. I've told you that before. Maybe you've never written it down. My name is Edmund. Ed.'

I realised it could not have been him. He would barely have been born.

'You may be confabulating,' he said. 'Like Dr Wilson explained.'

'Yes,' I said. 'I—'

'Or maybe you were attacked by someone with the same name?' He was making light of the situation, but in doing so revealed he had already worked out what occurred to me only later. I had woken that morning happy. Happy to be in bed with someone called Ed. But it was not a memory. It was a fantasy. Waking with this man called Ed was not something I had done in the past but—even though my conscious, waking mind didn't know who he was—something I wanted to do in the future. I want to sleep with Dr Nash.

And now, inadvertently, I have revealed the way I must feel about him.

He was professional, of course. We both pretended to attach no significance to what had happened. We walked back to the car and he drove me home, chatting about trivialities. At one point he said, 'We're going to the theatre tonight,' and I noted his careful use of the plural. Don't worry, I wanted to say. I know my place. But I didn't want him to think of me as bitter.

He told me he would call me tomorrow. 'If you want to continue?'

'Yes,' I said.

'Good. Next time I think we should visit somewhere else from your past: the care home you were moved to when you left Fisher Ward. Waring House is not too far from where you live. Shall I ring them?'

I wondered what good it might do, but then realised there were no other options. I cannot stop until I have learned the truth.

'Ring them,' I said.

Tuesday, November 20

It is morning. Ben has suggested that I clean the windows. 'I've written it on the board in the kitchen,' he said as he got into his car. I looked. *Wash windows* he had written, adding a tentative question mark. I wondered what he thought I did all day. He doesn't know I now spend hours reading my journal, and sometimes hours more writing in it. He does not know there are days when I see Dr Nash.

I wonder what I did before my days were taken up like this. *Wash windows*. Possibly some days I read things like that and feel resentful, but today I viewed it as nothing more sinister than the desire to keep me occupied. I thought how difficult it must be to live with me. Ben must worry constantly that I will get confused, and wander off, or worse. He has never told me that I started the fire, though I must have. He has forgiven me for that, just as he must have forgiven me for so much more. I realised that Ben must have known that I was having an affair—certainly once I'd been discovered in Brighton, if not before. How much strength it must have taken to look after me once I had lost my memory, with the knowledge that I had been intending to fuck someone else when it had happened. He had stood by me, where another man might have left me to rot.

I filled a red plastic bucket with hot water, adding a squirt of soap and a tiny drop of vinegar. How have I repaid him? I thought. I began to soap the kitchen window. I have been seeing doctors, visiting our old homes and the places I was treated after my accident, all without telling him. And why? Because he has made the decision to protect me from the truth? I took another cloth and polished the window to a shine.

Now I know the truth is even worse. This morning I woke with an almost overwhelming sense of guilt, thinking I had woken with a man who was not my husband. Later I discovered that I have betrayed him twice. The first time years ago, and now I have done it again—with my heart if nothing else—as I have developed a crush on a doctor who is trying to help me. A doctor who I know is much younger than I am, and has a girlfriend. And I have told him how I feel! I feel more than guilty. I feel stupid.

As I cleaned the glass, I make a decision. Even if Ben doesn't share my belief that my treatment will work, I can't believe he would deny me the opportunity to see for myself. Surely I can trust him with the truth? This can't go on. I will tell my husband. Tonight.

I wrote that an hour ago, but now I am not so sure. I think about Adam. I have read about the photographs in the box, yet there are no pictures of him on display. I can't believe anyone could lose a son and then remove all traces of him from his home. Can I trust a man who can do that? I read about the day on Parliament Hill when I had asked him straight. He had lied. I read it again. *We never had children?* I said, and he had replied, *No. No, we didn't.* Can he really have done that just to protect me?

It occurs to me that the reason he shortens explanations and changes stories is not to do with me at all. Perhaps it's so that he doesn't drive himself crazy with the constant repetition.

Later. I have just finished speaking to Dr Nash. I was dozing in the living room when the phone rang. For a moment I couldn't tell where I was. I thought I heard voices: one was mine, and the other sounded like Ben. He was saying, *You fucking bitch*, and worse. I screamed at him, in anger, and then in fear. A door slammed, the thud of a fist, breaking glass. Then I realised I was dreaming.

I opened my eyes. A chipped mug of cold coffee sat on the table in front of me, the phone buzzing nervously next to it. I picked it up.

It was Dr Nash. He introduced himself, though his voice had sounded familiar anyway. I told him that I'd read my journal.

'You know what we talked about yesterday?' he said. I felt a flash of shock. Horror. He had decided to tackle things, then. I felt a bubble of hope—perhaps he really had felt the same way I had, the same confused mix of desire and fear—but it didn't last. 'About going to the place where you lived after you left the ward?' he said. 'Waring House? I called them this morning. We can visit any time we like. We could go on Thursday.'

'That seems fine,' I said. It didn't matter to me when we went. I was not optimistic it would help.

I was about to say goodbye when I remembered what I had been writing before I dozed. I realised that my sleep couldn't have been deep, or else I would have forgotten everything.

'Dr Nash?' I said. 'Can I talk to you about Ben?'

'Of course.'

'I'm confused. He doesn't tell me about things. Adam. My novel. And he lies about other things. He tells me it was an accident that caused me to be like this.'

A pause. 'Why do you think he does this?' He emphasised the *you* rather than the *why*.

'He doesn't know I'm writing things down. He doesn't know I know any different. I suppose it's easier for him.'

'Just him?'

'No, for me, too. Or he thinks it is. But it isn't. It just means I don't know if I can trust him.'

'Christine, we're constantly changing facts to make things fit in with our preferred version of events. We do it automatically. If we tell ourselves something happened often enough we start to believe it, and then we actually remember it. Isn't that what Ben's doing?'

'But I feel like he's taking advantage of me. He thinks he can rewrite history in any way that he likes and I will never know. But I do know. And so I don't trust him.'

'So,' he said. 'What do you think you can do about it?'

I knew the answer already. I have read what I wrote this morning, over and over. About how I should trust him. 'I have to tell him I am writing my journal,' I said. 'I have to tell him I have been seeing you.'

I don't know what I expected. Disapproval? But when he spoke he said, 'I think you might be right.'

'You agree?'

'Yes,' he said. 'I've been thinking it might be wise. I had no idea that Ben's version of the past would be so different from what you're starting to remember. But it also occurs to me that we're getting only half the picture. From what you've said, more of your repressed memories are beginning to emerge. It might be helpful for you to talk with Ben about the past.'

'You think so?'

'Yes,' he said. 'Perhaps keeping our work from Ben was a mistake. Plus I spoke to a woman you became close to at Waring House. Nicole. She's only recently returned to work there, but she was so happy when she found out that you'd gone to live at home. She said no one could have loved you more than Ben. He came to see you pretty much every day and tried hard to be cheerful, despite everything. They all got to know him very well.' He paused. 'Why don't you suggest Ben comes with us? I probably ought to meet him anyway.'

'You've never met?'

'No,' he said. 'We only spoke briefly on the phone when I first approached him about meeting you. It didn't go too well . . .'

It struck me then, the reason he was suggesting I invite Ben. He wants to bring everything into the open, to make sure that the awkwardness of yesterday can never be repeated.

'OK.'

Then he said, 'Christine? You read your journal?'

'Yes.'

'I didn't ring this morning. I didn't tell you where it was.'

I realised I had gone to the wardrobe almost without thinking. I had found it myself. As if I had remembered it would be there.

'That's excellent,' he said.

I am writing this in bed. It is late, but Ben is in his office, across the landing. I can hear the clatter of the keyboard, the click of the mouse, the creak of his chair. I trust that I will hear him switch off his machine, that I will have time to hide my journal when he does. Despite what I agreed with Dr Nash, I don't want my husband to find out what I have been writing.

I talked to him this evening, as we sat in the dining room. 'Why did we never have children?'

'It never seemed to be the right time. And then it was too late.'

I was disappointed. He had got home late. We had eaten in near silence. I had asked him if everything was OK, but he had shrugged. 'It's been a long day,' was all he would tell me. Discussion was choked off before it had begun and I thought better of telling him about my journal and Dr Nash. Anxiety gnawed at me. I could feel the opportunity to speak slipping away. Eventually I could bear it no longer. 'But did we want children?' I said.

He sighed. 'Christine, do we have to?'

'I'm sorry,' I said. It might have been better to let it go but I couldn't do that. 'It's just that the oddest thing happened today. I remembered having a baby.'

He sat back in his chair. His eyes widened and then closed completely.

'Is it true?' I said. 'Did we have a baby?' If he lies now, I thought, then I don't know what I will do. Argue with him, I suppose. Tell him everything in one uncontrolled, catastrophic outpouring.

He opened his eyes and looked into mine. 'Yes,' he said. 'It's true.'

He told me about Adam, and relief flooded through me. Relief tinged with pain. All those years, lost for ever. Ben told me about Adam's birth, his childhood, his life. Where he'd gone to school, the nativity play he'd been in, his skills on the football pitch, his disappointment in his exam results. Girlfriends. The time an indiscreet roll-up had been mistaken for a joint. He seemed happy to be talking about his son.

'But there are no photographs of him,' I said. 'Anywhere.'

He looked uncomfortable. 'I know. You get upset.'

'Upset?'

He said nothing. He looked defeated, somehow. Drained. I felt guilty, for what I was doing to him, for what I did to him, every day.

'It's OK,' I said. 'I know he's dead.'

He looked surprised. 'You . . . know?'

I was about to tell him about my journal but I did not. His mood seemed fragile. It could wait. 'I just feel it.'

'That makes sense. I've told you about it before.'

Of course he had. Just as he had told me about Adam's life before. And yet one story felt real and the other did not. I realised I didn't believe that my son was dead.

'Tell me again,' I said.

He told me about the war, the roadside bomb. He talked about Adam's funeral, told me about the salvo of shots that had been fired over the coffin, the Union Jack that was draped over it. I tried to push my mind towards memories. Nothing would come.

'I want to go there,' I said. 'I want to see his grave.'

Without memory, I would have to see evidence that he was dead, or else forever carry around the hope that he was not.

I thought he might say no. Tell me it might upset me too much. What would I do then? How could I force him?

But he did not. 'We'll go at the weekend,' he said.

I stood at the sink, dipping the dishes Ben passed to me into hot, soapy water, passing them back to him to be dried. I forced myself to think of Adam's funeral, imagined myself looking at a coffin suspended over a hole in the ground. I tried to imagine the volley of shots, the lone bugler playing as we—his family, his friends—sobbed in silence. But I could not. It was not long ago, and yet I saw nothing.

I tried to imagine how I must have felt. I would have woken up that morning without any knowledge that I was even a mother; Ben must have first had to convince me that I had a son, and then that we were to spend that very afternoon burying him. I imagine not horror but numbness, disbelief. There is only so much that a mind can take and surely none can cope with that. I looked at Ben's reflection in the window. He would have had to cope with all that at a time when his own grief was at its most acute. It might have been kinder if he hadn't taken me to the funeral at all. I wondered if that was what he had done.

I still didn't know whether to tell him about Dr Nash. He looked tired, almost depressed. I couldn't help but feel I was to blame for his mood. I realised how much I cared for him. I couldn't say whether I loved him but that is because I don't really know what love is. Despite the nebulous memory I have of him, I feel love for Adam, feel that he is part of me and without him I am incomplete. For my mother, too. When my mind sees her, I feel a different love. A more complex bond, with caveats and reservations. But Ben? I find him attractive. Despite the lies he has told me I know that he has only my best interests at heart. But can I say I love him, when I am only distantly aware of having known him for more than a few hours?

I must make more effort, I decided. This journal could be a tool to improve both our lives, not just mine.

I was about to ask how he was when a plate clattered to the floor and shattered. Ben sank to the floor, cursing under his breath, snatching at the larger chunks.

'I'm sorry,' I said. 'I'm so clumsy!'

'Fuck!' He dropped the remains of the plate and began to suck the thumb of his left hand. Droplets of blood spattered the linoleum.

'Are you OK?' I said.

He looked up at me. 'I cut myself, that's all. Stupid fucking—'

'Let me see.' I reached for his hand.

'For fuck's sake!' he said, batting my hand away. 'Just leave it! OK?'

I was stunned. He hadn't shouted exactly, but neither had he made any attempt to hide his annoyance. We faced each other, balanced on the edge of an argument.

'I'm sorry,' I said, even though part of me resented it.

His face softened. 'I'm sorry, too.' He paused. 'I'll just go upstairs. Take a shower. OK?'

I heard the bathroom door close, a tap turn on. I gathered the pieces of the plate and put them in the bin, before sponging up the blood. When I had finished I went into the living room, where the TV was on.

The flip-top phone was ringing, muffled by my bag. Dr Nash. Above me I could hear the creak of floorboards as Ben moved from room to room upstairs. I didn't want him to hear me talking on a phone he doesn't know I have. I answered, whispering, 'Hello?'

'Christine, can you speak?' Dr Nash's voice was urgent. 'Have you spoken to Ben yet?'

'Yes,' I said. 'Sort of.'

'Did you tell him about your journal? About me?'

'No,' I said. 'I was about to. He's upstairs, I—what's wrong?'

'It's probably nothing to worry about. Nicole from Waring House just called to give me the phone number of your friend, Claire. She called there, wanting to talk to you.'

'I don't understand,' I said. 'Recently?'

'No,' he said. 'It was a couple of weeks after you left to live with Ben. She took Ben's number, but she called again later to say she couldn't get through to him. She asked for your address. They couldn't give it to her, of course, but said that she could leave her number in case you or Ben ever called. Nicole found a note in your file after we spoke this morning and she rang back to give the number to me.'

'But why didn't they just post it to me? Or to Ben?'

'Nicole said they did.'

'Ben handles all the mail,' I said.

'Has Ben given you Claire's number?'

'No. He said she moved away to New Zealand.'

'Well . . . it's not an international number.'

'So she moved back?'

'Nicole said Claire used to visit you all the time at Waring House. She never heard anything about her moving away to New Zealand.'

There must be a rational explanation, I thought. There has to be. I wanted him to stop talking, to undo the things he had said, but he did not.

'There's something else,' said Nash. 'Nicole was surprised that you were back living with Ben. I asked why.'

'OK,' I heard myself say. 'Go on.'

'She said that you and Ben were divorced.'

The room tipped. It didn't make sense. On the television, a blonde woman was screaming at an older man. I wanted to scream, too.

'She said that you and Ben were separated. Ben left you a year or so after you moved to Waring House.'

'Separated?' I said. 'You're sure?'

'That's what she said. She said she felt it might have had something to do with Claire. She wouldn't say anything else.'

'Claire?'

Even through my own confusion I could hear how difficult he was finding this conversation. 'I don't know why Ben isn't telling you everything,' he said. 'I did think he believed he was protecting you. But now I don't know. To not tell you that Claire is still local? To not mention your divorce? It doesn't seem right.' I said nothing. 'I thought maybe you should speak to Claire. She might have some answers. Do you have a pen?'

I reached for a corner of the newspaper and wrote down the number that he gave me. I heard Ben come onto the landing.

'Christine?' said Dr Nash. 'Don't say anything to Ben. Not until we've figured out what's going on. OK?'

I heard myself agree. He told me not to forget to write in this journal before I went to sleep. I wrote *Claire* next to the number, and tore it off and put it in my bag.

Ben came downstairs. I wanted to ask him if I was still in touch with Claire, but did not want to hear another lie.

'Are you all right?' he said. I nodded.

He looked relieved. 'I have work to do upstairs. I'll come to bed soon.'

I looked at him then. I didn't know who he was.

'Yes,' I said. 'I'll see you later.'

Wednesday, November 21

I have spent all morning reading this journal. And now I am in the bedroom, sitting in the bay, writing more. I have the phone in my lap. Why does it feel so difficult to dial Claire's number?

I want to ask Dr Nash what to do or, better, to ask him to do it for me. But for how long can I be a visitor in my own life? I need to take control. The thought crosses my mind that I may never see Dr Nash again now that I have told him of my feelings, but I don't let it take root. Either way, I need to speak to Claire myself.

But what will I say? There seems to be so much for us to talk about, and yet so little. I think of what Dr Nash had told me about why Ben and I separated. *Something to do with Claire.*

It all makes sense. Years ago, my husband divorced me, and now we are back together he is telling me that my best friend moved to the other side of the world before any of this happened. Is that why I can't call her? Because I am afraid that she might have more to hide? Is that why Ben seems less than keen for me to remember more? Is that even why he has been suggesting that treatment is futile, so that I will never be able to link memory to memory and know what has been happening?

I cannot imagine he would do that. Nobody would. I think of what Dr Nash told me about my time in the hospital. *You were claiming the doctors were conspiring against you,* he said. *Exhibiting symptoms of paranoia.*

I wonder if that is what I am doing now.

Suddenly a memory floods me. Claire and me, another party. 'Christ,' she is saying. 'Everyone's so bloody hung up on sex. It's just animals copulating, y'know? No matter how much we dress it up as something else.'

Is it possible that with me stuck in my own hell, Claire and Ben have sought solace in each other?

I have no idea where Ben goes every morning, or where he might stop off on the way home. And I have no opportunity to build suspicion on suspicion. Even if one day I were to discover Claire and Ben in bed, the next I would forget what I had seen. I am the perfect person on whom to cheat.

I think this and yet, somehow, I don't think this. I trust Ben and yet I don't.

I dialled the number, of course. It rang for a while, then there was a click, and a voice. 'Hi, please leave a message.'

I knew the voice at once. It was Claire's. Unmistakable.

I left her a message. 'Please call me,' I said. 'It's Christine.'

I went downstairs. I had done all I could do.

I waited for an hour that turned into two. I spent the time writing in my journal and made a sandwich. While I was in the kitchen the doorbell rang.

Through the frosted glass I could see the outline of a man wearing what looked like a suit. It was Dr Nash. I knew, partly because it could be no one else, but partly because I recognised him. His hair was short, parted, his tie loose and untidy.

'Christine? It's me. Dr Nash? Did you read your journal?'

'Yes, but . . . Did we have a meeting arranged?'

'Yes,' he said. 'Can I come in?'

I wasn't sure I wanted to invite him in. It seemed wrong somehow. A betrayal. But of what? Ben's trust? I didn't know how much that mattered to me any more.

I opened the door and took his jacket. 'In there,' I said, pointing to the living room and he went through.

I made us both a coffee and sat opposite him. He put his cup down on the table between us.

'You don't remember asking me to come round?' he said.

'No,' I said. 'When?'

'This morning. When I rang to tell you where to find your journal.'

I could remember nothing of him calling that morning and still can't.

'I don't remember,' I said. A panic began to rise within me.

Concern flashed on his face. 'Have you slept at all today?'

'No,' I said, 'I just can't remember. When was it?'

'Christine, please. It doesn't mean anything. You just forgot, that's all. Everyone forgets things sometimes.'

'But whole conversations? It must have only been a couple of hours ago!'

'Yes,' he said softly. 'But your memory has always been variable. Forgetting one thing doesn't mean that you're deteriorating. OK?'

I nodded, desperate to believe him.

'You asked me here because you wanted to speak to Claire, but weren't sure you could. And you wanted me to speak to Ben on your behalf.'

'I did?'

'You said you didn't think you could do it yourself.'

I didn't believe him. I must have found my journal myself. I hadn't asked him here today. I didn't want him to talk to Ben. Why would I, when I had decided to say nothing to Ben myself yet? And why would I tell him I needed him here to help me speak to Claire, when I had already phoned her myself and left a message?

I wondered what other reasons he might have for coming.

'Why are you really here?' I said. Possibly he just wanted to see inside the place where I live. Or possibly to see me, one more time, before I speak to Ben. 'Are you worried that Ben won't let me see you after I tell him?'

'No. I came because you asked me to. Besides, you've decided not to tell Ben that you're seeing me. Not until you've spoken to Claire. Remember?'

I shook my head. I didn't remember. 'Claire is fucking my husband.'

He looked shocked. 'Christine, I—'

'They've been having an affair for years. It explains everything. Why he tells me she moved away. Why I haven't seen her even though she's supposedly my best friend.'

'Christine, you're not thinking straight.' He came and sat beside me on the sofa. 'Ben loves you. I've spoken to him, when I wanted to persuade him to let me see you. He was totally loyal. He told me that he'd lost you once and didn't want to lose you again. That he'd watched you suffer whenever people tried to treat you. He loves you. He's trying to protect you.'

I thought of what I had read this morning. Of the divorce. 'But he left me. To be with her.'

'If that was true, why would he bring you back here? He would just have left you in Waring House. But he looks after you. Every day.'

I felt as if I understood his words, yet at the same time didn't. I felt the warmth his body gave off, saw the kindness in his eyes. He spoke, but I didn't hear what he said. I heard only one word. *Love.*

I didn't intend to do what I did. It happened suddenly. In a moment all I could feel were my lips on his, my arms around his neck. I wanted to tell him what I felt, but I did not, because to do so would have been to stop kissing him. I felt like a woman, finally. In control.

He did not push me away roughly. He was gentle. He simply removed his lips from mine, then my hands from where they had come to rest on his shoulder, and said softly, 'No.'

I was stunned. At what I had done? Or his reaction to it? I cannot say. It felt only that, for a moment, a new Christine had taken me over completely and then vanished. I was not horrified, though. I was glad. Glad that, because of her, something had happened.

'I'm sorry,' he said, and I couldn't tell what he felt. Anger? Pity? Regret? Perhaps the expression I saw was a mixture of all three. He was still holding my hands and he put them back in my lap, then let them go.

I didn't know what to do. 'Ed. I love you.'

'Christine,' he began, 'I—'

'Don't tell me you haven't felt it too. You know you love me.'

'Christine,' he said. 'Please, you're confused.'

I laughed. '"Confused"?'

'Yes,' he said. 'You don't love me. You remember we talked about confabulation? It's quite common with people who—'

'I know. With people who have no memory. Is that what you think this is?'

'It's possible. Perfectly possible.'

I hated him then. He thought he knew everything, knew me better than I did myself. All he really knew was my condition.

'I'm not stupid,' I said.

'I know that, Christine. I don't think you are. I just think—'

'You must love me. Why else have you been coming here so much? Driving me around London. Do you do that with all your patients?'

'I've been trying to help you,' he said.

'Is that all?'

'Well, no. I've been writing the scientific paper—'

'Studying me?'

'Sort of,' he said.

'But you didn't tell me that Ben and I were separated,' I said. 'Why?'

'I didn't know!' he said. 'It wasn't in your file, and Ben didn't tell me. I would have told you. If I'd known.'

'Would you?' I said. 'Like you told me about Adam?'

He looked hurt. 'Christine, please.'

'Why did you keep him from me?' I said. 'You're as bad as Ben!'

'We've been through this. Ben wasn't telling you about Adam. I couldn't tell you. It wouldn't have been ethical.'

I laughed. 'What is ethical about keeping him from me?'

'It was down to Ben to tell you about Adam. Not me. I suggested you keep a journal, so that you could write down what you'd learned.'

'How about the attack, then? You were quite happy for me to go on thinking I'd been involved in a hit-and-run accident!'

'Ben told you that. I didn't know that's what he was saying to you. How could I?'

I thought of orange-scented baths and hands around my throat. The feeling that I couldn't breathe. The man whose face remained a mystery. I began to cry. 'Then why did you tell me at all?' I said.

He spoke kindly. 'I didn't tell you that you were attacked. You remembered that yourself.' He was right, of course.

'I want you to leave,' I said. I was crying solidly now, yet felt curiously alive. I could barely remember what had been said, but it felt as if some dam within me had finally burst.

'Please,' I said. 'Please go.'

I expected him to argue. But he did not. 'If you're sure?' he said.

'Yes.' I turned towards the window, determined not to look at him again today, which for me will mean that by tomorrow I might as well never have seen him at all.

'I'll call you,' he said. 'Tomorrow? Your treatment. I—'

'Just go,' I said. 'Please.'

He said nothing else. I heard the door close behind him.

I sat there for a while. I felt empty and alone. Eventually I went upstairs. In the bathroom I looked at the photos. My husband. Ben. I have nothing, now. No one I can trust. No one I can turn to. I kept thinking of what Dr Nash had said. *He loves you. He's trying to protect you.* Protect me from what, though? From the truth. I thought the truth more important than anything. Maybe I am wrong.

I went into the study. I knew what I had to do. I had to know that I could trust him about this one thing.

The box was where I had described it, locked. I began to look. I told myself I wouldn't stop until I found the key. I searched the office first. The other drawers, the desk. I did it methodically, replacing everything where I had found it. I went into the bedroom. I looked in the drawers, digging beneath his underwear, the handkerchiefs, the vests and T-shirts. Nothing.

There were drawers in the bedside tables. I started with Ben's side of the bed. I opened the top drawer and rooted through its contents before opening the bottom drawer. At first I thought it was empty. I closed it gently, but as I did so I heard a tiny rattle. I opened it again, my heart already beating fast.

A key.

I sat on the floor with the open box. It was full. Photographs, mostly. Of Adam, and me. Some looked familiar but many not. I found his birth certificate, the letter he had written to Santa Claus. Handfuls of photos of him as a baby. The photo of him dressed as a cowboy, the school photographs— they were all here, as I had described them in my journal.

There were photographs of Ben and me, too: one in front of the Houses of Parliament, both smiling, but standing awkwardly, as if neither of us knows the other exists, another from our wedding, a formal shot. We are in front of a church under an overcast sky. We look happy, even more so in one that must have been taken on our honeymoon. We are in a restaurant, smiling, our faces flushed with the bite of the sun.

Relief began to flood through me. I stared at the photograph of the woman with her new husband and thought about how much I share with her. All of it is physical. Cells and tissue. DNA. She is a stranger. Yet, she is me, and I her, and I could see that she was in love with Ben, the man she has just married. He did not break the vows he made in the tiny church in Manchester. I looked at the photograph and love welled inside me again.

But still I carried on searching. I knew what I wanted to find, and what I dreaded finding. The one thing that would prove my husband wasn't lying.

At the bottom of the box, inside an envelope, was a photocopy of a news article. I knew what it was almost before I opened it, but still I shook as I read. *A British soldier who died escorting troops in Helmand Province, Afghanistan, has been named by the Ministry of Defence. Adam Wheeler was 19 years old. Born in London . . .* Clipped to it was a photograph. Flowers, arranged on a grave. The inscription read, *Adam Wheeler, 1987–2006.*

I doubled up in pain, too much pain even to cry. I closed my eyes, and saw in front of me a medal in a black velvet box. A coffin, a flag. I looked away and prayed the image would never return. There are memories I am better off without.

I began to tidy the papers away. I should have trusted him all along, I thought. I should have believed he was keeping things from me only because they are too painful to face every day. All he was doing was trying to spare me from this brutal truth. I put the box back in the filing cabinet, the key back in the drawer. I can look whenever I want now, I thought.

There was only one more thing I still had to do: I had to know why Ben had left me. I had to know what I had been doing in Brighton. I had to know who had stolen my life from me.

For the second time today, I dialled Claire's number.

Static. Then a two-tone ring. She will not answer, I thought. She has not responded to my message. She has something to hide, something to keep from me.

I almost felt glad. This was a conversation I wanted to have only in theory. I prepared myself for another invitation to leave a message.

A click. Then a voice. 'Hello?'

It was Claire. I knew it, instantly. Her voice felt as familiar as my own.

'Hello?' she said again.

Images flooded me. I saw her face, her hair cut short, wearing a beret. Laughing. I saw her at a wedding—my own, I suppose, dressed in emerald, pouring champagne. I saw her holding a child, giving him to me with the words *Dinner time!* I saw her sitting on the edge of a bed, talking to the figure lying in it, and realised the figure was me.

'Claire?' I said. 'It's me. Christine.'

Silence. Time stretched so that it seemed to last for ever.

'Chrissy!' she said. I heard her swallow, as if she had been eating. 'Chrissy! My God. Darling, is that really you?'

'Yes. It's me. It's Chrissy.'

'Jesus,' she said. 'Roger! Rog! It's Chrissy! On the phone! How are you? Where are you?'

'Oh, I'm at home,' I said.

'Home?'

'Yes.'

'With Ben?'

I felt suddenly defensive. 'Yes. Did you get my message?'

'Yep! I would have called you back but this is the land line and you didn't leave a number.' She hesitated, and for a moment I wondered if there were other reasons she had not returned my call. She went on. 'It's so good to hear your voice! Where are you living?'

'I don't know exactly.' I felt a surge of pleasure, certain that her question meant that she was not seeing Ben, followed by the realisation that she might be asking me so that I don't suspect the truth. I wanted so much to trust her—to know that Ben had not left me because of something he had found in her, because doing so meant that I could trust my husband as well. 'Crouch End?' I said.

'Right,' she said. 'So how's it going?'

'Well, you know,' I said. 'I can't remember a bloody thing.'

We both laughed. It felt good, this eruption of an emotion that wasn't grief, but it was short-lived, followed by silence.

'So what's happening with you?' she said, eventually.

'I don't know,' I said. 'It's difficult . . .'

I must have sounded upset, because she said quickly, 'Chrissy darling, whatever's wrong?'

'Nothing,' I said. 'I'm fine. I just feel confused. I think I've done something stupid.'

'Oh, I'm sure that's not true.' Another silence and then she said, 'Listen. Can I speak to Ben?'

'He's out. At work.'

'Right,' said Claire. Another silence.

'I need to see you,' I said.

'"Need"?' she said. 'Not "want"?'

'No,' I began. 'Obviously I want . . .'

'Relax, Chrissy, I'm kidding. I want to see you, too. I'm dying to.'

I felt relieved. I had had the idea that our talk might end with a polite goodbye and another avenue into my past would slam shut for ever.

'Thank you,' I said. 'Thank you.'

'I've been missing you so much. Every day I've been waiting for this bloody phone to ring, hoping it would be you, never thinking it would be.' She paused. 'How . . . how is your memory now?'

'Better than it has been, I think. But I still don't remember much.' I thought of all the things I'd written down, all the images of me and Claire. 'I remember a party. Fireworks on a rooftop. You painting. Me studying. But nothing after that, really.'

'Ah!' she said. 'The big night! That seems like a long time ago. There's a lot I need to fill you in on. A lot.'

I wondered what she meant, but didn't ask her. It can wait, I thought. There were more important things I needed to know.

'Did you ever move away?' I said. 'Abroad?'

She laughed. 'Yeah, for about six months. I met this bloke, years ago. It was a disaster.'

'Where did you go?'

'Barcelona,' she replied. 'Why?'

'They said you'd been to New Zealand. They must have made a mistake.'

'New Zealand? Nope. Not been there. Ever.'

So Ben had lied to me about that, too. I couldn't think of a reason he would feel the need to remove Claire from my life so thoroughly. Was it like everything else, for my own benefit? It was something else I would have to ask him, when we had the conversation I now knew we must. When I tell him all that I know and how I have found it out.

We spoke some more. Claire told me she had married, then divorced, and was now living with Roger. 'He's an academic,' she said. 'Psychology. Bugger wants me to marry him, which I shan't in a hurry. But I love him.'

It felt good to talk to her, to listen to her voice. It seemed easy, familiar. Almost like coming home. She demanded little, seeming to understand that I had little to give.

'So,' she said, 'Tell me about Ben. How long have you been, well . . .?'

'Back together?' I said. 'I really don't know. I didn't even know we'd ever been apart.'

'I tried to call him this afternoon, after you rang. I guessed that he must have given you my number. He didn't answer, but then I only have an old work number. They said he's not there any more.'

I felt a creeping dread. I felt sure she was lying.

'Do you speak to him often?' I said.

'No. Not for a few years.' A new tone entered her voice. Hushed. I didn't like it. 'I've been so worried about you.'

I was afraid that Claire would tell Ben I had called her before I had a chance to speak to him.

'Please don't ring him,' I said. 'Don't tell him I've called you.'

She sighed heavily, then sounded cross. 'Look, what is going on?'

I couldn't bring myself to mention Adam, but I told her about Dr Nash, and the memory of the hotel room, and how Ben insists I had a car accident.

'I think he's not telling me the truth because he knows it would upset me. What might I have been doing in Brighton, Claire?'

Silence stretched between us. 'If you really want to know, I'll tell you. Or as much as I know, anyway. But not over the phone. When we meet. I promise.'

'When can you come over?' I said. 'Today?'

'I'd rather not come to you,' she said. 'It's better if we meet somewhere else. I can take you for a coffee?' There was a jollity in her voice, but it seemed forced.

I wondered what she was frightened of, but said, 'OK.'

'Alexandra Palace?' she said. 'You should be able to get there easily enough from Crouch End.'

'OK,' I said.

'Cool. Friday? I'll meet you at eleven. Is that OK?'

I told her it was. It would have to be. She told me which buses I would need and I wrote the details on a slip of paper.

'Ben?' I said. He was sitting in the armchair in the living room. He looked tired, as if he'd not slept well. 'Do you trust me?' I said.

His eyes sparked into life, lit with love, but also something else. Something that looked almost like fear. Not surprising, I suppose; the question is usually asked before an admission that such trust is misplaced.

'Of course, darling,' he said. He came over and perched on the arm of my chair, taking one of my hands between his. 'Of course.'

'Do you talk to Claire?'

He looked down into my eyes. 'Claire? You remember her?'

'Vaguely,' I said.

He glanced away. 'I think she moved away years ago.'

'Are you sure?' I asked. I could not believe he was still lying to me. This, surely, would be an easy thing to be honest about? The fact that Claire was still local would cause me no pain, might even be something that—were I to see her—would help my memory to improve. So why the dishonesty? Suspicion entered my head but I pushed it away. 'Where did she go?'

'I don't remember. New Zealand, I think. Or Australia.'

I took a gamble. 'I have this odd memory that she was thinking of moving to Barcelona.' He said nothing. 'You're sure it wasn't there?'

He squeezed my hand. A consolation. 'It's probably your imagination.'

'It felt real, though. You're certain it wasn't Barcelona?'

'No. It was definitely Australia. Adelaide, I think.' He shook his head. 'Claire. I haven't thought of her for years and years.'

I wanted to slap him. 'Ben,' I said, 'I've spoken to her.'

I didn't know how he would react. He did nothing, then his eyes flared.

'When?' His voice was hard as glass.

I could either tell him the truth, or admit that I have been writing the story of my days. 'This afternoon. She called me.'

'She called you?' he said. 'How?'

I decided to lie. 'She said you'd given her my number.'

'That's ridiculous! How could I? You're sure it was her?'

'She said you spoke occasionally. Until fairly recently.'

He let go of my hand and stood up. 'She said what?'

'She told me that the two of you had been in contact until a few years ago.'

He leaned in close. 'This woman just phoned you out of the blue? You're sure it was even her?'

'Oh, Ben! Who else could it have been?' I had never thought this conversation would be easy, but it seemed infused with a seriousness I didn't like.

He shrugged his shoulders. 'There have been people who have tried to get hold of you in the past. Journalists. People who have read about you and what happened and want your side of the story, or even just to nose around and find out how bad you really are. They've pretended to be other people just to get you to talk.'

'Ben, she was my best friend for years. I recognised her voice.'

His face sagged, defeated. 'You have been speaking to her, haven't you?' He looked up. His face was red, his eyes moist. 'OK,' he said. 'OK. I have spoken to Claire. She asked me to keep in touch with her, to let her know how you are. We speak every few months, just briefly.'

'Why didn't you tell me?' He said nothing. 'Why?' Silence. 'You just decided it was easier to pretend she'd moved away? Just like you pretended I'd never written a novel?'

'Chris,' he began, then, 'What—'

'It's not fair, Ben,' I said. 'You have no right to keep these things to yourself. To tell me lies just because it's easier for you. No right.'

He stood up. 'Easier for me?' he said, his voice rising. 'You're wrong, Christine. Wrong. None of this is easy for me. I don't tell you you've written a novel because I can't bear to see the pain when you realise you will never write another. I told you that Claire lives abroad because I can't stand to hear the pain in your voice when you realise that she abandoned you in that place. Did she tell you that?'

I thought, No, she didn't, and in fact today I read in my journal that she used to visit me all the time.

'Did she tell you that she stopped visiting as soon as she realised that fifteen minutes after she left you'd forgotten she even existed? It was me who stood by you, Chris. Me who was praying for you to be well enough that I could bring you here, to live with me in safety. I didn't lie to you because it was easy for me. Don't you ever make the mistake of thinking that I did.'

I remembered reading what Dr Nash had told me. I looked him in the eye. 'Claire said you divorced me.'

He froze, then stepped back, as if he'd been punched. His mouth opened, then closed. It was almost comical. At last a single word escaped. 'Bitch.' His face melted into fury. I thought he was going to hit me, but found I didn't care.

'Did you divorce me?' I said. 'Is it true?' I stood up. 'Tell me,' I said. 'Tell me!' We stood opposite each other. I didn't know what he was going to do, didn't know what I wanted him to do. I only knew I needed him to be honest. To tell me no more lies. 'I just want the truth.'

He fell to his knees in front of me, grasping for my hands. 'Darling—'

'Did you divorce me, Ben?' I shouted. He began to cry. 'Ben! She told me about Adam, too. She told me we had a son. I know he's dead.'

'I'm sorry,' he said. 'I'm so sorry. I thought it was for the best.' And then, through gentle sobs, he said he would tell me everything.

The light had faded completely. Ben switched on a lamp and we sat in its rosy glow, across the dining table. There was a pile of photographs between us, the same ones I had looked at earlier. I feigned surprise as he passed each one to me, telling me of its origins. He lingered on the photos of our wedding—telling me what an amazing day it had been, how beautiful I had looked—but then began to get upset. 'I never stopped loving you, Christine,' he said. 'You have to believe that. It was your illness. You had to go into that place and, well . . . I couldn't bear it. I would've followed you. I would've done anything to get you back. But I couldn't see you . . . they said it was for the best.'

'Who?' I said. 'Who said? The doctors?'

He was crying, his eyes circled with red. 'Yes. The doctors. They said it was for the best.' He wiped away a tear. 'I did as they told me. I wish I hadn't. I wish I'd fought for you. I was weak, stupid. I stopped seeing you for your own sake. I did it for you and our son. But I never divorced you. Not really. Not here.' He took my hand, pressing it to his shirt. 'In here, we've always been married.' I felt warm cotton, damp with sweat. The quick beat of his heart. *Love*.

I have been so foolish, I thought. I have allowed myself to believe he did these things to hurt me, when really he tells me he has done them out of love. I should not condemn him. Instead I should try to understand.

'I forgive you,' I said.

Thursday, November 22

Today, when I woke up, I saw a man sitting on a chair, watching me. I didn't know who he was, but I didn't panic. Some part of me knew that he had a right to be there.

'Who are you?' I said. He told me. I felt no horror, no disbelief. I understood. I went to the bathroom and approached my reflection as I might a long-forgotten relative. I dressed, getting used to my body's new dimensions, and then ate breakfast, dimly aware that, once, there might have been three places at the table. I kissed my husband goodbye and then, without knowing why, I opened the shoebox in the wardrobe, and found this journal. I knew straightaway what it was.

The truth of my situation now sits nearer the surface. It is possible that one day I will wake up and know it already? Even then, I know, I will never be normal. My history is incomplete. There are things about myself, my past, that no one can tell me. Not Dr Nash and not Ben, either. Things that happened before I met him. Things that happened after but that I chose not to share. Secrets.

But there is one person who might tell me the rest of the truth. Who I had been seeing in Brighton. The real reason my best friend vanished from my life. Tomorrow I will meet Claire.

Friday, November 23
I am writing this at home. I have read this journal through and I have seen Claire and between them they have told me all I need to know. Claire has promised me that she is back in my life now and will not leave again. In front of me is a tatty envelope with my name on it. An artefact that completes me. At last my past makes sense.

Soon, my husband will be home and I am looking forward to seeing him. I love him. I know that now.

I will get this story down and then, together, we will be able to make everything better.

It was a bright day as I got off the bus. The light was suffused with the blue coolness of winter, the ground hard. Claire had told me she would wait at the top of the hill, by the main steps up to the palace, and so I began to climb the gentle incline. It took longer than I expected and, still unused to my body's limitations, I had to rest as I neared the top.

The park opened out to an expanse of mowed grass, crisscrossed with tarmac. I realised I was nervous. I didn't know what to expect. How could I? In the images I had of Claire she was wearing a lot of black. Jeans, T-shirts. Heavy boots and a trench coat. Or else she was wearing a long skirt, tie-dyed, made of some material that I suppose would be described as 'floaty'. I could imagine neither vision representing her now—not at the age we have become—but had no idea what might have taken their place.

I was early. Without thinking, I told myself that Claire is always late, then wondered how I knew. There is so much, I thought, just under the surface.

I decided to wait on one of the benches. Long shadows extended across the grass. Over the trees rows of houses stretched away from me, packed claustrophobically close. With a start I realised that one of the houses I could see was the one in which I now lived.

I felt even more nervous, ridiculously so. Yet there was no reason. Claire had been my friend. My best friend. There was nothing to worry about. I was safe.

A shadow fell across my face and a woman stood over me. Tall, with a shock of ginger hair, she was wearing trousers and a sheepskin jacket. A little boy held her hand, a plastic football in the crook of his other arm.

'Sorry,' I said, and shuffled along the bench. The woman smiled.

'Chrissy!' The voice was Claire's. 'It's me.' Her face was furrowed where once it must have been smooth, her eyes had a downturn to them that was absent from my mental image, but it was *her*. She pushed the child towards me. 'This is Toby.'

The boy took a step forward. I smiled. My only thought was, Is this Adam? Even though I knew it couldn't be.

'Hello,' I said.

Toby shuffled his feet and murmured something I didn't catch, then turned to Claire and said, 'Can I go and play now?'

'Don't go out of sight.' He ran over to the park.

I didn't know if I would have preferred to turn and run myself, so vast was the chasm between Claire and me, but then she held out her arms. 'Chrissy,' she said, 'I've missed you so much.' The weight that had been pressing down on me vanished and I fell sobbing into her arms.

For the briefest of moments I felt as if I knew everything about her, and everything about myself, too. It was as if the emptiness, the void that sat at the centre of my soul, had been lit with light. A history—my history—flashed in front of me, but too quickly for me to do anything but snatch at it.

'I remember you,' I said, and then it was gone and the darkness swept in once more.

We sat on the bench and silently watched Toby playing football with a group of boys. I felt happy to be connected with my unknown past, yet there was an awkwardness between us that I could not shake.

'How are you?' I said in the end, and she laughed.

'I feel like hell,' she said. She opened her bag and took out a packet of tobacco and some rolling papers.

'What's wrong?'

She began to roll her cigarette, nodding towards her son. 'Oh, you know. Tobes has ADHD. He was up all night, and hence so was I.'

'ADHD?'

She smiled. 'Sorry. Attention deficit and hyperactivity disorder. We have to give him Ritalin, though I hate it. He's an absolute beast without it.'

I looked over at him, running in the distance. Another faulty brain in a healthy body.

'He's OK, though?'

'Yes,' she said, sighing. 'He's just exhausting sometimes. It's like the terrible twos never ended.'

I smiled. I knew what she meant, but only theoretically. 'Toby seems quite young?'

'Yes. I had him late. I wouldn't say he was an accident, but let's just say he was something of a shock.' She put the cigarette in her mouth. 'Do you remember Adam?'

'No,' I said. 'A few weeks ago I remembered that I had a son, and since I wrote about it I've been carrying the knowledge around, like a rock in my chest. But I don't remember anything about him.'

She sent a cloud of smoke skyward. 'That's a shame. Ben shows you pictures, though? Doesn't that help?'

I weighed up how much I should tell her. They seemed to have been friends once. I had to be careful but I felt an increasing need to speak, as well as hear, the truth.

'He does show me pictures, though he doesn't have any up around the house. He says I find them too upsetting. He keeps them hidden.'

She seemed surprised. 'Hidden? Really? You might not recognise him?'

'I suppose so.'

'I imagine that might be true,' she said. 'Now that he's gone.'

Gone, I thought. She said it as though he had just popped out for a few hours. I tried to imagine what it must have been like, to have seen my child every day. I tried to imagine waking every morning knowing who he was, being able to plan, to look forward to Christmas, to his birthday.

How ridiculous, I thought. I don't even know when his birthday is.

'Wouldn't you like to see him?'

My heart leaped. 'You have photographs?'

'Of course! Loads! I'll bring one next time, but—'

She was interrupted by a cry in the distance. Toby was running towards us crying.

'Fuck,' said Claire, under her breath. She stood up. 'Toby! What happened?' He kept running. 'I'll just go and sort him out.'

She went to her son and crouched down to ask what was wrong. I felt pleased. Not only that Claire would give me a photograph of Adam, but that she had said she would do so next time we met. We were going to be seeing more of each other. Then I realised that every time would once again seem like the first. The irony: I am prone to forgetting that I have no memory.

I realised, too, that the way she had spoken of Ben—some wistfulness—made me think that the idea of them having an affair was ridiculous.

She came back. 'Everything's fine. Slight misunderstanding over ownership of the ball. Shall we walk?' She turned to Toby. 'Ice cream?'

We began to walk towards the palace, Toby holding Claire's hand. They looked so alike, I thought, their eyes lit with the same fire.

'Do you still paint?'

'Hardly,' she said. 'I dabble. Our own walls are chock-full of my pictures, but nobody else has one. Unfortunately.'

I smiled. I didn't mention my novel, though I wanted to ask if she'd read it, what she thought. 'What do you do now, then?'

'I look after Toby mostly,' she said. 'He's home-schooled. None of the schools will take him. They say he's too disruptive.'

He seemed perfectly calm, holding his mother's hand. I couldn't imagine him being difficult.

'What was Adam like?' I said.

'As a child?' she said. 'He was a good boy. Very polite.'

'Was I a good mother? Was he happy?'

'Oh, Chrissy. Yes. Nobody was more loved than that boy. You were worried you might not be able to get pregnant but then along came Adam. You were so happy, both of you. And you loved being pregnant. I hated it. Bloated like a house and such dreadful sickness. But it was different with you. You glowed for the whole time you were carrying him.'

I tried to remember being pregnant and then to imagine it. I could do neither. I looked at Claire. 'And then?'

'The birth was wonderful. Ben was there, of course. He was a great father. When Adam said his first word Ben called everyone up and told them. The same when he began to crawl. And Christmas! So many toys!

I think that was just about the only thing I ever saw you argue about—how many toys Ben would buy for Adam. You were worried he'd be spoilt.'

'I would let him have anything he wanted now,' I said.

She looked at me sadly. 'I know,' she said. 'But be happy knowing that he didn't want for anything from you, ever.'

A van was parked on the footpath, selling ice creams, and Toby began to tug at his mother's arm. She gave him a note from her purse. 'Choose one thing! And wait for the change!'

'Claire,' I said, 'how old was Adam when I lost my memory?'

She smiled. 'He must have been three. Maybe four, just.'

I felt I was stepping into new territory. Into danger. But it was where I had to go. 'My doctor told me I was attacked in Brighton. Why was I there?' I looked at her, scanning her face. She seemed to be weighing up the options.

'I don't know for sure. Nobody does.'

Toby had his ice cream now and was unwrapping it, concentration scoring his face. Silence stretched in front of me.

'I was having an affair, wasn't I?'

Claire looked at me steadily. 'Yes. You were cheating on Ben.'

'Tell me,' I said.

'OK, but let's sit down. I'm gasping for a coffee.'

The cafeteria doubled as a bar. The chairs were steel, the tables plain. We sat opposite each other, warming our hands on our drinks.

'What happened?' I said again. 'I need to know.'

'It's not easy to say,' said Claire. She spoke slowly, as if picking her way through difficult terrain. 'I suppose it started not long after you had Adam. Once the initial excitement had worn off there was a period when things were extremely tough. You cried awfully. You worried you weren't bonding with the baby. All the usual stuff. And you couldn't get back into your work. You said you felt like a failure. Not a failure at motherhood—you could see how happy Adam was—but a failure as a writer. You and Ben were arguing, too. He offered to pay for a nanny but, well . . .'

'Well?'

'You said that was typical of him. To throw money at the problem. You had a point, but . . . Perhaps you weren't being terribly fair.'

Perhaps not, I thought. It struck me that back then we must have had money. What a drain on our resources my illness must have been.

I tried to picture myself, arguing with Ben, looking after a baby, trying to write. I imagined bottles of milk, or Adam at my breast. Dirty nappies. Craving sleep that was still hours away. But imaginings were all they were. Claire's story felt like it had nothing to do with me at all.

'So I had an affair?'

'I said I'd look after Adam two afternoons a week, so you could write. I insisted.' She took my hand in hers. 'It was my fault, Chrissy. I even suggested you go to a café.'

'A café?' I said.

'I thought it would be a good idea if you got out of the house. A few hours a week, away from everything. After a few weeks you seemed to get better. You said your work was going well. You started going to the café almost every day, taking Adam when I couldn't look after him. Then I noticed that you were dressing differently. The classic thing, though I didn't realise what it was at the time. Then Ben called me one evening. He said you were arguing more than ever and he didn't know what to do. You were off sex, too. I told him it was probably just because of the baby. But—'

I interrupted. 'I was seeing someone.'

'I asked you. You denied it at first and we had an argument, but after a while you told me the truth.'

The truth. Not glamorous, not exciting. I had turned into a living cliché, sleeping with someone I'd met in a café while my best friend was baby-sitting my child and my husband was earning the money to pay for the clothes I was wearing for someone other than him. I pictured the furtive phone calls, the aborted arrangements and the sordid afternoons spent in bed with a man who had seemed better—more exciting? attractive? a better lover?— than my husband. Was this the man I had been waiting for in that hotel room, the man who would attack me?

I closed my eyes. A flash of memory. Hands gripping my hair, around my throat. My head under water. I remember what I was thinking: I want to see my son one last time. I want to see my husband. I should never have done this to him. I will never be able to tell him I am sorry. Never.

I opened my eyes. Claire was squeezing my hand. 'Are you all right?'

'Tell me,' I said. 'Who was it?'

'You said you'd met someone else who went to the café regularly. He was nice, you said. Attractive. You hadn't been able to stop yourself.'

'What was his name?' I said.

'I don't know.'

'You must!' I said. 'Who did this to me?'

She looked into my eyes. 'Chrissy, you never told me his name. You didn't want me to know any details. Any more than I had to, at least.'

I felt another sliver of hope slip away. I would never know who did this to me. 'What happened?'

'I told you that you ought to stop seeing him. There was Adam to think about, as well as Ben. We fought. You were putting me in an impossible situation. Ben was my friend, too. You were asking me to lie to him.'

'What happened? How long did it go on for?'

She was silent, then said, 'I don't know. One day you announced it was over. You'd told this man you'd made a mistake. You said you were sorry.'

'I was lying?'

'I don't think so. You and I didn't lie to each other. A few weeks later you were found in Brighton. I have no idea what happened in that time.'

Perhaps it was those words—*I have no idea what happened in that time*—that set off the realisation that I may never know how I came to be attacked. A sound suddenly escaped me. Something between a gasp and a howl, it was the cry of an animal in pain. Everyone in the café turned to stare at me, at the mad woman with no memory. Claire grabbed my arm.

'Chrissy!' she said. 'What's wrong?'

I was sobbing now, my body heaving. Crying for all the years that I had lost, and for all those that I would continue to lose between now and the day that I died. Crying mostly, though, because I had brought all this on myself.

'I'm sorry,' I said. 'I'm sorry.'

Claire crouched beside me, her arm around my shoulder, and I rested my head against hers. 'It's all right, Chrissy darling. I'm here now. I'm here.'

We left the café. Toby had become boisterously noisy after my outburst and Claire said, 'I need to get some air.'

Now we sat on one of the benches that overlooked the park. Claire held my hands in hers, stroking them as if they were cold.

'Did I—' I began. 'Did I have lots of affairs?'

She shook her head. 'No. You were always faithful to Ben.'

I wondered what had been so special about the man in the café. Claire had said that I'd told her he was *nice. Attractive.* My husband was both of those things, I thought. If only I'd been content with what I had.

'Ben knew I was having an affair?'

'Not until you were found. At first it looked as though you might not even live. Later, Ben asked me if I knew why you'd been in Brighton. I told him. I'd already told the police all I knew. I had no choice but to tell Ben.'

Guilt punctured me once more as I thought of my husband trying to work out why his dying wife had turned up miles away from home.

'He forgave you, though,' said Claire. 'He never held it against you, ever. All he cared about was that you lived and that you got better. He would have given everything for that. Everything. Nothing else mattered.'

'Will you talk to him?' I said.

She smiled. 'Of course! But about what?'

'He's not telling me the truth,' I said. 'He's trying to protect me. He tells me what he thinks I can cope with.'

'Ben wouldn't do that,' she said. 'He loves you. He always has.'

'Well, he doesn't know I'm writing things down. He doesn't tell me about Adam, other than when I remember him and ask. He doesn't tell me he left me. He tells me you live on the other side of the world. Whatever he used to be like, he's given up on me. He doesn't want me to see a doctor because he doesn't think I will ever get better, but I've been seeing one in secret, a Dr Nash. I can't tell Ben.'

Claire looked disappointed. In me, I suppose. 'That's not good,' she said. 'You ought to tell him. He loves you. He trusts you.'

'I can't. He admitted he was still in touch with you only the other day. Until then he'd been saying he hadn't spoken to you in years.'

For the first time I could see that she was surprised.

'It's true,' I said. 'I need him to be honest with me. I don't know my own past. And only he can help me. I need him to help me.'

'Then you should just talk to him. Trust him.'

'But how can I?' I said. 'With all the things he's lied to me about?'

She squeezed my hands in hers. 'Believe me. You can sort everything out, but you have to tell him the truth. Tell him about Dr Nash. Tell him what you've been writing.'

Deep down, I knew she was right, but still I could not convince myself I should tell Ben about my journal.

'But he might want to read what I've written.'

Her eyes narrowed. 'There's nothing in there you wouldn't want him to see, is there?' I didn't reply. 'Is there?'

I looked away. We didn't speak, and then she opened her bag.

'I'm going to give you something. Ben gave it to me when he decided to leave you.' She took out an envelope and handed it to me. It was creased, but still sealed. 'He told me it explained everything.' I stared at it. My name was written on the front in capitals. 'He asked me to give it to you, if I ever thought you were well enough to read it.' I looked up at her, feeling excitement and fear. 'I think it's time you read it.'

I put it in my bag. Though I didn't know why, I didn't want to read it in front of Claire. Perhaps I was worried that she would be able to read its contents reflected in my face and they would no longer be mine to own.

'Thank you,' I said.

'Chrissy, there's a reason Ben tells you I moved away. I have to tell you something. About why we lost touch.'

I knew without her saying anything. The missing piece of the puzzle, the reason Ben had gone, the reason my best friend had disappeared from my life and my husband had lied about why this had happened. I had been right all along.

'Oh God. It's true. You're seeing Ben. You're fucking my husband.'

She looked up, horrified. 'No!' she said. 'Not now. But we were once.'

Of all the emotions I might have expected to feel, relief wasn't one of them. But I felt relieved. Because she was being honest? Because now I had an explanation for everything that I could believe? I'm not sure. But the anger that I may have felt was not there; neither was the pain. Perhaps I was just relieved that Ben had an infidelity to go with my own, that we were equal now. Quits.

'Tell me,' I whispered.

'We were always close,' she said, softly. 'The three of us, I mean. But there had never been anything between me and him. Never. After your accident I tried to help out. You can imagine how terribly difficult it was for Ben. Just on a practical level, having to look after Adam . . . We spent a lot of time together. But we didn't sleep together. Not then.'

'So when?' I said.

'Just before you were moved to Waring House. You were at your worst. Adam was being difficult. Things were tough. Ben wasn't coping. One night we got back from visiting you. I put Adam to bed. Ben was in the living room crying. "I can't do it," he kept saying. "I love her, but it's killing me." I sat next to him. And . . .'

I could see it all. The hand on the shoulder, then the hug. The mouths that find each other through the tears, the moment when guilt and the certainty that things must go no further gives way to lust and the certainty that they cannot stop. And then what? The sex. On the sofa? The floor? I do not want to know.

'I'm sorry,' she said. 'I never wanted it to happen. But it did, and . . . I felt so bad. So bad. We both did.'

'How long did it go on for?'

'A few weeks. We only . . . we only had sex a few times. It didn't feel right. We both felt so bad afterwards.'

'What happened?' I said. 'Who ended it?'

She shrugged, then whispered, 'Both of us. I decided I owed it to you—and Ben—to stay away from then on. It was guilt, I suppose.'

I looked at her. I still didn't feel angry. What she had told me felt as though it belonged to another time. Prehistory. I found it hard to believe it had anything to do with me at all.

Claire looked up. 'At first I was in touch with Adam, but then Ben must have told him what had happened. Adam told me to stay away from him and from you, too. But I couldn't. Ben had given me the letter, asked me to keep an eye on you. So I carried on visiting Waring House. Every few weeks at first, then every couple of months. But it upset you terribly. I know I was being selfish, but I couldn't just leave you there. I carried on coming. Just to check you were all right.'

'And you told Ben how I was?'

'We weren't in touch.'

'Is that why you haven't been visiting me at home? Because you don't want to see Ben?'

'No. A few months ago I visited Waring House and they told me you'd gone back to live with Ben. I knew Ben had moved. I asked them to give me your address but they wouldn't. They said they would give you my number and that if I wanted to write to you they would pass the letters on.'

'So you wrote?'

'I addressed the letter to Ben. I told him I was sorry, that I regretted what had happened. I begged him to let me see you.'

'But he told you you couldn't?'

'No. You wrote back, Chrissy. You said that you were feeling much better. You were happy with Ben.' She looked away, across the park. 'You said you didn't want to see me. That your memory would sometimes come back and when it did you knew I had betrayed you.' She wiped a tear from her eye. 'You told me it was better that you forgot me for ever and that I forgot you.'

I tried to imagine the anger I must have felt to write a letter like that, but realised maybe I hadn't felt angry at all. To me, Claire would hardly have existed, any friendship between us forgotten.

'I'm sorry,' I said. I couldn't imagine being able to remember her betrayal. Ben must have helped me write the letter.

She smiled. 'Don't apologise. You were right. But I didn't stop hoping you'd change your mind. I wanted to see you. To tell you the truth to your face.' I said nothing. 'I'm so sorry. Can you ever forgive me?'

I took her hand. How could I be angry with her? Or with Ben? My condition has placed an impossible burden on us all.

'Yes, I forgive you.'

We left soon after. At the bottom of the slope she turned to face me.

'Will I see you again?'

I smiled. 'I hope so!'

She looked relieved. 'I've missed you, Chrissy. You've no idea.'

It was true. I did have no idea. But with her, and this journal, there was a chance I could rebuild a life worth living. I thought of the letter in my bag. A message from the past. The final piece of the puzzle.

'I'll see you soon,' she said. 'Early next week. OK?'

'OK,' I said. She hugged me. She felt like my only friend, the only person I could rely on, along with Ben. My sister. I squeezed her hard. 'Thank you for telling me the truth,' I said. 'Thank you for everything. I love you.' When we parted, both of us were crying.

At home, I sat down to read Ben's letter. I felt nervous—would it tell me what I needed to know? I felt sure it would. Felt certain that with it, with Ben and Claire, I will have everything I need.

Darling Christine,

This is the hardest thing I have ever had to do. Already I've kicked off with a cliché, but you know I'm not a writer—that was always you!—so I'm sorry, but I'll do my best.

By the time you read this you'll know, but I've decided I have to leave you. I have tried so hard to find another way, but I can't.

You have to understand that I love you. This isn't about revenge, or anything like that. I haven't met anybody else. When you were in that coma I realised I didn't care what you were doing in Brighton, or who you were seeing. I just wanted you to come back to me.

And then you did, and I was so happy the day they told me you wouldn't die. Adam was just little, but I think he understood.

When we realised you had no memory of what had happened, I thought it was for the best. But then you started forgetting other things, too. At first it was the names of the people in the beds next to you, the doctors and nurses treating you. But you got worse. You forgot why you were in the hospital, why you weren't allowed to come home. You convinced yourself that the doctors were experimenting on you.

That's when things started to get difficult. You loved Adam so much. It shone out of your eyes when we arrived and you would know who he was straightaway. But then you started to believe that Adam had been away from you when he was a baby. Every time you saw him you thought it was the first time since he was a few months old. I would ask him to tell you when he last saw you and he would say, 'Yesterday, Mummy,' or 'Last week,' but you didn't believe him. 'What have you been telling him?' you'd say. You started accusing me of keeping you there. You thought another woman was raising Adam as her own while you were in the hospital. One day I arrived and you didn't recognise me. You grabbed Adam and ran to the door, to rescue him, I suppose; but he started screaming. He didn't understand. He started being really frightened of you.

One day I called the hospital. I asked them what you were like when I wasn't there. They said you were happy, talking to one of the other patients. Sometimes you played cards together. They said you were good at cards. They had to explain the rules to you every day, but then you could beat just about anybody.

'Does she remember me?' I said. 'Adam?'

'Not unless you're here,' they said.

I knew then that I would have to leave you. Because you will be happy, without me, without Adam. You won't know us and so you won't miss us.

I love you so much, Chrissy. You must understand that. But I have to give our son a life. Soon he will be old enough to understand what's

going on. I will not lie to him, Chris. I will tell him that although he
may want to see you very much it would be enormously upsetting for
him to do so. Maybe he will hate me. I hope not. But I want him to be
happy. And I want you to be happy, too. Even if you can find that
happiness only without me.

    I'm going to give this letter to Claire. I'll ask her to keep it and to
show it to you when you're well enough to understand it. I can't keep it
myself; I'll just brood over it, and won't be able to resist giving it to
you next month, or even next year. Too soon.

    I cannot pretend I don't hope that one day we can be together again.
The three of us. I have to believe that might happen or else I will die
from grief.

    Don't hate me. I love you.

    Ben

I read it again now. The paper feels crisp, as though it might have been written yesterday, but the envelope into which I slip it is soft, its edges frayed.
For years it waited for the right time to be read. Years that I spent not knowing who my husband was, not even knowing who I was.

    I slip the envelope between the pages of my journal. I am crying as
I write this, but I don't feel unhappy. I understand everything. Why he left
me, why he has been lying to me.

    He has not told me about the novel I wrote so that I will not be devastated
by the fact that I will never write another. He has been telling me my best
friend moved away to protect me from the fact that the two of them betrayed
me. He has been telling me that I was hit by a car, so that I don't have to
deal with the fact that I was attacked. He has been telling me that we never
had children, not only to protect me from the knowledge that my only son is
dead, but to protect me from having to deal with his death every day. And he
has not told me that he had to leave in order to find happiness.

    He must have thought that our separation would be for ever when he
wrote that letter, but he must also have hoped that it would not, or else why
write it? But it has not been for ever. Somehow my condition has improved,
and he came back for me.

    Everything seems different now. I have been wrong. I have made a mistake.
Again and again and again I have made it; who knows how many times?
My husband is my protector, yes, but also my lover. And now I realise that

I love him. I have always loved him and, if I have to learn to love him again every day, then so be it. That is what I will do.

Ben will be home soon and, when he arrives, I will tell him everything. I will tell him that I have met Claire—and Dr Nash and Dr Paxton—and that I have read his letter. I will tell him that I understand why he left me and that I forgive him. I will tell him that I know about the attack but that I no longer care who did this to me.

And I will tell him that I know about Adam. I know what happened to him and though the thought of facing it every day makes me cold with terror, that is what I must do. The memory of our son must be allowed to exist in this house, no matter how much pain that causes.

And I will tell him about this journal and I will show it to him, if he asks to see it. And then I can continue to use it. To create myself from nothing.

No more secrets, I will say to my husband. I love you, Ben, and I always will. We have wronged each other. But please forgive me. I am determined to make this up to you now.

And then, when there is nothing else between us but love, we can begin to find a way truly to be together.

I have called Dr Nash. 'I want to see you one more time,' I said. 'I want you to read my journal.' I think he was surprised, but he agreed.

'Come for it next week.' I said.

He said he would collect it on Tuesday.

PART THREE

Today

I turn the page but there is no more. The story ends there. I have been reading for hours. I am shaking, can barely breathe. I feel that I have not only lived an entire life in the past few hours but I have changed. I am not the same person who met Dr Nash this morning. I have a past now. I know what I have, and what I have lost.

I close the journal and the present begins to reassert itself. I look at the clock and there is a jolt of shock. Only now do I realise that it is the same clock as the one in the journal that I have been reading, that I am in the same living room, am the same person. Only now do I fully understand that the story I have been reading is mine.

I take my mug into the kitchen. On the wall is the wipe-clean board I had seen this morning, with the note that I had added myself: *Pack bag for tonight.* Something about it troubles me, but I can't work out why.

I think of Ben. How difficult life must have been for him. Never being certain how much I would remember, how much love I would be able to give him. But now I know enough for us both to live again. I wonder if I ever had the conversation with him that I had been planning. I must have, but I have not written about it. I have written nothing for a week. Perhaps I gave my journal to Dr Nash before I had the opportunity. Perhaps I felt there was no need to write in my book, now that I had shared it with Ben.

I turn back to the front of the journal. Three words, scratched onto the page beneath my name. *DON'T TRUST BEN.* I take a pen and cross them out.

Back in the living room I see the scrapbook on the table. Still there are no photographs of Adam. Still he didn't mention him to me this morning. I think of my novel and then look at the journal I am holding. A thought comes, unbidden. *What if I made it all up?*

I stand up. I need evidence. I need a link between what I have read and what I am living—a sign that the past I have been reading about is not one I have invented. I take the stairs two at a time.

The office is smaller than I imagined, but the cabinet is there, gun-metal grey. In the bottom drawer is a towel and beneath it a box. I grip it, convinced it will be either locked or empty.

It is neither. In it I find my novel. Not the copy Dr Nash had given me—there is no coffee ring on the front—so it must be one Ben has been keeping all along. Underneath it is a photograph. Me and Ben, smiling at the camera, a house in the background. It looks recent. On the back someone has written *Waring House.* It must have been taken on the day he brought me back here.

That's it, though. There are no other photographs. Not even the ones I have found here before and described in my journal. I look through the papers that are piled on the desk: magazines, software catalogues, a school timetable. There is a sealed envelope—which, on an impulse, I take—but there are no photographs of Adam.

I go downstairs and make myself a coffee. A phone rings in my bag and I answer it. Ben.

'Christine? Are you OK? Are you at home?'

'Yes,' I say. 'Yes. Thank you.'

'Have you been out today?' His voice sounds familiar, yet cold. I think back to the last time we spoke. I don't remember him mentioning that I had an appointment with Dr Nash. Perhaps he really doesn't know, or perhaps he is testing me, wondering whether I will tell him. I think of *Don't tell Ben* written next to the appointment. I must have written that before I knew I could trust him. I want to trust him now. No more lies.

'Yes,' I say. 'I've been to see a doctor.'

'Yes, I heard.' I register his lack of surprise. So he had known I was seeing Dr Nash. 'I just wanted to make sure you've remembered we're going away tonight, for our anniversary.'

'Of course,' I say, and add, 'I'm looking forward to it!' and I realise I am. It can be another beginning for us.

'I'll be home soon. Can you try to have our bags packed? There are two bags in the spare bedroom. In the wardrobe. Use those.'

'OK.'

'I love you,' he says, and then, after a moment too long, a moment in which he has already ended the call, I tell him that I love him too.

I go to the bathroom. I am an adult, I tell myself. I have a husband. I think back to what I have read of him fucking me.

Can I enjoy sex? I don't even know that. I flush the toilet and step out of my trousers. How alien my body is. How can I be happy giving it to someone else, when I don't recognise it myself?

I part my legs, lift my blouse and look down. I see the wiry shock of my pubic hair. I place my hand over my pubic mound. I brush the tip of my clitoris and press, moving my fingers gently, feeling a faint tingle.

I wonder what will happen, later.

The bags are where he said they would be. I take them into the bedroom and select clothes for us both.

I choose a dress, a skirt. Some trousers, a pair of jeans. I wonder what kind of couple we are, when we go on holiday. Whether we spend our evenings in restaurants or pubs. I wonder whether we walk, exploring the town and its surroundings. These are the things I have the rest of my life to find out. To enjoy.

As I place clothes in the cases I feel a jolt and see a vision. I see myself standing in front of a soft leather suitcase. I feel young again, like a teenager preparing for a date, wondering whether he'll ask me back to his house, whether we'll fuck. I feel that anticipation. I select blouses, stockings, underwear. Sexy underwear that is worn only with the anticipation of its removal. I put in a pair of heels. I don't like them, but this night is about fantasy. Only then do I move on to the functional things: perfume, shower gel, toothpaste. I want to look beautiful tonight for the man I love, for the man I have been so close to losing. I add bath salts. Orange blossom. I realise I am remembering the night I packed to go to Brighton.

The memory evaporates. I could not have known, back then, that I was packing for the man who would take everything from me.

I carry on packing for the man I still have.

I HEAR A CAR pull up outside. Ben is here. I feel nervous. I am not the same person he left this morning; I have learned my own story. I must ask him if he knows about my journal. If he has read it.

The lowest step creaks and I hear an exhalation as first one shoe is removed and then the other. He will be putting his slippers on now. I feel a surge of pleasure at knowing his rituals but, as he ascends the stairs, another emotion takes over. Fear. I think of what I wrote in the front of my journal. *DON'T TRUST BEN.*

He opens the bedroom door. 'Darling!' he says. Then he comes over and kisses me.

'How was your day?' I say.

He takes off his tie. 'Oh, let's not talk about that. We're on holiday!'

He begins to unbutton his shirt. I fight the instinct to look away, remind myself that he is my husband, that I love him.

'I packed the bags,' I say. 'I hope yours is OK. Only I wasn't exactly sure where we were going. So I didn't know what to pack.'

He turns and I wonder whether I catch a flash of annoyance in his eyes. 'I'll check. Thanks for making a start.' He pulls on a pair of faded blue jeans. I notice a perfect crease ironed down their front and the twenty-something me has to resist the urge to find him ridiculous.

'Ben?' I say. 'You know about Dr Nash?'

'Yes. You told me about it all. I know everything.'

'You don't mind? About me seeing him?'

'I wish you'd told me. But no. No, I don't mind.'

'And my journal? You know about my journal?'

'Yes,' he says. 'You told me. You said it helped.'

'Have you read it?'

'You said it was private. I would never look through your private things.'

'But you know that I know about Adam?'

I see him flinch, and I am surprised. I was expecting him to be happy that he would no longer have to tell me about his death, over and over again.

'Yes,' he says.

'There aren't any pictures,' I say. 'There are photos of me and you but still none of him.'

'I wanted to surprise you,' he says. He reaches under the bed and retrieves a photo album. 'I've put them in here.'

The album is heavy. Inside it is a pile of photographs.

'I wanted to put them in properly,' he says. 'To give it to you as a present tonight, but I didn't have time. I'm sorry.'

The photographs are not in any order. They must be the ones from the metal box. Adam as a baby, a young boy. One stands out. He is a young man, sitting next to a woman. 'His girlfriend?' I say.

'One of them,' says Ben. 'The one he was with the longest.'

She is pretty, blonde, her hair cut short. Adam is looking directly at the camera, laughing, and she is looking at him. They have a conspiratorial air, as though they have shared a joke with whoever is behind the lens. They are happy. 'What was her name?'

'She's called Helen.'

I wince as I realise I had thought of her in the past tense, imagined that she had died, too. 'Were they still together when he died?'

'Yes,' he says. 'They were thinking of getting engaged.'

She looks so young, so hungry, her eyes full of possibility. She doesn't yet know the pain in store for her.

'I'd like to meet her,' I say.

'We're not in touch,' he says. 'There were arguments.'

I can see he doesn't want to tell me. 'Before Adam died or after?'

'Both.'

What if Adam and I had fought, too? Surely he would have sided with his girlfriend over his mother?

'Were Adam and I close?' I say.

'Oh, yes,' says Ben. 'Until you lost your memory. Even then you were close, of course. As close as you could be.'

His words hit me like a punch. I realise that Adam was a toddler when he lost his mother to amnesia. I had never known my son's fiancée; every day I saw him would have been like the first.

I close the book. 'Can we bring it with us? I'd like to look at it later.'

WE GET INTO THE CAR. I check I have my handbag, my journal still within it. Ben has added a few things to the bag I packed for him and he has brought another bag—the leather satchel that he left with this morning—as well as two pairs of walking boots. I ask him how long the journey may take.

'Not too long, once we're out of London.'

A refusal to provide an answer, disguised as an answer itself. I wonder if years of telling me the same thing have bored him to the point where he can no longer bring himself to tell me anything.

He is a careful driver, that much I can see. I wonder if Adam drove. I suppose he must have done so to be in the army. Did he pick me up, his invalid mother, and take me on trips? Or did he decide there was no point?

We are on the motorway, heading out of the city. It has begun to rain; huge droplets smack into the windscreen. I am struggling inside. I want so much to think of my son as something other than abstract, but without a concrete memory of him I cannot. He might as well never have existed.

I close my eyes. I think back to what I read about our son this afternoon and an image explodes in front of me—Adam as a toddler pushing a blue tricycle along a path. But even as I marvel at it I know I am not remembering the thing that happened; I am remembering the image I formed in my mind as I read about it, and even that was a recollection of an earlier memory. Memories of memories.

Failing to remember my son, I do the only thing to quieten my sparking mind. I think of nothing. Nothing at all.

I OPEN MY EYES. I see the wet windscreen, and beyond it there are distant lights. I realise that I have been dozing. I am leaning against the window, my head twisted awkwardly. The car is silent, the engine off.

Ben is sitting next to me. He is awake, looking ahead. He doesn't seem to have noticed that I have woken up but continues to stare, his expression unreadable in the dark. I turn to see what he is looking at.

Beyond the rain-spattered windscreen is the bonnet of the car and beyond that a low wooden fence, dimly illuminated in the glow from the street-lamps behind us. Beyond the fence I see a blackness, huge and mysterious, in the middle of which hangs the moon, full and low.

'I love the sea,' he says, and I realise we are parked on a clifftop, have made it as far as the coast. 'Don't you?'

'I do,' I say. He is speaking as if we have never been to the coast before. Fear begins to burn within me but I resist it. 'You know that, darling.'

He sighs. 'You always used to, but you've changed. I wake up each day and I don't know how you're going to be.'

I can think of nothing to say. We both know how senseless it would be for me to try to defend myself. I am the last person who knows how much I change from day to day.

There is a single light in the distance. A boat, on the waves. 'We'll be all right, won't we, Chris?'

'Of course,' I say. 'This is a new beginning for us. I have my journal and Dr Nash will help me. I'm getting better, Ben. I know I am. And I'm in touch with Claire now and she can help me.' An idea comes to me. 'We can all get together, don't you think? Just like old times? The three of us. And her partner, Roger, I suppose. We can spend time together. It'll be fine.' It is my turn to be strong now. 'As long as we promise always to be honest with each other, everything is going to be OK.'

'You do love me, don't you, Chris?'

'Of course. Of course I do.'

'And you forgive me for leaving you? I didn't want to.'

'Ben. I understand. I forgive you.' I look into his eyes. They seem dull and lifeless. 'I love you.'

His voice drops to a whisper. 'Kiss me.'

I do as he asks, and then he whispers, 'Kiss me again.'

I kiss him a second time. But, even though he asks me to, I cannot kiss him a third time. Instead we gaze out to sea. Just the two of us. Together.

We sit there for what feels like hours. Ben scans the water, as if looking for some answer in the dark. I wonder why he has brought us here.

'Is it really our wedding anniversary?' I say.

'No. It's the anniversary of the night we met.'

The moon is rising high in the sky. I begin to worry that we will stay out all night. I affect a yawn.

'I'm sleepy,' I say. 'Can we go to our hotel?'

'Of course. Sorry.' He starts the car. 'We'll go there right now.'

The coast road dips and rises as the lights of a town draw near. A marina appears with its moored boats and shops and nightclubs, and every building seems to be a hotel. The streets are busy; it is not as late as I had thought. A pier juts into the water, flooded with light and with an amusement park at its end. I can see a domed pavilion, a roller coaster, a helter-skelter.

An anxiety I cannot name begins to form in my chest.

'We're here,' says Ben, as we stop outside a terraced house. There is lettering on the canopy over the door. *Rialto Guest House*. There are steps up to the front door, an ornate fence separating the building from the road.

I am gripped with an intense fear.

'Have we been here before?' I say. 'It looks familiar.'

He shakes his head. 'We might have stayed somewhere near here once. You're probably remembering that.'

We get out of the car. There is a bar next to the hotel and through its windows I can see throngs of drinkers and a dance floor. Music thuds.

'We'll check in, and then I'll come back for the luggage. OK?'

I go up the steps and through the door into the lobby. There is a sign on the reception desk: NO VACANCIES.

'You've booked?' I say, when Ben joins me. We are standing in a hallway.

'Yes, of course,' says Ben. 'Don't worry.' He rings the bell.

A young man comes from somewhere at the back of the house. He is tall and awkward, and greets us as though he was expecting us. I wait while he and Ben complete the formalities.

It is clear the hotel has seen better days. The carpet is threadbare and the paintwork around the doorways scuffed and marked.

'I'll take you to the room now, shall I?' says the tall man. I realise he is talking to me; Ben is on his way back outside to get the bags.

'Yes,' I say. 'Thank you.'

He hands me a key and we go up the stairs. On the first landing are several bedrooms but we walk past them and up another flight. The house seems to shrink as we go higher. We pass another bedroom and stand at the bottom of a final flight of stairs.

'Your room is up there,' he says. 'It's the only one.'

I thank him and climb to our room.

I open the door. The room is dark and bigger than I was expecting, up here at the top of the house. The music from the club next door thuds, reduced to a dull, crunching bass. I stand still. Fear has gripped me again. Something is *wrong*. I am filled with an overwhelming terror of what will happen when I switch on the light.

What will happen if I leave? I could walk back along the corridor, past Ben if necessary, and out of the hotel. But they would find me and bring me back. And what would I tell them? That the woman who remembers nothing had a feeling she didn't like? They would think me ridiculous.

I have come here to be reconciled with my husband. I am safe with Ben. And so I switch on the light.

There is nothing to be frightened of. The room is unimpressive. The carpet is a mushroom-grey, the curtains and wallpaper both in a floral pattern, though they don't match. The dresser is battered, with a faded painting of a bird above it, and the bed is covered with an orange bedspread in a diamond design.

The fear has burned itself down to dread.

I close the door behind me and try to calm myself. I am being stupid.

The window is open. I go over to close it and look out across the rooftops. I see the cool moon hanging in the sky and, in the distance, the sea. I can make out the helter-skelter, the flashing lights. And then I see the words over the entrance. *Brighton Pier.*

BEN HAS BROUGHT ME to Brighton, to the place of my disaster. But why? Does he think I am more likely to remember what happened if I am back in the town in which my life was ripped from me? Does he think that I will remember who did this to me?

I remember reading that Dr Nash had suggested I come here and I had told him no.

There are footsteps on the stairs, voices. The tall man must be bringing Ben here, to our room. What should I tell him? That he is wrong and being here will not help? That I want to go home?

I go towards the door. I will help to bring the bags through, and then I will unpack and we will sleep, and then tomorrow—

Tomorrow I will know nothing again. That must be what Ben has in his satchel. Photographs. The scrapbook. He will have to explain who he is and where we are all over again.

I try to calm myself. Tonight I will put my journal under the pillow and tomorrow I will find it and read it. Everything will be fine.

I can hear Ben on the landing. He is talking to the tall man, discussing arrangements for breakfast. 'We'd probably like it in our room,' I hear him say. I go towards the door and then I see, to my right, a bathroom with the door open. A bath, a toilet, a basin. But it is the floor that fills me with horror. It is tiled and the pattern is unusual; black and white alternate in crazed diagonals.

I recognise the pattern.

It is not only Brighton that I have recognised.

I have been here before. In this room.

I SAY NOTHING as Ben comes in, but my mind spins. Is this the room in which I was attacked? Why didn't he tell me we were coming here? How can he go from not even wanting to tell me about the assault to bringing me to the room in which it happened?

He looks at me. 'Are you all right, love?' he says. I nod and say yes, but the word feels as though it has been forced out of me. He takes my arm, squeezing the flesh just a little too tightly. 'You're sure?'

'Yes,' I say. Why is he doing this? He must know where we are. 'I just feel a little tired.'

And then it hits me. Dr Nash must have something to do with this. Perhaps Ben called him after I told him about our meetings. Perhaps some time during the past week—the week I know nothing about—they planned it all.

'Why don't you lie down?' says Ben.

'I think I will.' I turn towards the bed, removing my shoes as I do so. Dr Nash might have been lying about everything. As I lie down, I picture him dialling Ben after he'd said goodbye to me, telling him about my progress.

'Good girl,' says Ben. 'I'll go and get some champagne. There's a shop, I think. It's not far.'

I turn to face him and he kisses me, puts his hand in my hair, strokes my back. I fight the urge to pull away. His hand comes to rest on the top of my buttock. I swallow hard.

I cannot trust anybody. Not my husband. Not the man who has claimed to be helping me. They have been working together. How dare they? I think. *How dare they!*

He turns and leaves the room. 'I'll just lock the door,' he says, as he closes it behind him. 'You can't be too careful . . .' I hear the key turn and begin to panic. Is he really going to buy champagne? Or is he meeting Dr Nash? I cannot believe he has brought me to this room without telling me —another lie to go with all the others. I hear him go down the stairs.

Thoughts race as if, in a mind devoid of memory, each idea has too much space to grow. I stand up, enraged. I cannot face the thought of him coming back, pouring champagne, getting into bed with me. Neither can I face the thought of his hands on me in the night, pawing at me, encouraging me to give myself to him. How can I, when there is no me to give?

I would do anything, I think. Anything, except for that.

I cannot stay here. I try to work out how much time I have. Ten minutes? Five? I go to Ben's bag and open it. I don't know why; perhaps I intend to find the car keys, to force the door and go out into the rainy street. Although I'm not even certain I can drive. Or perhaps I mean to find a picture of Adam; I know they're in there. I will take just one and then I will leave the room and run. I will run and run, and then I will call Claire, or anybody, and beg them to help me.

I dig my hands deep in the bag. I feel an envelope. I take it out and see that it is the one I found in the office at home. I must have put it in Ben's bag as I packed, intending to remind him it had not been opened. The word *Private* has been written on the front. I tear it open.

Paper. I recognise it. The faint blue lines, the red margins. These pages are the same as those in my journal. And then I see my own handwriting.

I have not read all of my story. There is more. Pages and pages more. I find my journal. I had not noticed before, but after the final page of writing a whole section has been removed, cut with a scalpel or a razor blade, close to the spine.

Cut out by Ben.

I sit on the floor, the pages spread in front of me. This is the missing week of my life. I read the rest of my story.

THE FIRST ENTRY is dated. *Friday, November 23*. The same day I met Claire. I must have written it that evening, after speaking to Ben. Perhaps we had had the conversation I was anticipating after all.

I sit here, it begins, *on the floor of the bathroom. Tissues are balled around me, soaked with tears, and blood. Blood drips into my eye as fast as I can wipe it away. The skin above my eye is cut, and my lip, too.*

I want to sleep. To find a safe place and rest, like an animal. That is what I am. An animal. Living from moment to moment, trying to make sense of the world in which I find myself.

I read back over the paragraph, my eyes drawn to the word *blood*. What had happened?

I begin to read quickly. I don't know when Ben will get back and can't risk him taking these pages before I have read them.

We ate in the lounge and, when we had finished, I asked if he would turn the television off. 'I need to talk to you,' I said.

'Darling,' said Ben, putting his plate on the table, a lump of meat on the side, peas floating in thin gravy. 'What's this about? What's wrong?'

'Ben, I know you've been lying to me.'

I saw him flinch. 'What do you mean? I haven't been lying to you.'

I felt a surge of anger. 'Ben,' I said, 'I know about Adam.'

His face changed. 'What?'

'I know we had a son. I know he died in Afghanistan.'

'How do you know that?'

'You told me weeks ago. I came downstairs and told you that I had remembered we had had a son, and then we sat down and you told me how he'd been killed. You showed me some photographs. Photos of me and him, a letter to Santa Claus—' Grief washed over me. I stopped talking.

Ben was staring at me. 'You remembered? How?'

'I've been writing things down. For a few weeks.'

'Where?' he said. He had begun to raise his voice, as if in anger, though I didn't understand what he might be angry about. 'Where have you been writing things down?'

'I've been keeping a journal.'

'For how long?'

'I don't know exactly. A couple of weeks.'

'Can I see it?'

I felt petulant and angry. 'Not yet.'

He was furious. 'Where is it? Show it to me.'

'Ben, it's private. I wouldn't feel comfortable with you reading it.'

'Why not?' he said. 'Have you written about me?'

'Of course I have.'

'What have you written? What have you said?'

I thought of all the ways I have betrayed him. The things I have said to Dr Nash, and thought about him. The ways in which I have distrusted my husband. I thought of the lies I have told, the days I have seen Dr Nash—and Claire—and told him nothing.

'Lots of things, Ben. I've written lots of things.'

'But why have you been writing things down?'

I could not believe he had to ask me that question. 'I want to make sense of my life,' I said.

'Are you unhappy? Don't you want to be with me, here?'

Why did he feel that wanting to make sense of my fractured life meant that I wanted to change it in some way?

'I don't know,' I said. 'What is happiness? I'm happy when I wake up, I think. But I'm not happy when I look in the mirror and see that I'm twenty years older than I was expecting. I'm not happy when I realise that all those years have been lost. So I suppose a lot of the time I'm not happy, but it's not your fault. I'm happy with you. I love you. I need you.'

He sat next to me. His voice softened. 'I'm sorry. I hate the fact that everything was ruined just because of that car accident.'

I felt anger rise in me again, but clamped it down. I had no right to be angry with him; he did not know what I had learned and what I hadn't.

'I know what happened. It wasn't a car accident. I was attacked.'

He looked at me, his eyes expressionless. 'What attack?'

I raised my voice. 'Stop it! Don't keep lying to me! I know there was no car accident. I know what happened. Denying it doesn't get us anywhere.'

He stood up. He looked huge, looming over me, blocking my vision.

'Who told you? Was it that bitch Claire shooting her ugly fat mouth off?'

'Ben—' I began.

'She's always hated me. She'd do anything to poison you against me.'

'It wasn't Claire,' I said. 'I've been seeing a doctor. He told me.'

He was perfectly motionless. When he eventually spoke, his voice was so low I struggled to make out the words.

'What do you mean, a doctor?'

'His name is Dr Nash. Apparently he contacted me a few weeks ago.'

'Saying what?'

'I don't know. I don't think I wrote down what he said.'

'And he encouraged you to write things down?'

'Yes. And we've been doing some tests. I had a scan—'

'A scan?' His voice was louder again.

'An MRI. He said it might help. They didn't really have them when I was first ill. Or they weren't as sophisticated as they are now—'

'Where have you been doing these tests?'

'In his office,' I said. 'I don't remember exactly.'

'How have you been getting there? How did someone like you get to a doctor's office?' His voice was pinched and urgent now. 'How?'

I tried to speak calmly. 'He's been collecting me from here. Driving me—'

What happened next was not what I was expecting. A dull moan began in Ben's throat. It built quickly until, unable to hold it in any more, he let out a screech, like iron nails on glass.

'Ben!' I said. 'What's wrong?'

I worried he was having some kind of attack and put my hand out for him to hold on to. He ignored it, steadying himself against the wall. His face was bright red, his eyes wide, spittle at the corners of his mouth.

'You stupid fucking bitch,' he said, his face inches from mine. 'How long has this been going on, you slut?'

'Nothing's going on!' I said. Fear welled within me. It did a slow roll on the surface and then sank again. I could smell the food on his breath. Meat, and onion. Spittle flew, striking me in the face, the lips.

'You're sleeping with him. Don't lie to me.'

The backs of my legs pressed against the edge of the sofa and I tried to move along it, to get away from him, but he grabbed my shoulders and shook them. 'You've always been the same,' he said. 'A stupid lying bitch. What have you been doing? Sneaking off while I've been at work? Or have you been having him round here?'

I felt his fingers and nails digging into my skin through my blouse.

'You're hurting me!' I shouted. 'Ben! Stop it!'

He loosened his grip a fraction. It didn't seem possible that the man gripping my shoulders could be the same man who had written the letter that Claire had given me. How could we have reached this level of distrust?

'I'm not sleeping with him,' I said. 'He's helping me get better so that I can live a normal life. Here, with you. Don't you want that?'

His eyes began darting around the room.

'Ben? Talk to me! Don't you want me to get better? Isn't that what you've always hoped for?' He began to shake his head, rocking it from side to side.

Hot tears ran down my cheeks, but I spoke through them, my voice fracturing into sobs. 'I met Claire. She gave me your letter. I've read it, Ben. After all these years. I've read it.'

There is a stain there, on the page. Ink, mixed with water. I must have been crying as I wrote. I carried on reading.

Perhaps I thought he'd fall into my arms, sobbing with relief. And then we would sit and talk things through. Perhaps I would go upstairs and get the letter and we would read it together, and begin the slow process of rebuilding our lives.

Instead, there was an instant in which everything was quiet. I didn't even hear the ticking of the clock. It was as if life was suspended, hovering on the cusp between one state and another.

Then Ben drew away from me. I was aware of a blur out of the corner of my eye and my head cracked to one side. Pain radiated from my jaw. I fell and the back of my head connected with something hard and sharp. I cried out. There was another blow, and then another. I closed my eyes, waiting for the next—but instead I heard footsteps moving away, and a door slamming. Ben had left.

I swallowed, and tasted blood.

I made sure he was gone, then came upstairs and found my journal. Blood dripped from my split lip. I don't know where my husband is, or if he will come back, or whether I want him to. But I need him to. Without him I can't live.

I am scared. I want to see Claire.

I stop reading and my hand goes to my forehead. It feels tender. The bruise I saw this morning, the one I covered up with make-up. Ben had hit me. I look back at the date. It was one week ago. One week spent believing that everything was all right.

I look in the mirror. The bruise is still there. A faint blue contusion. Proof that what I wrote is true. I look at the pages in my hand and it hits me. *He wanted me to find them.* He knows that even if I read them today, I will have forgotten them tomorrow.

Suddenly I hear him on the stairs and realise fully that I am in this hotel room with the man who has hit me. I hear the key in the lock.

I stand up, push the pages under the pillows on the bed and lie down on it quickly. He comes into the room, clutching a bottle. 'I could only get Cava,' he says. 'OK?'

He puts the bottle on the dresser. 'I think I'll take a shower,' he whispers, and goes into the bathroom.

When he has closed the door I pull out the pages. I don't have long—surely he will not be more than five minutes. My eyes flick down the page, not even registering all the words but seeing enough.

That was hours ago. I have been sitting in the darkened hallway, a slip of paper in one hand, a telephone in the other. There was no answer, just an endless ringing. I wonder if she has turned off her answering machine. I try again. And again. Claire is not there to help me.

I looked in my bag and found the phone that Dr Nash had given me. His home number was written in the front of my journal. It rang and rang, and then was silent. I tried again. The same.

I sat there for a while, looking at the front door, half hoping to see Ben's shadowy figure, half fearing it.

Eventually I went upstairs and got into bed and wrote this. In a moment I will close this book and hide it, and then switch off the light and sleep.

And then I will forget and this journal will be all that is left.

I look at the next page with dread, fearing I will find it blank, but it is not.

Monday, November 26
He hit me on Friday. Two days, and I have written nothing. For all that time, did I believe things were all right? My face is bruised and sore. Today he said that I fell and I believed him. Why wouldn't I? He'd already had to explain who I was. I kissed him as he left for work. And then I came in here, found this journal, and learned the truth.

I realise I have not mentioned Dr Nash. Had he abandoned me? Had I found the journal without his help? Or had I stopped hiding it? I read on.

Later, I called Claire. There was no answer, and so I looked at my journal, unable to concentrate, unable to write. I tried her again. She answered just after lunch time.

'I need to see you,' I said. 'Can you come over?'

'Is everything OK, Chrissy? You read the letter?'

I took a deep breath and my voice dropped to a whisper. 'Ben hit me.' I heard a gasp of surprise. 'The other night. I'm bruised. He told me I'd fallen, but I wrote down that he hit me.'

'Chrissy, there is no way Ben would hit you. He isn't capable of it.'

Doubt flooded me. Was it possible I'd made it all up?

'But I wrote it in my journal,' I said.

'Why do you think he hit you?'

I thought back to what I had written. 'I told him that I've been keeping a journal. I said I had been seeing you and Dr Nash. I told him I knew about Adam. I told him you'd given me the letter he'd written, that I'd read it. And then he hit me.'

'He just hit you?'

'He said I was a bitch.' I felt a sob rise in my chest. 'He—he accused me of sleeping with Dr Nash. I said I wasn't, then he hit me.'

A silence, then Claire said, 'Has he ever hit you before?'

I had no way of knowing. It was possible that ours had always been an abusive relationship.

'I don't know,' I said.

'It's difficult to imagine Ben hurting anything, but I suppose it's not impossible. It's just so hard to imagine. He's the one who convinced me that fish have as much right to life as an animal with legs.'

I felt a chill. 'Ben's vegetarian?'

'Vegan,' she said, laughing. 'Don't tell me you didn't know?'

I thought of the night he'd hit me. A lump of meat, I'd written.

'Ben eats meat,' I said. 'He's not vegetarian. Maybe he's changed?'

'Right,' Claire said. She sounded angry. 'I'm ringing him. I'm sorting this out. Where is he?'

'He'll be at the school, I suppose.'

'Do you mean the university? Is he lecturing now?'

'No,' I said. 'He works at a school near here. I can't remember the name.'

'What does he do there?'

'A teacher. He's head of chemistry, I think.' I felt guilty at not knowing what my husband does for a living. 'I don't remember.'

'I'm sorry, Chrissy. I didn't mean to upset you. Could you find out the name of the school? I'd like to speak to him.'

I went upstairs. The office was tidy, piles of papers arranged across the desk. It did not take long to find some headed paper.

'It's St Anne's,' I said. 'You want the number?'

She said she'd find it out herself. 'I'll call you back.'

I sat down, my legs shaking. What if Claire and Ben were still sleeping together? Maybe she was calling him now, warning him. She suspects, *she might be saying.* Be careful.

I remembered reading my journal earlier. Dr Nash had told me that I had once claimed the doctors were conspiring against me. A tendency to confabulate. Everything in my journal might be fantasy. Paranoia.

I thought of what they'd told me on the ward, that I was occasionally violent. I realised it might have been me who caused the fight on Friday night. Did I lash out at Ben? Perhaps he hit back and then I took a pen and explained it all away with a fiction.

What if all this means I'm getting worse again? I went cold, suddenly convinced that this was why Dr Nash had wanted to take me to Waring House. To prepare me for my return.

All I can do is wait for Claire to call me back.

Is that what's happening now? Will Ben try to take me back to Waring House? I look over to the bathroom door. I will not let him.

There is one final entry, written later that same day.

Monday, November 26—6.55 p.m.

Claire called me after less than half an hour. And now my mind swings from one thing to the other: I know what to do. I don't know what to do. But there's a third thought—I am in danger.

She sounded hesitant. 'Chrissy, I called Ben at school.'

Her tone frightened me. I sat down. 'What did he say?'

'I didn't speak to him. I just wanted to make sure he worked there.'

'Why?' I said. 'Don't you trust him?'

'He's lied about other things. You know he trained to be an architect? The last time I spoke to him he was setting up his own practice. I thought it was odd he should be working in a school.'

'What did they say?'

'They said they couldn't disturb him. He was in a class.'

I felt relief. He hadn't lied about that, at least.

'I told them I wanted to send him a letter and asked for his official title.'
'And?' I said.
'They said he was a lab assistant.'
'Are you sure?' I said. My mind raced to think of a reason for this new lie. Was it possible he was embarrassed? Worried what I would think if I knew he had gone from being a successful architect to a lab assistant in a local school? Did he really think I was so shallow?
'Oh God,' I said. 'It's my fault! It's the strain of having to look after me. He must be having a breakdown. Maybe he doesn't even know himself what's true and what's not.' I began to cry. 'It must be unbearable. He even has to go through all that grief on his own, every day.'
'What grief?'
'Adam,' I said. I felt pain at having to say his name.
'What about Adam?'
Oh God, I thought. She doesn't know. Ben hasn't told her.
'He's dead,' I said.
She gasped. 'Dead? When? How?'
'I think it was last year. He was killed in Afghanistan.'
'Chrissy, what would Adam be doing in Afghanistan?'
'He was in the army,' I said, but even as I spoke I was starting to doubt what I was saying.
'Chrissy darling, Adam hasn't been in the army. He's never been to Afghanistan. He's living in Birmingham with someone called Helen. He works with computers. He hasn't forgiven me still, but I ring him occasionally. I'm his godmother, remember?'
It took me a moment to work out why she was using the present tense, and as I did so she said it. 'I rang him after we met last week. He wasn't there, but I spoke to Helen. She said she'd ask him to ring me back. Adam is alive.'

I stop reading. I feel light. Empty. Dare I believe it? I read on, only dimly aware that no longer do I hear the sound of Ben's shower.

'He's alive? But I saw a newspaper clipping. It said he'd been killed.'
'It can't have been real, Chrissy.'
Images entered my head, of Adam as he might be now, fragments of scenes I may have missed, but none would hold. The only thing I could think was that my son is alive.

'Where is he?' I said. 'Where is he? I want to see him!'

'Chrissy, stay calm.'

I am hysterical. I take a breath. 'Why doesn't he visit me?'

'Birmingham is a fair way away,' she said, her voice soft. 'But maybe he does come, when he can.'

I fell silent. She was right. I have been keeping my journal for only a couple of weeks. Before that, anything could have happened.

'I need to see him,' I said. 'Do you think that can be arranged?'

'I don't see why not. But if Ben is really telling you that he's dead then we ought to speak to him first.'

'He'll be home soon. Will you come over and help me sort it out?'

'Of course,' she said. 'We'll talk to Ben, I promise. Something's not right.'

Her tone bothered me, but I felt excited that I might soon meet my son. I wanted to see his photograph right away. A thought began to form.

'Claire,' I said, 'did we have a fire?'

She sounded confused. 'A fire?'

'We have very few photographs of Adam or of our wedding. Ben said we lost them in a fire in our old home years ago.'

'No photographs of Adam?'

'Not many. Hardly any of him other than when he was a baby. A toddler. And none of holidays, not even our honeymoon.'

'Chrissy,' she said. Her voice was measured. I thought I detected some new emotion. Fear. 'Describe Ben to me.'

'What about the fire?' I said. 'Tell me about that.'

'There was no fire years ago. Ben would have told me. Now, describe Ben. Is he tall?'

'Not particularly.'

'Black hair?'

My mind went blank. I went back upstairs. The photographs were pinned around the mirror. Me and my husband. Happy. Together.

'His hair looks kind of brown,' I said. I heard a car pull up outside. 'I think Ben's home.'

'Shit,' said Claire. 'Quick. Does he have a scar?'

'A scar?' I said. 'Where?'

'Across one cheek. He had an accident rock climbing.'

I scanned a photograph of me and my husband sitting at a breakfast table. Apart from a hint of stubble, his cheeks were unblemished.

I heard the front door open.
'No,' I said. 'No, he doesn't.'
A sound. Somewhere between a gasp and a sigh.
'The man you're living with,' Claire said. 'I don't know who it is. But it's not Ben.'

Terror hits. I hear the toilet flush, but can do nothing but read on.

I don't know what happened then. I can't piece it together. Claire began talking, almost shouting. 'Fuck!' she said, over and over. My mind was spinning with panic. I heard the front door shut, the click of the lock.
'I'm in the bathroom,' I shouted to the man I had thought was my husband. My voice sounded cracked. Desperate. 'I'll be down in a minute.'
'I'll come round,' said Claire. 'I'm getting you out of there.'
'Everything OK, darling?' shouted the man who is not Ben.
I heard his footsteps on the stairs and lowered my voice. 'Come tomorrow. While he's at work. I'll pack my things.'
'OK,' she said. 'But write in your journal. Don't forget.'
I thought of my journal, hidden in the wardrobe. I must pretend nothing is wrong until I can write down the danger I am in.
I ended the call as he pushed open the bathroom door.

IT ENDS THERE. Frantic, I fan through the last few pages but they are blank. Ben had found the journal, removed the pages, and Claire had not come for me. When Dr Nash collected the journal—on Tuesday 27th, it must have been—I had not known anything was wrong.

I look up. Ben, or the man pretending to be Ben, has come out of the shower. He is standing in the doorway, looking at me. I don't know how long he has been there, watching me read. His eyes hold nothing more than a sort of vacancy.

I drop the papers. 'You!' I say. 'Who are you? Answer me!' My voice has an authority to it, but one that I do not feel.

My mind reels as I try to work out who he could be. Someone from Waring House, perhaps. A patient? Nothing makes any sense.

'I'm Ben.' He speaks slowly, as if trying to make me understand the obvious. 'Your husband.'

I move away from him. Claire's words come back to me. *But it's not Ben.*

I realise I am not remembering reading about her saying those words; I am remembering the incident itself. I can remember the panic in her voice.

I am remembering.

'You're not Ben,' I say. 'Claire told me! Who are you?'

'Remember the pictures, though? Look, I brought them.'

He reaches for his bag on the floor. He picks out a few curled photographs. 'This is us. Look. Me and you.' The photograph shows us sitting on a boat, on a river or canal. We both look young, our skin taut, our eyes unlined and wide with happiness. 'We've been together for years, Chris.'

He holds up another picture. We are much older now. It looks recent. We are standing outside a church. The day is overcast and he is wearing a suit. I am wearing a hat that I am holding as if it is in danger of blowing off.

'That was just a few weeks ago,' he says. 'Some friends of ours invited us to their daughter's wedding.'

I remember reading what Claire had said when I told her I had found a newspaper clipping about Adam's death. *It can't have been real.*

'Show me one of Adam,' I say. 'Go on! Show me just one picture of him.'

He takes out the picture of Adam with Helen. The one I have already seen. 'Show me a picture of Adam with you in it. You must have some if you're his father?'

'I don't have one with me. They must be at the house.'

'What father wouldn't have pictures of himself with his son? And what kind of father would tell his wife that their son was dead when he isn't? Admit it! You're not Adam's father! Ben is.' Even as I said the name, an image came to me. A man with narrow, dark-rimmed glasses and black hair. I say his name again, as if to lock the image in my mind. 'Ben.'

The name has an effect on the man standing in front of me. 'You don't need Adam,' he says. 'You have me now. You don't need Adam. You don't need Ben.'

At his words I sink to the floor. He smiles.

'Don't be upset,' he says, brightly. 'What does it matter? I love you. That's all that's important, surely. I love you and you love me.' He crouches down, holding out his hands towards me. 'Come to me.'

I shift farther back, hit something solid and feel the radiator behind me. He advances slowly.

'Who are you?' I try to keep my voice even. 'What do you want?'

He stops moving. He is crouched in front of me. If he were to reach out he could touch my foot, my knee. If he were to move closer I might be able to kick him, should I need to, though I am not sure I could reach and, in any case, am barefoot.

'I don't want anything,' he says. 'I just want us to be happy like we used to be. Do you remember?'

Remember. For a moment I think he is being sarcastic. 'How can I remember? I've never met you before!'

I see his face collapse in on itself. 'But you love me,' he says. 'I read it, in your journal.'

'My journal!' I know he must have known about it—how else did he remove those pages?—but now I realise he must have been reading it since I first told him about it a week ago. 'How long have you been reading my journal?'

He doesn't seem to have heard me. He raises his voice, as if in triumph. 'Tell me you don't love me.' I say nothing. 'See? You can't. Because you do. You always have done.'

He rocks back, and the two of us sit on the floor, opposite each other. 'I remember when we met,' he says. 'You were always writing. You used to go to the same café every day. You always sat in the window. Sometimes you had a child with you, but usually not. I thought you looked so beautiful. I used to walk past you on my way to catch the bus, and I started to look forward to my walk home so that I could catch a glimpse of you. I used to try and guess what you might be wearing, or whether you'd have your hair pulled back or loose, or whether you'd have a cake or a sandwich.'

I remember Claire telling me about the café and know that he is speaking the truth. 'One day, you weren't there. I waited until I saw you coming down the street, pushing a buggy, and when you got to the café door you seemed to have trouble going through it. I held the door for you. And you smiled at me. You looked so beautiful, Christine. I wanted to kiss you, and I stood behind you in the queue. You spoke to me as we waited. I wondered if I should ask you whether it would be OK for me to sit with you, but by the time I'd got my tea you were chatting to someone, so I sat on my own.

'After that I used to go to the café almost every day. And you noticed me. You began to say hello. Then one time there were no free tables and you said, "Why don't you sit here?" and you pointed opposite you. Do you remember?'

I shake my head. I want to find out everything he has to say.

'You said you'd had a book published but you were struggling with your second one. I asked what it was about, but you wouldn't tell me. "It's fiction," you said, "supposedly" and you looked very sad, so I offered to buy you another cup of coffee. After that we started to meet quite regularly.'

I begin to see it all. The casual meeting, the exchange of a drink. The appeal of confiding in a stranger, one who doesn't take sides because he can't. The gradual acceptance into confidence, leading to . . . what?

I have seen the photographs taken years ago. He was attractive, better-looking than most; it is not difficult to see what drew me. At some point I must have started thinking about what clothes I would wear when I went to the café, whether to add a dash of perfume. And, one day, one or the other of us must have suggested we go for a walk, or to a bar, and our friendship slipped over a line, into something infinitely more dangerous.

I try to imagine it and, as I do, I begin to remember.

The two of us in bed, naked. Me turning to him as he begins to kiss me again. 'Mike!' I am saying. 'Stop it! You have to leave soon. Ben's back later and I have to pick Adam up.' But he doesn't listen. Instead he leans in, his moustachioed face on mine, and we are kissing again, forgetting about everything, about my husband, about my child. I realise that a memory of this day has come to me before in the kitchen of the house I once shared with my husband. I had not been remembering my husband, but my lover. That's why he had to leave—because the man I was married to would be returning home.

He is still crouching in front of me.

'Mike,' I say. 'Your name is Mike.'

'You remember!' he says. He is pleased. 'Chris! You remember!'

Hate bubbles up in me. 'I remember your name. Nothing else.'

'You don't remember how much in love we were?'

'No,' I say. 'I don't think I could ever have loved you, or surely I would remember more.'

I say it to hurt him, but his reaction surprises me. 'You don't remember Ben, though, do you? You can't have loved him. And not Adam, either.'

'You're sick,' I say. 'Of course I loved him. He was my son!'

'Is. Is your son. But you wouldn't recognise him if he walked in now, would you? And where is he? And where is Ben? They walked out on you, Christine. I'm the only one who never stopped loving you. Not even when you left me.'

Then it hits me, finally. How else could he have known about this room, about so much of my past?

'Oh my God,' I say. 'It was you who attacked me!'

He moves over to me then. He wraps his arms around me and begins to stroke my hair. 'Christine darling,' he murmurs, 'don't think about it. It'll just upset you.'

I try to push him off me but he is strong. He squeezes me tighter, rocking me as if soothing a baby. 'My love, you should never have left me. None of this would have happened if you hadn't gone.'

Memory comes again.

We are sitting in a car, at night. I am crying.

'You don't mean it,' he says. 'You can't.'

'I'm sorry. I love Ben. We have our problems, yes, but he's the person I am meant to be with. I'm sorry.'

I am aware that I am trying to keep things simple, so that he will understand. I have come to realise that complicated things confuse him. He likes order. Things mixing in precise ratios with predictable results.

'It's because I came round to your house, isn't it? I just wanted to explain to your husband—'

I interrupt him. 'Ben. You can say his name. It's Ben.'

'Ben,' he says, as if finding the word unpleasant. 'I wanted to tell him that you love me now. That you want to be with me.'

'Even if it were true—which it isn't—it's not you who should be saying that to him. It's me. You had no right to turn up at the house.'

As I speak I think about what a lucky escape I have had. Ben was in the shower and I was able to persuade Mike that he ought to go home. That night I decided I had to end the affair.

'I have to go now,' I say. I open the car door, step out.

He leans across to look at me. I think how attractive he is, that if he had been less damaged my marriage might have been in real trouble. 'Will I see you again?' he says.

'No,' I reply. 'It's over.'

Yet here we are all these years later. I begin to scream.

'Darling,' he says. 'Calm down.' He puts his hand over my mouth and I scream louder. My head smacks backwards, connects with the radiator behind me. The music from the club next door is louder now. They will never hear me. I scream again.

'Stop it!' he says.

My head hits the warm metal again and I begin to sob. 'Let me go,' I plead. He relaxes his grip a little, though not enough for me to wriggle free. 'How did you find me?'

'I never lost you,' he says. 'I watched over you. Always.'

'You visited me in the hospital? Waring House?'

'They wouldn't have let me. But I would sometimes tell them I was there to see someone else, or that I was a volunteer. Just so that I could see you. At that last place it was easier. All those windows . . .'

I go cold. 'You watched me?'

'I had to know you were all right, Chris. When I found out that bastard had left you, I couldn't just leave you in that place. I knew you'd want to be with me. Who else would have looked after you?'

I wonder what lies he must have told for them to let him take me, then remember reading what Dr Nash had told me about the woman from Waring House. *She was so happy when she found out you'd gone back to live with Ben.* An image forms. My hand in Mike's as he signs a form. A woman behind a desk says, 'We'll miss you, Christine, but you'll be happy at home with your husband.'

'My God!' I say now. 'How long have you been pretending to be Ben?'

His face falls. He looks upset. 'Do you think I wanted to do that? I had to. It was the only way.'

His arms relax, slightly, and an odd thing happens. My mind stops spinning, and, although I remain terrified, I am infused with a bizarre sense of complete calm. A small voice in my head comes from nowhere. *I will beat him. I will get away. I have to.*

'Mike?' I say. 'I do understand, you know. It must have been difficult.'

He looks up at me. 'You do?'

'Yes, of course. I'm grateful to you for coming for me. For giving me a home. For looking after me.'

'Really?'

'Yes. Just think where I'd be if you hadn't. I couldn't bear it.'

I sense him soften. The pressure on my arms and shoulder lessens and is accompanied by a subtle sensation of stroking that I find almost more distasteful, but I know is more likely to lead to my escape. I need to get away. That same voice comes in again. *I will escape.* I move my head to face him, and begin to stroke the back of his hand where it rests on my shoulder.

'Why not let me go and then we can talk about what we should do?'

'How about Claire, though? She knows I'm not Ben. You told her.'

'She won't remember that,' I say, desperately.

He laughs, a hollow, choked sound. 'You always treated me like I was stupid. I'm not, you know. I know what's going to happen! You told her. You ruined everything!'

'No,' I say quickly. 'I can tell her I was confused. That I'd forgotten who you were. That I thought you were Ben, but I was wrong.'

'She'd never believe you. Why did you have to call her?' His face clouds with anger, he begins to shake me. 'Why?' he shouts. 'Why?'

'Ben,' I say. 'You're hurting me.'

He hits me. I hear the sound of his hand against my face before I feel the flash of pain.

'Don't you ever call me that again,' he spits. 'I'm sick of being Ben. You can call me Mike from now on. OK? That's why we came back here. So that we can put all that behind us. You wrote in your book that if you could only remember what happened here then you'd get your memory back. Well, we're here now. So remember!'

I am incredulous. 'You *want* me to remember?'

'Of course I do! I love you, Christine. I want you to remember how much you love me. I want us to be together again.' His face is inches from mine. I can smell sourness on his breath, and another smell, too. I wonder if he's been drinking. 'We're going to be OK, aren't we, Christine? We're going to move on.'

'Move on?' I say. 'Are you crazy?' He moves his hand to clamp it over my mouth and I realise that has left my arm free. I hit out, catching him by surprise. He falls backwards, letting go of my other arm as he does.

I stumble to my feet and head towards the door. He grabs my ankle and I come crashing down. My head hits a stool and my body twists awkwardly. Pain shoots up my back and I am afraid I have broken something. He pulls me towards him with a grunt and then his crushing weight is on top of me, his lips inches from my ear.

'Mike,' I sob. 'Mike—'

'You stupid bitch,' he says. One of his hands is round my throat; with the other he has grabbed a handful of my hair. He pulls my head back, jerking my neck up. 'Where did you think you were going to go, eh?' he says. He is snarling now, an animal. 'Where do you think you're going to run to? You can't drive. You don't know anybody. You don't even know who you are most of the time. You're pathetic.'

I start to cry, because he is right. Claire never came; I have no friends. I rely totally on the man who did this to me and, tomorrow morning, if I survive, I will have forgotten even this.

If I survive. The words echo through me as I realise what this man is capable of and that, this time, I may not get out of this room alive. Then I hear the voice again. *This is not the place you die.*

Lunging forward I grab the leg of the stool. It is heavy but I manage to twist round and heave it back over my head where I imagine Mike's head will be. It strikes something with a satisfying crack and there is a gasp in my ear. He lets go of my hair.

I look round. He has his hand to his forehead. Blood is beginning to trickle between his fingers. Later, I will think how I should have hit him again. I should have made sure he was incapacitated, that I could get away.

But I do not. I pull myself upright and then I stand, looking at him on the floor in front of me. No matter what I do now, I think, he has won. He has taken everything from me, even the ability to remember what he did to me. I turn towards the door.

With a grunt he launches himself at me. Together we slam into the dresser. 'Christine!' he says. 'Don't leave me!'

I reach out. If I can just open the door then, surely, someone will hear us?

He clings to my waist. Like some grotesque, two-headed monster we inch forward, me dragging him. 'Chris! I love you!' he says. The ridiculousness of his words spurs me on. Soon I will reach the door.

Then I remember that night all those years ago. Me, in this room, reaching out a hand towards the same door. I am happy. The air is tinged with the sweet smell of the roses in the bouquet that is on the bed. *I'll be with you around seven, my darling*, said the note that was pinned to them, and I am glad of the minutes I have had alone before he arrives. It has given me the opportunity to reflect on what a relief it has been to end the affair with Mike. Mike would never have done what Ben has done: arrange a surprise night away in a hotel to show me how much he loves me and that, despite our recent differences, this will never change.

I am touching the handle of the door, twisting it, pulling it towards me. We have a whole weekend in front of us.

'Darling,' I am starting to say, but the word is choked off. It's not Ben at the door. It's Mike. He is pushing past me and, even as I am asking him what he thinks he is doing—what right he has to lure me here, to this room, what he thinks he can achieve—I am thinking, You devious bastard! How dare you pretend to be my husband!

I look at the flowers, the bottle of champagne he holds in his hand. Everything smacks of romance. 'My God!' I am saying. 'You really thought you could just lure me here, give me flowers, and everything would go back to being like it was before? You're crazy, Mike. I'm leaving now. Going back to my husband and my son.'

I suppose that must have been when he first hit me but, after that, I don't know what happened. And now I am here again, in this room. We have turned full circle, though for me all the days between have been stolen. It is as though I never left.

I cannot reach the door. I begin to shout. 'Help! Help!'

'Quiet!' he says. 'Shut up!'

I shout louder and he swings me round. I fall and my skull hits something hard and unyielding. I realise he has pushed me into the bathroom. I twist my head and see the tiled floor stretching away from me. 'Mike!' I say. 'Don't . . .' But his hands are around my throat.

'Mike—' I gasp. I cannot breathe. Memory floods back. I can remember him holding my head under water. I remember waking up, in a white bed, wearing a hospital gown, and Ben sitting next to me, the real Ben. I remember a policewoman asking me questions I cannot answer. A little boy with blond hair and a tooth missing calling me Mummy. One after another the images flood through me. Mike grips me tighter, his eyes wild and unblinking as he squeezes my throat and I can remember it being so once before, in this room. 'How dare you!' he is saying, and I cannot work out which Mike it is who's speaking: the one here now or the one who exists in my memory.

'How dare you!' he says again. 'How dare you take my child!'

Then I remember. When he had attacked me all those years ago, I had been carrying a baby. Not Mike's but Ben's. The child that was going to be our new start together.

Neither of us had survived.

I MUST HAVE BLACKED OUT. When I regain consciousness I am sitting in a chair. I cannot move my hands. Mike is sitting opposite me, on the edge of the bed. He is holding something in his hand. I try to speak but cannot.

I realise something is in my mouth. It has been tied in place and my wrists are tied together, also my ankles.

This is what he wanted all along, I think. Me, silent and unmoving. He stares at me, right into my eyes. I feel nothing but hate.

'This isn't what I wanted,' he says. 'I thought we would come here and it might help you to remember how things used to be between us. And I could explain what happened here, all those years ago. I never meant for it to happen, Chris. I just get so angry, sometimes. I'm sorry. I ruined everything.'

There is so much more I used to want to know, yet I am exhausted. I feel as though I could close my eyes and will myself into oblivion, erasing everything. Yet I do not want to sleep tonight. And if I must sleep, then I do not want to wake up tomorrow.

'It was when you told me you were having a baby.' He speaks softly and I have to strain to hear what he is saying. 'I never thought I'd have a child. They all said—' He hesitates, deciding that some things are better not shared. 'You said it wasn't mine. But I knew it was. And I couldn't cope with the thought that you were going to take my baby away from me, that I might never see him. You think I'm not sorry for what I did? Every day you wake up and look at me and I know you don't know who I am. I can feel the disappointment and shame. That hurts. Knowing that you'd never sleep with me now if you had the choice. And then you go to the bathroom and I know that in a few minutes you will come back confused and in so much pain.'

He pauses. 'And now even that will be over soon. I've read your journal. I know your doctor will have worked it out by now. Claire, too. I know they'll try to take you away from me. But Ben doesn't want you. I do. Please, Chris, remember how much you loved me. You can tell them that you forgive me. For this. And then we can be together.'

I cannot believe he *wants* me to remember what he has done.

He smiles. 'Sometimes I think it might have been kinder if you'd died that night. Kinder for both of us. I would join you, Chris, if that's what you wanted. You could go first, and I promise you I would follow.' He looks at me, expectantly. 'Would you like that?'

I shake my head, try to speak, fail. I can hardly breathe.

'No?' He looks disappointed. 'I suppose any life is better than none.' I begin to cry. He shakes his head. 'Chris. This will all be fine. This book is the problem.' He holds up my journal. 'We were happy before you started writing this. We should just get rid of it, and you could tell them you were confused and we could go back to how it was before.'

He puts a metal bin from beneath the dresser on the floor between his legs. 'Easy.' He drops my journal into the bin and adds the last few pages that are littering the floor. 'We have to get rid of it once and for all.' He takes a box of matches out of his pocket.

I look at him in horror. 'No!' I try to say; nothing comes but a muffled grunt. He doesn't look at me as he sets fire to a page and drops it into the bin.

I watch my history begin to burn to ash. My journal, the letter from Ben, everything. I am nothing without that journal, I think. And he has won.

I launch my body at it. With my hands tied I hit it awkwardly, hearing something snap as I twist. Pain shoots up my arm. The bin falls over, scattering burning paper across the floor.

Mike cries out and falls to his knees, trying to put out the flames. I see that a burning shred has come to rest under the bed, unnoticed. Flames are beginning to lick at the edge of the bedspread but I can neither reach it nor cry out and so I simply watch the bedspread catch fire. The room will burn, I think, and Mike will burn, and I will burn, and no one will ever know what happened in this room, just like no one will ever know what happened all those years ago, and history will turn to ash and be replaced by conjecture.

I cough, a dry, heaving retch. I am beginning to choke. I think of my son. I will never see him now, though at least I'll die knowing he is alive and happy. I think of Ben. The man I married and then forgot. I want to tell him that now, at the end, I can remember him. I can remember meeting him at that rooftop party, and him proposing to me on a hill looking out over a city, and I can remember marrying him in the church in Manchester, having our photographs taken in the rain.

And, yes, I can remember loving him. I know that I do love him, and I always have.

Things go dark. I can't breathe. I can hear the lap of flames, and feel their heat on my lips and eyes. There were never going to be any happy endings for me. But that is all right.

I AM LYING DOWN. I have been asleep, but not for long. I can remember who I am, where I have been. I can hear noise, the roar of traffic, a siren that is neither rising nor falling in pitch but remaining constant. Something is over my mouth yet I find I can breathe. I am too frightened to open my eyes. I do not know what I will see. But I must. I have no choice but to face whatever my reality has become.

The light is bright. The walls are close by on each side, and they are shiny with metal and perspex. Everything is moving slightly, vibrating, including, I realise, the bed in which I am lying.

A man's face appears from somewhere behind me. He is wearing a green shirt. I don't recognise him. 'She's awake,' he says and more faces appear. I scan them quickly. Mike is not among them and I relax a little.

'Chrissy,' comes a woman's voice I recognise. 'We're on our way to the hospital. You've broken your collarbone but you're going to be all right. That man is dead. He can't hurt you any more.'

It's Claire. The same Claire I saw just the other day, not the young Claire I might expect to see after just waking up. She leans forward and whispers something in my ear. It sounds like 'I'm sorry.'

'I remember,' I say. 'I remember.'

A young man takes her place. He has a narrow face and is wearing thick-rimmed glasses. For a moment I think it is Ben, until I realise that Ben would be my age now.

'Mum?' he says. 'Mum?'

'Adam?' Words choke in my throat as he hugs me.

'Mum,' he says. 'Dad's coming. He'll be here soon.'

I pull him to me, breathe in the smell of my boy, and I am happy.

I CAN WAIT NO LONGER. I must sleep. I have a private room and so there is no need for me to observe the strict routines of the hospital, but I am exhausted. It is time.

I have spoken to Ben. To the man I really married. He told me that he flew in as soon as the police contacted him.

'When they realised you weren't living with the person Waring House thought you were living with, they traced me. I've been working in Italy for a few months.' He took my hand. 'I thought you were OK. I'm sorry . . .'

'You couldn't have known,' I said.

He looked away. 'I left you, Chrissy. I thought it was for the best. I thought it would help you. Help Adam. I thought I could only get on with my life if I divorced you. Adam didn't understand, even when I explained you wouldn't remember being married to me.'

'Did it?' I said. 'Did it help you to move on?'

He turned to me. 'I won't lie to you, Chrissy. There have been other women. At first nothing serious, then I met someone a couple of years ago. But that ended. She said I'd never stopped loving you.'

'And was she right?'

He did not reply and, fearing his answer, I said, 'So what happens now? Tomorrow? Will you take me back to Waring House?'

'No,' he said. 'She was right. I never stopped loving you. And I won't take you there again. Tomorrow, I want you to come home.'

NOW HE SITS in a chair next to me and, although he is already snoring, he still holds my hand. I can just make out his glasses, the scar running down the side of his face. My son has left the room to phone his girlfriend and whisper a good night to his unborn daughter, and my best friend is in the car park, smoking a cigarette. I am surrounded by the people I love.

Earlier, I spoke to Dr Nash. He told me I had left the care home almost four months ago, a little while after Mike had started visiting, claiming to be Ben. I had left voluntarily. When I left, I took with me the few photographs and personal possessions that I still had.

'That was why Mike had those pictures?' I said. 'The ones of me and Adam. The letter to Santa Claus? Adam's birth certificate?'

'Yes,' said Dr Nash. 'At some point, Mike must have destroyed all the pictures that showed you with Ben. The staff turnover at Waring House is high and they had no idea what your husband really looked like.'

'But how would he have got access to the photographs?'

'They were in an album in your room. He might even have slipped in a few photographs of himself. He must have had some of the two of you taken when you were seeing each other, years ago. The staff were convinced that the man visiting you was the same one as in the album.'

Dr Nash looked tired and guilty. I hoped he didn't blame himself for any of what had happened. He had rescued me.

'How did you find me?' I said.

He explained that Claire had been frantic with worry after we'd spoken, but she had waited for me to call the next day. 'When you didn't call, Claire tried to phone you, but she only had the number for the mobile phone I had given you, and Mike had taken that. I should have known something was wrong when I called you on that number this morning and you didn't answer. But I didn't think. I just called you on your other phone . . .'

'It's OK,' I said. 'Go on.'

'Mike must have removed the pages from your journal that night. That was why you didn't think anything was wrong when you gave me the journal on Tuesday. It's fair to assume he'd been reading your journal for at least the past week or so, probably longer.'

I think of this man discovering my journal, reading it every day. Why didn't he destroy it? Because I'd written that I loved him. And because that was what he wanted me to carry on believing.

Or maybe I am being too kind. Maybe he just wanted me to see it burn.

'Claire didn't call the police?'

'She did. But it was a few days before they took it seriously. In the meantime, she'd got hold of Adam and he'd told her that Ben had been abroad and that, as far as he knew, you were still in Waring House. She contacted them and they gave Adam my number as I'm a doctor. Claire got through to me only this afternoon. She convinced me something was wrong and finding out that Adam was alive confirmed it. We came to see you at home, but by then you'd left for Brighton.'

'How did you know to find me there?'

'You told me this morning that Ben—sorry, Mike—had told you that you were going away to the coast for the weekend. Once Claire told me what was going on I guessed where he was taking you.'

'But you told me Adam was dead,' I said. 'You said he'd been killed. And you told me there'd been a fire, too.'

He smiled sadly. 'Because that's what you told me. I told you the truth as I believed it. It was the same with the fire. I believed there'd been one, because that's what you told me.'

'But I remembered Adam's funeral,' I said. 'His coffin . . .'

Again the sad smile. 'Your imagination . . .'

'But I saw pictures. That man'—I found it impossible to say Mike's name—'showed me pictures of me and him together, of us getting married. I found a picture of a gravestone. It had Adam's name—'

'He must have faked them,' he said. 'It's quite easy to mock up photos these days on a computer. It's quite likely that some of the photos you thought were of the two of you were also faked.'

I thought of the times I had written that Mike was in his office. Working. Is that what he'd been doing?

'Are you OK?' said Dr Nash.

'I think so.' I looked at him and realised I could picture him in a different suit, with his hair cut much shorter.

'I can remember things,' I said.

'What things?'

'I remember you with a different haircut,' I said. 'And I recognised Ben, too. And I can remember seeing Claire the other day. We went to the café at Alexandra Palace. She has a son called Toby.'

'Have you read your journal today?'

'Yes, but I can remember things that I didn't write down. I remember the earrings that Claire was wearing. And I remember that Toby was wearing a blue parka and had cartoons on his socks. I didn't write those things down. I remember them.'

He looked pleased. 'Dr Paxton did say he could find no obvious organic cause for your amnesia. That it seemed likely that it was at least partly caused by the emotional trauma of what had happened to you. I suppose it's possible that another trauma might reverse that, at least to some degree.'

I leaped on what he was suggesting. 'So I might be cured?' I said.

He looked at me intently, weighing up what to say. 'It's unlikely. There's been a degree of improvement over the past few weeks, but nothing like a complete return of memory. But it is possible.'

'Doesn't the fact that I remember what happened a week ago mean that I can form new memories again? And keep them?'

He spoke hesitantly. 'It would suggest that, yes. But the effect may well be temporary. We won't know until tomorrow.'

'When I wake up?'

'It's entirely possible that after you sleep tonight all the memories you have from today will be gone. All the new ones and all the old ones.'

'It might be exactly the same as when I woke up this morning?'

'Yes,' he said. 'It might.'

That I might wake up and have forgotten Adam and Ben seemed too much to contemplate. It felt like it would be a living death.

'Keep your journal, Christine,' he said. 'You still have it?'

I shook my head. 'He burned it. That's what caused the fire.'

'That's a shame. But it doesn't really matter. You can begin another. The people who love you have come back to you.'

'But I want to have come back to them, too,' I said.

We talked for a little while longer but he was keen to leave me with my family. I know he was only trying to prepare me for the worst. But I have to believe that he is wrong. That my memory is back. I have to believe that.

I look at my sleeping husband. I remember again us meeting, that night of the party, the night I watched the fireworks with Claire on the roof. I remember him asking me to marry him on holiday in Verona and the rush of excitement I'd felt as I said yes. And our wedding too, our marriage, our life. I remember it all. I smile.

'I love you,' I whisper, and I close my eyes, and I sleep.

s.j. watson

Profile

Born:
1971. Stourbridge, West Midlands.

Education:
Read Physics at the University of Birmingham.

Jobs:
Worked in various hospitals and specialised in the diagnosis and treatment of hearing-impaired children.

Favourite writer:
Margaret Atwood. I love the breadth of her work.

Writing tip:
Write one word at a time. Put the hours in. Don't be too hard on yourself.

Secret of his success:
Luck.

Website:
www.sjwatson-books.com

You attended the Faber Academy's first six-month-long 'Writing a Novel' course. Did you enjoy it?

I loved every moment of it, and really can't praise it highly enough! I met, and learned from, some wonderful writers, and I made some lifelong friends. I learned so much—everything from how to capture the essence of a character to how to write a synopsis and pitch your book to an agent—but it was also incredible just to be surrounded by people who took their writing as seriously as I did, and who understood what the writing life involves.

What writing regime do you follow?

I wrote *Before I Go to Sleep* while working part-time in the NHS, so as well as writing pretty solidly on my 'writing days' I used to grab the odd hour whenever I could at weekends and in the evenings. I'm not a great believer in the rituals around writing—I think it's important to remember that really one can write anywhere and with any instrument—so while a lot of the book was written either at my dining-room table or at the library in the Barbican, a huge amount was written on trains, in various hotel rooms and in a not insignificant number of cafés and bars!

Where did the idea for *Before I Go To Sleep* come from?

I was reading about a man called Henry Molaison who suffered severe amnesia following an operation he underwent when he was twenty-seven. He died at the age of eighty-two, and for all that time could form no new memories. I was struck by the image of that old man waking up and looking in the mirror, fully expecting a twenty-seven-year-old to be gazing back at him. I realised how vital our memories are to our sense of self, and from that seed the whole novel began to grow.

What was the most challenging element of the novel?

I decided to tell the story in the first person, from the point of view of someone who has severe amnesia. That presented some tricky technical challenges, particularly as I edited the book. I had to keep a close eye on the things my character knew at any given time, and the things she didn't.

Why did you write it from a female perspective?

I did toy with the idea of writing the novel from a male perspective. But I realised very quickly it would have been a very different story and I wouldn't have been able to explore some of the ideas I'd been thinking about for a while. Also there was an element in it of me wanting to get as far away as possible from my own life as I could. Although now the book has been finished for a couple of years, I can see there are bits of me everywhere!

You published the novel with just your initials 'S. J.' instead of your Christian names. Was this your way of putting Christine's voice to the test?

Yes. I did feel the whole book would fall apart if the voice didn't sound authentic, so it is really nice when people come up to me at events and say, 'I'm really sorry, I thought you were a woman.' They apologise and my answer is always, 'Please don't apologise, it's incredibly flattering—in the field of writing at least.'

How much research did you do?

I did a fair bit of research for *Before I Go to Sleep* as I wanted it to be as medically and scientifically accurate as it could be, and I also wanted to try to understand what it must be like living with a memory problem. So most of my research was around that. But also there's a lot of observation involved, and I'm always looking for details. Everywhere I go I'm thinking 'What makes this café different?' or 'How could I bring that person to life on the page? What is unique about them?' I've never really gone to extreme lengths to research a scene, though for my new book I might have to!

What do you hope people take away with them after reading your novel?

It's a thriller, and there are a few surprises along the way, so I hope people finish the book with a feeling that they've been on an exciting journey. But I also wanted to ask some questions about identity, about what makes us who we are, and also about ageing and the nature of love, so my hope is that people will be thinking about those kind of issues, too.

How has life changed for you since the success of your debut novel?

I'm lucky enough that I can now focus on writing as a full-time job, rather than trying to fit my writing in around the rest of my life.

SIEGE

SIMON KERNICK

THE STANHOPE HOTEL, PARK LANE,

LONDON.

For duty manager, Elena Serenko, it's just a routine

day in the 5-star hotel.

Upstairs in their hotel rooms, a young woman awaits

her lover; an American family prepare for an evening

out; a sick man contemplates his own mortality; and a

skilled and dangerous killer is settling an old score.

But then terror strikes the Stanhope as a group of

ruthless gunmen burst into the building, shooting

indiscriminately and taking hostages.

Will anyone make it out alive?

THURSDAY MORNING
ONE

07.45

They killed her as soon as she opened the front door. It was all very easy. Bull was dressed in a navy-blue Royal Mail cap and sweater, looking just like any ordinary postman, and he was carrying a box with the Amazon logo on the side in front of him, so the girl didn't suspect a thing.

Fox was standing just out of sight. He was dressed similarly to Bull, and was wearing a backpack. He also had a semiautomatic pistol with a suppressor attached down by his side, so that no one walking past the front gate would see it. He brought the pistol up as the girl came into view, and before she had a chance to acknowledge his presence, he pulled the trigger, shooting her in the temple. Thanks to the suppressor the noise it made was little more than a loud pop. The girl fell back against the doorframe, and Bull dropped the empty box and caught her under the arms as her legs gave way.

Moving past him, Fox produced a balaclava from his pocket and pulled it over his head as he walked through the hallway, the gun outstretched in front of him. He was making for the back of the house. Behind him he could hear Bull dragging the dead girl into the hallway and closing the door.

'Who is it, Magda?' a male voice called out from the kitchen.

'Nobody move,' said Fox, striding into the room.

A well-built middle-aged man in a shirt and tie sat at the table holding a mug of tea. Opposite him were a boy and a girl in different school uniforms. The kids were twins but they didn't look much alike. The boy was tall for fifteen, with the same broad shoulders as his father, and a shock of boy-band blond hair, while the girl was small and dumpy, and looked much younger. All three of them stared at Fox with shocked expressions.

'I'm afraid Magda's dead,' said Fox, pointing the gun at the father, his hand perfectly steady. 'Now, everyone needs to cooperate, or they die too. And that means stay absolutely still.'

Nobody moved a muscle.

Bull joined him in the room. He was wearing his balaclava now and he stood near the doorway, waiting for orders. As the name suggested, Bull was a big guy. He was also dim-witted and did what he was told without question, which was why he'd been chosen for this particular job. That and the fact that he didn't seem to possess any obvious compassion for or empathy with his fellow human beings.

'Please,' said the father, meeting Fox's gaze and keeping his voice calm, 'take what you want and leave. We haven't got much.'

Fox glared at him. The father had been a police sergeant for seventeen years before being invalided out when he'd been stabbed on duty three years earlier, and he was therefore used to being in control of confrontations, which made him potentially dangerous. Fox's finger tightened on the trigger. 'Don't say another word or I'll put a bullet in your gut. Understand? Nod once for yes.'

The father nodded once, giving his two children a look of reassurance.

'Stand up, turn round and face the wall.'

'Don't hurt my dad,' said the boy, who Fox knew was called Oliver.

'No one gets hurt if you all do as you're told.' Fox's tone was cold but even. He knew it was essential that he didn't give off any sign of weakness, but also that he didn't do anything to panic the prisoners. It was all a very delicate balancing act. For the moment, they had to be kept alive.

'We're not going to offer any resistance,' said the father, getting up and facing the window. 'But can you tell me what this is all about?'

'No.'

'We're just an ordinary family.'

Well, you're not, thought Fox, otherwise we wouldn't be here. But he didn't say that. Instead he said, 'Because it's early in the morning, I'm going to pretend that you're still only half awake and didn't hear me the first time. If you talk again, I will shoot you. I'd prefer to have three of you alive, but I can just as easily manage with two.'

That was when the father belatedly seemed to realise that he was dealing with professionals and fell silent once again.

Fox slipped the backpack off and threw it to Bull, who unzipped it and pulled out plastic flexi-cuffs and ankle restraints. He went over to the father, pulled his hands roughly behind his back and started to put on the cuffs.

'I'm not pointing the gun at you any more,' Fox told him, moving his gun arm to the left, 'I'm pointing it at your son's head. Remember that.'

The father stiffened, and seemed about to say something, then settled for a simple nod.

'Where's your phone?'

'In my pocket.'

'Thank you. If you'd be kind enough to get it, Bull.'

Bull nodded, fastened the father's ankles, then did a quick search of his pockets, coming up with an iPhone 4, which he handed to Fox.

'What's the code to unlock it?'

The father told him. Fox pocketed the phone and wrote the number down on the inside of his forearm.

'Right, kids, your turn. Up against the wall, next to your dad.'

For a few seconds the twins didn't move. The girl—Fox had been told her name was India—was staring down at the table, while Oliver was breathing heavily and clenching and unclenching his fists. He got up first, giving Fox a defiant look, before going over to stand to the right of his dad. Fox admired his guts. It took something to pull a face at a man who's pointing a gun at you. India was a different story. She remained glued to her seat, and Bull had to lift her to her feet and shove her bodily against the wall.

When all three had been restrained and were standing in a forlorn row with their backs to him, Fox took out the father's iPhone and took a photo of them. Then he told them to turn round and took another one. India was looking weepy; the father was looking scared but in a manly, lantern-jawed way; Oliver was still glaring from beneath his blond hair.

He got them to turn round again so they were facing away from him, and handed the gun to Bull. 'Cover them,' he said. 'Anyone moves, shoot them in the leg.'

Pulling off his balaclava, Fox went back out towards the front door, stepping over Magda's body, which Bull had propped up against the wall, walked out of the house and down to where he'd parked the van.

The street was fairly quiet. It was an affluent area of detached 1950s homes and Fox guessed that people minded their own business here. Fox backed the van through the gates and up the gravel driveway, stopping just outside the front door. He opened the van's rear doors and went back inside the house.

'OK, we're all going for a short drive,' he announced as he entered the kitchen, pleased to see that nobody had moved.

'Can you tell us where we're going?' asked the father.

'Unfortunately not, but I can confirm that your stay will be temporary. By this evening you'll be released, and this will be an unpleasant memory.'

As he finished speaking, he pulled the Taser from his backpack, clipped on the cartridge, and let the father have it with the two electrodes. He went down with an almighty crash, and the kids both jumped.

'What are you doing to my dad?' yelled Oliver.

'Keeping him quiet for a moment,' said Fox calmly.

He grabbed Oliver by the collar of his school blazer and dragged him out into the hallway. At the same time, Bull wrapped one of his huge arms round a now near-hysterical India's neck and, shoving the gun in her back, brought her out behind.

Oliver gasped when he saw Magda's corpse.

'She's dead,' he said with the first hint of a wail.

Before he could say another word, Fox kicked his legs from under him and forced him to the floor, so that his and Magda's shoulders were almost touching. Bull forced India down next to Magda on the other side, pushing the end of the suppressor into her forehead to help things along. She'd stopped crying now but still looked suitably distraught.

Fox pulled out the father's iPhone and took two photos of the three of them together, then switched the setting to video as Bull slowly moved the gun from one child to the other. The message was obvious.

When that was done, Fox put hoods on the kids, securing them in place with duct tape, and led them out one by one to the van. He made them lie next to each other on the floor, checking their pockets to make sure they weren't carrying mobiles before locking the van doors. He also switched off the father's iPhone. Fox knew how easy it was to trace mobiles.

Finally Fox turned to Bull. 'You know what to do,' he said. 'It's time.'

Bull nodded, and the two of them went back inside.

The father was still lying on the floor, already beginning to recover from the Taser. Bull sat down on his chest, his knees pinning the father's arms down, and pushed the end of the suppressor into his face. The father's eyes widened in alarm and he tried to move his head. Bull pulled the trigger.

It had never been the plan to take the father along with them. The kids were far more useful to them than he was.

'Now you're one of us,' Fox said as Bull got slowly to his feet.

Bull smiled. He looked pleased.

Fox took the gun from him, slipping it into the back of his trousers, and checked his watch. 07.51. Bang on schedule.

But as they walked back to the front of the van, Fox ran into the first complication of the day. An old lady with a mad head of white hair was walking a couple of ratlike dogs past the open gates. Straightaway she slowed down and clocked him and Bull with a long stare that said (a) she'd not seen them round these parts before, and (b) because of this she was noting all their physical details just in case they were up to no good.

She was going to have to die too.

Relying on the fact that he was a fairly ordinary-looking white man in his mid-thirties and therefore not all that threatening for an old suburban lady, Fox smiled broadly. 'Excuse me,' he called out, striding down towards her, his gun hidden from view, 'I wonder if you can help us?'

His plan was simple. Pull her inside the gate, break her neck, and hide the body in the bushes. Then throttle the yappy little hounds.

The old lady stopped, but she was looking past Fox towards the van and Bull. That was the flaw in the plan. Bull. He was sure the big oaf was giving the old bitch one of his dead-eyed glares.

Fox was closing in on her. He kept talking, trying to allay her suspicions. 'We're meant to be delivering a washing machine, but there's no answer . . .'

Three more seconds and she'd be his.

But the old lady suddenly looked scared. 'I'm sorry I can't help,' she said quickly, and before he could put out a hand to grab her she turned on her heel and hurried beyond the gate, just as a UPS truck came past, slowing down to negotiate the parked cars on either side of the road.

Fox cursed and walked quickly back to the van.

'You didn't give her one of your looks, did you?' he said to Bull, getting in alongside him.

Bull shook his head, his expression defensive. 'I didn't look at her at all, Fox. Honest.' His voice was deep yet with an irritating childlike whine to it.

Fox sighed, then started the engine and pulled out of the drive.

The old lady was twenty yards away now. It was almost light, way too risky for them to try anything now, so he drove off in the opposite direction, hoping that by the time she realised the significance of what she'd just seen it would be far too late for her to do anything about it.

It started to rain, that cold November drizzle that goes right through to the bones, and as Fox looked up at the leaden grey sky he thought that it really was an awful day. And for many people, not least the ones in the back of the van, it was soon going to get a whole lot worse.

15.05

So she'd finally done it. Got engaged. She was twenty-eight years old—near enough an old woman in the eyes of her parents' generation. In fact, her mother had already had three children by the time she'd turned twenty-eight. But unlike her mother, who'd married young and stayed at home to raise her family, Elena Serenko had put everything into her career. In the ten years since she'd come to London from Poland she'd risen from a night receptionist in a rundown dump in Catford to the youngest duty manager at the 320-room Stanhope Hotel on Park Lane, one of the West End's most prestigious five-star establishments. Not a bad achievement for a girl from rural Krasnystaw.

And now, after all that, it looked like she would be leaving. Her boyfriend of eighteen months—sorry, fiancé—Rod was Australian, and he wanted them to go out there to live. His family home was in a coastal town south of Sydney, and she knew how much he missed the sunshine and the ocean. When Rod had proposed to her the previous evening, she'd replied with a delighted yes, because she truly loved him. He'd then dropped his second bombshell, saying he wanted to be home for Christmas. For good. With her.

But Christmas was only five weeks away, which meant she'd have to give in her notice within the next few days. She'd asked Rod for a couple of days to think about it, as it was all so sudden, and because of the man he was, he'd agreed. But as she walked across the Stanhope's grand lobby Elena Serenko made up her mind. Just like that. She wasn't normally impulsive, but as soon as the decision was made she knew it was the right one.

The thought filled her with a mix of nervousness and excitement, and she vowed to call Rod and tell him the good news as soon as she had a spare moment. Right now, though, she had work to do.

Elena made a quick check of the mezzanine floor to ensure that the ballroom had been cleaned properly after the three-day conference that had finished in there that morning (it had, and it looked immaculate), then slipped into the satellite kitchen behind it.

Like all big hotels, the Stanhope had a number of satellite kitchens situated at points in the building where food from the main kitchens on the ground floor could be reheated before being served to guests. The kitchen behind the ballroom contained a walk-in store cupboard, which was a favourite among certain members of staff for taking a sneaky nap in, because there was a crawlspace beneath the bottom shelf where a person could lie out straight and not be seen. Pretty much everyone had put their head down there at one time or another.

Feeling oddly mischievous, Elena tiptoed over to the store cupboard door and gently opened it, bending down in the near-darkness so she could see inside the space, although from the sound of gentle snoring she already knew there was someone in there.

She smiled. It was Clinton, the ancient maintenance man who'd been with the hotel for more than thirty years. He was on his back, his tool belt by his side, his ample belly inflating and deflating as he slept like a baby.

If it had been anyone else, Elena would have woken them up and given them a talking to, but Clinton was a hard worker, she was in a good mood, and he looked so damn peaceful down there she couldn't bring herself to do it. So she left him there, closing the door gently behind her.

15.25

The Westfield Centre in Shepherd's Bush is London's largest shopping mall. It opened for business on October 30, 2008 and contains 255 stores spread over 150,000 square metres of retail space—equivalent to thirty football pitches. An underground car park with 4,500 spaces is situated directly beneath the centre, and although there were still more than five weeks to go until Christmas, spaces were already few and far between as Dragon drove the white Ford Transit van onto the car park's upper level. By a stroke of luck he managed to find a space next to the pedestrian walkway, barely fifty metres from the entrance to the lifts. Out of the corner of his eye he saw a harassed-looking woman in expensive designer clothes unload two preschool boys from her 4x4, and shove them into a double-pushchair.

In the back of the van were sixteen 47-kilo cylinders of propane gas piled on top of one another in groups of four. Wedged between the cylinders and the front seats of the van was a rucksack containing a specially modified mobile phone set to vibrate, a battery pack and a 3-kilo lump of C4 plastic explosives. When a call was made to the phone, the vibrations would complete the electrical circuit, thereby setting off the detonator and igniting the

C4, which in turn would ignite the propane gas, causing a huge fireball.

Casualties wouldn't be particularly high since the bomb would hit only those people passing by and the blast wouldn't have the force to cause any damage within the centre itself. But that wasn't the point. The point was to cause panic and chaos among the civilians in the immediate area, and to stretch and divide the resources of the security services so that they'd be less quick to react when the main operation got underway.

NOTHING EVER PREPARES YOU for it. The moment the consultant walks into the room and closes the door quietly behind him, and you see that look on his face. The grim resignation as he prepares to give you the news you've been waiting for, ever since he did the tests. And you know the news is bad.

The consultant takes a deep breath, and—'I'm afraid there's nothing we can do, Mr Dalston. Your particular cancer is inoperable.'

Strangely, you don't react. You just sit there, and now that the words have been spoken, you feel a sense of bleak calm. There is, at least, no more suspense.

The consultant, a dapper little Asian man called Mr Farouk who always wears brightly coloured bow ties, starts talking about chemotherapy and the opportunity it provides to prolong life, but you're not really listening. You ask only one question. The obvious one. The one we'd all ask straightaway.

'How long?'

With chemotherapy, as long as two years, although Mr Farouk is quick to point out there are no guarantees.

'And without chemotherapy?'

'In my opinion, an absolute maximum of six months.'

And that's it. The death sentence has been passed.

In the end, Martin Dalston had decided against chemotherapy. He had read up enough about advanced liver cancer and didn't see the point, mainly because the end result was always going to be the same. It felt too much like prolonging the agony. When he'd told his ex-wife and their seventeen-year-old son, they'd both tried to persuade him to reconsider. He wanted to enjoy his last days, he told them, even though the words had sounded empty as soon as he'd spoken them. Sue had been remarried for two years, so those last days weren't really going to involve her.

Robert was different. Until he'd become a teenager, he and his father had been very close. They'd grown apart as the marriage had descended into its death spiral, with Robert regularly siding with his mother in their arguments, or ignoring both of them. But the news of Martin's cancer had brought them back together. They'd taken a week out to go to Spain, a fishing trip to the Ebro river, where they'd bonded over good food and good conversation.

And then the sickness had started: the intense bouts of abdominal pain, the chronic tiredness, the nausea and, finally, the weight loss. Martin knew he was fading. Given his views on treatment, he had only two alternatives. One: let the cancer take him at its own pace, with Robert there by his side helplessly watching him as he deteriorated. Or two: end matters himself.

Martin had never been a particularly brave man. But perhaps, he thought, as he walked into the lobby of the Stanhope Hotel that afternoon, there was an inner steel in him after all. Because today was going to be the last day of his life and he felt remarkably calm about it.

Room 315, which he'd booked four days earlier, was ready for him. The pretty young receptionist smiled and wished him a pleasant stay in lightly accented English, and he thanked her with a smile of his own, and said he would, before heading for the lifts.

For the first time, he felt guilty about doing what he was about to do in a public place like a hotel room, where his body would inevitably be discovered by an unfortunate member of staff. He could, he supposed, have done it in the poky little flat he called home, but somehow that seemed far too much like a lonely end. There was something comforting about having other people near him when he went, even if they were strangers.

When he got to the door of 315, he stopped as the memories came flooding back. Memories of the only time he'd truly been in love—indeed, truly happy—and he felt an intense wave of emotion wash over him. This had been their place, twenty-two years ago. He thought of her now, all those thousands of miles away, and wondered if she was even still alive. In the past few weeks he'd seriously considered making contact to let her know what had happened to him, but in the end he'd held back. There was too much scope for disappointment. Carrie Wilson was the past, and it was far better simply to have her as a lingering, beautiful memory.

THE RENDEZVOUS was an empty warehouse on the Park Royal industrial estate just north of the A40 that had been hired on a three-month lease by an untraceable offshore company registered in the United Arab Emirates.

Fox was the first to arrive, at 15.40. It took him five minutes to get through the complex set of locks they'd added to maximise security. Once he was inside, he did a quick sweep of the main loading-bay area with a bug finder. Once he was satisfied that the place was clean, he put a call in to Bull using one of the three mobiles he was carrying. He'd left Bull with the kids at a rented house three miles away that morning.

Bull answered with a simple 'yeah' on the second ring.

'It's me,' said Fox, pacing the warehouse floor. 'Everything all right?'

'All good. I just checked up on them now.'

He sounded alert enough, and Fox was sure he wouldn't hesitate to do what needed to be done when the time came. Fox ended the call and switched off the phone.

There was an office at the end of a narrow corridor leading from the loading bay, and he unlocked the door and went inside, switching on the lights. At the far end of the room, hidden behind a pile of boxes, was a large padlocked crate. As he did every time he came here, Fox checked the contents, making sure that nothing had been tampered with.

The weaponry for the operation originated from Kosovo. It consisted of eight AK-47 assault rifles, six Glock 17 pistols with suppressors, grenades, body armour and 25 kilos of C4 explosive, along with detonators and thousands of rounds of ammunition. It had been bought from a group of former members of the Kosovo Liberation Army in a deal arranged by the client, before being smuggled into Scotland. From there, the crate had been collected by Fox and several other members of the team, and driven to London.

Because the C4 had still been in powder form, Fox had delivered it separately to a lockup in Forest Gate, along with the detonators, where it had been collected by the people whose job it was to turn it into bombs. Fox had no idea of their identity. Then, two weeks later, he'd received a text telling him to go back to the lockup, where six identical black North Face backpacks and a small suitcase were waiting for him, all of them now converted into deadly weapons.

Fox pulled out one of the Kevlar vests, grabbed a set of stained navy-blue decorator's overalls from a built-in cupboard next to the door, and got changed, packing the civilian clothes he'd come here in, and which he'd be needing later, into a backpack. Fox could feel the excitement building in him now. This was it. The culmination of months of planning. Success, and the whole world was his. Failure, and it would be his last day on earth.

Death or glory. The choice was that stark. It reminded him of his time in the army, in those all too rare moments when he'd seen action. It was that feeling of being totally and utterly alive. He loved the thrill of violence, always had. And today, for the first time in far too long, he was going to get the chance to experience that thrill on a grand scale.

Down the corridor, he heard the sound of the rear loading doors opening, and he smiled. The others were beginning to arrive.

CAT MANOLIS paced the hotel room, wondering if it was work or the interminably heavy London traffic that was delaying her lover.

Their affair had started innocently enough. The occasional shared smile as they passed each other in the corridor at work, or in the gym beneath the building, where they both worked out. It had been weeks before he'd asked her out for a coffee. Everything had had to be so secret. It was the same old thing. He was trapped in a loveless marriage, a handsome, charismatic man in need of female attention, possessed of the kind of power that was always such an aphrodisiac, even to a woman barely half his age.

They'd met for coffee one Saturday morning in a pretty little café on the South Bank. He'd made an excuse to his wife, telling her he had to come into town, and they'd spent a snatched couple of hours together. They'd walked along the banks of the Thames, and Cat had put her arm through his as they talked. She'd told him about her upbringing in Nice, how she'd married a man who was the love of her life, only to lose him a week before her twenty-fourth birthday. It was grief, then, that had brought her to London five years earlier. He'd seemed genuinely touched by her story.

'I care for you very much,' he'd said when it was time for them to part.

They'd kissed passionately. When they'd finally broken apart, they'd promised to meet again as soon as circumstances allowed.

Since then they'd had three separate trysts—all involving coffee, followed by a walk—and all the time they'd been moving towards this day. When they would finally sleep together for the first time.

Cat was dressed seductively in a simple sleeveless black dress that finished just above the knee, sheer black hold-up stockings, and black court shoes with four-inch heels. Usually she dressed far more modestly and, as she stopped and looked at herself in the room's full-length mirror, she felt a frisson of excitement. She looked good. There was no doubt about it. Michael would melt when he saw her.

If, of course, he turned up.

16.00

'If we want to survive, then we have to operate like a well-oiled machine. That means obeying orders when they're given. Innocent people are going to die. But that's not our problem. They're collateral damage in a war. At no point can you forget that, or suddenly develop an attack of conscience, because if you hesitate about pulling the trigger, or refuse, then the penalty's immediate death. No exceptions. We can't afford for the machine to break down. If it does, we're all dead, or worse still, in the hands of the enemy, which means the rest of our lives in prison. And I'm not going to let that happen. Clear?'

Fox looked in turn at each of the four men facing him, watching for any signs of doubt in their eyes, but none of them gave anything away. All of them had worked for him in the past, and they had three things in common. One: extensive military experience in a combat role. Two: no spouses or dependants. And three, and most important of all: they were all disaffected individuals who harboured a rage against the many perceived injustices in the world—a rage that had manifested itself in the heady mix of violent extremism. There were other motives at play too, which explained why they'd chosen to become involved—money, boredom, a desire once again to see real action—but it was the rage that was the most important, because it would be this that drove them to do what was needed today.

There were two he considered totally reliable. One was Dragon, the ex-sapper he'd picked to drive the van bomb to the Westfield. He was on the run from prison, where he was being held on remand on a number of explosives charges. He'd run down and killed a ten-year-old boy in a hijacked car during the course of his escape, as well as seriously injuring a prison officer, and he was facing the rest of his life inside if he was recaptured.

The other was Leopard, a short, wiry former marine who'd ended up being court-martialled in Afghanistan for breaking the British Army's ultra-strict rules of engagement by carrying out an unauthorised kill on two members of a Taliban mortar team. He'd served more than two years inside on manslaughter charges—just, in his mind, for doing his job—and the burning anger he felt at his treatment was authentic.

Tiger, a typically Aryan Dane who'd received extensive shrapnel injuries while serving in Afghanistan and walked with an aggressive limp, also had plenty of ruthlessness, but Fox was a lot less sure of his reliability. A one-time member of a neo-Nazi group, Tiger had grown up with an almost psychotic hatred of Jews, and after his experience in Afghanistan had added

Muslims to his list of sworn enemies, along with politicians and, as far as Fox could tell, pretty much everyone else who didn't agree with him.

And then there was Bear, the so-called 'man with the face'. Fox trusted Bear the least. And yet he owed him the most. Bear had once saved his life when they were serving together in Al-Amarah back in 2005 by spotting an IED half buried in a ditch as the platoon was passing by on patrol. Fox had been closest to it and would have taken the brunt of the blast, but Bear had shouted a warning and jumped on his back, sending them both sprawling into the dirt just as it was detonated. Fox had been temporarily deafened by the blast but was otherwise unhurt. Bear had been less lucky. A jagged, burning piece of shrapnel had struck him on the side of the face. Fox had managed to pull it free. The shrapnel had burned away most of the flesh just beneath the eye to the jaw line, leaving him permanently disfigured, and bitterly resentful of the politicians he'd always blamed for it.

Bear had worked with Fox since those army days, and Fox knew that he was a proven killer, but he was still concerned that, when it came down to it, Bear wouldn't be able to murder an innocent person in cold blood.

Fox turned to the sixth man in the room, standing next to him. 'Now, I'm going to hand you over to Wolf, who you've all met before. I just want to reiterate that he's the client's representative, and in overall command of the operation on the ground, while I'm acting as his second-in-command. You refer to him, as you refer to me, and each other, by code name rather than rank, and never, at any point, use real names. Understood?'

The men nodded, and Wolf took a step forward. He was a short, squat man, well into his forties, with dark skin and a pockmarked face that, combined with his lacquered, dyed-black hair, gave him more than a passing resemblance to the former Panamanian dictator, General Noriega.

'In the next fifteen minutes, you are all going to be half a million dollars richer,' he announced in a clear, strong Arabic accent. 'As soon as I give the word, the money will be sent to your nominated bank accounts. The remainder, one and a half million dollars, will be paid at nine o'clock tomorrow morning, on successful completion of the job. Before I give the word for the first instalment, however, I need proof that we are all committed.'

Wolf reached into his overalls pocket and produced a mobile phone.

'We all know about the decoy bomb in the Westfield Shopping Centre car park that Dragon delivered. The man who presses the call button on this phone will detonate it. I understand that we'll be able to hear the explosion in here, as we're only a mile away.' He paused for a moment, watching them carefully. 'So, my friends, who wants to make the call?'

Dragon spoke up. 'I drove the van, I'll do it.' He put out a hand.

He looked like he'd do it too, thought Fox. So did Tiger, the psychotic Dane, who was standing there with an expression of utter boredom on his face. Leopard wore an impassive expression. He'd do it too, if he had to. Bear, though, was sweating. Wolf noticed it too, Fox could tell.

Bear lowered his eyes, trying not to draw attention to himself, but it didn't work.

Wolf lobbed the phone over to him. 'You do it.'

Bear caught it in one gloved hand, looked at it, then looked at Fox, the expression in his eyes demanding 'you owe me, help me out here'.

But Fox couldn't. There would be no favouritism on his part.

Bear took a deep, very loud breath, his finger hovering over the button.

Fox's voice cut across the room. 'We said no hesitation.'

He and Bear stared at each other as if locked in a silent battle of wills.

Fox saw Wolf slip a pistol from his waistband and hold it down by his side. Bear was unarmed. All of them were except him and Wolf.

Wolf's gloved finger tensed on the trigger.

Bear pressed the call button in one swift decisive movement.

The silence in the room was absolute.

And then they heard it. A dull thud coming from the south.

Fox straightened up and took a deep breath. There was no going back now. The operation had begun.

16.05

The man called Scope heard it in the cramped flat he'd been renting for the past month. A faint but distinctive boom. It was a sound that would always remind him of heat and death. He ignored it. He guessed it was probably just a crane dropping its load on one of the many building sites that dotted this surprisingly drab part of west London.

He finished dressing and looked at himself in the mirror. The face that stared back at him was lined and gaunt, with skin that was dark and weather-beaten from the sun. He bore the haunted look of a man who'd seen and done far too much and there was a hardness in his flint-grey eyes that was impossible to disguise. Still, he was going to have to try.

He produced a pair of horn-rimmed glasses from the breast pocket of his cheap black suit and put them on, adopting a polite, almost obsequious expression. 'Good afternoon, sir,' he said, addressing the mirror with a respectful, customer-oriented smile. 'May I have a word? It's about a small discrepancy on your latest bill.' Not perfect, but it would have to do.

Turning away, he picked up the small tools he was going to need from the coffee table, and secreted them about his person. Finally, he slipped the hotel name tag introducing him as 'Mr Cotelli, Manager' into his breast pocket and headed for the front door of the rental flat.

He made his way down to the street, hailed the first passing cab and asked the driver to take him to the Stanhope Hotel.

ELENA WAS HUNTING DOWN one of the room-service waiters, a new addition to the team called Armin, who'd gone AWOL. There had been three separate complaints about missing room-service meals and, according to the kitchen, Armin was responsible for at least two of the missing meals. She'd asked the catering manager, Rav, to check the male toilets on each floor, but so far he hadn't shown up there either.

As she headed onto the fire-exit staircase, hoping finally to call Rod, she heard someone talking on the steps above her. Looking up, she saw a young room-service waiter on the phone by the third-floor doors. His tray was on the floor in front of him. She'd never met Armin before, but she'd have bet a week's wages it was him. Elena marched up to him.

He quickly ended his call and replaced the phone in his pocket.

'Armin,' she snapped, reading his name tag. 'Where have you been? Rooms 422 and 608 haven't received their food orders.' She looked down at the full tray at his feet. 'I assume that's them.'

Armin looked her up and down dismissively. 'Sorry,' he said in heavily accented English, sounding like he didn't mean it. 'I was on the phone.'

'Who to?'

He hesitated before answering. 'A friend.'

'You shouldn't be calling your friends in office hours. Especially when you're in the middle of delivering room-service orders. Don't you want this job? Because there are plenty of people out there who do.'

Armin looked her right in the eye, and there was such naked rage in his expression that she took a step back. 'I said I was sorry,' he said quietly. 'I'll deliver the order now.' He picked up the tray and continued up the stairs, leaving Elena staring after him.

She took a deep breath. The confrontation had really shaken her. She could tell from the way he'd spoken that he despised her. Yet she'd never even met him before. She turned and started back down the stairs, determined to have a word with Rav and get him to sack Armin the moment his shift was finished.

16.28

The First Great Western from Bristol Temple Meads crawled snakelike into Paddington Station, two minutes behind schedule.

The young man was one of the first to his feet, picking up his rucksack from the floor in front of him. He hauled it over his shoulders, making sure the detonation cord was out of sight but within easy reach, and headed for the exit door at the end of the carriage.

There was a bottleneck forming as the tiny corridor between carriages became thronged with passengers, and he was forced to stop next to the luggage rack, only feet from the trolley suitcase containing five kilos of explosives rigged up to a battery pack and mobile phone. No one had noticed him bringing it on earlier, and by the time anyone realised that it had been left behind it would be too late.

The train came to a stop and the doors opened. Immediately, the bottleneck eased as the passengers exited one at a time. When it came to the young man's turn, he took a quick look up the platform at the wall of people pouring down the platform towards him from the rear coaches, then stepped down and joined them.

This was it. The time. He'd been building up to it for months now. Ever since the cowardly dogs of NATO had declared war on his country and tried to divide its peoples so that they could steal the oil that was rightfully theirs. And now he had the honour of being one of the few chosen to strike back.

The young man had been travelling on the train's third carriage, and when he was level with the beginning of the first carriage he took his phone from his pocket and speed-dialled the number on the screen.

The sound of the explosion was deafening. Even though he'd steeled himself against it, and was wearing noise-suppressing headphones, he was still pushed forward and fell to one knee.

For a long time, no one moved. This was the moment of shock, when everyone's senses were so scrambled they didn't know how to react. And then the screams started.

Slipping the phone back into his jacket pocket, he got to his feet and took a first look at the mayhem behind him.

Thick black smoke and claws of flame billowed out of a huge hole in the side of the train. There were a lot of people lying unmoving on the platform, while others were on their hands and knees, clutching at injuries. He couldn't tell how many because his view was blocked by people—some trying to help, others simply milling about with shocked, terrified expressions, and a few sensible ones making a dash towards the exits and safety.

The young man took no pleasure from the scene, but he felt no guilt either. This was war. And in war, there were always civilian casualties.

The station staff had opened the ticket gates now and were yelling at people to get away from the source of the explosion, while a couple of overwhelmed-looking police officers shouted for people to leave the station but to stay calm, even though their own faces seemed to radiate panic.

Immediately, there was a rush for the exits. On the public address system an announcement started up, playing on a loop: 'All passengers must evacuate the station now. Please follow the instructions of staff.'

The young man knew where they were being sent. It was common knowledge that the meeting point in the event of an emergency was on the slip road next to the taxi rank on the southern side of the station.

When it came to his turn, he hurried through the turnstile, following the barked commands of the police officers as they ushered him to the right, towards the exit. His last walk on Planet Earth.

It wasn't particularly inspiring, taking in the giant overhead signs carrying the arrival and departure times of the trains, the information centre, the bland-looking shops . . . all temples of a Western consumerism he despised. He wouldn't miss this place. A far better one awaited him, as it awaited all good warriors.

A crowd of people were waiting on the slip road outside the station, while a far smaller number of station staff in fluorescent jackets tried to keep them adequately marshalled.

The young man reached round behind his back and gently tugged the detonation cord free from his rucksack. His body throbbed with anticipation. His palms were lined with sweat. For the first time, perhaps in his life, his whole world was in perfect focus.

The crowd seemed to part naturally, allowing him to move inside it. One of the staff urged him to keep moving. But he didn't. He slowed right down.

He was in the middle of it now, only feet away from a man talking loudly into a phone. But he hardly saw the man. He hardly saw any of them. This was it. The time. He stood up ramrod straight, the detonation cord gripped firmly in his hand.

Someone saw him. A middle-aged woman with bleached blonde hair. No more than five feet away. She cried out. One single, howled word: 'Jesus!'

The man on the phone looked round and seemed to realise what was going on. Instinctively he moved towards the young man, his hand outstretched. But he was too late. The young man was ready.

'For God and my people!' he cried out, and yanked the detonation cord.

THEY LEFT THE WAREHOUSE in a white Transit van with Andrews Maintenance Services written on the side. Fox was driving, with Wolf in the passenger seat next to him, while the other four were hidden away in the back behind a grimy curtain, along with the bulk of the weaponry.

The van was just passing Notting Hill Gate tube station when Fox heard the faint boom of the explosion through the open window. That'll be the train bomb, he thought. He took a quick breath as the enormity of what he was involved in was brought home to him.

Two minutes later, just as they came towards Lancaster Gate, they heard the second blast.

Wolf nodded slowly. Fox had never met the man who'd just turned himself into a walking bomb but he knew he was one of Wolf's protégés. He watched as Wolf reached for his phone and dialled a number.

'It's out of service,' he said. 'He's gone.'

'I can just imagine what it's like in Scotland Yard's control room now,' said Fox.

'It's time to rain down some more havoc,' Wolf responded, putting the phone on loudspeaker as he dialled another number.

A woman's voice came on the line. '*Evening Standard*, Julie Peters.'

'In the past five minutes two bombs have exploded at Paddington railway station,' Wolf announced, using his heavy Middle Eastern accent to maximum effect. 'One on the First Great Western train from Bristol, the other a martyrdom operation by a young mujahideen warrior on the concourse. These bombings, and the bombing at the Westfield Shopping Centre, were carried out by the Pan-Arab Army of God in direct retaliation for Britain's involvement in the NATO attacks on Arab nations and their occupation of

Muslim lands. There are four more bombs planted on trains coming into Waterloo, St Pancras, Fenchurch Street and Liverpool Street. We give you this warning to show that we are prepared to negotiate.'

'And what is it you want?' asked Julie Peters breathlessly, but Wolf had already ended the call. He switched off the phone and removed the SIM card, which he flung out of the open window.

Fox knew that Wolf had given the *Evening Standard* reporter enough information about the bombings to confirm that he was involved in them, so his warning would be taken seriously, and a vague warning of multiple potential targets would stretch resources to the absolute limit.

And it would be all for nothing. There were no more bombs on trains. They weren't needed. Their real target was somewhere else entirely.

'WHAT WAS THAT, MOM?'

'I don't know, honey,' said Abby Levinson, giving her son a reassuring smile as they walked back towards the hotel. 'Probably nothing.'

But the heavy bang had unnerved her. She looked across at her father, who was walking next to the road on the other side of Ethan, and now it was his turn to give her a reassuring look.

'Definitely nothing,' he said, ruffling Ethan's hair. 'You always hear stuff like this in big cities. New York's much noisier than London.'

'Is New York nicer?' asked Ethan.

His grandpa laughed. 'I'm biased. I grew up there. But I like both.'

It had been a fun, if exhausting, day. A visit to the London Dungeon, lunch at McDonald's, the London Eye, and finally the Aquarium. Ethan had had a great time. It had been almost a year to the day since his father had left the family home and Ethan had taken his absence hard. This trip, combining the Thanksgiving holiday with his seventh birthday, was a way of taking his mind off his father and having some fun.

The second bang stopped Abby dead in her tracks. It was louder than the first. Other passers-by had stopped too, and they were now looking in the direction the noise had come from.

'And what do you think *that* was, Mom?'

Abby didn't answer her son. She was watching a thin plume of smoke rising up through the rain and gathering dusk, somewhere beyond the other side of Hyde Park. A police car raced through the traffic past Marble Arch with sirens blaring. It was heading in the direction of the smoke.

'Whatever it is, it's nothing to do with us,' Ethan's grandpa replied over the noise of the siren. 'Come on, let's get inside.'

He put a protective arm round both their shoulders, steering them towards home, and even though he was barely as tall as her and almost seventy-five years old, his touch made her feel a little safer.

Trying hard not to grip her son's hand too hard, Abby hurried past the tall concierge and into the warmth and security of the Stanhope Hotel.

TWO

Newly promoted Deputy Assistant Commissioner Arley Dale was bored. She was chairing a meeting between community leaders and senior officers from Operation Trident, the unit that dealt with so-called black-on-black gun crime in the city. The meeting had dragged on for close to two hours now and nothing of any substance had been achieved.

Arley was also distracted. Twenty minutes earlier, her secretary, Ann, had interrupted the meeting to inform her that there'd been an explosion in the underground car park of the Westfield Shopping Centre. There'd been no further details available at the time, and Arley had asked to be kept informed as they came in. If the explosion turned out to be suspicious, then as the most senior officer of the Met's Specialist Crime Directorate on duty, she'd be involved in implementing the Major Incident Plan in response.

The knock on the door interrupted her thoughts.

It was Ann, her secretary, again. 'Ma'am, you're needed urgently.'

'I'm afraid I have to go,' Arley announced to the attendees. 'I'll leave you in the capable hands of DCS Russell.'

'The explosion at the Westfield has been confirmed as a bomb,' said Ann when they were out in the corridor.

'What do we know about casualties?'

'So far we've got reports of six people injured, but no fatalities.'

'Thank God for that.'

'That's not all,' Ann continued. 'There have been two more explosions at Paddington Station. Initial reports say they're both bombs. The commissioner wants you in the control room right away.'

Arley had been with the Met for over twenty years. She was used to crises, and knew how to handle them. 'I'm on my way,' she said, already feeling the adrenalin as it pumped through her system, shaking her out of the torpor of the meeting.

HE WASN'T GOING TO COME. In her hotel room, Cat was about to light a cigarette when there was a loud knock on the door.

It was Michael, his presence immediately filling the doorway. He was a big man with big, rugged features who'd worked hard to keep himself in shape, and even though he was in his early fifties, he wore the years easily.

He grinned and took her in his arms and kissed her. 'I need you, Cat,' he whispered. 'God, I need you so, so badly.'

'You've got me,' she whispered back. 'And we've got all night.'

They walked crablike together towards the bed, his hand running up her leg to the stocking top, his breathing getting faster now.

She felt his phone vibrate in his trouser pocket. He ignored it. So did she.

By the time it had stopped vibrating they were standing against the bottom of the bed. Almost immediately, his phone started up again.

'Damn,' he cursed. 'I'd better see what they want.' He gave Cat an apologetic look and turned away. 'What is it?' he demanded brusquely.

As he listened to what was being said, his shoulders slumped visibly.

Cat stepped away and reached under the pillow on her side of the bed.

'All right,' said Michael at last, 'I'll be there as soon as I can.' He ended the call and turned round with a frustrated sigh. 'I'm truly sorry about this, Cat, but there's been some kind of terrorist incident— '

'I know,' answered Cat, her voice perfectly calm as she brought the gun round from behind her back and pointed it right between his eyes.

Michael stared at her in utter disbelief. His phone fell to the floor. 'What on earth are you doing?' he asked.

Cat stared back coldly. 'Don't ask questions. Just do as I say.'

'But I've just told you, there's a major terrorist incident going on and—'

'And I told you, I know. There's been a bomb at the Westfield Shopping Centre, and two more at Paddington.'

Michael's eyes widened. 'God, how the hell—'

'Because I'm involved. Now sit down in the chair by the bed, and no more talking.' She cocked the pistol and tightened her finger on the trigger.

'Now look here, Cat, I'm sure we can sort this out,' he said, as if he was confident that she could be reasoned with, which was typical of him. Michael Prior was a man used to getting his own way.

'There's nothing to sort out. I'm a soldier of the Pan-Arab Army of God and you are my prisoner.'

Michael sat down heavily in the tub chair next to the window.

'If you put the gun down, we can sort this out, I promise. It's not too late.'

Cat could hear the strain in his voice. 'And if you keep talking, I'll shoot you in the kneecap, and I won't miss. I've had extensive training with the Glock 17, and the suppressor does a very good job of keeping the noise down. My orders are to keep you alive, but no one's going to care if you can't walk.' She kept her voice totally calm, as she'd been trained to do.

Keeping the gun on him, she reached into a Harrods bag she'd brought with her, pulled out two pairs of ankle restraints, and lobbed them over to him. 'Put these on—one hoop round each ankle, the other round each of the front chair legs. Make sure they're locked, then throw the keys on the bed.'

He caught them easily, but rather than put them on he made one last effort to salvage the situation. 'Come on, Cat,' he said, looking at her imploringly. 'We have something together, don't we? Something special. Let's not destroy it. I'm in love with you, darling. Remember that.'

Cat shook her head. What fools men could be sometimes. 'You make my skin crawl, Michael. I was given orders to draw you into a relationship, and that's what I've done. Now put those restraints on before I lose patience.'

She watched the realisation that he'd been utterly suckered finally sink in. He looked upset, which pleased her. She'd done her job well. Michael must have seen the contempt in her face, because he finally did as he'd been told.

When he'd finished she came up behind him and made him put his hands behind his back. 'The Glock's trained on your right shoulder blade, so don't try anything,' she said, putting a pair of handcuffs on his wrists and locking them with her free hand. Michael was now completely helpless.

'But I've seen your background details,' he said, the confusion in his voice obvious. 'How could this have happened?'

She smiled coldly. 'The woman you employed does not exist. Catherine Manolis died in Nice in October 1985, aged twenty-three months. Her identity was stolen and used to apply for false identity documents. We tailored her to suit the job application, and no one spotted it.'

Michael sighed. 'So, everything you told me about your upbringing was rubbish. You're not a widow at all.'

'Oh yes,' she told him, her voice hardening, 'I'm definitely a widow. My husband was murdered last year defending his country against men like you. Except while he was fighting on the front line you were sitting far away behind a desk giving orders.'

'But Cat, you must understand, I had nothing to do with that. I was—'

Before he could finish the sentence, she stuffed a ball gag into his mouth. When she'd finished gagging him, she pulled out his mobile phone and switched it off. It would be switched on again later and moved to different places in the hotel to confuse any rescuers trying to locate him.

She then pulled out her own phone and speed-dialled a number. 'I have the prize,' she said, 'and it's ready to be opened.'

And Michael Prior truly was a prize. But then, a director of MI6 was always going to be.

16.40

Wolf put down his mobile and turned to Fox. As he did so, some of the hardness left his face.

Every man has a weakness, thought Fox, and, like a lot of men, Wolf's was the opposite sex. The woman on the other end of the line had him wrapped round her little finger, and that worried Fox. He had the feeling that when the op began in earnest she might well cause problems.

'Cat's got him,' Wolf said as Fox turned the van out of the traffic chaos of Park Lane and down one of the side streets. 'The MI6 man is ours.'

'Good. She's done well.'

Fox drove the van round the back of the Stanhope Hotel, parking a few yards short of the delivery entrance. Fox could almost feel the adrenalin surging round the interior as each of them prepared for the assault.

Wolf put his mobile on loudspeaker and called Panther, their inside man in the Stanhope. Panther was Cat's brother, Armin. Both Fox and Wolf had met him on a number of occasions as they endeavoured to find out everything they could about the hotel. He was an unpleasant little bastard who resented the fact that he might have to take orders from Fox, a foreigner he neither knew nor respected, but in the three weeks he'd been working at the Stanhope as a room-service waiter he'd been an invaluable source of information.

It had been no problem getting him the job. He possessed good-quality fake papers supplied by his embassy, entitling him to work in the UK, and the fact that he had no experience was clearly of no consequence. What mattered to the hotel's management was that he had a valid work permit and, more importantly, was prepared to work hard for the appalling wages.

Panther answered immediately.

'What's the situation in there?' Wolf asked.

'Everything's good. The kitchens are beginning to get busy. About twenty to twenty-five staff inside.'

'What's the security on the gate like? Can you see?'

'Just the usual guy, Kwame. He's sat down reading the paper.'

Wolf and Fox exchanged glances, then Fox turned to the men in the back. They were all sat up straight in anticipation, cocking their weapons.

'OK, get the back door open,' ordered Wolf. 'We're coming in.'

'Right,' Fox said, 'we all know what we're doing. This is crowd control, not a shooting fest. We want them scared but not panicking. But if anyone resists or makes a bolt for it, take them down. Got that?'

Every man grunted his agreement.

Fox pulled the van away from the kerb and into an archway that led through to a rear courtyard where the Stanhope received all its deliveries. As the van approached the security gate, Kwame put his paper down and got up from the chair. He was only a young guy—twenty-five, twenty-six.

As he walked up to the driver's-side window, Fox pulled a gun from the seat pocket beside him and pointed it at his face. 'Open the gate.'

Kwame nodded rapidly and immediately put a code into a keypad on the gatepost that lifted the gate automatically, before shoving his hands in the air just so no one was in any doubt that he was being cooperative.

Not that it made any difference. Fox held his gun arm ramrod straight and shot him in the eye, before accelerating into the courtyard.

Panther had already opened the double doors that led through to the kitchens, and it looked like he was talking to someone behind him.

Fox swung the van round in a wide semicircle and backed it up to where Panther stood in the open doorway, looking over to where Kwame's body lay unmoving on the ground. Anyone passing along the street outside would see it, but it no longer mattered. They'd arrived, and soon the whole world would know about what they were doing.

He cut the engine, removed the cap and glasses disguise he'd been wearing, and pulled on a balaclava. Then, grabbing his AK-47 and backpack from behind the seat, he leaped out of the van along with the others, feeling a tremendous exhilaration. It was time for war.

THE STANHOPE'S MAIN KITCHEN was situated on the ground floor, directly below the main ballroom on the mezzanine floor, yet well out of sight of the lobby. It was reached through a soundproofed door marked STAFF ONLY, and as soon as Elena was through it she was assailed by the smell and noise of preparations for the evening food service.

Her mood hadn't improved much. Having mollified the guests who'd originally complained about the late arrival of their room-service orders with complimentary champagne, she'd just been informed by reception that there were two more similar complaints. Elena had decided to get it sorted out once and for all with the catering manager.

She spotted a familiar face—Faisal, the Jordanian cook—and he gave her a big grin. 'Miss Serenko. Looking beautiful as always. How are you?'

'Why thank you, Faisal,' replied Elena, feeling better immediately. 'I'm fine, thanks. Have you seen Rav? I need a word with him.'

'I think he's out the back telling off one of the employees.' He was about to say something else when there was a loud commotion coming from behind the door that led to the kitchen's delivery area. As everyone turned towards it, another sound rang out. One that was unmistakeable. A gunshot.

No one moved. It was just too unexpected for anyone to react.

And then the door opened and Elena let out a shocked gasp as Rav stumbled through it. He was clutching his stomach, where a dark-red stain was visibly spreading across the white of his shirt. As he collapsed, another figure filled the doorway. It was Armin, the room-service waiter, and he was holding a smoking handgun out in front of him.

A young pot washer Elena vaguely recognised was standing a few feet away from Armin, and he leaped at him, going for his gun. But Armin was quicker. He swung round and opened fire, his bullets sending the pot washer crashing backwards.

More men strode into the room, one after another, dressed identically in balaclavas and dark clothing. All were carrying assault rifles.

'Everyone down on the floor now!' screamed the first of the men, pointing his rifle straight at Elena's chest.

For an interminably long, slow moment, she was completely mesmerised by the scene in front of her, then Faisal grabbed her by the collar of her jacket and pulled her to the floor. A second later the noise of automatic rifle fire from more than one weapon erupted around the kitchen, and as Elena hit the floor, she heard Faisal cry out and saw him collapse to his knees. He swayed unsteadily as more bullets tore up his back like angry geysers, and then he pitched over sideways, landing on Elena's feet, already dead.

The whole thing had lasted barely ten seconds, and it had taken Elena a good portion of that time to come to terms with what was going on; but now that she had, she experienced an icy, stomach-wrenching terror followed immediately by a desperate desire to survive. Knowing she had to get out of the line of fire, she scrambled on her hands and knees behind one of the kitchen units as another burst of rifle fire reverberated around the room.

Leaning back against the unit she realised she was trapped. It was a good ten feet to the door that led back into the lobby, most of it over exposed ground. She'd never make it. She was going to die. Elena caught the eye of another member of staff, an Irishman called Aidan. He was squatting down on his haunches next to a unit a few feet away, looking scared but calm. He tried to give her a reassuring look.

The shooting had stopped. Somehow, Elena found the silence even more terrifying than the noise because she had no idea what was going to happen next. She heard more shouting coming from the gunmen, telling people to get down and stay down, followed by footsteps coming closer.

She held her breath and pushed back against the metal, hoping it would somehow open up to conceal her, praying for God's help.

The footsteps stopped. Out of the corner of her eye she could see a pair of scuffed black shoes, only feet away. On her side of the unit. Slowly, experiencing a cold dread that seemed to turn her body to jelly, she looked up.

Armin stared back at her coldly, no feeling at all in his dark eyes. Then he looked beyond her towards Aidan.

Aidan looked at Armin calmly and there was defiance in his eyes. 'There's no need,' he said, his voice steady.

The gun kicked violently as Armin pulled the trigger, hitting Aidan in the head. He gasped once and toppled silently to the floor.

Seeing him go like that—his life, his dreams, his secrets, snuffed out in an instant—was such a huge shock that Elena hardly noticed Armin turn his gaze back to her. He was smiling as his finger tightened on the trigger.

Surprisingly, she felt perfectly calm. If this was her time, so be it. She thought of Rod. Of the life they could have had together . . . the sun, the sea, children, because she'd always wanted children. A boy and a girl.

And then one of the balaclava-clad gunmen appeared. 'What's going on?' he demanded in a Middle Eastern accent.

'That one tried to run away,' Armin lied, motioning dismissively towards Aidan's body. 'And this one's the manager.'

The masked gunman looked down at Elena. 'All right, on your feet. You're coming with us.' He leaned down and grabbed her by the hair, yanking her roughly to her feet, which was when she saw that there were five other gunmen dotted around the room.

God, Elena thought, beginning to panic again. What the hell is going on?

'Grab anyone that's still alive and bring them through,' the man holding her shouted. 'Fox—you, Panther and Leopard are the vanguard. Now, let's take the rest of this place. And remember, hold your fire and shoot only when you have to. We want to keep as many people alive as possible.'

With that he shoved the rifle in Elena's side and dragged her towards the door that led through to the rest of the hotel.

THE PLAN CALLED FOR the utmost speed when taking control of the building. Already things had got out of hand with the assault on the kitchen. Panther had gone crazy, shooting dead at least three people and panicking the others, several of whom had tried to escape. The result had been more people shot down by other members of the team. Fox knew it was time to restore discipline, otherwise they'd provoke an early assault from the security forces, which would mess up everything.

As Wolf took hold of the hotel manager, an attractive blonde in a smart trouser suit, and began barking out orders, Fox grabbed Panther by the collar of his waiter's uniform. He thrust his face in close to the other man. 'No more unauthorised shooting, or you die too. Understand?'

Panther's eyes blazed with anger, but Fox was undaunted. The little shit might be Wolf's fellow countryman, but he still had to know who was boss. 'Understand?'

Panther nodded, and Fox motioned for him and the ex-marine Leopard to follow as he ran through the door that led into the lobby, holding his AK-47 out in front of him.

The kitchen was supposedly soundproofed, but as Fox moved into the lobby the first guests were already hurrying towards the main doors.

'Everyone on the floor!' Fox yelled. 'Now!'

Almost all of them obeyed, but one guy, a businessman in a suit, who'd almost made it to the doors, clearly decided to take the risk and keep going. There was no way Fox could let him go. It would be a show of weakness, and he was too pumped up for that anyway. Flipping the AK to his shoulder, he took aim and fired a single burst of automatic weapon fire into the man's back. The force drove the target into the door with an angry thud and a second later he collapsed.

Fox looked around the room. 'Anyone else try anything, they die too.'

No one did. They lay still, faces squashed into the expensive-looking burgundy carpet. There'd be no further resistance here.

Fox motioned for Panther to stand guard over their new hostages and took Leopard through the adjacent corridor and into the main bar and restaurant area, where there was now outright panic. People were running around looking desperately for a way out. Unfortunately for them their only obvious means of exit was through the main lobby of the hotel. It was one of the reasons they'd picked the Stanhope. It was easy to corral their prey.

Fox estimated that there were about fifty people in all in the restaurant and bar, a manageable mix of afternoon teas, business drinks and the first of the after-work crowd. An hour later and there'd have been too many, an hour earlier, too few. Like everything else about the op, they'd planned the timing of the assault carefully. Publicity-wise, five p.m. GMT was perfect. Their audience would be eating breakfast in LA, getting ready for lunch in New York, heading home from work in Europe, and sitting down to dinner all across the Arab world. Even in Pakistan, India and beyond people would be up and tuning in to what was happening on a billion television sets. Soon the whole world would know about them. It was an intoxicating thought.

Once again, Fox yelled at everyone to get down on the floor, putting a burst of fire into the ceiling to encourage them.

There were a few screams, and everyone hit the deck.

When they were done, Fox walked into the room and began his prepared speech, delivered in a non-specific eastern European accent he'd been working on. 'Please do not be alarmed. You've been taken hostage by the Pan-Arab Army of God. As long as you cooperate, no harm will come to you, and you will be released when our demands are met.'

'What are your demands?' came a male voice from somewhere in the middle of the restaurant.

'Who said that?' demanded Fox, taking a couple of steps forward.

A balding businessman reluctantly put up an arm.

'Get up.'

Slowly the businessman got to his feet, palms outstretched in the universal gesture of nonconfrontation. 'It's just I may be able to help. I'm a—'

Fox shot him in the chest. He knew that the cardinal rule of hostage-taking was to establish total control over your hostages, and that meant eliminating any challenges to your authority quickly and ruthlessly.

Screams and terrified gasps immediately filled the room but Fox ignored them and kept on talking. 'As I was saying, you will all be released when our demands to the British government are met. In the meantime, you are to do exactly what you are told. Any failure to comply, or any attempt to escape, will result in the same punishment I've just meted out to Mr Loudmouth here. Do you all understand?'

There was a low and not particularly enthusiastic murmur of agreement.

'On my command you are all to get to your feet and form two orderly lines. You'll then follow me out of the room, and in silence please. My colleague here will be bringing up the rear. We're going to go upstairs to the next floor. Anyone trying to stay behind will be shot on sight. If you want to live, you're going to have to do as we say.'

Within seconds the hostages had got themselves into two long, roughly even lines, including several people who'd come out from where they'd been hiding behind the bar.

Fox gestured for the two people at the front of the lines to follow him, then backed slowly out of the room, keeping his gun trained on them.

Wolf and the others were already in the lobby and in the process of taking the remainder of the hostages, including the traumatised kitchen staff, up the marble staircase that led to the next floor and the hotel's ballroom.

The ballroom was the perfect location for holding the hostages. It was a cavernous place with no windows or natural light, and like the main restaurant and bar area, there was only one way in or out, making escape impossible and severely limiting the scope of an assault by the security services to free them. Once again, it was why they'd chosen the Stanhope.

The hostages were largely calm and quiet as they were shepherded over to the far end of the room and made to sit down. There were about eighty altogether, and all adults, which made things a little easier. After the earlier shootings, no one was asking any questions or trying to engage in amateur negotiation. A couple of the kitchen staff had minor injuries, but none was seriously wounded. All the seriously wounded were still in the kitchen, and they were going to have to be finished off since there were neither the resources nor, to be frank, the desire to do anything to save them.

When everyone was sitting down and four of the men had formed a guard around them, Wolf approached the group, still holding the blonde hotel manager by the collar of her jacket. He forced her to her knees in front of him and stood legs apart, chest puffed out, looking every inch the man in charge, as he delivered his own speech to the assembled hostages, which was pretty much a rehash of Fox's but with an added harangue about the crimes of the West, and the UK in particular, against the Muslim world. He finished by ordering everyone to turn off their mobile phones and put them on the floor where they could be seen.

The first part of the operation was complete. The hotel was under their control and the hostages were subdued.

Fox looked at his watch. The time was 16.55.

ELENA GASPED as the man holding her, whom she assumed was the leader, pulled her to her feet. His grip hurt, but she was getting used to it now. In fact she'd calmed down a great deal. She'd always been practical and right now she knew she had to deal with the current situation and do her best to stay alive. And that meant cooperating. These men might be animals—to kill Rav, Faisal, Aidan and the others in cold blood like they'd done, they had to be—but for the moment at least they'd stopped shooting.

The man the leader had addressed earlier as Fox took the rucksack from his back and placed it in the middle of the hostages. He opened it up, fiddled about inside for a few seconds, then removed what looked like a roll of cable, which he trailed across the floor over to one of the other gunmen. She saw that there was a press-down lever attached to the roll, which the other gunman put his foot on. She'd seen something similar once on a TV programme about the Beslan siege, and her heart lurched as she realised that it was a detonation device and that the rucksack contained a bomb.

Elena didn't resist as the leader marched her across the ballroom floor and into the satellite kitchen. They were followed by Fox, who'd collected rucksacks from two of the other gunmen. As soon as they were inside, the leader told her to face the wall, with her hands in the air.

She felt a spasm of pure terror. Were they going to shoot her?

But the two men started peppering her with questions. Where were the master key cards to the rooms kept? What was the password for the hotel's electronic guest register? Where was the CCTV camera control room?

Elena answered each question honestly, but when the leader asked her how to disable the hotel's sprinkler system, she hesitated. There could be only one reason why they'd want to know this: so that if it came to it they could set the place on fire. Her mind went back to the Mumbai sieges of 2008, the flames and thick black smoke billowing out from the upper windows of the grand old buildings.

'Answer,' demanded the leader, 'or I'll shoot you through the kneecap.'

'There's a box on the wall in the storage room on the ground floor,' she said. 'There's a lever inside that you pull down to disconnect it manually.'

'And is the box locked?'

She nodded. 'Yes. So's the storage room. The keys to both are in the safe.'

'I'll take her down there with me,' said Fox. 'I need to secure the downstairs area.'

Fox took her by the arm and led her towards the door.

As she was ushered out of the room, Elena glanced briefly back towards the store cupboard. She wondered if Clinton the handyman was still in there, and if he was, whether they'd find him. Armin had obviously told them about the satellite kitchen, but she wasn't sure he'd know about the secret sleeping spot. She hoped not. She liked Clinton. She wanted him to live.

Fox didn't speak as he hurried her down the staircase. As they strode across the lobby, she saw the body of the businessman lying just inside the main doors. It was dark outside now, but there were two figures standing just beyond the doors, and she could tell by their fluorescent jackets that they were police officers. As soon as they saw Fox they took a step back.

Fox told her to get down as he raised the assault rifle to his shoulder.

She fell to her knees, shutting her eyes, as a heavy burst of automatic weapon fire filled the air. He pulled her up again and, as she opened her eyes, she saw that the bullets had peppered the glass of several of the doors close to where the policemen had been, but that neither of them had been hit. She wondered whether he'd deliberately missed them, and if so, why.

'OK, let's go,' he said, hauling Elena to her feet. 'I want the front doors locked. Have you got the keys on you?'

'No, they're kept in the main safe,' she said, knowing there was no point lying since Armin would already have told them most of what they needed to know about the workings of the Stanhope.

'And you know the combination.'

Again she told the truth. 'Yes.'

'I want all the master key cards too. The ones that'll open every room.'

'I can get them.'

He looked at her closely for a moment, and she saw that beneath the balaclava he had pale blue eyes. This surprised her. Because she'd assumed that people claiming to represent an organisation called the Pan-Arab Army of God would all be Arabs. Yet Fox was clearly white. He spoke with an eastern European accent, so perhaps he was a Muslim from the south.

'I got engaged today,' she said quickly.

He didn't answer. Instead, he tightened his grip on her arm and walked across the lobby, stopping beside one of the leather sofas to deposit a rucksack beneath the glass coffee table in front of it, before continuing over to the door that led behind the main reception desk. With Fox following closely behind, Elena walked round the back of the desk and into the CCTV control room where the main safe was kept.

While she opened the safe and took out the keys, she watched Fox as he stared at the bank of screens on the wall.

'Why isn't this camera working?' he said, pointing to the only blank screen.

Elena frowned. The hotel's CCTV system was generally reliable. 'I don't know,' she answered. 'It must be faulty.'

'Where is it?'

'Up on the top floor. Where the suites are.'

He nodded slowly, then took the key cards and told her to turn off all the lights in the front section of the lobby, which she did manually from behind the reception counter. Finally, he ordered her to lock the hotel's front doors.

That was the hard part. Being so close to freedom. People looked at her, some pointing, as she went from one door to the other, stepping over the body of the dead man as she imprisoned herself, the gunmen and the hotel guests inside. The outside was so, so near. All she had to do was fling open one of the doors, run for her life in a zigzag motion, keeping low like they did in the movies, and she'd be free. But she knew she'd never make it.

Elena put her key in the last door and twisted it. There was no prospect of escape for anyone now.

TEN FLOORS ABOVE Fox and Elena, the man called Scope watched as police cars stopped on either side of the hotel, blocking the traffic in both directions, creating a car-free zone right in front of the main entrance.

Another police car pulled up slightly behind the others, and three guys got out. They went round the back of the car and opened the boot, pulling out what looked like MP5 submachine guns. Proper firepower.

Something big was going on, and for a moment Scope thought it might have something to do with what he'd done here, except he was sure it couldn't be. He'd worked efficiently and there'd been no noise.

No, whatever this was, it was way bigger than him. Already he could see more police cars, along with a fire engine and two ambulances, driving into Hyde Park and taking up position a hundred yards distant, while in the sky overhead a helicopter with search beam made tight circles. He wondered what the hell was happening. The problem was, he had to get out, and soon. And with all these police around it wasn't going to be easy.

He walked back through the suite's lounge, stepping round the bodies. He removed the manager's badge and left the room, slipping off his gloves as he started down the corridor.

MARTIN DALSTON took another long sip from his glass of pinot noir and placed it on the bedside table next to the three bottles of pills and the two envelopes containing the letters to his ex-wife and his son.

He looked at the rope with noose attached that he'd hung from the large picture hook on the opposite wall. He still wasn't sure the hook would take his skinny ten stones.

Typically for a man who'd always liked to keep his options open, Martin had chosen two different ways to die. Hanging was the quick method, although, thanks to the height of the hook, it would mean him keeping his legs bent and off the floor as the rope either throttled him or broke his neck, something that would require the kind of self-discipline he wasn't at all sure he possessed. The slow, more painless method was the drugs—a combination of barbiturates, oxazepam and aspirin that he'd been assured would send him gently to sleep.

After much thinking, he'd come up with a simple plan: take the pills, lie back on the bed, and keep the rope in sight as he drifted off, so that he'd always know how painful the alternative was.

Strangely, he'd been looking forward to this afternoon. To have the opportunity to relive the happiest two weeks of his life, and to savour all the things that could have happened if he'd followed his dreams and made a life with Carrie Wilson, rather than taking the sensible option and marrying Sue, was a guilty pleasure.

But so far his reminiscing had been disturbed by the constant noise of sirens going past the window in both directions. A few minutes earlier there'd been a lot of shouting inside the hotel; he even thought he'd heard some shots, although he wasn't entirely sure.

He thought about getting up to see what all the fuss was about, but quickly dismissed the idea. The world outside the door to room 315 was no longer relevant. He picked up the wine glass and took another long sip of the pinot noir. Soon it would be time to start taking the first of the pills.

17.11

Room 1600, the Operations Control Centre on the sixteenth floor of the New Scotland Yard building, was bedlam. Of the twenty or so officers and staff crowded inside, many of them talking on phones, DAC Arley Dale was the most senior, and she had the Herculean task of coordinating the evacuation of the entire London transportation system, as well as all major public buildings, in response to the bombs at Westfield and Paddington Station. No one knew where the next bomb would strike, or how far to extend the evacuation, and now matters had been further complicated by multiple reports of an attack on the Stanhope Hotel in Park Lane.

A bank of TV screens showing real-time CCTV footage of central London took up the whole of one wall, and they recorded vividly the problems the police faced. All the major roads were gridlocked. On a screen somewhere in the middle, a thick pall of smoke could be seen above Paddington Station. The latest reliable report said that there were already thirteen dead and as many as sixty injured at Paddington, while the number of injured had risen to nine at Westfield, although thankfully there were still no fatalities. But for Arley, what it all meant was that there was no point taking risks with public safety.

'We need to make a decision on the Gherkin, ma'am,' said a young male officer. 'We've just had a second bomb threat against it.'

'Evacuate it,' she answered. 'In fact, evacuate every building we get a threat against.'

'Ma'am?' Her secretary, Ann, was tapping her on the shoulder. 'You're wanted in the commissioner's office. DCS Stevens will take over in here.'

Arley went out into the corridor. Like most police officers, she craved the excitement of a crisis, and she had a cool enough head to cope with one, which was the main reason she'd travelled as far as she had in the Met.

Chief Commissioner Derek Phillips was one of the good guys, a copper's copper with the best interests of the people beneath him at heart, but Arley sometimes wondered if he had the decisiveness to deal with a major incident. He was standing behind his immense glass desk when Arley walked in.

'Thanks for coming so promptly,' he said. 'How are things in 1600?'

'We're under the cosh, sir. Do you have any more information on the Stanhope attack?'

'Apparently a group of gunmen have broken into the building and are taking hostages. There are unconfirmed reports of casualties, and we do know that shots were fired from inside the hotel at the first officers on the scene. That was about twenty minutes ago. But so far the picture of what's actually going on is very patchy. Chris Matthews, the chief inspector down at Paddington Green, is on the scene. He's put a cordon in place and set up an RP in Hyde Park, but he's being hampered by all the gridlock round there. It looks like everyone's trying to leave the city at once.'

'I can't say I blame them. We're getting a lot of claims of responsibility for what's happening, but nothing's confirmed.'

'I've just been on to Hendon. They say one call stands out. It was made to the *Evening Standard* at four thirty-four p.m., just after the Paddington bombs had gone off. It came from a mobile in the western Hyde Park area, which is a good three-quarters of a mile from the scene.'

'So there's no way the caller could have known about the bombs unless he was responsible for them?'

'Exactly. It was too quick to have been a hoax. The caller claimed to be from an organisation called the Pan-Arab Army of God. No one at Counter Terrorism Command seems to have heard of them, so we're guessing they're new boys. The caller said something about the attacks being in retaliation for British and NATO interference in Arab and other Muslim countries. He also claimed that there were bombs at other London mainline railway stations. Have you had any other reports of bombs going off?'

Arley shook her head. 'Plenty of scares, but nothing else.'

'Thank God for that. We're stretched enough as it is.'

Arley filled him in on the evacuation plans she was putting in place.

'You're doing a good job,' he told her, sounding like he meant it. 'But I need you out in the field. It looks like it's turning into a siege situation at the Stanhope. The PM's convening a meeting of COBRA for six p.m. In the meantime, we have to respond fast. We're using the usual structure. I'm Gold Commander. Assistant Commissioner Jacobs is Silver. We'll both be based here. I want you as Bronze, running things on site at the Stanhope.'

Arley was pleased to be Bronze Commander, though a little awed by the size of the task ahead. 'I'll get down there as soon as I can but you know what the traffic's like. It may take me some time.'

'We haven't got time. There's a helicopter waiting to take you there now.'

The phone on Commissioner Phillips's desk rang. He picked up the receiver, listened, then replaced it. His expression was grim. 'That was Hendon. They've just had a call from a wounded kitchen worker inside the building. He told them that there are at least half a dozen masked gunmen in the building, and that there are three people dead. And that's just in the kitchen. They were still talking to him when there was the sound of gunfire and he was cut off. It sounded like he was shot.'

Arley nodded. The situation already appeared to be running out of control. 'If we've got gunmen firing indiscriminately, it sounds as though it's going to have to be handed over to the military sooner rather than later.'

'That's why I want you on the scene. Get going, and good luck.'

FOX STOOD OVER the body of the kitchen worker, his AK-47 still smoking, and shook his head angrily. He hadn't wanted to kill him, but the guy had been on the phone to the emergency services, doubtless giving them important information as to the number of gunmen, as well as letting them know there were multiple casualties.

Beside him, Dragon, the man who'd left the bomb at the Westfield, sighed. A former sapper, he was the explosives expert, and Fox had brought him with him to help secure the rear of the hotel.

'What did that prick think he was doing going on a shooting fest like that?' said Dragon in his deep Welsh accent. He was referring to the actions of Panther, the inside man at the hotel, and his words matched Fox's own thoughts. 'It's stuff like that that brings on an early assault.'

'I'll speak to Wolf. Get him to keep an eye on him.'

'He's dangerous. Fucking Arabs. You can't trust them.'

'It's Arabs who are paying our wages,' Fox reminded him. 'Come on. We need to get this area locked down.'

He went over to the main kitchen window and looked out. They'd killed the lights so that no one from outside could see what they were doing, but it didn't look like there was anyone watching them. The building at the other end of the courtyard, a vacant office block with no windows looking back towards the hotel, blocked the view from the road. The only way of seeing or getting in was through the archway beneath the office block where the body of the security guard Fox had shot earlier still lay. The street beyond it looked empty. Fox assumed that the police would still be evacuating the area around the Stanhope so for the moment it was safe to work.

The rear of the hotel was their most vulnerable point. If there was an attack, Special Forces would come in through the kitchen and fan out into the building. He and Wolf didn't have the manpower to put guards down here so it was essential to make entry as difficult for them as possible.

Dragon had brought one of the rucksack bombs with him, and while he prepared it in one of the wheelie bins in the delivery area, Fox locked all the external doors using the manager's keys and booby-trapped each of them with a grenade. They worked quickly and in silence. Six minutes later, having wheeled the bin out into the courtyard and placed it against the wall among half a dozen others, they were done. It was 17.22, and still the street beyond the archway was empty.

'Jesus, I don't know how I got involved in something as risky as this,' said Dragon.

Fox grinned. He liked Dragon. The guy was no-nonsense. 'Because you're on the run and wanted for murder. You don't have a lot of options.'

'But I've just basically helped seal myself in a building with half the Met outside. I didn't even walk into a trap. I made it for myself.'

'It's all part of the plan,' said Fox. 'Cause maximum chaos, maximum embarrassment to the government and the establishment, and then, pfff! We disappear into the ether, two million dollars richer.'

Dragon grunted. 'That's the theory, anyway.'

'If it wasn't risky, you wouldn't be getting paid two million,' Fox told him, stepping over one of the bodies and heading for the door.

They walked back through the darkness of the lobby then went round the back of reception. Ultimately, the most important part of the plan was not just getting into the hotel, it was getting out afterwards without getting caught, and they had a plan for that as well. Using the password he'd been given by the hotel manager, Fox logged into the guest reservation database on one of the tabletop PCs. He pulled a piece of paper from his pocket containing a list of fake IDs and which operatives they applied to, and while Dragon watched he matched their names to empty rooms, making a note of the number of each one as he did so.

'How the hell did you manage to get into the system so easily?' Dragon asked him when he'd finished.

'The manager told me.'

'That's the blonde girl in the suit, right? The good-looking one.'

'That's right.'

'That's a pity. I'm assuming we're going to have to make sure she doesn't tell the authorities that she gave you the password to the computer system.'

Fox nodded, thinking about what she'd told him about getting engaged. She seemed a nice girl. 'You're right,' he said. 'She's going to have to die.'

THREE

Elena sat on the ballroom floor along with the other hostages while four of the gunmen, including Armin, stood in a semicircle guarding them.

What scared Elena the most was how well organised the gunmen were. They seemed to know exactly what they were doing, and they were so damn calm. Especially the one called Fox, the white man who'd dragged her around the lobby while he set traps and disabled both the lifts and the sprinkler system. She'd just seen him come back up, along with one of the other gunmen, carrying more bags. They'd gone straight into the satellite kitchen, which they seemed to be using as some kind of HQ.

She wondered what it was they really wanted. She was sure they had to be on some sort of suicide mission. Why else would they disable the sprinkler system unless they planned to set the hotel ablaze?

The door to the satellite kitchen opened suddenly and the leader and Fox came out. They strode over to the other terrorists, one after another, and spoke to them in hushed tones.

Then the leader approached Elena and yanked her to her feet by her arm. 'You're coming with us,' he snapped in his thick Middle Eastern accent.

'Where?' she asked before she could stop herself.

'Don't ask questions, bitch. Move.' Grabbing her by the collar, he shoved the barrel of his assault rifle into her back and made her walk towards the exit. 'Take us to room 316. Use the staircase.'

Elena did as she was told, conscious that three more gunmen, including Armin and Fox, were also coming with her.

The third-floor corridor was completely silent as Elena led the gunmen through. She wondered how many people were hiding terrified behind their doors. The hotel was currently booked to over eighty per cent capacity, so there would be quite a few of them.

'Which side's room 316?'

She pointed right.

'In a few minutes' time you're going to tell the people on this floor to come out of their rooms and line up outside. But first I want you to see exactly what, and who, you're dealing with.'

Elena felt a growing sense of dread as they stopped outside room 316 and Wolf knocked four times on the door.

A second later it was opened from the inside by a young woman about Elena's age, with black hair and olive skin. She was barefoot and wearing a figure-hugging black dress. She looked completely normal, except for one thing: she was holding a pistol with a silencer attached to it.

'Welcome,' she said in lightly accented English.

Elena looked past her and saw a grey-haired man tied to the tub chair beside the bed. He had a gag in his mouth and he looked pale and terrified.

They filed into the room and she saw the woman and Armin exchange small smiles. They obviously knew each other.

The leader ordered Elena to stand against the far wall. He then walked over to the man in the chair and, pulling a pistol from his waistband, shoved the gun against his forehead.

'Hello, Mr Prior,' he said. He turned to Armin. 'Get everything set up. I want this recorded and put online straightaway in case they switch us off.'

Elena watched as Armin pulled a laptop out of the rucksack he was carrying and connected it via a cable to a camera. At the same time, the leader removed what looked like a large belt with pouches along its entire length. Then she saw the wires poking out of the pouches and the old-style battery-operated alarm clock in the middle.

The leader looped the belt over their prisoner and the chair so that the bomb was resting across his chest with the alarm clock dead centre, while the woman pulled on a balaclava and went over to join him.

As Armin lifted the camera and began filming, the woman put the barrel of her pistol against the man's temple. He sat still, his eyes wide, sweat forming on his forehead. She spoke directly into the camera, her voice confident. 'The man sitting here is Michael Prior, a director of MI6. His job is to oversee the surveillance, arrest, torture and imprisonment of Muslims all over the world, and both he and his government are responsible for the ongoing slaughter of Arab and Muslim civilians. We, as members of the Pan-Arab Army of God, have taken him into our custody, along with a number of other British citizens, and we demand that the British government immediately cease all its current military, political and economic operations against Muslim and Arab countries. Unless our demands are met in full, he will be executed tonight, at midnight GMT, and this building will go up in flames, along with everyone in it.'

Elena felt her heart sink as the woman stopped speaking, and Armin lowered the camera and started typing on the laptop.

'OK,' he said after a few moments. 'We've got the footage online.'

This was the cue for the leader to start giving orders again. He told the woman to take the laptop and go downstairs to the ballroom to reinforce the others. Then he ordered the rest of the men out into the corridor.

Finally, he grabbed Elena roughly by the arm. 'We need more hostages,' he said. 'And you're going to get them for us.'

IT WAS ALL GOING so damn wrong, thought Martin Dalston as he lay behind the double bed, trying to keep as still as possible. One minute he'd been sipping the pinot noir, the pills still in their containers, the next he'd heard the commotion coming from the room next door, followed by people talking just outside his door. He'd tried to ignore it, but then he'd heard a woman introducing herself as the Stanhope's duty manager. She was saying that the hotel had been taken over by a group called the Pan-Arab Army of God, that they had master key cards to all the bedrooms, and that everyone had to come out of their rooms, otherwise they would be shot immediately.

The whole thing seemed so surreal that at first he'd thought it was some bizarre joke, but then he'd ventured over to the window and peered out, which was when he saw the flashing lights of dozens and dozens of emergency vehicles blocking the road in both directions. That was when he'd knelt down behind the bed.

Martin was scared. Terrified. Irrationally so, really, given that within the next few hours he'd fully intended to kill himself anyway. But the thing was, he wanted to die at a time and by a method of his own choosing, with happy memories filling his consciousness. Not at the hands of terrorists.

He could hear the sound of doors opening farther down the corridor, barked orders, and the nervous whispers of frightened people. Martin felt his stomach knot. He knew if he didn't go out he risked being shot. Even so, he didn't move, hoping that the terrorists wouldn't search all the rooms.

'Please, this is your last chance to come out of the rooms.' The manager's voice was coming down the corridor, loud and clear. Getting closer.

Martin remained absolutely still. There was no way he was going out. He could hear muffled voices right outside the door.

And then it began to open, and he could hear movement.

God, they were inside his room. He held his breath. With his eyes tightly shut, he felt rather than heard the man stop at the end of the bed, and he knew he'd been seen. He heard the sound of a gun being cocked, loud in the silence of the room, and he gritted his teeth, waiting for it all to be over.

'Open your eyes.'

The words were delivered calmly in an eastern European accent that, for some reason, didn't sound quite right. Martin gasped and looked up into the eyes of a masked man in a balaclava, pointing a rifle down at him.

The man turned round. 'See, I told you there'd be more of them hiding.'

'Kill him,' ordered a voice in a foreign accent, its tone terrifyingly casual.

But the gunman didn't fire. 'We need more hostages,' he said. 'And if we shoot too many guests, we'll make the security forces jumpy.'

'As you wish,' grunted the other man dismissively.

The gunman flicked his gun upwards and Martin got to his feet unsteadily, unsure whether to feel relief, gloom or terror.

He could now see the other gunman. He was small and dark, heavily built, also dressed in black. Beside him was the hotel manager. She was tall and pretty, with blonde hair and a kind face. She was staring, horrified, at the noose hanging from the picture hook.

Their eyes met briefly, and Martin experienced a deep sense of humiliation as his deeply personal plans were exposed to the world.

And then he was being pushed into the corridor along with the manager and maybe a dozen guests of varying ages, including a crying girl, who was no more than ten. There were four gunmen in all, all masked, and the leader—the man who'd ordered his killing—didn't look happy at all.

'There must be more people on this floor,' he snapped, grabbing the manager and pointing his gun at her.

'Most of the rooms are taken,' she answered quickly, 'but it doesn't mean that they're occupied. A lot of our guests will be out.'

'There should be more.' The leader turned to two of the other gunmen, one of whom was Armin. 'You have your key cards. Clear the rooms one by one. Take people alive unless they resist. If they try to fight back, kill them.'

FOR MORE THAN TEN MINUTES after leaving the suite on the top floor of the Stanhope, Scope had tried to get out of the building. The lifts were all out of order, and when he'd started down the fire-exit stairs he'd run into one of the hotel staff coming the other way. The kid had told him that there was some sort of terrorist attack going on. He didn't have too many details, other than that he'd seen some dead bodies and at least two men with assault rifles.

The kid had said he was going up to the restaurant on the ninth floor, where apparently there were some good hiding places. He'd suggested Scope join him, but Scope had declined, figuring he'd take his chances. But he'd got only a couple of floors down when he'd heard a burst of automatic gunfire coming from somewhere in the building, followed a few seconds later by people coming up the staircase far below. At that point he'd decided that, given that he was armed with only a knife, maybe discretion was the better part of valour. At least until he knew what he was up against.

He'd returned to the suite and put on the TV. Sure enough, Sky News was showing live footage of the front of the hotel, and the scrolling headline was reporting the presence of armed men inside.

He was trapped. And the bodies in the suite were already beginning to smell. He thought about his options for a couple of minutes, before concluding that he had only two: stay where he was and sit it out until the cavalry arrived, or try to make a break for it. He drew the knife, kept it down by his side, and made his way back to the fire-exit stairs.

'WE OUGHT TO LEAVE,' whispered Abby Levinson, squeezing her son's hand.

Her dad shook his head emphatically. 'No. We stay where we are.'

'But you heard what the manager was saying. They'll shoot us if we stay in our rooms.'

'They'll shoot us if we leave.' He looked at her imploringly. 'We're Jewish, and they're Arab extremists with guns. We're the enemy. At least if we stay in here, we have a chance.'

'Why do they want to kill us?' asked Ethan quietly.

'Because they're bad men,' said his grandpa, putting a reassuring hand on his shoulder. 'There are hundreds of rooms in this hotel. They won't be able to search all of them.' He leaned forward and cupped Abby's face in his hands. 'Have I ever lied to you? Have I ever given you reason not to trust me?'

'No.' And he hadn't. Dad had always been there for her.

'Then please,' he continued, 'do as I say.'

'OK,' she whispered. 'We'll do as you say.' She squeezed Ethan that bit harder. 'It's going to be all right, baby.'

Breaking away from them, her father picked up the tub chair in the corner of the room and manoeuvred it towards the door. Abby helped him and they tried to prop it under the handle so it wouldn't open from the outside, but the back of the chair fell a good couple of inches short.

Abby froze. She could hear footfalls outside in the corridor coming closer. Her father heard them too and he mouthed at her to take Ethan and go into the bathroom. Picking up a glass vase from the desk, he stood behind the door. The footfalls stopped.

Slowly, silently, Abby crept away from the door, putting a finger to her mouth to warn Ethan to stay quiet, and led him into the bathroom.

Ethan looked up at her with wide, frightened eyes as she closed the bathroom door, and she gave him as reassuring a look as she could muster.

Then she heard a key card being inserted in the door to their room and the handle turning. Her heart pounding, she put a hand over Ethan's mouth.

The door was opening now, and she could hear the tub chair scuffing against the carpet as it was pushed out of the way. She peeked round the bathroom door and saw her father holding the vase above his head. The door continued to open. And that was when she noticed it: the narrow gap between the door and the doorframe widening at the hinges. Whoever was on the other side would be able to see her father standing inside. She opened her mouth to say something, willing her father to turn round—

The shots exploded in the room—two of them, one after the other—and her dad fell back, dropping the vase and crashing into the bedside table. His legs went from under him and he collapsed to the carpet with a dull thud.

'Grandpa!' cried Ethan, struggling out of his mother's grip.

'No, Ethan, stop!' Abby tried to pull him back into the bathroom, desperate for him not to give them away. But it was too late. He broke away from her and ran towards his grandpa, just as the door was flung open and a man in a balaclava, dressed in what looked like a hotel waiter's uniform, came into the room. Behind him the door clicked shut, trapping them inside.

'You hurt my grandpa!' Ethan shouted, moving towards him.

The man raised his gun. 'Stop him or I'll shoot the little bastard.'

Abby grabbed Ethan and pulled him to her, with all the strength she could muster. 'I've got him. Don't shoot. Please.'

'Shut the boy in the toilet,' he said. 'Or I'll kill him now.' His pistol was pointed at Ethan's head.

Ethan had stopped struggling but she could tell he was sobbing behind the hand she'd placed over his mouth. Her father lay in front of them, his head almost at her feet. He'd been hit in the upper body, and blood was soaking through his shirt, but he still seemed to be breathing.

'Come on, Ethan,' she whispered. 'We've got to go into the bathroom.'

'Not you. Just him. Get him in there now.'

Something had changed in the gunman's voice. Whatever was going to happen to her, she didn't want her son to see it, so she pulled him inside the bathroom, then whispered in his ear. 'I want you to stay in here until I call you, OK? Please. Otherwise he'll hurt me.'

It was emotional blackmail of the worst kind, but what choice did she have? She shut the door and turned to face the gunman.

He stood in the middle of the room, his pistol aimed at her chest. 'Turn round and lift up your dress, or you and the brat die together.'

IN THE STAIRWELL, Scope was level with the third floor when he heard two gunshots, followed by a woman's scream. He stopped and listened. He knew he ought to keep going. He had only a knife, but he'd never been one to walk away from someone in obvious danger. It just wasn't in his DNA.

He opened the stairwell door and stepped into the corridor, looking both ways. To his left, he could hear voices coming from behind one of the doors. It sounded like a man was barking orders and a woman was pleading with him. Scope strode over to the door, and put his ear to it. There was another noise—a kid, quite young by the sound of him, crying.

Sliding the homemade lock-picking device he'd brought with him out of his pocket, Scope pushed it into the narrow gap between the door and the frame and lowered it carefully onto the lock. He tensed as he gave the door a firm shove, the click of the bolt being released sounding loud in his ears. Scope pushed the door open.

An old man lay on his back on the floor next to a double bed. His white shirt was stained red where he'd been shot. At the far end of the room stood the gunman. He had his back to Scope, and it was clear he hadn't heard the door opening. He was pointing a pistol down at a woman who was on her knees just inside the entrance to the bathroom, with her arms round a child.

'You had your chance, whore. Now you die.'

'Kill me, but please let my son go,' the woman was saying.

Scope took a long, silent step into the room. The woman saw him then, her expression changing before she could stop it.

The gunman started to turn round and Scope charged him, ending his run in a flying headlong dive that sent him and the gunman crashing into the far wall. The gunman struggled violently as Scope grabbed his gun hand by the wrist and yanked it upwards so that the barrel was pointing up in the air. The gun went off, the bullet ricocheting off the ceiling. Eyes blazing with rage, the gunman drove his head forward, trying to slam it into Scope's face, but Scope turned, bringing up his knife hand and driving the blade deep into the gunman's side so that it pierced his heart.

The room erupted in noise as the gunman's finger involuntarily squeezed the trigger, sending two more bullets into the ceiling. Scope stabbed him a second time, then a third, ignoring the ringing in his ears, waiting until the gunman's body relaxed in his arms before letting him slip to the floor.

Behind him the bedroom door swung open. Scope wheeled round in time to see a second gunman enter, this one carrying an AK-47. He was saying something, but Scope couldn't catch it above the ringing in his ears.

Scope threw the knife just as the guy raised his gun to fire. At the same time he ducked down and weaved away.

The knife hit the guy in the chest, blade first, embedding itself about an inch in, and though the force of the blow made him take a step back, he didn't fall. Instead, with the knife sticking out of his chest, he raised the AK to fire, which was when Scope realised that he was wearing body armour.

But Scope was fast. He drove himself into the gunman, grabbing his AK by the stock as the gunman opened up with a burst of fire. The kick from the barrel sent shock waves up Scope's arm, but he managed to push it out of the way so that the bullets flew high and wide, then he fell on the gunman.

With a roar, the gunman threw Scope off, sending him crashing back into the tub chair by the door. But Scope held on to the rifle with both hands, knowing that as soon as he let go of it he was a dead man.

The gunman yanked on the AK, trying to twist it out of Scope's hands.

But Scope clung on, letting himself be taken by the momentum for a couple of seconds so that his adversary thought he had the upper hand. Then he dug his heels into the carpet, forcing the gunman to fall into him, before wrapping a leg round one of his ankles and tripping him up. The gunman fell onto the bed, relinquishing his grip on the AK, and swung round to face Scope, at the same time pulling the knife from his chest.

Scope slammed the stock of the AK into the gunman's face.

The gunman howled in pain as his nose exploded. Scope came forward fast and drove the butt of the AK into his face a second time. This time, however, there was real power behind the blow, and it drove the gunman's head back against the wall. Scope came in close, using the AK as a club to hit him again and again until the stock fell apart in his hands and the gunman slid silently down the wall.

Scope put his hands on his knees and took some deep breaths before retrieving his knife and turning back towards the woman and the boy.

That was when he saw that the woman had been hit.

She was sitting back against the bathroom doorframe clutching her leg just above the knee, her face contorted with pain as blood seeped through her fingers. The boy was holding on to her, sobbing.

Scope went over and knelt beside her, gently prising open her fingers so he could see the wound. Blood leaked out steadily from a five-pence-sized hole three inches above the kneecap, and as he probed round the back of her leg he felt a larger, more ragged hole where the bullet had exited, and this was bleeding more heavily. Scope knew that the ammo used in the AK-47 could cause extensive tissue damage, but from the close positioning of the two holes it looked like this could be a relatively superficial hit.

'You're going to be OK,' he said. 'I'm going to dress the wound.'

She nodded tightly, her eyes focusing on him, and he was relieved to see that she didn't appear to have gone into shock yet.

'I understand,' she said through gritted teeth.

Grabbing a hand towel from the bathroom, he tied it round her leg to soak up the blood and restrict its flow, careful not to make the knot too tight. As he did so, he took in her appearance for the first time. She was in her late thirties, good-looking but rail-thin, with shoulder-length black hair, dark oval eyes, and skin that should have looked tanned but was now an anaemic grey thanks to the shock of her ordeal.

Scope knew he had to get this woman and her son out of the hotel fast, but he also knew that, once outside, they'd tell the authorities what he'd done, which would attract a lot of unwelcome attention. He didn't want anyone linking him with what had happened in the suite upstairs.

He looked at the boy, who couldn't have been more than seven years old, and who was staring at Scope curiously. He had the same colouring as his mother, but his face was rounder and he had a dimple on his chin that somehow made him look even more vulnerable than he was.

Scope turned to the woman. 'We've got to go.' His fight with the gunmen had made a hell of a lot of noise and it wouldn't be long before more of them turned up to investigate.

'It hurts,' she whispered, closing her eyes.

'It's not as bad as it looks. I promise you. Now, stay awake for me, OK?'

She nodded weakly.

'She's been shot,' said the boy, his voice high and panicked. 'People who get shot always die, don't they?'

'No, most survive,' Scope told him firmly.

'How do you know?'

'I just do.'

'Is Grandpa dead?'

'I'm afraid he is. I'm sorry.'

'The bad man killed him. He was trying to protect us.'

Scope spoke slowly, his tone reassuring. 'That's because he loved you, but the bad man's dead too. He won't be able to hurt anyone again, ever.'

The boy's dark eyes burned angrily. 'I'm glad you killed him.'

'How did the bad man get in here?'

'He had a key.'

So they had key cards to the rooms. Masters probably. It showed a level of planning that was worrying.

Scope got up and took the pistol from the man in the waiter's uniform. It was a Glock 17. He checked the number of bullets. Three. He gave the guy a quick pat down but he wasn't carrying any spare ammo. He took both gunmen's key cards and went back to where the woman was lying.

Her eyes were closing as Scope picked her up in his arms as gently as he could. 'What's your name?' he asked her.

'Abby.'

'We're going to get help, Abby. I want you to stay with us, OK?'

'OK,' she groaned in response.

'And what's your name, son?'

'Ethan,' said the boy.

'I want you to follow me and your mum, Ethan, and try to make as little noise as possible. You think you can do that?'

The boy nodded. 'But what about Grandpa? I don't want to leave him.'

'We've got to for the moment, but the police'll be coming back in for him very soon. Now don't say another word, OK?'

'OK.'

Conscious of the fact that if they were ambushed he wouldn't have a chance of fighting back, Scope carried Abby out of the room, Ethan following. It was completely silent in the corridor as he made his way over to the emergency staircase. He took a brief look through the door's frosted glass, saw nothing on the other side, and led Ethan into the stairwell.

They'd just started down when Scope heard someone hurrying down the stairs a few floors above them. It might just have been a frightened guest, but there was also a good chance it was another of the gunmen.

Gesturing for Ethan to follow, he hurried down the steps to the second floor, opened the exit door and turned right down the corridor, trying to put as much distance as possible between them and the emergency staircase.

As soon as they'd turned the corner, Scope stopped outside the nearest room and carefully placed Abby on the floor, propping her up against the wall, while he fished in his pocket for one of the hotel key cards. He inserted the key card, and while Ethan held the door open, Scope lifted his mother up again and took her inside.

The room was empty, and in the semidarkness Scope saw that the bed hadn't been slept in. As he placed Abby on it, he noticed that the blood from her wound had seeped through the towel.

Clearly now in shock, she asked him where they were.

'In one of the other rooms. We should be safe here for now.'

'But we need to get outside.'

'I know. But right now, it's too dangerous.'

He moved away from the bed, switched on the lights, and pushed a chair across the door, positioning it so that the back was just beneath the handle, then got another towel from the bathroom to replace the first. As he wrapped it round Abby's leg, he noticed her staring up at him.

'Who are you?' she asked him. 'The way you dealt with those men . . .'

He returned her stare. 'I'm the man who's keeping you alive,' he answered.

17.50

A cold wind blew over Park Lane and, with impeccable timing, an icy drizzle began to fall as DAC Arley Dale stood at the police rendezvous point—a marked Land Rover Freelander 2 from Traffic parked in the middle of the road twenty yards west of the hotel. Two mobile incident rooms were en route from different locations but both were stuck in traffic. With her was Chief Inspector Chris Matthews of Paddington Green Station, who'd been coordinating the initial response to the crisis.

Matthews was bald and underweight and looked like he ran marathons every day. He had the kind of severe face that scares criminals, children and probably a lot of other people too, but Arley had the feeling that if you pressed the right buttons you'd see a much softer side. He was highly competent too, and right then, that was by far the most important thing.

'I've got the inner cordon in place all round the hotel,' Matthews explained, 'but I'm short of CO19 officers.'

'They'll be here soon. We've got them coming from all over. But I also want a central and an outer cordon set up, so we can get civilians and camera crews as far back as possible.'

'I haven't got the manpower at the moment, ma'am. All my spare resources are carrying out an evacuation of the surrounding buildings.'

'Evening all,' came a voice behind them. 'DCI John Cheney, Counter Terrorism Command.'

Arley and Matthews both turned round and were confronted with a tall, good-looking man in his mid-forties with a full head of natural blond hair.

'I've been sent here to give what assistance I can,' said Cheney, as he and Matthews shook hands. 'My speciality's foreign terror groups.'

He turned to Arley and she gave him a thin smile. 'Hello, John.'

'You two know each other?' asked Matthews.

'From a long time back,' said Arley, shaking hands formally.

And it had been a long time. Getting close to twenty years. She'd still been a uniformed constable and he'd been a handsome young DC. For a few short weeks she and John Cheney had embarked on a passionate affair until the point she found out that he was sleeping with at least two other women. At the time, Arley had been truly gutted. She'd been infatuated, but, having had her fingers burned, she'd turned her back on him, and in the years since they'd seen each other only a handful of times at official functions.

Seeing him now, she felt nothing. It had all been too long ago. Getting straight down to business, Arley gave him a brief rundown of events so far.

'Have we had any claims of responsibility?' he asked.

'We think they may be from an organisation called the Pan-Arab Army of God. Have you come across them before?'

Cheney shook his head. 'Never heard of them.'

Arley rolled her eyes. 'That's useful.'

'It's also no great surprise. These terrorist groups chop and change their names and personnel all the time. New ones are always appearing. Do we know if they want to negotiate?'

Arley looked up towards the hotel. 'They've been in there an hour, and they're making no move to get out or to blow the place up, and they said something in the call to the *Standard* about being prepared to negotiate, so I'm guessing they must want to talk at some point. But to be brutally honest, we haven't got a clue what they're up to in there.'

'We need to listen in to them,' Cheney said. 'I've got contacts over at GCHQ. I can get on to them and see if they can set something up remotely.'

'That'd be a help,' said Arley.

At that moment, Chris Matthews's mobile rang.

'The first of the incident rooms is here,' he told her, shouting above the shrieking of a police siren as a riot van pulled into the top of Park Lane.

Not before time, thought Arley, as the rain began to come down even harder.

THE STANHOPE'S Park View Restaurant was on the ninth floor of the hotel and had floor-to-ceiling windows right across its western side, which looked out on to a spacious roof terrace and beyond that to Hyde Park.

Tonight all the blinds were drawn, and tables and chairs had been piled up against the windows by Elena and the other hostages to create a space in the middle of the floor. They were sitting in that space now, a frightened, confused, largely silent group of about twenty people bolstered in number by a group of guests and staff members who'd been discovered hiding in the adjoining kitchen. In the middle of the group, only a few feet from where Elena sat, was a rucksack bomb. She wondered why they'd been brought up here, a long way from the other hostages in the ballroom.

There were two gunmen in the restaurant: the man who seemed to be the leader, whom she now knew was called Wolf, and his sidekick, the man who'd accompanied her to the lobby earlier, Fox. Both of them were holding assault rifles, and Wolf's foot was on the pedal connected by wires to the rucksack bomb. They'd even set up a portable TV next to them so they could use the news channels to keep tabs on what was going on outside.

On the way up, Elena had tried to speak to Fox, to establish some kind of rapport, but he'd told her to shut up, and the tension in his tone had persuaded her that it wasn't a good idea to carry on talking.

There were three young children among the hostages, two girls of about six and eight and a boy of about twelve who was dressed in his school uniform and who'd been one of those hiding in the kitchen, along with his parents. Both the boy and one of the little girls were sobbing quietly—a sound that wrenched at Elena's heart. It sickened her that these innocents were caught up in this nightmare.

Before she'd had a chance to think about what she was doing, she stood up. Wolf and Fox immediately turned her way, and Wolf raised his gun.

'Sit down,' he ordered.

'Please,' she said, still standing, 'let the children and their mothers go. There'll still be plenty of us left behind.'

'Sit down.'

'But they've done nothing to you. Please. Have some heart.'

Wolf took three steps forward and put the rifle to his shoulder.

For a terrible second, Elena thought he was going to shoot her, even though she'd been banking on the fact that, as the most senior member of the Stanhope's staff on duty, she was a lot more useful to them alive.

'I'll tell you one more time: sit down.'

Reluctantly, and with anger coursing through her, she did as she was told.

Wolf lowered the gun, and Elena saw him glance at the three young children in turn. 'If you all cooperate, and if your government cares enough about you,' he said at last, 'then you will all be freed. But in the meantime you will suffer the way so many of the world's people have suffered at your hands. You will be given no food or water, and you will not be allowed to leave the room. You will speak only when spoken to by one of us. Anyone who speaks out of turn from now on will be shot immediately.' He glared at Elena. 'Including you. Do you understand?'

There were a few nods and murmurs. Elena didn't say anything. She held Wolf's gaze.

'Do you understand?' he demanded as he stared straight at Elena.

She nodded, hating him. 'Yes.'

'Good. Are there any guests staying in the suites?'

'Yes. One of them is occupied, the Garden Suite.'

Wolf turned away. Elena looked round at the other hostages, and saw the fear in their faces. She caught the eye of the man next to her. It was the man who'd had the rope in his room. Elena gave him a supportive smile, trying to forget the fact that he'd been planning to commit suicide in her hotel—an act she considered incredibly selfish, given that one of her staff members would have had to deal with the aftermath. He smiled back weakly, and it was clear that he knew what she was thinking and was ashamed.

She turned away, and thought of Rod. He would almost certainly have heard what was happening at the hotel and would be terribly worried. For the first time she wondered whether she'd ever see him again. It made her feel sick to think that this could be it for her—the end.

Fox LOOKED AROUND the restaurant at the group of hostages sitting silently on the floor, a smaller and more manageable number than downstairs, then tensed as Wolf put a gloved hand on his shoulder.

'What's keeping those two downstairs?' Wolf asked. 'Go and get them. I'll be all right here.'

Fox used the emergency staircase to get back to the third floor. When he came out into the third-floor corridor, it was silent. Too silent. There was no sign of either of the men, or any of the people they were meant to be rounding up. Fox looked up and down the empty corridor, his finger tensing on the trigger of his AK-47 as his concern grew.

That was when he heard it. A scraping sound coming from inside one of the nearby rooms. He walked slowly towards the source of the noise, stopping at the room from where it was coming.

A small dark patch was spreading out from under the door, only just visible against the burgundy of the carpet.

Keeping his finger on the AK's trigger, he pushed the key card in the reader and, in one rapid movement, kicked open the door.

It flew back only a foot because it was being blocked by a man lying across it like a human draught excluder. It was one of his own men, the ex-marine Leopard, and his balaclava-clad head had been smashed to a bloody pulp. Blood bubbles formed in his open mouth as he tried to breathe.

Fox kicked the door again, harder this time, shunting the body back until it opened completely. Stepping over Leopard's body, he went inside and saw

Panther, propped up against the wall on the other side of the room. His head was slumped forward, his shirt drenched in blood.

Fox felt someone touch him and looked down sharply. Leopard had lifted one of his gloved hands, and the material had briefly touched his leg.

He sighed. Leopard had been a good soldier, but he was no use to him now. He pushed the barrel of the AK against his head and pulled the trigger.

The hand dropped down with a thud, and the rasping breaths stopped.

Fox looked around the room. Leopard's AK was lying on the bed, its stock smashed so badly that the trigger guard was hanging off, rendering the weapon useless. Near the bed on the floor the body of an old man lay on its side. He'd been shot, but there was no way, given his build and the damage done to Leopard and Panther, that he was responsible for their deaths.

Fox checked the bathroom and the corner cupboard but they were both empty. There were a few kids' toys on the floor—and a black leather handbag sitting on the table on the far side of the bed. Fox picked up the handbag and looked inside, quickly locating an American driving licence in the name of Abigail Ruth Levinson. She looked skinny and petite in the photo, which made Fox pretty sure she wasn't the killer either. Someone else was involved. Someone who clearly knew what he was doing.

His hand brushed against something in the handbag, and he pulled out a clear plastic bag containing what looked like stubby blue pens. He looked more closely and saw that the pens contained insulin. So, she was a diabetic, and one who had to inject herself as well. Which meant she'd be needing them again at some point soon.

He slipped the package into the pocket of his overalls and threw the bag on the floor. It was possible that Abigail and the boy were not known to the killer, and therefore no longer with him, but if they were, and he had her insulin, then it might prove useful at some point.

However, in the end, that was scant consolation. Already two of their number were dead, and the Glock that Panther had been carrying was missing. Fox sighed. They now had a real problem on their hands.

SCOPE MIGHT HAVE LEARNED first aid during his days in the military, but he was no doctor, and although the wound didn't look that serious, he couldn't tell for certain.

He looked down at the Glock in his hand. Three bullets. That was all he had. Enough for an emergency, nothing else. He knew they were going to have to wait to be rescued. Breaking out would be next to impossible with a young kid and a wounded woman.

He pushed the gun into the back of his trousers and went over to the bed. Abby looked pale and listless, and he could see she was in a lot of pain.

'How are you feeling?'

'I feel numb, and it hurts . . .' She stopped, and Scope could tell that she was making an effort to keep things together for Ethan's sake. 'But I'm OK. When do you think the police will have us out of here?'

'I don't know. It could be a while.'

'Then I've got a bit of a problem. I'm a Type One diabetic, and the insulin's back in my room. I forgot about it in all the commotion.'

Scope nodded slowly. 'When do you need to inject yourself again?'

'When I next eat. Ideally, it should be about seven thirty, but I could hold on a while after that.'

'Will the gunshot wound affect the timing?'

'I don't think so.'

'Don't worry,' Scope said, 'I'll go back to your room and get it, but if you're OK, I'll leave it until things have calmed down. The terrorists will have discovered the two I killed by now, and they're not going to be pleased.'

'Of course.' She smiled weakly. 'Thank you for doing this for us.'

'It's fine. I'll make sure you and your son stay safe, I promise.'

But even as he spoke the words he wondered if he wasn't making a big mistake by playing the Good Samaritan.

A SERVICE LIFT, the only one they'd kept in operation, linked the hotel's main kitchen to the two satellite kitchens on the mezzanine and ninth floors, and Fox travelled up on it now, along with the Welsh sapper Dragon and the Dane, Tiger, whom he'd collected from the ballroom. He'd told them what had happened to the other two men. Neither man was too sad to see the back of Panther, but they'd both known and trained with Leopard, and his death had unnerved them, as had the fact that his killer was still somewhere in the hotel.

'The plan's flexible enough to deal with eventualities like this,' said Fox as they came out of the lift on the ninth floor and moved into the kitchen next to the Park View Restaurant. 'We'll find him.'

Dragon and Tiger were professional enough not to argue with this, but Wolf didn't react in quite the same way when Fox gave him the bad news.

'What do you mean, they're dead?' he hissed, the shock clear in his eyes.

'Someone killed them both,' repeated Fox. 'Whoever it is, he definitely knows what he's doing.'

'And what about the MI6 man?'

'I haven't had a chance to check. I wanted to let you know what had happened straightaway. I'll go down there in a minute, but I'm sure there's no problem. No one except us knows he's there.'

'Do that. We don't want to lose him.' Wolf shook his head in disbelief. 'Has anyone told Cat about her brother?'

'No, I thought that was best left to you.'

'This is very bad news. I knew Panther well. He was a good man.'

Which was something he definitely hadn't been, Fox thought. 'I'm not happy either. Leopard was one of mine. But right now we've got a much bigger problem. There's someone in the hotel not connected to us who knows how to kill people, and he's armed with Panther's Glock.'

'Could it be the police or the SAS?'

Fox shook his head. 'No. If it was the SAS, I'd be dead now. Chances are we all would. This is a guest. It has to be.'

Wolf said nothing for a minute, but Fox could see him struggle for control. 'OK,' he said at last. 'We need to clear the top floor and secure it. Then I'll tell Cat what has happened to her brother.'

Leaving Dragon and Tiger guarding the hostages, Wolf and Fox used the emergency staircase to walk the one floor up to where the Stanhope's suites were situated. As soon as they were through the staircase doors, the opulence hit them. Expensive Persian rugs covered the mahogany floor, while paintings lined the walls, and fresh flowers sprang from china vases.

Fox despised the fact that the wealthy thought they were above everyone else just because they had money. When he and his fellow soldiers had been stuck in a barracks in the flea-ridden hellhole of Al-Amarah in Iraq, the rich hadn't given a shit about them. Instead they'd continued spending their millions while Fox fought to protect them. And when he'd come back from the war, having given ten hard years' service to his country, what had they, or the politicians, or any of the bastards, done for him?

Nothing. There'd been no jobs above minimum wage. There'd been no occupational training. Fox knew of two men who'd wilted under the strain and committed suicide. But not Fox. He hadn't wilted. He'd shown ambition, setting up a firm providing security to private companies in Iraq and

Afghanistan. He'd done well financially, selling his company at a decent profit to a bigger outfit and remaining onboard as a consultant.

But for Fox, there was far more to life than making money. He burned with anger at the way his country had been sold down the river by politicians who'd opened the floodgates to millions of immigrants, who'd helped to create a soft, fat people whose poor were more interested in claiming benefits and watching reality TV than in doing anything to stop the rot all around them. Fox wanted to wake people up. He wanted to cause chaos and terror, to smash the old established order and pave the way for a new, more honourable society. It was this desire that had pushed him into extremism, and into the arms of others who shared his views.

An introduction from one of his extremist contacts had put him in touch with Ahmed Jarrod, aka Wolf, a man with rich backers and an exciting and lucrative proposition. Wolf wanted Fox to set up a small, hand-picked team of mercenaries to carry out a terrorist attack on the UK. It would be an opportunity for Wolf's backers (whom Fox assumed were an Arab government) to get revenge on the UK for its interference in their affairs. For Fox, who knew that Muslim extremists would get the blame for this, it was the perfect opportunity to divide and infuriate the British people, and give the establishment the bloody nose it so richly deserved. The irony of fighting alongside the type of people he despised in a battle against his own people was not lost on him. But in common with all other extremists, he was convinced his actions were necessary, and served a greater good.

They stopped outside the Garden Suite. Fox raised his rifle and unlocked the door, excited by the shock he was about to deliver.

Fox saw it immediately. An outstretched arm, hanging out from behind one of the interior doors. It belonged to a man, and it looked like there was a small patch of blood on his sleeve.

Wrinkling his nose against the stale smell, Fox entered the suite, Wolf following behind. Keeping his gun pointed in front of him, Fox walked slowly through the foyer, and into the sitting room. It was then that he saw the full extent of the carnage.

There were three men in the room and they were all sprawled out on the shagpile carpet. The one in the doorway, a well-built, well-dressed man in his early thirties, had had his throat cut, as had another guy, bigger, black, with a bald head and a sharp suit, who was lying on his back ten feet away. The third one looked Greek. He was older, with a thick head of dyed-black curly hair and an open-necked shirt and medallion combination. Fox could see he'd been stabbed a number of times in the upper body. He took a deep breath. It reminded him of what Panther had looked like downstairs.

He lifted the man's head up and saw that he too had a neck wound. The blood hadn't yet coagulated, meaning he hadn't been dead long.

He stood up, puzzled. It looked like Jack the Ripper had set to work in this room, yet he knew for a fact that none of his people had been up here. There were also very few signs of a struggle. It looked to Fox like all the men had been caught by surprise, and had died within seconds of each other. It meant that whoever had killed them was good.

'Well?' said Wolf, coming into the room behind him.

Fox looked around the room one more time. 'This is the work of the man who killed Leopard and Panther, I'm sure of it. And he's a pro. We need to ask the manager who it was who was staying here. That might give us some indication as to who we're dealing with.'

Closing the door of the suite, they made their way back to the emergency staircase. Wolf waited while Fox set a grenade booby trap behind the door. If Special Forces landed on the roof and came in through the top-floor windows, their arrival would be announced with a loud bang.

'Don't say anything about what's happened up here,' said Wolf as they headed down the stairs. 'We don't want to panic the men.'

Fox nodded. For once he agreed with him.

As they walked back into the Park View Restaurant, Wolf nodded curtly at Dragon and Tiger, then called the hotel manager over.

She stood up reluctantly, and Wolf and Fox moved her to one side so that the other two couldn't hear what was being said.

'Do you have any soldiers staying here?' Wolf whispered.

'Not that I know of, but I don't always know the details of the guest lists.'

'Do any of your staff have military training?'

'I don't think so.'

Fox could see that her curiosity was piqued. 'Who's staying upstairs in the Garden Suite?' he asked.

'Mr Miller. He's had the suite for most of the past two months. I think he's going through a divorce.'

'What does he do for a living?'

'I think he's some sort of businessman, but he keeps himself to himself.'

'And does he have bodyguards?'

She nodded. 'Yes, I believe he does. But that's not unusual. We have a number of clients—'

'Has he got any enemies?'

The manager looked puzzled. 'No, why? Has anything happened?'

'All right,' snapped Wolf, pushing her away. 'Sit back down, and don't say a word to anyone.'

'We need to make a change of plan,' said Fox when she'd returned to where she'd been sitting. 'We've lost two men, which leaves us with six. It's not enough to hold hostages securely in three locations. We should keep the MI6 man apart, but we need to take the ones in here down to the ballroom.'

'But the whole point is to keep them in different places. That way it's far harder for the security forces to launch an assault.'

'I know that,' said Fox. 'But if we keep the hostages up here we're splitting our resources too much. In fact, it makes it *easier* for them to launch an assault. By now they'll know we've brought people up here—it'll have been caught on the TV cameras. But with the blinds down, they won't know we've moved them, so they'll still think we've got them in separate places.'

Wolf shook his head emphatically. 'No,' he said. 'We stick to the plan. We'll keep Dragon and Tiger up here, and Cat and Bear in the ballroom.' He stopped and looked at his watch, his eyes lighting up. 'It's nearly twenty past,' he said. 'Time we began negotiations.'

18.21

Arley was talking to Chief Inspector Chris Matthews outside the command centre—which consisted of two mobile incident rooms side by side, surrounded by a cluster of police vehicles—trying to organise an HQ for the hundred or so Special Forces and their support teams, whose arrival was imminent, when she saw the helicopter coming in. She immediately excused herself and started across the park towards the landing pad.

Riz Mohammed was one of the most successful negotiators in the Met. He had the right mix of hardness and empathy to get under the skin of hostage-takers, and in ten years in the job he'd never lost a hostage. He also had the priceless asset of being a Muslim.

Arley watched as Riz emerged from the cockpit door.

'Hello, ma'am, how are you?' he said, shaking her hand with a firm grip.

As the head of Specialist Operations, the Met's Kidnap Unit fell under Arley's overall control, and she'd worked with Riz several times before.

'I've been better. Thanks for coming, Riz. I know it's your day off.'

'Can you give me a rundown of what's happening?' Riz asked her as they walked towards the command centre.

'Things are still sketchy, but we've definitely got multiple gunmen, large numbers of hostages in at least two different areas of the building, a lot of people trapped in their rooms, and there've been reports of sporadic shooting inside the hotel for the past forty-five minutes. What makes it even more critical is that one of the hostages is the Head of the Directorate of Requirements and Production at MI6 and one of its top people.'

'You're joking. What the hell's he doing in there?'

'We don't know yet. The hostage-takers have released a film of him tied up in one of the rooms. It's been picked up by Al-Jazeera and a number of Islamist web sites. One of the hostage-takers is holding a gun to his head and saying that if their demands aren't met they'll execute him at midnight.'

'Of course. What are their demands?'

'The broadcast called for all British operations against Muslim and Arab countries to stop, but they haven't made direct contact yet. We've tried calling the hotel on the external lines but there's been no response.'

Riz nodded. 'I'm assuming this is connected with the bomb attacks at the Westfield and Paddington.'

'We think so, so it's obvious they're not too worried about taking human life. Also, when they attacked the hotel they killed several people in the kitchen, and opened fire on the first officers at the scene.'

'That's not going to help the negotiations. I was told they're from an organisation called the Pan-Arab Army of God. Does that mean they're Islamic extremists?'

'We don't know anything about them yet but, given what we've got so far, we've got to assume that, yes.'

She saw the concern on his face when she said this. Islamic extremists were notoriously tricky to negotiate with because they were unpredictable and far less concerned with staying alive than the average hostage-taker.

'I'm sorry, Riz. But if anyone's got a chance of turning this round, it's you.'

He sighed. 'I'll do my absolute best, but I'm no miracle worker.'

'I know,' she said. 'None of us is. We've just got to hope we can conjure up something.'

Arley's mobile rang. It was Gold Commander, Commissioner Phillips—the first time she'd heard from him for over half an hour.

'Has your negotiator turned up yet?' he asked.

'I've just collected him. We're outside the incident room.'

'You need to hurry. We've had contact. A man with a Middle Eastern accent has just phoned, saying he's the commander of the Pan-Arab Army of God forces in the Stanhope Hotel. He's demanded to speak to me personally in the next fifteen minutes, or his men are going to kill a hostage.'

'You haven't spoken to him, sir, have you?' she asked, thinking it would be a complete breach of procedure if he had.

'Of course not,' he answered gruffly. 'That's your negotiator's job. The call was made from a land line in the kitchen on the mezzanine floor, and it was logged at 18.20. That's six minutes ago.'

'What instructions shall I give our negotiator?'

Phillips paused. 'That's the thing, Arley. They're very specific. I've just been on the phone to the Prime Minister, and he's very concerned.'

'We all are, sir.'

'Not just about the situation with the civilian hostages.' Phillips spoke slowly and carefully, the concern in his voice becoming steadily more obvious. 'Can you move away, so there's no risk you're being overheard?'

'Of course.' She excused herself from Riz and walked a few yards away.

'Apparently the MI6 man Michael Prior has some information that, should it fall into the wrong hands, would be disastrous for the country. There's no reason to believe that the terrorists know he has this information—only a handful of people do know about it—but it's absolutely essential your negotiator speaks to him. He's got to insist on it.'

'But how are we going to find out whether Prior's given away information without alerting the people holding him?' she asked.

'Prior has two prearranged code words. He'll use one if he has been compromised, and the other if he hasn't. They're both on your desk in the incident room. As far as anyone else is concerned, the code words are simply to find out if he's been mistreated or not. Is all that clear?'

'It's clear,' she said, not liking the sound of his voice at all.

FOX SLIPPED INTO ROOM 316, shutting the door quietly behind him and bolting it from the inside.

Michael Prior was still in the tub chair, staring at Fox from behind the gag.

'You know they wanted to kill you on film,' said Fox, reverting to his normal accent as he threw his rifle on the bed and pulled off his backpack.

He leaned round behind Prior's head and unstrapped the ball gag.

'If you let me go, I'll do everything I can to minimise your prison sentence.' Prior's voice was deep and authoritative, accustomed to giving orders.

Fox ignored him. 'They wanted to shoot you dead as a show of strength to the UK government. I stopped them.' Fox sat down on the bed. 'I told the man holding the gun to your head that you were more useful to them alive.'

'You keep saying "them" and "they". If you're not a part of them, then who are you?'

'That doesn't really matter right now. What matters is that you have information that I need.'

Prior's eyes widened just a little. 'I know a lot less than you think.'

'Don't try to bullshit me. We haven't got time. I need a name. A name that only you and a handful of other people know.'

Prior swallowed, and Fox could tell that he knew exactly who he was referring to. 'I thought this was a terrorist attack.'

Fox stood up. 'It is. Now, we can do this the hard way, or we can do it the easy way, but the result's going to be the same. You're going to give up that name, and if you do it quickly, then it'll be a lot less painful.'

'Please, if you have any decency or patriotism . . .'

He stopped talking as Fox produced a scalpel from the backpack.

'Give me the name and as soon as I've verified it I'll unstrap the bomb, untie you, and let you go. You'll probably make it out alive.'

'I can't. Please. I'll give you any information you want, but not that.'

'Last chance,' said Fox. 'Then I'll have to replace the gag while I go to work on you.'

He lifted the scalpel, and Michael Prior's eyes grew wide with fear.

FOUR

18.29

The interior of the mobile incident room was long, narrow and windowless, like the inside of a shipping container. A bank of TV screens—some blank, others showing rolling news footage of the Stanhope Hotel—lined one side, beneath which were half a dozen work stations.

There were three other people in the room when Arley and Riz Mohammed walked in. Will Verran and Janine Sabbagh were both police technicians whom Arley had only just met. Janine was a petite blonde-haired South African in her mid-thirties with dark eyes and a friendly smile, while Will was a tall, lanky twenty-something with a boyish face. Their responsibility was to keep open the channels of communication between Arley and all the other people and agencies involved in the operation.

The third person was John Cheney. He'd removed his jacket and was down to his shirtsleeves as he stood talking on one of the phones. He gave them a nod as they walked in, sizing up Riz with watchful eyes.

Arley saw the surprised look cross Riz's face when he saw the three of them. It was clear he thought there'd be more people inside the police's forward control room.

'We've got officers in the incident room next door but most of our non-front-line resources are remaining off-site,' she explained as she introduced him to the others. 'Mainly because it's so difficult to get down here with the traffic, and'—she swept an arm round—'obviously there's not a great deal of room. But we're in touch with everyone we need to be, and we have video-conferencing facilities set up. Right, Janine?'

'We've got a video link to the Scotland Yard control room, which means they'll be able to see and hear us in here,' said Janine. 'And we're establishing one to the chief commissioner's office so he can listen in on the call.'

Arley turned to Riz. 'Don't forget, you've got to insist on speaking to Prior. The code words he'll use are written down there. Anything else you need before you make the call?'

'The most important thing for me is to know who I'm dealing with,' said Riz, addressing the room. 'If we can ID any of the hostage-takers, particularly those in charge, it'll be a huge help.'

'We've got MI5 and CTC checking the voice records from the calls to see if they match any known suspects,' said Arley, 'and GCHQ are listening in on all the mobile phone conversations taking place inside the building.' Turning to Cheney she asked, 'What are the people calling out from the hotel saying about the hostage-takers? Are they speaking English? If so, with local or foreign accents?'

'The leader's speaking with an Arab accent,' said Cheney, 'and we've got phonetics experts trying to place it to a specific locality, but they haven't come back to us yet. As to the rest of the hostage-takers, we believe they're a mixture of Middle Eastern and eastern European accents.'

'OK,' said Will Verran, 'we've got live feed to the commissioner's office.'

One of the blank screens lit up, showing Derek Phillips sitting at his desk, watching them. 'Are we ready to make the call?' he asked, checking his watch. 'We're only two minutes off the hostage-taker's deadline.'

'We're ready now, sir,' Arley answered, before turning to Riz. 'It's all yours.' She pointed at a handset on the desk in front of him. 'That's the phone to use. It's a secure land line. Press one and it'll get you straight through to the phone the terrorist leader made his original call from.'

Riz picked up the phone. Everyone in the room was watching him. The phone rang six times before it was picked up.

'Who am I speaking to?' The voice at the other end of the phone sounded clear in the confines of the office.

'My name's Rizwan Mohammed. I work for the Metropolitan Police's Kidnap Unit. Is this the commander of the Pan-Arab Army of God at the Stanhope Hotel?'

'I said I wanted to speak to the chief commissioner of the Metropolitan Police. Get him on the phone in the next five minutes or a hostage dies.'

'I'm afraid I can't do that. I'm the representative of the police and security forces. You're going to have to talk to me.'

'Then a hostage dies, and one will die every five minutes until he comes on the line.'

'That's not going to help you get what you want,' Riz said calmly, but the line had already gone dead.

Arley looked up at the screen showing Phillips's desk, and was surprised to see he was no longer sitting in it, and the audio feed was turned off.

'Do you think he'll carry out his threat?' Arley asked Riz.

He shook his head. 'I don't think so, but in any case we can't give in to him. Not at this stage. Otherwise he'll be running rings round us. The hostage-taker always wants to establish control, and every negotiator knows that you can't let him. We have to be the ones calling the shots.'

Arley knew this, but like most police officers who'd got as far as she had, she was a political animal with big ambitions, and she was aware that her actions tonight would put her in the spotlight. 'But if he starts killing hostages and it comes out that it was because we wouldn't let him speak to Commissioner Phillips, it won't look good.'

'And if we start letting him order us around this early in the negotiations then the chances are there'll be more people dead later on.'

There was silence as they both weighed up their options.

'Let me try him again,' Riz said at last.

'OK. It's your call.'

This time the phone was picked up straightaway. 'Yes?'

'It's Rizwan Mohammed again. Look, I know we can resolve this peacefully. Why don't you tell me what you want?'

'I want to talk to the man in charge.'

'And I want you to know that if you talk to me, your message will be responded to at the highest level. Do you mind if I ask your name?'

'You may call me Wolf.'

'OK, Wolf. Are you the leader of the hostage-takers?'

'I am,' he said, and Arley could hear the pride in his voice.

'And what is it that you want?'

There was a pause and what sounded like the rumpling of paper at the other end of the phone before Wolf started speaking again. He was clearly reading from a prepared text. 'We want a commitment from the British government that British crusader forces will cease their hostilities against all Arab and Muslim lands, and remove their representatives from Arab and all Islamic soil within sixty days. We want a public statement from the Prime Minister promising that Britain will henceforth keep out of Arab and Islamic affairs, and end its involvement in the so-called War on Terror.'

There was another silence.

'Those are very ambitious demands,' Riz said at last.

'We are very ambitious people. And we have a hotel full of prisoners, including a director of MI6. This puts us in a position of strength. Not you.'

'Before we go forward, I need to speak to Michael Prior to ensure that he's in good health.'

'You do not make demands of me. I make demands of you.'

'And I will do all I can to meet those demands. But I need to speak to him.'

'We'll consider it.'

'It's going to be extremely difficult to get my government to move on your demands if you don't let me talk to him.'

'I told you: we'll consider it.'

'Please do. It'll be seen as a real gesture of goodwill by the British government.'

Riz looked up at Arley. His expression said: what more can I do? On the screen, she saw that Phillips had returned to his desk and was listening. He made no move to speak, so Arley mouthed the words 'leave it' to Riz.

'Also, we want the Internet kept on,' Wolf continued. 'If you take away our access, a hostage will die every five minutes until you reinstate it. Do you understand that?'

'Yes, but it's not going to help negotiations if you start killing people.'

'Then do as I say and no one will get hurt. You have until midnight to meet all our demands. If they haven't been met by then, we will execute your MI6 man and then one hostage every five minutes until they are. And for your information, we have rigged the building, including the areas where we're holding the prisoners, with explosive devices, none of which needs to be detonated by mobile phone. If your forces make any attempt to storm the building we will detonate all the devices, and kill the hostages, and ourselves if necessary. We are warriors, and we are prepared to die.'

Riz tensed at these words. It was exactly what they'd all feared.

'We understand there are wounded people inside,' Riz said at last. 'We'd like to send ambulance crews in to bring them out.'

'There are no wounded people here.'

'That's not our understanding. We'd also like the release of all the children too. It will do your cause no good at all if any of them get killed. I'm sure you remember what happened in Beslan. All those children dying did untold damage to the Chechen cause.'

'What do you know about the Chechen cause?'

'Enough to know that the Chechen leadership acknowledged that Beslan was a failure. I'm sure the Pan-Arab Army of God don't want that to happen.'

'Don't lecture me.'

'I'm not,' said Riz. 'But it will help your cause if you're merciful.'

'We will consider your request,' said Wolf impatiently. 'Do not make contact unless you have good news. I'm well aware of the kinds of stalling tactics negotiators use, and we're not going to tolerate them.'

The line went dead.

Arley took a deep breath as the tension slowly seeped out of the room, and put a supportive hand on Riz's shoulder. 'You handled that well.'

Riz sat back in his seat and stretched. 'That wasn't easy.'

On the screen, Arley saw Commissioner Phillips talking to someone off camera. The audio feed was turned off. Then he turned back and addressed the room. 'I've just received word from the PM's office that all mobile phone coverage and Internet access is to be switched off inside the Stanhope with immediate effect.'

'What?' asked Riz. 'They specifically demanded the Internet be kept on.'

'I know they did,' said Phillips. 'But these are the PM's direct orders. He's not prepared to let them make propaganda videos or communicate with the outside world from inside the hotel without us knowing about it. He's currently hosting a meeting of COBRA, so it's likely to be a group decision.' He addressed Riz directly. 'You can tell them we'll restore the Internet as soon as we speak to Prior.'

Riz looked concerned. 'It's a very risky course of action we're taking. Their commander is not talking like a desperate man. He's talking like a man who's holding lots of cards. He's part of a well-organised team. And we already know they're quite prepared to kill innocent people. My feeling is that if we push them, they'll react violently.'

Phillips sighed. 'We have to make a stand and face the consequences.'

'We have another major problem as well,' said Arley. 'We can't actually meet any of their demands. The government doesn't negotiate with terrorists.'

Riz nodded. 'I believe the hostage-takers know that.'

Arley frowned. 'So, why make the demands in the first place?'

'Because they've planned this very carefully. First of all, by making demands, it extends the publicity they and their organisation can get out of their operation. Also, it helps to shift the onus of blame on to the British government, because if we refuse to negotiate and turn down every demand flat, we're going to end up catching a lot of the flak if things go wrong.'

'There must be a way of bringing this to a peaceful conclusion,' Arley objected.

'Anyone can be negotiated with,' Riz replied. 'The fact is he's already backed down a little by speaking to me. The key is to keep pushing him. One thing I know about Islamic culture, being a Muslim myself, is the importance of family. I know it's a long shot, but if we can ID him and get members of his family involved in the negotiations, then we might be able to sway him from the present course.'

'We're doing everything we can to ID him,' said Cheney. 'But even if we do manage it, there's a small something that we seem to have overlooked.'

Arley turned his way. 'What's that, John?'

'The man we're speaking to made some pretty major demands but at no point did he do what almost all hijackers do when they're trapped. He didn't ask for safe passage out. Not for himself or any of his men.' He paused, and Arley felt the tension in the room cranking up again. 'Which suggests to me that neither he, nor they, have any intention of leaving that place alive.'

AS SOON AS FOX had the information he needed from Michael Prior, he used the laptop from his backpack to log into a Hotmail account that only he and one other person had access to, where he left a three-word message in the drafts section: *I have it*. Leaving a message in the drafts folder was an old anti-surveillance trick. It meant the content couldn't be monitored or read by the security forces, since no message was ever actually sent over the Internet.

He knew he had to move fast. Leaving Prior behind, he exited room 316 and took the emergency stairs to the second floor, where he stopped at room 202. Before he'd tampered with the guest reservation database, 202 had been empty. Now it was registered to Mr Robert Durran, a freelance architect who was on the first night of a two-night stay.

Using the master key card, Fox let himself into the room. The lights were off and the curtains open, letting in the flashing lights of all the emergency services vehicles gathered across the street.

Fox unzipped the rucksack and removed the clothes and shoes he'd been wearing when he arrived at the Park Royal rendezvous earlier that afternoon. Next he pulled out a wallet containing a driving licence, passport and credit cards in the name of Robert Durran, as well as several hundred pounds in cash, from an internal pocket. He slipped the wallet into the front pocket of the trousers, then carefully placed the whole bundle under the bed, pushing it in so that it was well out of sight.

Finally, he looked round the room and, satisfied that his contingency plan was in place, headed back to join the others.

In the ballroom, Bear and Cat were sitting on chairs a few yards apart, watching the hostages. Both of them turned round as he entered the room. Cat gave him a bored look, which meant that Wolf had yet to tell her about the death of her brother, while Bear gave him a nod, which he returned.

Only a handful of the hostages looked up. There were seventy-seven of them in all, forty-six men and thirty-one women, and Fox had to admit they were an acquiescent bunch. Seated quietly at the far end of the room, their heads were down and they were behaving exactly as they'd been ordered to.

Fox walked past them and into the satellite kitchen.

Wolf was sitting alone at the far end next to the phone in the kitchen drinking a coffee. He turned round as Fox entered. 'I've spoken to the negotiator and given him our demands. They want to speak to Prior.'

'We need to be careful about that,' said Fox. 'They'll be trying to pinpoint his location in the building. If you let them speak to him, they'll know exactly where he is.'

'We can always move him.'

'True. But we're already two men down so we can't just shift him from room to room. It means manpower and logistics, not to mention risk.'

Wolf frowned. 'So you think we shouldn't?'

'We don't have anything to gain from it. Let them sweat a little. And in the meantime, let's release the children. That'll give them something to work with, and help to stave off any chance of an early assault.'

'OK,' said Wolf slowly. 'That's what we'll do. But I'm not releasing any of their parents. I don't want them giving anything away about us.'

Fox agreed with him. The minute any hostages were released, the police would be on them like a shot, trying to extract any information they could about what was going on inside the Stanhope—information that would later be handed over to the military for when they staged their inevitable assault. Children, however, would be of only limited help.

'I'm guessing you haven't told Cat about her brother yet?' he asked.

'Not yet, no.'

'She's not going to take it well.'

'Of course she isn't, you fool.' Wolf looked agitated. 'I'll handle her. She listens to me. Take over out there and send her in.'

CLINTON BONNER was dying to urinate. A weak bladder had been a constant companion ever since he'd hit his fifties, over a decade before, and right now it was tormenting him with a vengeance.

He was in the walk-in cupboard of the ballroom's satellite kitchen, lying in the same spot he'd been in for more than three hours now—the crawl-space beneath the left-hand bottom shelf. When he'd sneaked in there to have a quick nap it was 3.30 on a normal November afternoon. He'd slept for well over an hour, and when he'd woken up at ten to five, already needing the loo, his whole world had changed.

The first thing he remembered was the faint rat-a-tat-tat of automatic gunfire coming from downstairs, then lots and lots of shouting and screaming. His instincts had told him to stay put until it stopped.

The shooting had finally stopped, but the shouting hadn't. It had got closer until it seemed to be coming from the ballroom, barely ten yards from where he was lying. Clinton had lain there until he'd heard voices, quieter and calmer now, inside the satellite kitchen. What he'd heard had been truly terrifying. It was obvious armed men had taken over the Stanhope.

That had been some time ago now. Clinton sneaked a peek at his watch, sheltering the green light with his hand, and saw that it was five to seven, almost an hour and a half since the end of his shift. His wife, Nancy, would be worried sick—which was why he'd sent her a text earlier, telling her he was safe and hidden away, but couldn't talk. He'd then switched off the phone, not prepared to risk the fact that it might make a noise and betray his location to the men who'd taken over the hotel.

His bladder felt like it was bursting. He tried to think of something else, but nothing seemed to work. He considered wetting his pants. Almost did it. But the fear that the odour might give him away held him back.

The talking outside had stopped but he could still hear movement. Someone was there, just beyond the door. Someone prepared to kill him.

He heard footsteps approaching, and he felt the fear rise in his chest as they stopped outside. And then the door opened and light flooded in.

Clinton held his breath, pushing himself as far into the crawlspace as possible, silently praying that the intruder wouldn't look down.

The intruder was inside the store cupboard now, rummaging around on the shelves, his booted feet only inches from Clinton's face.

Clinton desperately wanted to breathe. To breathe and to pee. Terror coursed through him as he realised that he could be just seconds from the end of his life. *Please, God. Don't let me be discovered.*

Which was when Clinton felt the wetness running down his leg as his bladder finally gave way. *Oh God, no. Please.*

His eyes filled with tears as he tried to stop himself. But he couldn't seem to manage it, and now he could hear the urine dripping onto the floor, forming a puddle that any second now was going to be discovered.

The man grunted as he dropped a can of something onto the floor. It rolled towards Clinton and he reached out a finger and rolled it back out, away from the crawlspace, praying the man wouldn't look down and see the growing puddle, or pick up the strong odour of urine that seemed to Clinton to be overwhelming. At last, Clinton managed to stop the flow of urine, but still he didn't dare breathe, even though his lungs were close to bursting.

Finally, the man turned and walked out of the store cupboard, carrying a case of bottled mineral water under one arm. He didn't shut the door, allowing Clinton to catch a look at him for the first time as he placed it down on one of the worktops, and pulled one of the bottles free. He was short and squat, with a wide froglike face peppered with acne scars. What truly scared Clinton, though, was the fact that if he could see the man, then the man could surely see him.

Then Clinton heard the kitchen door open more widely and a moment later a woman came into view, pulling off a black balaclava. She was dark-haired and pretty, and wearing a surprisingly sexy black dress underneath a thick bomber jacket. She had a handgun down by her side.

The man said something in Arabic and walked over to her.

A few seconds later the woman let out a wild animal howl that filled the room before storming into view, a hand covering her face. The man pulled her back and they continued to talk in hushed voices for several minutes more before she broke free from him and paced the room in ferocious, intense silence. On three separate occasions she passed just in front of the open cupboard door, but was thankfully too preoccupied to look inside.

Finally, she stopped. 'I want him alive,' she hissed, speaking in English for the first time. 'And I want to be the one who slices his balls off.'

'You shall have him, I promise you that.'

'When?'

'Later. There are things we need to do first.'

'Like what?'

'We have to release the children.'

'That is more important than finding the man who murdered my brother?'

'We need to give a sign of goodwill. When we have done that, we will look for this man. Remember, this whole building will burn tonight, and he will burn with it.'

'I want them all to burn,' she said, walking into view. Her face was no longer pretty but set hard and merciless, and her dark eyes blazed with a terrible anger. 'I want to kill as many of these dogs as possible.' She was looking past the man now, right towards where Clinton was lying.

'Something smells strange in here,' she said, wrinkling her nose.

Clinton almost cried out with fear as he heard those words.

The man turned round, and now he too was looking straight at Clinton. He frowned. 'It's something in there.'

Clinton didn't move. It was over. He was going to die.

The man was walking towards him, his rifle dangling from his arm. Getting closer and closer. And then, in one single terrifying movement, he slammed the door shut, plunging Clinton back into welcome darkness.

19.05

Arley Dale was drinking a cup of coffee and thinking about having a ciga-rette. In the past few minutes, things in the mobile incident room had quietened right down, and the phones had stopped ringing. Riz Mohammed and John Cheney were going through lists of terror organisations, searching for anything that might provide a link to the Pan-Arab Army of God.

The orders from Commissioner Phillips, and from the Prime Minister himself, who as Platinum Commander was in overall charge of the operation, were to attempt a negotiated settlement, but they were also hedging their bets. A full squadron of SAS troops had arrived a few minutes earlier, ready to stage a rapid assault on the hotel if the situation deteriorated.

Arley needed to call the SAS leader and give him a briefing, but she decided to have a cigarette first, figuring she'd earned it. She went outside, walking away from the office and the police vehicles as she lit up.

Her mobile rang, and she sighed, wondering what had happened now.

It was Howard, her husband. She'd left a message on his phone close to two hours back now to let him know that she was involved in the siege at the Stanhope, and it had taken him this long to get back to her. Doubtless he'd been busy getting supper ready and hadn't wanted to disturb her.

But the voice at the other end wasn't Howard's. It belonged to a man with a foreign accent. 'We have your family,' he told her.

Arley felt a physical lurch of terror that almost knocked her over. 'Hold on,' she said, moving farther away from the police vehicles.

'Your au pair is dead,' continued the caller, his tone matter of fact, 'and your husband, son and daughter are being held in a secure location.'

'What do you want?' Arley whispered into the phone.

'I'm going to send you a video of your children with the au pair. Then I'm going to call you back. Do not try to trace me. I am in contact every fifteen minutes with the man holding your family. If he doesn't hear from me for more than half an hour he has strict instructions to execute all of them.'

'I'm not going to do anything stupid, I promise,' she said. But she was already talking into a dead phone.

234 | SIMON KERNICK

For perhaps the longest few minutes of her life she stood in the cold staring at the phone, ignoring everything around her, before it bleeped to say she'd received a text message from Howard with a video attached. Taking a deep breath, she opened the message and pressed play on the video.

It lasted barely thirty seconds but it was enough to confirm that the people holding her family were utterly ruthless. The frightened expressions on the faces of her children as they were forced to sit either side of Magda's dead body made her want to throw up. Don't panic, she told herself. Think.

The phone rang again, Howard's name coming up on the screen.

'You've seen the video?' asked the caller.

'Yes. What do you want?'

'I understand you are in charge of the police operation at the Stanhope Hotel.' It was a statement, not a question. 'You're going to find out the SAS's plan of attack, and when they're aiming to penetrate the building. If your information is correct, your family will be released unharmed.'

'There is no plan of attack,' she whispered urgently into the phone. 'We're still at the negotiating stage.'

'There will be an attack,' said the man. 'And you will find out the details.'

'I don't think you understand. Even if an attack did go ahead it would be a military operation, which means I won't be party to any of their plans.'

'Then you will need to find a way, Mrs Dale. This phone is now going to be switched off. I will call you again when the time is right. If you ever want to see your family again, you'll tell us everything we need to know.'

THE PARK VIEW RESTAURANT was hot and silent. Elena glanced up at the two guards. The taller of the two was sitting down with his foot dangling above the detonation pedal for the bomb that had been placed in the middle of the group, only a few feet from where Elena sat. He was watching them carefully. The other guard was smaller and had a pronounced limp. He spoke with a Scandinavian accent. He seemed more agitated and unpleasant.

The Scandinavian guard left the room, which eased the tense atmosphere a little. Elena shifted position on the floor so that she was sitting with her arms clasped round her knees. She was trying to get comfortable. The man next to Elena, the one who'd fashioned a noose in his room, caught her eye and gave her a reassuring smile.

She smiled back, curiosity getting the better of her. Here was a normal-looking middle-aged man and he'd come here to die a lonely, bleak death.

'Are you here alone?' she whispered to him. She glanced up as she spoke to make sure the tall guard hadn't heard her. It didn't look like he had.

He nodded, looking ashamed. 'Yes, I am.'

They were silent for a few moments after that, then he sighed. 'I have to admit, I came here to die,' he whispered. 'But not like this.'

'Forgive me for asking, but why do you want to die?'

'Because I'm going to die soon anyway. I've got cancer.'

Elena's jaw tightened. 'I'm sorry. I shouldn't have asked.'

'It's OK,' he said, and they both fell silent.

'What's your name?' she asked him eventually.

'Martin.'

'I'm Elena.'

'I'm sorry about choosing your hotel to finish things in,' he continued. 'The Stanhope has a very special place in my heart.'

Elena was curious. 'Why?'

He paused. 'I came here with a girl once. Twenty-two years ago now. Her name was Carrie. She was the love of my life.' He shook his head sadly. 'I should have stayed with her. I know it sounds clichéd, but don't ever let anything get in the way of love, Elena. It's the most important thing there is.'

She thought of Rod, and it made her feel happy briefly. 'I know.'

'You're engaged?' he whispered, looking down at her new ring.

'Yes. He proposed last night.'

'God, I'm sorry. Not that you got engaged, but . . .' He looked around. 'Because of all this. You don't deserve it.'

'None of us does.'

'What's going on over there?' The voice cut through the quiet of the room. 'You were told to keep your mouths shut.' It was the Scandinavian guard. He'd come back into the room and was limping over to them.

He stopped in front of them. 'What were you talking about?'

'I was just asking if she was OK,' said Martin. 'That's all.'

'What did I tell you, shithead? No talking.' He kicked Martin hard in the chest, knocking him backwards. Martin went down hard on to his side, gasping for air, and the Scandinavian immediately kicked him again. 'Talk again and I'll really make you suffer,' he sneered, before turning away.

'Coward,' said Elena, unable to stop the words coming out of her mouth.

The Scandinavian stopped. Then, very slowly, turned round. 'What did you say?' he hissed, pushing the rifle against her forehead.

Elena swallowed. 'He's ill. And he can't fight back.'

'Please, leave her,' she heard Martin say. 'She didn't mean it.'

For several seconds, nothing happened. Elena realised with dread that the Scandinavian was debating whether or not to pull the trigger. She closed her eyes. If the end was about to come, then she prayed it would be quick.

Then she heard the door from the kitchen opening. Instinctively she opened her eyes and saw the terrorist leader, Wolf, walk into the room accompanied by the woman from downstairs. Both of them were masked and armed—he with an assault rifle, she with a handgun—and right then, Elena was hugely relieved to see them, because the Scandinavian immediately lowered his gun and retreated as Wolf beckoned him over. There followed a hushed debate in the corner involving the four hostage-takers.

Elena leaned down and helped Martin back up. His face was twisted in pain, and he'd gone so pale that she thought he might vomit.

Still struggling for breath, he gestured for her to come closer. 'You shouldn't have done that,' he whispered. 'You could have been killed.'

'I hate bullies,' she whispered back, putting a hand on his arm.

Wolf stood in front of the hostages. 'As a gesture of goodwill, we're going to release the children. They are to come with us now. They will be released through the front doors of the hotel in the next fifteen minutes.'

The mother of a little girl raised a hand. 'Are parents able to go with their children? My daughter needs me.'

'No. They go alone. But we will release them safely. You have our word.'

The mother started to speak, then thought better of it. Holding her daughter close, she whispered in her ear, tears streaming down her face. The daughter immediately tightened her grip, but the mother pushed her away, promising they'd be together again very soon. Across the room, three other sets of parents said goodbye to their children: the eight-year-old girl, the boy of about twelve in his school uniform and a Japanese boy closer to sixteen.

'He's not going,' said Wolf, pointing to the Japanese boy as he got up.

The boy stopped, and both his parents got to their feet.

'Please, sir,' said his mother, 'let him go. He's very young.'

'Not young enough. In my country, he'd be considered a man. Sit down.'

The mother kept pleading but Wolf stared at her coldly and told her that he'd shoot them unless they did as they'd been instructed. The husband gently took hold of his wife and son, a sorrowful expression on his face, and they sat down slowly, the mother's sobs quickly subsiding.

19.18

Arley Dale stood in the cold night air of Hyde Park, still stunned by the phone call she'd just received. In the space of a few cruel minutes her whole world had become a nightmare from which it seemed there was no escape.

If she told the man holding her children the details and timing of any SAS entry into the Stanhope she would be betraying them, perhaps even sending the soldiers to their deaths. She would effectively be committing treason. She would also almost certainly be found out, which would mean losing her career, her life as she knew it, and her liberty. Even if a judge took into account the extenuating circumstances behind her betrayal, she could still spend the next ten years of her life in prison.

But if she didn't do what the caller wanted, what then? There was, of course, the possibility that if she told her bosses they could keep things under wraps while the full resources of the Met were thrown into the hunt for Howard and the children. But the problem was, her family could be anywhere. And there was nothing to suggest that the terrorists wouldn't kill Howard, Oliver and India if it suited them. And as soon as they realised that she'd given them false information about any attack (which she'd have to do if she confided in Commissioner Phillips) they would take their revenge.

She also knew that, even if she did cooperate, there was absolutely no guarantee that her loved ones would be released. In fact, it would be far simpler for the terrorists to kill them.

She couldn't believe what was happening to her. How on earth had they got to her family? How did they know she'd be involved with the Stanhope Hotel siege? It wasn't as if the Met's major incident command structure was decided in advance. It simply depended on who was available and on duty when an incident happened. But they had known. Just as they seemed to know that the SAS would be launching a rescue operation later that night.

Arley felt sick as she lit a cigarette with shaking hands. She pictured Oliver and India. How would she ever live with herself if they died? And she thought of Howard. She loved him too, of course, but not in the same desperate, all-encompassing way she loved her children

She dragged hard on the cigarette. Weighing up her options. *What options?* Unless . . . She looked down at her phone. There was one person who might be able to help her; one person she felt she could trust with this, the darkest of secrets. It was a hard call to make, but she knew it was worth the risk. In the end, she'd destroy anyone, whoever it was, to save her children.

TINA BOYD had never been a conventional police officer. In a career of sailing close to the wind she'd been shot twice, kidnapped once, and had even killed violent murderers herself on two occasions—although both men had deserved what they got in her opinion. She'd also planted evidence on suspects, had assaulted quite a few, had been suspended twice, and had finally been fired earlier in the year after an unofficial case she was working on in the Philippines had ended with a lot of dead bodies. In short, Tina Boyd was trouble to anyone mad enough to get involved with her.

But she had one unique selling point, which was the reason she'd lasted as long as she had in the Met: she got results. Not necessarily by the book. But the statistics didn't lie. Of the thirty-nine major investigations she'd been a part of, or had led, her clear-up rate was one hundred per cent.

Ultimately, though, nothing had been able to stand in the way of her own volatility and lack of discipline, and now, nine months on from parting acrimoniously with the Met, she was scraping by doing unofficial private detective work, and the occasional bit of consultancy for film companies. But ask her if she regretted anything and her answer would always be the same.

Everything I did, I did for the right reasons.

Although, as she sat in her living room watching events unfold at the Stanhope Hotel on the TV, Tina realised how much she missed her old life.

Tina's mobile rang just as the PM appeared on the screen for a news conference. She picked it up and frowned at the screen. Arley Dale.

They'd been friends once—or perhaps acquaintances was a better word for it. Tina didn't have many friends. In fact, she was actually surprised she still had Arley's number stored. They hadn't spoken in months.

When she'd been suspended eighteen months earlier, Arley had supported her, saying the Met needed more strong women like Tina. But she'd been noticeable by her absence in February when Tina had finally got the push, which was fair enough. You can only stick your neck out so far when the other person insists on hanging one-handed from the parapet. Especially when you're a high-flying DAC in the Met. Tina picked up. 'Arley? How are you?'

A pause. Then five words, laced with desperation. 'You've got to help me.'

ARLEY TOOK A DEEP BREATH. She was taking an immense risk confiding in Tina Boyd, but she knew too that she was extremely short on alternatives.

'I'm in real trouble,' she whispered into the phone, keeping one eye on the incident room, 'and I don't know where else to turn.'

'What is it?'

There was no sarcasm in Tina's voice. Just genuine interest.

So Arley told her everything that had happened, keeping it as brief and businesslike as possible.

'Jesus,' said Tina when she'd finished. 'You've got to tell your superiors. You can't deal with something like this on your own.'

'I can't, Tina. The government will sacrifice my family if they have to. They won't let their safety stand in the way of an assault on the hotel.'

'But why are you calling me?'

'I want you to find them. I know it's a long shot—'

'It's more than a long shot, Arley. It's a physical impossibility. I'm one woman who no longer has a warrant card or access to any police resources.'

'I've got access to resources.' Arley could hear the desperation in her own voice. 'I'll give you every assistance I can.'

'We haven't spoken for nearly a year.'

'I know we haven't. And I know I should have helped you over that Philippines thing. But you're a bloody good detective, Tina. One of the best I've ever come across. And you get things done. Where are you now?'

'I'm at home.'

'That's near Ridge, isn't it?'

'That's right.'

'Well, that's only twenty minutes away from me. I live in Mill Hill.'

'I know where you are. You could have called, or visited couldn't you? In an unofficial capacity, so that it wouldn't have affected your career.'

'I'm sorry. I truly am. But they have my family.'

'I still don't see what I can do.'

'I know I'm putting you on the spot, Tina. But you're the only person I know who might just be able to find them.'

Silence at the other end. Then, 'When did you last have contact with them?'

'This morning. I left the house at seven thirty. They were all there then.'

'Nothing suspicious? No unfamiliar vehicles? Anything like that?'

Arley wrenched her mind back to earlier that morning. 'No. Nothing.'

Tina was silent again. 'I'll go over there. But listen, Arley. I would think really carefully about telling your bosses about this because the chances are I'll turn up nothing. You have to understand that.'

'I do. Just please, please, do what you can. And call me, will you? As soon as you find out anything at all.'

SCOPE SAT ON THE FLOOR against the bed, Ethan beside him. Abby had drifted off to sleep, and after checking that she was all right, Scope had let her be.

'When are the police coming?' Ethan asked for the hundredth time.

Scope knew how he felt. The slow turn of the minutes was hugely frustrating. 'They'll come as soon as they can,' he answered, yet again. 'They just need to find out where the bad guys are so they can come in here and save us.'

'They need to hurry up. Mom's really sick.' Ethan's face was white and strained. 'I wish my dad was here.'

'Where is he?'

'He left home. Last year.'

'Do you still see him?'

Ethan shook his head. 'No. Mom says he still loves me, but he's very busy. He calls me sometimes, though.'

'I'm sure he misses you.'

'I miss him.'

Scope wished he'd seen more of his own daughter when he'd had the chance. And yet, like Ethan's dad, he'd left home and his family, and since then he'd lost count of the number of times he'd wondered how different things might have been if they'd all stayed together. He remembered Mary Ann as a laughing two-year-old running around the back garden on tiny legs while he and Jennifer looked on with the broad, dopey smiles of new parents full of love for the beautiful creature they'd created.

'Grandpa brought us here as a treat. I've never been to London before. And I don't want to come again now. Never.'

'Where are you from?'

'Florida. Near Disneyworld. Have you ever been to Disneyworld?'

'No, can't say I ever have.'

'Where are you from? You've got a funny accent.'

'A place called Manchester, and it's not funny.'

'What are you doing here?'

Scope thought of the three men upstairs. 'Visiting friends.'

Ethan was silent a moment, his face scrunched up in thought. 'Why are those men killing people?' he said at last. 'They killed Grandpa. Why?'

'Some people like hurting other people for no reason. There aren't very many of them, and you were very unlucky to have run into some today. I'm sorry for you.'

Ethan's eyes flashed. 'I'm glad you killed them,' he said defiantly.

Scope nodded. So was he.

'Are you a policeman?'

'No.'

'A soldier?'

'You ask a lot of questions.'

'I think you're a soldier,' said Ethan. 'Thank you for helping us.'

'You should never walk by and leave people who are in trouble.'

But even as he said this, Scope wasn't sure he believed it. Helping Abby and Ethan had already caused him a hell of a lot of grief.

Scope's attention was caught by something on the TV. The camera had suddenly panned from a reporter to the front entrance of the hotel. As Scope watched, the far left door was slowly opened and a masked terrorist in navy overalls appeared in the doorway with a small group of children. The terrorist then disappeared back inside, locking the door and leaving the kids standing on the front step, holding hands and looking confused.

Two armed police officers, accompanied by a pair of paramedics, rushed over, and led the children away from the hotel entrance.

'What's happening?' asked Ethan, who was also watching the TV.

'I think they might be releasing some of the hostages.'

'Can we go too?' For the first time, there was excitement in Ethan's voice.

'I'm not sure,' said Scope, trying to figure out a plan of action, knowing that there was no guarantee they would let Ethan go. But knowing too that he couldn't simply sit here waiting for events to unfold, not with Abby injured and in need of insulin. He sighed.

The last thing he wanted to do was draw more attention to himself, not after what had gone on upstairs.

IN THE INCIDENT ROOM, Riz Mohammed was grinning as he and the others watched the screen that showed the three children being released.

'Well done, Riz,' said John Cheney. 'That was some good negotiating.'

Janine and Will were both on their feet, smiling and adding their own words of encouragement, and Arley had to force herself to do the same, even though she was finding it almost impossible to concentrate.

'The children are going to need debriefing as soon as they've been checked out at St Mary's,' she said. 'John, can you get CTC to send their people over there, and then let us know what, if anything, they find out?'

Cheney nodded, and Arley was amazed at her own capacity for carrying on in the midst of this, the worst personal crisis of her life.

One of the secure phones rang in the incident room and Janine picked it up.

'Gold for you, ma'am.'

Decision time. Arley picked up the phone at the far end of the office.

'It's good news about the children being released,' said Commissioner Phillips without preamble. 'Congratulations are in order to you and your negotiator.'

Tell him. Tell him now.

'Thank you, sir,' she replied, her voice sounding hollow.

'But the PM and I are still very concerned that your negotiator hasn't yet been able to speak to Michael Prior. We need to find out urgently whether he's been compromised.'

'I can understand that, sir, but if we insist, we risk antagonising them or letting them know that we're really worried about what he might say.'

'Which is why we're preparing for a possible armed intervention.'

Oh Jesus. The assault the caller was talking about.

'Are we handing over control of the scene to the military?' she asked.

'Not yet. The PM's very keen for a negotiated settlement.'

'So am I. Especially now that we've secured the release of some of the hostages peacefully.'

'But we're also going to have to review our options if Michael Prior remains unaccounted for. Do we have any news on where he might be?'

'According to calls made to his phone, he was initially being held in one of the guest rooms somewhere on the third floor, but the phone signal was last picked up on the ground floor. We don't know where the phone is now, because we no longer have coverage within the building. And, of course, there's no guarantee it's with him anyway.'

'So, we don't have a clue, basically,' said Phillips, sounding irritated.

A silence stretched between them. 'No,' she responded tightly, 'I'm afraid we don't, sir.'

'Are you all right, Arley? You sound very tense.'

Last chance. Tell him.

'It's a tense situation, sir.'

'Well, you were picked because you're calm and level-headed, and it would be a great help to all of us if you didn't forget that.'

FIVE

20.02

Tina Boyd drove slowly past the Dale family home. There were no lights on inside and none of the curtains at the front of the house had been drawn, which was the first thing you'd do if you didn't want anyone seeing inside.

An Audi estate, which Tina presumed belonged to Arley's husband Howard, was the only car in the driveway. She continued driving, checking to see if any of the cars parked on either side of the road were occupied.

When Tina was satisfied that the street was clear, she found a parking space about thirty yards farther on and got out. She walked back towards the Dales' house but instead of turning into their drive, she turned into the one next door. She crept by the side of the house and tried the side gate, which was locked. She clambered over it and into the back garden.

A high evergreen hedge separated the two properties, and Tina had to force her way through it before emerging on the other side at the back of the Dales' house. There were no curtains closed on this side either. She stayed in the shadows of the hedge for a full minute, watching for any signs of life.

Nothing and no one moved. There were no lights coming from inside to signify someone watching the TV. No sounds either. Just the distant hum of traffic. She gave it another thirty seconds, then slowly approached the nearest window, which looked straight into a kitchen diner.

Straightaway she saw the body lying there. A dark pool of blood had formed round the upper part of the body. Tina had never seen a photo of Howard but she was certain it was him.

She took a step back. This was the time to call the police. If she went inside, she'd be contaminating a crime scene, and giving herself a whole lot of trouble. It was also possible that the kids were still in the house—and if they were, they were almost certainly dead too.

With a long sigh, she put on her gloves and retrieved the spare keys from the potting shed, where Arley had said they'd be, and opened the kitchen door. As she stepped inside, she was greeted by telltale sour smell of death. She crouched down beside the body and felt for a pulse as a formality. She wasn't surprised when there was no sign of one.

To make absolutely sure this was Arley's husband, Tina crept into the hallway looking for family photos, which was when she saw the second body, propped up against the wall. This would be Magda, the Dale family au pair. Arley had told Tina that she'd been killed by the kidnappers.

There was a family portrait on the opposite wall. Arley, her two teenage children and Howard, a big bluff smiling man standing a good head taller than the others, and without doubt the corpse she'd just seen in the kitchen.

'Jesus,' whispered Tina in the gloom, feeling the kind of intense righteous anger she hadn't experienced in a long, long time. She wanted to get the people responsible for this. She wanted to make them pay.

She searched the rest of the house, but there was no sign of the two children. Both they and the kidnappers were gone, just as she'd expected. She checked for anything that might give her some clue as to the kidnappers' identity, or their final destination, but nothing sprang out at her.

All of which left Tina with a stark choice. The chances of her finding Arley's children were slim in the extreme. The best course of action was to persuade Arley to tell her colleagues what was going on. But she wasn't at all sure that Arley would. And Tina knew she was almost certainly right not to. Neither the Met nor the government would put her two children before the lives of the hostages in the Stanhope.

Tina let herself out of the house, pulling from her jeans pocket a fake warrant card she used sometimes for PI work. She'd made her decision.

20.20

In the ballroom, Fox was on guard duty with Bear. He and Bear were sitting on chairs twenty feet apart, and well back from the hostages. Bear's foot rested on the detonation pedal for the bomb that sat in the middle of the hostages, and Fox hoped that none of them would work out that there was no way he or Bear would detonate it, given that they were sat right in the path of any shrapnel. In fact, the bomb, like all but two of the others, was set to a timer and would explode at 23.00 hours, not before. Both the pedal and the det cords were there for show only.

Still keeping a firm grip on his rifle, Fox slid the pack from his back and, as casually as possible, removed his laptop. He wanted to check that the individual he'd left a message for earlier in the drafts section of the Hotmail account had received it and responded with a message of his own.

But when he tried to go online, the computer didn't respond. He tried again but it definitely wasn't working. The bastards had cut them off.

This was a real problem. He wasn't so worried about his own private message. He knew it was there, so a response was less important. However, one of the key components of their plan was knowing where and when the security forces would launch their attack. This information was also going to be provided through the drafts section of a separate Hotmail account so that it couldn't be read by the authorities. But if they didn't have an Internet connection, they wouldn't get it, and they'd lose a key advantage.

He tried one more time, got the same result, and replaced the laptop in the backpack as he got to his feet.

Bear gave him a questioning look. 'Is there a problem?' he whispered.

'I just need to see Wolf quickly. I'll be back in a minute.' And then louder, so the hostages could hear, he said, 'Anyone moves, put a hole in them.'

'DID YOU MANAGE to get the insulin pens?' Abby asked groggily. She looked tired but in OK shape, and was drinking from a bottle of water while Ethan knelt beside her, holding her hand.

'I'm afraid they weren't there,' said Scope, shutting the door behind him and putting the chair back against it.

'But they were in my black handbag by the side of the bed. I'm sure of it.'

'Your handbag was on the floor, and it looked like someone had been through it.'

'Who?'

'I'm guessing one of the terrorists. He was probably looking for clues about who killed his friends.'

A wave of panic crossed Abby's face.

'Don't worry,' he said. 'We'll sort something out.'

'What, though? I'm going to need that insulin soon, as well as something to eat, otherwise my blood sugar levels are going to start getting too high.'

'What happens then?'

Abby looked down at Ethan. It was clear she didn't want to worry him. 'If they keep going up, then it could be a problem, but I should be good for a few hours yet.' She squeezed her son's hand and forced a smile.

'Mum, you'll be OK,' said Ethan, before turning to Scope. 'Won't she?'

Scope nodded, but something in Abby's expression worried him. He didn't know a lot about Type One diabetes, but he was pretty sure the consequences would be serious if she didn't get her insulin soon. 'Leave it with me,' he said. 'I'll sort it.'

He grabbed the hotel phone, walked it as far as possible from the bed, and dialled the emergency services.

As soon as the operator picked up, Scope asked to speak to a paramedic. He was put through to a male paramedic who identified himself as Steve.

Scope briefly explained the situation, keeping his voice low. 'We need that insulin fast. She told me she thinks she's good until about ten, so we've got an hour and a half maximum.' This was a lie, but he knew he needed to inject a sense of urgency into the situation. 'In a hotel this size they must keep medical supplies somewhere on-site. I just need to find out where.'

'I can't help you there,' responded Steve.

'That's where you're wrong. You can find out for me. Someone in the emergency services will be in touch with the hotel's owners, and they'll know. You've got to ask to be put through to someone at the scene.'

'It'll take time.'

'We haven't got time, Steve,' Scope whispered. 'There's a woman in here who's going to die if she doesn't get her insulin, and her seven-year-old son's going to have to witness it.'

Steve sighed. 'I'll see what I can do, but it's not going to happen just like that. This whole thing is bedlam and I'm only a lowly paramedic.'

'Do what you can, and do it fast. Have you got a number I can get you on?'

Steve hesitated for a moment, then gave Scope his mobile phone number.

'I'll call you in fifteen minutes,' Scope told him.

20.29

The SAS team had been billeted two streets south of Park Lane, well away from the TV cameras, which had been placed around the perimeter of Hyde Park—from where they had a clear shot of the front of the Stanhope.

It was a six-minute walk to the team's temporary base from the mobile incident room but Arley did it in four. The office was large and open-plan and full of casually dressed men unpacking kit. There must have been thirty of them in all that she could see. In one corner, a table had been set up and three men were bent over one of three laptops that had been lined up in a row, along with several telephones. One of them was older than the others—probably about forty-five, with greying hair and a lined, weatherbeaten face. He was dressed in jeans and an open-necked shirt.

'Major Standard?'

He looked up and gave her an appraising look.

'I'm DAC Arley Dale,' she said, forcing a smile. 'I'm in charge of the emergency services on the ground.'

'And I'm the man in charge of this lot.' He put out a hand. 'Good to meet you, DAC Dale.'

'Please, call me Arley. I just wanted to give you a brief face-to-face rundown of what we've got so far.'

Standard nodded, and Arley thought he seemed a nice guy, which somehow made what she was about to do worse.

'We've had some information,' he said, 'but not a great deal.'

'There isn't a great deal to be had. We've got a previously unknown group of men of Middle Eastern and possibly eastern European origin who are making some very ambitious demands, and who we believe are linked to the bombs at the Westfield and Paddington.'

'Were they suicide bombs?'

'We think one of the two at Paddington was.'

'That makes things a little tricky,' said Standard with admirable under-statement. 'Our understanding is that they're holding one group of hostages in a restaurant on the ninth floor.'

'That's right. They've released a handful of children, and we've managed to get some limited information from the oldest of them, a boy of twelve. He says there are about thirty hostages in the restaurant guarded by two terrorists armed with assault rifles. The terrorists have access to a TV showing the news, so they can see what's going on outside. Because they keep the blinds down the whole time, we can't see their exact locations.'

Standard nodded thoughtfully and, though he was trying to hide it, Arley could see he wasn't liking the information he was receiving.

'They also have a rucksack that they claim contains a bomb, which they've placed in the middle of the hostages, and one of them always keeps his foot close to the detonator.'

Standard nodded again. 'And there's another group being held in the ballroom on the mezzanine floor. Is that right?'

'That's what we believe, yes, but we have no idea of numbers, of the hostages or the hostage-takers. According to GCHQ, the hostage-takers aren't communicating by radio, and there's no mobile phone signal inside the hotel, so it's impossible to track them. Our negotiations are being held on the telephone in the kitchen next door to the ballroom, so we think that's the terrorists' command centre.'

'What about Michael Prior? Do we have any idea where he's being held?'

Arley shook her head. 'All I can tell you is that as of five p.m. he was being held in one of the guest rooms on the third floor at the front of the hotel, but we haven't been able to find out which one because he wasn't booked into the hotel under his own name, and neither his wife nor his office knew he was there. Since then his mobile phone's moved within the building, and it's now been switched off. We've asked the lead hostage-taker for permission to speak to him, but so far it hasn't been forthcoming.'

Standard sighed. 'It sounds like they are very well organised. What about their state of mind? Do they come across as agitated, or desperate?'

'We've been dealing with one man, who calls himself Wolf, and he seems remarkably calm. I'm hoping we can negotiate a peaceful solution.'

'We're all hoping that.'

'We've got the TV cameras well back from the scene and we're operating a complete no-fly zone in central London, but if you go in from the roof or the front, your actions will be seen live on TV. With the technology they've got these days, there's no way round that.'

'I'm aware of that,' said Standard with a frown.

'Right now, the situation's calm, but if things deteriorate rapidly, what's your plan for penetrating the building?'

There it was. The life-or-death question. She asked it calmly enough, but all the time she was thinking of Howard, Oliver and India.

'If things go totally awry and we have to go in at a moment's notice, our IA—the immediate action plan—is a multi-entry assault via the roof and neighbouring buildings. But I have to tell you, it's a very risky strategy, given the way the terrorists have split the hostages, and our lack of knowledge of their numbers. Or what booby traps, if any, they've laid.'

'We can't afford large numbers of civilian casualties.'

'We know that,' said Standard. 'Which is why we're currently formulating a more subtle surprise attack. But we received the digital plans for the building only in the past ten minutes, so it's going to take time.'

Arley needed more than this. Much more. 'The hostage-takers claim to have booby-trapped the whole building,' she said, 'including the ground-floor entrances. And we know they've got ready access to explosives.'

'In that case, we'd be looking at a silent entry through windows on the mezzanine floor into guest rooms on either side of the ballroom. That way we're almost certain to bypass any booby traps they've set. The idea would be to take out the terrorists in the ballroom, then continue through the building, securing it floor by floor, before engaging the hostage-takers in the restaurant. The terrorists think they're being clever by not communicating by radio, but in a surprise attack like this it would count against them.'

'What about Michael Prior? How do you intend to find him?'

'We're still working on that, but if you can get a location for him, it would be a huge step forward.'

'We'll do everything we can,' Arley replied, feeling a knot in her stomach. Somehow they had to find a way to end the siege without the SAS having to go in. Somehow, too, Tina Boyd had to find her family and bring them home safely. Both things were still possible. They had to be.

Allowing herself to see the tiniest chink of hope, she stepped out of the office and into the street as her mobile rang.

'Are you on your own?' asked Tina.

'Yes. What have you got?'

'I've got bad news, and I've got good news. The bad news is bad, and there's no easy way to say it.'

Arley felt her stomach lurch. 'Go on.'

'Your husband's dead. I found his body in your house.'

The news was a terrible shock, but Arley didn't have time to process it. 'What about the twins?'

'There's no sign of them. I think they must have been taken this morning, not long after you left. Your husband's been dead quite a long time.'

'Christ . . .'

'The better news is I've just come from one of your neighbours, a Mrs Thompson. She saw two men in a red van leaving your house just before eight o'clock this morning. She noted the registration number.'

Arley felt a rush of hope. 'Give me the number,' she said, pulling a notebook and pen from her pocket. 'I'll get on to the ANPR guys.'

'Arley, you know as well as I do that as soon as you make the request there'll be a paper trail leading back to you, and you might have to answer some very awkward questions later.'

'Right now, that's the least of my worries.'

'Have the kidnappers been back in contact?'

'Not yet, no.'

'They will be,' said Tina. 'You know, we shouldn't be doing this alone. A single registration number isn't going to lead us straight to your kids.'

'Look, Tina, I can't afford to tell anyone else what's going on.' She paused. 'These people know so much I'm beginning to wonder if it's an inside job. The thing is, I don't know who I can trust.'

'You're going to have to put your trust in somebody.'

'And I have done. You.'

'I'm not enough, Arley. If the SAS go in and you give their plans to the terrorists, you'll have a lot of blood on your hands. And so will I.'

'I know, but just let me see what this registration number gives us. Where are you now?'

'Just down the road from your house.'

'Can you stay there for the moment? I'll call back as soon as I can.'

'OK. And while you're at it, try and get a trace on your husband's mobile too. It might help me pin down a location for your children.'

'OK, I'll do it. And Tina?'

'What?'

'Thank you.' She felt herself beginning to well up as the emotions of the evening fought to get the better of her.

Tina sighed. 'Just get on with it, Arley. Time's not on our side.'

20.38

As soon as Arley stepped back inside the mobile incident room, she knew that something was wrong.

'I've just tried calling you, ma'am,' said Riz Mohammed. Like everyone else in the room, his expression was tense.

'What's happened?' she asked, telling herself to remain calm.

'I've just had a call from the man called Wolf. Either we switch the Internet service back on inside the hotel or they kill a hostage publicly. They've given us fifteen minutes to comply. And the call came in at 20.35.'

Arley shook her head. 'Have either Gold or Silver been informed?'

'I relayed the message to Gold,' said Riz. 'We're waiting for him to come back to us.'

'What's your assessment, Riz?'

'Wolf sounded a lot more stressed than he did when we first talked to him. I'd say we've got to take this threat very seriously.'

Arley's gaze found Cheney, the most senior person in the room after her. 'What's your take, John?'

'I agree with Riz. It's serious. Are the SAS ready to go in yet?'

Arley felt her guts clench. 'I don't believe so, no.'

'Then we should let them have their Internet connection back. They probably only want to bang out one of their propaganda videos, and it's not worth sacrificing a life not to let them. Not if we're not ready for an assault.'

'I think it would do a lot to help calm the situation,' added Riz.

Arley was wholeheartedly in agreement, but what she knew and the other two didn't was that Michael Prior possessed highly sensitive information that the government were desperate to keep inside the building.

At that moment, Commissioner Phillips appeared on one of the screens as he sat back down at his desk in his office at Scotland Yard.

'I've just spoken with the PM,' he said, 'and it's been agreed that Internet access can be restored to the hotel, as long as we are able to speak to Michael Prior and ascertain that he's in good health.'

Arley felt a rush of relief. 'We'll get on to them straightaway, sir.'

Riz picked up the secure phone and the incident room fell silent.

The phone rang twice before being picked up.

'We still haven't got Internet access,' said Wolf angrily. 'Don't you care about your hostages?'

'Of course we do,' said Riz. 'But we need something in return.'

'What?'

'We need to speak to Michael Prior.'

'He's not available.'

'Is there a specific reason why we can't talk to him?'

'Yes. Because we don't take orders from you.'

'But I'm not ordering, Wolf. I'm asking you to allow us to talk to him. If you do that, we'll restore the Internet immediately. I promise you that.'

'Just turn the damn thing on. Now. I gave you an ultimatum, and you're ignoring it. Your deadline runs out in ten minutes. After that, a hostage dies. And then one dies every five minutes until you reconnect us.'

'This is not going to help anyone,' Riz said, working hard to keep his voice calm, but Wolf had already hung up on him. He exhaled loudly, and looked at Arley. 'Do you want me to call back?'

Arley wanted to shout: *Yes, call back, do whatever you can to delay things*. If a hostage was executed then the SAS would go in and that would be the end of everything.

But it was Phillips who answered him. 'No. We can't show weakness here. We have to call his bluff.'

'I'm pretty certain he's going to do it, sir,' said Riz. 'And it's very likely he'll kill other hostages until he gets what he wants.'

'And I have orders from the Prime Minister not to restore access until we speak to Prior.'

Arley's body was rigid with tension. She desperately wanted to throw up. 'Doesn't the PM realise the kind of flak he's going to get if the family of the hostage find out that he or she died because we wouldn't let the man holding them have a bloody Internet connection?'

'This is a matter of national security, DAC Dale,' the commissioner said coldly. 'I'm sorry, but on this we're going to have to stand firm.'

20.50

You're never so alive as when you're on the verge of death. Martin Dalston remembered reading that somewhere once. And the thing was, it was true. He felt more alive than he'd felt in years. He wanted to survive this night. He wanted to tell his friends all about it over a pint.

It was quiet in the restaurant. The thirty or so hostages looked tired and drawn, but an uneasy calm seemed to have descended on everyone. The guards had become visibly more relaxed, and occasionally one would disappear into the kitchen for a few minutes, leaving the other on guard alone.

Keeping his head down, he looked over and caught Elena's eye. He smiled at her and she smiled back. 'Tell me something,' she whispered, stealing a glance towards the guard to check that he wasn't looking at them. 'What happened to Carrie? If she was the love of your life, why did it end?'

'Because I was a fool.'

'Tell me about her.'

'She was beautiful. We met in Australia when I was travelling after university. That's where she was from.'

Elena's eyes lit up. 'That's where my fiancé Rod's from too. We're going to move there at Christmas.'

Martin grinned. 'You'll love it. I loved it. Carrie and I bought a clapped-out Beetle and travelled the whole country. It was the best time of my life. When my visa ran out I had to come back here. But we were still together, and we kept in touch. She was going to move to the UK for a couple of years, and a few months later she came over on business. She added a week to her stay and we spent it driving all over England. That's when we came here for a romantic weekend.' He smiled to himself.

'It sounds lovely,' whispered Elena.

Martin sighed. 'It was, but she had to go back to Oz, and although she applied for jobs over here, it was in the midst of a recession and there wasn't anything. She didn't want to come without a job so she asked me to go over there. I was working as an accountant and I think I probably could have got something over there, but I dithered. Our conversations got fewer, I kept delaying a decision, even though I was desperate to go, and finally the conversations stopped altogether. She stopped taking my calls, and then she sent me a letter. It said that she'd met someone else.' He paused. 'That was twenty-two years and two months ago, and we haven't spoken since.'

Elena put a hand on his arm. 'Sometimes things just aren't meant to be.'

Martin felt tears well up and forced them back down. He looked away, which was when he caught the eye of a well-built man in his mid-twenties who was sitting on his own a few feet away. He was dressed in a crumpled suit and had the lived-in, slightly puffy face of a rugby player. The man looked at him and gave a very small nod. There was a grim determination in his face, as if he'd recently come to an important decision.

Martin looked away quickly. He knew the man was thinking about some kind of escape attempt, and he wanted no part in it. It was far too dangerous, and he didn't think he had the physical strength to take on the guards. Deliberately, he lowered his head and stared at the floor.

The sound of a lift door opening interrupted his thoughts, and he looked up to see the leader of the hostage-takers march into the room followed by the female terrorist. They were both holding handguns with silencers attached, and the Scandinavian was just behind them. Something about their demeanour told Martin that their presence meant bad news.

They stopped and conversed with the other guard in hushed tones, occasionally looking over at the hostages; then, as Martin watched, the leader handed the woman a balaclava, which she quickly pulled over her head.

The tension in the room seemed to mount substantially. Something was about to happen. Martin and Elena exchanged glances but neither spoke.

The woman pulled up one of the six blinds that covered the restaurant's window. She secured the drawstring then stepped to one side, facing the hostages, the gun pointed at a forty-five-degree angle in front of her—a pose that, with the balaclava, gave her the appearance of an executioner.

'Your government does not want to help you,' announced the terrorist leader, stepping forward, his tone angry. 'You are not important to them.

None of us here wants violence, but we have to make your government listen to us.' He paused. 'And for that reason, one of you has to die.'

A collective gasp went up. Someone cried out, a strangled 'oh God', but otherwise there were no hysterics. Just a cold, silent sense of shock.

Keeping his gun in front of him, the leader walked out among them, his eyes scanning the group as he hunted for a victim.

Martin stared at the floor, every nerve in his body taut, every sense heightened, more alive than he'd ever been. More terrified too.

I don't want to die. Not yet. I want to see Robert, my only son, one more time. I want to phone Carrie and tell her that I've never stopped loving her.

He could sense rather than hear the footfalls as they came closer. He could hear breathing right above him, knew that the leader was there. Only inches from him. He didn't move. Just waited. Praying.

'You,' said the leader, and Martin felt a hand grip him firmly by the shoulder.

His prayers, it seemed, hadn't been answered.

ARLEY DALE stared at the ops room screens. Three of them were showing close-ups of the Park View Restaurant, where the recently opened blind was giving the whole world a narrow view inside. Behind the piled-up tables and chairs, Arley could clearly see hostages sitting on the bare floor, and a masked gunman moving among them. As she watched, the gunman leaned down, pulled a middle-aged man to his feet, and put a gun to his temple. The man looked terrified as the Sky News camera panned in on him.

'CO19 have a moving target inside the building,' said Chief Inspector Chris Matthews. 'They have a clear shot at him, ma'am. They can take him down now.'

Everyone in the room was looking at Arley.

The gunman was leading the hostage towards the window now. On the TV screen Arley could see resignation in the hostage's demeanour. So could five hundred million other people. He was about to die, and only she could stop it.

'Ma'am?'

She thought of her children, thought of everything she had to lose personally, and knew there was only one decision she could make.

'Tell them to keep their guns trained, but not to fire,' she said. 'We can't risk the gunmen shooting other hostages as well. I'm sorry.'

MARTIN DIDN'T RESIST when he was hauled to his feet and felt the pressure of the gun barrel against his head. In fact, a strange calm descended upon him. In a few seconds' time it would all be over. He would leave his life, and his cancer, behind. He would be free. He closed his eyes, allowing himself to be guided towards the place where he knew he would die.

And then there was a sudden commotion, and he was pitched forward.

Martin's eyes flew open and he saw the young rugby player who'd looked at him a few minutes earlier struggling violently with the terrorist leader.

'Help me!' he yelled, a desperation in his voice, as he, Martin and the terrorist stumbled around together. The rugby player was holding on to the terrorist's wrist, forcing his gun up in the air. The gun went off with a loud pop, and someone screamed.

'Help me!'

Martin knew that this was it—his chance to do something—but everything was happening so fast that he didn't have time to react before the woman took three quick steps forward, and calmly shot the rugby player in the upper body, the force of the bullet knocking them all backwards.

'Everyone stay down!' she screamed. 'Move and you die!'

No one moved except the rugby player, who let out a tortured gasp as if he'd been winded, and fell to his knees, clutching at his arm.

The terrorist leader threw Martin to the floor, then swung round and kicked the rugby player hard in the chest. 'You want to die, uh? You want to die? You *can* fucking die!' He grabbed him round his neck, dragging him to his feet. Still cursing him, he slammed him up against one of the restaurant tables in front of the uncovered window and forced the gun into the base of his skull. The rugby player cried out. The next second, there was another loud pop, and blood splattered against the window.

Immediately he stopped struggling and, as the leader let go of him and stepped aside, Martin could clearly see the wound in the back of his head. Slowly the dead man slipped from the table and fell to the floor.

'That's what happens when you try to escape!' the leader shouted, turning on the rest of them. 'Do you understand?' He was shaking with rage and spraying spittle as he talked. 'He stays here as a warning to the rest of you.'

He looked down at Martin, who looked back steadily. For three seconds they stared at each other, and Martin could hear his heart beating in his chest. Then the leader turned away and he and the woman strode past the two guards and out of the room, leaving the rest of them in stunned silence.

CAT AND WOLF walked into the kitchen next to the ballroom. Wolf immediately checked the laptop. 'They still haven't turned it back on, the bastards. I'll phone the negotiator and let him know another will die.'

'If they're so desperate to speak to Prior, let them.'

'We don't want to give away his location.'

'Then let me record a message from him and we'll play it down the phone to the negotiator. That way they will realise he's still alive but they won't know where he is.'

'That's a good idea,' Wolf said. 'Do it now and I'll tell the negotiator that we'll let them hear from him soon, as long as they put the Internet back on.'

With a nod of acknowledgement, Cat left the room. She was looking forward to seeing Michael Prior again. She'd extract a message from him, of course, but she'd also make him suffer a little as well, to ease the rage that was coursing through her heart at the thought that her brother's killer was still alive and somewhere in the hotel.

When she was out in the silence of the corridor, her grip tightened on the gun. She kept it down by her side and out of sight, in case she ran into one of the guests, or, if she was really lucky, the man who'd killed her brother. Her frustration at not knowing how to find him in this maze of rooms was increasing the more time went on, and her rage meant she would take it out on whoever crossed her path. As far as she was concerned, all the people in this hotel were the enemy, and deserved whatever fate God chose to dish out to them. In two hours' time, the Stanhope would go up in flames, and Cat would go up with it, dying a martyr's death, taking as many of the enemy with her as possible. It was a prospect that excited her.

Pausing outside the room where they were holding Prior, she opened the door. Then she saw him. Michael Prior was dead. But that wasn't what grabbed Cat's attention. It was the fact that his left eye had been gouged out.

ARLEY FELT SICK. Events were now running completely out of her control. Watching the hostage die on-screen had given her a terrible premonition of what might be happening right now to her children.

'We don't want anyone else dying, Wolf,' Riz Mohammed was saying. 'It will only hurt your cause.'

But Wolf was shouting down the phone. 'Then turn the Internet back on!'

'I'll do everything I can, I promise, but don't hurt anyone else.'

'You have five minutes. Five minutes, do you hear?'

'And you'll let us speak to Michael Prior?'

'If you put the Internet back on, yes.'

'I'll see what I can do. Give me ten minutes. Can you do that?'

'OK. You have ten minutes. But after that, another hostage dies.'

The line went dead, and the incident room fell silent.

On the screen, Commissioner Phillips's seat in his office was empty, although Arley had heard from her immediate superior, A. C. Jacobs. He'd told her to stall the terrorists while Phillips talked to the Prime Minister about their next course of action.

Riz turned to Arley. 'We're going to have to give in and buy ourselves some time. He's said we can speak to Prior so we're making some progress.'

'I agree,' said Arley, trying to hold things together.

'For what it's worth, you did the right thing earlier,' said John Cheney. 'With the hostage. There was nothing else you could have done.'

The others in the room murmured their agreement.

Arley nodded, acknowledging Cheney's comments. Her face, she knew, said it all. She might have been doing everything she could to hide her torment, but there was no way she could disguise it completely. She was glad that he thought it was the dead hostage that was bothering her.

She sat down as Phillips reappeared at his desk. He looked grim-faced.

'I've just been told by Silver that the lead terrorist has given permission for us to speak to Michael Prior,' he said, addressing the room. 'Because of this, the Prime Minister has given permission to re-establish the Internet connection inside the hotel with immediate effect.'

Arley flinched as relief, however temporary, flooded through her.

'However, the PM also believes there's now no alternative to a rescue mission to free the hostages. Responsibility for this has now officially been passed to the military. Arley, you and your colleagues need to continue doing everything you can to keep the terrorists from killing any more hostages, while the SAS plan the logistics of their operation.'

Arley nodded slowly, accepting the inevitable, conscious that her phone was ringing. She pulled it out and saw Howard's grinning face filling the screen, which meant only one thing. Her family's kidnappers were calling.

'ARE YOU IN THE CONTROL ROOM?' asked the man on the other end of the phone, his voice calm.

Arley walked across the grass, away from the incident room, glancing over her shoulder to check she wasn't being followed. 'Not any more.'

'Is the Internet coming back on?'

She desperately wanted to reason with him, to tell him to please release her children, but she'd been around long enough to know that pleading wasn't going to work. 'It should have come back on by now.'

'And what are the plans for an assault?'

'All I know is that the military have taken control of the operation.'

'Does this mean it's imminent?'

She knew there was no point lying. 'Not necessarily, no.'

'The phrase "not necessarily" is of no use to us. We need to know what's being planned. So do you, if you ever want to see your family again.'

Arley took a deep breath. 'The military have only just taken control, and it'll take them some time to organise a rescue operation. I'll make sure I know their plans.' She considered adding that she'd already had a meeting with the SAS commander, but held back. There was no point giving this man anything until it became absolutely necessary.

'I'm going to keep this phone on for the next fifteen minutes. The moment you have an update, call me. Do you understand?'

'I do.'

'If you try to trick us in any way, your family will die. Remember that.'

Arley slowly removed the phone from her ear and looked back towards the incident room, wondering if her absence, and the manner in which she'd taken the call, was arousing suspicion among her colleagues.

Her phone bleeped. She had a message from the people running the ANPR database at Hendon, and she felt a surge of hope mixed with dread.

21.12

Tina lit a cigarette and turned on the car's engine to stay warm. She wondered what the hell she was doing, risking her neck to help a woman she hadn't spoken to in months, and who was an acquaintance at best. So far tonight she'd impersonated a police officer, interfered with a crime scene, and withheld vital information in what was shaping up to be one of the biggest single crimes in modern policing history.

But she never did anything by halves. And so far she still believed that she was doing the right thing, although the more she thought about it, the more the doubts gnawed away at her. She understood why Arley hadn't wanted to say anything to her bosses, but Tina herself didn't want to be responsible for the deaths of any SAS men. After all, they had families too.

Her phone rang. It was Arley.

'What have you got?' Tina asked her.

'The vehicle with the registration you gave me was last picked up on the ANPR cameras in Willesden,' stated Arley. 'That was at eight twenty-seven a.m. this morning, and it hasn't moved within camera-range since. And it's definitely the same vehicle because it was caught on camera a few hundred metres from our house at five to eight.'

'How big's the area it could be in?'

'About four hundred metres by six hundred. And it's high-density residential. The Hendon guys are contacting the local council to see if there are any other cameras that might narrow it down, but that's going to take time.'

'Driving there's going to take time too, and unless I strike bloody lucky, I could still be looking around for it tomorrow morning.'

'It doesn't look like there's much off-road parking or garages,' said Arley.

Tina didn't share her optimism. 'Any news on the location of your husband's phone?'

'It's been switched off most of the day, but on those occasions it has been on, it's been nowhere near Willesden.'

'Have any calls been made on it today?'

'Only the ones to my mobile.'

Tina suppressed a frustrated sigh. The man dealing with Arley was being careful to give away as little information as possible. 'You need to get me a map of the area where the van could be. I've just set up an anonymous Hotmail account. Send it to me there.' Tina gave her the address.

'Will you be able to go over there right away?'

'Yes, but it still might take me time when I get there.' She thought for a moment. 'Listen, I've got an idea. The next time you speak to the kidnapper, demand proof of life. Demand to speak to your family. Say that if you don't, you won't cooperate.'

'What if he doesn't go for it?'

'Make him go for it. You haven't got anything to lose.'

'I've got everything to lose, Tina. My children, for God's sake.'

'But you need to know they're still alive. And you need to make him want to keep them alive so that you do what he wants. And the only way you're going to do that is by being firm. It's the only way.'

'OK,' said Arley uncertainly. 'But wait, he doesn't have the children. He told me he was in contact every fifteen minutes with the man holding them.'

'That doesn't change anything. Insist on speaking to your family—not just the children, or he'll know you know that Howard's dead. And if he won't go with that—which I suspect he won't—demand that he send a video message from them, and insist that one of the children says something that tells you that the footage has been taken after you demanded it.'

'But how will that help us locate them? He's obviously using a different phone to stay in touch with the man holding the twins.'

'The man who makes the video will send it via a phone to the man you're in contact with. He won't have time to do it all through email. I reckon your man will get him to send the video to Howard's phone so that he can send it straight on to you, and as soon as he does that we've got the other guy's number, and we'll be able to track his location.'

'But he'll see through it, surely? It seems too obvious.'

'Not if you sound frightened enough. He'll think you genuinely want to hear from them, which of course you do. And remember, he'll be under pressure himself by now, and people under pressure make mistakes.'

There was silence. 'Unless they're already dead,' said Arley at last.

'We can't think like that,' Tina said. 'I'm on my way to Willesden.'

21.20

Graham Jones should have been home for dinner at eight at the absolute latest. He'd told his wife that morning before he left for work that he had a business meeting in Birmingham, which was why he'd be home at eight rather than the usual time of six.

In truth, since 1.30 that afternoon he had been in the Stanhope Hotel, ensconced in a room on the fifth floor with his lover of more than two years. Like Graham, Victor Grayson was married with children and couldn't afford for his secret to come out—at least not until his children had grown up and left home.

For the past four hours they'd been trapped in their room as the dramatic events of the siege played out around them. Victor had stayed remarkably calm, saying that they should stay in the room and wait for help to arrive. But then Victor had the advantage of not being expected home until much later. His wife seemed to be a lot more laid-back than Graham's wife Carol, who these days acted as if she was permanently suspicious of him, even though he was sure she had no idea about Victor.

As time kept ticking by, so the chances of his secret being exposed to the world grew greater. Surprisingly, it was this, rather than being caught by the terrorists who'd taken over the hotel, that scared him the most. He knew how long sieges could last. Days in some cases. He couldn't have that. He had to get out. Make a break for it somehow.

Victor had told him not to be so stupid. That he'd be risking his neck for no good reason. 'Text her,' he'd suggested. 'Say you're stuck on the train.'

But when he'd tried to text, the message had bounced back. He'd tried again every fifteen minutes until eventually he'd realised that the signal had been cut deliberately, leaving him with no means of communication with the outside world, other than the hotel phone, and if he used that he'd have to whisper and the stress he was suffering from would be obvious.

Which was how Graham now found himself alone in the hotel lobby, having walked all the way down the emergency staircase from the fifth floor. Keeping close to the side of the main staircase for cover, he looked over towards the hotel's front doors, wondering if there was someone guarding them. He couldn't see anyone, but that didn't mean no one was there. And there was another problem. He was pretty sure Carol would be watching events on the TV. If he went out the front of the hotel, she might see him on TV, and even if she didn't, someone would, and his secret would be out.

He'd go out the back. That would be easier. He knew that the Stanhope backed on to narrow streets where TV cameras would almost certainly be prohibited. He could get out without being seen, at least in public.

Graham made his way across the floor and through a door marked STAFF ONLY. Straightaway his nostrils were assailed by an appalling stench. Holding his breath, he made his way down a dark corridor, then through another door, and into the hotel kitchens. The smell was far worse in there and it took him only seconds to realise why, as his eyes became accustomed to the gloom. There were bodies, three of them as far as he could see, lying on the floor in pools of blood. A wave of nausea overcame him and he had to put his hand on one of the worktops to steady himself.

Plucking up courage, he skirted around them and tried the windows that led out on to an empty courtyard behind the building, only to find them all locked. To his right was a fire door with a push-lever handle. It had to lead outside, and it wouldn't be locked. Graham hurried over to it, forcing down the lever and pushing it open in one movement, hardly hearing the clunk as the fully primed grenade dropped to the floor.

FOX STOOD in the ballroom satellite kitchen, waiting impassively while Wolf ranted and raved.

'You were the last person to see him alive, Fox. If it wasn't you who killed him, who was it?'

'I have no idea. And why on earth would I want to gouge his eye out?'

'I don't know, but it was your idea for us to kidnap him in the first place—' Wolf stopped in mid flow, interrupted by a dull boom coming from below. 'What was that?'

'It sounded like a grenade,' said Fox, immediately tensing. 'I set a couple of them as booby traps on the exit doors to the kitchen.'

Wolf checked the portable TV, then leaned over the laptop. 'Are we under attack already? You said it would take them time to strike.'

'What's the TV showing?'

'Just the front of the hotel. It all looks the same.'

There was an edge of panic to Wolf's voice, and Fox knew he was going to have to take charge.

'If they've come in via the kitchen, then they're on their way up now. Come with me.'

Fox walked rapidly out of the kitchen with Wolf behind him. Cat and Bear were guarding the increasingly restless-looking hostages, and they both turned round when they heard the door open.

'Everything's all right,' Fox called out, more for the benefit of the hostages than anyone else. 'One of the booby traps went off accidentally.'

Keeping a firm grip on his AK-47, he opened the ballroom doors and went over to the top of the main mezzanine-floor staircase. He looked down into the empty hotel lobby. If this was an attack the SAS would have been slowed down by the booby-trapped grenade. There was no sign of them yet.

He heard Wolf come up behind him.

'Is anything happening?' he whispered.

Fox pointed his AK-47 down the stairs. 'Nothing yet.'

They waited a full minute. In the background, Fox could hear the faint ringing of the phone in the satellite kitchen. It seemed the negotiators were trying to make contact. If this was a full-scale, multi-entry attack, then where the hell was everybody?

'I don't think that was the SAS,' said Fox at last, still watching the lobby.

'Then what was it?'

'I'm not sure. We need to investigate.'

'Are you going to go downstairs?' asked Wolf.

Fox turned round. 'I've got a better idea. Send Cat. She looks like a civilian, so if it is the military, or the police—and I'm pretty damn sure it's neither of them—they won't open fire on her.'

Wolf's eyes narrowed and he looked at Fox suspiciously. Fox knew that, after the discovery of Michael Prior's body, Wolf no longer trusted him. Fox's suggestion could easily be construed as a plan to get rid of Cat, yet it wasn't. Sending her down seemed to him the logical thing to do. She was relatively inconspicuous, unlike the rest of them.

'All right,' Wolf said with a sigh. 'We'll send Cat down.'

SIX

21.26

In the incident room, events had taken an unexpected turn. Officers inside the inner cordon had heard the explosion at the rear of the Stanhope, and the officer who'd called it in said he could see a thin plume of smoke.

Arley glanced at her watch. Her fifteen-minute deadline for calling the kidnappers was up, and she was going to have to make contact again. But she needed more time. Tina needed more time.

One of the secure phones started ringing and Will Verran, the young police technician, picked up. 'It's Major Standard for you, ma'am.'

She took the receiver. 'Major Standard.'

'Hello, Arley,' said the major. 'There's been an explosion at the back of the Stanhope on the ground floor. My understanding is it's some kind of ordnance. Have you had any explanation for it from the terrorists?'

'Not yet, sir. But it happened only a few minutes ago, and we're going to keep trying them. It seems it might be some kind of one-off incident.'

'Perhaps,' said Standard. 'And you've nothing new on Prior's location?'

'Nothing yet, but as I mentioned earlier, the lead terrorist calling himself Wolf has promised we can speak to him. As soon as we do, I'll let you know.'

'Good. We're ready to go in at short notice now.'

'It may be worth waiting until we can speak to Prior.'

'Keep trying to talk to him, but if you're still having no joy in fifteen minutes, let me know. We may have to reassess.'

She handed the phone back to Will and left the incident room without a word, knowing that her actions were beginning to look odd, but no longer caring. She'd got barely ten feet from the building when she dialled Howard's number.

'I said fifteen minutes,' snapped the kidnapper. 'Not twenty.'

'I was on the phone to the man in charge of the SAS operation,' she whispered into the phone. 'It was a long conversation.'

'And you have the details of their assault, yes?'

'I do.'

'When will it be happening?'

'Not yet. At the moment they're waiting until we can find a location inside the building for Prior.'

'That seems reasonable. Tell me the plan for the assault.'

'Not until I get visual proof that my family are still alive. Right now. Otherwise I give you nothing.'

'You're not in a position to make threats,' he hissed into the phone.

'It's not a threat. I just need to see my family.'

'I'm not with your family, so it won't be possible.'

'Then speak to whoever is and sort something out fast, because otherwise I'm not going to go through with this.'

'I hope this isn't some sort of trick to determine their whereabouts. Because if it is—'

'It isn't, I promise. I just need to see that they're still alive. And to prove it, I want to hear my daughter say the name of her former primary school.'

'Impossible. You'll do as you're told.'

'No,' she said firmly. 'I won't. Not unless I hear from them.'

There was a pause at the other end of the phone. 'I'll see what I can do,' the man said at last, and the line went dead.

Arley took a deep breath, turning round, and almost jumped out of her skin. John Cheney was standing right behind her, and immediately she wondered what he'd heard of her conversation.

'Is everything OK, Arley?' he asked her.

She stared at him for a long moment, wondering whether she should tell him everything. He'd always had a solid, reliable air about him. She almost said something, then remembered that the reliability hadn't stopped him cheating on her. It was just too risky to let another person in on her secret.

'Everything's fine, thanks, John. Give me a moment and I'll be back in.'

Cheney nodded. 'Of course,' he said, giving her an appraising look that lasted a second too long, before starting back towards the incident room.

She watched him go, paranoid thoughts flying crazily through her mind. How much had he heard? Was he going to say something to Commissioner Phillips about her ability as a boss?

And most prevalent of all: *How long have I got left to save my children?*

21.31

Scope cursed as he slammed down the phone receiver.

'Still no luck?' asked Abby.

He sighed. 'No. The lines out are all still busy.'

This had been the problem for more than half an hour now, ever since the terrorists had killed a hostage in the upstairs restaurant, in full view of the TV cameras. It seemed that plenty of the guests trapped in their rooms had seen it too and were panicking and phoning out. Luckily, Ethan had fallen asleep just before the killing happened, and had been sleeping ever since.

Abby was sitting up on the bed, her leg propped up on the pillow, but she looked awful. Her face was thin and drawn, its complexion fish-grey.

He asked her if she was all right.

'I'm going to need my next dose and food soon. I'm feeling pretty weak.'

'Tell me honestly,' said Scope. 'What happens if you don't get it?'

'At some point, my blood sugar will get so high that I'll start fitting. If it's still untreated, then eventually I could die.' She smiled tightly. 'But that's a way off yet, I promise. Do you think they'll have insulin on the premises?'

He nodded. 'I'm sure of it. It's a big hotel.'

'If something happens to me, please will you promise me that you'll get Ethan out of here safely?'

Scope stopped in front of the bed, looking down at her, touched by her vulnerability. 'Nothing's going to happen to you, I promise. If I have to, I'll go out there and find the insulin myself.'

'No,' she said emphatically. 'I want you to look after Ethan.'

Scope wondered how much time she had left until she started to deteriorate seriously. For the first time it struck him that he might not be able to save her.

'You know,' continued Abby, 'we know almost nothing about you, but I can tell by your eyes that things have happened to you. Bad things.'

'Bad things happen to everyone,' said Scope, not liking her gaze, or the questions it seemed to want to pose.

'I don't feel so great.' She slurred the words, and as Scope hurried over to her, she closed her eyes and fell sideways onto the bed.

Cursing silently, he checked her breathing. Shallow, but enough.

'Abby?' he said quietly, giving her cheek a gentle tap. 'Abby?'

There was no response, so he laid her gently on her side. He stood back up and immediately dialled Steve's number again, willing it to ring.

It did. And kept ringing.

'Answer, you bastard,' he hissed, through gritted teeth. 'Answer.'

'Steve Grantham.'

'Steve, I've been trying to reach you. Have you found out where the insulin is in here?'

'Yes. There's a medical station behind the reception area, but it's kept locked. The keys are in a strongbox, also behind reception, but only the duty manager has the key to it.'

'But they have insulin, right?'

'Yes, they do. In standard pen form.'

'Thanks, Steve. I appreciate your help.'

'Listen, it sounds extremely risky going down there. It might be best to stay where you are. I'm sure this situation will be resolved soon.'

'Are you? I'm not.'

Steve sighed. 'You're not going to be any help to anyone if you're hurt.'

'I'll take my chances,' said Scope, and hung up.

Ethan lay fast asleep beside his mother. He looked so peaceful that Scope wondered whether he should wake him or not. But if Ethan woke up and saw Scope gone, that would panic him even more.

He put a hand on Ethan's shoulder and roused him.

Ethan looked up at Scope groggily, and smiled. 'I was asleep.'

Scope smiled back. 'I'm going to get the insulin. I know where it is now.'

'Is Mom OK? It's getting late, isn't it?' He put a hand on her shoulder.

'She's asleep, and she needs it soon. That's why I'm going to get it.'

'What if something happens to you?'

'It won't. I'm a soldier. And I've been a soldier a long time. I'm good at what I do. Nothing will happen to me.'

Ethan looked relieved. 'Good.'

'When I come back, it'll be like the last time I left the room. I'll knock on the door five times: bang, bang, bang, bang, bang. That'll tell you it's me. Then I'm going to let myself in. In the meantime, you do like I told you.

Anyone knocks on the door that doesn't use the code, ignore them and don't say a word, even if they beg to come in. Do you understand?'

He nodded. 'What if they force their way in, like before?'

'I'm pretty sure they won't, but if anyone does, hide behind the bed. But I won't be long. I promise.'

Ethan looked scared but determined. 'Do you promise you'll be back?'

'Yeah,' said Scope, meaning it. 'I promise.'

THE SHUFFLING SOUND was coming from beyond one of the doors. Cat listened. The sound came again, then a low moan. Someone was still alive.

She moved through the gloom of the hotel's main ground-floor kitchen, keeping her gun hidden under her jacket, just in case it was a trap. Stepping over the body of a young man, she looked through the window to the rear courtyard, being careful to stay well back, but couldn't see anyone.

The moaning grew louder as she opened the door, and stepped into a narrow corridor that led through to the delivery entrance.

A badly burned man was lying on his back on the floor, his clothes in shreds, his face blackened. Beyond him was what was left of the fire door. It was obvious that he'd been trying to leave the hotel and been caught in one of Fox's booby traps. 'Help me,' the man whispered, his voice a hoarse rattle.

Removing the gun from where she'd hidden it, Cat pointed it at his head. 'Don't shoot me,' he whispered weakly. 'I've got children.'

Cat stared down at him dispassionately. Then, without a word, she pulled the trigger, the bullet passing directly through one eye.

Having found no one else in the kitchen, Cat crept back, listening out just in case there was anyone else for her to deal with. But the silence was total. And then, as she opened the door leading back into the main part of the hotel, she saw the man on the other side of the lobby, heading towards the reception counter. Even though he had his back to her, and the lighting was fairly dim, she could see that he was holding a gun. She could also see that he was dressed in a suit, which meant he wasn't one of their group. Which could mean only one thing: this was the man who'd murdered her brother.

A burst of intense rage shot through her veins and she raised her gun, aiming towards the back of his head, following him as he walked. Then she lowered it. He was at least thirty yards away—too far to guarantee a direct hit. And anyway, a bullet in the back was far too easy a death for a man like him. No, this one was going to die slowly, and at her pleasure.

SCOPE WAS TEN FEET from the reception area when he heard a door close behind him. He swung round fast, holding the pistol two-handed in a classic shooting position, and saw a young woman standing at the other end of the lobby. Her hands were thrust high in the air and she looked scared stiff.

'Please,' she said in a whisper. 'You're not one of the gunmen, are you?'

Scope let her come towards him. She was young. Late twenties, very attractive, and would have looked faintly vampish in her black dress and stockings if it wasn't for the bomber jacket she was wearing over the top.

'Stop right there,' he said when she was ten feet away. 'Where have you come from?'

'I was hiding in the kitchen,' she answered. 'I heard a noise in the lobby, looked round from behind the door, and saw you. Are you a police officer?'

Scope shook his head, beginning to relax, although he still pointed the gun at her. 'I'm not, but my advice is get out now.' He motioned towards the hotel's front doors. 'Quickly.'

'I can't,' she whispered. 'The doors are locked, and I think they may have booby-trapped them. Look.'

He looked back quickly and saw a holdall tucked away next to the leftmost door. It had two command wires attached that ran across the floor. 'Then you need to get back to your hiding place. It'll be safer there.'

'I can't stay in the kitchen. There are bodies everywhere. Can't I come with you?'

Having someone else to look after was the last thing Scope needed, but it seemed he had little choice. 'OK,' he sighed. 'Follow me.'

'Where are we going?'

'I've got someone upstairs who needs insulin urgently. I'm looking for the room where they're storing it.' He went over and opened the door next to the reception area. 'Are you coming?'

She nodded, and followed him inside as he walked through a corridor that ran past the reception bay and into a small foyer with doors going off on three sides. The nearest one had a sign on it identifying it as the medical room. Luckily it was unlocked. He flicked on the lights and glanced back to check that the girl was still following him. She gave him a small smile.

The medical room was small, with a treatment area consisting of a bed and chair, which took up most of the floor space, and a set of locked glass cupboards filled with various substances lining the upper walls.

Scope smiled when he saw the set of keys sitting on the room's only worktop. This was going to be easier than he'd thought. He slipped the gun into the waistband of his suit, but as he went to pick up the keys, a worrying thought struck him. For someone as scared as the woman behind him should be, she'd seemed extraordinarily calm and together.

Which was the moment when he saw her reflection in one of the glass cabinets. She was standing in the doorway, pulling a pistol with suppressor attached from beneath her jacket, her teeth bared in a snarl.

Scope dived to the floor in one rapid movement, just at the moment the girl fired, her bullet shattering the glass on one of the cabinets and immediately setting off a piercing alarm. Twisting his body round as he fell, he yanked out his own gun and let off a single round in her general direction in a desperate effort to prevent her getting an accurate shot at him.

But she was quick too and she'd already jumped out of sight behind the door, firing off two more rounds that narrowly missed his head.

He leaped to his feet, charged forward, and came out of the room in a roll, just in time to see the girl vault over the reception counter. Tightening his finger on the trigger, he took aim. But he was too late. She was gone.

For a few seconds he didn't move, waiting to see if she'd reappear. But he also knew that the shots would have alerted the other terrorists so he couldn't afford to hang around. He got slowly to his feet, assessing the situation. He'd come close to making a fatal mistake by being way too careless, which wasn't like him. But he genuinely hadn't expected a pretty girl in Western clothes to be part of a group of extremists. It was bizarre. But then everything about this whole day had been bizarre, including the fact that he'd already killed five men—two more than he'd planned to.

His problem now was that not only was he trapped, he'd also given away his position. He went back into the medical room and took a quick look round, scanning the glass cabinets for insulin pens, but there was too much stuff in them. It was going to take a good five minutes to find what he was looking for, and right now he simply didn't have the time.

Putting the keys from the worktop in his back pocket, Scope crept towards the reception counter, keeping low, knowing that the woman would be waiting for him to reappear. He had two shots left. He was going to have to make them count.

He jumped up fast from behind the counter and saw her straightaway behind a leather tub chair, resting her pistol against the arm. He fired a single shot at her position, making no attempt to duck back down, even though all his instincts were telling him to get out of the way of her aim.

The girl fired back, but she was already ducking down behind the chair to give herself better cover, and Scope took the tiny respite this offered to jump over the counter, taking off at a run down the lobby towards the back of the hotel, still keeping his gun pointing in the girl's general direction.

She was up fast, cracking off three quick shots that were pretty damn close to him. He fired his last bullet back, aiming from the hip, not expecting to hit anything, hoping just to buy himself a little time.

It worked. She ducked again, and by the time she was back up he was almost level with the central staircase, running in a zigzag and keeping low, putting some much-needed distance between them.

Which was the moment when he glanced up and saw the masked gunman at the top of the staircase, aiming his AK-47 down at him.

The wall just above Scope's head erupted as the bullets stitched across it, and from somewhere behind him he heard more shooting as the girl tried to take him out. Adrenalin surged through him and he put his head down and kept running, knowing that the gunman's angle was extremely tight.

More shots ricocheted off the carpet just beside him but he ignored them, kept going, and a second later he was past the staircase and out of range and sight of the gunman. The girl tried to bring him down with more shots, but he was moving too fast, and two seconds later he was out of sight and charging down the hallway in the direction of the restaurants and the emergency staircase, knowing that he'd failed Ethan and Abby.

He might have been unarmed and running for his life, but he couldn't go back yet. Not until he'd got the drugs.

21.39

From his vantage point at the top of the main staircase, Fox saw Cat race after the fugitive, her face a mask of fury.

He yelled at her to come back but she'd already disappeared from view. Knowing she'd almost certainly get herself killed, he ran down the stairs, taking them three at a time, annoyed with himself for missing the guy.

He raced round the corner, reloading the rifle as he went, catching up with Cat in the main restaurant. She was standing near the bar, gun outstretched, looking around for her quarry. It was clear she'd lost him.

'We need to get back upstairs quickly,' he told her, conscious of the fact that all the gunfire would have spooked the hostages in the ballroom.

'But he's here somewhere,' she hissed. 'He must be. I'm going to find him.'

'He could have made for the stairs or one of the ground-floor rooms. And if he has gone through that door, you could be walking into a trap.'

She turned on him, her dark eyes radiating fury. 'He murdered my brother. I owe him. But someone like you . . . a *mercenary*'—she spat out the word—'wouldn't understand that, would you?'

'What I understand is that all this gunfire's going to bring the SAS down on us fast. We need to defend our positions, which means sticking together. Was he the one who caused the explosion in the kitchen?'

'No. That was someone else trying to escape.'

'So what was this guy doing in reception?'

'He was trying to find some medicine for another guest.'

'Insulin?'

She frowned. 'How do you know?'

'I found some in the room where your brother and Leopard were killed. I took it with me. It means he'll have to break cover again soon. Come on.'

21.45

Arley Dale stood in the middle of the cramped incident room desperately waiting for proof that her son and daughter were still alive, while all around her was chaos. The phones inside the room were ringing off the hook with reports about the eruption of gunfire coming from various points inside the hotel. And all the time, its sound like a death knell, the incessant ringing of the terrorist's phone over the loudspeaker, as Riz Mohammed waited for Wolf to give them an explanation of exactly what was going on in there. Something that might just delay an assault and give Arley breathing space.

She was already late in calling back Major Standard to give him an update on their failed attempts to speak to Michael Prior, and she was dreading making the call now. With the deadline looming, and still no sign of Prior, Arley was sure that Standard would begin the assault.

The ringing stopped and Wolf's voice filled the room, sounding agitated. 'Everything is fine in here,' he said, before Riz had a chance to speak. 'We had some problems with a couple of the hostages, but all is back under control.'

'Has anyone been hurt?'

'No. They were warning shots only. Everything is fine.'

'You promised me we could speak to Michael Prior. Is he there?'

Wolf hesitated. 'Not at the moment.'

'Why not?'

'Because we haven't had time to get him. You can talk to him soon.'

'You said that over half an hour ago. We need to speak to him now.'

'And I need you to meet our demands. How is that going, uh?'

'All your demands are currently under discussion. I believe we have until midnight to meet them.'

Wolf hesitated again, clearly thinking. As he did so, Arley felt the mobile in her pocket vibrate with the arrival of a text. She desperately wanted to look at it, but knew that to do so at this juncture would raise all kinds of suspicions among the other people in the room.

'I will let you speak to Prior in the next half an hour,' said Wolf finally. 'You have my word on it.' The line went dead.

Commander Phillips, who was patched into the incident room, took a very deep breath. 'Mr Mohammed, you're an experienced negotiator. Tell me frankly, do you think this man Wolf is going to let us speak to Prior?'

'No, I don't. For some reason, he seems to be stalling.'

'Why might that be?'

'I honestly don't know, but the only reason I can think of is that Prior's been incapacitated.'

'You mean he's dead?'

'It's certainly possible.'

'We don't think he's been compromised, sir,' said John Cheney. 'GCHQ haven't picked up any coded messages being sent out of the Stanhope containing classified information.'

'That's one thing, I suppose,' said Phillips. 'But because we can't get hold of him, we can't get a location for him inside the building, which was the reason for holding up the assault. Therefore, we need to get on to the military and tell them that there's no longer any point waiting to go in.'

Arley felt her heart sink. 'I'll call Major Standard and inform him, sir. Janine, can you get him for me?' she added, before Phillips had a chance to interrupt. If anyone was going to speak to Standard, it was her. She was aware of the mobile ringing in her pocket, but flicked it on to silent.

'You're through to Major Standard on line four, ma'am,' said Janine.

Arley picked up the receiver, conscious that all eyes on the room were on her. Briefly she explained the situation.

'Thank you for keeping me informed, Arley,' said Major Standard, with a warmth that pained her. He was a good man, and she was going to betray his trust and help send his men to their deaths. She knew this was her last chance to say something. *But they have your children.*

'Are you sticking to your original plan of attack?' she asked, trying to sound as casual as possible, knowing he was under no obligation to tell her.

'Yes, we are. We haven't had enough time or information to formulate anything substantial, so we'll be going in round the back, out of the glare of the cameras, and making a silent entry. It's now exactly 21.49 according to my watch. At 22.05, I want your negotiator to call the lead hostage-taker, Wolf, and tell him that the British government will be making an announcement to the world's media at 23.00 hours tonight, and that it's a potential breakthrough. Are you clear on that?'

'Absolutely.'

'And make sure he keeps Wolf talking. After that, I'll contact you the moment we need police and emergency medical back-up.'

'Of course. I'll have everyone on full standby.'

She put down the phone and looked round the room. On the screen, Commissioner Phillips was no longer patched into the incident room, and instead was talking silently on his phone.

Sixteen minutes. She had sixteen minutes.

'Well,' she said. 'It's out of our hands now. I need another cigarette.'

Trying to be as casual as possible, Arley went outside, lighting a cigarette with fumbling hands as she checked her mobile. She'd received a text from Howard's phone containing a video attachment, plus two missed calls.

She took a deep breath and opened the attachment. It lasted barely ten seconds but it was enough to make her stomach churn. Oliver and India were sitting on the floor side by side, their hands bound behind their backs. Oliver's mouth and eyes were bound with grey duct tape, while India's eyes were covered, but a piece of duct tape hung down from her cheek where it had been torn away from her mouth. 'Go on,' prompted an unseen, muffled voice.

'My primary school was St Mary's,' said India. 'And I really want to come home, Mum. So does Olly.'

Oliver made a noise behind his gag but then the film ended, leaving Arley staring at the screen, trying to control her breathing, wanting to throw up.

But there was hope. They were still alive.

The screen lit up and Arley pressed the answer button.

'Your turn,' said her tormentor. 'Tell me the assault plan.'

The time for doubts about her course of action was gone. Now all that mattered was keeping her children alive until Tina could locate them. Speaking quietly, she began to give him the details of Major Standard's plan.

'When are they going in?' he demanded.

'Our negotiator's going to make a call to Wolf at 22.05. This'll be a decoy, so I believe the attack will be starting then.'

'Thank you. We will talk again soon.'

'Hold on, I haven't finished yet—' But she was talking to a dead phone. 'Shit,' she cursed, suddenly feeling the terrible vulnerability that comes when you've played all your cards. She'd betrayed her colleagues and her country, and at that moment she had nothing to show for it.

And only one hope. That Tina's hunch was right and the man who'd filmed her children had sent the footage directly to Howard's phone, because if he had, then she could get a location for him.

The only person who could trace the calls was Phil Rochelle, the police coordinator at Hendon whose job it was to speak to the mobile phone companies on behalf of the Met. Arley had already spoken to him earlier that evening and got him to run a continuous trace on Howard's number. She dialled his number, praying that he had something useful for her.

He answered on the second ring. 'Hello, Phil. Have you had any phone traffic to the mobile you're tracking for us?'

'Your husband's. Yes, I have. Two calls were made on it to your phone in the past few minutes. And a call was received on it a few minutes before that from another mobile phone.'

'Do you have the number of that other mobile phone?'

'Yes, I do.'

'Good,' she said, trying to stay calm. 'We need a current location on it.'

'I'm going to need to know what this is about. We're talking about your husband's mobile here, and there is the very real matter of protocol.'

'I'm afraid the matter is top secret, but I can tell you it's to do with the current situation at the Stanhope Hotel and the earlier bomb attacks.'

'With all due respect, I'm still not sure what this has to do with your husband's mobile phone.'

'And I can't give you the answers right now because we're in the middle of an ongoing and fluid situation.'

'Then I'm going to need authorisation from the Home Secretary, or the chief commissioner at the very least.'

This was what Arley had most feared. It was always going to be a huge gamble trying to convince someone like Rochelle, a by-the-book man if ever there was one, that her husband's mobile records were essential to the Stanhope siege. But it was also too late to stop now.

'Neither the Home Secretary nor Chief Commissioner Phillips is available right now, Phil. Believe it or not, they're bunkered up in the Cabinet briefing room with the PM and the heads of the security services trying to deal with this crisis. As Bronze Commander, I am in charge of the situation on the ground, and I am requesting immediate assistance. If you refuse to give it, you may well find yourself having to explain why to the inevitable public inquiry. So, are you going to risk lives, or are you going to help save them?'

She could hear her heart thumping as she waited for his response.

He sighed. 'I'll have the location of the phone in the next few minutes.'

'Thank you. Please make it top priority.' Arley ended the call and took a deep breath, fighting down a wave of nausea.

With Phil Rochelle's information, they could use armed police to free the twins rather than having to rely on an alcoholic female ex-cop. They could even probably delay any assault on the hotel while they secured the area where the twins were being held and took down the bastard holding them.

But once again she stopped herself. Because there was every chance that they wouldn't delay the assault. Or that they'd try to negotiate with the kidnapper rather than make an immediate arrest. Whichever way Arley cared to look at it, her children were expendable to the authorities, and she couldn't allow that. She had to do this her way, whatever the consequences might be.

21.56

'She says we've got less than ten minutes,' said Fox.

'And you think this is the true plan?' Wolf asked.

'We've got this woman's kids at gunpoint. It'll be the true plan.'

'I want you and Bear to organise the first line of defence against our attackers,' said Wolf. 'Cat and I will remain here guarding the hostages. And your two operatives in the restaurant upstairs will hold their positions there. You'll need to hold off the attacking forces at least until I can get through to the negotiator and tell him that unless the assault stops, we will blow up the building. Do you think that will be enough to make them pull back?'

'If they lose the element of surprise and the authorities realise we're still in control of the situation, they'll have to stop the assault.'

Wolf looked excited. 'Which will leave them totally humiliated. We are doing good work here, Fox. The British government will fall over this.'

'Let's hope so,' said Fox, although right then he was far more interested in getting out of the building alive, which was no sure thing.

As they hurried from the kitchen, Fox felt the adrenalin pumping through him. Zero hour was approaching—the time when he'd finally earn his money. The plan had always been to trigger an assault on the building. It was why they'd set a midnight deadline while timing the bombs inside the hotel to detonate an hour earlier. They'd never expected to last until midnight. Ideally, the assault would have come just before 23.00. That way they could repel the SAS forces, thus heaping public humiliation on the British government, and use the subsequent timed explosions (which could also be blamed on the government) as cover to escape from the building.

Instead, they were going to have to put up with the assault coming nearly an hour earlier, which would mean a nerve-jangling climax to the siege as they tried to keep the security forces at bay. But it was still manageable, as was the fact that they were operating two men short. The most important thing was that, unlike the SAS, they still possessed the element of surprise.

SCOPE WORKED as quietly and methodically as he could under the circumstances, going through each of the medicine cupboards one at a time.

He'd taken a huge risk coming back as he knew the terrorists were aware how much he needed the insulin. He'd been only feet away from them, hidden behind the bar in the ground-floor restaurant, while they'd discussed the fact that they could take him out when he emerged from cover to find it.

Right now, Scope was relying on the fact that the terrorists were too busy upstairs, and too short of numbers, to send someone down here. But if he was wrong then he was trapped, and almost certainly dead. Strangely, though, it wasn't death he was scared of. He'd faced that on many occasions in his time as a soldier. And in truth, since Mary Ann had gone, life had ceased to be anything other than a simple mission for revenge.

No, what he feared was failure. He had to save Abby and her son. He cared about them now, had bonded with them, which was something he hadn't done with anyone in a long time. The world was a hard, brutal place; it had destroyed his daughter, and it had come close to destroying him. But so far it hadn't, and right then he was determined to keep it that way.

He found the insulin pens in a box at the back of the middle cupboard.

Feeling a sudden burst of elation, he ripped open the box and pulled out a handful of the pens, shoving them in his trouser pocket.

Then, holding his knife by the blade, in case he ran into one of the terrorists, he exited the room at a run, praying he wasn't too late.

'WHAT THE HELL WAS THAT?' Bear had stopped in the middle of the lobby.

'What the hell was what?' demanded Fox.

'I thought I heard a noise behind reception.'

Fox briefly wondered if it was the man he and Cat had just had a firefight with. He stopped too, but couldn't hear anything.

'It's nothing,' he said, although he tightened his grip on the gun. 'Come on. We need to hurry.' He had no desire to help Cat avenge her brother, and if this guy, whoever he was, was out the back trying to find insulin, then that was fine too, because it kept him out of their hair. 'Just keep down,' he hissed as they moved through the STAFF ONLY doors and into the gloom of the main kitchen, before stopping at the windows looking out on to the courtyard. It was raining outside and the cobblestones were shiny and wet.

The two men crouched low and Fox scanned the area, squinting in the darkness. When he was satisfied that the courtyard was empty he reached down and carefully retrieved the button detonator he'd left underneath the worktop earlier. 'In a few minutes the military will come through there,' he said, pointing towards the archway they'd driven through earlier. 'They'll head over to the wall here and rendezvous underneath the mezzanine-floor windows. What they don't know is there's a bomb hidden. It's about twenty feet to the left of us. It's a simple low-tech command wire device so any radio-jamming gear they've got won't be able to stop it from detonating. Your job's to man this position. You don't move, you don't lose concentration. Do any of those things and we're all dead.'

'You don't have to tell me that, Fox. How long have we worked together?'

'I know. But we're up against the best in the world here. We can't afford to make even the smallest mistake.'

'Sure. I know.'

'When you see movement through the arch, and you've confirmed it's enemy forces, you get down, count to twenty, so they've got time to come into the courtyard in numbers, then press the button. And make sure you're behind the kitchen units, because it's going to be a big bang.'

He gave the detonator to Bear, then pulled a pair of noise-suppressing headphones from his backpack. 'You might want to wear these when you set off the bomb. I'm going to be upstairs. As soon as I hear it go off, I'll open up with the AK and chuck out a couple of grenades. If you get the chance, unload a few rounds yourself, but then make your way back to the mezzanine floor using the emergency staircase. We'll rendezvous there.'

'What if they keep coming? They're not going to give up just like that.'

'They'll be sitting ducks out there so they're going to want to get back and regroup. Also, as soon as Wolf hears all the commotion, he's going to get on to the negotiator and threaten to kill all the hostages unless they pull back.' He patted Bear on the shoulder. 'They'll pull back. Remember, they've had hardly any time to prepare for this. They'll be making mistakes too.'

Bear grinned. 'Reminds me of the old days,' he whispered, peering out into the gloom. 'Waiting for the enemy to appear.'

'And we got out of that OK, didn't we? We'll get out of this too. Then we can all retire.' Fox got to his feet, keeping low. 'Rendezvous back in the mezzanine foyer. I'll be waiting for you there. Good luck.'

He slipped back through the kitchen and headed upstairs.

Barely a minute later he was inside the Meadow Room on the mezzanine floor. He stood in the corner of the room, the AK-47 in his hands, and looked round the edge of the curtain, into the courtyard below.

This was it. The culmination of months of training and planning. One more hour and he'd either be very rich or dead. He looked at his watch. 22.01.

22.01

Tina was driving round the maze of rain-soaked residential streets where the van she was looking for was supposed to be parked, as she had been for over twenty minutes now, when her phone rang.

'They sent me a video from Howard's phone,' Arley announced breathlessly. 'My children were alive ten minutes ago.'

'That's brilliant news. Were there any details that could be of use to us?'

'Only that it was shot inside a house.'

'And a location?'

'I've just emailed it to you. It's not exact, but it's down to a twenty- or thirty-metre area around Pride Street, within the same location as the van.'

'I drove down Pride Street two minutes ago and I didn't see a van, but I'll have another look now. But listen, Arley, I'm not risking my neck here. I'm unarmed. I'll see if I can find the house, but that's it.'

'If you can find proof that the kids are there, that's all I need. Then the security forces can deal with it. But I need to know for sure. Please. We're so close.' The desperation was clear in her voice.

'Have the SAS made the decision to go into the hotel yet?' asked Tina, knowing that if they had, she was going to have to make this thing public.

'Not yet, but it's going to come soon.'

'OK. Leave things with me, and make sure you get the ANPR people to get in touch with you if that van starts moving. I'll call you the moment I have something.'

Tina ended the call and pulled over. Her laptop was open on the seat next to her and she picked it up and checked the Hotmail account, opening the attachment from Arley's email of three minutes earlier.

It showed a small-scale street map of the area she was in with an irregular red circle over a section of Pride Street that was two hundred yards west of her current location. Pride Street backed on to a railway track, and Tina could see that there was a track running behind the houses with another house at the end of it, next to the railway line—one she hadn't seen earlier on the bigger map. The house was just inside the red circle, and it struck Tina that it was isolated enough for the kidnappers to have got the children out of the back of the van without attracting attention.

She pulled back out again and accelerated towards the railway line. She almost missed the narrow turning with the dead-end sign that, according to the map, led down to the house she was interested in. Slowing up, she caught a glimpse of a high-wire fence about thirty yards distant just as a train passed on the other side of it with a steady rumble.

She continued farther down the street, found a spot and parked. Taking a deep breath, she grabbed the can of pepper spray she'd bought in France from the glove compartment, as well as an eight-inch piece of lead piping—both totally illegal for a civilian to be in possession of. She slipped the pepper spray into her coat pocket and the lead piping into the back of her jeans, and then got out and hurried along the street.

The turning down to the house was little more than a muddy track, with overgrown brambles and scrub on either side. Tina followed the track as it turned at a narrow angle in front of the barbed-wire fence before ending at the entrance to a rundown cottage that was almost entirely obscured by high vegetation. Parked in the narrow carport in front of the cottage, beyond two ancient wrought-iron gates, was the red van they were looking for.

Tina stopped. There were lights on in the ground floor of the cottage and all the curtains were drawn. This was the place, she knew it.

She should have got straight back on the phone to Arley and told her that she'd done as much as she could. But she didn't. Instead she switched her phone to vibrate and climbed over the gates, tiptoeing across the gravel until she was level with the driver's window of the van. She peered inside. The front was empty, while the rear was hidden by a makeshift curtain, and she couldn't see or hear anything. Satisfied it was empty, she approached the cottage along the edge of the driveway, keeping close to the undergrowth before stopping outside the first of the ground-floor windows. She put her ear to the glass and heard the sound of a TV.

Slowly, carefully, Tina made her way round the back of the cottage. A back door led into an unlit utility room, and beyond that Tina could see a narrow hallway with a staircase and the glow of lights at one end. Nothing moved inside, but there was definitely someone in there.

Putting on her gloves, Tina tried the back door and wasn't surprised to find it locked. It didn't matter. She'd been trained in covert entry years before when she was in SOCA, and she'd brought a set of picks with her.

Even so, she paused. The man who'd kidnapped Arley's children was armed and extremely dangerous. All her instincts told her to hold back, but in the end it made no difference. She wanted to find those kids and make them safe. If anything happened to them because she hadn't done all she could . . . Well, she found it hard enough to live with herself anyway.

Reaching into her pocket, she pulled out the picks; in thirty seconds she had the door unlocked. Slowly, she turned the handle and crept inside.

LIAM ROY SHETLAND, code-named Bull, had been buzzing all day. He'd finally killed a man. Put a gun against his head and pulled the trigger.

It was one of the most amazing things he'd ever experienced. He'd been reliving every detail in his head ever since. Which was just as well really, because otherwise the day would have been shit boring, hanging round on his own baby-sitting a couple of brats, and without even a PlayStation or the net to keep him occupied. Just a tiny little telly with nothing but Freeview.

The handler should be calling him any time now, telling him he could leave. His instructions were simple. He was to drive the van as close as he could to the Stanhope Hotel, and park it in as public a place as possible. There was a bomb in the back, set to go off at 11 p.m., and he needed to be well away from it when it blew. Fox had given him a rucksack containing a smaller bomb, and his job was to take this and continue towards the Stanhope on foot. When he got to the outer cordon where the crowds and TV cameras were gathered, he'd been told to get rid of the bag somewhere among them, and then get the hell out, because the rucksack bomb was timed to go off at 11.15. Liam was pleased he'd been given such responsibility by Fox, who was a bloke he seriously admired.

His mobile bleeped and he checked the screen. It was a text from the handler. All it said was WE'RE READY. Liam smiled, leaning over and picking up the gun from the table next to him. It was time to do the kids.

TINA WAS HALFWAY UP the staircase when she heard what she was sure was the bleep of a phone coming from beyond the half-open door that led into the living room—the only room downstairs she hadn't yet checked for signs of the children. A couple of seconds later, it was followed by the sound of a man clearing his throat loudly and moving around.

Making a snap decision, she continued up the last few stairs as quickly as she could, gritting her teeth when one of them creaked loudly, and darted behind the wall at the top just as the living room door opened.

There were three doors up here, two on her side of the landing, one on the other. Tiptoeing across the carpet, she opened the nearest one and stepped inside, and was immediately assailed by the smell of urine.

They were both on the floor in the middle of the empty room, lying on their fronts, trussed up from head to foot with duct tape like caterpillar larvae. As she gently closed the door behind her, they both started wriggling and making moaning noises beneath their gags.

'It's OK,' Tina whispered, feeling a huge sense of relief. 'I'm here to help. Your mum sent me. You've just got to stay quiet for a second.'

They both fell silent and stopped moving. Tina crouched down beside the girl, whose name she'd forgotten, and, after putting down the weapons, removed the duct tape covering her mouth as gently as she could, before doing the same with the tape covering her eyes. This way the girl could see who she was dealing with. She blinked up at Tina with wide, frightened eyes, and Tina smiled back at her reassuringly, putting a finger to her lips.

'Do you know how many men are holding you here?' she whispered.

'Two came to our house this morning,' the girl answered. 'They both had guns. I haven't heard any talking down there, so I don't know if they're both still here, but one definitely is. He was up here a little while ago.'

'OK. Now, I'm going to untie you both and then we're going to go out of the window as quietly as possible. Understand?'

The girl nodded. She looked incredibly relieved that Tina was there. Next to her, the boy, whom Tina remembered was called Oliver, rolled onto his side to face her and made a noise behind his gag.

She leaned over and began to remove the tape round his eyes, at the same time pulling out her phone so she could text Arley the news.

And then she heard it. The stair that had creaked earlier when she'd been coming up had creaked again. Even louder this time. Another stair creaked, and she stopped. The man was on his way up.

SEVEN

22.05

Arley watched as Riz picked up the phone. A second later he was connected to Wolf's phone in the satellite kitchen on the mezzanine floor, the sound of it ringing over the loudspeaker, filling the tense silence in the room. This was it. The decoy call. No one spoke as they waited.

Arley stood in the middle of the room, wearing a mike and earpiece connecting her to the mobile in her pocket. The moment it rang with news from Tina she'd call Major Standard in the SAS control room and tell him what she'd done. It would mean the immediate loss of her job, and the possibility of a whole raft of criminal charges, but in truth she didn't give a hoot about any of that. All she wanted was her children back with her safe and sound, and to stop the assault on the hotel. Everything else was irrelevant.

'We've got some movement in Worth Street at the back of the hotel,' said Will Verran. A few minutes earlier he'd connected the incident room to a police camera that had been set up on Worth Street, just inside the inner cordon, and he was watching the screen that showed it.

Arley peered at the screen. She could see a line of dark figures moving through the shadows on the pavement towards the Stanhope's delivery entrance, before stopping behind a parked lorry, where they were hidden from view. This was the assault force. She'd run out of time.

Call me, Tina. Please, just call.

TINA STOOD BACK against the bedroom wall, just behind the door, wondering what the hell the guy was doing. He'd been up here close to two minutes now, yet he hadn't come in. She'd got the two kids lying back on their fronts so that he wouldn't notice anything amiss when he eventually came in, but now she was wondering whether she should have tried to get them out of the window and to safety. But then she heard the flushing of a toilet and knew she'd made the right decision. He was coming.

She could hear his heavy footfalls on the landing, stopping outside the door. The boy moaned as the door opened and the light was switched on.

Tina held her breath, blinking against the light, her hand tight on the pepper spray canister. She'd replaced the lead piping in the back of her jeans because she needed a free hand in case the guy was armed. She needed to blind him, and for that, the spray was perfect.

Her heart hammered as he moved through the open door. She knew she had to be quick. She was going to get only one chance.

And then he was in the room, a huge hulk of a man holding a pistol. He turned to shut the door and Tina charged into him sideways on, her free hand grabbing his gun arm by the wrist as the force of her attack knocked him back against the wall. She thrust the pepper spray into his face and pressed the button, sending clouds of chilli powder straight into his eyes.

He screamed in pain, and she tried to drive her forehead into his nose, but he was already turning his head, and she caught only his cheek. It didn't stop her. She butted him again and again, as she reached into the back of her jeans, yanking out the lead piping. But then he ripped his gun hand free of hers, grabbed her by the throat in an iron grip that cut her breath like a knife, before literally throwing her across the room. Her head slammed into the wall with a dizzying thud and then she was on her back on the floor.

'Bitch!' he howled, swinging the gun round in a jerky arc as he pawed at his eyes. A shot rang out, the bullet ricocheting off the floor and into the ceiling. His gun hand jerked crazily as he searched for a target. The kids were wriggling about wildly, trying to get out of the line of fire. Suddenly the weapon was pointing at a spot right between Oliver's shoulder blades.

Tina's head was spinning but she knew she had to act, because it looked like he was going to pull the trigger. She still had hold of the lead piping, and, using her free hand to propel herself off the floor, she leaped to her feet.

He swung round to face her, still blinking wildly but managing to take aim. His finger tightened on the trigger just as she threw the lead piping.

It struck him full in the face and his nose erupted, sending blood squirting all over his mouth. Crying out, he lost his footing, his shot going high and wide, and, as he tried to right himself, Tina charged, driving a knee into his groin, and her head into his ruined nose.

This time he screamed. Not just in pain, but also in fear, and she sensed him weakening under the ferocity of her assault. But he still had a gun, and as he brought it up to aim it at her she grabbed desperately for the barrel and yanked with all the strength she had. The gun came free and flew across the room, clattering into the corner without discharging, and Tina pressed her advantage, kicking, punching and butting her adversary in a bid to beat him into submission. With an angry roar, he literally lifted her up and threw her off him, sending her crashing to the floor.

He stumbled across the room in the direction of the gun. She had to get up. To keep fighting. Rolling over, she jumped to her feet and was immediately assailed by an intense dizziness. But she held herself together, and as it cleared she saw him bending over to pick up the gun, his back to her.

Tina saw the lead piping on the floor. Operating entirely on instinct, she grabbed it and ran at her adversary, lifting the weapon above her head.

He could hear her coming, and he straightened with the gun in his hand, already turning towards her. But it was too late. She brought the lead piping down into his temple with all the force she could muster. He went down heavily, making no sound at all, and Tina fell over him, landing on the carpet. For a good ten seconds she didn't move as she fought to get her breath back. Then slowly she got to her feet, feeling in her pocket for her phone.

22.09

Arley felt her personal mobile vibrate as she watched the black-clad men on the TV screen disappearing one by one into the archway leading to the back of the Stanhope. It was Tina.

'What's happening?' she demanded, concerned only for news.

Tina's voice was full of exhaustion. 'I've got your kids. They're safe.'

Arley wanted to faint with the sudden burst of euphoria she experienced at that moment, but there was no time for that. 'Thank you,' she said simply. 'I'll call you back in five minutes.' She pocketed her mobile and grabbed one of the secure phones, speed-dialling through to the SAS control room.

An unfamiliar voice picked up, introducing himself as Captain Hunter. Arley spoke rapidly, 'This is DAC Arley Dale, Bronze Commander. Stop the attack. I have reliable information that your men are walking into an ambush.'

'It's too late,' said the other man. 'They're going in.'

'They can't. Get them back.'

'I'm not going to do that. This is a military operation.'

'Then let me speak to Major Standard. It's a matter of life and death.'

The captain told her to hold. Arley could only pray she wasn't too late.

FROM HIS POSITION in the Meadow Room on the mezzanine floor, Fox saw them as they emerged one by one from the darkness under the arch, fanning out into the courtyard. The enemy.

He slipped back out of sight, his AK-47 down by his side as he counted to twenty in his head, waiting for Bear to detonate the bomb.

Even though he'd braced himself for the impact, Fox jumped when the bomb exploded, the force of the blast shaking the windows. But his reactions were still lightning fast. Taking advantage of the seconds of chaos and disorientation that always follow an explosion, he looked out of the window and opened fire into the thick cloud of rapidly rising smoke.

As the glass exploded, he strafed the courtyard with bullets, before he was forced to leap back out of sight to avoid a burst of returning fire. Fox was already pulling a grenade from his belt. He yanked out the pin, counted to three and lobbed it out of the window, hearing it explode just as it hit the ground. At the same time, amid the wild ringing in his ears, he heard Bear's AK-47 open up from the ground floor—a single long burst followed by the crackle of returning fire and the whump of a stun grenade.

Jumping to his feet, Fox reloaded his AK and went into the next-door function room, pulling a second grenade from his belt. He strode over to the window and unleashed a burst of gunfire into the glass, before pulling the pin and flinging the grenade out through the hole he'd created.

As it exploded, he let loose another burst of fire, unable to resist taking a quick look at the carnage. He stiffened, confused. Because other than a few small fires and the remnants of the smoke, the courtyard was empty. There were no bodies at all. The ambush had failed.

22.13

'How on earth did you know that was going to happen, Arley?' asked Major Standard.

'I had good information,' said Arley into the phone. 'The point is, did it work? Did you pull your men out in time? It sounded like there was quite a firefight over there.' From their position in the mobile incident room two hundred yards away, they were unable to see what was happening, but they'd all heard the explosions interspersed with the gunfire easily enough.

'Yes. Every man's been accounted for. We had to return fire to cover the retreat, but I don't know if we hit any of the terrorists or not. I need to speak to your source urgently. I want to know how he knew about our movements, and what he can tell us about the terrorists inside the building. Do you have a name and number for him?'

'No,' lied Arley, improvising. 'He called from a callbox.'

'Then who is he? And why did he call you?'

'He's an informant through an MI5 source. He was put on to me because I'm the police commander on the scene. I'll try to get through to him now.'

'Do that. It's urgent I speak to him. We can't make another move on the building until we've got some idea what we're up against.'

'I've still got our negotiator trying to get hold of Wolf,' said Arley. 'He hasn't been answering. What do you want our man to say if he does?'

'Get him to tell Wolf it was a mistake and there was no attack. And get me that contact now, Arley. That's an order.'

'Yes sir,' she said, hanging up and repeating Standard's instruction to Riz.

It was just in time, because barely twenty seconds later the phone in the hotel's satellite kitchen, which had been ringing off the hook for close to ten minutes, was finally picked up, and Wolf was on the line.

'Stop the attack now!' he was shouting, his voice filled with fear and anger. 'If you don't, we will detonate the bomb in the ballroom and kill all the hostages. You have one minute to comply. Do you understand?'

'Yes, I do,' answered Riz. 'But there's been some mistake because there hasn't been an attack.'

'What are you talking about? What were the explosions and all the shooting, then?'

'I don't know,' Riz replied. 'But my understanding is that two members of the SAS were watching the rear of the hotel when some of your operatives opened fire on them. They then immediately retreated.'

'Bullshit. That can't be right. They were attacking us.' But there was the first hint of doubt in his voice.

'It wasn't an attack, Wolf,' said Riz, the calmness in his voice a contrast to the terrorist's. 'I can promise you that. We genuinely want to negotiate.'

'Your men shouldn't have been round the back of here anyway. What were they doing there?'

'They were simply keeping an eye on things.'

'Tell them to stay away. Do you understand that? If we see any more of them again, we kill ten hostages.'

The line went dead, and Riz took a deep breath. 'Bloody hell, that was close. He's not happy.'

'It could have been one hell of a lot worse,' murmured Arley.

'So, who's this contact of yours?' asked John Cheney, frowning as he posed the question everyone in the room wanted an answer to.

'I can't talk about it right now,' she said dismissively. 'It's classified.'

'That's ridiculous,' complained Cheney.

'That's the way it is. No more discussion.' But even as she spoke the words, she knew she was on the verge of being found out.

'WHAT'S HAPPENING?' asked Ethan, his face etched with fear, as he sat on the bed next to his mother.

'It's all right,' Scope told him, putting a protective arm round his shoulder as the last of the explosions and gunfire faded away. 'We're safe here.'

'What about Mom?'

'Your mum's going to be all right too.'

But as they looked down at her, Scope wasn't at all sure he was right. It had been five minutes since he'd roused her and injected the insulin. He'd managed to get her to take a few sips from a Lucozade bottle he'd found in the minibar, but she'd almost immediately thrown it up, and she was barely conscious. She needed proper medical treatment urgently.

He looked over at the TV, wondering what on earth all the fighting had signified. The rolling headline at the bottom of the TV screen said that explosions and gunfire had been heard inside.

Tell me something I don't know, he thought.

Another headline appeared: UNOFFICIAL SOURCE SAYS NO ASSAULT TAKING PLACE, NEGOTIATIONS CONTINUING

This was bad. More than that, it was almost unheard of. There'd definitely been some kind of attack, but it seemed it had been abandoned, which put him, Ethan and especially Abby in a dangerous position.

'What's going on?' asked Ethan.

'We're getting out of here,' Scope said. 'Right now.'

'WHAT THE HELL HAPPENED?' demanded Fox as he and Bear came together at the top of the central staircase. 'We didn't get any of them.'

'I saw them come in,' said Bear. 'There were loads of them. I kept my head down and counted to twenty, then blew the thing. Just like you said.'

'Well, it didn't work.'

'They must have been pulled back. If they'd been within twenty yards of that bomb, they'd have been blown to pieces. Are you sure none of them was killed?'

'Well, there aren't any bodies out there,' snapped Fox. 'Come on, we'd better give Wolf the good news.'

As they went through the doors, Fox could see that the hostages were looking extremely agitated, while both Wolf and Cat kept watch on them, weapons at the ready.

Hearing their return, Wolf stepped back, still keeping his gun trained on the hostages, until he was level with Fox and Bear. He looked furious. 'I called the negotiator. He says there was no attack.'

'There was. At least one person fired at me. And they threw a stun grenade.'

'Someone fired at me as well,' added Bear.

'Did you get any of them?'

Fox shook his head. 'No. They were definitely ordered back.'

'So someone told them about our ambush. Your plan failed, Fox. You've made us look like fools.'

'No, I haven't. They came in. We fired at them. They left. Which meant it was a victory to us.'

'But you didn't kill any of them.'

'It doesn't matter,' said Fox, who was beginning to get heartily sick of Wolf. 'The point is, we're still in control, and holding the military at bay. All we have to do is keep this up for another three-quarters of an hour and then the hotel goes up in flames and we make our escape. Just as we've always planned. We can still say we repulsed their attack. It's still a victory.'

'Except we didn't humiliate them. That's what we always wanted. To make the great SAS look like amateurs.'

'I think they've been pretty badly humiliated already,' he said, meeting Wolf's hard stare with a far harder one of his own. 'And right now, it's the best you're going to get.'

Wolf grunted. 'All right. You and Bear watch the hostages. I need to speak to the negotiator again.' He turned away, motioning for Cat to follow, while Fox and Bear took up positions standing twenty feet apart.

Their plans had been thrown off course, but if Fox kept calm, soon most of these people would be dead, and he'd be on his way to a new life.

TINA HAD WRAPPED the children in blankets she'd found in one of the cupboards and they were now sitting at the kitchen table taking it in turns to speak to their mother on her mobile. They were both in tears, and by the sounds of things, Arley was too. Tina couldn't blame any of them.

She left them in there, putting up a finger to say she'd be back in one minute, then returned to the bedroom where the kidnapper lay face down on the carpet. She felt for a pulse but there was nothing. He was dead.

She went back downstairs and made her way into the living room, where the kidnapper had been sitting when she arrived. A rucksack was on the sofa and she went over to it, wondering if there'd be a clue to his identity in there. She pulled open the rucksack and stopped dead when she saw the battery pack and wires, realising she was staring at a bomb.

Slowly, very carefully, she stepped away from the device, knowing she had to get the kids out of there. As she turned towards the door, she glanced briefly at the TV, and saw the rolling headlines saying that explosions and gunfire were audible from the back of the Stanhope hotel and that unofficial sources suggested a rescue attempt by Special Forces was being repelled.

So there *had* been an assault on the building by the SAS, and it seemed that things had gone badly wrong, which meant only one thing: Arley must have told the terrorists of their plans, despite Tina's warning to her about having blood on their hands as a result.

Oliver was speaking on the phone when Tina came back into the kitchen. 'I need to speak to your mum urgently,' she said, taking the phone from him. 'And we need to get out of here right now.'

'What's going on, Tina?' asked Arley.

'Give me a minute,' she answered, pushing the kids out of the front door and onto the driveway, ignoring their questions. It occurred to her that there might be further devices in the house, and that the van might contain some kind of bomb too. 'I've just seen the news on the TV. So the SAS went in. You all but promised me you wouldn't let that happen.'

'They did go in, but I managed to get a message to them to abort the attack. They pulled back just in time, and none of them was hurt.'

'Are you sure? Because there's no point lying to me now, Arley.'

'I swear it, Tina. There were no casualties.'

'Surely they must want to know how you came by the information.'

'They do. It's something I'm going to have to deal with when this is over. Listen, Tina, I won't implicate you, I promise.'

'It's too late. You already have. And I've killed a man here. I can hardly try to hide it. That just implicates me more.'

'God, I don't know what to say, I really don't.'

Nor did Tina. There was a long silence while both women processed the events of the night and their inevitable repercussions.

'It's all over for me, Tina,' said Arley quietly.

'I know it is.'

'And I know how this must sound, but can I ask you one final favour?'

Tina almost laughed. 'Jesus, you've got chutzpah, I'll give you that.'

'I need to see my children while I'm still free. I need to tell them about their father. And I want to do it face to face.'

'I don't see how that's going to be possible,' said Tina as she ushered Oliver and India down the muddy track outside the cottage.

'My mother lives in Pinner. If I text you the address, please can you take them there? I know I've asked a lot of you.'

'You've asked everything of me.'

'I know. And I'm begging you . . . please.'

'I need to phone the police. There are bombs in the house where I found your kids, as well as a body, and we need to get the area sealed off.' Tina sighed, looking at Arley's children. 'Then I'll take them to your mother.'

MARTIN DALSTON was feeling nauseous and tense, although he wasn't sure how much of this was due to his illness and how much to the atmosphere inside the restaurant. Ten or so minutes ago they'd heard explosions and shooting coming from somewhere in the building. The taller of the two terrorists, the one Martin had overheard referred to as Dragon, had told them in advance to expect some gunfire, but that the situation was under control.

But it seemed it wasn't fully, because both terrorists were now on their feet, their body language riddled with tension as they kept their rifles trained on the hostages, screaming threats the moment someone so much as changed position on the floor. Dragon kept exchanging nervous glances with the other guard, the one with the Scandinavian accent. Both were checking their watches every few seconds, as if they were waiting for something.

Their erratic behaviour, and the uncertainty of the situation, was also affecting the hostages. One person in particular, a white-haired businessman in his sixties, only a few feet away from Martin, had started to breathe very heavily in the past few minutes, and it looked like he might be having a panic attack. His breathing was getting louder and more laboured, and he bent forward, one hand on his chest. Martin could see he was in a bad way, and he wanted to do something to help.

Elena was looking over at him now, a concerned yet helpless expression on her face. She wanted to help too. Martin could see that. But she wasn't going to. None of them was, including Martin himself.

He suddenly felt a terrible anger, not just towards the terrorists, but towards himself, for not doing something. He might be unarmed, physically weak and desperately thirsty, but he had one huge advantage over all the hostages: he had nothing left to live for.

The businessman suddenly cried out in pain and fell over, clutching at his chest with both hands as he began to hyperventilate.

Martin knew that for once in his life he had to stand up and be counted. 'This man needs help urgently,' he shouted at the two terrorists. 'Please. You've got to help him.'

Other hostages murmured in agreement, their confidence boosted by Martin's actions.

'Leave him, he'll be all right,' said Dragon dismissively.

'He won't be all right unless he gets some kind of medical attention.'

Martin crawled over to the man on his hands and knees, feeling liberated now that he was actually doing something, and put a steadying hand on his arm. The man stared up at him with wide, frightened eyes, but he was still conscious, and Martin had no idea whether he was experiencing a panic attack or something more serious.

'Get back!' yelled the Scandinavian. 'You were told to leave him alone.'

But Martin was defiant. 'He needs some water. Come on. Please. Have some kind of humanity.'

The Scandinavian marched over. 'You want to see my humanity?' he sneered. 'Yeah? I'll show you my fucking humanity.'

He grabbed Martin by the shirt and yanked him out of the way. Then, with barely a moment's hesitation, he took a step back, pointed his assault rifle down at the businessman's chest, and pulled the trigger, shooting him three times in rapid succession. The man's desperate, rasping breathing suddenly stopped, just like that, and he lay still.

The Scandinavian turned to Martin, his bright blue eyes alive with excitement. 'There. That's my humanity. Anyone else move, and they get the same. And that includes you.' He aimed the rifle at Martin's head. 'Get it?'

Martin looked down. Said nothing.

'Good. Now shut up. All of you.'

The gunman turned away, walking back towards his colleague.

Which was when Martin Dalston leaped to his feet, fury sweeping through him in a physical wave that gave him a strength he'd never experienced before. He charged at the Scandinavian, grabbing him in a bear hug and biting him as hard as he could in the exposed flesh of his neck.

The Scandinavian let out a startled yelp and tried to throw him off, but the adrenalin was pumping through Martin and he held on tight. He knew that the moment he fell off, he was dead. Then, out of the corner of his eye, he saw a flash of blonde. Elena was on her feet and leaping towards him too, her momentum knocking all three of them to the floor.

A burst of gunfire filled the room as the assault rifle discharged, but Martin had no time to see who, if anyone, had been hit. The Scandinavian had rolled onto him as he struggled to break free from his two attackers. Martin was gouging at his eyes and face, while Elena fought with him from the front, the weight of their two bodies crushing down on him.

Another burst of gunfire filled the room, as Dragon fired into the air. He was shouting for people to sit down. 'Get back, or I'll blow the bomb!'

It was difficult to see from Martin's position on the floor, but it looked like more people had got to their feet to join in the resistance, but even as he watched, he could see Dragon looking more confident, as if he could see that his orders were being obeyed. Above him, the Scandinavian threw off Elena, and tried once again to wrench himself away from Martin's grip, but still Martin held on like grim death, even though he could feel his strength fading. And now Dragon was coming over, his rifle pointed at Elena, who was on her hands and knees looking terrified. Which was the moment when a figure appeared out of the corner door behind Dragon and charged him.

Scope had never intended to be a hero. His plan had been to try to get on to the hotel roof from where he hoped to be able to summon some kind of help, but as he, Abby and Ethan had reached the ninth floor on the emergency staircase, with its sign for the Park View Restaurant, he'd heard the sound of shouting and gunfire, and reassessed. He could have carried on going but he remembered from the news that the terrorists had been holding hostages in the restaurant, and that the restaurant itself led out on to a flat roof terrace, which probably represented a better escape route.

Having sat Abby down and instructed Ethan to look after her, he'd made his way along towards the restaurant, and through the glass in the door had witnessed a scene of chaos. One gunman was struggling on the floor with several hostages, while another was shouting at the remainder of the group. His foot was resting on a pedal detonator and he was threatening to use it.

As Scope watched, the gunman on the floor threw off one of the people he was struggling with, a blonde-haired woman, while the second one took his foot off the detonator and started walking into the crowd.

Immediately, Scope saw his chance. Pulling out his knife, he threw open the door and ran into the room.

At the last second, the second gunman—a big guy with broad, muscular shoulders—heard him and swung round fast, finger tensing on the trigger. But he was too late. Still sprinting, Scope dived at him, using one hand to knock the rifle to one side, and the other to ram the knife into his neck.

Momentum sent them both hurtling through the crowd, the blood spurting from the gunman's severed jugular vein. They hit the floor hard, with Scope on top, and the gunman made a final grunt as the last of the air escaped his lungs, Scope turned round, just in time to see the other one hauling himself heavily to his feet, kicking off a smaller man who was trying to drag him back down.

The blonde woman jumped up and made a lunge at the gunman, grabbing for his weapon, but he slammed the barrel into her face, knocking her backwards to the floor, before swinging the rifle round towards Scope.

Scope yanked the AK-47 from the dead man's hands and rolled round to face him, but even as he did so he knew he was too late. The gunman had already steadied his aim and was ready to fire. But the smaller guy grabbed him round the legs again, knocking him slightly off balance, just as he fired a burst of shots. Scope felt them pass close to the left side of his face, and started firing himself. The AK was set to single shot, and he put two into the gunman's torso, knocking him backwards. Then, remembering that one of the terrorists he'd taken out earlier had been wearing a bulletproof vest, Scope shot at the gunman's head. One round missed and a second hit him in the shoulder, before the third took him through the cheekbone. The gunman began to sway, before toppling to the carpet with a loud thud.

Scope clambered to his feet, knowing that they all had to get out of there before the other terrorists arrived. The hostages were all looking at him, including the blonde girl who'd helped save his life, and who was now holding her nose as blood poured out of it. Scope looked at the smaller guy—the other person who'd helped save his life. He was panting hard and his face was pale. Scope nodded at him, and mouthed the word 'thanks'.

'All right, we've got to leave now,' he shouted.

'What about that rucksack?' one of the hostages shouted back. 'It's got a bomb in it.'

'I'll deal with it,' said Scope. 'The rest of you, get the hell out.'

The blonde woman got to her feet. 'Follow me,' she said. 'We can go on to the roof terrace outside. The doors should be unlocked.'

No one needed asking twice. As they scattered the tables and chairs piled up against the windows and pulled up the blinds, Scope picked up the rucksack, knowing there was no time for caution, and placed it round the other side of the restaurant, out of sight of the windows. Then, slinging the AK-47 over his shoulder, he ran back towards the staircase.

It was time to get Abby and Ethan.

CAT HEARD THE SHOTS from the satellite kitchen next to the ballroom. Beside her, Wolf was on the phone talking loudly to the negotiator. 'We have waited for the British government to come back to us on our demands, and all you have done is send in SAS men rather than trying to negotiate in good faith.'

There was a second burst of gunfire from high up in the hotel and Wolf stopped talking and cocked his head.

'I thought you said there was no attack!' he shouted. 'What is all that shooting?' Then he frowned. 'What do you mean it's not you?'

The noise of more shooting tore down the staircase, and Cat glanced over at the TV on the worktop. It was showing live news footage of the Park View Restaurant on the ninth floor. A number of the blinds had been pulled up and people were pouring through the open French windows that led out on to the roof terrace. The two men supposed to be guarding them, Dragon and Tiger, were nowhere to be seen.

When Wolf saw what was happening on the TV, his face darkened. 'Keep your people back!' he shouted at the negotiator. 'Do you understand?' Then he slammed down the phone and turned to Cat. 'What's going on up there?'

'I don't know,' she said coldly. 'But we have to stop them. It'll be the work of the bastard who killed my brother.' As she spoke the words, she felt a rush of anger, and her grip on the pistol tightened. She had to find him.

Wolf shook his head angrily. 'It doesn't matter now. They'll be sending the SAS in again. We need to get out of here.'

'How? We're half an hour early. The bombs won't blow, and we'll be caught. This wasn't part of the plan.'

'We have to try.'

Cat was annoyed by his weakness. 'Be a man, Wolf. It's time for us to make a last stand. Let's go up there and fight.'

'I *am* a man,' he said indignantly. 'But the plan was to escape.'

'Mine wasn't. I never expected to leave alive, and I'm surprised you did. We must kill as many of the enemy as possible. For our country. For our leader. For our religion.' She lifted her pistol in a defiant gesture, and patted the pockets of her jacket. 'We have the weapons. Let us make them pay.'

FOX WAS IN THE BALLROOM when he heard the gunfire.

'What the hell's going on up there?' hissed Bear.

Whatever it was, it had to be serious. Their hostages had heard it too, and their tension levels were rising once again. The problem was they numbered close to eighty, and with only him and Bear guarding them, all it took was a concerted effort and they'd be overrun in seconds.

'Do you think the SAS are attacking again?'

Fox shook his head. 'I don't think so. Let's just stay calm. I don't want this lot to know you're worried.'

The shooting stopped, but it didn't make Fox feel any better. It had almost certainly come from the Park View Restaurant. Either Dragon and Tiger had the situation back under control, or they were dead.

At that moment Cat marched in, with Wolf following. But they didn't come over. Instead, they made straight for the ballroom door.

'Shit,' cursed Bear. 'Now what are they doing?'

'Watch the hostages,' snapped Fox as he caught Wolf's eye.

Wolf put up two fingers to suggest he and Cat would be back in a couple of minutes, and then they were out of the door.

Fox knew instantly they weren't coming back. There was something too purposeful in their manner. Which meant it was time to make a decision. If they stayed put, they risked being trapped there. If they abandoned their stations, they ran the risk of not being paid the balance of the money for the job. But with the information he had, Fox didn't actually need that money.

Bear was standing a few feet away, looking at Fox expectantly.

Fox made his decision. 'All right. Let's go.'

He fired a burst of shots over the top of the hostages, and as they cried out and covered their heads, he and Bear turned and ran for the door.

It took a few seconds for the hostages to realise what was happening, but when they did, some jumped to their feet. Someone shouted that the terrorists were going to detonate the rucksack bomb that was still right in the middle of them, causing a panicked rush after Fox and Bear.

As Fox reached the door, he turned round and unleashed another burst of fire, scattering the hostages as he tried to buy himself and Bear a few extra seconds. Then they were through the door and out into the corridor.

Fox couldn't hear any movement coming from the ground floor but it wouldn't be long before the SAS came blasting through the doors. Yanking a grenade from his belt, he pulled the pin and rolled it down the central staircase, keen to cause as much mayhem as possible, then he and Bear sprinted through the doors in the direction of the emergency staircase.

Ahead of them, the corridor was empty, but behind he could hear the panicked shouts of the hostages as they fought their way through the door, followed by the loud blast of the grenade. In a few minutes, this whole place was going to be a screaming mass of people trying to get out, and SAS men trying to get in, which was exactly what Fox had planned. It would have been helpful if the bombs they'd set on timer had accompanied their escape, but it probably wouldn't matter. There was just one more thing to do.

As they ran up the emergency staircase to the second floor, where they'd stashed their civilian clothes and fake IDs in separate rooms, Fox pulled out his pistol, and in one swift movement shot Bear twice in the face, not even stopping to watch as the other man grunted and fell back down the steps. He didn't feel bad about killing the man who'd saved his life in Iraq all those years before. For Fox, it was all business. The fewer people who knew about him the better. Especially ones with big mouths like Bear.

Fox used his master key card to open room 202, from where he would shortly emerge as Robert Durran, freelance architect and guest in the hotel, and join all the other fleeing guests unlucky enough to have been caught up in the terrible events of that day.

As SCOPE gently laid Abby down on the roof terrace, helped by Ethan, she was beginning to come round again and blinking against the search beam of the police helicopter circling overhead.

'You're still at the hotel, but you're going to be OK,' Scope told her. 'There are people coming to help you.'

So far, though, with the exception of the helicopter, the cavalry hadn't actually arrived. The twenty-five or so hostages mingled uncertainly on the terrace, nobody really sure what was going on. Scope wasn't too worried. The rescuers would be here soon enough, and now that Abby was awake, there was less urgency.

He grinned at Ethan. 'See? Your mum's going to be all right.'

But as Ethan grinned back, a long burst of gunfire came from somewhere in the building, followed by a loud explosion, and a few seconds later a couple carrying two young children, who must have come from one of the guest rooms, hurried through the double doors onto the terrace.

'There are terrorists coming!' said the woman breathlessly.

'They're shooting at everyone and everything,' added her husband.

Scope stood up. 'How many of them are there?'

'I don't know, but they're not far away.'

A worried murmur went up among the crowd. Scope picked up Abby and took her over to the far end of the terrace, where she'd be seen and dealt with by the rescuers when they finally arrived.

'Stay here with your mum, Ethan. I'm going back inside.'

Ethan looked scared. 'But you might get hurt. Don't leave us. You keep leaving.'

Scope smiled. 'And I keep coming back. Remember that.'

He looked around for the blonde manager and saw her holding a bloodied tissue to her nose as she directed people back from the edge of the terrace. 'I'm going to try and hold them back,' he told her, 'but can you look after those two over there and make sure they get to safety?'

'Of course. But be careful.'

'And you.'

Turning away, he ran back into the restaurant. He'd stashed the AK-47 under a chair to avoid getting mistaken for one of the terrorists by the security forces, and he grabbed it now, keeping it down by his side as he strode over to the doors leading back to the emergency staircase. He peered through the glass and immediately saw a young man in bare feet sprinting

298 | SIMON KERNICK

along the corridor towards him. He stepped aside as the guy came charging through without even slowing down and ran towards the open terrace doors.

More gunfire rang out, and this time it was really close. As Scope peered through the glass, he saw a man stagger out of the emergency staircase door, halfway along the corridor. He'd clearly been shot and was clutching at his side. Unable to keep his balance, he went down on his knees.

Holding the rifle out in front of him, Scope kicked open the door and went out to help him.

At exactly the same moment, the side door flew open again, and a man in a balaclava and boiler suit came storming through, already firing into the injured man, who pitched forward with a strangled scream.

The man turned Scope's way. He was short and well-built, moving with a confidence that came when you had a gun in your hand and the people you were hunting didn't. But the moment he saw Scope he took an instinctive, startled step back, and hesitated for just half a second too long.

In one fluid movement, Scope put the rifle to his shoulder and opened up on fully automatic.

The masked gunman flew backwards, firing from the hip, his bullets ricocheting off the ceiling, and Scope charged him. The gunman went down on his back and lay still, but Scope knew there was a good chance he was wearing a flak jacket, and faking it. He'd been hit in the chest, and was still holding on to his weapon with one hand.

Scope stopped ten feet short of him and took aim at his head.

The gunman realised at the last second that he'd miscalculated and brought round his weapon to fire, but he was too late. Scope shot him twice in the face and the rifle dropped out of his hand as he died.

Scope opened the door to the emergency staircase. There was no longer any shooting, just a lot of shouting, and doors slamming coming from farther down the steps. It was obvious that those guests who'd barricaded themselves into their rooms had seen images on the TV of their fellow guests escaping and were following suit.

He turned to go, eager to leave himself.

And then he heard a pained cry coming from the next floor down.

'Is anyone down there?' Scope called out, still keeping his finger tight on the trigger, knowing it could easily be a trick.

'Help me,' came a young, female voice. English accent. 'I've been hurt.'

Scope started down the staircase. 'Stay there,' he said. 'I'm coming.'

He saw her as he came round the corner on to the next set of steps. She was about twenty, no more, a pretty Asian girl in a waitress's uniform, standing in the middle of the stairwell with her arms down by her side. She was shaking, although Scope couldn't see any sign of injury. There was another girl, partially obscured, lying in a foetal position behind her.

Scope frowned. He couldn't see the face of the girl lying down, but she was wearing a black dress.

The Asian girl opened her mouth to say something, her eyes wide with fear, and then her face seemed to explode as the stairwell erupted in the noise of gunfire.

Scope tried to jump out of the way as the girl pitched forward, landing heavily on the stairs, but he was too late. He just had time to register the pretty dark-haired woman who'd tried to kill him earlier, sitting up in the corner of the stairwell and firing at him with her pistol, before a bullet struck him in the shoulder, spinning him round. One more caught him in the back, and he was slammed hard into the staircase face first. He felt his own rifle clatter down the steps as he instinctively released it.

There was no pain, just a massive sense of shock. He tried to move, but couldn't. Then he felt a hand on his suit jacket, pulling him over, and he was looking into a pair of dark, hate-filled eyes.

'Good,' hissed the woman with a cruel smile. 'You're still alive.' She lifted the knife, holding it millimetres from his right eye. 'Now you're all mine.'

MARTIN DALSTON knew he should have stayed with the others out on the roof terrace, but when he saw the man who'd saved them all earlier run back inside the hotel to try to keep the remaining terrorists at bay, he wanted to help him. He wanted to do something valuable before he died, something that would make his son proud of him, and now he had an opportunity.

He went back into the restaurant, hearing gunfire coming from the corridor, but Martin didn't hesitate. He ran through the doors into the corridor.

Two bodies lay on the floor about halfway down. One, by his outfit, was clearly a terrorist, while the other was a guest. The shooting had stopped now. There was just silence, and Martin wondered where the man had disappeared to. He walked towards the emergency staircase.

As he opened the door to the staircase, he heard the words straight-away. Spat out of her mouth and dripping with hate, 'Does that hurt, yes? Does it?'

Martin froze. He recognised that voice. It belonged to the cruellest terrorist of them all. The beautiful dark-haired woman.

'Fuck you,' came the grunted reply.

It was the man from the restaurant. He was clearly in immense pain, the defiance in his voice tinged with resignation.

'I can make you scream. Perhaps if I cut this eye out, just—'

And then Martin was running down the stairs, letting out some kind of weird battle cry. He came sprinting round the corner, saw the man lying on his back, bleeding badly, unable to move, while she crouched over him, a knife in her hand. She was looking up, having heard his approach, but he was so quick that she hadn't had time to grab her gun, which he could see was lying on the stairs next to her.

He had two choices: hesitate and die, or keep going and probably die. He chose the latter, diving straight into the woman, his momentum making up for his lack of weight and power, and the two of them crashed down the stairs and into the stairwell.

As they rolled onto the floor, Martin kept her in a tight bear hug so that she couldn't use her knife. But she was stronger than he was and she wriggled ferociously in his grip, screaming and cursing into his face.

And then they were rolling down the next set of steps and Martin could feel the wind being taken out of him. As they hit the bottom, she pulled her knife hand free, rolled on top of him, and thrust the blade at his chest. The knife caught him somewhere in the upper body—he couldn't see where. He felt a tremendous shock, and then the whole world seemed to slow right down. He felt his head fall back against the floor and his hands slip to his sides. Almost immediately his vision began to darken, and the woman became hazy in appearance as she got to her feet, still holding the knife.

And then he heard the sound of bullets echoing round the stairwell and the woman cried out and crashed backwards into the wall. More shots rang out and the woman slid down the wall, leaving a long dark stain behind.

Everything was now utterly silent, and Martin began to feel very, very tired. A face appeared in his fading vision. He thought it was the man he'd just rescued, but he couldn't be sure. The man was saying something to him, but Martin couldn't hear what it was. He closed his eyes and felt himself letting go, pulling away like a boat from a harbour, heading slowly out to sea.

His last thoughts as he died were not of Carrie, or what could have been. They were of his son, and his wife. Of what was.

22.28

Elena stood in the wind and the rain at the edge of the roof terrace. The fire brigade had put up two ladders and a cherry picker, and were in the process of evacuating the hostages. Behind her, the first thin plumes of smoke were drifting out through the restaurant double doors, but nothing moved in there, and the shooting had stopped.

She'd seen Martin go running in there a few minutes ago, after the other man—the one who looked like a soldier—but neither of them had emerged, and she was beginning to fear the worst. She didn't want to leave without them, but at the same time she desperately wanted to get back to Rod. And she needed to have her nose looked at.

A steadily growing roar filled the air and, as Elena watched, a huge military helicopter came into view, and stopped just metres above her, dropping down long rope lines. A few seconds later, two dozen armed men abseiled down onto the terrace, pausing only to gather together in groups of four.

And then, beyond them, Elena saw a figure stumbling through the restaurant in the direction of the French windows. He was wearing a suit, and she immediately recognised him as the man Martin had gone in after.

The armed men saw him too, and one group of four approached him, weapons outstretched, the search beams attached to the sights homing in on his face.

The man stopped in the doorway, shielding his eyes with his hand as the men in black barked orders at him. Then he tottered and fell onto one knee.

'He's hurt!' shouted one of the men, and they descended on him quickly, moving him rapidly to one side as their colleagues poured through the French windows and into the restaurant.

Elena ran over and saw that they'd laid him out on his back. Two of them were frisking him for weapons, even though it was clear that he was badly injured. 'Please,' she said, 'he's not a terrorist. He attacked the terrorists in the restaurant. He saved our lives.'

'Get back, ma'am, please,' said one of the men.

Behind him, his colleagues had finished their frisking and two of them had lifted the man to his feet. As they led him past Elena, her eyes met his.

'Where's Martin?' she asked him. 'I saw him go down to look for you.'

'He didn't make it,' said the man in the suit. 'I'm very sorry.'

And then he was being helped into the cherry picker, where two firemen waited to take him.

'Come on, ma'am, you need to come too.'

Elena looked up towards the sky, and for a long moment she forgot everything and simply savoured the feel of the rain on her face.

The nightmare had ended. She was free.

22.32

As they emerged from the front of the hotel, the hostages were searched individually by SAS teams stationed just outside. The injured were moved to one side to be treated by paramedics, the remainder were funnelled into a narrow corridor—formed by two lines of police tape, and flanked by armed officers—which ended in a large tent that had been erected earlier in the middle of Park Lane. The tent was a processing centre where the hostages would need to provide ID and an explanation of what they were doing in the hotel, in order to sift out anyone who might have been involved in the attack.

Fox wasn't unduly nervous as he joined one of the queues, even though armed CO19 cops and SAS men were positioned around the interior to make sure no one tried to make a break for it. He was dressed in a crumpled suit, with smoke marks on his face, and he looked just like any other civilian.

There were only a couple of people in front of him, and as he waited, he checked his new civilian phone, which had been registered in the name Robert Durran two weeks earlier. There was reception, and he felt confident enough to send a text to a number he'd memorised earlier. The content was innocent enough: HAVE MADE IT OUT! TOMORROW AT 10. I HAVE GREAT NEWS. RD XXX. Fox didn't think anyone would bother checking his phone, but if they did he would tell them that, having made it out of the hotel in one piece, he now wanted to propose to his fiancée.

In reality, TOMORROW AT 10 represented his payday, the time when he would hand over to his contact the information given to him under torture by Michael Prior, in exchange for five million dollars. The information was simply a name, nothing more. But it happened to be the name of a very senior member of the Chinese government who was providing high-level intelligence to MI6, and very likely the CIA. This man's identity was so secret that, including Fox himself, probably no more than half a dozen people knew it, which made the information very valuable indeed. Fox suspected his contact, the same right-wing extremist who'd put him in touch with Wolf all those months ago, was selling it on for far more money, but that wasn't his concern. He'd be rich enough after this to retire to the home he was having built for himself in the tropics, and never be seen or heard from again, which was just the way he liked it.

It was his turn at the desk. Two officious-looking uniformed cops sat there, while a CO19 with an MP5 stood behind them.

'Name please, sir,' said the first one.

'Robert Durran.'

'Were you a guest in the Stanhope?'

'Yes. Room 202.'

The second one typed something on the laptop, and nodded to the first, who asked Fox if he had any ID.

'Yes, I do.' But as he reached into his pocket for the wallet, he heard a commotion behind him.

'I know him,' said an older-looking black man in dungaree overalls who was standing a couple of people back in the next line. 'He's one of them,' he continued, pointing at Fox. 'He's one of the terrorists. I was hiding in the crawlspace in the ballroom kitchen. I heard him speaking in there loads of times. It's him. I'm sure of it.'

Everyone was looking at Fox now. He could have tried to brazen things out, but it wouldn't take the authorities long to work out the truth if they delved deeper into his background. Which left him with only one option.

He turned and bolted for the exit, knowing he was never going to make it. He was trapped and unarmed, but he knew he couldn't surrender and face the rest of his days behind bars. That would be too much.

He heard the angry shouts of armed officers screaming at everyone to get down, saw the guns pointing at him from every direction.

And then someone in one of the lines threw out a leg and Fox pitched forward over it, his mobile clattering across the tarmac.

In the next second, he felt someone jump on his back, knees first, screaming and shouting. Fox gasped in pain as the wind was taken out of him. It was one of the hostages. As Fox tried to struggle free from his grip, a great shout rose up from the other hostages, and they fell upon him, tearing at his hair and face and screaming abuse as they dragged him to his feet.

He felt a surge of panic as he was kicked and punched and scratched. These people were going to tear him apart limb from limb—he could hear the bloodlust in their voices. Someone spat at his face; someone else tried to gouge out his eyes. But then the people moved away, and once again he was being slammed back to the ground, except this time he felt the cold metal of gun barrels being pushed against his head. Unable to stop himself, he threw up, just as someone took a photo of him lying with his face in the dirt, completing his humiliation. With his vision blurred from the attempt to gouge out his eyes, he heard rather than saw someone pick up his mobile from the ground, and shout something about the text he'd just sent.

It didn't matter. None of it mattered any more. He was caught.

THE MOMENT ARLEY walked back in the room, everyone turned her way.

'Ma'am, where the hell have you been?' John Cheney asked incredulously. He looked more stressed than she'd seen him all night. 'The SAS have gone in and we've got hostages coming out.'

'Silver Commander's on the line from 1600, ma'am,' said Janine.

Riz Mohammed had the phone to his ear, but he was shaking his head. 'I'm getting no answer at all. I have no idea what's going on in the hotel.'

Arley looked around. She felt numb. She had her children back, and for that she was truly thankful in a way she couldn't describe, but now that they were safe the enormity of her losses bore down on her like a lead weight.

She turned to Janine. 'Can you tell Silver that I wish to be relieved of my post. I'd recommend that Chris Matthews take over for the duration. Thanks to each and every one of you for all your efforts tonight.'

There was a stunned silence lasting a good three seconds, before Cheney finally broke it. 'Arley? Ma'am? You can't just leave in the middle of a crisis like this. It's bloody madness.'

Arley gave him a hard stare. 'I'm sorry. There's nothing else I can do.'

Cheney started to say something else, but she'd already turned her back and was walking out the door, knowing it was only a matter of time before her colleagues realised what she'd done, but knowing too that she had to see Oliver and India before she was arrested.

But she'd barely gone ten yards across the grass in the direction of the outer cordon when she heard footsteps behind her. It was Cheney.

She stopped, facing him. 'Leave me alone, John.'

'At least tell me what's going on, Arley. You've been behaving strangely all night. And who exactly was your mysterious source who knew that the SAS were walking into an ambush?'

'You'll find out soon enough.'

'Come on. We go back a long way. I may be able to help.'

She didn't know if he could or not, but before she had time to think about it, she was talking. 'My children were kidnapped by the terrorists who organised this siege. They used me to tell them the plans for an assault on the building. I almost sent those SAS men to their deaths.'

'Jesus. What stopped you?'

'The kids escaped,' lied Arley, knowing she had to protect Tina's role.

'So, there was no informant?'

'No, there wasn't.'

'I'm sorry. If there's anything I can do.'

'You can cover my tracks, and give me some time. I need to go and see my children. I need to tell them about Howard.'

Cheney nodded. 'I understand. And I'll do what I can.'

Arley managed a tight smile. 'Thanks, John.'

'Good luck, Arley.'

They looked at each other for a long moment. Then she turned away and started walking, her pace quickening on the wet grass. And then, suddenly, she stopped, feeling a growing sense of dread. She turned round and watched John Cheney walk back towards the incident room. Which could mean only one thing. He already knew.

'HOW THE HELL did you know about Howard?'

They were just a few yards from the mobile office, the area around them almost deserted now that all the available officers had gone forward to deal with the hostages.

When he turned round, Cheney looked so shocked and confused that a part of her doubted the accusation she was throwing at him. 'I don't understand what you're talking about,' he said.

'I told you that I had to tell my children what had happened to him, and you said you understood. You didn't ask what happened to him. That means you must have known he was dead.'

'Arley, I think all this stress is getting to you.'

'It's not. You know something.'

All night she'd wondered how the terrorists had known so much about the police operation. It stood to reason that they had an inside man. Cheney wouldn't have been able to get hold of the SAS plans himself. Nor would he have wanted to when he could use Arley to do it for him, and therefore keep suspicion firmly away from himself.

'I ought to have you arrested right now,' said Cheney angrily. 'And if there was anyone around here, I would. But right now, someone's got to take responsibility for the operation now that it's been compromised. Just go and see your children while you still can.' He turned away from her.

'You'll get found out,' she called after him. 'When they arrest me, I'll tell them to investigate you. And they will. They'll want to know how the terrorists knew I was going to be a commander today.'

'Anyone could have guessed it if they'd known you were on duty.'

'You won't have been that good at covering your tracks, John,' she continued, ignoring his protests.

'Come on, Arley,' Cheney sighed, turning back round and walking up to her. 'This is ridiculous.'

At the last second, she saw him glance out of the corner of his eye to check that there was still no one around, and knew immediately what was going to happen next.

His grabbed her roughly by the throat, squeezing as hard as he could as he tried to drag her behind one of the empty squad cars. But Arley reacted fast, grabbing his crotch and twisting with all the strength she had. His grip loosened and they both fell over, Cheney on top. They struggled violently on the ground, Arley driven on by anger as she scratched and kicked him, but Cheney was a big man and his hands were still round her throat, applying more and more pressure, and Arley began to feel herself passing out.

'What's going on?'

It was Janine Sabbagh, standing over them.

Cheney immediately released his grip and Arley gasped for air.

'It's not what it looks like, Janine,' said Cheney, rolling off her. 'DAC Dale was resisting arrest.'

'It seemed like you were trying to strangle her,' said Janine.

'He was trying to kill me,' Arley gasped, getting shakily to her feet.

'Don't be stupid,' snapped Cheney. 'Get back inside, Janine. I'll handle this.'

'No, stay here, please.'

'Look, I don't know what's going on here,' Janine said uncertainly.

There was a shout from behind her and Chief Inspector Chris Matthews came running into view, accompanied by three CO19 officers. 'I need to see both your phones,' he said, addressing Arley and Cheney. 'In fact I need to see the phones of everyone here. We've just traced a mobile phone contacted a few minutes ago by one of the terrorists to this exact area.'

'It'll belong to him,' said Arley, recovering herself now.

'I don't know what you're talking about,' spat Cheney.

Matthews put out a hand, and one of the CO19s raised his MP5. 'I need to see the phones now.'

Arley saw Cheney tense just before he made a run for it. As he took off into the darkness away from Matthews and the others, she leaped forward and rugby-tackled him, sending him to the ground with a satisfying thud.

Matthews was on him like a whippet, followed by the CO19 officers, and Cheney's struggles ceased as his hands were cuffed behind his back.

'Do me a favour, ma'am,' said Matthews, turning to Arley, 'and tell me what's going on here.'

'This man's working with the terrorists,' she answered. 'I discovered his identity and he tried to kill me. Get him into the incident room and we'll organise a vehicle to take him down to Paddington Green for questioning.'

Matthews and the others hauled Cheney to his feet, and Cheney point-edly ignored Arley's gaze as he was led back to the incident room. Only Janine lingered. She looked at Arley strangely, as if there were still a lot of unanswered questions, which there were. Then she too turned away.

Arley pulled out her phone, putting it to her ear as if about to make a call, then she started walking briskly across Hyde Park towards the outer cordon, before finally breaking into a run. It was time to see her children.

23.17

Tina stood on the doorstep of Arley's mother's house, looking at the empty wet street. Lights were on in all of the houses, and Tina was pretty sure that behind every curtain people were watching events unfolding at the Stanhope.

On the way over here in the car, she'd heard the news that all the gunmen were supposedly now dead or captured and Special Forces were in the building, clearing it room by room, floor by floor, while bomb-disposal teams had dealt with a number of suspect devices. Tina knew that her actions had almost certainly saved the lives of SAS operatives, but it had been a close-run thing, and, given everything else she'd done, including killing a man, it might not be enough to save her from prison.

But Tina didn't regret what she'd done. A man had once told her that you should judge your actions by how much good they do; if the good outweighed the bad, then those actions were worth it. And tonight, the good she'd done far outweighed the bad.

She stubbed her cigarette out, and rubbed her hands against the cold. She could do with warming up but she had no desire to go back inside, where Arley's mum would only keep bombarding her with questions.

A black cab turned into the street, stopping directly outside. It was Arley, still in her DAC finery, although it was looking somewhat dishevelled.

After paying the cab driver, Arley walked up the steps to where Tina was standing. She took a deep breath, and threw her arms round Tina. 'Thank you so much for what you've done. I don't know how I can ever repay you.'

Tina pulled away gently. 'Save the hugs for the children, Arley. You haven't got much time.'

Arley took a step back. 'Have you called the police?'

'I have, but I haven't told them where to find us. I'm going to need to call them again now and tell them to come here.'

'Can't you leave it for a little while?'

Tina shook her head. 'I left a crime scene containing the body of the man I killed. I can't afford to avoid them. Neither can you right now.'

Arley gave an understanding nod. 'Then I guess I'd better hurry up.'

Tina stepped aside to let her past. She didn't envy Arley, having to tell her children that they'd lost their father. But they were good, brave kids and they would have family around them. And at least, unlike many of the victims of that day, they still had their lives in front of them.

Lighting another cigarette, she walked slowly up the street, waiting until she finished it before making the call. Then she walked back down to the house and sat down on the bottom of the steps to wait.

SIXTEEN DAYS LATER

I t was a mild afternoon for December, but raining steadily, and already very dark, as the mourners filed slowly out of the church. Beyond the wall stood a very wet-looking camera crew—the only sign that the funeral of Martin Dalston was any more than just a run-of-the-mill event. He was by no means the first victim of the terrorist attack on the Stanhope to be buried, but there was a rumour that he was in line for a posthumous bravery award, which probably explained the presence of the camera crew.

Scope had stood at the back of the church, keeping well out of sight, and consequently he was one of the first people out. He wore a beanie hat with a scarf pulled up over half his face, so that no one would recognise him, but unfortunately the walking stick he was having to use was a bit of a giveaway. During the week he'd spent in hospital the police and the staff had kept the media at bay, but since then everyone had been trying to get some sort of comment from him. Scope knew he was a big story—the guy who'd taken on the terrorists and saved the lives of dozens of hostages. They'd dug up and picked over his past. His eighteen-year military service, including two tours each in Iraq and Afghanistan, marriage to his childhood sweetheart, and fatherhood at nineteen, the affairs, the messy divorce and the tragedy of his daughter.

That was the part Scope hated about it the most. Dredging up what had happened to Mary Ann for the entertainment of the masses. He didn't want anyone knowing about her. He was surprised, though, that the media hadn't delved further into what had happened after her death. If they had, they'd have discovered an explosive story that would have satisfied even the most jaded reader. Maybe one day they would, and he'd be found out. But there was no point in him worrying about that now. He'd done what he had to do.

It was a two-hundred-yard walk back to where he'd parked his car, and his progress was slow. He'd looked for Abby and Ethan in the church but didn't think they'd been there, which was probably for the best, although he would've liked to have seen Ethan again one more time. He'd received a card from them when he was in hospital, thanking him for all he'd done. It had had a Florida postmark, and Ethan had enclosed a picture he'd drawn of Scope as an action man with immense biceps, an ill-fitting suit and a very big gun. Scope had put it on the table by his hospital bed, and he had it now, packed up among his belongings.

As he reached the car and felt in his pocket for the keys, someone tapped him on the shoulder. He turned round and saw that it was the blonde manager from the hotel, whose name, he'd found out, was Elena Serenko.

'Hello,' she said, with a shy smile. 'I thought I saw you inside the church.'

'I was trying to keep a low profile. I guess it didn't work.'

'The cane doesn't help. How are your injuries?'

'I'm on the mend. I was very lucky. I got hit twice and no major internal damage, but I'm going to be walking with this for a while yet.'

'I wanted to say thank you again for what you did for us in the hotel.'

'Thank you too. You helped save my life.'

There was an awkward silence, and Scope had the idea that she wanted to say something else.

'Are you going back to the wake?' she asked.

'No. I came only to pay my respects. He was a good man.'

'Do you know I knew him for only a few hours but I feel like I found out so much about him. Does that make sense?'

'You can find out a lot about someone in that time. Especially in difficult circumstances.'

There was another awkward silence, this one longer. Scope was about to say something when Elena started speaking again. 'We had a guest in one of the suites at the Stanhope called Mr Miller. He'd been there for a while, and I have to admit, I didn't like him very much. On the day of the terrorist attack, he was killed, along with his two bodyguards. But the thing is, the terrorists didn't kill them. I know that because I heard them talking about it.' She frowned. 'I don't know how to say this,' she continued, looking embarrassed again, 'but did you know anything about him?'

For a moment, Scope wanted to tell her everything. But he knew it would put Elena in a terrible position. He smiled. 'I'm sorry, I can't help you with that one. I don't know how I'd have fitted it in.' He looked at her steadily, and he could tell she knew he was lying. 'Have you told the police about it?'

She looked down. 'No. The police have plenty to keep them busy as it is, and anyway, I'm off to Australia with my fiancé very soon.' She smiled, and looked him in the eye. 'We're about to start a new life.'

He smiled back. 'Good luck. If I had my time again, I think I'd do the same thing.'

This time there were no awkward pauses. She thanked him almost formally, and said goodbye.

Scope watched her go, feeling very lonely. He thought of Mary Ann and the trail of revenge that had led to that fateful day at the Stanhope Hotel.

When she'd died of an overdose of unusually pure heroin aged barely eighteen, the news had devastated him. His ex-wife had died six months later in a car accident, hitting a tree on a country road late at night. Scope had often wondered whether it was suicide, and concluded that it probably had been. He could easily have gone the same way too, almost did on more than one occasion when the pain and the loneliness had got too much.

But slowly he'd pulled himself together, and as he'd done so, he'd begun to feel a new emotion. Anger. He realised, almost with surprise, that he wanted to make those who'd contributed to Mary Ann's death pay, and he'd set about planning how to make this happen.

It was two years from the moment he'd put a bullet in the man who'd sold the fatal dose to when he'd finally got to the individual at the top of the pile.

Frank Miller was running his business from a suite in the Stanhope, ever since a messy divorce of his own. Miller didn't get his hands dirty. A middle-aged businessman, he was a multimillionaire with interests in construction, retail and property. He was also one of the biggest importers of heroin into the UK, with contacts in Turkey and Afghanistan.

Scope had spent months planning that particular killing, and it had all gone incredibly smoothly. Neither Miller nor his bodyguards had been expecting a thing, and they'd died within seconds of each other. Even so, Scope had still expected to get caught for this particular crime. His luck had held well for a long time, but three killings in a big London hotel was always going to be a risk too far. And yet, because of everything else that had happened in the Stanhope that day, their deaths were being treated as directly connected to the terrorist attack.

So now, three years after her death, Mary Ann could finally rest in peace.

He took a last look up and down the road, shivering against the cold, wondering whether he would ever be brought to book for what he'd done. In the end, it was out of his hands. He slowly got back into his car, threw his stick on the seat and, with a deep breath, drove away from the church, and the mourners, and the past.

simon kernick

Profile

Born:
Slough, 1966.
Education:
Read Humanities at
Brighton Polytechnic.
Jobs:
Labourer in a road-building
gang, barman, stockroom
assistant, fruit picker,
Christmas Tree uprooter
(his second favourite job

of all time after writing),
computer software
salesman.
Books:
The Business of Dying,
The Murder Exchange,
The Crime Trade, A Good
Day to Die, Relentless,
Severed, Deadline, Target,
The Last 10 Seconds,
The Payback.

Did you always want to write?

Yes. Particularly crime books—so I wrote two in my spare time: one in 1995–6, the other in 1998. Sadly, neither was met with much of a welcome (in fact I think every agent in the country rejected number two: a huge gangster tome entitled *Fine Night for a Killing*). But I persevered, embarking finally on *The Business of Dying*, the story of a London detective who moonlights as a hitman, which was finally completed in early 2001. After another couple of rejections, I managed to get an agent, and in September of that year, much to my amazement, the book was sold to a publisher.

Siege is your eleventh published novel. Do you find it gets easier or harder to write each new book?

One of the problems I always have when I'm starting out on a new story is confidence. I'm terrified that what I'm producing isn't good, or pacy enough. Or is worse than the book before. Often, when I'm at my desk plugging away, I'll stop what I'm doing, stare at the screen and think: This isn't going to work, I'm going to have to come up with a new idea, followed by a general panic which lasts anything from a minute to a few hours. The key is to ignore the fear and keep going.

What was your inspiration for Siege?

Like everyone else, I was shocked by the brutality of the Mumbai attacks of November 2008, and the utter ruthlessness of the men who took over the hotels, indiscriminately slaughtering the guests. At the time, though, it didn't make me want to write a book about a hotel siege. However, in the summer of 2010 I was staying in a big old hotel in Taba Heights, Egypt, very close to the Israeli border, and the idea for *Siege* hit me. There was a large raised sundeck twenty feet above the pool from where I had a panoramic view of all the hotel grounds and the Red Sea beyond, and it occurred to me that if a group of terrorists were to storm through the hotel entrance, where two bored and not very efficient-looking security staff stood guard, we'd all be caught like rats in a trap, since there was no way out of the hotel except through the front. Almost immediately after that, I had a vision of a man, possibly a criminal, who was already inside the hotel and up to no good when the terrorists struck—someone who'd be prepared and able to fight back. I knew then I had a story.

How concerned were you about fictionalising terror on the streets of London?

To be honest, I thought long and hard before putting pen to paper. I think most writers are nervous about creating any story with a strong terrorist connection because of the possibility of being overtaken by real events. I wanted to set the book in London, using a fictionalised West End hotel, but I was mindful of the fact that the UK's been on heightened alert for most of the past decade, and that only a year ago intelligence came out of Pakistan warning of a plot to carry out a Mumbai-style attack in London. In the end, though, I decided it was worth taking the risk.

How difficult a book was *Siege* to plot?

I was keenly aware that a 'siege' scenario isn't necessarily a good format for a book, because after the big bang opening there's often plenty of time in the middle when very little happens, as both hostage-takers and the police get down to negotiations. That was why I added the Arley Dale subplot. After months of planning, I'd created this huge, forty-page, chapter-by-chapter synopsis which told the story from start to finish. But almost as soon as I started writing I ran into complications. Because of the sheer number of characters, the logistics of the plot—choreographing where people were so that they ended up in the right places after the climactic scenes—became a bit of a nightmare. Also, trying to make the police response realistic was a challenge, helped by a talk with a senior officer in Counter Terrorism Command and other research.

So your characters changed as you wrote?

Yes, changes were made constantly. In one draft, Abby and Ethan were captured, and Scope (who was originally an American hitman) gave himself up to the terrorists so that they could be freed. He was then tortured for several hours before making an escape. I later changed this because it seemed implausible that the terrorists would keep Scope alive. Elena, too, nearly didn't make it to the end. She was originally executed by Cat about halfway through, but I liked her too much, so she came back. That's one of the fun things about being a writer—being able to commute people's death sentences!

Women and
Children First

Gill Paul

The magnificent *Titanic* left Southampton on her maiden voyage on April 10, 1912. Just five days later, after hitting an iceberg, she sank to the bottom of the Atlantic Ocean.

Gill Paul's factually accurate, vivid novel brings to life imaginary characters such as Reg Parton, a handsome young steward; Annie McGeown, an Irish mother of four; Juliette Mason-Parker, a debutante with a shameful secret; and Mr Grayling, a mysterious American millionaire. As the *Titanic* sinks all must fight for their lives, but for the survivors the struggle is just beginning . . .

Prologue

Reg's hands were shaking so hard he couldn't hold the newspaper still enough to read. He sat on his bunk and smoothed the pages open on the shabby grey blanket. Lists of names in tiny type covered their surface, organised into uneven columns of surnames, forenames, the class in which each person had travelled and, finally, their country of origin.

Straight away he saw an error: Luigi Gatti was listed as Spanish rather than Italian. How could he trust this list if they could make such a simple mistake? Was anything in it reliable?

His finger moved down the page. There was Colonel Astor. All that money couldn't buy him a place on the other, shorter list: the list of survivors. There was Bill, who had slept in the next bunk to his, and Ethel from the pantry, the one they called Fat Ethel. If only they'd been kinder . . .

A couple of columns across, his heart began pounding hard. It was a most peculiar feeling to see yourself listed as dead. He looked away and refocused his eyes just outside the window where he could see unfurling buds on the topmost branches of a linden tree. For a few minutes he breathed quietly, until he felt able to look at the newspaper again.

The first name that appeared before his eyes now was 'Grayling, Margaret, 1st class, American'. His eyes filled with tears for the generous woman who had been his favourite passenger as into his head came the peculiar scene he had witnessed between her husband and a striking young girl on the boat deck. Everything in his mind was now divided into 'before' and 'after', and that had been before: exactly forty-eight hours before the unthinkable happened.

Chapter One

It was one in the morning and first-class victualling steward Reg Parton should have been asleep in his bunk, but a restlessness had taken him to the ship's galley where he knew Mr Joughin, the chief baker, would be pulling steaming trays of bread out of the ovens. Joughin was a good sort and always ready to slip him a fresh roll or two.

The ship was almost twelve hours out of Queenstown, on the southern tip of Ireland, and gliding her way across the Atlantic. The *Titanic* was a beautiful beast, with everything brand new and sparkling. It was nice being on a maiden voyage—there was the sense of every surface being untouched and pristine, and this ship was the most magnificent he'd ever seen. Woodwork gleamed, chandeliers shot pinpricks of light around the vast salons, and every surface was clad in gilt, mosaic or milky mother-of-pearl.

Reg had been on board for two days and he'd spent all his off-duty time exploring. There were ten separate decks, each almost 300 yards long. Every deck had a different layout of interminable corridors with faceless doors and he'd got lost more times than he could count. It would take months to get to know this ship properly.

Second Officer Lightoller put his head round the door of the galley. 'Tea for the bridge, Mr Joughin,' he said, without so much as a glance at Reg.

'Right you are, sir.'

Lightoller disappeared and Mr Joughin began to set a tea tray. 'Where's that bloody Fred when you need him?' the cook said. 'He went for a fag half an hour ago and hasn't come back. Who's going to take this tray?'

'I'll do it!' Reg nearly jumped with excitement. 'Please let me.' He was dying to see the bridge with all its gleaming, state-of-the-art equipment. Maybe Captain Smith would even be there.

'It's not your place,' Joughin grumbled. 'It should be Fred.'

'But he's not here. They won't notice who brings their tea. Let me do it.'

'Go on with you, then.'

Reg took the elevator up to the boat deck and walked to the short flight of steps that led up to the bridge. The moon was waning, the night was so black there was no dividing line between sea and sky, and the few stars were distant dots in some other galaxy. Lights had been turned to a dim glow as the 1,300 passengers slept below.

When Reg entered the bridge, he was disappointed to see that it wasn't the captain on duty but another officer—one he didn't recognise—who was standing alone by the wheel gazing out at the ocean ahead. If it had been Captain Smith, he could have asked him questions about all the buttons and levers and dials. He'd sailed under the captain two years earlier, had been his personal dining steward on the voyage, and he'd found the grizzly bearded old man to be a genial, fatherly sort who had encouraged Reg's curiosity.

'Put the tray down there,' said the officer, pointing vaguely.

'Thank you, sir,' Reg said, before turning to leave.

Reg stopped just outside the bridge, gazing down the length of the vessel, past the huge funnels and towards the stern. It was a floating hotel, like the Ritz at sea. Of course, he'd never been to the Ritz Hotel, but he'd read all about it in the papers when it had opened six years earlier. One day he would like to visit.

A movement caught his eye and he turned to see a girl standing behind one of the lifeboats, right next to the railing. Her back was to him but he could see that she was very slim, with copper hair secured by a diamond clasp, and wearing a shimmery white dress. She was holding something bulky and brown and, if he wasn't mistaken, furry. Could it be an animal, perhaps a pet dog? It seemed rather large for that.

She turned and Reg shrank back, not wanting to be caught, but she didn't once glance up towards the bridge. She was gazing beyond the lifeboat towards the entrance to the Grand Staircase, looking agitated. Suddenly, she turned back towards the ocean, lifted her brown bundle and tossed it right over the railing. Reg jumped in horror and opened his mouth to yell, the thought that it might be a dog foremost in his mind but, as it flapped in the air, he saw that it was a coat. A fur coat. Why would anyone do that? It was a gesture of such extravagant abandon that he was struck dumb.

The girl glanced over her shoulder, presumably to check whether anyone had witnessed her bizarre behaviour. In the lamplight, her face looked exquisite, flawless, though her robe plunged at the front in the most revealing manner Reg had ever seen on an upper-class lady. Yet, there was no doubt that she was upper class. Everything about her seemed expensive.

But what was she up to? She leaned against the railing and bent over to look at the ocean seventy-five feet below. Reg took a step towards her. Was she planning to jump? Or just trying to see where her coat had landed?

As he stood there, Reg noticed the figure of a man coming up the Grand Staircase and emerging onto the deck. The man walked past a lamp and Reg saw that it was Mr Grayling, an American whose table he waited on in the first-class dining saloon. He strode directly towards the girl. As she saw him approach, she gave a little cry, and threw herself into his arms.

He held her close for a while then he leaned back to cup her chin in his hands. He said something to her, but Reg could only catch the word 'Sorry' before he enveloped her in his arms and kissed her full on the mouth.

An awful fact nagged at Reg's brain as he stood watching. Mr Grayling was married to a woman Reg knew and liked, and who was with him on this trip. He'd waited on Mrs Grayling on a Mediterranean cruise last year, when she'd been travelling with a woman friend, and they'd had several friendly conversations. Reg had been touched when she had remembered him: she was nicer than any other passenger in first class, where familiarity with the staff was frowned upon. How could Mr Grayling betray her? What kind of a man would bring his mistress onto the same ship as his wife?

The lovers slipped behind the lifeboat, still caught up in their embrace, and Reg decided he had best get a move on before he was spotted. He knew to his cost that if a first-class passenger made a complaint against a steward it would always be believed, no matter how unjust the circumstances. On his last voyage, an elderly gentleman had lost a silver cigar case and accused Reg of stealing it. Reg's belongings had been searched and, of course, it wasn't found. It finally turned up under a table in the smoking room, but the incident had already been recorded in his particulars at the White Star Line office and nothing would make them remove it.

Reg walked down the steps with a heavy footfall, so no one could accuse him of sneaking around. When he reached the Grand Staircase, he didn't look back but hurried down. He caught the elevator to D Deck, then descended a further flight of stairs to Scotland Road, a corridor stretching half the length of the ship, where he had a berth in a dormitory with twenty-seven other saloon stewards. It was one thirty, and he had precisely four hours to sleep before it was time to get up and prepare for breakfast service.

LADY JULIETTE MASON-PARKER knelt on the bathroom floor, acid scorching her throat and the taste of vomit in her mouth. The floor was tiled with a black and white diagonal diamond-within-diamond motif. Everything on the *Titanic* seemed meticulously designed; even the bathroom fittings were real marble. It seemed remarkable to her that the ship could stay afloat with the weight of all its fixtures and fittings: the library full of books, the swimming pool, the enormous pieces of mahogany furniture. It was much more luxurious than their draughty family pile in Gloucestershire.

In the next room, her mother slept soundly, occasionally snuffling and murmuring in her sleep. The last thing Juliette wanted was for her to wake and start fussing. If ever there was a woman who enjoyed fussing, it was Lady Mason-Parker. She had been irritating Juliette beyond measure on this voyage. If it wasn't her endless advice on which hat to wear for breakfast, and which gown was suitable for walking on the promenade, then it was her lectures on how to ensnare a husband with methods that Juliette considered had gone out with Jane Austen. So far mother and daughter hadn't argued outright, but tetchy barbs had been fired back and forth.

Juliette rose tentatively, holding on to the basin, and regarded herself in the mirror. Her eyes had bruised circles underneath and her skin without make-up had a faint greenish tinge. She would never get a husband looking like this; certainly not the rich American one her mother had in mind. And there was the added complication that it had to be done within a couple of months, from first meeting to marriage ceremony. The problem was that Juliette was pregnant. It was only eight weeks since the one and only time she'd had intercourse, but the signs were unmistakable.

When she first caught her daughter throwing up and prised the truth out of her, Lady Mason-Parker had swung into action like a military commander. 'We need to find you a husband straight away. English men dither so, but a rich American would be ideal. They would be over the moon to get themselves a real English Lady for a wife, and they tend to be more impulsive than Englishmen when they fall in love.'

Juliette was horrified. 'Mother, you can't be serious! I'm not interested in tricking some poor Yankee into holy matrimony. It's hideously immoral.'

'What you did to get yourself into this condition was immoral. Getting married is the way to fix it, and your husband will be delighted to have a child so soon. It will prove you're good breeding stock.'

'I'm not a farm animal! And I refuse to cooperate with your schemes.'

Juliette's protests were in vain, however. Her mother had booked them a passage on the *Titanic*'s maiden voyage, calculating that the ship would be overflowing with eligible American millionaires. Since they had sailed, she had occupied herself making enquiries of crusty dowagers and arranging introductions to crass Americans who sold automobile components or garden fencing. Juliette had no choice but to converse with the men in question, but at some stage she would find a way to put them off. Mentioning her support for women's suffrage seemed a foolproof method. And, quite apart from the dishonesty of tricking someone into marriage, Juliette didn't want to be legally entwined with an American millionaire. She liked Gloucestershire and her horses and her friends, and had a strong suspicion she wouldn't like living in America. If only this whole unfortunate pregnancy could be over as quickly as possible then life could go back to normal.

She favoured Plan B, which was that, in the event her mother failed to entice some rich gent to propose to her during the crossing, they would rent a small house in upstate New York, sit out the remainder of the pregnancy, then have the baby adopted. Juliette could return to England with no one any the wiser. Even her own father and brother had no idea about her pregnancy; they thought she and her mother were simply visiting some distant American cousins. And as for the baby's father, he would never find out.

Charles Wood was their local member of parliament, and quite high up in the Liberal party. Juliette had been introduced to him because of her charity fundraising work, and one weekend he had invited her to a house party on his estate. It was there that Juliette had allowed Charles to come to her bedroom. She had been flattered by his interest in her and stupidly developed a crush on a married man without a thought for the consequences.

There had been no point in telling Charles. What could he have done? In the unlikely event he offered to divorce his wife and marry her, he would have destroyed his parliamentary career: in 1912, no one would countenance a divorced MP. Besides, her mother had much grander plans for her eldest daughter. either Juliette must marry money or she must marry landed gentry, as her younger brother would inherit the Mason-Parker estate. She had been born to a titled family and must uphold the standards set by her own upbringing, which meant no commoner was good enough unless he happened to be sufficiently wealthy to make such criteria insignificant.

Juliette dabbed a little toothpowder onto her brush and scrubbed her teeth, then rinsed. She wouldn't let herself think about the creature growing in her belly because she knew it would be the undoing of her. Her baby would go to decent people and have a happy life and one day, when Juliette was married to a man she loved, she would have children of her own.

She crept back into bed and pulled the satin coverlet up to her chin. How she wished she could forward time to when they would be on the return voyage to Southampton, footloose and unencumbered.

ANNIE MCGEOWN sat on the edge of a bunk and watched her four children breathing. They were so peaceful now, like little angels. Shame it hadn't been that way earlier. They'd only been on the ship for twelve hours since boarding at Queenstown, but the eldest boys were running riot, feeling cooped up in the limited space. Back home she could kick them out into the fields between meals, but here there was just the third-class outdoor deck and the long corridors, where they got told off for making a racket.

Oh, but they were lucky, though. Look at this place! They had a cabin of their own with real sprung mattresses on the bunks. There was a tiny port-hole and even a washbasin crammed in between the beds. And the food! It was the best she'd eaten in her life, no question. She'd felt so grand, sitting with her brood in the restaurant, waiters serving them with three courses at dinner. Any more than a week of eating like that and she'd be the size of a house when she got to America and met up with Seamus again.

It was a year and a half since she'd seen her husband, and even that was only for a month, when he'd managed to wangle a cheap passage and come back to Cork for a visit. He'd never met his youngest and didn't know any of the children well, because he'd been out in New York for five years, working on the railways and saving enough money to afford a good home there. And now at last he was ready for them to be reunited. He'd leased a three-room apartment in a place called Kingsbridge, a suburb of New York where there were lots of other Irish. In his last letter, he'd sent the money for their tickets: thirty-five pounds and five shillings, a vast sum. But in America, Seamus earned two pounds a week: Annie didn't even know anyone who got two pounds a *month* in Ireland!

It was a new life for all of them. Their children would better themselves and get good jobs one day. The only bitter-sweet edge was the sadness Annie felt for the relatives she'd left behind: her elderly mam, her brothers and sisters and cousins. Would she ever see them again?

Look on the bright side, Annie, she urged herself. *Here you are on the most luxurious ship in the world and in five days you'll be with yer man again.* She felt excited at the thought. Married thirteen years and she still felt as much passion for him as the day they were wed.

The people in third class were friendly as well. Earlier that evening, after dinner, there had been a quick knock on the door of her cabin. She'd opened it to find three women about her age grouped outside.

'I'm Eileen Dooley,' one said. 'This is Kathleen and Mary. We noticed you earlier with your brood. Aw, will you look at them all peaceful now, God bless them.' The other women poked their heads round the cabin door for a peek. 'Anyway, we're going for a cup of tea while our menfolk are in the smoking room, and we thought you might want to come along, too.'

'That's neighbourly of you, but I'm worried about leaving the little ones in a strange place,' she said. 'What if they wake up?'

'Your eldest looks old enough to cope. What age is he?'

'Finbarr's ten.'

'Sure and they'll be fine. Turn the key in the door so they can't run off and get up to shenanigans.'

Annie hesitated, then said, 'Aw, they're all out for the count here, so I'll just come for a quick brew.'

They'd led her to the third-class general room, where there were polished tables and chairs, teak wall panels and white ceramic fittings.

'Aren't you the brave wan travelling on your own with the children like that?' Eileen told Annie. 'We're a big group. Fourteen of us, all from Mayo, so we're company for each other. You'll have to sit with us for your meals or those children will drive you to drink by the time we reach America.'

'I'd love to,' Annie said. She'd been feeling a bit shy on the ship, not sure about the correct etiquette. Which bits of the ship were they allowed to wander in and which were off limits? Now there were some people she could ask, who said they had crossed on these ships before and could tell her what to do. They seemed a lovely bunch.

When she got back to her cabin, the children were still sound asleep. She climbed into bed, shifting the baby, little Ciaran, over beside the wall so he couldn't fall out. Strange to think that on the other side of that wall were thousands and thousands of miles of ocean, and up above them only stars. She said her prayers in her head, before dropping off to sleep.

REG LAY AWAKE mulling over what he'd seen on the boat deck. Of course, he knew that rich men had affairs. He'd sometimes see them sneaking shoeless out of the wrong cabins when he passed in the early morning on his way to the dining saloon. He knew from gossiping with the other lads in the mess that Mr Guggenheim had his mistress on board with him, a young French singer called Madame Aubart, while his wife was back home in New York. These things happened.

Was that the case with Mr Grayling and the girl? He had a large fortune made in South American mining. Did he buy her expensive gifts in return for her favours? Somehow it didn't fit with the scene Reg had witnessed. The girl had an air about her, as if she had grown up with wealth. And if it wasn't about money, why would a stunning girl like her be having an affair with a man who must be more than twice her age? Reg guessed she wasn't any older than himself, and he was twenty-one. It certainly couldn't have been physical attraction because Mr Grayling wasn't a looker. He was a round-faced gent with sleek greying hair and a waxed moustache, who gave the impression of a sea-lion when first you met him. It disturbed Reg to visualise him pressed against the girl's slender frame.

It wasn't just the physical side that disturbed him, but also his loyalty to Mrs Grayling. She had been friendly to Reg from the first day of her cruise the previous year. One afternoon, she had eaten lunch alone because her friend felt poorly and, afterwards, while Reg was clearing the plates, they had got into conversation.

'Where's home for you, Reg?' she had asked.

'Southampton, ma'am.'

'Do you live with your family? Or your wife?'

'I live with my mum and three younger brothers. I've got a girlfriend, Florence, but we're not married.'

'And do you love her? My goodness, listen to me,' Mrs Grayling laughed. 'Tell me to mind my own business if you don't want to answer.'

'No, it's fine.' For some reason, Reg didn't mind the directness of her questioning, although he never talked to anyone else in this way. 'I do love her, but I just don't know if I'm ready for marriage and I think that's what she wants. Her friend Lizzie got engaged recently and I could tell by the way Florence looked at me when she told me about it that she would like me to propose.'

'Why don't you feel ready?'

Reg considered. 'Before I get married and have kids I want to be confident that I'll have enough money to be able to put food on the table for them. Working on ships, you only get a contract for each voyage and you can never be sure you'll ever be hired again. That worries me.'

There was more. Reg dreamed of bettering himself and being able to afford some of the luxuries his wealthy passengers enjoyed.

'I want to get my own car one day,' he'd told Florence. 'Have you ever seen a picture of a Lozier? A bargain at only seven and a half thousand pounds!'

'You admire the rich more than I do,' Florence mused. 'You're more impressed by them.'

He suspected it was true. Not the ones who'd simply inherited their wealth, but the self-made millionaires from America; the ones who had started car dealerships and hotels and property empires. He wished he could make enough money to have a better life, but there was nothing he could do besides wait on table. So they carried on as they were.

'Marriage is a tricky thing,' Mrs Grayling had told him. 'It's hard work and sometimes it feels as though you are the only one trying.' Her grey-blue eyes had depths of sadness in them. 'But it sounds as though you had better not let that girl slip away. You should hang on to her. Take my advice.'

A year after that exchange, Reg was overjoyed when he spotted Mrs Grayling's name on the passenger list. He asked the chief steward, Mr Latimer, if he could wait on her table. As soon as she had walked in to dinner on the first evening and seen him holding her chair for her, she had exclaimed, 'Reg! How wonderful you're here. Tell me, how is the lovely Florence?'

He had been touched to the core that such a grand lady would remember anything about his life. 'She's fine, thank you, ma'am,' he said.

'And are you married yet?'

'Not yet,' he said with a grin.

'But still together?'

Reg nodded.

'Good. I'm delighted to see you again.'

Now, two nights after that, Reg had seen Mrs Grayling's husband with the woman on the boat deck and the knowledge weighed heavily on him. Should he tell Mrs Grayling? Or do something about it himself? But what?

THE NEXT MORNING, at breakfast, Reg couldn't meet Mrs Grayling's eye, scared that something in his countenance might give away what he had seen on the boat deck. The situation was compounded when he overheard Mr Grayling being irascible with his wife. He seemed a bad-tempered sort, forever complaining about something: his food wasn't hot enough, or the people at the next table were making too much noise.

'Will you try out the gymnasium today, George?' she asked. 'You could have a Turkish bath afterwards. It's supposed to have glorious mosaics.'

'Have you taken leave of your senses? When have you ever known me go to a gymnasium or a Turkish bath?' Mr Grayling's tone was impatient, and Reg couldn't help noticing the hurt look on Mrs Grayling's face.

'I plan to stroll along the promenade this morning, then perhaps I shall write some postcards,' she told her husband. 'How about you, dear?'

'I haven't made up my mind but when I do, I'll be sure to inform you.'

His tone was heavy with sarcasm and Reg flinched. Mr Grayling seemed to be in a particularly foul mood this morning, which was rum considering that, from what Reg had seen, he was having his cake and eating it.

He wasn't the only grumpy one that morning. At one of Reg's tables there was a young Canadian couple, Mr and Mrs Howson: the wife was a silly, giggling girl who kept making eyes at Reg right under her husband's irritated nose. Maybe she was trying to show hubbie that she was attractive to other men, but it put Reg in a very awkward situation. He tried to be strictly formal and avoid any eye contact, but it was embarrassing, and he moved away from their table as quickly as he could.

As he worked, he kept watch for the girl from the boat deck to arrive. He was curious to find out whether she was travelling with a husband or, if she was unmarried, who was chaperoning her. First class was full of beautiful women. Even at breakfast, they wore fancy gowns in expensive velvets and silks with lace trimmings, and they all had hats with feathers and bows pinned to their heads. It was a regular fashion parade.

Breakfast service ended at 10.30 a.m. There had been no sign of the girl from the boat deck. Reg cleared the plates from his tables, then caught his friend John's eye and motioned with two fingers to his lips that he would meet him down in the stewards' mess for a fag.

'You'll never guess what I saw last night!' Reg told John after they'd both exhaled the first drag. 'One of my passengers, Mr Grayling, fooling around on the boat deck with a girl less than half his age, while his wife is in their suite just a couple of decks below.'

John was unsurprised. 'Goes on all the time. These people have different rules to you and me. It's not just the men, either. The women do it as well.'

'Get away with you.' Reg frowned.

'Colonel Astor's first wife had an affair and the whole of New York knew about it. They say his daughter isn't really his. Now he's got divorced and married again and they're all pointing the finger and saying he shouldn't have remarried, yet his wife was the one that started it.'

'They sit in your section, don't they? She's eighteen, I heard, and he's nearly fifty. I don't know why a girl would want to do that.'

John rolled his eyes comically. 'Hundred million dollars in the bank? I'd marry him for that!'

'I don't think you're his type, somehow.' John would never win any beauty contests, but he was the nicest chap you could ever hope to meet. They'd been friends since Reg's first voyage, and it was like having a brother on board.

Reg had hoped John would have some advice for him regarding Mr Grayling's infidelity and, in particular, if there was anything he should do about it. 'You should have seen this girl who was with him on the boat deck,' he reiterated. 'She was the bee's knees. It just didn't make sense, somehow.'

AFTER BREAKFAST, Margaret Grayling found a deckchair on the promenade and sat staring out at the ocean with a huge lump in her throat, her eyes watering in the salt breeze. George, her husband, had been more than usually difficult during this voyage. He'd always been a cold man but he would never have spoken discourteously to her in front of the servants at home, and yet he was prepared to do so in front of a steward on the *Titanic*.

In private, George had renewed his demands that she should divorce him, but the idea was anathema to her. It was against every religious principle she held dear. They had been married in the sight of God and the minister had clearly said, 'What God hath joined together, let no man cast asunder.' How could she go against God's commandment?

George didn't share her religious beliefs and seemed to think she was merely worried about what society might say. Divorce would cause a scandal, and there was no question that both parties were stigmatised by it, even when one was blameless. But Margaret had never given much weight to others' opinions and had more or less stopped appearing in society seven years earlier, after great tragedy had rent her life apart.

Theirs had never been a passionate marriage, but it had produced a daughter, a gentle, artistic girl called Alice, who was the sun around which they both revolved and the cement that kept their marriage civil and sometimes even happy throughout the seventeen years of her life. When Alice died of scarlet fever in February 1905, everything had collapsed inwards.

In the cruellest of all the cruel things George had ever hurled at her, he had screamed that she had been responsible for killing their daughter, and from that fatal wound their marriage had never recovered.

Rationally, Margaret knew it was simply not true. She and Alice had visited friends of hers and, two days after the visit, it transpired that one of the friends had succumbed to scarlet fever, despite showing no signs of it when they were there. And then Alice had developed a sore throat and pink cheeks and a sand-papery rash on her chest and neck. Her friend recovered within a week but Alice's condition had continued to deteriorate. She struggled for breath and was rarely fully conscious during her last days. George had paid for the advice of every specialist in New York and beyond, but to no avail.

A solitary tear trickled down Margaret's cheek. Grief like that never left you. It abated sometimes, just for a while, then returned to thump you in the gut. It was something she would always live with. But George had turned all his grief into anger directed towards his wife.

She'd hoped this trip to Europe would achieve some kind of rapprochement. She'd begged him to bring her along, hoping to re-ignite some companionship at least, but to no avail. Nothing had been gained by the trip.

Should she go against God's will and give George his divorce so that each had a chance of happiness in the future? The more she observed other marriages, the more she believed that women seemed most content when they lived on their own.

AT LUNCHEON, first-class passengers could choose from a set menu with soup, fish, chicken, eggs or beef; they could have items from the grill, such as mutton chops or sirloin steak, or they could select from a buffet with salad, cold cuts and seafood dishes, such as salmon mayonnaise or potted shrimp.

Most of the ladies had changed since breakfast. First thing in the morning they wore skirts and blouses but for lunch they wore suits with long jackets, topped with the obligatory hat. Reg thought it was silly wearing a hat to a meal because they kept having to flick back long floaty feathers and ribbons.

The Howsons sat down at their table and Reg spread the napkin on Mrs Howson's lap in a swift fluttering motion, without touching her or encroaching on her line of sight, just as he'd been taught. Straight away, she began bothering him with her dozens of inane questions.

'Have you ever been skiing, Reg? You'd love it. You should visit Calgary some time and we'll take you out on the slopes.'

'Thank you, ma'am, but my work keeps me too busy.'

'You must play some sports. What do you play, Reg?'

'I like a bit of football when I'm back home.'

'What in God's name is football?'

'It's a game with two teams where you kick a ball into a goal, ma'am.'

The husband sat scowling throughout their exchange; then as soon as Reg left the table, he heard the hiss of their argument: 'It's vulgar to talk to the staff like that. You shouldn't be overfamiliar. Didn't your mother teach you anything?'

The tension grew as they ate, and Reg tried to keep clear of them. When he came to collect their plates, Mrs Howson's face was pink with fury. 'My husband thinks I shouldn't fraternise with you, Reg. What do you think?'

'Oh, shut up,' her husband snapped. 'Leave the poor boy alone.'

Reg was balancing their plates and a serving dish on one arm as he scooped a stray piece of cauliflower from the tablecloth. Mrs Howson turned and yanked the pocket of his jacket just at a moment when he was twisted at an awkward angle, leaning sideways towards the table.

'I'll talk to him if I feel like it,' he heard her saying as he struggled to regain his balance, but it was no use. He managed to twirl at the last moment so that the dishes fell to the floor behind her, rather than into her lap, but the dining salon fell silent at the resounding crash of breaking crockery.

Instantly, Reg sprang into action, crouching down and picking up the jagged pieces. John appeared by his side with a dustpan and brush and between them they had the floor spotless again in less than a minute. But the chief steward, Latimer, was watching and as Reg scurried past towards the galley, he said in a cold voice, 'Wait behind after service.'

Reg was glad to see that the Howsons had left when he emerged from the galley, but Mrs Grayling was sitting at their table. Reg approached to ask if he could fetch anything for her.

'I saw what happened with those plates,' she told him. 'It wasn't your fault. Will you get into trouble?'

'Please don't worry on my behalf, ma'am.'

'I could explain to the chief steward what I saw, if that would help.'

'Thank you,' Reg said. 'But I simply lost my balance. I'm sorry if the noise disturbed you.'

She looked at him with her kind eyes. 'They'll make you pay for the breakages, won't they? Please will you at least let me give you the money?'

'We're not supposed to accept money from passengers, but thank you very much for the offer.' For a moment, Reg felt like crying under her maternal gaze. She was much nicer than his own mum, who'd never had any time for him: she couldn't wait to send him out to work so he could contribute to the household coffers, which seemed to be his only value to her.

'Nonsense. Plenty of the other staff members accept tips, and you will accept one from me. I insist. I'll slip it to you quietly some time before we reach New York, but for now I don't want to hear any more about it.' She stood up to bring an end to the conversation. 'I'll see you at dinner.'

'Thank you, ma'am.' Reg held her chair for her, wrestling with a powerful wave of embarrassment mixed with gratitude.

He would accept the money, he decided, after Old Latimer told him that the three porcelain plates he had broken cost two and six each. Reg's wages were only two shillings and four-pence per day, so that breakage would cost him more than three days' wages.

'Worse than that,' he told John later, 'it's going on my report. I explained what happened but he wasn't having it. It's one law for them and another for us, and I'm fed up to the back teeth with it.'

'It's just the way it is. No point fighting the system.'

'It's alright for you with your squeaky-clean record. I'm trying to better myself and all I get are setbacks.'

'It'll be fine so long as you keep your nose clean from now on. They won't do anything about this one misdemeanour.' His face broke into a grin. 'Anyway, I wish I had your problems with all the lasses fancying me,' he said. 'You've always got lasses chasing after you. It must be your dark, brooding looks.'

'What a load of rot!' Reg punched his arm. That kind of attention was discomfiting. He hated it. Florence didn't flirt with other men. He'd known as soon as he met her that she was different; not at all like these first-class ladies with their airs and graces, who flirted with him as though he was their plaything. They were dangerous, women like Mrs Howson and the girl on the boat deck. If you knew what was good for you, you'd keep out of their way.

THE STEWARDS were free from the end of lunch service, at around three o'clock, until just before dinner began at six. They ate a meal in the mess on E Deck, usually whatever was left over from the third-class dinner, then had a couple of hours free. Reg liked to walk around the ship, exploring.

That Saturday, he started up on A Deck and wandered into the first-class smoking room, where there was a card game in progress. He then walked down the stairs to B Deck.

A few young folk were relaxing in the Café Parisien and, as he walked past, one of them called out, 'I say, could you fetch us some pink gins?'

'Of course, sir.' Reg moved away and passed on the order to one of the French stewards employed there. Every room on the *Titanic* was an exquisite copy of something or other, and this was supposed to be a Parisian pavement café, so the staff were all French (or at least spoke in mock French accents). He glanced along the length of the room, wondering if the girl from the boat deck might be spending her time there, but there was no sign of her.

He worked his way along the B Deck corridor and, level by level, wandered down into the depths of the ship. He ended up on G Deck, where the post office was situated, next to the squash court. Suddenly there was a commotion. A door leading to the boiler room opened and an engineer emerged holding two scrawny children by their arms. Spotting Reg, he called over, 'Can you find out where these two come from? I just caught them sneaking around the engines without a by your leave.' He shook the boys' arms, but they were giggling and didn't look in the least abashed. 'If I catch you in here again, I'll have you scrubbing the decks,' he warned them.

Reg wasn't looking at the boys, though. Over the engineer's shoulder, he caught a glimpse of a huge machine with all its pistons and cylinders and shafts, which provided the power that made the ship move. It emitted impressive hissing and clanking noises, and Reg could well understand why the two boys had sneaked in for a look.

'Which class are you in, lads?'

They looked at each other. 'Third,' the older one said. 'With me mam and baby brother and sister.' The accent was Irish.

'What're your names?'

'I'm Finbarr and he's Patrick.'

'I bet you don't know your cabin number,' Reg challenged. 'Young lads like you would never remember.'

'We do, too. It's E107.' The older one was doing all the talking.

'Let's go up there, then. Your mum'll be worried about you.'

On the way, he told them what he knew boys would want to know: that the ship had two, four-cylinder triple-expansion steam engines that drove the propellers, and a low-pressure turbine that recycled steam from the engines. He told them that it had a maximum speed of twenty-three knots but that they were currently only doing about twenty-one. He told them the length and the breadth and the tonnage of the ship, and he was still talking when they arrived up on E Deck outside number 107.

Hearing voices, Annie McGeown opened the door and immediately grabbed her sons and pulled them into the cabin.

'What have they been doing? Oh, I hope they haven't been up to mischief and causing trouble?'

'Not at all,' Reg told her. 'We were just having a chat about the ship.' He saw the boys' expressions of surprise when they realised he wasn't going to tell on them for going in the engine room. 'They're clever lads,' he continued. 'I bet they do well at school.'

'I'm so grateful to you, Mr . . .'

'Parton. Reg Parton.'

'I'm Annie McGeown. I wonder, could I ask you a question? Is there somewhere I can warm the baby's milk? I filled his bottle from a jug at lunch so I could give him a feed later, but he doesn't like it cold. I haven't seen any other babies down here, and I don't want to cause a fuss.'

'I can pop down the corridor to our mess and get someone to do it straight away,' Reg replied. 'Tell you what—why don't your two eldest come with me and they can bring it back again?'

This was readily agreed and Reg led the boys along the corridor. He showed them where the crew dorms were, and the storerooms and the mess, then he took them to meet Mr Joughin, who warmed the bottle and gave the excited boys a teacake each. Finally, Reg showed them back to the gateway into third-class aft, and pointed them in the direction of their cabin.

'Will we see you again?' Finbarr asked wistfully.

'I should think so,' Reg smiled. 'I'll keep an eye out for you.'

'Grand!' Finbarr breathed, and Reg realised with amusement that they looked up to him. They must be the only people on the ship who did.

Once they'd gone, he wandered back to his berth for a lie-down. He had a Sherlock Holmes novel with him but he wasn't in the mood for it. There was a steward lying on a nearby bunk.

'You work in Gatti's, don't you?' Reg asked him. Gatti's was the à la carte restaurant on board, run by Luigi Gatti, who also ran the restaurants at the Ritz in London.

The chap nodded. 'Why do you ask?'

'I don't suppose you have a girl who comes in there, really slender, with copper-coloured hair? She's beautiful, about twenty-ish I'd say. I saw her on deck last night in a silvery-white dress, very low neckline, but she hasn't been into our restaurant so I thought maybe she eats in yours.'

The Gatti's waiter shook his head. 'They are mostly older couples in ours. I can't think of a girl like you describe.'

'Reg is in love!' Bill, in the bunk next to him, teased, and this was met by a chorus of whistles.

''Course I'm not.' Reg was regretting opening his mouth. 'I just wondered why she never comes to the dining saloon.'

'She might eat in the Parisien or the Verandah,' one chap suggested. 'Lots of the young ones eat in the Parisien.'

'Perhaps she's not in first class?' someone else suggested.

Reg considered it for a brief second, but there was no question in his mind. 'She's definitely in first. Keep your eyes peeled for me, will you?'

'For you? Not if I see her first,' Bill rejoined, and they all chuckled at the idea. In reality, none of them would ever try flirting with an upper-class lady. It wasn't the way things worked. You were born to a certain station and that's where you stayed.

Chapter Two

By dinner time on Saturday evening, Juliette was restless in her gilded prison. No matter how large the ship, there was no escape from the exasperating presence of her mother and from the burden of class expectations, which were magnified a thousand times on board. Brought up with a brother who was close in age, Juliette enjoyed tennis, cricket and tree-climbing rather than needlepoint and bridge. She liked male conversations about politics and exploration and technology, but when she had tried to engage their companions in the reception room outside the dining saloon in speculation about what might have happened to Captain Scott, her mother was desperate to change the subject.

'Really, Juliette, I'm sure the ladies don't wish to talk about such things.'

Now, Juliette found herself seated between a taciturn, middle-aged American called Mr Grayling, who was accompanied by his wife, and a Canadian couple who weren't speaking to each other. On the other side of the table, the conversation was about the speed of the ship, and Juliette listened with increasing interest.

'I do wonder if they are going for a record crossing,' remarked one gent. 'They say we covered five hundred and nineteen miles yesterday, which is rather more than the day before.'

'Would that mean we'd get into New York early?' his wife asked.

'In theory, yes. So it could be Tuesday evening rather than Wednesday morning.'

'That would be a bore. Our chauffeur won't be there till Wednesday.'

The Canadian woman, Mrs Howson, joined in. 'You could send him a Marconi-gram. I sent my sister one yesterday, saying "You'll never guess where I am!" She'll be astonished when she gets it.'

Mrs Grayling asked how Marconi-grams reached the people concerned, and one gent took it upon himself to explain about radio waves and how they were sent from ship to ship, then on to base stations on shore.

'How clever!' Mrs Grayling remarked. 'What will they think of next?'

'I imagine they will think of a way of using the telephone across an ocean. That will rather change the world, won't it?'

'I can't see it happening in our lifetime. How would they run the telephone wire along the ocean floor?'

'Do you have a telephone yet?' Mrs Howson interrupted. 'It's very convenient, but the operator always listens. It's most off-putting.'

Mrs Grayling said that her telephone always gave her a start when it rang. 'It's so loud and shrill. I'm not sure I like it. You use it more than I do, darling.' She had turned to Mr Grayling, trying to include him in the conversation. 'What do you think?'

'Technology has never been your strong suit, has it, my dear?' He looked round the other guests at the table. 'She doesn't like to touch the light switches in case she electrocutes herself.'

Juliette was astonished by his patronising tone.

'But there was that case in the *New York Times*,' Mrs Grayling protested. 'It can happen.'

'I read that story,' another gent burst in gallantly. 'It *was* alarming.'

Juliette was interested to hear that so many Americans had telephones and electric lights in their homes. Back in Gloucestershire, they had neither.

After dinner, as the ladies rose to leave the saloon, Juliette caught eyes with a man at the next table. He was sandy-haired, with an intelligent face. He gave a slight smile and she smiled back, but it was over in an instant.

She followed her mother to the reading room and once they were seated, Lady Mason-Parker regarded her with a twinkle.

'Mrs Grayling has invited us to dine with them the week after we arrive in New York. Isn't that kind?'

'Very kind,' Juliette replied suspiciously. 'Will it just be the four of us?'

'She said she might try to find some young people to join us. That would make it more fun for you, I expect.'

It was an ambush, pure and simple. Juliette wondered which poor dupe was to be seated next to her. Would he be told that she was a titled English Lady looking for a husband? Probably. She dreaded the evening already.

Claiming slight nausea, Juliette got up to return to their cabin. She stopped on the outdoor promenade to look out at the inky ocean and the star-speckled sky. She felt as though she were being punished for the brief affair with Charles Wood; something that really didn't feel as though it were her fault. *He* had been the one who seduced *her*. The life she was being forced to lead as a result was suffocating her.

REG SCANNED the dining saloon once again for the boat-deck girl, as he now thought of her, but yet again she wasn't there.

The Howsons were arguing again. *What is it about my tables that attracted the unhappily married*, Reg wondered. If he married Florence, would they end up bickering like that? He couldn't bear to live that way.

Towards nine o'clock, the dining room was thinning out and Reg noticed that Mrs Grayling was sitting on her own at the table again. He assumed Mr Grayling had gone to the smoking room for a brandy.

'Would you like me to bring you something else, ma'am?'

She smiled. 'No, I'm fine. I've been watching you and it makes me quite exhausted to see how hard you work. You don't stop for a second, do you?' She glanced over to where the chief steward stood at the entrance. He wasn't looking their way. She said, 'Hold out your hand.'

Reg did as she asked, holding it out flat. Her gloved hand came down on top of his and she placed something there, then bent his fingers over so that it wouldn't show.

'This is from me, not my husband. It's to say that I'm grateful for the way you've been looking after us. I'm going down to my room now and we won't mention it again.'

Reg pulled back her chair. 'Thank you very much, ma'am,' he said, quietly. 'It means a lot to me.'

'You're very welcome, Reg. I'll see you at breakfast.'

Reg could feel that there was some kind of banknote in his palm. He put it directly into his trouser pocket and only fished it out later when he went to the lav. He nearly fell backwards with shock. It was a five-pound note. He whistled out loud: he'd never even held one of those in his hands before. Straight away, he decided not to tell anyone, not even John, because it would make the others jealous. They might even report him and he'd be forced to hand it back. He would keep it in his trouser pocket and never be separated from it. There was too much chance of pilfering if he left it unsupervised with his few possessions in the dorm.

Good old Mrs Grayling. How could he ever thank her? With money like this, maybe he could get a stall and sell meat pies to the seamen who came ashore at Southampton. Where would he make his pies, though? His mum would never let him use her kitchen and he'd have no income to pay rent on a place of his own.

Reg felt restless and unsettled. He was twenty-one years old and still waiting for his life to begin, but he didn't even know what it was he really wanted. John wasn't ambitious like him, and he was probably a happier person as a result. All John wanted was to find a good woman to marry, and maybe to make it up the ranks to be a sommelier or chief steward one day— although Reg couldn't see that happening because he was rather too coarse in his looks. They liked their head waiting staff to be easier on the eye. Reg could have done it, but he was insubordinate at heart. He followed the White Star Line rules but sometimes felt as though his head might explode. He'd rather be his own boss one day.

Maybe too much contact with the rich had spoiled him, giving him airs above his station. Face facts: the only thing he was good at was waiting on table; the only money he had was a five-pound note. He should accept his lot, go home and put down a deposit on a nice engagement ring for Florence. But he knew he wasn't going to do that; it was not what the money had come to him for. It was his chance to do something that would change his life once and for all.

AS PASSENGERS BEGAN ARRIVING for breakfast on Sunday morning, Reg rehearsed in his head some way in which he could thank Mrs Grayling for her generosity. But when Mr Grayling arrived and walked over to the table, he was alone. Reg hurried to pull out his chair.

'Would you like to wait for Mrs Grayling before ordering, sir?' Reg asked.

'My wife's unwell. She won't be taking breakfast today.'

Reg immediately felt concerned. 'I'm sorry to hear that. Shall I ask the ship's doctor to call on her?'

Mr Grayling shook his head. 'It's just a touch of seasickness. She'll sleep it off in no time. Now I think I'll have the lamb collops this morning.'

'Very good, sir.' As he walked away to place the order, Reg thought cynically that Mrs Grayling's illness would be very convenient for Mr Grayling and his young mistress.

Reg was tired and after breakfast service finished, he nipped back to the dorm for a nap. John and some of the others had gone to the church service and Reg reckoned he'd be woken by the lads making a racket when they got back, and there would be time to have a bite to eat before lunch service. He was wrong, though, because John thumped his shoulder when there were just five minutes left to rush upstairs to work.

'I thought you needed your beauty sleep,' he explained.

'I'm starving,' Reg said. 'I need my grub more than I need my kip.'

'Sorry, man; thought you'd eaten earlier.'

The occupants of Reg's tables arrived all at once, and he had a flurry of trying to take their orders without anyone waiting for too long. Mr Grayling was once again unaccompanied and in answer to Reg's enquiry, said he was sure that his wife would be better in time for dinner that evening.

Everyone placed complicated orders for starters, soups, mains, side dishes and puddings. As Reg carried plate after heaped plate of piping hot meals to tables, hunger gnawed at his belly.

One o'clock came and went, then one thirty, and then two. By two fifteen, Reg only had a couple of tables left, and one of them was on desserts. He cleared the main course plates from the other, deftly stacking them with the fullest on top; as he did so, he noticed an untouched piece of filet mignon in gravy. Reg's belly gurgled like a rusty old water tank.

He crossed the room, pushed open the swing door into the pantry and headed towards the washing-up area. The pantry was crowded but everyone was busy with their own tasks. Reg balanced his plates on the table, had one more swift look round the room, then lifted the filet mignon and took a bite. The texture was like velvet. But his mouth was full and the filet mignon still in his hand as Latimer strode into the pantry and came straight over.

'What are you doing, Parton?'

Reg tried to slip the piece of meat under his tongue and speak normally. 'Nothing, thir,' the words came out, then he started coughing and had to spit the meat into his hand. It hadn't melted in his mouth after all.

'Any guests passing by could have glanced in at the door and seen you guzzling their leftovers like a wretched dog. This will go on your report, Parton. I thought you would have been more careful after yesterday, but it seems you don't care about your position here.'

Reg hung his head and whispered, 'I do care, sir. I'm sorry.'

'Get back out to your tables.' Latimer marched off.

Reg was sunk in gloom. He was booked to wait first class on the *Titanic*'s return voyage to Southampton; after that he would almost certainly be relegated to second or third class. They expected impeccable standards in first.

'BAD LUCK, MAN,' John said, once they were standing in the dinner queue in the mess. 'We all do it from time to time, but it's rotten that you should be caught straight after that eejit woman got you into trouble yesterday.'

Reg sighed. 'I dunno, John, I think I've just about had enough of this life. I can't see me going on like this, year in, year out.'

John was shocked. 'You've got a great career here. Everyone wants our jobs. Why not talk to the Tiger and explain what happened when you dropped the plates? He could maybe talk to Latimer and sort things out for you.'

The Tiger was the name given to the captain's personal dining steward, the role Reg had filled on a previous voyage with Captain Smith.

Reg decided this was a good idea. If he mentioned it to Captain Smith, he was sure the captain would sort things out. The captain liked him.

After he'd finished his bowl of stew, Reg turned down John's offer of a game of rummy and went to walk his dinner off. He went along the port side cabins on B Deck, his feet slowing outside the door to the Graylings' state room. He knew from the passenger list that they were in B78. He listened hard but there was no sound from within. Should he knock and ask if he could fetch anything for Mrs Grayling? But that was the bedroom steward's job, and he wasn't sure who their bedroom steward was. Crew on a ship like this could get bad-tempered if you tried to do their job for them.

He walked on. When he reached the end of B Deck, he walked back along the other side, then descended a staircase to C. Ahead of him, he was suddenly surprised to see a girl from one of his tables in the dining saloon rushing towards him with her hand over her mouth. She gave a cry and bent double. Reg hurried over and saw that she was retching: a small pool of vomit was on the carpet at her feet. She looked up at him and they caught eyes before a fresh convulsion seized her.

'Here. Please use this, ma'am,' he said, handing her his handkerchief.

She grabbed it and held it to her mouth, her eyes signalling thanks.

'May I walk you to your cabin?' he asked.

She nodded. 'It's C43. But what about . . .?' She motioned towards the mess on the carpet.

'I'll have someone see to that, ma'am.'

She took his arm and leaned against him as they walked down the passageway and round the corner to her cabin.

'Shall I ask a doctor to call on you?' Reg asked.

'No, really,' she said. 'I'm fine now, thank you.' She peered at him properly. 'I know you from the dining saloon, don't I? What's your name?'

'It's Reg Parton, ma'am. Reginald, my mum calls me.'

'My name's Juliette Mason-Parker. Well, I expect I'll see you later at dinner. Goodbye for now.'

After seeing her safely inside her cabin, Reg hurried back along the corridor but, when he reached the spot, someone had already cleaned up the mess, leaving a barely discernible damp patch on the carpet.

PERHAPS IT WAS the Wideners' party for the captain, or perhaps it was because there were only two nights left before they reached New York, but all the ladies seemed to have made a special effort with their appearance that evening. The younger ones wore quite daring décolleté gowns in vibrant shades; the older matriarchs appeared to have been unable to decide which jewels to wear and had just piled on the lot. Diamonds and precious stones glittered in tiaras, necklaces, earrings and bracelets.

The chef had pulled out all the stops, serving ten courses and several options for most: oysters, salmon mousse, the infamous filet mignon, roast duckling, roast squab, foie gras, éclairs. There were going to be a few groaning waistbands, a few people groping for indigestion remedies in the middle of the night.

To Reg's surprise, Lady Juliette Mason-Parker was at dinner, looking fetching in an ivory gown trimmed with lace at the sleeves and neckline.

'I trust you are feeling better, my lady,' Reg said quietly, as he fluttered her napkin onto her lap.

'Yes, thank you so much,' she whispered, and gave him a quick smile with her eyes. It was obvious she didn't want her mother or anyone else at the table to hear of her misadventure.

Again Mr Grayling came into the dining saloon on his own. When Reg asked about Mrs Grayling's condition, he didn't have much to say.

The Howsons had wangled an invitation to the Wideners' party, so Reg didn't have to serve them, but he found all his other passengers in celebratory mood. Bottles of champagne, Madeira, Château Lafite and aged cognac were opened and quaffed, and the noise level in the room rose as the levels in the glasses dropped. Faces reddened and smiles broadened. The Wallace Hartley trio played ragtime classics out in the reception room and a couple of young men did a Turkey Trot on their way into the saloon that had diners laughing and applauding.

Behind the scenes, Reg kept his head down and worked hard, hoping to impress the chief steward with his diligence. It was after ten by the time the last diners drifted away to the smoking room or the reading room, or to one of the cafés to continue the party.

'I'm gasping for a smoke. You coming?' John asked.

'Let's go outside,' Reg suggested. 'I fancy a breath of fresh air.'

They stopped by the dorm to pick up their cigarettes, then made their way outside. The second they stepped through the doorway in their thin uniform jackets, they clutched their arms and shivered. 'Bloody hell. It's chilly out here,' Reg said. 'The temperature's plummeted since this afternoon.'

'We must be getting close to Iceberg Alley,' John said, peering out into the pitch black. 'Wonder if we'll see any.'

'Only if you fancy sitting out here all night. I can just about manage five minutes for a smoke then I'm going in before my bits freeze off.'

When they had finished smoking, they made their way down to the mess and had a cup of tea with some of the other stewards, but most were too tired for conversation, and the two men were in their bunks by eleven. Reg dropped off to sleep rapidly. It had been a long five days.

At eleven forty, Reg woke suddenly and sat bolt upright when his berth was jolted, as if a giant hand had shoved it. He felt the ship juddering and heard a drawn-out scraping sound. He'd been on steamers for seven years and he knew right away that it was odd. It would take a lot of force for such a huge structure to be rocked in that way.

'What the bloody hell was that?' someone asked.

Reg was already out of bed and pulling on his trousers.

Chapter Three

The engines had stopped almost immediately, and the silence that followed was eerie. They'd got used to the constant roar down there on E Deck and modulated their voices to be heard above it, so the next person who spoke sounded unnaturally loud.

'We definitely hit something. Maybe it was a whale,' Bill speculated.

'Poor thing. It's going to have one hell of a sore head,' someone else chipped in, and the mood of slight alarm lifted.

Reg knew it wasn't a whale, though. A whale wouldn't account for that unearthly scraping sound. As he tied his shoelaces, he was turning over two theories in his head. Either it was a problem with a propeller, or they'd hit something hard. Maybe another ship. Maybe an iceberg. Whichever it was, he had an overwhelming urge to get out on deck and see it.

'Where are you going, man?' John asked sleepily.

'I'll find out what's happened and come back and let you know.' Reg grabbed his jacket and before John could reply, he'd hurried out of the dorm and along the corridor to the staff deck at the front of the ship.

As soon as he opened the door and stepped outside, he found his answer. Small chunks of ice littered the deck, most of them no bigger than his clenched fist. A seaman was idly kicking some around.

'That was a close shave,' he commented, when he noticed Reg standing there. 'Big as the Rock of Gibraltar, she was. Came out of nowhere.'

'We hit her, though,' Reg said, peering backwards over the rail to try to see the berg, but the night was too black. He couldn't make out a thing.

'Just a side swipe. It'll be two or three hours before we're on our way again, though,' the seaman was saying. 'Captain Smith isn't one for cutting corners, so it'll be a full inspection, prow to stern.'

Reg nodded goodbye to the seaman and headed up to the boat deck. There were bound to be officers on deck and by eavesdropping on their conversations, he'd get more information.

There were lots of people standing around but the first person Reg recognised was Second Officer Lightoller. He was a stern, very formal man, always impeccably turned out, but now he was dressed only in pyjamas. He made an incongruous sight striding across the deck towards the officers' quarters in his bedroom slippers. Small groups of crew and passengers stood around talking in low voices, waiting and wondering, or peering into the dark trying to see what they had struck. A man pointed out to sea and several more turned to follow the direction of his finger. Reg wandered over to see what had attracted their attention.

'She looks as though she's stopped for the night,' he heard someone say and, glancing towards the horizon, he thought he could just make out tiny pinpricks of light: there was another ship out there. It was good to know they weren't completely alone in the vast darkness—just in case.

Just then, he saw Captain Smith coming down the steps from the bridge and he hurried over to try and hear what was said. Before Reg got there, however, an order was given and several men scurried towards the lifeboats and began unfastening the tarpaulin covers. Why were they preparing the boats? It must be bad news. Then he told himself it was most likely a precaution.

Near the entrance to the Grand Staircase, the captain was hailed by Colonel Astor. This time Reg was close enough to make out his words: 'We're putting women and children into the lifeboats. I suggest you and your wife go below and don your life preservers and some warm clothing.'

'Thank you for your frankness,' Astor said, and the captain strode off.

We must be holed, Reg decided, *and they want to get passengers off for their own safety while we carry out the repairs.* Lots of doubts assailed him, though. They hadn't had a lifeboat drill on the *Titanic*. No one would know where to go. Most other ships made the passengers take part in a mock evacuation during the first day on board, but no one had bothered on this voyage. Now it meant they risked chaos.

And why women and children first? Surely they would remain calmer with their menfolk by their sides? Of course, there weren't enough boats for every passenger to have a place all at once, but he imagined the ship he'd seen on the horizon would be radioed to come and pick them up so the lifeboats could return for more. If it came to that.

He felt charged up, anxious to be doing something to help, so he walked across to the officer who was overseeing the preparation of the lifeboats.

'What can I do, sir? Can I help with the boats?'

The officer glanced at his steward's jacket. 'Go and rouse passengers. Tell them to make their way up here wearing warm clothes and life preservers. No panic, though. Tell them it's nothing to worry about.'

ANNIE MCGEOWN was lying in her bunk unable to get to sleep. She'd been imagining the new home they would have in New York. All Seamus had told her was that it had three rooms—three!—and a yard out the back where the children could play.

She felt the ship turn sharply, then there was a jolt, and a noise that seemed to her like the sound of the big cogwheels grinding the corn at Dunemark Watermill. That was her first thought: *why do they have a watermill at sea?* She got up and crept to the porthole but outside all was black.

The engine noise had stopped abruptly and now the only sounds were her children snuffling in their sleep. *Something's broken in the engine*, she thought. *I hope it won't make us late arriving in New York.*

In the corridor outside, she heard voices. People were emerging from their cabins to discuss the reason for the unscheduled stop. When she heard voices she recognised as belonging to her friends from Mayo, she pulled her coat on over the top of her nightdress and quietly eased the door open.

'What happened?' Annie looked from one to the other and they shrugged, but a man further along the corridor had more answers.

'We hit an iceberg. There's a small hole in the front of the prow but they've closed the watertight doors so the water won't flood in.'

'Mother of God,' Annie exclaimed. 'Are you sure? Who told you that?' She peered at the speaker, who was wearing an overcoat and cap, his face indistinguishable in the dim lighting.

'I've come from downstairs. There's an inch of water on G Deck but the damage is contained. They'll mop the floors and we can all go back to sleep.'

'Holy Jesus,' Kathleen gasped, crossing herself. 'You think we're going to go back to sleep while the ship's taking on water?'

The man sounded impatient. 'It's not taking on water any more. They've closed off that area and we're right as rain. That's why she's unsinkable.'

Annie felt her guts twisting. What would Seamus do if he was here?

'You alright, love?' Eileen asked, taking her arm. 'You look shook up.'

'I wish my husband was here. He'd know what to do.'

'You're with us, now. Our men will look out for you.'

'You won't go anywhere without me? I'd never find my way around this place. It's the most I can do finding my way to the dining room and back again.' Annie tried to speak lightly, but her voice caught in her throat.

Eileen put an arm round her shoulders and gave her a quick squeeze. 'I promise we won't go anywhere without you. We should all go back to bed. If anything more happens, they'll come and let us know.'

Annie thanked them and let herself back into the cabin. The children were still asleep, their breathing barely detectable. She smoothed a curly lock back from the forehead of little Roisin, her precious daughter.

Finbarr started dreaming. She could tell from a change in his breathing, some little sighing noises, a slight restlessness. Finbarr was the main reason they were moving. From the day he started school, he had been bright beyond his years and Annie could tell there wasn't enough the teachers back home could teach him. They would do better by Finbarr in America— the land of opportunity, everyone called it.

As REG WALKED along B Deck, passengers were beginning to emerge from their cabins, fiddling with the ties on their cork life preservers.

'Do we need to put these on now?' someone asked him.

'No, just take them up on deck with you,' he improvised. He wasn't sure if that was the correct advice but reasoned that the officers on deck would soon set them straight.

Since he seemed to be in possession of information, a few people crowded round him with more queries.

'Is it true that the ship's taking on water?'

'No, sir, not that I've heard.' He wondered where they had got that from.

'Do we all have to get in the lifeboats? Are they safe?'

'Safe as houses,' Reg told them. 'The captain will decide whether they're to be lowered or not.'

Once they had assured themselves that he knew little more than they did, the group dispersed and Reg continued along the corridor to the Graylings' suite. Most other doors were ajar, evidence that the room steward for the floor had already knocked and passed on the message. Reg arrived at their door and listened, but couldn't hear any sound from within. Were they there? He knocked and waited, but no one came. He knocked again, more loudly this time. Still there was no reply. Finally, he tried the handle and found the door locked. That was odd. No one locked their doors on board. Still, he assumed it meant they had gone up to the boat deck already.

Reg made his way down to C Deck, but the stewards appeared to have roused everyone there as well. There was nothing for him to do here.

As he passed the first-class restaurant, he noted the time. It was only fifty-five minutes since the collision, but it felt like hours. Time seemed to have slowed down—or could the clock have stopped?

Descending the staff stairs to E Deck, Reg noted that the steps seemed to be at a strange angle. The ship was listing, he realised. His heart began to beat just a bit harder. That seemed to imply they *were* taking on water. Maybe that passenger had been right.

There was no one in the dorm. No John, no Bill. Someone had come and given them instructions, and Reg felt a little panicky that he hadn't been where he was supposed to be and now he'd been separated from his fellow workers. Before leaving the dorm, he went to his bunk and retrieved his passport and a St Christopher that Florence had once given him, which he kept under his pillow. He checked his trouser pocket and made sure the five-pound note was still there. Then he reached under the bunk and grabbed his life preserver. Clutching it to his chest, he hurried out of the door and back up the stairs, two at a time, all five floors to the boat deck.

When Reg emerged panting for breath on deck, lifeboats were being loaded. A nearby boat was hanging on its davits, suspended over the side. Fifth Officer Lowe was standing with one foot in the boat and one on the railing as he helped an elderly woman to step in. Others hung back, glued to their partners, unwilling to commit themselves to a wooden rowing boat hanging seventy-five feet above the surface of the ocean.

'Who's next? Any more women or children here?' Lowe called out. 'We're about to lower away.'

As Reg watched, a slender figure suddenly appeared, clutching a velvet cloak around her. Her back was to Reg but as she stepped up to the rail, she turned and he saw that it was the beautiful girl from the boat deck, the one who had thrown her fur coat overboard. She skipped, light as air, into the boat as if this was a fun new game, rather than a mid-Atlantic emergency.

As the crew began to untie the ropes, another figure stepped forward.

'Room for one more?' asked a man's voice. It was Mr Grayling. Without waiting for an answer he stepped smartly up to the rail and climbed straight over into the boat, where he sat down beside the girl and smiled at her.

'But it's women and children first!' Reg wanted to call out. He looked at Officer Lowe, waiting for him to issue a reprimand, but instead he gave his men the order to start lowering.

Reg hurried over to the rail as the boat began to descend jerkily towards the glinting ocean surface so far below. The girl was holding onto Mr Grayling's sleeve and saying something to him that Reg couldn't hear. But where was Mrs Grayling? He scanned the occupants of the lifeboat but there was no sign of her. As the lifeboat disappeared into the gloom, Reg took a mental note of the number on the side: Lifeboat 5.

He peered out towards the horizon. Where was the ship they were going to offload passengers onto? Surely it should have drawn closer? It must be round on the port side, he guessed. He hoped they wouldn't take too long transferring passengers and sending the lifeboats back: the *Titanic* was beginning to feel distinctly queer underfoot. He put on his life preserver.

WHEN SHE WOKE, for a few seconds Juliette couldn't remember where she was. Her mother was shaking her shoulder.

'We have to get up, dear. The captain wants us all up on deck: something about an accident. It's nothing serious but we have to get into the lifeboats. I hope it won't take too long.'

Juliette heard the wardrobe doors being opened. Her mother said, 'I thought you could wear the tweed coat with cherry velvet trim over your blue wool dress. They're probably the warmest clothes you have with you.'

'What's the time?' Juliette asked.

'Twelve thirty. Hurry now. The steward is coming back for us in five minutes and you've got your hairpins in.'

There was no option but to get up and drag herself over to her dresser to start pulling out the pins from her hair. She then wound it into a quick chignon, and got dressed. When the steward arrived she was bent double, fastening the fiddly buttons on her boots.

'Please put on your life preservers, ladies.' He retrieved them from the top of the wardrobe and demonstrated how to slip them over their heads and tie the ribbons around the side.

Rubbing her eyes, Juliette followed as he led them up the Grand Staircase to the boat deck. As they emerged she heard the orchestra playing a ragtime classic and she saw groups of first-class passengers hovering:

Benjamin Guggenheim talking to his valet, and the Howsons standing with several other couples she recognised but hadn't been introduced to.

'This way, please.' Their room steward beckoned them towards a lifeboat that was being filled. 'Fifth Officer Lowe will take care of you.'

'Please allow me to assist you into a boat, ma'am.' Lowe extended an arm to Lady Mason-Parker.

'Is it strictly necessary, officer? My daughter hasn't been feeling at all well. She's still queasy and this won't do her any good.'

'I'm afraid it's captain's orders, ma'am. We'll get you and your daughter safely back to bed as soon as we can.'

'Oh, well, really,' Lady Mason-Parker grumbled, but something about his polite accent and smart officer's uniform made her obey.

There were four other women in the boat as they stepped in, and Lady Mason-Parker nodded in greeting before taking a seat right at the back. Juliette followed her, still groggy from her sudden awakening from deep sleep. She watched as their boat filled up with women, none of whom she knew. Turning, she caught an unguarded expression on her mother's face: she was afraid.

'Lower away,' someone shouted, and their boat lurched down about five feet and tipped to the side, causing several women to scream in terror. Juliette gripped her mother's arm, her throat too tight to make a sound.

They must know what they're doing, Juliette tried to assure herself. She counted five men on the boat and around forty women. Were there sufficient men to row and steer? Where had they been told to go?

Suddenly there was a white flash in the sky far above and, shortly afterwards, another, then another.

'Those are rockets,' her mother said quietly. 'They're trying to attract the attention of other ships.'

Juliette felt goose bumps all over. 'What does that mean?'

'I wish I had brought our jewellery. I could kick myself for leaving it behind in the cabin.'

'Do you think we are being transferred to another ship? If so, I'm sure they'll have our luggage sent on.'

'If it's possible, I'm sure they will,' her mother replied, in a tone that suggested she thought otherwise.

The lifeboat lurched downwards, past lit portholes with no one behind them, until there was a bump as they hit the ocean.

'Man the oars,' Lowe shouted, and their craft began to glide away from the side of the *Titanic* that towered above them like a smooth, vertiginous rock face.

'ANNIE? IT'S EILEEN.' The words were accompanied by urgent knocking. 'We're to go up on deck.'

Annie flung the door open. 'What's happening?'

'You'll have to wake the little ones. A steward just told us all to get dressed in warm clothing and put on our life preservers and make our way up to the boat deck. I'll be back for you in five minutes, love.'

Annie didn't allow herself to think. She shook Finbarr and Patrick awake and gave them their clothes to put on. Startled by the sharp edge to her voice and too sleepy for questions, they obeyed. Annie dressed her little girl while she slept and then dressed herself quickly, just pulling on the first items that came to hand. She had all her papers and money in her handbag so now she just had to get a change of clothes for the baby, and some nappies and a bottle.

'You ready, Annie?'

There was Eileen at the cabin door, and one of the men behind her, whom she remembered as Kathleen's brother but whose name she didn't know. 'Would you like me to carry one of the children?' he asked.

'Oh, would you?' Annie asked. 'That'd be a big help.' She picked up the still-sleeping Roisin and handed her over.

'You'll need your life preservers. They're under the bunks.' Eileen squeezed into the cabin and crouched down to haul them out, then helped the boys to pull theirs over their heads.

'Where are we going?' Finbarr asked in a puzzled tone.

'Finbarr, not now.' Annie knew that his stream of questions would continue ceaselessly once you let him get started.

The life preservers were miles too big for her youngest two, so she pulled on her own and left theirs behind. Maybe someone up on deck would have smaller ones they could use. 'That's us all set,' she said, picking up the baby in one arm and her handbag in the other.

'They're waiting for us by the stairs,' Kathleen's brother told her.

Just along the corridor was the staircase they normally used to go down to the dining saloon, and there the rest of the Mayo party was waiting.

'A steward said they're not ready for us up there yet,' someone said. 'The gate up to D Deck is closed. He said he'd come back for us when it's time.'

'I don't know about you but I'm not hanging about down here,' someone else replied. 'If they're loading lifeboats, I'm going straight up there.'

'But you can't get through this way.'

Annie's stomach was in knots. She reached for Patrick's hand and gripped it tightly as the men went into a huddle to discuss the situation. Groups of passengers were heading in different directions but no one seemed to know what they were supposed to do. There wasn't a crew member in sight.

Kathleen's brother came over with Roisin still sound asleep on his shoulder, oblivious to the commotion. 'We're planning to go down through the crew area to the third-class outdoor deck. There's a ladder from there up to the boat deck. We'll give you a hand with the kids, so don't worry about that.'

'Are you sure it's alright?' Annie asked. 'Shouldn't we wait for the stewards to come and get us?' She didn't like to break the rules.

'They're going to be busy with all these folk.' He gestured around as at that moment, a large crowd swarmed up the stairs from below, all chattering in a mixture of languages.

'There's a foot of water down there,' someone called in English, and Annie's mind was made up.

'I'll come with you then,' she said. 'Thank you.'

They pushed forwards down the now-crowded corridor and through a gate into the staff quarters. Annie struggled to stay right behind Kathleen's brother. He was walking fast.

'See in there, Ma?' Finbarr called over the voices. 'That's where Reg took us, it's where he sleeps. Reg said this is called Scotland Road.'

'Keep up, Finbarr. Stop dawdling and yammering.' Annie was exasperated by the effort of rushing with Ciaran in her arms, her bulky handbag dangling from her elbow, Patrick's little fingers in hers, and keeping sight of Roisin and the man carrying her.

At last they reached a staircase that led upward, with no gate blocking it. A mass of people was already on the stairs and Annie was scared that if one toppled, they would all fall down and crush those below.

'Keep a tight grip on each other's hands, boys,' she told them and, glancing down, she saw their scared little faces. *It must be terrifying to be caught up in such a mob.* 'We just need to get up these stairs to the deck. Stick right beside me.'

As soon as she stepped onto the stairs someone pushed in behind her and she had to nudge backwards with the sharp point of her elbow to make space to haul Patrick up onto the step. She held his hand so tightly she knew she was hurting him but there was no choice. Under her breath, she began to pray. 'Holy Mary, mother of God, help us please.'

They moved slowly but steadily upwards. She saw the doorway to the open air up ahead and Kathleen's brother was through it. He turned back and waved at her and pointed to indicate he was going to the left.

'Wait for me,' she wanted to shout, but he had already vanished.

When she reached the top, she peered to the left and saw Eileen climbing a big metal tower. Her heart sank: it wasn't a ladder at all, but a crane for loading cargo, and at the top she would have to shimmy along the beam and over a railing onto the boat deck. She hurried across.

'I'll never manage that with the children in tow,' she cried.

'Eoghan here will take the babby for you and I'll manage this little 'un.' Kathleen's brother nodded his chin at Roisin. 'The boys can climb by themselves if they've got a man right behind in case they slip.'

Annie looked up. It seemed a long way. 'What do you think, boys?' She turned round, and her heart skipped a beat. There was no sign of Finbarr.

'Where's your brother?' she screamed at Patrick. 'Where is he?'

'I don't know,' he murmured. 'I tried to tell you but you didn't hear me.'

'When did you let go of his hand?'

'On the stairs. I couldn't hold on.'

Annie fought her way back to the top of the stairs and screamed, 'Finbarr!' She scanned the crowd: Finbarr wouldn't have the strength to haul himself up if he got knocked to the floor with all these people tramping over him. '*Finbarr!* Can anybody see a boy with black hair?'

Most people ignored her but a few turned to look, then shook their heads. 'Sorry, no.'

Kathleen's brother tapped Annie on the arm. 'I'll go back and find him. You go with the others. Take the other three up and I'll meet you at the top.'

'I'm not leaving without Finbarr.' She was wild with anxiety.

'Of course you're not, love. He'll turn up any second. Come on, now.' He pulled her back to where the others still stood around the foot of the crane.

'I've lost my eldest,' she told them, choking back tears.

'I'm going to look for him,' Kathleen's brother explained. 'Someone take this wee girl.' He handed Roisin over to Eoghan.

'But you don't know what he looks like,' Annie protested.

''Course I do. Black hair, skinny legs, cheeky smile. I'll find him. I'll see yous all up at the boats.' He turned and strode off towards the stairs, pushing his way through the crowds coming in the opposite direction.

'Come on, love. They'll be right behind us,' Kathleen urged Annie. 'We'll get your children up there. I'll take this fella.' She nodded at Patrick.

'Come on, Annie,' a man's voice urged. 'I'll take the babby for you.'

The man took Ciaran from her arms and started climbing. Annie let Kathleen help Patrick onto the crane and waited until he was a few steps up before getting on behind him. It was hard to climb with her bulky skirts wrapped round her legs, slowing her.

When Annie reached the top of the crane, she sat astride the boom and inched her way along, then someone helped her to swing her legs over onto the boat deck. As soon as she was on her feet, she turned to peer down to the third-class deck and the doorway beyond. With a tight feeling in her chest, she scrutinised each new head that emerged and prayed her boy would appear any moment.

REG MADE HIS WAY over to the port side of the boat deck and scanned the horizon, but there was no sign of the other ship he had spotted earlier. The implications of this struck him immediately: if there wasn't another ship to empty the lifeboats into, then most people would have to remain on the *Titanic* until help arrived. But how much longer would that be? They were obviously taking on water. You could feel a distinct list to port now.

Second Officer Lightoller, now properly attired in his uniform, was in charge of loading the boats on the port side and Reg soon realised he was being much stricter than Officer Lowe in his application of the 'women and children' rule. Only a handful of seamen got into his boats—just sufficient to row them—and the rest of the occupants were women.

Reg walked to the railing to peer out at the boats that had been launched. Several were only half full. Why hadn't they filled them up at least?

'Reg!' He turned at the sound of his own name and was overjoyed to see John running towards him. 'Where the hell have you been, man?'

'I've been wandering around. It's hard to know what to do for the best.'

'She's going to sink, you know,' John said gravely, and Reg felt a plummeting sensation at the shock of his words.

'How do you know?'

'An engineer from the boiler room told us. He says straight after the collision the water was gushing in and they had to run for their lives. They closed all the bulkheads but the hole is too big and the water's flooding in.'

'Christ! How long have we got?'

'A couple of hours, he told me, but that was maybe an hour ago. There's help on the way, but it's not certain anyone'll get here in time.'

'I thought I saw a ship on the horizon earlier but it's gone now.'

'It's such a black night, it's hard to see anything. But listen, Reg, you and me, we're never gonna get into a lifeboat so we need a plan.'

Reg tried to still the panic in his chest, in his head, so he could think clearly. 'These lifeboats are pulling away half full. If we could only get to one of them when the ship goes down, they'd have to take us on board. We've got an advantage here, John. We're both strong swimmers.'

'Aye, remember that time we got caught in a current off Malta and were getting swept out to sea? I thought I was a goner, but you said, "Just keep swimming" and we did and we made it. That's what we'll do. We'll just keep swimming. But it's going to be bloody freezing in there!'

They looked at each other and Reg saw that the defiant words were at odds with the terror in John's eyes. His own were probably the same, but being with John gave him courage. They'd make it if they stuck together.

'Hey, you! Stewards!' Reg turned to see Lightoller beckoning them over. They hurried across. 'One of you go down to the galley. Joughin's baking some bread. Bring up any batches that are ready and distribute them among the lifeboats. And the other, find the captain and give him this message.' He handed a folded piece of paper to John. 'Be quick about it.'

The last thing Reg wanted was to go below again but as John was clutching the message it looked as though it had to be him. 'I'll meet you by the captain's bridge as soon as I'm done,' he told John. 'Good luck.'

'You, too.' John gave a quick smile then went off on his errand.

Reg ran all the way down the Grand Staircase to D Deck. Joughin was sitting by the bread oven in the galley, looking bleary-eyed.

'Hello, young Reg. Did your belly bring you down here? It always seems to let you know when I've got fresh bread on the go.'

His words were slurred and Reg caught the smell of whisky on his breath.

'I've to take some bread up to the boats.'

Joughin waved an arm at a batch of loaves that was cooling on racks. 'Take all you can manage. It would be a shame for it to go to waste.'

'Are you coming up to the boats soon?' Reg asked.

'By and by,' Joughin grinned. 'By and by.'

Reg grabbed some white towels to protect his hands and lifted a rack of a dozen hot loaves. 'I'll see you up there, then,' he said. 'Good luck, sir.'

He hurried back as fast as he could while balancing the rack of bread. Lightoller nodded and motioned for a seaman to take the tray; Reg didn't see what happened to it after that. He'd meant to break off a piece for himself and John but his stomach was in knots and he wasn't remotely hungry.

There was only one lifeboat left on the port side now, and Reg heard an argument among an Irish crowd nearby.

'Annie, will you see sense? Finbarr could be off on another boat already. Take this one and save yourself and the children.'

'I can't leave him. He's my first-born, my angel.' Her voice was sharp, desperate. She whirled round and saw Reg. 'Oh!' she exclaimed. 'You're the one who brought the boys back that day. Do you remember?'

'Yes, of course I do, ma'am.'

'My Finbarr is lost. This lady's brother has gone to look for him and everyone says I should get on a boat. I don't know what to do.' A baby cried continuously in her arms, and two scared children clung to her skirt.

Reg swallowed hard. 'Your friends are right, ma'am. You should get on the boat to save these three little ones. Finbarr is a smart boy. I expect he'll find his own way to a boat. Where did you see him last?'

'In the corridor they call Scotland Road. Finbarr was showing me the dorm where you sleep, then we got crushed on the way up the stairs at the end and when I got to the top he wasn't with us any more.'

Reg took a deep breath. All he wanted was to go and find John and look out for himself, but he couldn't walk away from this woman's distress. 'I tell you what . . . If you get on this boat now, I'll go and find Finbarr. I'll look after him and we'll catch up with you later. How about that?'

'It's not right for me to leave without him. It's not right.'

'Ma'am, it's your duty.' Reg steered her towards Lightoller. 'You have to protect your little ones. I'll find your boy, I promise I will.'

She looked up at him with such trust and faith that he felt dreadful. He couldn't promise any such thing with all the chaos and confusion. He just knew he had to make her save her other children.

'A woman and three little ones, sir,' he called to Lightoller, who immediately picked up the girl and passed her to a seaman on the lifeboat.

Reg turned to Annie. 'Come along, ma'am. They're about to lower away.'

Annie looked at him. 'Please find my boy and bring him to me safe.'

'I will,' he said. 'Trust me, I will.'

He watched as she was helped on board, then turned to begin his search.

REG RAN OVER to the top of the Grand Staircase. 'Finbarr!' he yelled, but his voice was lost in the din of anxious voices, distant crashing noises, and the strains of the orchestra who were still, unbelievably, playing their hearts out. The whole deck was slanted towards the bow, and Reg could clearly see she was sinking nose first. Oh God, where were those rescue ships?

He swallowed his panic and scanned the boat deck methodically, section by section, looking for Finbarr and looking for John as well, but there was no sign of either. He jumped down the steps and pushed his way through to the railing that overlooked the third-class open area. There were groups of passengers huddled down there but none of them was Finbarr. With a sinking heart, Reg realised there was nothing for it but to go back down to E Deck himself and have one last look along Scotland Road.

The staff staircase was listing so badly that he had to cling to the banister with one hand and balance on the edges of the steps. *His mother will never know if I turn back now,* Reg thought. *I could just say I didn't manage to find him.* The idea was incredibly tempting, but then he remembered the boy's eager face and knew he couldn't abandon him.

As E Deck came into sight, Reg saw it was submerged under inches of water. Little waves were lapping up the stairs, and he swore. 'Finbarr!' he yelled and listened hard, but there was no answer. 'Finbarr!'

He decided he would wade halfway along as far as the stewards' dorm, then turn back. There was a current pulling him along Scotland Road, and he hooked his fingers around doorjambs so as not to be swept off his feet by the water. 'Fin-barr!' he shouted.

He was about to give up when he heard a faint cry of 'Help!' coming from further down Scotland Road.

'Is that you, Finbarr?' he called.

'Yes!' came the reply.

Reg waded further along the corridor as far as the elevators. A metal gate was pulled shut across the stairs to F Deck and Finbarr was trapped behind that gate, up to his waist in water. His face was bright scarlet with crying. The poor kid was scared out of his wits.

'How on earth did you get in there?' Reg exclaimed, trying to make his voice sound calm. 'Your mum's been going crazy looking for you.'

'I lost me ma in the crush and someone said there was water coming in down below and I wanted to see it. But I got lost and I couldn't find the way back up again.' Finbarr was sobbing and stuttering with emotion.

Reg wrenched at the gate, but it wouldn't move. The floor catch on his side needed to be released, and he groped under the water to find it. 'We'll soon get you up on deck,' he soothed.

The catch sprang loose and he pulled at the gate, using all his strength to drag it across against the weight of the water until there was just enough of a gap to haul Finbarr through.

'Where's Ma? Is she mad at me?'

'She's not mad, just worried. We've to get upstairs to the boat deck now. Quick as you can.'

'Is the ship sinking?' Finbarr asked.

There was no point in lying. 'Yes, it is. But don't worry, because help is on the way. It might even be there by the time we reach the deck.' Reg felt cheered by his own words but, seconds later, the ship gave a huge judder, causing a wave to sweep along Scotland Road, nearly knocking them off their feet. They clung to door frames until they got to the staff staircase.

'Start heading up,' he told Finbarr. 'I'll be right behind you.'

When they emerged onto the boat deck, they had to grab hold of the nearest railing: the deck was at such a slant that anything unsecured was hurtling down towards the bow. There were folk huddled on the stairs to the bridge and around the base of it, but no sign of John.

While Reg hesitated, there was a deafening crash deep within the bowels of the ship. Something gave way and they were suddenly thrown back against the doorway to the stairs. Seconds later, a huge wave washed over the boat deck, sweeping several people over the side into the ocean. Their terrified screams hung in the air.

Finbarr grabbed Reg's arm. 'What's going to happen to us?' he sobbed.

Reg felt like sobbing himself, but having someone else to look after made him calm. 'OK, Finbarr, this is how it is. I don't think we'll make it to a boat on deck. We'll have to jump into the water and then one will pick us up. You're wearing your life preserver so that's good. It means you'll stay afloat. I need you to listen to me very carefully and do exactly what I say.'

Finbarr nodded, his face so trusting that Reg felt a lump in his throat.

'First, we're going to make our way over to that railing. That's where we'll jump from. We'll just run and grab hold of it. Are you ready? Go!'

Finbarr dashed first and Reg followed directly behind him. When he reached the edge, he saw they were still around thirty feet above the water: too high to risk it. Some people were already floating on the surface but none looked as though they had survived the drop. The nearest lifeboats were about fifty or sixty feet away. He reckoned they could make that, so long as the boy stayed calm and didn't thrash around in panic.

'We mustn't jump too soon or it will be too far to fall. I'm going to tie our life preservers together so we don't get separated. When I say jump, you jump.' As he spoke, he unfastened the ties at the side of his own life preserver and looped them through Finbarr's, tightening all the knots carefully. 'As you jump, put your arms right up in the air so you hit the water feet first in a straight line, like a pencil.' Reg demonstrated. They'd been shown this in staff training. If you didn't do that, the impact could force the life preserver upwards and break your neck. 'Do you understand?'

Finbarr nodded, too overcome for speech.

'Once we're in the water, we'll find the nearest lifeboat and, later, when the rescue ships come, we'll get you back together with your mum.' *Oh God,* Reg prayed silently. *Please make it true.*

Something odd was happening below decks. With a sharp crack, the bow of the ship disappeared completely and the stern upended. Simultaneously, the ground disappeared from beneath their feet so they were left hanging by their arms from the railings. The deck was almost vertical now, and the water was close by. Reg heard screams as people all around them fell away into the bubbling whirlpool below.

'Pull up and swing your feet over the edge,' Reg yelled at Finbarr, and with his free hand he pushed the boy's legs to demonstrate what he meant. He did the same himself, and now they were poised, maybe twenty feet above the ocean. Out of the corner of his eye, he saw a collapsible being washed overboard.

'See that boat?' he shouted to Finbarr. 'When I count to three, we're going to jump in that direction. Are you ready?'

He looked at the boy, and Finbarr nodded. Reg grinned, to give him courage, and Finbarr smiled back.

'One, two, three . . . jump!'

Together they made their leap out into the blackness.

Chapter Four

The water came faster than Reg had expected and he shot down through it like an arrow. There was no time to notice the cold: he was conscious only of the pressure pounding in his ears. Just when his lungs were fit to burst, his head broke the surface and he sucked in huge gulps of air.

That's when he began to feel the excruciating cold biting into the back of his neck, his hands, his legs. His flesh felt raw with it. *Just keep swimming. Just keep swimming*, he told himself, and then his next thought was to look around for the boy. The knots between their life preservers hadn't survived the impact with the water but he couldn't be far off.

'Finbarr?' Reg called. 'Fin-barr!' he called as loud as he could. He turned in each direction yelling the boy's name and scanning the water, but there was no sign. What could have happened to him? Reg began shuddering with the cold and knew that if he didn't start swimming soon, he would die.

Suddenly the ocean moved. Reg was pulled under again and he struggled to find the surface. He opened his eyes but all around was black. Panic set in and he kicked out with all his might. After all this effort, was he going to drown anyway? His lungs were agony. *Don't panic, don't panic.* Just when he thought he was lost for sure, he found the surface and gulped the air again.

He trod water for a minute, trying to breathe his fill, and then he looked around to get his bearings. He turned one way then the other and a new horror filled him. Where was the ship? She had gone. Disappeared. In the water there were bits of fractured wood, life preservers—some with people in them and some without—a deckchair, a barrel of some kind. But no *Titanic*. How could something so enormous have simply vanished?

He tried to lift himself higher out of the water to spot a lifeboat but found he had little strength left. It was ebbing from him as the cold gnawed into his muscles and bones. He turned ninety degrees and scanned the horizon, then another ninety, then again, and finally he spotted a collapsible. It was upside down in the water and half a dozen men were sitting on it.

If I can get there, I'll be safe, Reg thought. Like that time in Malta, he knew he had to keep swimming. Easy to say, but his arms felt as though they belonged to someone else, and he had lost any sensation in his legs. He was working as hard as he could and didn't seem to be moving at all. *I have to do this,* he spoke sternly to himself. *I have to live. I'm only young and I haven't done anything yet.* He wanted to start his own business, buy a car and get married. He couldn't die before he'd achieved all those things. His arms and legs had stiffened up, making it harder than ever to move forwards, but he pictured himself in his car, driving down a road on a sunny day with Florence by his side, laughing. *Just keep swimming, just keep swimming. Not far now, you can do it.*

By the time he reached the collapsible there were a dozen men on it, some standing, some sitting and one, just near Reg, who was lying with his leg trailing over the edge. Reg grabbed hold of that leg for something to haul himself up by and the man said 'Hey!' but that was all. Reg tried to get a grip on the wooden slats but there was nothing to hold so he used the body of the man and, with the last of his strength, he crawled onto the boat.

Instantly he was out of the water, he felt colder. His teeth were chattering and he couldn't stop shaking.

'Stand up. You're taking too much room,' someone nagged him.

His legs were so wobbly he wasn't sure he could make it and he had to grab hold of another man to steady himself. Once upright, he looked at the scene around him and blinked. As far as the eye could see, the ocean was littered with bodies and broken pieces of the ship. He couldn't see any other lifeboats. Suddenly he remembered Finbarr, and began to yell his name.

'Shut up, you,' someone growled.

Reg called even louder. Guilt pierced his heart like a knife. He had promised to protect Finbarr, and instead he had saved himself.

Someone else was climbing onto their raft, and Reg was delighted to recognise Second Officer Lightoller. They would be alright now, because Lightoller would take charge. He'd tell them what to do. First, it was imperative that he told Lightoller about the boy.

'Excuse me, sir,' he called. 'Excuse me, Officer Lightoller.'

'Who are you?'

'Reg Parton, sir. There's an Irish boy, a passenger, in the water nearby. I promised his mother I'd look after him. We have to find him.'

'Everyone who can, on their feet,' Lightoller ordered, and Reg thought with relief that he was getting them all to search for Finbarr. 'Easy does it. Lean towards me, men.'

The boat wobbled and almost overturned, but every time it tipped in one direction, Lightoller gave an order and they managed to lean and steady it. *He's looking for Finbarr now. He's bound to find him,* Reg told himself, and it was a while before he realised that Lightoller was simply directing their movements so that the collapsible didn't capsize.

More swimmers came towards them but were told they couldn't climb aboard or the boat would sink. One man tried his luck and was beaten off with an oar. He fell back into the ocean with a groan of despair. The cries for help gradually subsided as swimmers realised there was no one to come to their rescue and they needed all their breath simply to keep moving.

'Finbarr!' Reg called his name one last time, but without any hope. It had taken all the strength of his twenty-one years and all his skill as a swimmer to make it this far. A skinny little lad of ten wouldn't have stood a chance.

ANNIE SAT HUDDLED on a bench in Lifeboat 13, so traumatised she couldn't move. Baby Ciaran was crying, Roisin was sucking her thumb and whimpering, and Patrick was white as a ghost, but Annie was enveloped in a sense of dread so heavy that it made her oblivious to everything around her.

She had done a wicked, evil thing leaving Finbarr behind on the ship: Seamus would never forgive her if any harm came to him. She should have sent the other three on a lifeboat and stayed behind to find Finbarr herself. Why hadn't she thought of that? It hadn't been fair to put such pressure on Kathleen's brother and on that young steward. Neither of them knew the boy. They might search for a while but then they'd give up because, after all, he was nothing to them. But she would not have given up until she'd found him.

She kept turning to look back at the ship, although they were too far away now to make out the faces of those on the decks. It was obvious the vessel was fatally damaged because of the slant at which it sat in the water, its bow almost submerged. Was Finbarr one of those little black figures she could see on deck? Why weren't they launching any more lifeboats? Could he maybe have disembarked on the other side? Pray God that he had.

When she turned again she could see that the huge vessel had upended itself in the water, like a broken child's toy. Some of the little black figures, mere dots, were slipping and falling overboard, and their cries for help reached her ears and pierced her soul. What kind of a mother was she that she left her son to go through this on his own?

She couldn't take her eyes off the ship. The lights flickered off, then on again, and it seemed as if it might stay poised there, providing refuge for those left on board. 'Please God, please,' Annie repeated over and over. If it could just stay like that, there was hope.

But then it began to slip, smoothly and quietly, into the oily blackness. In just a few seconds it was gone completely and they were plunged into almost complete darkness. There was no moon that night, no lamps on the lifeboats, just the dim glow of the stars to see by.

There was a delay before the wave of sound reached her: a prolonged howl of anguish unlike anything she had ever heard.

All those people on deck had plummeted into the North Atlantic, all those tiny specks swallowed up by the water that must be close to freezing point. 'We must go back,' she insisted to the men who were rowing their boat. 'My son might be in there.'

'We've no room, ma'am,' a seaman replied. 'We're full to bursting and the boat would be overwhelmed if we went back. Every man and his brother would try to climb aboard and we'd all drown.'

'He's small for his age. He's only ten. We must go back.' She pressed them, trying to get them to understand.

'He'll be on another boat already,' a woman told her kindly. 'There were places for all the women and children. Those in the water are grown men and pray God they will find something to float on until help arrives.'

'Oh, please can we go back just in case?' Annie wailed.

She strained her ears to listen, trying to pick out individual voices. There were cries of 'Help me!' and 'My God!' and a couple of times she thought she heard shouts of 'Ma', but none with the distinctive Cork accent. Gradually the cries got fewer and further between.

Annie knew that if her son had got onto a boat, he would be alive, but if he had toppled into the ocean he had no chance. He couldn't make his way to a lifeboat because he had never learned to swim.

As JULIETTE WATCHED the *Titanic* sliding beneath the water, she heard the piteous screams of the men pitched from the ship into the ocean.

'We must go back and save as many as we can,' a woman declared.

'Not yet,' Officer Lowe told her. 'We'd be overwhelmed by swimmers.'

An argument broke out, with some passengers urging Lowe to turn back while others claimed it was too dangerous. Juliette listened, unsure what to think. Her mother was being uncharacteristically silent.

Lowe seemed to have a plan, however. He called to the men rowing some other craft and the five boats converged and were tethered together.

'Ladies, I'd like to transfer you into these other boats so that I can go and pick up survivors,' Lowe announced. There was a collective gasp of fear, so he continued: 'There's no need to be alarmed. We'll hold the boats very steady so there can be no risk of falling. The ocean is very calm.'

Juliette's heart was beating hard. Some months previously, she had been trained in lifesaving by the Red Cross—she had been asked if she would like to attend a one-day lifesaving course, and she had agreed. Should she mention this to Officer Lowe? For the life of her, she didn't think she could remember a single thing they had taught her, though.

Women had begun stepping across to the other boats, causing theirs to rock alarmingly in the water. Juliette's mother stood to take her turn and she shrieked as two seamen lifted her by the elbows into an adjoining boat.

Juliette stood up, still wrestling with her decision. Should she say anything? Officer Lowe reached a hand towards her and the words spilled out: 'I have Red Cross training . . . maybe I could be of assistance?'

'Good,' he nodded, appraising her. 'Stay here then.'

She sat down, feeling sick. Now she would be expected to know what to do, to save lives, and she couldn't think of anything useful. Her mother looked across at her and seemed surprised, but didn't say anything.

Once most of the women had been distributed among the four other boats and only a few were left on the boat, Lowe ordered his men to row back towards the area where they could still hear voices crying out for help. Juliette ran through her scant knowledge: check if they are breathing, feel for a pulse. Goodness knew what would be required.

When they reached the first figure in the water, Lowe leaned over to check for vital signs but quickly decided there was no hope. They stopped again and again, but none was alive. The groans and cries were getting fewer and weaker as men succumbed to the brutal water temperature.

Then Lowe found a man who was still breathing, semiconscious, and all the crew gathered to help haul him into the boat.

Juliette sprang into action. She placed her fingers on his neck and felt a pulse, a faint one. She took off his life preserver, loosened his collar to help him breathe more easily and started rubbing his arms and chest vigorously in an attempt to warm him. He was young, in his twenties, clean-shaven.

'Mother,' he mumbled at one point.

'I'm here,' she whispered. 'You're safe.'

Three more men were hauled on board and some other women took care of them, following Juliette's lead.

Juliette sat on the floor of the boat and pulled the man's head onto her lap, so she could more easily continue to warm and soothe him.

Lowe circled the area several times and checked dozens of bodies floating in the water but no more were pulled on board. *They're all dead,* Juliette realised. She had no idea of the number of casualties but guessed it must be in the hundreds. The extent of the disaster was unimaginable. There were floating life preservers as far as the eye could see, most of them holding a body suspended inside. She bent down and hugged the man on her lap, trying to transmit her own body warmth to him. *There's nothing I can do for the ones out there,* she decided, *but I am going to save this man if it's the last thing I do.* 'Hold on,' she whispered to him. 'Help will be here soon.' She brushed the dark hair back from his forehead and kissed his brow gently, and he murmured something unintelligible in reply.

REG WAS SHIVERING convulsively and if it hadn't been for the men who surrounded him, he would have fallen and slipped over the edge of the collapsible. He had no feeling at all in his feet and that bothered him. There was a very real danger he could lose them to frostbite.

All was quiet now, apart from Lightoller's occasional orders for them to lean to the left or to the right. Oars were virtually useless on an upturned boat, so they drifted aimlessly through the blackness.

The night seemed interminable. Reg focused on the act of staying upright. His legs were like jelly and he knew he was leaning on his neighbours too heavily because they nudged him and snapped that he should get off the boat and swim for it if he couldn't stand up by himself.

Reg looked out across the ocean. There weren't so many floating bodies now; they must have drifted away on the current. On the horizon he could see faint grey dawn arriving. Gradually he became aware that the other men were talking among themselves: quietly at first, then more animatedly. What were they saying?

'I reckon she's twenty minutes away.'

'Less than that.'

Reg looked out towards the horizon and first he saw an iceberg, glistening in pale pink rays of sunlight. And then the sun rose a little further over the horizon and he made out an indistinct glowing shape and his heart gave a little skip. He kept his eyes glued to that shape as it got bigger and closer and soon there was no doubt. It was a ship. He was going to live.

'WAS THAT A SHOOTING STAR?'

Juliette looked up. A carpet of stars was blinking against the black sky but she couldn't see any trails. And then she saw what they were talking about: a white starburst that exploded outwards then petered down towards the water.

'It's a rocket!' Lowe declared. 'It must be the *Carpathia*.'

'Is that a ship come to rescue us?' one woman asked.

Lowe told her that it was and Juliette leant down to whisper the news to the man on her lap. 'Not long now,' she told him. 'We'll soon be there.'

It was getting lighter and, as she looked out over the edge of the boat, she saw other lifeboats dotted in the water around them, all full of huddled figures. She counted six boats, each of them crammed with survivors. Maybe more people had lived than she thought.

It was another half-hour before they pulled alongside the *Carpathia*. Some of her crew began helping them on board. She saw there was a rope ladder stretching upwards. 'Will you manage to climb, ma'am, or would you like us to lower a chair?' someone asked her.

'I can climb myself, but what about this man? Look after him first, please. He needs help.'

A *Carpathia* crew member came on board and crouched to assess the condition of her patient. After a minute, he looked up gravely. 'I'm sorry, ma'am, but he's gone.'

It was like a punch in the heart. 'He can't be. He's not, he's alive!' she insisted. She grabbed his wrist and felt for the faint pulse she had detected not long before. She shook him by the shoulders. 'He was alive just now, I swear.' Tears came to her eyes. 'Oh God, he has to be alive.'

'Let me help you on board.' The seaman took her hand and raised her to her feet. She stepped across onto the rope ladder and began to climb; and that's when she started to sob in earnest.

THROUGHOUT THE NIGHT, Annie sat still and silent, her chest tight with fear. Roisin and Patrick snuggled into her sides and slept fitfully, the baby lay cradled and snuffling in her arms, but she remained wide awake, her ears alert for a Cork accent on one of the boats they occasionally drifted near.

As dawn broke and the *Carpathia* was sighted, she felt a mixture of hope and fear. Now she would know for sure if Finbarr had reached a lifeboat. Their boat pulled up alongside the *Carpathia* and the crew lowered a sling for baby Ciaran. She nestled him into it and he was hauled up to an opening in the ship's side, then it came back down for Roisin, who started crying.

'Can you climb by yourself?' she asked Patrick, conscious these were the first words she had spoken to him since the *Titanic* had sunk. He nodded.

She climbed the ladder directly behind him. Immediately she reached the deck, she demanded of the crew there: 'Have you seen a young Irish boy, black hair, so high?' She held her hand at a height just a few inches taller than Patrick.

'Yours is one of the first boats but there are lots more coming,' a crew member told her. 'If you go upstairs they've got blankets and hot food and drinks. We need to keep this area clear.'

She led the children up the stairs he indicated, where an elderly American couple approached them. 'You poor things, you've been through such an ordeal,' the woman said. 'Would you like to rest in our cabin? We're in first class. There's room for you all to have a proper sleep.'

'It's kind of you,' Annie said, 'but I have to keep watch in case I miss my eldest son.'

The couple conferred with each other in low voices and then went off, but five minutes later they were back, carrying blankets and bearing a tray with three steaming cups of tea, a jug of warm milk and a bowl of sugar.

Annie's eyes filled with tears at their kindness. 'God bless you,' she said.

The woman wrapped a blanket around Roisin and stirred sugar into a cup of tea for her. Annie found the baby's bottle in her handbag and filled it with the milk. Patrick sipped some tea as well but Annie wouldn't touch it herself. It wouldn't feel right to take any sustenance until she knew where Finbarr was.

As each boat approached, her eyes moved from head to head, quickly at first, and then more methodically. Each time she realised he wasn't on board, she switched her attention to the next boat that was drawing near.

A particularly crowded boat appeared and she suddenly saw Reg, ready to disembark. Her heart skipped a beat as her eyes roved the faces in the throng but there was no Finbarr. Had Reg not found him? He made his way to the rope ladder and she could see he was having a lot of trouble climbing.

He was in a shocking state, white-faced, blue-lipped, with his clothes frozen to his skin. Annie grabbed the children and rushed down to meet him. He saw them and straight away shook his head.

'I'm so sorry. I found him, then I lost him again.'

'What happened?' she breathed.

'I tied him to me as the ship went down and we jumped but the knots broke and I couldn't find him in the water.'

Annie felt like lashing out at him. *Why had he survived and not her son? How could he find him then let him go again?* Instead, her knees collapsed beneath her and she sank to the floor, the babe still in her arms.

'Ma!' Patrick yelled in terror. Roisin screamed, a shrill, horrible sound.

I can't break down, she realised. *It's not an option. I have to pull myself together for the sake of these three.*

Someone appeared with smelling salts, but she waved them away. A woman took the baby from her while she leaned on a gentleman's arm to get to her feet. Reg had disappeared, led off by the crew to see the doctor.

Now I know the worst, she thought. *I just have to find out if there is any way that I can carry on living.* At that moment, it didn't feel as though there ever would be.

IN THE DOCTOR'S CONSULTING ROOM, Reg was stripped of his wet clothes and wrapped in blankets. A nurse manoeuvred him into a chair and lifted his feet into a basin of warm water. Still he had no sensation in them.

'We'll find some dry clothes for you,' she said, giving him a cup of hot tea. 'Once you've warmed up a bit.'

People were bustling around and he wanted to nod off to sleep, but he felt too stricken with guilt. The sight of Annie's face, the way she collapsed when he told her that Finbarr was lost, would stay with him for ever.

His feet were starting to hurt now, as if they were being jabbed by hundreds of needles.

'That's good,' the doctor said. 'The circulation is returning. A couple more minutes then I'll dry them and put on sterile dressings.'

I don't deserve this, Reg thought. *They wouldn't be so kind if they knew.*

The nurse brought a set of clothes for him: a grey suit, a white shirt and some socks and underwear. He wondered whose they were but didn't ask.

'Where are my other clothes?' he asked, and the nurse showed him a pile by the door.

'We'll launder them and you can pick them up tomorrow,' she said.

Reg slipped his fingers into his trouser pocket and felt something soggy. Very carefully, he extracted Mrs Grayling's five-pound note and placed it in the inside pocket of his new jacket, making sure it was flat. In the other pocket he found the remnants of his passport and the St Christopher Florence had given him, and transferred them to his new trousers.

The doctor applied bandages to his feet, then told him, 'There's space downstairs in the crew dorm. Go and have a sleep.'

Reg nodded, but had no intention of sleeping before he found John. Holding his shoes, he limped painfully out of the surgery.

The ship was unfamiliar and much plainer than the *Titanic*. Reg hobbled into a lounge. Survivors from the *Titanic* were huddled in every chair, wrapped in blankets and talking in hushed tones. He walked through, scanning all the faces, but they were passengers rather than crew. In one corner he recognised the Howsons and slunk past, careful not to catch their attention. He couldn't face talking to them.

'Where have the *Titanic* crew gone?' he asked a *Carpathia* steward.

'There's some down below in crew quarters. Do you want me to take you down?' The lad spoke so kindly that Reg felt tears spring to his eyes.

'I can find it.'

The steward showed him the entrance to their staff staircase and patted him on the back. He found the crew dorms and walked round, peering down at the heads on the pillows. He recognised a few *Titanic* crew members he knew by sight but none he knew to talk to, and no John.

He turned and hobbled slowly, painfully, back up the stairs again. When he reached the lounge, he continued out onto the observation deck.

There were some *Titanic* passengers there, either sitting on deckchairs or standing by the railings looking out across the water. He continued further along the deck and there, by the railing, was Mr Grayling. They caught eyes, and Mr Grayling nodded to Reg.

'I hope Mrs Grayling is alright, sir,' Reg ventured, approaching.

'I haven't been able to find her yet,' he replied gravely 'I put her on a lifeboat and then we became separated. I expect she's here somewhere.'

It was on the tip of Reg's tongue to mention that he had seen Mr Grayling boarding Lifeboat 5, but he didn't. It wasn't his place. 'If she got on a lifeboat, I'm sure she'll be fine, sir. I'm very glad to hear it.'

'If you bump into her, do tell her I'm looking for her.'

Reg agreed that he would but he felt cross with Mr Grayling. Why was he standing out on deck rather than searching for his wife? It wasn't right.

Reg walked on, his feet hurting badly, searching for John. He asked each member of the *Titanic* crew he came across, but no one had seen him.

There was a hard nugget of panic deep behind his breastbone. *What if John hasn't made it?* Why should he have survived and John hadn't? It was random, arbitrary and unspeakably cruel. If it turned out that John was dead, Reg thought he would rather swap places with him. He would rather be dead himself than carry on living in such a hostile, unpredictable world.

ANNIE STOOD ON DECK watching until the last lifeboat had been unloaded. Then, as the *Carpathia*'s engines started and the ship sailed in a big circle around the area where the *Titanic* had disappeared, Annie's eyes never once left the water. If she could find his body and take it back to Seamus, that would be something.

The kindly American couple took her and the three children to a dining room where the tables were set for breakfast. The American lady, who had introduced herself as Mildred Clarke, helped them order and got a steward to fill a bottle with warm milk for Ciaran.

As the children ate, Reg limped into the room. He hesitated and looked as though he was about to turn on his heel when he saw Annie, but she held out her hand to him. It wasn't his fault Finbarr had died, not really. It was unfair to blame him. He was only a boy himself.

'Have you eaten? Would you like some food?' she asked.

'I can't eat,' he said, his voice a husky whisper.

'No, me neither.' She hesitated. 'Do you feel able to tell me what happened? There's no rush. Just when you can manage.'

Reg nodded, his eyes cast down. 'Now is fine.'

They moved to an unoccupied table, leaving the children sitting with Mildred. Reg began to talk in a voice that was shaking with emotion.

'Was he scared?' Annie asked. She wanted every last detail.

'He was scared when I found him but, just before the jump, he seemed fine. He trusted me. He was sure I was going to save him.' Reg's hands were trembling and he couldn't meet her eye.

Annie placed her hand on his. 'He thought you were quite the hero after that day you took them to the galley. I'm so glad he had you for comfort, and that he wasn't alone at the end.' She tried to smile.

Reg was distraught. 'I don't know what happened. He just didn't surface from the jump. I looked for as long as I could but he didn't appear.'

'Didn't he tell you?' Annie asked. 'Finbarr couldn't swim.'

At that, Reg broke down. 'I didn't know,' he sobbed. 'He didn't say.'

'It wouldn't have changed anything,' she said, rubbing his back. 'He's in God's hands now.' If she said it often enough, maybe the time would come when she was able to believe it. 'We're all in God's hands.'

JULIETTE FOUND that she couldn't stop crying. A *Carpathia* passenger came over to her and asked, 'Have you lost your husband, dear?' and Juliette had to explain that she wasn't married and that she hadn't lost anyone. *Control yourself*, she urged. *Pull yourself together.* But the tiniest thing would set her off again.

The Howsons came to sit with her and her mother in the lounge. Juliette noticed that their former hostility towards each other was long forgotten: they held hands now, grateful not to be widowed, and full of news about those who had survived and those who hadn't.

'Colonel Astor is lost and his wife is quite inconsolable. She's pregnant, you know. It's tragic for the little one, who'll never know its father.'

Juliette thought with distaste that Vera Howson appeared almost to be enjoying her role as emissary of bad news.

Juliette's mother joined in. 'What are they going to do about compensating us? I've lost some priceless family jewellery. If only the steward had said to bring it with us onto the lifeboats, it could have been saved.'

'There will have to be compensation,' Bert Howson agreed.

Juliette felt sick listening to them as they reduced the whole disaster to a financial transaction. She stood up abruptly and announced that she was going outside for some fresh air.

Out on deck, she stood gazing across the water. They were speeding towards New York now, and would be arriving on Thursday, only a day later than scheduled. Though life could carry on as before, she felt that she would never be the same again. She felt as though she had been a naive child before. She'd never understood the nature of the world; never before felt the sheer fragility of existence.

'Are you alright?' a man's voice asked, and she looked up to see a fellow passenger. She recognised him as the man with the sandy hair who had smiled at her as she left the dining saloon after that last dinner.

'I haven't lost a loved one, if that's what you mean. But no, I'm not alright.' Tears filled her eyes yet again. 'I can't seem to stop crying, and then I feel guilty because I have no right to cry when the ship is full of people who have lost those to whom they were closest in the world. How about you? Did your wife survive? Your family?'

'I'm not married and I was travelling alone. You mustn't feel guilty for crying. You are in shock—we all are. It will take some time before anything feels normal again.' He had a warm voice, and an American accent, but not a broad one. He sounded cultured.

Tears rolled down Juliette's cheeks and she opened her handbag to search for her handkerchief.

'Normally I would be able to offer you my own handkerchief but I'm afraid these are not my clothes. I was given them by a nice woman who underestimated my size somewhat.' He opened the jacket to show how the waistcoat buttons were straining across his chest.

Juliette smiled through her tears. 'What happened to your own clothes?'

'Wet from my swim. They'll be dry in the morning, I'm assured.'

Juliette gasped. 'You were in the water and survived?' She told him about the man she had looked after, and her shock when a sailor from the *Carpathia* pronounced him dead.

'It sounds as though nothing you could have done would have made any difference. But no wonder you are still in shock.'

Juliette's eyes welled up again and she dabbed at them.

'My name is Robert Graham,' he introduced himself. 'And you, I know, are Lady Juliette Mason-Parker. I noticed you in the dining saloon and someone at our dinner table told me your name. Are you travelling with your mother? Do you have no male escort?'

Juliette shook her head. 'My father is back home in England.'

'In that case, I would be honoured if you would allow me to be of assistance to you and your mother on the ship.'

'Thank you so much. We might well take you up on that. In fact, perhaps you could advise me how we can send a Marconi-gram to my father to tell him we are alive? I don't want him to worry.'

'I'll see to it straight away. I've already sent one to my mother. Would you care to come with me and choose the wording yourself?'

He offered her his arm. As they walked to the Marconi office, Juliette could feel the reassuring warmth of his arm through the fabric of his jacket.

REG WAS BADLY SHAKEN by his conversation with Annie. He felt sick and dizzy with exhaustion but he needed to find John.

A *Carpathia* crewman was walking round with a list of names. *That's it!* Reg thought. *He will know if John is here. I need to get him to check his list.*

The man was talking to another group of passengers, but Reg waited patiently to attract his attention. At last he turned towards Reg.

'Passenger or crew?' he asked.

'Crew.'

'Name?'

'John Hitchens.'

He scanned the list then wrote the name down. 'What job?'

'First-class victualling steward.'

He wrote that down as well. 'You need some kip,' he told Reg. 'Go down to our dorms and pick any bed that doesn't already have someone in it.'

But I don't want to sleep. I want to find John, Reg thought. The man had turned to walk away, though, and Reg realised he still didn't know if John was on the list. His brain felt as though it was full of fog.

Reg turned into a carpeted corridor with cabins leading off. Was this the first-class area? While he was hesitating, a cabin door opened and Mr Grayling emerged and stared at him.

'What are you doing here?' he demanded.

'I was looking for someone, a friend of mine.'

'I see.' He frowned. 'Well, I still haven't found my wife and I'm becoming rather alarmed. I don't suppose you have come across her?'

'Oh, no!' Reg cried in despair. 'She must be here. Where could she be?'

Mr Grayling looked surprised. 'I wasn't aware you were so fond of her.'

Reg nodded. 'I am.' He looked at the floor. 'She's been very good to me.'

'I suppose she gave you a ridiculously generous tip. She's like that.' He tutted. 'I can't imagine what's happened to her, unless she got off the life-boat I put her on to go back to our cabin for something. Did you see her at all after the collision?'

Reg shook his head. 'I knocked on your door but there was no one there.'

'You didn't go in?'

'It was locked.'

Mr Grayling looked startled for a moment, but recovered himself quickly. 'Yes, of course. It would have been. I see. I suppose . . . I'm afraid I'm beginning to think the worst.' His voice was grave but emotionless.

Tears came to Reg's eyes. 'There's a man going round with a list,' he suggested. 'Maybe she's on it?'

'The roll call? I've already checked that.'

Reg smeared the tears from his eyes with his sleeve. Poor Mrs Grayling. Why would she have got off her lifeboat? What had been so important?

'You're in a bad way, my boy. Look, your feet are bleeding. You should go and rest somewhere. Shall I call for someone to help you?'

'I'm fine,' Reg mumbled. 'You're right. I'll go and rest now. Thank you, sir.' Then he added, 'I do hope you find Mrs Grayling.'

He turned and hobbled back the way he had come, going over the conversation in his head. How could Mr Grayling be so calm about the loss of his wife? She deserved much better.

And then something else Mr Grayling had said came to mind. He had talked about a roll call. That's what the list was, and Reg's name wouldn't be on it because he had given John's name instead of his own. *Idiot!* He'd have to find the man with the list and get him to change it. Not until he'd had some rest, though. Somehow he made it to the crew dormitory, selected a bed, and was unconscious as soon as his head hit the pillow.

THE *CARPATHIA* had been sailing towards the Mediterranean with almost all her cabins occupied, so it was a crush for the 711 *Titanic* survivors to be fed and found places to wash and rest.

It seemed that most of Juliette's acquaintances from the ship had survived, but Robert was with her when she heard the news that Mrs Grayling was not among them.

'How could that be?' she exclaimed, distraught. 'I thought all the first-class women were escorted to lifeboats by their room stewards?' She couldn't fathom what might have happened.

'Something went wrong, I suppose. I believe she was one of only four first-class ladies to perish. I expect her last moments will remain a mystery.'

'Yet her husband survived. Why did he not attend to her safety?'

'You were fond of her, I see,' Robert commented.

'In truth, I didn't know her well, but she had invited us to dine with her on arrival in New York.'

Tears had come to Juliette's eyes again and to distract her, Robert continued, 'Speaking of our arrival in New York, do you have a hotel reservation?'

'I believe we are staying at the Plaza.'

'Then I would be honoured if you would allow me to escort you there on arrival. My driver will be waiting at the dock.'

'Oh, please. Yes.' The prospect of trying to find a taxi in an unfamiliar city was daunting. And she didn't want to be separated from Robert on arrival. She felt safe with him around.

WHEN REG OPENED HIS EYES, he was momentarily confused to find himself on a lower bunk, instead of the top one above a sleeping John. And then it all came back to him in a great rush: the horror of struggling for his life in the water; the stricken look on Annie's face when he told her he hadn't managed to save her son; the absence of John: missing, almost certainly dead. It was unbearable. *What on earth am I going to do now?* he thought.

'Are you OK?' someone asked. 'It's just that you were moaning.'

Reg raised his head and saw it was a steward from second class, whose name he didn't know. 'I'm OK,' he managed to say. 'What day is it?'

'Tuesday. They say we dock in New York on Thursday night, then we're being loaded straight onto another ship, the *Cedric*, for the journey home.'

Reg was filled with horror at the idea. Another transatlantic voyage straight away would be more than he could bear. What if the *Cedric* hit an iceberg and the whole thing happened again? Reg turned his face to the wall. He knew that after tomorrow evening, he never wanted to set foot on a ship again. He felt numb, but his brain was racing, trying to think of a way he could manage on his own if he left White Star Line. He had his wages for this voyage and he had Mrs Grayling's five pounds, but would that be enough to rent a room somewhere and tide him over until he found a job? If he made a fresh start in America, he wouldn't ever have to go back on a ship. That was his overriding concern. He considered what kind of job he might be able to get in New York. Perhaps as a waiter in a topnotch restaurant. But he would need a reference to get a position. If only his record at White Star Line didn't have those blemishes on it: breaking crockery, eating a passenger's leftovers, and then that accusation of theft from the previous year. It didn't occur to Reg to wonder whether Latimer had already recorded his recent misdemeanours, and if so whether the record had survived.

For most of the day, Reg lay in the bunk turning over the problems in his head, but without finding a solution. It was as though his brain was encased in fog; it felt as though the answer was somewhere nearby but he couldn't quite reach it.

As darkness fell, hunger forced him to get up and go to the staff mess. They were serving stew with mashed potatoes and he let them pile his plate high. He began to eat and was surprised how much better he felt after only a couple of forkfuls.

As he ate, he looked around the room and spotted the man who had been taking the roll call the day before. *I should talk to him later, give him my real name*, Reg thought. But then another idea sprang into his head, and it was so obvious he was amazed he hadn't thought of it before. He was already on the survivors list as John . . . so why not continue to be John? On arrival in New York, he could use John's name when he looked for work, and when the restaurant manager called White Star for a reference, he would be told that John's record was spotless. It was a perfect plan.

Of course, he would need to write to his mum and Florence to explain. They would try to persuade him to come back, but he'd have to make them understand that he simply couldn't cross the ocean again. Maybe in a year or so he'd feel differently, but for now he simply had no choice.

He would have to write to John's family as well, to tell them he was using John's name just while he got on his feet. It would be a tricky letter to write but surely they wouldn't mind when he explained his reasons? He felt sure John wouldn't have minded.

REG RETURNED to the doctor's surgery to have the bloodied bandages on his feet changed. Underneath, the toes were purple and swollen, with blackened nails. 'Keep clean dressings on them,' the doctor advised. 'They will form blisters as the tissue heals and if you don't keep them clean, they could become gangrenous.' Reg found he could get his shoes on again so long as he didn't fasten the laces. He didn't bother to pick up his steward's uniform, though: he wouldn't need it any more. The grey suit he'd been given would be of much more use to him in New York.

The *Titanic*'s crew were told that they would disembark after all the passengers had left, at which time they would be taken to the *Lapland*, another vessel on the pier. They would be assigned cabins there while they waited for the ship that would take them back to England.

Reg felt like a prisoner. Once they had docked, he couldn't bear being stuck on the water a moment longer. He wanted to flee the *Carpathia* onto dry land and take his chances in the city.

When the third-class passengers lined up to disembark, Reg slipped into the queue, just behind an Eastern European family. With his dark hair, he thought he could pass for one of them, and so it was. They were waved through and he walked with them down the pier towards the exit.

The street door opened and Reg shrank back at the flashing lights and sounds that were like explosions, like the rockets that had been fired on the *Titanic*. He pressed his hands to his ears, feeling confused and scared.

'Are you alright?' a woman's voice asked.

'What are those lights? And the noise?'

'That's photographers taking pictures. Their flares provide light so the images come out.' She looked at Reg and took in his pale skin and wide, staring eyes. 'Are you on your own? Is anyone meeting you?'

'I don't know anyone in New York,' he said. 'I don't know where to go.'

She nodded. 'Don't worry. I'll fix you up. I'm Madeleine Butterworth from the Women's Relief Committee and we're here precisely to help people like you. Do you have a job to go to? Do you have any money?'

Reg decided not to mention Mrs Grayling's fiver. That was his emergency fund. He shook his head. 'No, but I'll look for a job as soon as I can.'

'You look done in,' the woman remarked. 'I'm going to take you to a hostel on East 25th Street and get you some cash to tide you over. I assume you've lost all your belongings? And your papers?'

Reg nodded. He had the fragments of his own passport, but he needed papers in John's name.

'Fine,' she said. 'I'll take your details while we're in the automobile.'

Reg blinked. He had never been in a car in his life before.

'We'll have to run the gauntlet of the photographers. Are you up to it?'

He agreed he could cope and they walked through the door, Reg covering his face with his hands so his picture wouldn't be taken. A row of black automobiles stood waiting. Madeleine Butterworth spoke to the driver of the one at the front and they climbed in.

She smiled at Reg. 'You see? We women of New York will look after you. Every family that possesses an automobile has sent it down to help the survivors. Now' she pulled out a notebook 'what is your name?'

'John Hitchens,' Reg told her. The lie made him blush, but if she was going to help him to get new papers, then John it had to be.

'Where are you from, John?'

'Newcastle originally, but I've been away from home a while.'

'And what class were you travelling in?'

Reg hesitated. 'Actually, I was crew. A first-class victualling steward.'

'Didn't White Star Line arrange somewhere for their crew to stay tonight? That's outrageous.'

'They did,' Reg admitted, 'but it was on another ship and I couldn't face it. I can't go back to sea. I want to get a job and stay here in New York.'

'I'm not surprised,' she said. 'I can't begin to imagine what you've all been through. Well, I'm here to help. I can give you four dollars tonight, which should be enough to tide you over for a few days. Come to our offices at the pier tomorrow and I'll see what else I can do for you.'

Their car pulled up outside a tall grey building with lots of windows, and Madeleine Butterworth cried, 'Here we are!' She walked into the vestibule with him and had a word with the superintendent.

He was shown upstairs to a dormitory where at least a dozen other men were tucked up in bunks. Reg realised it must be late because all were sound asleep. He took off his jacket, transferred his money to his trouser pocket, just in case, and climbed into the bed. He knew he would sleep, his exhaustion was so profound.

As he lay waiting for unconsciousness, Reg suddenly felt as if he were cast adrift and floating; as if he was utterly alone in the world, accountable to no one, and with no future obligations. He decided he wouldn't even go to meet Madeleine Butterworth the next day. He would cut himself off from everything else in his life up to that point and reinvent himself, not as Reg Parton, but as John Hitchens. With John's help, he would recover from the strange fogginess in his head and the heaviness in his limbs, and he would make a success of his life. Somehow. When he felt strong enough.

Chapter Five

Reg got a shock when he looked at himself in the mirror the next morning: it was as if someone else was looking back at him. His chin stubble had almost become a beard, which made him look much older than his years.

After breakfast, he went to a drugstore down the street and bought a razor, some soap, a toothbrush and hair oil. On the way back, he spotted a newspaper seller. 'TITANIC: SURVIVORS' STORIES' read one headline, and underneath a smaller headline said, 'Heard death chorus for over an hour'. Reg shuddered. It seemed some survivors had been quick to tell their stories to the press, but he didn't want to read their descriptions. He wanted hard facts, so he decided to buy the *New York Times*, which promised a full list of the living and dead. Clutching his paper, he walked back to the hostel and went up to the dormitory, which was empty now, and opened the newspaper. He found he was shaking so hard he had to sit down.

There was the list in black and white newsprint: Reginald Parton, first-class victualling steward was listed among the dead. It was the strangest feeling. Then a terrible thought occurred to him. Would the same list have appeared in the English newspapers? Florence would be devastated. He was sure his mother would only miss the money he brought home, but his brothers would be upset. He had to write to them straight away.

He thought of Florence's freckled skin, her gentleness, and felt a pang of longing for her. If only she were there right at that moment, he could have buried his face in her neck and held her tight. But their relationship felt like something from his distant past. He was a different person now. He felt confused, and sad, and desperately lonely, but what option did he have?

I'll find out how to send a telegram, he decided. If he sent it that day, they should get it before they'd made funeral arrangements. After that, he could shut all his memories of Southampton away while he tried to make a life for himself in New York. He'd need all the strength he could muster.

He looked at the other names of those lost: Mrs Grayling, Bill, Ethel, Captain Smith, of course . . . Almost everyone he had known personally was dead. It was unthinkable. Unbelievable.

He closed the newspaper abruptly, and went to the bathroom for a shower and a shave. He brushed his teeth and combed oil through his hair, then considered his appearance; he didn't look too bad now. Perhaps he could try to find a job straight away? As soon as he'd sent his telegram.

The hostel superintendent told him that the main Western Union office was on Broadway, just before Times Square. He suggested catching a tram but Reg preferred to walk. Towering buildings lined the street, which was full of trams, carriages and automobiles. The pavements were thick with people, all of whom seemed to have urgent business to attend to.

At the Western Union office he was directed into a hall where clerks in uniform sat behind a long counter.

'Next!' One of them waved him over.

'How much does it cost to send a telegram to England?' he asked.

'Three dollars, twelve cents for ten words.'

The fellow had a nasal accent and spoke so quickly that it took Reg a few moments to understand what he'd said, then he flushed. He had spent over a dollar in the drugstore so didn't have enough American money left. He felt close to tears. Why was everything so difficult?

'Could you change an English five-pound note?' he asked, pulling the salt-marked note from his pocket. 'I'm sorry, it got a bit wet.'

The man took in Reg's countenance and the state of the money. 'Would you mind telling me how it got in this condition?' he asked, gently now.

'I was on the *Titanic*,' Reg told him. 'We arrived in port last night. I want to tell my mum I'm alright.'

'In that case, sir, we wouldn't dream of taking your money. Please write your telegram on this form and we'll send it free of charge.'

Reg felt overwhelmed. 'Thank you,' he said. 'Thank you so much.'

Now he had to think of what to say. His mind went blank. He decided to write to Florence and ask her to pass the message on to his family. He scribbled down the bare facts, trying to keep it brief. He filled in the address and passed it to the clerk.

'Don't you want to give a return address so she can get back to you?'

'I don't have one yet,' Reg said.

'OK, I'll send this straight away. Good luck, buddy.'

Reg hesitated. He should really send a telegram to John's mother as well. He remembered seeing their address on John's payslip one time and he knew it was West Road, Newcastle, but he didn't recall the number. The telegraph boy would be bound to know the family, though. But what should he say? 'I'm sorry but your son didn't make it and I'm using his name.' He couldn't put that in a telegram. He'd write a letter instead, explaining all the circumstances, and post it as soon as possible.

He left the building, then continued up to Times Square. One of the streets running off was labelled Seventh Avenue, and it reminded Reg that he had meant to make his way to Fifth Avenue, where he'd heard there were lots of restaurants. He had to start looking for work. He asked a passer-by for directions and just two blocks down 42nd Street, he came upon Fifth Avenue. There were several restaurants lining the road, but they didn't have the grandeur he sought. He had full silver-service training and he might as well use it. Presumably the smarter the place, the better the pay.

He stopped when he got to the crossroads with 44th Street, because there were two very fancy restaurants facing each other on opposite corners. The nearest one, Delmonico's, had awnings over a pillared entrance, and through the windows he could see chandeliers and crisp white tablecloths. It looked as though lunch service was over, and the staff were clearing up.

He took a deep breath and marched purposefully up the steps and in through the front door. Inside, he saw someone by a lectern who he assumed must be the maître d'.

'Excuse me, I'm looking for work,' he began. 'Who should I speak to?'

The man raised his head and sneered at him. 'Did you just use the front entrance? Who do you think you are?'

'I'm sorry, I didn't realise there was any other entrance.'

'Get out. Scram.' He waved his hand in dismissal, and Reg hurried back out to the street, feeling as though he might faint. *You don't want to work somewhere that employs the likes of him, anyway. Just try the next place.*

Opposite, there was another restaurant entrance, just as smart-looking and sumptuous as Delmonico's. It was called Sherry's. It seemed worth a try but he didn't want to make the same mistake again, so he walked down the alleyway at the side of the building, past huge waste bins, until he came to some back steps where a man in a white chef's hat was smoking.

'Excuse me, do you know if there's any work for waiting staff?' he asked.

'There might be. What's your experience?'

'I was a first-class victualling steward on the *Titanic*. We just got in last night. I don't want to go to sea any more so I'm looking for work.'

'Jesus Christ! You poor kid! Come on in and have a bite to eat, and I'll get the manager to have a word with you.'

Reg followed him up the steps and into a vast kitchen, all shiny and modern, where sous-chefs stood preparing food at their stations.

'We've got some roast lamb left over from luncheon, or some duck. What would you like?' the chef asked Reg.

'Lamb would be very nice, thank you.'

'Aren't you polite? Listen to his accent, boys! He's from the *Titanic*.'

As he sat at a table in the kitchen eating, the kitchen staff gathered round to ask questions. When they heard he had survived on the upturned collapsible, their admiration knew no bounds. They'd read about the collapsible in that morning's papers because Harold Bride, one of the *Titanic*'s radio operators who had also survived on it, had told his story to the press.

When he pushed his plate away, the chef went to fetch the restaurant manager, Mr Timothy, a slight man in spectacles.

'Are you sure you are able to work?' he asked. 'You must be pretty shook up from your experience. Don't you want some time off?'

'I want to stay busy to take my mind off it,' Reg replied.

'I guess you've done silver service?' Reg nodded. 'We'll need to check your references with White Star but as far as I'm concerned, you're on for a try-out. What did you say your name was?'

'John Hitchens.' The lie was becoming easier.

'Come back tomorrow morning at ten sharp and you can work the lunch service. We're open six days and the salary is five bucks a week. We'll provide a uniform, but make sure you look shipshape.' He winced. 'Sorry, not a good choice of words. You know what I mean.'

Before he left, Reg asked Mr Timothy for a sheet of paper and a pencil, saying he had to write home. He continued a few more blocks up the road to Central Park and found a bench where he could write to John's family.

ON ARRIVAL at New York's Pier 54, Robert Graham led Juliette and her mother past the photographers to where his driver was waiting in his car.

They drove uptown to the Plaza Hotel. 'It's gigantic,' Juliette exclaimed as they pulled up outside. 'It's quite the largest building I've ever seen.'

'I believe it has twenty storeys,' Robert told her, 'but it's not New York's tallest building, by any means.'

'So long as it's comfortable,' Lady Mason-Parker grumbled. 'I hardly slept a wink in that hard, narrow bunk on the *Carpathia*.'

Robert helped them to check in and, as he said goodnight, he asked Juliette if he might come by the following afternoon to see that all was well.

'Oh, please do,' she cried, unable to disguise her eagerness. For four days they had spent most of their waking hours together and she knew she would miss his calm presence and the reassuring sense that no matter what happened, he could deal with it. She began to miss him the minute he left.

The Plaza was a lovely hotel. The rooms were large and opulent, decorated in the rococo style, with cream walls and gold swirl carvings on balustrades. The service was impeccable, too. A tray of tea and cakes was brought to their room within five minutes of it being requested.

Next morning at breakfast, they spotted some other *Titanic* survivors, the

Duff Gordons, in the dining room. Ordinarily, Lady Mason-Parker would not have socialised with Lady Duff Gordon since she was a divorcée, but these were extraordinary times. They hit it off immediately, and retired to the lounge for coffee together after breakfast. It meant that Juliette didn't feel guilty leaving her mother behind when Robert came to call later.

'Where would you like to go?' he asked. 'I am at your disposal.'

'Actually, I enjoy walking. Could we take a stroll somewhere?'

'Of course.' He offered his arm. 'Central Park is just across the road.'

As they walked, they talked about their lives. He told her that he ran a small investment company. He lived with his mother and sister near Washington Square, and they socialised with New York's finest families—although he wasn't much of a one for fancy parties, finding the conversation rather superficial. Juliette agreed, although in truth they didn't attend many such parties at home, leading a more countrified existence.

'You said that you are planning to visit your family in upstate New York,' Robert commented. 'When must you leave for that visit?'

Juliette remembered, with a start, the lie she had told him to explain their trip. 'Not straight away. My mother has sent a telegram and we'll wait to hear. But for the time being we will stay in New York.'

'I hope you will do me the honour of letting me show you around and perhaps do some sightseeing? You must tell me if you would like to go to the opera, or shopping, or to museums. What are your favourite hobbies?'

'At home my favourite pastime is horse riding, but I suppose that's not possible in a city.'

'You really like to ride?' He seemed delighted. 'I have stables at Poughkeepsie, just outside New York. Perhaps I could take you there?' He smiled at her obvious pleasure. 'And now I'm going to take you to a café where they serve rainbow sandwiches. Have you ever had any such thing? No? Then come this way.'

REG POURED HIS HEART OUT in the letter to John's mother, describing the last time he had seen John, and telling her that no one knew what had happened to him. He explained why he was using her son's name, and apologised for any distress this had caused to his family. Finally, he wrote about how much he missed John, and sent his condolences on their loss. Then he found a post office and posted it, and immediately felt a sense of relief.

On the way back to the hostel, Reg bought himself a new white shirt, some fresh socks and underwear. He also treated himself to a sandwich called a 'hot dog', after questioning the vendor carefully to ensure that the meat it contained had nothing to do with dogs.

Still he felt very shaky. Anxieties were screeching through his head. What if he turned up at the restaurant tomorrow and the police were waiting to arrest him for giving the wrong name on the *Titanic*? What if White Star Line sued him for dereliction of duty? What if there was an inquest into Finbarr's death and it was found that he had been the cause of it? All these worries hammered at the inside of his skull, making him feel dizzy and sick.

When he reached Sherry's the next day, though, Mr Timothy was remarkably friendly. 'I spoke to White Star Line and they said you are a model employee. I didn't know where you were staying, so they said they will send your final pay packet to the restaurant here. They're also sending temporary documents so that I can apply for immigration for you. Is that OK?'

Reg nodded, amazed it was proceeding so smoothly.

Mr Timothy gave him a uniform of a black shirt, trousers and a white apron, then showed him the routine: the cutlery, linen and plate cupboards, the hot press, the cold buffet and the dessert trolley.

There was time for a smoke out the back before service, and someone offered Reg a cigarette. He accepted and the other waiters gathered round, eager to bombard him with questions about the *Titanic* again.

'There's a big stink in the papers about men who barged onto lifeboats so there was no room for the ladies. Did you see any of that?' someone asked.

'Yes,' Reg admitted. 'But I also saw lifeboats go off half full. It wasn't very well organised.'

'Where was the captain? Wasn't he in charge?'

'I don't know what he was doing. I think they were hoping another ship would arrive to pick us up. I thought I saw one, but it never appeared.'

'How long were you in the water?' someone else asked.

'I don't know,' Reg replied honestly. 'It felt like a long time.'

'Did you know anybody who died?'

Reg looked this last questioner in the eye. 'I hardly know anyone who didn't die.'

There was a hushed silence and one of the other waiters said, 'Give him a break. Think about what he's just been through.' He turned to Reg. 'My name's Tony. I'll be working the tables next to you at luncheon, so give me a nod if you need a hand or don't know where something is kept.'

'Thanks.' Reg managed a smile. 'I'll probably take you up on that.'

In fact, it went fine. The training on the *Titanic* had been so rigorous that Reg's standards were higher than those that prevailed in Sherry's, and the manager gave him several approving nods. Word spread among the diners that he was a survivor from the sinking and several shook his hand and gave him a generous tip.

'Where are you sleeping?' Tony asked at the end of the first evening shift. 'Do you have to go far?'

When Reg said he was staying down at East 25th Street, Tony exclaimed, 'That's crazy! There's a spare room at our place if you're interested. It's a buck seventy-five a week, breakfast and laundry included, and it's only a couple of blocks away. Do you want to come and look around tomorrow?'

Reg agreed that he would. It was extraordinary how quickly everything was falling into place.

ANNIE HAD BEEN DREADING the moment she stepped off the ship in New York and had to tell Seamus what had happened to Finbarr.

It wasn't till eleven at night that the call went out for third-class passengers to disembark. Slowly, Annie picked up the baby, looped her handbag over her elbow and got Roisin to hold onto her coat on one side, while Patrick held the other. She looked over to where third-class families were queuing but there were too many faces to pick Seamus from the crowd.

He found her, though. The minute they stepped off the ship he rushed over to them, joy written all over his face. It was heartbreaking to watch his broad smile fade as he first of all met her eyes and read the expression on her face, then looked at Patrick, Roisin and the baby. His eyes travelled over her shoulder and he searched the area behind them, then he looked at Annie again and it was as if something inside him broke in two.

'No!' he yelled with such anguish that people turned to stare.

'I'm so sorry,' Annie whispered.

He pulled her to him, wrapped his arms around her and buried his face in her neck. He was shaking with uncontrollable grief, unable to speak, as all their plans for the future were swept away in a devastating roll of the dice.

The apartment that Seamus had found for Annie and his children was built on a hillside and separated from other apartment buildings by step streets. When they came out of Pier 54, a kind woman ushered them into an automobile, which drove them all the way to Kingsbridge and stopped on the street below. Finbarr would have loved his first-ever ride in an automobile, bouncing around full of questions. Everything would have been exciting, and they would all have raced up the steps for a first glimpse of the new place. Instead, they trudged slowly, wearily, and Annie's legs were aching by the time she reached the top of the flight of steps to the apartment house.

Seamus took out a key and unlocked the first doorway they came to. As he swung the door open and lit a candle, she watched his face and knew how much he would have been looking forward to this moment.

The apartment seemed nice. The room at the front had a tall window with a view right down the step street and across their neighbours' rooftops. It was a good size and, what's more, it was clean.

'Some women from the church cleaned it for us,' Seamus said, reading her mind. 'It's a lovely community.'

'Isn't that nice of them?' Annie looked around the room, then lit another candle and wandered through to the kitchen. *Pretend,* she told herself. *You have to learn to pretend.*

'Isn't this grand?' she said. 'Much better than my kitchen back home.' The two bedrooms already had single beds in them and she nearly broke down when she saw the one for Finbarr. 'It's lovely,' she told Seamus. 'You've done well.'

'I said I would take you down to meet the priest, Father Kelly, just as soon as we've settled in. I was thinking . . . Maybe he could say a mass for Finbarr.' Annie could see it was hard for him to say his boy's name.

'I'd like that, but we need to buy some clothes first. We've only got the ones we're standing up in and I can't meet my new priest looking like this.'

'Yes, of course.'

They were tiptoeing round each other, scared of saying an insensitive word that might cause any additional grief. *Just look after the practicalities,* Annie thought. *That's all I can do.*

When they fell into bed and at last she was in Seamus's arms, tears came to her eyes for the first time, but she fought them back because she didn't want to upset him. Possibly he was doing the same thing, because they lay there without words, feeling the warm familiarity of each other's bodies.

WHEN JULIETTE TOLD HER MOTHER that Robert wanted to take her to Poughkeepsie to visit his stables, Lady Mason-Parker was pleased, because it looked as though her daughter was getting closer to this man by the day.

Her discreet enquiries had ascertained that he was an extremely suitable match. She had one concern, though.

'When you see these horses, you know you will want to ride them. And you mustn't. All that bouncing around in the saddle would be terrible for the baby. I think I should come to Poughkeepsie as chaperone in case you are tempted to take any risks.'

'No, absolutely not,' Juliette said. 'There's no reason why I shouldn't ride and, anyway, I can't bear the way you talk to Robert, always boasting about our connections and titled ancestors. It's vulgar.'

'I won't be spoken to like this. Apologise at once!'

Juliette apologised, and managed to marshal all her skills of tact and diplomacy to talk her mother out of chaperoning her. In fact, she sensed that Lady Mason-Parker hadn't really wanted to come. Since they had been in New York, she had shown no interest in seeing what the city had to offer.

'I've taken a lease on a house in Saratoga Springs,' she announced at breakfast one morning. 'That's in upstate New York. We'll be leaving three weeks on Friday. I don't see how you can keep your secret any longer than that. Unless, of course, wedding bells are in the air. Are they?'

'Mother, you know they are not. Robert is a good friend and I refuse to trick him into marrying me.'

Lady Mason-Parker sighed. 'Well, you can't expect the "friendship" to be sustained through six months' absence. He will find someone else to befriend as soon as your back is turned.'

Juliette knew it was true. She had an ache in the pit of her stomach when she thought of Robert falling for someone else, but what could she do? *Oh, foolish, foolish girl!* Why had she ever succumbed to the charms of Charles Wood, which now looked so meagre compared to those of Robert Graham?

On the day of their Poughkeepsie trip, the sun was shining. Robert's chauffeur rolled the car's hood back and the two-hour drive passed quickly.

'We've had a letter from our relatives,' Juliette told Robert on the way, 'and I'm afraid we must leave the city to join them in three weeks. I'm sorry, because I have greatly enjoyed our time together.'

'Where do your relatives live?' he asked.

'Just outside Saratoga Springs.'

'But that's perfect!' Robert exclaimed. 'My sister has some friends who live there, and she plans to spend part of the summer with them. I will invite myself to join the party and then I will be able to visit you.' He frowned, noting Juliette's screwed-up face. 'If you would like me to, that is.'

Juliette had to think on her feet. 'I'm afraid that won't be possible. You see, our relatives are very elderly and Mother and I have to assist them with some pressing business of a personal nature. We have promised to devote ourselves entirely to them in order to solve a particular family problem.'

He was puzzled. 'Surely you will be able to slip away for a couple of hours of an afternoon? They can't demand all of your time.'

'But they will. I'm sorry, Robert. I know I will miss you. But we can write to each other, if you are willing. I'd like to keep in touch.'

She changed the subject. Soon they were chatting animatedly on a wide range of subjects, and in no time they were pulling into a large stable yard with twelve horses leaning over stable doors and several grooms at work.

'Oh, they're beautiful!' she exclaimed. 'Just look at them.'

Robert led her around, introducing each horse in turn, and she stroked their noses and spoke softly to them. They were obviously well cared for.

When they reached a gentle bay, Robert said, 'This is Patty. She's our calmest mare and I thought you might like to ride out on her.'

Juliette looked longingly. 'She won't mind an unfamiliar rider?'

'She has never thrown anyone in her entire life. You would be the first! And I have a sidesaddle you can use.' He eyed her long skirt.

'In fact, I much prefer to ride astride. I don't suppose you have some breeches I could borrow?'

Robert grinned. 'I thought you would. You can use my sister's breeches.'

It was a tight squeeze to get into the breeches, but the hacking jacket she wore over the top disguised her belly.

Juliette mounted the mare and for the first time in months, she felt a sensation of perfect happiness, galloping through glorious countryside under a warm sun.

At dusk, it was time to drive back to the city. As Robert took Juliette's hand and helped her into the automobile, he had a soft look in his eyes and his gaze lingered on her in a way that made her shiver with pleasure. She knew he was falling for her, just as she was falling for him.

ON SUNDAYS, when Reg wasn't working, he explored the city street by street, learning it by heart. It was lonely spending so much time on his own, but he resisted the other waiters' attempts at friendship and sank deeper inside himself, constantly mulling over what had happened on the *Titanic*.

The White Star Line had sent a month's salary as severance pay to Sherry's, along with the official documents in John's name. Would they send Reg's final salary to his mother? He hoped so.

How would Florence be coping? He knew he must write to her soon but what would he say? He couldn't ask her to come out and join him, much as he would like to, because he had nothing to offer. He felt like the burnt-out shell of the person he had once been. How could she love a man who had saved himself and failed to save Finbarr?

His hours at the restaurant were eleven in the morning till midnight, with a couple of hours' break when the waiters could eat a meal and have a smoke and a gossip. Reg liked the routine, and when he first heard about a possible strike among New York waiters, he paid no attention. One day, Tony spelled it out for him, though.

'We want to join the International Hotel Workers' Union so they can protect our rights, but management is against it. The point is,' Tony said, 'that the Negroes are coming up to New York from the South and taking our jobs for a whole lot less pay.'

'What are you planning to do?'

'Well, we're threatening an all-out strike. It would hit the restaurant trade so bad I bet they'd cave in before a week's out. It wouldn't last too long.'

Reg knew that strikers didn't get paid, and although he had some savings put by they wouldn't last indefinitely. So far he had eight pounds, ten shillings in English money, and a few dollars in American currency, but he was hoping to use it to better himself somehow.

In the back of his mind, he had an idea that he might start his own small restaurant one day. Maybe he could specialise in English dishes, like tripe or steak and kidney pudding. The Americans seemed fascinated by all things English. His new employer, Mr Sherry, had started as a waiter after all, so it wasn't entirely far-fetched.

Also, he was reluctant to get into a dispute with Mr Sherry, and the manager, Mr Timothy, who had been so kind and understanding towards him. How could he reward them by going on strike? He decided to keep his head down and hope it all blew over before long.

Far from blowing over, however, the talk of a strike got louder and more strident until, towards the end of May, the staff of seventeen New York restaurants, including Sherry's, told their managers that they would walk out if their demands weren't met. Reg's anxiety grew with each day that passed.

One evening, he was asked to wait on a couple who were eating in a private dining room upstairs. 'Be discreet,' the manager instructed him. 'Just take the order and don't stop to talk.'

That suited Reg fine. He climbed the stairs to the private room, opened the door and stopped dead in his tracks. Inside, holding hands across the table, were Mr Grayling and the beautiful girl from the boat deck.

'My goodness! What brings you here?' Mr Grayling looked startled and quickly pulled his hand away from the girl's.

'I work here, sir. I decided I couldn't face another Atlantic crossing so soon after the *Titanic*, so I found a job on dry land.'

'You were on the *Titanic*?' the girl asked. She had an upper-class English accent. 'So were we. Aren't we all the lucky ones to have survived? It was such an adventure.'

Close up she was even more stunning than he remembered: her eyes an intense blue and sparkling like sapphires, her hair a deep copper colour, her lips painted in a Cupid's bow. But how could she be so vacuous as to describe the sinking of the *Titanic* as 'an adventure'?

Reg gave Mr Grayling a menu. 'This is Miss Hamilton,' he told Reg. 'We met on the *Carpathia* and are just catching up . . . I'm afraid I've forgotten your name.'

Reg hesitated, thrown by the lie, and unsure whether Mr Grayling might know his real name. 'John Hitchens,' he said, and tensed for the reaction.

'Of course! I remember now.' He turned to Miss Hamilton. 'John was our dining saloon steward. It's a small world, isn't it?'

He'd got away with it, thank goodness. 'I hope you didn't lose any loved ones on the ship, ma'am?' Reg asked politely.

'No, thank God!' She gave a tinkle of a laugh and some ostrich feathers in her headdress swayed. 'We were very lucky.'

'I'll give you both a moment to decide on your order,' Reg told them and backed out of the room. His brow was damp with sweat and his hands shook. He leant against the wall in the corridor to catch his breath. It was bizarre to bump into someone from his old life, and it took him right back to the *Titanic*'s grand dining saloon. He could almost feel Latimer's eyes on him and hear the gay chatter of the first-class passengers. Then he felt angry. It was only six weeks since the *Titanic* sank. What was Mr Grayling doing dining out with another woman? Perhaps that was why they were in a private room. There had been some stories in the press castigating Mr Grayling for surviving while his wife did not, so the last thing he'd want would be to be caught courting a girl less than half his age. The scandal would finish him off in the city.

When he went back in to take their order, he could tell they had been talking about him. He tried to seem as though he was in a hurry when he brought in their entrées, turning and heading straight back to the kitchen.

When he brought their main courses, though, Mr Grayling stopped him and asked whether he was going to go on strike with the other waiters. Reg answered honestly.

'I don't rightly know, sir. I can't afford to live without any wages coming in, but I don't want to let my fellow workers down, either. I'm hoping it will be resolved before it comes to that.' Reg bowed, then turned and left the room.

At the end of the meal, when Reg brought the bill, Mr Grayling said, 'I have an offer for you, John, that might help you out of your present difficulty. You seem a very dedicated worker and I would be delighted to offer you a job at my residence in Madison Avenue. I see from the newspapers that waiters at top establishments earn about five dollars a week. Well, I would give you ten. What do you say to that?'

Reg was astonished. 'Thank you, sir. I don't know what to say.'

'I run a very happy household and I'm sure they would be pleased to welcome you. We're close to Central Park, and you would eat well because I have a French chef. I imagine it could see you through the strike and perhaps help you to build up a nest egg. I know my wife was fond of you, and I believe I should support you in her memory. She would want me to.'

Reg wanted to refuse, but couldn't think of a way to do so politely, so he hesitated. 'That's very kind of you, sir, but I've never worked in service before,' he said eventually.

'I assume Sunday is your day off. Why don't you come over at three and look around? You could let me know your answer after that.' He handed Reg his card. 'I'll see you on Sunday.'

A DATE WAS SET for Juliette and her mother to take tea with Robert's mother and one of his sisters at their family home. Lady Mason-Parker reacted with great excitement.

'If they approve of you, he'll certainly propose. Gentlemen don't invite you home to meet their mothers unless they have serious intentions.' She eyed Juliette up and down. 'We must get you a tighter corset. He might not notice your swollen belly but the women certainly would, and if they put two and two together your chances will go up in smoke.' Her mother sighed. 'If only you had made Robert fall in love with you a bit sooner, it would have been possible to convince him the child was his. I fear it is getting rather late in the day now. But maybe . . .'

'I would never have tricked him. Never.'

'You and your misplaced sense of morality. You'll be the death of me.'

When they arrived at the tall, brownstone house Robert shared with his mother and sister, a footman showed them into a large, sunny drawing room decorated in blue, with handsome velvet chairs. Robert's sister Eugenie came over to shake their hands, then introduced them to her mother.

'It's a great pleasure to meet you at last. Robert has told us all about the close friendship you've developed since meeting on the *Carpathia*. We are so grateful that he had someone to talk to during those awful first few days when you must all have been in terrible shock. Please, sit down.'

Lady Mason-Parker smiled graciously. 'Robert has been invaluable to us, helping to solve all the tricky little problems that arise when you lose your luggage and need to replenish it in a foreign country. He almost feels like a new member of our family.'

Juliette willed her mother to stop talking. They had barely sat down and already she was dropping hints. Above the fireplace there was a painting of a pot of white flowers with some yellow pears around the base. 'What a beautiful picture!' exclaimed Juliette. 'It looks just like a Cézanne.'

Robert's mother smiled. 'You obviously know your art. Yes, it is a Cézanne. We're very lucky to have it.' She launched into the story of how they came to possess it, and Juliette sighed with relief at her lucky guess, which had successfully redirected the conversation.

The whole meeting lasted under two hours but Juliette was on edge the whole time, certain she would inadvertently give herself away. Either that or her mother would alienate the Grahams with her snobbishness and pushiness. But, at last, Robert arrived to convey them back to their hotel and the farewells seemed genuine and affectionate.

Robert was silent throughout the journey but, at the entrance to the Plaza Hotel, he asked if he might take Juliette out for dinner that evening.

'He'll check what his mother and sister say, and when they tell him they adore you, he will propose,' Lady Mason-Parker predicted.

'No, he won't,' Juliette frowned, but there was a kernel of hope inside her.

With this thought in mind, Juliette was nervous going down to meet Robert that evening, and her hands were shaking as he helped her into the automobile. Conversation between them felt unusually stilted, although he assured her that she had been a great hit with the Graham family women. *If he proposes, I must confess straight away that I am pregnant*, she decided. *I will lose him, but at least he will respect my honesty.* It seemed the only decent thing to do—and yet, she couldn't bear to lose him. She would never be able to see him again, a prospect that felt unbearable. Wasn't there any way she could put him off and ask him to wait six months for her hand? If he proposed, that was. Maybe he wouldn't.

In fact, they had barely sat down in the restaurant before Robert opened his heart. 'You must know how I feel about you.' He gazed into her eyes. 'I think about you day and night and can hardly concentrate on my work.' He took her hand across the table. 'I might have waited longer to speak but I can't bear the thought of you disappearing to some gloomy relatives for the whole summer. I love you with all my heart. If only you will consent to marry me before you leave for Saratoga Springs, then I will become a member of your family and can help to solve your relatives' problems. Please say yes.'

She covered her face with her hands. 'Oh God, I can't tell you how difficult this is. I love you too, but I can't invite you to my relatives' this summer. I simply can't. Mother and I have to do this on our own.'

Robert looked crestfallen. 'I fear that I will lose you during such a long separation. You will forget me and in the fall you'll return to your family in England and I'll never see you again.'

'That won't happen. I swear.' How could she convince him?

'Would you consider setting up home with me in the States? Would you not be homesick?'

'I'd be happy to live wherever you were. I want to be with you, Robert. I do. Please believe me. I just can't be with you this summer.'

He kissed the back of her hand. 'In that case, let's get married before you leave. The weeks will be easier to bear if you are my wife and I know for sure that you will come back to me.'

Juliette felt giddy with delight. 'Yes,' she gasped. 'Oh, yes, let's!' It seemed the answer to all her worries.

But then, she began to see problems. 'There's no time to organise a wedding. My father and brother would be terribly disappointed not to be invited, and my mother will have a huge list of acquaintances to be included. I don't see how we could manage it with less than three weeks before we go.'

'They can all wait,' Robert said, in a husky tone that brought goose bumps to her skin. 'I want to marry *you*. We can go to City Hall next week and get legally married without telling anyone else. We can simply tell them that we are engaged, and we could then have a formal wedding in England. That's traditional, isn't it? The wedding is at the bride's local church?'

'Is it really possible to get married at City Hall without giving more notice? I don't mind if you would rather just get engaged for now.'

The passion of his response amazed her. 'I want you, Juliette. I want you so much that I can't wait six months. Please say you'll marry me.' He fished in the pocket of his waistcoat and pulled out a small box. He opened the lid and she could see the glitter of a diamond inside.

'I will,' she said firmly. 'I can't wait, either.'

He leaned over the table to kiss her on the lips, and she thought she was going to faint with happiness.

ANNIE FOUND LIFE in Kingsbridge a struggle. The practicalities were easy enough: Father Kelly got Patrick into a good Catholic school, and he introduced her to a local woman who would look after the little ones sometimes to give her a break. She was a country girl, though, and she missed the green fields, trees and birdsong of her home in Cork.

The one blessing was that she felt Finbarr around her a lot of the time. She heard his voice in her head, and sensed that he was content. When the others weren't there, she kept up a running monologue with him: 'Why do you think this dough won't rise, Finbarr? What do they put in their strange American flour?' 'How long do you think it will be before my old knees give out, what with climbing these steps twice a day, sometimes more?' But during the bad moments, the burden of her loss came crashing back and she crouched in a corner of the apartment sobbing so hard she made herself hoarse. She never let Seamus or the children see her like that; she only succumbed to it on her own.

Father Kelly encouraged her to make friends and become involved in the local community, so she donated some loaves to a yard sale to raise funds for the church, and she helped arrange the flowers in the church.

'You've got an eye for colour, Annie,' Father Kelly told her, and she repeated the compliment to Seamus that evening.

'You should do some embroidery to show him,' her husband suggested. 'I haven't seen you embroidering since you got here. Maybe you should, because it always seemed to make you peaceful.'

She turned her head away. *How can I be peaceful when my son is drowned?* But Seamus was right. She used to feel at peace when she was absorbed in her creations. Maybe she could start by making a sampler for Father Kelly to thank him for his kindness to her family.

It was good to have a project to throw herself into, and she spent all her spare moments on it. Seamus was right. It definitely made her feel more peaceful. The work was absorbing and didn't leave her much time to think, but she always felt as though Finbarr was around while she was embroidering. Roisin and Ciaran would play on the floor nearby, Patrick was at school and Seamus at work. She looked forward to those moments when she was at peace with the world.

'Is it alright where you are?' she asked Finbarr one time, in her thoughts.

Immediately an answer came: 'Ma, it's wonderful here. I'm with yer da and he sends his love. He's been looking out for me since I arrived.'

Annie's father had died ten years earlier, when Finbarr was just a baby. 'That's good. It's nice to think of the two of you together.'

She smiled at the image and carried on with her stitching.

Chapter Six

The night following Mr Grayling's offer of employment, Reg lay in bed wondering what to do. Why had he offered such a thing? Was it really because he felt sorry for Reg as a fellow survivor? Or was he trying to buy his silence? The last thing he would want was Reg gossiping about his new romance so soon after his wife's death. *Before it, in fact.*

Reg had formed a distinctly unfavourable impression of Mr Grayling's character since encountering him on the *Titanic*, and he didn't want to be under obligation to such a man. Yet he had agreed to go to his house on Sunday. And he had better go, or else Mr Grayling might complain about him to the restaurant. He could get him fired with one telephone call.

Reg had more or less made up his mind he was going to turn down the offer, but at work on Saturday, a union representative came to the restaurant for a word with the staff. 'These goldbricks aren't even listening,' he said, referring to the restaurant bosses. 'They've got trainloads of Negroes lined up down South. We have to be ready to walk out for the long haul. The only way to beat them is to stick together. Are you with us on this?'

'Yeah!' 'Too right!' The waiters at Sherry's were a vociferous crowd.

Reg shrank back, his chest tight with nerves. The following afternoon, he made his way to the address in Madison Avenue that Mr Grayling had given him. He found the tradesman's entrance and rang the bell. It was opened by a tall, skinny man in a chef's hat.

'*Ah, bonjour!* You are the new footman from the *Titanic*, yes?'

This was obviously the French chef Mr Grayling had mentioned. He had a heavy foreign accent. Reg nodded shyly. 'Maybe.'

'You look good. That is a start. Come this way.'

The chef led him up some stairs to a hallway, where he introduced him to a man in wire spectacles who seemed to be the butler, a Mr Frank.

'John Hitchens? I've been expecting you. Let me take you upstairs first and we can work our way down.' He smiled in a friendly fashion. 'Perhaps there will be a cup of coffee on offer when we get to the kitchen.'

Right at the very top of the house, there was a room with a slanted sky-light window through which Reg could see clear blue sky. As well as a bed there was a writing desk, an armchair, a wardrobe and a china washbowl.

'You'd share a washroom with Alphonse, the chef, but otherwise you'd have this floor to yourself.'

It was quiet up there, a million miles away from the hustle and bustle of the rooming house where he lived. *I could think up here, clear my head.*

'Your duties would be to serve breakfast, luncheon and dinner to Mr Grayling, when he is at home, and occasionally afternoon tea if there is a visitor. Between times, you would help Alphonse with food preparation, but most days you are likely to have several hours free. Would that suit you?'

Reg nodded. *Yes, it would.* 'And the wages?'

'Mr Grayling said he agreed that with you. Ten dollars a week.'

At least I'd be safe here, Reg thought.

Down in the kitchen he was given coffee in a cup, and a piece of cake. A girl came in wearing a maid's uniform, and was introduced as Molly. She had reddish-blonde curly hair and a broad smile. 'Are you the guy from the *Titanic?*' she asked. 'What a shocker that was. I hope you're going to work here. We need someone new to talk to. It's easy work. Alphonse and I will look after you. Come on, say you'll take the job, John, won't you?'

'Yes,' Reg said. 'Yes, I rather think I will.'

ROBERT CAME TO CALL on Juliette every afternoon before her departure to Saratogo Springs, and he took her out for dinner each evening. Every second was precious as they talked about the house they would buy in New York, the honeymoon—both had a hankering to see the Egyptian Pyramids—and their English wedding. He had applied for a licence for them to marry in secret at City Hall and when it arrived, he made an appointment for an afternoon just four days before she was leaving for the country.

'Are you sure you want to do this, my love? I don't mean to pressure you,' Robert said gently. 'The haste is merely born of my insecurity that you might change your mind during our long separation. But as I get to know you better, I see you wouldn't trifle with me.'

Juliette blushed. 'I understand your reasons, and mine are the same. Let's get married now so that neither of us has any doubt about the other's commitment. Leaving you behind would otherwise be unbearable.'

And so it was that at four o'clock on a Monday afternoon in early June, they rode in Robert's car down to the south of Manhattan. The simple ceremony in City Hall lasted only fifteen minutes before the city clerk pronounced them husband and wife.

Straight afterwards, they went to the Waldorf Astoria for a glass of champagne in its plush drawing room.

What have I done? Juliette wondered, feeling light-headed. But she had no regrets when she looked at the wonderful man who sat beside her on a velvet sofa, gazing into her eyes. She was so much in love with Robert, and so perfectly happy, that she wanted the moment to last for ever.

He paid for a room and, when the door closed behind them, they devoured each other with kisses. They slipped under the bedcovers to make love, and afterwards lay wrapped in each other's limbs, kissing and talking softly. At one o'clock in the morning, they knew they must get Juliette back to her hotel or risk arousing Lady Mason-Parker's suspicions.

'I never thought a love like this was possible,' Robert whispered as he said good night. 'You have made me the happiest man in the world.'

REG WAS ASTONISHED but pleased when he saw a story in the *New York Times* that Lady Juliette Mason-Parker and Mr Robert Graham had become engaged to be married after meeting on the *Carpathia*. It was heartening to hear of love blossoming out of tragedy like that.

He would have liked to discuss it with the other waiters at Sherry's, but he wasn't very popular after announcing that he was leaving. Mr Timothy was understanding, but Tony implied that he was something of a traitor. Fortunately he only had to work a week's notice, then he packed his few belongings and headed uptown.

Molly answered his knock at the back door and led him up to his room, chatting all the way. 'We're so glad you took the job. Me and Alphonse are dying to hear all about the *Titanic*. Mr Grayling doesn't talk about it much, but Miss Hamilton sometimes spills the beans when you get her alone.'

'Does Miss Hamilton live here?'

'No, of course not. She lives in a hotel. She's here all the time, though. Mr Grayling's been helping her get back on her feet. Well, that's what he says. If you ask me, it's really the opposite.' She giggled at her own joke.

'But I'd have thought Mr Grayling would be in full mourning.'

'Mrs Grayling was a good mistress and a nice lady, but we aren't allowed to talk about her now. Mr Grayling's orders.'

Molly watched as Reg hung his only spare shirt in the wardrobe, and put his one spare pair of socks in a drawer.

'Is that all you got? You'd better buy some more clothes because Mrs Oliver only does the laundry once a week, on Mondays.'

When he'd finished, she took him downstairs to meet Alphonse properly. 'He can be a bit grouchy at times,' she said, 'but he's a topnotch chef.'

Alphonse shook Reg's hand, and asked if he would like something to eat. Reg was feeling peckish so he said yes, and was served a delicious savoury tart. It was as good as anything he'd had at Sherry's.

The butler, Mr Frank, came in to tell them that Miss Hamilton would be dining with them that evening. When he saw Reg, he shook his hand and welcomed him to the house. 'When you've finished eating, I'll show you round and explain your duties.'

The public rooms were decorated in old-fashioned, dark fabrics and seemed gloomy, especially as the shutters were pulled across. On the first floor, he was shown Mr Grayling's office, and Mr Frank pointed to a couple of doors that were locked, and not in use at present.

'Were they Mrs Grayling's rooms?' Reg asked.

'Did you meet her?' Mr Frank asked, giving him a curious look.

'Yes, I was very fond of her.'

Mr Frank nodded. 'I was as well. But Mr Grayling doesn't want the staff gossiping about her. He's dealing with his bereavement in his own way and has asked for our discretion. I hope you'll respect his wishes.'

That evening, Reg laid the table for two and was there to hold a chair for Miss Hamilton when she and Mr Grayling came in for dinner. She looked stunning in a slim black satin sheath, with diamonds dripping from her ears and looped around her slender neck. Her copper hair was swept back by a silvery headband, revealing her near-perfect heart-shaped face.

'I'm so glad George managed to tempt you away from Sherry's,' she told Reg. 'We *Titanic* survivors have to stick together.'

'Yes, ma'am,' Reg agreed.

'Where are you from, John?' she asked, and he had a moment of panic. If he said Newcastle, she would realise he was lying, because he didn't have a Geordie accent, but if he said Southampton, would Mr Grayling remember when he looked at his immigration papers, and find him out in a lie?

'I was living in Southampton before we sailed,' he compromised, hating the deception all over again. 'But my folks come from the north.'

She was barely listening to his response, though, because all her attention was focused on Mr Grayling. He looked mesmerised by the sparkle of her diamonds and the perfection of her features, like a man in a trance.

After the couple had retired to the drawing room, Reg went out to sit on the back door step for a cigarette. Molly came to join him.

'Are you OK, John?' she asked. 'You seem down in the dumps. It must be really lonely for you, going through such a bad experience and then not having anybody you can talk to about it. I hope we can be friends.'

Her face was tilted towards him and she was staring straight into his eyes, her face just inches from his. Reg sensed she would have let him kiss her if he'd tried, but the thought made him feel disloyal to Florence.

'Yes, I hope so, too,' he replied. He finished his cigarette and ground it out under his heel before standing up to go back inside.

THE MORNING OF THEIR DEPARTURE for Saratoga Springs, Robert joined Juliette and her mother for a farewell breakfast in the Plaza, at which Lady Mason-Parker chatted interminably about the wedding plans—the flowers, the hymns, the guests; details that neither of them cared about.

Juliette barely spoke, afraid that her tears might start to flow. Robert held her hand and stroked it gently, sensing her distress. It wasn't just that she would miss his conversation and caresses; without him, she would feel lonely and vulnerable in this foreign country. Her mother would be useless if anything went wrong, while Robert was eminently capable.

Porters carried their bags to the waiting car, and Lady Mason-Parker tactfully went ahead to give them time for a last embrace.

'Goodbye, my beautiful wife,' Robert whispered to her.

'I'll write to you on arrival,' she promised.

As their car pulled out into the New York traffic, Juliette finally gave in to the tears.

A COUPLE OF DAYS after starting work for Mr Grayling, Reg took a tray of coffee to him in his study. He was sitting behind a large leather-topped desk with a newspaper open in front of him.

'Put the tray there, please,' Mr Grayling said, making a space for it on the desk. 'And take a seat.' He indicated a chair on the other side of the desk.

Reg hesitated, then sat down.

'How are you finding it here? It's not too dull for you, I hope?'

'It's perfect, sir. I enjoy the peace and quiet.'

Mr Grayling was examining him in a way that made him feel uncomfortable. 'Do you still think about that night on the *Titanic*?'

'All the time, sir.'

'It's hard reading about it in the newspapers, don't you find? The inquiries seem interminable and the press dig up one story after another. You never did find that friend you were looking for on the *Carpathia*, did you?' Reg shook his head. 'Were you very close?'

'We'd been working on the same ships together for seven years. I was closer to him than to anyone in the world. But you lost your wife, sir. I don't know how I would have coped with that.'

Mr Grayling leant his chin on his hand. 'It's been tough, I don't mind telling you, and it's been made ten times worse by the scurrilous newspaper stories about me. Have you seen any of them?'

'Not really, no, sir,' Reg lied.

'There are all kinds of fabrications about me being a coward and saving my own skin while leaving my wife behind. It's terribly hurtful, and unfair.'

'The newspapers condemn any men who survived, sir. It's not just you.'

'Tell me, John, how did *you* make it into a lifeboat?'

Reg told him about jumping overboard and swimming to the collapsible, but he omitted any mention of Finbarr.

'And you were injured, weren't you?' Mr Grayling asked. 'I remember your feet were bleeding. Are they quite recovered now?'

'Yes, thank you, sir. I had frostbite, but they're fine now.'

'Good, I'm glad.' He paused. 'There was so much confusion on the boat deck that I haven't been able to establish exactly what happened to my wife. It would be extremely helpful if I could find someone who saw me helping her into a lifeboat and heard when the officer refused me permission to enter it myself.'

'Do you remember the number of the lifeboat, sir? They've compiled lists of who was in each boat.'

Mr Grayling shook his head. 'I wasn't thinking straight. I suppose I was concerned for myself, and then I got a place in a boat on the other side, and —well, you know the rest. I just wish . . . John, I am going to ask you a favour. You are under no obligation to agree, but it would make me very happy if you would give an interview to a reporter and tell him about the general air of confusion on the boat deck during the last hours of the *Titanic*. Explain how difficult it was to stay with your loved ones.'

Reg froze with horror. He'd done his best to avoid attracting attention to himself and now Mr Grayling wanted him to talk to the press. What if they wanted a picture? 'I'm very shy, sir. I wouldn't know what to say . . .'

'I could arrange for someone sympathetic to come to the house here. It would only take five minutes of your time, no more.'

'Would they want to take a photograph, sir? I really wouldn't like to have my photograph taken.'

'There's no need for a picture if you don't want one. I'll arrange an appointment for later in the week, then. Thank you, John. There's just one other thing . . .' Once again he paused, as if planning what he was going to say next. 'It would be best if you avoid mentioning Miss Hamilton. You know what reporters are like: they might leap to the wrong conclusion.'

Reg gazed down at his lap.

'Miss Hamilton has been consoling me in the loss of my wife . . . I value her opinions and judgment highly. She's a very sensible woman.'

Not from what I've seen, Reg thought, feeling awkward. It was almost as if Mr Grayling felt the need to justify himself to him, which was strange from a man in his position.

'Mr Frank will let you know when the reporter will be coming. Thank you. That will be all.'

He returned to his newspaper, and Reg hurried from the room. *What on earth have I agreed to?* he worried. *I'll really have to keep my wits about me so I don't give myself away. How long must I live this lie?*

THE REPORTER THAT CAME to interview Reg was called Carl Bannerman. Mr Frank led him into the front drawing room and Reg followed, feeling very self-conscious. They sat opposite each other in armchairs by the fireplace and Mr Frank offered them refreshments.

After Mr Frank had left the room, Carl began with some questions about Reg's background, which Reg answered as briefly as possible.

'And you became friends with the Graylings when you waited on them in the first-class saloon?'

Reg hesitated. He couldn't say that Mr Grayling had been a friend. 'I'd met Mrs Grayling the previous year on a cruise. She was very nice to me.'

Carl moved on quickly to ask about the night of the sinking. 'I bet you were terrified when you realised the ship was going to sink. You must have been out of your mind with worry.'

Reg agreed that he had been and Carl scribbled it down.

'And there were people hurrying around on the boat deck, but nobody to tell you what you were supposed to do.'

'That's right.'

'I bet you helped show the passengers to the boats, didn't you?' Reg nodded. 'But lots of the women didn't want to get on without their husbands?' He nodded again. 'Do you think that's why Mrs Grayling got off the boat her husband had helped her into? Was she going to look for him to make sure he was safe?'

'I don't know exactly. She was a very kind lady and she always worried about other people.'

'Maybe she gave up her place for someone who needed it more? A pregnant lady, maybe, or somebody with a little child?'

'It's possible,' Reg agreed doubtfully, and Carl wrote that down.

'Now tell me about your escape, John. You were on the upturned collapsible, weren't you? What was it like?'

'It was hard. I thought we weren't going to make it.'

'You were injured, I hear. Your feet were bleeding.'

'It was just frostbite. They're OK now.'

'But you could have eventually lost your feet to gangrene if you'd been out there any longer. You are lucky to be alive.'

Reg felt tears come to his eyes and blinked them away furiously, but he saw Carl writing something down. 'Yes, I suppose so.'

'I bet you really appreciate Mr Grayling giving you a job here.'

'I didn't want to go back to sea again,' Reg explained. 'I couldn't face it.'

'I'm not surprised,' Carl said, then looked up and smiled. 'Terrific. That's all I need from you.'

Reg was surprised because he felt he'd hardly opened his mouth. 'When will the story come out?'

'It's hard to say because it depends on what else is going on, but I'll write it this afternoon so it could be tomorrow or the next day. Thanks a lot.' He put his notebook and pencil away, and looked at Reg closely. 'Off the record, are you OK? I'm talking to lots of *Titanic* survivors and they're all shot to pieces. It must have been hell out there.'

'Yes, it was,' Reg told him. 'I'm fine. Just trying to keep myself busy.'

'Well, you take it easy. Look after yourself.'

They shook hands, then Carl hurried off to his next appointment.

That evening, as he sat on the back step with Molly after dinner, Reg couldn't help commenting, 'I find it strange that Mr Grayling is not in formal mourning. Back in England, husbands mourn their wives for at least a year, yet he dines out and entertains Miss Hamilton most evenings.'

Molly lowered her voice and inched closer. 'They weren't happily married.' She shook her head for emphasis. 'I used to hear him biting her head off and her crying sometimes. Did you know they had a daughter who died?'

Reg hadn't known. 'That's awful. Poor Mrs Grayling.'

'It was seven years ago, so you'd think she would have got over it. But I heard he wanted another kid and she was too old to give him one.'

He raised his eyebrows. 'Where do you get all this, Molly?'

She sniffed. 'I pick stuff up as I go along. My mom knew about them before I even started working here. She says Mr Grayling only married her for her money. It was her cash that helped him to set up his company.'

'Had you ever seen Miss Hamilton here before Mrs Grayling died?' Reg now asked.

Molly was surprised. 'Don't be an idiot! They met on the *Carpathia*.'

Reg threw caution to the wind. 'No, they didn't. I saw them together before we hit the berg. *And* I saw them getting on a lifeboat together.'

'You're kidding! They were fooling around while she was still alive?'

Reg nodded. 'Yes, they were. I don't know whether Mrs Grayling knew about it or not, but I'm sure they were.'

'That's incredible. Oh my gosh, no wonder he didn't have any time for his wife with such a gorgeous gal on the side. He's crazy about Miss Hamilton. Alphonse and I reckon they'll probably get married. It's kinda handy that Mrs Grayling is out of the way and they don't need to get divorced. Say, you don't think they bumped her off somehow, do you?'

'Molly! Don't be ridiculous!'

'Well, it's pretty easy for them now she's not around any more.'

The thought had never occurred to Reg before, and at first it seemed far-fetched, but in bed that night he began to wonder. Why hadn't he seen Mrs Grayling that last day on board the ship, or on the boat deck, or in a lifeboat? Was she already dead by the time they struck the iceberg? Were they planning to throw her body overboard in the dead of night? The image of Miss Hamilton tossing her fur coat over the railings on the boat deck came back to him. Was that a dress rehearsal? Was she checking how an object would fall when thrown from there? He shivered. If that were true, he was living in the house of a murderer.

Don't be silly. You're getting carried away, he told himself. But a niggling doubt had taken root in his head.

MR FRANK CAME INTO THE KITCHEN holding a newspaper. 'Your article's on page five, John. I thought you would like to see it.'

Reg sat at the table to read, with Alphonse peering over his shoulder.

'MILLIONAIRE'S WIFE GAVE UP HER PLACE IN LIFEBOAT', the headline read. Underneath, the article claimed that Mrs Grayling had been seated in a lifeboat that was full and ready to be lowered when a young woman who was pregnant and carrying a small child appeared. 'Give my place to her,' Mrs Grayling had cried, and leapt out of the boat. 'I will find my beloved husband and our fates will be entwined for ever.'

Unbeknownst to her, however, her husband had been ordered to board a lifeboat on the other side of the ship, and so she drowned while he was saved. All this was witnessed, according to the reporter, by a first-class steward called John Hitchens, whom they had befriended on board. In a unique twist of fate, the story continued, after the *Carpathia* docked Mr Grayling bumped into John, who had been badly injured, and offered him work at his luxury mansion, which is when the truth came out.

Reg winced. 'That's not what I said at all.'

'Reporters write what they want to write, *n'est ce pas*?' Alphonse said.

Mr Grayling seemed very pleased when Reg took him the newspaper. 'Well done, John. I appreciate it.'

I bet you do, Reg thought. *Especially if I'm helping you to cover up a murder.*

Molly seemed to have got the bit between her teeth and had more questions to ask. 'Did you even see Mrs Grayling near the lifeboats?' she wanted to know, and Reg admitted that he hadn't. He mentioned knocking on the door of their cabin and getting no reply, then trying the handle and finding it locked.

'That sure is suspicious.' Molly frowned. 'Where the heck was she?'

'It might be possible to work out which lifeboat she was on,' Reg mused, 'because I saw Mr Grayling and Miss Hamilton getting onto Lifeboat Five, which was quite an early one to launch, and he says he put Mrs Grayling in a boat on the other side *before* that. Hang on a moment.'

He ran all the way up to his room at the top of the house and retrieved a page he had torn out of a newspaper that estimated the time at which each boat had been lowered and who had been on them. He sat down beside Molly at the kitchen table and they pored over it together.

'Boat Five was lowered from the starboard side at twelve fifty-five. The first one to leave the port side, at around the same time, was Lifeboat Six. Look, it was full of women: Helen Churchill Candee and Elizabeth Jane Rothschild.' He read a few more names from the list.

'My sister works for the Rothschilds,' Molly said thoughtfully. 'She's a maid, like me. She wasn't with them on the *Titanic*, but she can probably ask Mrs Rothschild if she saw Mrs Grayling on the lifeboat. I think they knew each other.'

'What harm can it do?' Reg agreed.

'I'm going to see my sister on Sunday so I'll ask her then.'

Suddenly Alphonse banged a mixing bowl down on the table, making them jump. 'This is gossip,' he snarled. 'I hate gossip in my kitchen. It makes the sauce curdle. Don't you have any work to do?'

THAT EVENING, Mr Grayling and Miss Hamilton were dining out, so after the staff had eaten Reg was at a loose end. It was sunny and he decided to go for a walk in Central Park but by the time he had crossed the street, he found he was sweating so he turned back to leave his jacket at the house.

He entered by the back door and walked up to the cloakroom on the ground floor where outdoor clothing was kept. As he opened the door, Molly jumped back with a cry of surprise and Reg saw that she was holding one of Mr Grayling's wallets in her hand.

'What are you doing?' he asked.

'Mr Grayling . . . wanted me to find something . . .' she began.

'But he's not here.'

'He . . . erm, asked me before he left.' Reg looked down and saw that she was holding a dollar bill.

'I'll split it with you,' she said quickly. 'He never notices. He keeps wallets in all his coats and he never knows how much money he's got in them. Here—take this.' Reg backed away.

'I won't tell on you, Molly, but I don't want anything to do with this. You should be careful, because he'll call the police if you're caught . . .'

Molly cocked her head to one side. 'You're a nice guy, John. You're a good influence on me. Look! I'm putting it back.' She pushed the money into the wallet and replaced it in Mr Grayling's coat.

Reg took his jacket off and, as he stretched his arms up to hang it on a peg, Molly slipped her arms around his waist and pressed her body against him. 'I like you,' she whispered. 'I like you a lot.' Flustered, Reg was unable to move away before she leaned in and gave him a lingering kiss on the lips.

She had a sweet smell about her, and her touch felt good, but when she tilted her head back to look at him quizzically, he said, 'Molly, we can't do this. I'm sure Mr Frank wouldn't like it. It could get complicated.'

'We don't have to tell the world, do we? I like you, you seem to like me, and if we kiss and hug every now and then, it's not exactly a crime, is it?'

Before he could answer she kissed him again, and this time he couldn't help responding. It felt wonderful to be in a woman's arms.

A SIGN ANNOUNCED 'Welcome to Saratoga Springs, district of Saratoga County' and Juliette was surprised to find they were in a town, with hotels, shops, a racecourse and several bathhouses advertising health treatments with the local spring water. It seemed an attractive area, but quite different from the backwater she and her mother had been led to expect.

The house they pulled up in front of was isolated, down a dirt track and within a large flower-filled garden. It had a shady verandah out front with a swinging seat on it and, inside, the rooms were freshly painted and sunny. A local woman called Edna had been hired to shop, cook and clean for them, and she was waiting to greet them.

Edna brought them tea on the verandah, and Juliette asked her mother about the relatives they had told everyone they were visiting.

'I promised to write to Robert on arrival,' she explained. 'But what can I say? I suppose I must describe these elderly relatives we are supposed to be staying with. How can I not?'

'I will have to do the same when I write to your father and brother. I haven't seen them since I was a child, but they are the son and daughter of my grandmother's cousin and have lived in America all their lives.'

Together they invented a likely kind of house, very dark, and brimming with antiques, and two frail grey-haired people, a brother and sister, seeing out their final days together.

'I'm only just beginning to realise all the lies we are going to have to tell!' Lady Mason-Parker exclaimed. 'I must keep a note or I'll forget.'

'I'm sorry, Mother,' Juliette said. 'Truly I am. This has been horrid for you too, and we still have five months to go.'

The day after their arrival, a doctor came to examine Juliette. He took her blood pressure, felt her stomach and asked a number of questions about her diet and sleeping patterns, unable to conceal his disapproval of her.

'I've been getting a strange fluttery sensation in my belly,' she told him. 'But I expect it's nerves brought on by the journey.'

'On the contrary,' the doctor said. 'What you feel is the baby kicking.'

Juliette started back in her chair, open-mouthed with surprise. 'Really?' Until that point she had given the baby little thought, but if it was kicking her, she would have to start accepting it was a real living creature.

In bed that night, she couldn't sleep. The baby was kicking, and she stroked her belly trying to soothe it. Every letter she wrote to Robert that summer would contain yet more lies. There was nothing she could write that was true, apart from the fact that she missed him.

It all felt horribly wrong, but she knew that she had no choice. She just wished time would speed up and the months would pass quickly, so that it would all soon be over.

ANNIE HADN'T REALISED how hot it would be in New York in the summer. The only place where it was cool was in the church, and she looked forward to her daily visit. As well as looking after the flowers, she volunteered to sweep the floors on alternate days.

'How are you managing, Annie?' Father Kelly asked one day. He was around fifty, with wispy silver hair and kind blue eyes, and she had known at first glance that he was a good man: someone she could trust.

'This heat is something else!' she exclaimed. 'I don't know how you all cope with it.'

'Personally, I stay indoors. But I meant to ask how you are in yourself?'

'There're good days and bad days, Father.' She felt the tears coming and attacked a cobweb in the corner of a pew to drive them away.

'On the good days, what is it that makes them good? Is there something you can pinpoint that might help on the bad ones?'

'Well . . .' she hesitated. 'I don't know if the Church would think this wrong or not, but I talk to Finbarr in my head. Sometimes it really feels as if he is there, answering me.' She stopped to control herself, determined not to cry, then continued. 'I suppose the good days are the ones when I feel he is here with me, and the bad days are the ones when I can't feel him.'

'I wouldn't call that wrong, if it brings you comfort.' He paused, choosing his words carefully. 'Do you believe that Finbarr's spirit is genuinely with you on those good days?'

'I wonder about it, Father. It feels as though he is, not just from his words in my head, but also a sense of his presence around me. Sometimes I think I can even smell the scent of his hair. But I know that the brain can play tricks when you are grieving, and maybe mine is letting me believe his spirit is here so as to get me through this period. I know it's against the teachings of the Church, but I want to believe it.'

'Of course you do. You are right that the Church has pronounced against spiritualism, but I think that's because they are concerned about the charlatans and showmen it attracts. Tell me, when you talk to Finbarr in your head, does he answer you directly?'

'Not always, but a lot of the time it appears he does.'

'And do you talk to any other spirits in your head?'

'Goodness no, Father. I wouldn't do that.' Annie was shocked.

He sat down on the end of a pew. 'I am going to speak to you in confidence now, but I have attended a séance at which my mother's spirit came through.' Annie stared at him in astonishment. 'There was no doubt it was her. She called me Figgy, which was her pet name for me when I was a boy. My Christian name is Fergus but when I was little I used to call myself Figgy and it stuck. That's something no one here could possibly have known. It was a profound experience for me and it forced me to re-examine my beliefs and the teachings of the Church. But I found that nowhere in the Bible does it say it is a sin to contact those who are in heaven.' Father Kelly paused, then continued. 'I expect there are only a few people who have what they call the "second sight", but if such a gift is given to them by God, and so long as they use it responsibly, I can't see any harm in it. Was there no one else in the family who had the second sight?'

'I don't think so, Father.' Annie shook her head, running through all the aunties and grandparents she could remember.

'I wonder if you might be willing to talk to any of my other parishioners who are struggling to cope with a bereavement? The combination of the wisdom you have gained from your own experience, plus your ability to talk to spirits, could surely help folk through their dark times. Is it something you would consider, Annie?'

'Oh, really, Father, I don't feel I could be any use . . .'

'Of course you could! Think how much comfort you have gained from talking to Finbarr. You have the power in your hands to give that same comfort to others who are grieving. It would be a Christian thing to do.'

Despite her unease, Annie promised she would think it over.

REG HAD VERY MIXED FEELINGS about his flirtation with Molly. On the one hand, he enjoyed their stolen kisses in corners. It made the working day more interesting and fun, and she was a pretty girl. On the other hand, he was worried about anyone else in the house finding out. And he didn't entirely trust Molly since finding her stealing from Mr Grayling's wallet. If she could do that, what else was she capable of? And might she drag him into trouble with her? Above all, Reg knew she wasn't his type. He liked girls who were quieter and more refined. Like Florence.

He had told Molly about his idea of opening a restaurant one day and straight away she had said she'd like to help. 'I could be your maître d' and greet all the diners when they come. I'd be good at that. Everybody says I'm a friendly girl. Don't you think I'm friendly?'

Reg agreed that she was. He didn't tell her he was planning a small-scale venture, too humble for a maître d', and that when he pictured it, he certainly couldn't see Molly there.

Meanwhile, Molly remained obsessed by Miss Hamilton and Mr Grayling's behaviour on board the *Titanic* and, while they waited for her sister to report back about Lifeboat 6, she asked Reg many more questions.

'Where was Miss Hamilton's cabin? Was it near the Graylings'?'

Reg didn't know, but he fetched his newspaper with the list of survivors to confirm that she had been in first class. He ran his finger down the page, but the alphabetical list leapt from Hamalainen to Hansen.

'This is strange,' he told Molly. 'She's not listed here.'

'No kidding! I guess if you are a married man's mistress, you don't use your real name. But who is she then?'

Reg looked at the page that listed the occupants of the lifeboats, and there in Lifeboat 5 was Mr Grayling's name—but which one was his glamorous companion? Several women were listed as travelling alone, but some sounded German, two had obviously Jewish names and when he cross-referred between lists he found that the rest appeared to have left family behind on the ship. Perhaps, like him, Miss Hamilton hadn't given her real name to the man doing the roll call on the *Carpathia*? Perhaps she wasn't on any records. The full list of passengers and their cabin allocations didn't appear to have survived, so there was no way of checking.

'I'm going to keep an eye on her from now on,' Molly averred. 'I'll figure it out if it's the last thing I do.'

Miss Hamilton was spending increasing amounts of time at the house, and was even found there sometimes when Mr Grayling was out. One blazing hot afternoon she rang the bell and asked Reg to bring her some iced lemonade in the drawing room. When he arrived with the tray he found her sprawled against cushions, fanning herself by the open window.

Reg put the lemonade on a table by her side. 'Will that be all, miss?'

'I was just thinking about the *Titanic*,' she said. 'Has it changed you, John? Has it made you a different person?'

More than you could ever know, he thought. 'I suppose so. I've decided to stay in America instead of going home.'

She wasn't listening to him, caught up in her own thoughts.

'How long do you think one should know a woman before proposing marriage to her?' she asked. 'What is your opinion?'

He felt embarrassed by this personal line of questioning. 'I can't rightly say, miss, seeing as I'm not married myself. I suppose some people wait a year or so?' She made a tutting sound and he felt she wanted another answer, so he continued: 'I heard that Lady Mason-Parker, who was on the *Titanic*, has become engaged to a gentleman she met on the *Carpathia*. The announcement was in the newspaper.'

'Dowdy old Juliette? Really? Who on earth is marrying her?'

Reg was surprised to hear that they knew each other. 'A Mr Robert Graham. He's American.'

'Well, well. *She* didn't waste any time.'

Emboldened by her candour, Reg asked how she knew Juliette.

'We used to have a few friends in common back in England.'

'You didn't see her on the *Titanic*? I never noticed you in the first-class dining saloon, miss.'

She gave him a sharp look. 'I stayed in my cabin for most of the voyage. There are times when you want to escape from society . . .'

'I saw you one night,' Reg volunteered. He would never have been so forward with an upper-class lady if she hadn't introduced the conversational tone and seemed to want to chat. 'I was on the way down from the bridge and I saw you throwing your fur coat overboard. I nearly came to offer assistance because it seemed such a strange thing to do.'

She was alert now, listening carefully. 'If you must know, it was a present from an old beau and I couldn't bear the associations. It made my flesh crawl.' She shuddered. 'Were you watching me for long?'

Reg coloured. 'No, miss, I was taking tea to the bridge, so I couldn't stop.' He didn't want Mr Grayling to know he had seen them kissing.

Suddenly her eyes narrowed, as if she felt she had given too much away. 'That will be all,' she said, and gave a little wave of dismissal.

'Thank you, miss.' Reg bowed and left the room.

REG HAD BEEN TRYING to avoid gossiping with Molly, but when she came back from meeting her sister, who worked in the Rothschild residence, she drew him to one side in the hallway.

'Mrs Grayling wasn't on Lifeboat Six,' she hissed urgently. 'Apparently Mrs Rothschild was one of the first ones to get on board and she didn't see her all night. What do you think about that?'

Reg got goose bumps all up his arms. If Mrs Grayling hadn't been on that boat, which one could she have been on? He knew that all the others on the starboard side all left *after* Lifeboat 5, the one that Mr Grayling was on.

'Mrs Grayling must have been sitting in another boat that was delayed for some reason,' he suggested.

'You can believe that if you want to. I know what I think,' was all Molly said, darkly.

The next afternoon, when Reg had a few hours off, he went for a long walk. As he returned to the house, Mrs Oliver was polishing the brass fittings on the front door.

'You've got visitors,' she called to Reg. 'They're waiting in the kitchen.'

Surprised, Reg opened the back door and walked through to the kitchen. Sitting at the table were a woman and a girl he had never seen before. Alphonse had given them coffee and cake.

'Is our John with you?' the woman asked, in a broad Geordie accent.

Reg's knees gave way and he clutched at the kitchen sink.

'This is John,' Molly said, to fill the stunned silence in the kitchen.

'No, John Hitchens, I mean. He was on the *Titanic*. White Star Line told us he was working at Sherry's and Sherry's told us he was working here.'

Everyone turned to look at Reg. For a moment he considered running out of the back door, and keeping on running for as long as he could.

'He's my son,' the woman explained, 'but I haven't heard from him since the sinking, even though I know he survived. He's on the list of survivors.'

Reg couldn't speak for the colossal weight of shame. How could he have been so stupid? What had he done to this poor woman?

'This is John Hitchens,' Molly said carefully, 'and he was on the *Titanic*.' She turned to Reg. 'Did two of you have the same name? It would be terrible if it turns out they've come all this way for the wrong guy.'

At last Reg found his voice. 'Alphonse, Molly, do you think you could leave us alone for a while? I need to talk to Mrs Hitchens on her own.'

As the door closed behind them, Reg slumped in a chair and leaned his head in his hands. He couldn't bear to look the visitors in the eye.

'I am so sorry,' he said. 'I wrote to you. Didn't you get the letter?'

'What letter?'

'I sent it to you at West Road, Newcastle, but I didn't know the number. I was sure it would get there.'

'West Road is one of the longest roads in the city. We never got any letter from you. What did it say?'

Reg could barely speak for his shame. 'I can't tell you how sorry I am.

I've done something unforgivable and I didn't even realise it till now. John was my best friend and I took his name after the sinking. I've been pretending to be him. But I'm not. My name is Reg Parton.'

The woman was shaking her head in bafflement. 'I don't understand. Why would you do that?'

'I wanted to get work in New York and John had a clean record while I didn't.'

'So where is John then? Whose record is he using?'

The girl spoke for the first time. 'He's dead, isn't he? That's why you used his name. That's what you wrote to tell us.'

Reg nodded slowly. 'I'm so sorry. I don't know what happened to him when the ship went down, but he didn't make it onto the *Carpathia*.'

'He must be here,' John's mother insisted. 'We've come all the way from Newcastle to find him because White Star told us he was here.'

'That's because they believe that I am John. I don't know what I was thinking of. I can't begin to explain this to you . . .'

What was wrong with him? It was unbelievably cruel to steal a dead man's identity.

'I'm his sister, Mary,' the girl explained. 'Are you absolutely sure he couldn't be alive somewhere else? Maybe he took another name as well.'

'I searched the *Carpathia* from top to bottom. I was devastated when I couldn't find him. He was my best friend in the world.'

'I know. He mentioned you in letters.' The girl gave a huge sigh and it caught in her throat and turned into a sob. 'He was very fond of you.'

John's mother still couldn't believe it. 'White Star told us he was here. There must be some mistake. We've spent all the money we had in the world coming to find him. We thought he must be too shook up to get in touch. We sent letters to White Star but he never replied.'

'I didn't get the letters,' Reg told them. 'If I had, I'd have written back and told you the truth. I'll reimburse you for your fares. I'll give you all my savings and I'll keep sending you money until I've paid off everything you've spent. I promise.'

John's mother was pale and her face tight as the truth began to dawn on her. 'I don't want your *money*,' she cried. 'I want my *son*!'

Mary was crying silently, and Reg felt such a deep shame that he wished himself dead. He couldn't think straight. His head was full of fog and he'd made all the wrong decisions. He'd left his brain in the North Atlantic.

'I wish there was something I could do, something I could say, to make this better, but there isn't. I would do anything,' he pleaded.

'Bring me back my son!' John's mother shouted, angry now, and Mr Frank opened the kitchen door and stepped into the room.

'What's going on?' he asked quietly.

'He's impersonating my son John! We've come all this way and John is dead. I don't know how he could do that.' John's mother started crying, with huge sobs that made her chest heave. Her daughter tugged at her arm and said, 'Let's go back to the hotel, Ma. We need to be alone.'

Mr Frank barely glanced at Reg, just addressing them. 'Ladies, please allow me to get our driver to take you to your hotel. You are too distressed to walk the streets. Come with me and I'll show you out at the front.'

The women rose to their feet and Reg watched them go. John's sister gave him one long look of reproach, but he was frozen to the spot. He sat there without moving for more than ten minutes. He could hear Mr Frank talking to the women in the hall upstairs, then the front door opening.

He was in a hole so deep that he didn't believe he would ever be able to climb out again. How could he have been so thoughtless? He'd blithely assumed the postman would deliver that letter and hadn't bothered to check. He could have written to them care of White Star in Southampton—that would have reached them—but instead he'd just put them out of his mind. It was evil, that's what it was. He deserved to die. Just as soon as he could, he decided he would find a way to kill himself. That was the only solution.

Mr Frank was tight-lipped when he came back into the kitchen. 'I think we'd better go upstairs and explain this to Mr Grayling, don't you?'

MR GRAYLING was in his office. Mr Frank tapped on the door and led Reg in.

'Excuse me, sir. Can you spare a few moments?'

'Of course. Sit down,' Mr Grayling said.

Mr Frank pointed Reg towards a chair then sat himself and explained why they were there. Mr Grayling asked Reg to tell him the whole story, and Reg told him everything, from how he gave John's name to the man taking the roll call by mistake, to how he couldn't live this lie any longer. When he finished, Mr Grayling frowned and sat back in his chair.

'What's your real name?' he asked sternly.

Reg told him.

'And tell me about your record with White Star. Was it so bad?'

Reg explained about his misdemeanours, and Mr Grayling exchanged a look with Mr Frank.

'I see,' he said. 'I should dismiss you on the spot for lying to us. Don't you agree, Mr Frank?'

Mr Frank said nothing, but the two men continued to look at each other.

'However, I feel a sense of responsibility for you now. Everyone who was on the *Titanic* is struggling to come to terms with it, and I see you are having more trouble than most. But if you are to remain in my employment I need to be sure you will not tell me any more lies.'

Reg was trembling. 'I . . . I can't carry on, sir.'

'You have to carry on, Reg,' Mr Frank told him firmly, but his tone wasn't unkind. 'You have to keep working so you can repay these women every penny they've spent coming here, including the cost of their hotel and sustenance. I told them I will send you there to talk to them tomorrow.'

'I can't.' Reg's eyes welled up. 'They can have all my savings, all my wages, but I can't face them again.'

'It's the very least you can do,' Mr Frank told him. 'When they get over the shock, they are going to want to hear the whole story of what happened to John. You owe it to them to tell them every last detail.'

Reg covered his face with his hands and started to cry bitterly. He was crying for what he'd done to John's family, and crying for himself but, most of all, he was crying because he missed John.

Mr Grayling spoke to Mr Frank. 'I think we need to keep an eye on him tonight. He's in a bad way. And he's not the only person I've heard about who took on a different identity on the ship.' He turned to Reg. 'Come, come, lad. Pull yourself together.'

Reg wiped his eyes and struggled to regain control.

Mr Grayling continued: 'So, tomorrow you will go and visit these women and tell them everything they want to know. You can't ever make it up to them fully, but they will be able to see how remorseful you are, and that will help.'

'Yes, sir. I will. You can be sure of that.'

'Next week we are going to my summer house on Long Island for a vacation and I think the sea air will do you good. Tonight you may take the evening off your duties. Go to your room and rest. Someone will bring your dinner on a tray, and I'll see you tomorrow.'

Reg went upstairs and lay on his bed, watching the sky gradually darken through the skylight. Molly came up with a tray of food and slammed it on the chest, snapping, 'Here you go, *Reg*,' in a tone that showed she had heard the news and was furious with him. He could see how it must look to her. He had kissed Molly on several occasions, yet he hadn't trusted her enough to tell her his name. No wonder she was cross.

He couldn't eat, couldn't take so much as a sip of water. Suicide was the most appealing of the options in front of him, but he couldn't do that until he had reimbursed the Hitchens family. *I thought I had reached the depths of misery on the* Carpathia, Reg thought. *But that was nothing compared to how I feel now.*

Chapter Seven

I n Saratoga Springs, the temperature shot up into the nineties and Juliette's belly grew bigger by the day. She went for short walks in the vicinity of the cottage but the air was thick with stinging insects and, before long, her face and hands were covered in swollen, itchy lumps.

The entire focus of Juliette's day lay in writing a letter to Robert and waiting for the mail to arrive so she could read his replies. They were her umbilical cord with the outside world, where people went out for dinner and rode horses and formed friendships and fell in love.

Robert wrote about his business, about the choking heat of the city, about a niece who was visiting town whom he had promised to show around, and about events in the news. At the end of his letters, Robert never failed to say how much he loved her and was looking forward to seeing her.

Juliette pored over the *New York Times* so she had interesting items to write back to him about. She wrote about her family, drawing character sketches of each. In one letter, she described the cynical way in which Venetia, an old acquaintance, had seduced her brother Wills two years previously, hoping to get him to propose—until she found out that the Mason-Parker estate had a lot of land but not enough cash to keep her in jewels, at which point she disappeared. Wills had been cynical about women since then, seeing them as scheming, heartless, untrustworthy creatures and had not entered into any further affairs of the heart.

When she finished the letter she sat back to read it through and was overcome with guilt. Wasn't she being a scheming, untrustworthy creature herself? The difference between her and Venetia was that she loved Robert whereas her erstwhile friend had only ever loved herself, but there were times when it felt like a fine line.

MR FRANK INSISTED that Mr Grayling's chauffeur drove Reg downtown to the hotel in which John's mother and sister were staying. He took with him all the money he had in the world: Mrs Grayling's five pounds, the three pounds ten shillings which were John's final salary from White Star, and almost fifty dollars he had saved on his own account. He reckoned that should cover the cost of their tickets across to America, but he would need to save as much again for the return trip and for their hotel bill.

The women were expecting him and he was shown into a dingy drawing room. They'd chosen a very cheap hotel. Both were red-eyed and looked as though they hadn't slept much, but Mary rose to shake his hand in greeting.

'I'm sorry if we got you into trouble at your work yesterday,' she began. 'We were in such shock we weren't thinking about your position.'

'Please,' Reg begged them. 'Please, whatever you do, don't apologise to me. If I were to apologise to you a million times it could never be enough for what I've done to you and your family.'

'Sit down, lad. You look all in,' John's mother commented. 'It was a bad night for us all. I know you and John were great pals.'

Mary asked, 'We don't want to upset you, but would you mind telling us what happened to John after the *Titanic* hit the iceberg?'

Reg told them about bumping into John on the boat deck and their hastily agreed plan. 'We'd said we'd meet at the captain's bridge but he wasn't there. And then the ship started to go under and we had to jump. I don't know where he was then.'

'He didn't make it to any of the lifeboats?'

Reg shook his head sadly. He explained as well as he could about the way his mind had been working when he gave John's name on the *Carpathia* and then decided to pretend to be John. He told them about his fear of the water now, which meant he couldn't return to England even if he wanted to. He described the fogginess in his head and the difficulty he had making decisions. 'I can't explain properly why I did all this,' he told them, 'but in a funny way, I feel as though the old Reg died on the *Titanic*: I haven't been myself since then. I'm scared of everything, and I never used to be. Life feels unreal. I'm so sorry,' he repeated. 'I know it can't compensate in any way, but I've brought all the money I have.' He handed it to Mary. 'If you give me your address, I'll send you more every month to cover the cost of your trip.'

The women looked at each other. 'We talked about it this morning and decided that we'll take this money from you, if only to make you feel better. We'll put it towards a headstone for John and get him a fancy one. He'd be happy you'd done that.'

Least you could do, man, Reg imagined him saying.

BACK AT THE HOUSE, Reg wasn't surprised to find that the story had got around and hardly anyone was speaking to him. Mr Frank asked if everything had gone as well as could be expected at the meeting, and Reg said yes. Molly and Alphonse turned their backs when he walked into the kitchen. The only thing Mr Grayling said to him was that he was taking legal advice on how to get Reg immigration papers in the correct name and that it might take a while to resolve. Reg gave him the surviving fragments of his old passport and thanked him humbly for his trouble.

That afternoon, when he had a couple of hours free, he decided to write to his mum and Florence. John's family weren't the only people he had hurt with his selfish actions. There were his mother, his brothers, and Florence.

'*Dear Mother*,' he wrote, then stopped. These were going to be the hardest letters he would ever have to write in his life. He eventually completed the letter to his mother—a simple recitation of the facts followed by a heartfelt apology for the distress he had caused—but found he couldn't write to Florence. He started dozens of times, then ripped the paper into pieces because it sounded wrong.

After Molly's initial condemnation about his deception, her curiosity got the better of her and she tried to wheedle the story of his assumed name out of Reg, but he saw her in a different light now. She was a dishonest, gossiping troublemaker, and he should never have kissed her or told her anything about Mr Grayling and Miss Hamilton. He resolved to keep his distance, but it was easier said than done when they worked in the same house.

'What if it turns out he was a murderer?' she said one day. 'If he killed Mrs Grayling, we need to know. Maybe none of us is safe in our beds.'

'That's a bit far-fetched, Molly. He's an upper-class gentleman and they simply don't do things like that.'

Molly sensed she had lost Reg's interest. He no longer followed her into cupboards for a quick kiss when she beckoned, and if she joined him on the back step he quickly finished his cigarette and came indoors. All the same he was surprised when, the day before they were due to leave for Long Island, he walked into the kitchen and found her kissing Alphonse. As she broke away, Molly gave Reg a calculating look.

That night, Reg lay in bed thinking about Molly, with all her tricks and subterfuges, and it made him miss Florence terribly. She would never have played any of those games and it wasn't fair that Reg was being dishonest with her. He got out of bed and wrote to her in a great burst of emotion.

Dear Florence,

I'm sorry I haven't written before. I wanted to write lots of times but I couldn't do it because I couldn't bear you to hate me. I wish I could make you understand what I've been through but I'm no writer, as you know.

Do you remember saying to me once that when I'm upset I crawl inside my shell and hide from the world? Well, that's what I've been doing. On the Carpathia, *the man who took the roll call thought I was John, so I pretended to be him and got a job here using John's identity and references. John had died. I don't know what I was thinking. It was a terrible thing to do.*

I think about you a lot and wish I could talk to you again but I can't face getting on a ship. The thought is terrifying. I have no choice but to stay here for now. Anyway, I'm not the person you used to know. I'm very shook up and I don't know if I'll ever get better again. I miss you and will always cherish the memories of the times we had together.

I hope that you find someone who can give you everything you deserve. I'll always love you and wish nothing but the best for you.

Your loving Reg

As soon as he finished, he addressed the envelope without including a return address and put it with the letter to his mother. He'd ask Mr Frank to post them both in the morning. Mr Frank was staying behind with a small staff to look after the New York house while they were at Long Island.

MR GRAYLING had two automobiles and he and Miss Hamilton were travelling in the front one, while five members of staff, including Reg, Molly and Alphonse, came along behind. They headed downtown through the

New York traffic onto a huge bridge that crossed the East River to Long Island. The buildings started thinning out and Reg could see green fields and trees. The air smelled cleaner and fresher as they sped away from the city smog. They stopped at a diner for luncheon, and Reg ordered a hot dog. He'd developed a taste for them.

'Oh, look, they've got Pepsi-Cola!' Molly said. 'I'm going to try one of those. Did you know it's supposed to be good for you? It gives you energy.'

Reg ordered one, too. He wasn't sure if it gave him energy or not, but he felt relaxed as they continued the journey and he smelled the first hint of salt in the air. The ocean came into view, a deceptively warm shade of blue stretching out to the horizon, quite different from the oil-black, freezing water in which Reg had almost drowned back in April. He shivered.

At last they pulled up outside a white, two-storey clapboard house surrounded by a lawn and a low, white picket fence. There was a long verandah on the ocean side and the garden butted right onto the beach, whose pale sand was licked by frilly white waves.

Mr Grayling hadn't been to the house since the previous summer but the caretaker, a man named Fred, lived there all year round to keep an eye on it. When Reg came in through the kitchen entrance carrying his bag, it was Fred who showed him to his room on the first floor, near the garage.

When he went back into the kitchen, Alphonse was unpacking a big box of provisions he'd brought from New York, so Reg set to helping him. Then he wandered round the summer house, coming across a few items that he guessed must have belonged to its former mistress: under a cupboard on the verandah was a pair of faded blue canvas plimsolls with grains of sand still inside; on a bookshelf, some women's romance novels.

The next day, Alphonse was planning to boil some lobsters that had been hauled in from the bay.

'Find me the biggest pot you can,' he asked, so Reg got down on his hands and knees to explore the pot cupboard and there, in a corner at the very back, he found a child's rag doll.

Reg hauled out a large brass cauldron and took it to Alphonse, then went outside to where Fred was repairing a lobster pot in the yard.

'I found this,' he said, holding out the rag doll. 'Could it have belonged to the Graylings' daughter?'

Fred looked up and his eyes widened. 'Aw, heck, I was supposed to throw out all of Alice's things years ago.'

'Alice. Was that her name?'

Fred glanced around to check no one was listening. 'Yeah. Beautiful little thing, she was. When she died—must be seven years ago now—it broke their hearts clean in two.'

Reg remembered the sadness in Mrs Grayling's eyes. 'What happened?'

'Scarlet fever carried her off. That Miss Hamilton was a school friend of hers. Came here with the family the summer before she died. Those two were always giggling together, swimming and running along the beach.'

'Miss Hamilton!' Reg was flabbergasted. 'She was a family friend?'

'That's right. Everyone called her Vee back then, like the letter "V". They were at some fancy school together.'

'I wonder why she has come here with Mr Grayling? It must be strange for her to return to a place where she used to be so happy with her friend.'

'Over the years I've learned not to wonder about the affairs of upper-class folk. I have my own opinion about what's going on, and I have a hunch you do, too.' He winked. 'But we'll keep it quiet, won't we?'

Reg put the rag doll in the garbage can and went back to help Alphonse. This made the situation in the house all the more bizarre. How could Mr Grayling be having an affair with a friend of his daughter's?

THE DAYS WHEN JULIETTE could wear a corset were long gone. Her waist had completely disappeared and her belly bulged as if she had a plump cushion secured under her petticoat.

She could clearly feel the creature moving now, and was amazed at this life form that she was nurturing with her own cells. Juliette began to feel curious about the new little person who was forming inside her. What kind of personality would the child have? Who would it take after?

'Better not think about it,' her mother advised, 'or it will be harder to give it up when the time comes.'

There was precious little else to think about, though. Every morning, Juliette rose early and took a walk in the fields round the house before the heat of the sun became too fierce. She ate her breakfast, then sat on the verandah reading the newspaper. After luncheon, she would begin her letter to Robert, making it as entertaining as she could. His letter would arrive some time before afternoon tea, and she would reply to any questions he asked before sending the driver to the post office with hers.

One morning, she spotted her own name in the newspaper's gossip column. 'Lady Juliette Mason-Parker should consider cutting short her trip out of town and hurrying back to keep an eye on her fiancé, Mr Robert Graham. He was seen at the Poughkeepsie racetrack yesterday with the very fetching young actress, Miss Amy Manford, on his arm, and the pair seemed inseparable.'

The pain felt as though someone had plunged a knife into her chest.

He's slipping away from me, Juliette thought miserably. *We only had four days together as husband and wife. I can't lose him. It's not fair.*

FROM THE FIRST DAY at the summer house, Molly started flirting with Reg, trying to resurrect their former intimacy. He kept her at arm's length, not least because he didn't want to tread on Alphonse's toes, and she soon became frustrated at his lack of response.

'What a stuffed shirt you are!' she gibed. 'Come for a walk on the beach. It's a beautiful day and they're flying kites over in the next bay.' She kept on at him until eventually he agreed.

'OK, just for ten minutes,' he said. 'But I don't want to talk about Mr Grayling's affairs any more.'

'It wasn't Mr Grayling I wanted to talk to you about,' Molly said, as they set off. 'It was us. I'm sad that we're not friends any more, the way we used to be. I like you, Joh . . . I mean, Reg.' She laughed nervously. 'What do you reckon? Can we start again?'

Reg took a deep breath. 'Molly, I'm sorry. I shouldn't have fooled around with you before. Besides, I saw you with Alphonse. He seems keen on you.'

'Oh, *him!*' She waved her hand dismissively. 'He's always had a thing about me, but he's not my type. It's *you* I like.' She sniffed loudly, and he turned to see there were tears pooled in her eyes, ready to spill over. 'Do you think I have a chance with you?'

Reg knew he had to make himself clear once and for all. 'You deserve someone much better than me. You're pretty and clever and good at your job. You'll find a wonderful husband some day.'

'But I have lots of plans for us! Remember when you told me that you want to open your own restaurant some day and I said I would help you in front of house? I think we'd make a great team. Well, I've come up with a super idea for raising the money.' She turned to face him. 'We'll go to Mr Grayling and tell him that we know he didn't put his wife on a lifeboat on the *Titanic*. We know he was having an affair with a lady who is less than half his age. We know that there was no Miss Hamilton on the list of survivors, so she was using a fake name, which means she might be running away from something. We could say we suspect that he killed Mrs Grayling, but I don't think we need to. We'll have his attention by then. Anyway, we can say that if he doesn't pay up, we'll go to the newspapers and . . .'

'Stop!' Reg was shocked. 'Don't say another word.'

'I thought you'd be happy. It would take us years to save up enough money from our pay, but he has lots of money. He wouldn't exactly miss a few thousand bucks.'

'It's blackmail. You can't seriously think I would go along with this.' Reg regarded her with horror. 'Molly, what you are suggesting is wrong and dangerous and I would never be a party to it. Now please keep away from me.' He turned to head back to the house.

'You're kidding, aren't you?' she called after him. 'It would be so easy.'

He didn't reply but hurried along the sand, anxious to put physical distance between them. He noticed Alphonse standing on top of a dune and waved, but didn't go over to say hello.

ONE DAY, when Annie was tending to the flowers in the church, Father Kelly approached her and asked, 'I wonder if you might be willing to talk to one of my other parishioners who is struggling to cope with a bereavement? Her daughter died of cholera last year. She's still beside herself with sorrow. The poor woman just keeps repeating to me that little Dorothy won't be able to look after herself in heaven, and all the wisdom I can offer brings no relief. I told her about you and she has set her mind on meeting you and asking if you can contact her little girl. Would you consider it, Annie?'

'Oh, really, Father, I don't feel I could be any use . . .'

'Of course you could! Think how much comfort you have gained from talking to Finbarr. In this case, I know you could do so much good just by telling the woman that her daughter is safe in heaven. Will you do it?'

Annie had been brought up to believe that the parish priest was the next best thing to Jesus so, despite her misgivings, she said, 'All right, Father. If you think I can help.'

The priest arranged for the two women to meet at his house. The woman who came into the room that afternoon was shaking with nerves, and Annie's heart instantly went out to her. She smiled warmly and said, 'Please sit down. Take my hand.'

Father Kelly sat beside her and they all linked hands. Annie bowed her head, closed her eyes and focused, just as she'd read they do in séances. Instantly, she could hear the word 'Mama' in her head, with the accent on the second 'a', so she repeated it.

The woman gasped. 'That's what she called me. Just like that.'

Annie concentrated hard. 'I can see a tiny girl with a much older woman, perhaps her grandmother. She is sitting on her knee.'

'She must be with my mother,' the woman exclaimed.

Annie found some words in her brain and repeated them. 'Your mother says Dorothy is a little sweetheart. She says Dorothy comes to visit you when you are on your own at home. She puts her arms round you but she is not sure if you feel it.'

'I do. Many times I've thought I felt her but I didn't dare to hope.' Annie could hear the woman was crying, so decided to keep the séance brief.

'Your mother wants you to start living your life again. She says there's nothing you could have done to save Dorothy. You will always carry this sadness, but there will be happy times as well if you let them in. She and Dorothy will be with you forever, both in this world and the next.'

She opened her eyes and released the woman's hand to offer a handkerchief. They chatted for a while afterwards then, as she stood up to say goodbye, the woman grabbed Annie in a fierce embrace.

'You're a saint, so you are. You don't know what you've done for me.'

'I hope it helps,' Annie told her. 'You look after yourself now.'

In retrospect, she felt it had probably been the right thing to do, even though she felt drained. Father Kelly certainly thought so.

'You have great sensitivity and compassion,' he said. 'Seeing the way you handled her, I'd have no hesitation in recommending you to others.'

Once she had given one reading, the requests began to flood in: it seemed everyone in the parish knew someone in heaven they wanted her to contact. Annie was overwhelmed by the demand for her services, and because of her experiences on the *Titanic*, there were many requests for séances to contact those who had died the night of the sinking. Soon word of Annie's special talents spread beyond the little parish.

AT THE BEGINNING of August a storm blew up the Atlantic coast of America. At Mr Grayling's summer house, headache pills were consumed and nerves became frayed. In the middle of the afternoon, a shriek erupted from Miss Hamilton's bedroom followed by raised voices, and everyone rushed to see what was going on.

Miss Hamilton ran down the stairs crying, 'She's a thief! I caught her red-handed, George. I watched her tucking my diamond brooch into her bodice when she didn't know I was standing in the doorway.'

Molly stood at the top of the stairs. 'It's not true, sir. Miss Hamilton is mistaken. I was simply dusting the dresser.'

Reg knew from one look at Molly's pink cheeks that it *was* true, though.

Mr Grayling asked Molly to come into the drawing room and ordered everyone else back to their duties. Reg and Alphonse went into the kitchen, but they could hear what was being said through the wide-open windows.

'I've been suspicious for a while,' Miss Hamilton said. 'Remember I lost those sapphire earrings? And I've noticed that I never seem to have as much money in my purse as I thought I had.'

Molly stuttered in mock outrage. 'I have never in all my years in service taken a single thing that wasn't mine, sir. It's not in my nature.'

'But I *saw* you with my own eyes,' Miss Hamilton insisted.

Mr Grayling listened to both women before making up his mind. 'I'm afraid I'll have to let you go, Molly. You're lucky that I'm not going to call the police. I'll arrange for you to be driven back to New York this afternoon, and Mr Frank will supervise as you pack your belongings.'

'You can't fire me, sir,' Molly said, and something about her sly tone made Reg nervous. 'There are too many secrets around here that you wouldn't want me to let slip.'

'What on earth are you talking about?'

There was a pause before Molly took the plunge. 'I have a hunch that the newspapers would be very interested to hear that Reg saw you kissing Miss Hamilton on the *Titanic* before your wife's death. Except that she was travelling with a fake name, wasn't she? What is she trying to hide?'

Reg sat down hard on a kitchen chair, and sank his head into his hands. The volume rose and Reg heard the word 'blackmail' bandied around. Mr Grayling would be furious that he had blabbed. He was now part of this whether he liked it or not.

He got up and walked through the yard onto the beach. The wind was whipping the waves into swirling white foam and lifting clouds of sea spray. The air was darkening, and to the south the sky was purply black. He sat down on the sand to smoke a cigarette, but when the rain started to fall suddenly and heavily, he had to repair indoors. Reg bumped into Molly in the hall near the staff bathroom.

'Did you hear that?' she whispered. 'I'm being asked to leave, but he's giving me a hundred bucks as severance pay. If he thinks that's the end of it, he's got another think coming because I'll just come back and ask for more when that runs out. Come away with me, Reg, and we'll get old Grayling to subsidise our restaurant. That money would mean nothing to him.'

Reg stared at her, aghast. 'I don't want any part of this,' he told her. 'You're on your own.' He heard Alphonse coming down the hallway and stepped away from her.

'Are you alright, Molly?' Alphonse asked. 'Is he bothering you?'

She gave a little laugh. 'Oh, I'm fine. I'm staying here tonight because the driver doesn't want to drive in the storm. Bring me some dinner in my room, could you? I'm not working and I deserve a little treat.'

Alphonse agreed that he would, and she cooed 'Thank you, my hero.' She stood on tiptoe to kiss his cheek, making sure Reg could see. He turned away in disgust.

In bed that night, as the storm exploded into a frenzy of howling wind and horizontal rain, Reg lay awake, wondering how this new turn of events might affect him. Mr Grayling had every right to be upset since he had given Reg a second chance, only for him to turn out to be loose-tongued. Perhaps he would be fired the next morning.

He was beginning to drift off to sleep when he heard a sharp, high-pitched scream. He opened his eyes, fully alert. Through the noise of the storm, he made out angry voices but couldn't work out whose they were, then he heard another scream. It was coming from the garage, which was next to his room. Reg jumped out of bed, pulled some trousers and a jacket over his nightshirt, and hurried, barefoot, down the corridor.

The house was in silence. He opened the back door as quietly as he could and stepped outside. The wind buffeted him and rain plastered his hair to his head as he walked round to the garage entrance. The door was open and as he peered in, he saw Molly in the passenger seat of the car.

'Molly? What are you doing?' he called, over the noise of the wind. 'Are you alright?' She didn't turn round, didn't seem to hear him.

He took a step into the garage towards her, and was dimly aware of a movement over his left shoulder. Before he had time to turn, something heavy hit him on the head and he blacked out.

Somewhere in the depths of his brain, Reg became aware that he was in an automobile, being driven along a bumpy road. He was lying at an odd angle, virtually upside down and curled up. He couldn't force his eyes to open but he could hear the rattle of the motor and feel the vibrations and the roughness of the road surface. His head was knocking against something hard but he couldn't shift himself to a more comfortable position. It was a bizarre feeling to be vaguely aware of his surroundings but paralysed and unable to affect them, as if in a nightmare.

Who was driving? Was Molly still in the passenger seat?

The automobile stopped and he heard the door open and someone get out. He felt strong arms beneath his shoulders, lifting him upwards and hauling him over from the back seat into the front. He tried to resist but his muscles wouldn't obey. Still nothing was said.

The door slammed, and he felt the automobile rolling forwards. Suddenly the earth disappeared beneath it. There was a moment when Reg was flying through the air, then he was thrown backwards violently as they hit something hard, and cold water began to gush around him. The automobile somersaulted forwards and now he was submerged upside down in icy water, and knew he had to fight for his life.

It was pitch-black and he thrust out with his arms, frantically groping at the surroundings. The steering wheel was beneath him and something hard was directly above. On one side of him he felt a soft yet immoveable object, but on the other there was a narrow gap he could crawl through. His lungs were burning as he struggled to get free of the automobile.

Just keep swimming. Just keep swimming. It was as if he was back on the *Titanic* again and he only knew one thing: that he wanted to live.

Suddenly he realised his head was above water. He took a huge gulp of air just as a wave broke over him, making him choke and splutter. The moon glinted on the ocean and he saw that he wasn't far from shore, but the coastline was rocky and the current was dragging him out to sea.

As he was trying to work out what to do for the best a terrible thought occurred to him: had Molly been in the automobile with him? Had she been hit over the head as well? She had seemed unnaturally still and silent when he called to her from the garage door. Was she the unyielding obstacle he had felt beside him? He had to check.

He dived ten, twenty, thirty times, all around the area, until he had no strength left. There was no sign of the wreckage. If Molly was still down

426 | GILL PAUI

there, she couldn't possibly be alive. There was no more he could do, so he turned on his back and let the current pull him along, past the sharp black rocks and further up the coast to where he could see the glint of pale shingle. Using the last of his strength he swam towards the beach.

It was still raining, but not so fiercely. At the edge of the shingle, there was a wooden beach hut. Reg hurried up to it and yanked the door open, ripping it partly off its hinges. Inside there was a big pile of musty-smelling towels. He removed his jacket and trousers, and only then noticed that his shoes were missing. They must have come off in the automobile. He rubbed himself down with one towel, then wrapped himself up in some of the others and lay on the floor. Within seconds, he was sound asleep on the floor.

JULIETTE COULDN'T STOP torturing herself with visions of Robert escorting an actress around town. How could he believe that she wouldn't hear about it? How could he be so careless of her feelings? He was her husband after all. Suddenly she realised she didn't even have any proof that they were married: he had kept the sole copy of the marriage certificate for fear of her mother coming across it in her luggage.

In his letters, Robert always sounded busy. He was going into business with a man who had invented machines called 'air conditioners' that would cool the air in a room on a hot summer day. Robert was talking to manufacturers who could make them and department stores who would sell them. He seldom mentioned his social life, and the omission made Juliette suspicious. Surely he was doing something in the evenings? Did he eat at home on his own every night? Or was he dining with a certain attractive actress and that's why he didn't mention it in his letters?

Any patience she'd had was spent and impetuosity took over. She had to see him and ask him to his face what was going on. Of course, he would realise her condition straight away. He would have to decide whether he loved her enough to remain married to her when she was carrying another man's child. It was perhaps the greatest test of all. If he wanted a quiet divorce, she would give him one without complaint. So be it. She would rather lose him because of the mistake she had made in allowing Charles Wood to make love to her than lose him to another woman.

She went up to her room and packed a small overnight bag, then wrote a brief note to her mother, saying that she had gone to New York because she had to see Robert. She propped the note against her pillow then waited until she heard her mother in the kitchen talking to Edna before sneaking down the stairs. She crept out of the front door and hurried down to garage. The driver was there, waxing the car.

'I need to go to New York,' she told him. 'I'll make it worth your while if you will take me right now.'

She knew she was taking a huge gamble, but she needed to be honest with Robert if she was going to spend the rest of her life with him.

WHEN REG AWOKE, it was daylight outside and the storm had abated. Through the crack of the door, he could see the sky was pale grey and overcast, while the wet shingle was a dark tan colour. He tried to sit up but the movement brought on a pounding headache. The beach was deserted. He lay back and let the events of the previous night wash over him.

Was Molly dead in the wreck of the automobile? Reg was pretty sure that must be the case, and there was only one person who could be responsible: Mr Grayling. He had had no intention of letting Molly go after she made her blackmail threat. He probably intended to kill Reg as well. If it was true that he had murdered his wife on the *Titanic,* he couldn't risk anyone finding out, especially when he thought he had got away with it.

The question was, what should Reg do next? If he went to the police, would they believe him? If they found the wreck of the car and Molly's body was still in it, surely that was evidence enough? Alphonse would be able to back up his story that Molly had been trying to blackmail Mr Grayling; they'd both overheard the conversation.

But what if the police thought Reg was guilty? They might suspect he had murdered Molly after a lovers' tiff and driven the car off the road to hide the evidence. Reg had no love of the police. He knew that in England they always took the upper classes' word against that of the lower classes, and he assumed that it would be the same in America.

He found an old pair of deck shoes in the hut and put them on. They were several sizes too big, but better than nothing. His jacket and trousers were soaking wet and freezing but he pulled them on and peeked outside the beach hut. He spotted someone walking a dog on the beach. He ducked down, terrified. What if Mr Grayling had seen him swim clear of the wreck the previous night? He might be hunting for him to try and finish him off. Reg would have to stay out of sight.

As he scrabbled along the rocky slopes of the beach towards the road, he realised he was going to have to reinvent himself all over again. He would have to start from the bottom, accepting the kind of job where they didn't ask for a reference. It would help if he could at least retrieve his spare clothing from Mr Grayling's New York house. He might be able to slip unnoticed through the cellar window, which was usually left ajar to keep the wine cool. But first he had to get to New York somehow.

The first two automobiles that came along the road were black and shiny, similar to Mr Grayling's vehicles, so Reg kept out of sight. After a while, a yellow and green Ford truck came into view. As it drew near, Reg stood up and ran out to the roadside.

'Hey, mister!' he yelled, waving his arms in the air. 'Mister, please stop!' The driver pulled up. 'You want a lift?' he asked. 'Where y'all going?'

'New York City.'

'I'm only going as far as the Brooklyn Bridge. Any use?'

'That would be very kind. Thank you so much.' Reg climbed in and the driver pulled away.

JULIETTE SCRIBBLED a very simple note: '*Am in New York at the Plaza Hotel. Come as soon as possible,*' and gave it to her driver to take to Robert's house while she checked in to the hotel. She twisted her engagement ring so that the stone faced in towards her palm and requested a double room, saying that her husband would join her when he could. She was led up to a sumptuous room overlooking the park and she sat by a window to wait.

She was wearing a mauve silk dress that flared outwards from the bust, and she arranged the folds carefully so as to disguise her shape. He would discover her condition soon enough. If only there could be a warm embrace, perhaps a loving kiss before he noticed.

The hands of the clock were moving hideously slowly. Perhaps if he was in a business meeting, his butler had been unable to pass on the message so far. Perhaps he had stopped by his club after work. But the club must have a telephone. Surely he would get the message there?

Outside, the gas lamps were being lit in the street below. She lay down on the bed to rest, and when it reached nine o'clock without any sign of him, she began to cry. *What was I thinking?* She should never have come to New York. If he had fallen for an actress, the last thing she should be doing was humiliating herself by pursuing him.

She'd sent the driver back to their cottage so that her mother wasn't left without transport, but she decided that first thing in the morning, she would ask the hotel to arrange a car to take her back to Saratoga Springs. Once there, she would write to Robert and release him from their marriage.

IT WAS GETTING DARK as Reg made his way to the lodging house on East 25th Street, where he had stayed when the *Carpathia* docked. The superintendent recognised him and took him in without question.

When he woke the next morning, he lay in bed thinking about everything that had happened to him, and considered yet again whether he should go to the police. But he was still scared they wouldn't believe him, scared that he could end up in jail.

Over breakfast, he noticed the superintendent had a newspaper on his desk and asked if he could borrow it. On page five, his worst fears were realised. 'LOVEBIRDS STEAL CAR AND CRASH INTO OCEAN' read the headline. The story claimed that he and Molly had pilfered some money from Mr Grayling and escaped in his car, only to hurtle off the road at a notorious accident spot. Molly's body had been found in the wreckage, but they speculated that Reg had been swept away by the current.

Reg sat transfixed by horror. So it was true that Molly had been in the car. He was filled with rage against Mr Grayling. During all those weeks Reg had been living under the same roof as him, he hadn't been able to bring himself to believe he was working for a cold-blooded murderer. Now he realised his boss didn't care what he did so long as he got his own way.

And Reg was believed to be dead again, for the second time that year. At least it meant they weren't out hunting for him. But Molly, poor silly girl, had been found. He thought of their secret kisses and felt desperately sad for her. Alphonse would be in mourning as well.

After breakfast, Reg set out for the long walk uptown to Madison Avenue. He arrived at the house just after one, when the staff would be sitting down to luncheon. He crept round to the back door and slipped down to the cellar window. As usual, it was slightly ajar. His heart was pounding. If he were caught, he would tell Mr Frank the truth and throw himself on his mercy, but he didn't fancy his chances of a sympathetic hearing.

Once inside, Reg listened carefully at the cellar door before slipping up the steps into the hall, and then up the main staircase, storey by storey, to his bedroom. There was a bulky letter for him on the bed, from the immigration department. His new papers, in the name of Reg Parton, had come through.

He changed quickly into his spare suit, with clean socks and a shirt, and pulled on a pair of shoes. He bundled all his other possessions into a bag along with his passport and a few dollars he had saved.

Reg crept down the stairs as quietly as he could, but paused on the first floor. The door of Mr Grayling's office was ajar and a thought came to him. *I could go to the police if I had some evidence against him; if it wasn't just his word against mine.*

He tiptoed into the office and slid open the drawers of the desk. Inside the bottom one, right at the back, there was a small bundle of letters addressed to 'Mr George Grayling' and a small cloth bag with a key inside. He opened it and knew straight away what it was before reading the engraving on it: B78. It was the key to the Graylings' suite on the *Titanic*.

Why would he have thought to bring that with him when everyone was rushing to the lifeboats? Passengers never locked their doors on cruise ships. Did Mr Grayling really stop to worry about the risk of theft while the *Titanic* was sinking? That hardly seemed plausible. He must have locked the door because Mrs Grayling was lying in bed, either unconscious or dead, and he didn't want her to be found. The sinking of the *Titanic* had been extremely convenient for him. He'd hit her over the head, just as he'd done with Reg, but he didn't have to risk being caught when he tossed her body overboard because he could just let her go down with the ship. It was almost the perfect crime.

Mr Grayling might have thought he'd got away with it, but he should never have kept the key. That gave Reg enough evidence to go to the police.

He slipped the letters and key into his bag, crept back down to the cellar and out through the window. No one in the house heard a thing.

AS SOON AS JULIETTE WOKE the next day, she rang and asked a steward to enquire at the front desk whether a message had been left for her. When the reply came back that there was none, her spirits hit rock bottom.

'I'll be leaving the hotel this morning,' she told him. 'Please organise an automobile and driver to take me to Saratoga Springs.'

She didn't feel like eating but knew she had to for the baby's sake, so she rang for some baked eggs and corn bread.

'I'm afraid we can't get a driver for you until three this afternoon, ma'am,' the steward told her when he brought the food. 'Will that suffice?'

'It will have to,' she said. Her mother would be going out of her mind with worry, so she scribbled a telegram, which merely read: 'Back later this evening [stop] Juliette' and gave it to the steward, along with a tip.

She couldn't bear to sit cooped up in the hotel room a moment longer, so she decided to go for a walk in Central Park. If she met someone who recognised her and her pregnancy was revealed, so be it.

The weather was cool and fresh, and sunlight rippled through the leaves. She wanted to walk and walk and keep walking. It was her first taste of freedom in months. She was slightly nervous to be there alone, but reckoned that if she stuck to a main path she should be safe.

After a while, she began to feel thirsty. She remembered passing the café where Robert had bought her some rainbow sandwiches, so headed back in that direction.

As Juliette entered the café, she was aware of a young man sitting with his head bent over a letter, but it wasn't until she sat down and looked closely that she realised she knew him.

'Reg!' she exclaimed. 'It's you, isn't it? How are you?'

He looked alarmed, and quickly folded the letter he'd been holding. 'Excuse me, miss. I'm fine, thank you.' She saw him noticing her belly.

'I don't suppose I could join you? I feel rather awkward on my own.'

Reg leaped up to pull out a chair for her, embarrassed to be caught reading one of Mr Grayling's letters.

'I'm leaving in a couple of hours but I wanted to see the park first. It's beautiful, isn't it . . .' Her voice tailed off as her attention was caught by the letter Reg had been reading. 'My God, that's Venetia Hamilton's signature, isn't it? Why on earth would you have a letter from her?'

Reg coloured as he pulled it towards him. 'She is living with Mr Grayling, and I've been working for him. Do you remember him from the *Titanic*? They've been having an affair.'

Juliette snorted. 'But he's twice her age. I suppose it must be his money. Venetia only likes men with loads of money.' She rolled her eyes. 'Honestly, her reputation is atrocious; I imagine she decided to try America.' She glanced at the letter again. 'Are you delivering this for her?' she asked.

'No.' He hesitated for a moment, then he decided to tell her about seeing Miss Hamilton with Mr Grayling on the *Titanic*'s boat deck, and then watching him help her into a lifeboat on the night of the sinking.

'She was on the ship? But we never saw her.'

'I believe she must have stayed in her cabin. She told me when we were talking about the voyage that she wasn't in the mood for society.'

'I bet she wasn't! She had just jilted Lord Beaufort, left him standing at the altar, and no one on board would have given her the time of day. And before that she'd done the same to my brother, William.'

A waiter came by and Reg offered Juliette a drink, but she wouldn't let him. 'You'll need your money for whatever you decide to do next. Perhaps you would be so good as to escort me back to the Plaza Hotel?'

They chatted as they walked. Reg plucked up the courage to ask when the baby was due, and she waved her hand and said, 'Oh, not for ages yet.' Then she asked: 'What are your plans? Will you stay in New York?'

'I don't know,' Reg said. 'I've been feeling homesick, but the thought of the voyage is daunting.' He fingered the St Christopher in his pocket. 'And I don't think I have much to go back to.'

Chapter Eight

When Juliette walked into the Plaza's reception hall, Robert Graham jumped to his feet and rushed across the room to throw his arms around her.

'Darling, what's happened? Are you alright?' he asked. Feeling the bump between them, he looked down. There was a moment when she watched the truth sink in, then he exclaimed, 'Oh, my love, is it really possible? But that's marvellous news!' He kissed her on the lips, oblivious to the hotel staff milling around. 'I've always wanted to be a father, but I never dreamed it would happen so soon. Thank you. Thank you with all my heart.'

Juliette was dazed. How could he believe that their one night of passion two months ago could have made her so pregnant?

'Where have you been?' she asked. 'I'd quite given up hope of seeing you, and have a car booked to take me back to Saratoga Springs at three.'

'Didn't you receive my message? I was in California, trying to find premises for some new branches of the air conditioner company. I rushed back on the very next train when I heard you were here, but I asked my butler to send a message telling you I wouldn't arrive until today.'

'I didn't receive any message.' She was confused.

'You didn't? But that's preposterous.' He marched over to the reception desk. 'Do you have any messages for Lady Juliette Mason-Parker?'

The clerk looked at his pile of messages and instantly pulled one out. 'Yes, sir, I do.'

'And why didn't you pass it on?'

Suddenly Juliette realised what had happened and tugged at his arm. 'I checked in as Mrs Robert Graham. What an idiot I am!'

'Goodness, no, I should have guessed you might do that. Oh, poor you.' He smiled tenderly. 'What must you have thought?'

Juliette blushed, remembering how badly she had misjudged him.

'Might we not spend some time together now that I've dashed across an entire continent to see you? Must you really leave at three?'

She cancelled the driver and they went to her room. As soon as the door closed behind them, Robert started kissing her and her entire body strained towards him. They moved sideways towards the bed, entwined in each other, lips on lips and legs wrapped around legs. All thoughts of actresses left Juliette's head as she dissolved into passion. She couldn't stop kissing, couldn't stop touching him, and he was the same.

As they lay in each other's arms afterwards, Juliette waited for him to comment on the advanced stage of her pregnancy, but instead he stroked her face and told her how much he had missed her.

'You didn't mention what brought you to town,' he questioned.

'I came to ask you a question.' She took a deep breath. 'Who exactly is Amy Manford and what is she to you?'

'My niece,' he replied, straight away. 'Why?'

She stared at him, bemused. 'The gossip columns kept saying that you had been seen at the races and having dinner with an attractive actress . . . I wondered why you didn't mention it. That's all.'

He frowned. 'I'm sure I told you that my niece was in town and I was showing her around. I had no idea that she wants to be an actress. It's possible she has mentioned that ambition to her friends but I doubt my sister will allow it.' Suddenly he grinned. 'You were jealous, weren't you?'

'Of course! Why didn't you write to tell me the papers were wrong?'

Still grinning, he touched the end of her nose lightly with his finger. 'I have never read one of those columns in my life and don't intend to start. They are pure fiction. Were you really upset by them?'

Juliette was embarrassed. 'Well . . . a little.'

'But at least it has meant we are together now. How are your relatives? Must you rush back today? Might I not claim you for a while longer?'

'I think you might,' she breathed. She lay back in his arms in a glow of perfect happiness. He began to run his hand slowly over her belly, feeling its expanse, exploring its contours but, just at that moment, the baby chose to kick. She felt his hand falter and when she looked up into his face, he was frowning. Now was the moment when she had to confess.

Before she could speak, Robert rolled over and got out of bed. 'Please excuse me, but I have some business I must attend to this afternoon,' he said coolly, and started to pull on his clothes.

'Shall I see you later?' she asked.

'Yes, of course. I'll pick you up at six for dinner. The staff should be able to prepare something at the house. We don't want to . . .'

He didn't finish the sentence, but Juliette knew what he had been about to say. They couldn't risk being seen in public.

He's guessed, she thought, as he hurried out of the room and closed the door. *It's over. If only I had been brave enough to tell him myself.*

It wouldn't have made any difference, though. How could any man accept another man's child?

REG'S HEART WAS POUNDING as he walked into the police station on West 54th and Eighth Avenue.

'My n-name is Reg Parton. I was in the c-car that crashed off the road in Long Island, Mr G-Grayling's car, but I didn't steal it,' he stuttered.

'Hold on a second. Do you mean that car crash where two of Mr Grayling's employees died?'

'Yes, I'm one of them. Reg. I escaped.'

'Well, I'll be damned!' The policeman at the front desk looked Reg up and down. 'Please come with me. I'll find somebody to talk to you.'

Reg was led into an interview room to wait. There was a clock on the wall and the minutes ticked by slowly. Half past two. Three o'clock. At ten past three, the door opened and a very tall man with silver-grey hair and a reddish complexion walked in.

'Reg Parton?' He held out his hand so Reg shook it. 'Detective O'Halloran. Sorry to keep you waiting. You told the sergeant that you escaped from the car that went into the ocean off Long Island?'

'That's right, but it wasn't me who stole it. I was hit over the head and bundled into it. Look!' He parted his hair with his fingers to show the gash.

'That's OK. Sit yourself down. We know it wasn't you. We've got the man responsible. He walked into a police station and confessed.'

'Mr Grayling did?'

The detective gave him an odd look. 'No, Alphonse Labreche. The chef.'

'It can't be true!' Reg was stunned.

'Yes, it seems it was a classic crime of passion. He was in love with Molly, she was leading him down the garden path and he couldn't take it any more. After he strangled her, you happened to walk in and he had to shut you up, too. He's broken up with guilt.'

'Alphonse,' Reg repeated, as if in a daze. How could he not have realised Alphonse loved Molly? He must have been seething inside as he watched her pursuing Reg during all those weeks. And then on the night of the storm, he snapped. Poor Molly, and poor Alphonse as well.

'Are you OK? We should get somebody to look at that cut on your head.'

'I'm fine. I'm just astonished. Alphonse wasn't a bad person.'

'You'd be surprised what being spurned can do to a guy. I've seen it over and over again. So you escaped from the automobile after it crashed in the water?' Reg nodded. 'What did you do then?'

'I thought Molly might still be in there so I dived down over and over trying to find her. It was useless, though; the current kept pulling me away.'

'Apparently that stretch of water is nasty in a storm. It's damn lucky you managed to save yourself, never mind anybody else. Besides, it's thought she was already dead before she hit the water. Why didn't you go back to Mr Grayling's when you came ashore?'

'I was scared.'

'What were you scared of?'

Reg chose his words carefully. 'Molly had been trying to blackmail him about the young woman who was staying with us at the summer house. Her name is Venetia Hamilton.'

The detective whistled. It seemed there was a lot more to this case than he'd thought. 'So what grounds were there for the blackmail?'

'You know his wife died on the *Titanic*?' The detective nodded. 'Well, I think he might have killed her.' Reg explained that she hadn't been seen during the final day, that their suite door was locked and that he saw Mr Grayling and Miss Hamilton escaping together. 'Then I found this in the house.' He handed over the key, and put the letters on the table.

'Whoa! That's some accusation you're making. Mr Grayling told us that Miss Hamilton is a friend of his late daughter's and he's been looking after her while she gets over a broken engagement.'

Reg pursed his lips. 'I think you'll find a different story in these letters.'

O'Halloran picked up the letters thoughtfully. 'I'll have a look through these and if I think there's a case I'll bring Mr Grayling down to the precinct. Meanwhile, let me find somebody to come and look at your head.'

The doctor put three metal stitches in Reg's gash, and the pain was teeth-clenching. When he'd finished, O'Halloran came back in to chat. 'Mr Grayling's on his way back to Manhattan at the moment, so we'll call him later. You've had quite a year, young Reg. Saved from the *Titanic*, then this happens. I guess you lost friends on board, did you?'

Reg nodded. 'My best friend, John.'

The detective nodded. 'It leaves a big hole inside, don't it? My best buddy was stabbed on duty last year. There's not a day goes by when I don't think about him.' He patted Reg's arm. 'There's an Irish woman in Kingsbridge, where I live, who they say can talk to the spirits of people who died on the *Titanic*. They reckon she's pretty good. Annie McGeown.'

'Really? Annie? I knew her.'

'Is that so? What's she like? A bit of a loony?'

'Not at all. She was a nice woman. Very kind.'

When it began to get dark outside, Detective O'Halloran telephoned Mr Grayling's number and was told that he had just arrived home.

'Can you request that he comes down to the Eighth Avenue precinct? Tell him to ask for Detective O'Halloran. Yes, right away, please.'

Reg imagined Mr Grayling's expression when he got the message. It wouldn't be well received, he was sure.

REG FELT SCARED about being in the same building as Mr Grayling. Any moment now, he might find himself arrested for theft of the items from his desk. Even in the best-case scenario he would be out of a job, with no prospect of a reference to help him get a new one. He was back at square one, and didn't think he could find the energy to raise himself up yet again.

The door opened and Detective O'Halloran came in and sat down.

'Mr Grayling is insisting that he took his wife to a lifeboat on the *Titanic*, and he thinks their door must have been locked by a steward. He says the stewards had keys for all the rooms in their section. Is that the case?'

Reg agreed that it was.

'So he wouldn't have left a body there all day in case the steward came in and found it, would he? There sure is evidence in those letters that he was romantically involved with Miss Hamilton and had been looking for a divorce. But without a body, there's no suggestion of any crime.'

He could see Reg wasn't happy with this conclusion.

'Hey, I think you're wrong about him. He seems like a decent kind of guy. He was all made up when he heard that you escaped from the crash, and he wants to have a word with you.'

'No!' Reg cried. 'I can't.'

'Why not? I'll be in the room. You should hear what he has to say.'

Reg couldn't stop shaking as he was led to the interview room where Mr Grayling sat waiting. He flinched as his boss stood to greet him.

'Thank God you're alright, Reg. I'm told you have a head wound. Has it been properly taken care of?'

'Yes, thank you, sir,' Reg replied quietly.

Mr Grayling fixed his eyes on him. 'I can understand why you have a low opinion of me, but I want you to know that I've only ever felt protective towards you. My wife thought very highly of you and if you were of a mind to come back and work for me, I'd be happy to have you.'

Reg looked at the floor and shook his head.

'Otherwise, I'd like to give you a reference and some severance pay to help tide you over. Do you have any plans? Do you intend to go back to England? Because I would be happy to pay for a ticket for you.'

Reg still couldn't meet his eye. And he didn't want to accept anything from him. But suddenly going back home to Florence seemed like the only thing he wanted to do. 'I can work my own passage, sir.'

'Nonsense! I'm going to leave a ticket in your name at the Cunard office. I believe the *Lusitania* is sailing in four days' time. Would that suit? If you don't want it, they will let you change it for another sailing, or cash it in. Please accept this as your rightful due, Reg.'

'Thank you, sir.'

'Do you need somewhere to stay? You're welcome to your old room . . .'

'No, I have somewhere.'

'In that case I suppose I'll say goodbye—and good luck to you, Reg.' Mr Grayling held out his hand.

Reg didn't want to shake hands. He knew Mr Grayling was lying. If he had shown his wife to a lifeboat and she got back out again, someone would have mentioned it by now, either in the press or at the inquiries. But he was a polite boy, there was a policeman present, and it seemed awkward not to shake. He took Mr Grayling's hand then let go again as fast as he could.

LATER THAT NIGHT, George Grayling sat at his desk with a glass of cognac by his elbow, fingering the key with the number B78 engraved on it. *Margaret should never have come to Italy with me*, he brooded. *Why did she come?*

Had she perhaps suspected he was going to see another woman? She kept trying to 'save' their marriage, no matter how cruelly he behaved towards her. If she had only given him a divorce, she would be alive today.

He knew he'd been bad-tempered with her on the *Titanic* as he skipped between Venetia, who was safely ensconced in a stateroom on C Deck, and his marital suite up on B. He had resented having to return to Margaret in the early hours of the morning when Venetia dismissed him. He was bored with his wife's conversation and couldn't abide the time he spent eating meals in her company. Why did she not bow gracefully to the inevitable?

Her stubbornness had made him cross. As far as he could see, she had been the only obstacle that had stood between him and the exquisite Venetia. And with luck, Venetia could have given him another child.

Except now everything was ruined. He picked up the cognac and swallowed a mouthful, feeling the warmth of it in his gullet.

There was a knock on the door and Mr Frank looked in. 'May I get you anything before I turn in for the night, sir?' He noticed the expression on his boss's face. 'Are you alright, sir?'

'No,' Mr Grayling admitted. 'I'm not. Come in, Frank. Sit down. Have a drink with me.'

Mr Frank poured himself some cognac. 'Thank you, sir.'

'Did you know that Venetia has left me?' He shook his head in disbelief.

Mr Frank pursed his lips. 'I heard. I'm sorry, sir.'

'I loved her, Frank. I was going to marry her and have a child with her. I thought she felt the same way, but she was playing me for an old fool. She let me shower her with money and gifts before announcing that she's going back to Europe. I'm left with no one: no wife, no daughter, no Venetia. She said she couldn't be associated with the scandal of poor Molly being killed, but it wasn't that. She was bored. I could feel it in my bones.'

'She's still young, sir. It was quiet for her here, in the house.'

'I suppose I've always known deep down it wouldn't work. New York society would have mocked us.'

Mr Frank sipped his cognac, with an impassive expression. 'I take it you met her long before you sailed on the *Titanic*.'

'I know you disapprove, Frank, but you must understand that Margaret and I never had a passionate marriage. I married for money, not for love, so it's ironic that when I fell in love with Venetia, she only wanted me for my money.' He gave a harsh little laugh. He realised that the alcohol combined with his disappointment was making him loose-tongued. *Why was he talking to a member of staff about this? But who else could he talk to?*

'Did you plan to divorce Mrs Grayling?'

'She wouldn't let me. God knows I asked her . . .' He reached across the desk for the decanter and refilled his glass. 'Reg thinks I killed her. Can you believe it? Me? A murderer? He went to the police about it!' Mr Grayling exclaimed. 'That's why I was called down to the precinct tonight.'

'It seems incredible. I expect that's why they let you go again so quickly.'

'I still can't get over the fact he thought I'd murdered my wife to avoid the scandal of a divorce. In his opinion, I was capable of that . . .' He shook his head, and his words were slurred as he spoke. 'And yet, as it turned out, it almost amounted to the same thing. I might as well have killed her.'

Mr Frank frowned. 'Sir, you're tired. Perhaps you should go to bed.'

'No! I have to tell someone and you know me, Frank. You know I'm not a bad person. OK, I lied, but it's not what Reg thinks. I could never have killed her in cold blood. You believe me, don't you?'

'Yes, of course I do.'

'She'd been ill all that last day on the *Titanic*. Christ, the sound of her vomiting turned my stomach but still I dropped in every few hours to make sure she wasn't in need of anything. You see? I was a good husband in some respects. When I checked on her after dinner she was sound asleep, with a bottle of sleeping potion beside her, so I assumed she had taken some and was out for the night. I went to Venetia's room.'

He closed his eyes and imagined himself back there, in Venetia's dazzling presence. They had drunk champagne and talked and laughed. She kept him at arm's length, though. 'What kind of girl do you think I am?' she asked coyly. 'You'll get nothing more from me without a ring on my finger.'

And he was content just to be in her presence, allowed to gaze at her perfect features. She was intoxicating and he knew he was addicted to her.

Mr Frank cleared his throat, interrupting the reverie. 'Are you saying you were with Miss Hamilton when the ship hit the iceberg?'

'It was just a slight jolt. Venetia was anxious but I told her that it wouldn't be anything serious. Then a steward came and told us to come up to the boat deck with our life preservers. Just a precaution, he said.'

It was the same steward who had brought Venetia's meals to her: he must have guessed their arrangement was illicit but never gave so much as a hint of it in his composure. He had showed them how to fasten their life preservers, then led them up the Grand Staircase to the boat deck. Venetia had kept her head bowed, her face shadowed by a hat, and walked behind him for fear of being recognised by any of the English passengers.

'I *specifically* asked him whether all passengers would be brought up on deck by their room stewards and he assured me that they would. Assured me. I told him that I had a friend who was asleep in a room on B Deck and he said not to worry, that my friend would be fine. It just didn't occur to me to worry about Margaret after that.'

'So you didn't go back for her.' Mr Frank's voice was cold.

'It all happened so fast! You don't understand. They insisted that Venetia get into a lifeboat and she begged me to come, too. She was scared. They said women and children were going first but then they started to lower away and there were loads of places left, so I just got on.' He took a greedy swallow of his drink. 'You must believe me, Frank. I wouldn't have done it if that steward hadn't *assured* me that Margaret would be on another boat. It was his fault. Besides, no one said the ship was sinking.'

The butler's face was impassive. 'I suppose it was only when you reached the *Carpathia* that you realised Mrs Grayling hadn't made it.'

'I walked all round the ship but couldn't see any sign of her. It was horrible, Frank. You've got no idea what it was like for me. And then I bumped into Reg, and he told me that he had tried the door of our suite on the *Titanic* and found it locked.' A sob burst from his throat. 'That's when the terrible truth struck me: I'd locked the door when I went out.' He pushed the key across the desk. 'I only did it because I wanted her to sleep undisturbed.' He began to sob properly, covering his face with his hands, shoulders heaving.

Mr Frank picked up the key and looked at it. He felt disgust for the man sitting opposite. What kind of person would leave his wife to fend for herself on a sinking ship?

As ARRANGED, Robert came to the hotel at six. He took Juliette's arm to help her downstairs and out to his automobile.

'I'm not an invalid,' she said, trying to keep her tone light, although she was terrified about what the evening might bring.

'You must take care in your condition,' he replied. His voice was kind but not passionate, no longer the voice of a lover.

During the drive, she longed to touch him, to put her hand on his, but didn't dare. Her lips still tingled with his kisses, but everything between them had changed. As soon as they got to his house, she would explain that she was six months pregnant, not two, and offer him a quick and easy annulment. It was the only vaguely honourable route left to her.

The butler showed them straight in to dinner, and when finally they were alone, it was Robert who spoke first. 'Where are you hoping to have the child? Will you go back to England for the birth?'

'I was planning to have the baby in Saratoga Springs,' she said in a whisper, then took a deep breath and uttered the fateful words: 'It's due in November.' He looked so sad, she wished she could take back the words as soon as they'd been spoken. 'I'm sorry.'

Robert nodded and cleared his throat. 'Will you stay with your relatives for the remaining months?'

She shook her head. 'We have no relatives there. Mother and I have been staying in a rented cottage. I'm so sorry I've lied to you, Robert. I never intended this to happen, not any of it.'

'Yet you married me without saying anything. That's what I can't understand.' From his tone, Juliette could tell he was bitterly hurt.

'I couldn't bear to lose you. I planned to have the baby in Saratoga Springs, give it up for adoption and come back to you as if nothing had happened. It was a ridiculous plan, I know, but I prayed you would never find out. I swear I am not a dishonest person by nature. But you must have such a low opinion of me now.'

'I am surprised by you, indeed. When I guessed this afternoon that your pregnancy was more advanced than would have been possible with my child, I was shocked. I needed time to think. I didn't want to blurt out in the heat of the moment words that I might later live to regret.'

Juliette felt desperately ashamed. He was a decent, honest man and she had behaved unspeakably. 'Please let me explain,' she begged. 'I am not a woman of such loose morals as the bare facts might lead you to assume.'

He reached across the table and put his finger to her lips. 'No. I don't want to know. I will never tell you whether I considered marrying any other woman before I met you, and I don't want to know about all the many men who must have been head over heels in love with you. Do you understand what I'm saying?'

Juliette was confused. Was he implying that he would stay married to her? How could he?

He continued: 'I have always wanted to be a father. I also want to be with you, so I have decided that I will be a father to this baby and that we will tell everyone it is ours.' He reached across the table to squeeze her hand. 'In future, God willing, we will have more children of our own who will be brothers and sisters to it.'

Joy flooded Juliette's whole body. 'But how will we manage? What will people say?'

'I'm going to have to spend a lot of time in California over the coming months while I set up the new companies. I suggest we take a house out there and hire a nurse to live with us. You can have the baby there and your mother may accompany us if she wishes.' Juliette was gazing at him in astonishment. 'When the baby is old enough, we'll make a trip back to England and you can introduce me to the rest of your family then.'

Juliette sat back and watched him, full of wonder. He loved her so much that he was prepared to accept that she was having another man's child. It seemed extraordinary to her and, at the same time, quite wonderful.

'Can you ever forgive me?' she asked.

He gazed deep into her eyes. He still looked sad but there was love there as well. 'I wish you had told me before, of course, but think I can understand why you made the choices you made.' He lifted her fingers to his lips and kissed them. 'I love you, Juliette. You are my wife and I want to spend my life with you. Of course I forgive you.'

AFTER DROPPING PATRICK at school and picking up her groceries from the market each morning, Annie would drop in to the church to pray, then wander round it weeding out from the vases any blooms that had passed their best. It was while she was occupied with this one day that Reg came into the church and spotted her.

'Mrs McGeown?' he said tentatively.

'Will you look at that! If it's not Reg. My, but it's good to see you.' She meant it. She'd often thought of him, and felt grateful that Finbarr had been so well cared for in his final minutes. 'Did you come to see me?'

'Yes, I wanted to say goodbye. I'm going back to England. And I wondered if I might have a talk with you, if you have a minute to spare.'

He wants a reading. He's heard about the séances for relatives of Titanic *victims. Probably for his friend John. I suppose I can do that for him.* Out loud, she said, 'It would be much appreciated if you would help me up the steps to my house with my bags of shopping. My knees have been giving me trouble so I like to take it slow and easy.'

Reg carried her bags for her while she hauled herself up the step street. She led him into her sitting room and made some tea, then sat down opposite him. 'Now, did you come about your friend, John? Do you want me to try and contact him?'

'No . . . It's not that. There were some first-class passengers on board called Mr and Mrs Grayling. He survived and she didn't. I think he might have killed her and locked her in their suite. I've been to the police but there's not enough evidence to charge him. I suppose . . . I just hate to see him getting away with it.'

Annie nodded. 'You want me to try and speak to her.'

'I don't really know why I came. I'm not even sure I believe in all this.'

'I'll tell you a secret: I'm not sure I believe myself.' She smiled conspiratorially. 'But I can tell you it helps. I know it has lifted me out of blackness in the moments when I thought I was going mad, and other people tell me it has helped them to pull through. Well, we will try to contact your Mrs Grayling, but no promises, mind.'

She pulled a small table between them, lit a candle, then indicated that Reg should give her his hands. She closed her eyes and began to concentrate.

The first words that came into her head didn't sound as though they came from an upper-class woman: 'What are you doing here, man? Why don't you get yourself back home, marry some nice girl and have children before you get too long in the tooth? Call your handsomest boy after me.'

'It's John,' Reg breathed. The hairs stood up on the back of his neck. Annie's voice was still hers, but to his ears it had the ring of John's about it: a slight Geordie inflection. It was uncanny.

Next she spoke in her own voice. 'Is there a Mrs Grayling who was on the *Titanic*?' She paused for a long time. Then she began to hear a very distant voice. 'Tell Reg not to worry. I'm happy now. I'm glad to be here.'

'Is she with her daughter Alice?' Reg asked.

'Of course. Mothers always meet their children on the other side.'

'Can you ask if her husband killed her?'

Annie focused hard. 'She says, "My husband is foolish but he is not a bad man." I think that's your answer.'

Reg gave a deep sigh. If it were true, he could stop worrying. It sounded like the kind of thing Mrs Grayling might say. He hoped it was.

Annie listened a while longer but there was nothing more so she opened her eyes and let go of his hands. 'Was that what you needed to know?'

'I think so. Thank you.'

'It's good to see you, Reg. You're quite the hero, I believe. My husband said he read about you in the papers. You were in a car that crashed into the sea and you kept diving down, trying to save the girl in the passenger seat. It made us remember how brave you were in trying to save our son.'

Reg blushed to the roots of his hair. 'Please don't say that. I'm no hero. Officers Lightoller and Lowe, they're the heroes. I only saved myself.'

'And yet you *are* brave. I can see it in your soul.'

On his way back on the train, Reg wasn't sure why he had gone to see Annie. Spiritualism had to be nonsense. Yet he felt better for going. He felt as though he'd done all he could.

When Seamus got in from his work that evening, Annie told him about Reg's visit. He listened to her description of the conversation as he ate his chipped beef and mash.

'He didn't come here to talk to spirits,' he said when she'd finished. 'He came to check that we don't blame him for Finbarr dying. The spirits were an excuse.'

Annie remembered that Reg had looked nervous in the church when he first arrived, and how relieved he'd seemed by her greeting. 'I've never blamed him. Well, maybe just for a second after I got the news, but not once I'd heard his story.'

'No, but he's a good lad and if I put myself in his shoes, that's what I'd worry about. He can go home now knowing he has your blessing.'

Annie was suddenly overwhelmed by love for Seamus. He was so good and steady and wise. She got up and walked round the table and embraced him from behind, burying her face in his neck.

'There's something I've never told you, Annie,' he said in a low voice, 'and I should have. I've often thought about what happened on the *Titanic* that night and gone over things in my head again and again, and I want you to know that in your place, I'd have done exactly the same as you did. That's all.' He raised his fork and carried on eating.

'Thank you,' she whispered slowly.

WHEN REG TURNED UP at the Cunard Line office to see if Mr Grayling had left him a ticket as promised, he was astonished to find there was a first-class reservation in his name, together with a letter addressed to him.

Reg went to sit on a bench in the shipping office and tore it open. Two sides of the paper were covered in small, neat handwriting and the signature at the end read 'Algernon Frank'. He started reading.

The letter began with an account of Mr Grayling's confession about his part in his wife's death. '*In vino veritas*,' Mr Frank wrote, and Reg realised it was the truth. Everything fitted into place at last: that's why he'd had the key; that's why she hadn't been seen on any lifeboat.

'On reflection, I have decided that I can no longer continue in Mr Grayling's employment. His wife was a wonderful woman, and I always felt it was wrong that we weren't all in formal mourning for her. Now I know the full circumstances, I cannot contemplate staying in the service of such a man. Mr Grayling understands and says he will write me a reference for my next position.'

The letter finished by wishing Reg all the very best for the future, whatever he decided to do.

He folded it and put it back in the envelope, deep in thought. If only he had knocked harder on Mrs Grayling's door, or insisted that the room steward open it and check, then he could have saved her. But the room steward on B Deck had told him the Graylings must have gone already. It wasn't the steward's fault, and it wasn't Reg's fault; it was her husband's. Mr Grayling wasn't evil, but he was weak and selfish and, from the sounds of it, self-pitying.

Reg decided he would accept the ticket. For a moment, he pictured himself sleeping in a four-poster bed, sitting in the first-class dining saloon being served by someone just like himself—but it was ridiculous. He didn't belong there.

He went back to the counter and asked the clerk: 'How much was this ticket, and how much is a third-class cabin?'

The difference between the two was $4,000, which was about £800 in

British money. With that kind of cash he could pay back the rest of the money he owed John's family, and start a business back in Southampton. But what kind of business?

The idea came to him straight away. He'd been thinking of opening a British-style restaurant in Manhattan, but why not open an American one back home instead? He could serve hot dogs and Pepsi-Cola. If he liked them, surely other English people would, too?

ON HIS LAST DAY in New York, Reg got up early. He went to a soda fountain to ask who supplied them with Pepsi-Cola. He took a subway to the address he was given and asked to speak with the manager.

'I'm starting my own café in Southampton, England, and I'd like to import some Pepsi-Cola,' he said.

Instantly, the manager fetched some requisition forms, a list of prices, shipping costs and import licences. 'I'll do you a good deal if you order at least a thousand bottles,' he promised.

Reg agreed a price for a thousand and paid cash on the spot. He'd pick up the shipment from Southampton docks in three weeks' time.

He was nervous getting on the *Lusitania* the next morning. She was much smaller than the *Titanic*, but the third-class accommodation was smart and clean. Everyone sat at long tables in the dining saloon and the food was standard fare but perfectly adequate.

The minute they set sail, Reg made his way up to the wireless room to send a Marconi-gram to his mother. He chewed the end of his pencil for ages trying to think of something appropriate, but in the end he just wrote: 'Arriving Tuesday evening on Lusitania [stop] Reg'. It cost twelve shillings.

He had thought he wouldn't want to go out on deck, but in fact his feet led him there straight away. He stood at the railing and watched as they sailed past Governor's Island, Ellis Island and the Statue of Liberty, out towards the open ocean. It was a clear, sunny day in early September and light sparkled on the water, giving a festive feel.

The crossing to Southampton took seven days. Reg didn't socialise with other passengers but he wasn't lonely. He sat with his notebook making plans for the new business, drawing sketches of the seating arrangement he'd like. Sometimes he wondered what reception he could expect from his family as he apologised to them for his lost five months. Was that really all it had been since he had set sail on the *Titanic*? It felt like a lifetime.

He was standing on deck when the tugs guided them into harbour. Suddenly the air was filled with the deafening sound of pent-up steam being released as the engines were turned off, and it was only then that he realised there was some kind of celebration under way on the dock. He could hear whistles being blown and see flags being waved frantically in the air. He followed the noise to its source and saw a group of around thirty people jumping up and down, yelling and waving their arms. Some of the *Lusitania*'s passengers began to wave back.

Progress was slow as the tugboat captains manoeuvred round buoys, steering clear of other ships. Reg was about to go below to collect his belongings when something about the animated group caught his attention. They had a white banner with words painted on it in huge black letters, and he couldn't believe it when he got close enough to make out what it said: 'WELCOME HOME REG'. He focused hard and, gradually, he realised the group was his family and friends. There was his mum, his brothers. None of them had seen him yet but they were making so much noise he couldn't miss them.

Right at the front of the crowd, standing slightly apart, was a girl in a blue coat and with a lurch he knew who it was: Florence. Just as he realised that, she spotted him, even though they were still a hundred yards apart and the decks were lined with hundreds of other passengers. He could tell she'd seen him from the way she suddenly stood very still. In that magical moment, frozen in time, he knew as surely as he had ever known anything that he wanted to marry her.

Then she turned to the others and he saw her pointing towards him. They all began screaming his name and blowing their penny whistles even more frantically. The private moment was over for now, but he sensed with a warm, certain feeling inside, that there were going to be many more.

gill **paul**

Profile

Born:
Glasgow.
Home:
Hampstead Heath,
London.
Novels:
Enticement (2000),
Compulsion (2001),
*Women and Children
First* (2012).

Nonfiction:
Perfect Detox (2009),
Titanic *Love Stories* (2011),
Stop Smoking (2012).
Favourite ways to relax:
Exotic travel, swimming in
the open-air pond on
Hampstead Heath, theatre,
cinema, cooking and
catching up with friends.

What drew you towards the *Titanic* disaster as subject matter for a novel?
Both my grandfathers worked in the shipbuilding industry on the River Clyde, so I'd
heard about the *Titanic* from an early age. But it was when I saw the film *A Night to
Remember*, as a teenager, that the extraordinariness of the story really got under my
skin. The fact that the people on board had just two hours and forty minutes—between
the collision and the sinking—to make decisions that would determine their chances of
survival meant it was a true test of character. Ideal territory for a novelist.

How did the plot for *Women and Children First* develop?
I knew from the start that I wanted to explore the experience from the point of view of
different characters, and also that I wanted to follow them for a while afterwards to see
how they coped, particularly since it seems certain that many survivors suffered from
what we would now call post-traumatic stress disorder.

Can you tell us about the creation of the hero, Reg?
The stories of the crew aren't so often told and that's why I chose one of the stewards
as my main character. I wanted someone who both interacted with, and watched,
passengers rather than an engineer in the boiler room, say. Flicking through photos of
the *Titanic*'s crew, I came across one of a young man with movie-star looks. He was
twenty-one years old, from Southampton, worked as a steward in the first-class dining
saloon, but didn't survive the sinking. I had him in mind as I wrote about Reg.

Which of the real-life passengers fascinated you the most?

Eloise Smith is a favourite because, although she was only eighteen, she was very courageous in her testimony to the American Inquiry, and a feisty critic of Bruce Ismay, managing director of the White Star Line, the company that ran the *Titanic*. She also had a life like a soap opera: widowed at eighteen, had a son at nineteen by the husband she lost on the *Titanic*, then married the man who had comforted her on the *Carpathia*. (It didn't last, of course).

How did you research the details of that fateful night?
I read everything I could get my hands on: books, old newspapers and websites. For over three years now, I've just totally immersed myself.

Have you ever sailed on an ocean liner, or would you like to?
No, it doesn't appeal to me. Funny that!

You studied Medicine at Glasgow University before deciding that being a doctor wasn't your thing. What put you off?
I started Medicine at the age of seventeen, largely because my father was a medical researcher and I had a vague idea that I might try to discover a cure for cancer or something equally important. I soon found the reality of dealing with sick people very difficult to cope with and, embarrassingly, I never quite got over my squeamishness.

And how did you get from Medicine to becoming a writer?
I did an Arts degree, worked in publishing, built up my own little publishing-related company, then sold it, buying me enough time to write my first novel.

You've written several health books. Do you tend to lead a healthy lifestyle?
Yes, on the whole. I eat well and exercise regularly, but I do enjoy the odd glass of wine. And I'm a workaholic, which is not necessarily very good for me.

You've produced two other published novels apart from *Women and Children First*. Which do you prefer writing, fiction or nonfiction, and why?
Fiction is harder than nonfiction because there's no formula for making a novel work. You need to feel your way and sense how the story should go, but it's enormously rewarding when it falls into place. I enjoy nonfiction as well because I get to learn about a variety of different subjects. So I like them both.

Where do you live, and is it with family and pets?
I live in north London with my partner but no pets. I travel too much to have pets.

Is there anywhere else in the world that you'd like to call home?
I'm Scottish born and bred and proud of it. Scotland will always feel like home.

Have you done anything extraordinary in your life to date?
Riding an elephant through a eucalyptus forest in southern India was pretty special.

What would you most like to be remembered for?
Being a good friend to a wide circle of people.

Years ago, Ken Nichols was a neighbour and friend of lawyer Brady Coyne. But a lot has happened in the intervening years. Relationships have ended and begun, and both their lives are very different now. Still, it's fun for the two friends to catch up over a drink for old times' sake. Then Brady gets a call that changes everything, turning a meeting with a friend from the past into an investigation of a present-day murder.

ONE

I spotted Ken Nichols about the same time he spotted me. He was sitting at the end of the hotel bar and when I started towards him he grinned and raised what looked like a Martini glass.

I took the stool beside him. He held out his hand, and I shook it.

'Glad you could make it, Brady,' Ken said. 'It's good to see you. What's it been?'

'Ten years,' I said. 'At least.'

He was wearing a pearl-coloured, button-down shirt under a pale blue linen jacket, with faded blue jeans and battered boat shoes. He had a good tan, as if he played golf year-round. His black hair was now speckled with grey and cut shorter than I remembered.

Ken had big ears and a meandering nose and a mouth that was a little too wide for his face. He grinned easily, he loved animals, and when he spoke, I could still detect the Blue Ridge Mountains of his childhood in his voice. Ken Nichols was an easy guy to like.

He was a veterinarian, and back when we were neighbours in Wellesley, Ken was the one who gave my dogs rabies and distemper shots, and I was the lawyer who handled legal work for his business. We used to play in the same foursome on Sundays, and invited each other's families for cookouts on summer weekends.

Then Ken got divorced, dissolved his veterinary practice and moved to Baltimore, and shortly after that, I got divorced too.

We'd been out of touch ever since, but Ken and I used to be pretty good friends, and when he called me earlier in the week, saying he was coming up to Massachusetts to attend this veterinarian convention in the big hotel in Natick and would love to meet me for a drink if I could sneak away, just for old times' sake, I agreed instantly. Friends, old or new, were always worth sneaking away for.

'You're looking good,' I said to him.

'I work out,' he said. 'You get to a certain age, you've got to take care of the machine, you know what I mean?'

'Yeah,' I said. 'I know. Change the oil, replace the filters, rotate the tyres. I should do something about my brake pads, but . . .'

He smiled. 'Same old Brady.' He showed me his empty Martini glass. 'So what'll you have? The usual? Jack, rocks?'

I smiled and nodded. 'You remembered.'

'Some things never change.'

The bartender must have been listening, because he came over and said, 'Gentlemen?'

'Another for me,' Ken said, 'and a Jack Daniel's on the rocks for my friend.'

After the bartender turned away, Ken said, 'So how's your golf game these days?'

'I quit a few years ago,' I said. 'It came down to golf or fishing, and I picked fishing. You're still playing, I bet.'

He nodded. 'I joined a country club outside Baltimore, and—' He stopped when a cell phone began buzzing on the bar top beside his elbow. Ken picked it up and looked at it, flipped it open, and said, 'Clem? That you, man?' He listened for a minute, frowned down at his wristwatch, then lifted his head and gazed around the room. 'Yeah, OK,' he said. 'I see you. Wait there.'

He snapped the phone shut and looked at me. 'I'm sorry,' he said. 'I've got to do something. It'll take just a minute.'

I waved my hand. 'Don't worry about it.'

The area where I was sitting consisted of a short bar top with a dozen stools plus five or six small tables, all crowded into one corner of an open area off the hotel lobby. People—mostly vets, I assumed—were milling around and lounging on sofas, some with laptops propped open, some looking up at a wide-screen TV mounted on the wall that was showing a Red Sox game.

As I watched, Ken weaved through the crowd to the other side of the room and went up to a man who was leaning against the wall with his arms folded over his chest. The man had a neatly trimmed dark beard streaked with grey and a high shiny forehead. He was wearing a dark suit with a maroon tie. He looked to be in his late forties, early fifties, about the same age as Ken. He kept his arms folded as Ken approached him.

Ken held out his hand. The man grinned, and they shook. Ken said something, and the other guy frowned and gave his head a shake. Ken shrugged and said something else, and the man looked up and turned his head towards the bar. His eyes found me across the room, and he lifted his chin and smiled at me as if he knew me.

I nodded. Maybe I was supposed to recognise him, but I didn't.

The man turned back to Ken, reached out, put his hand on Ken's arm, pushed his face close to Ken's, and began talking.

After a minute or two, Ken nodded and stepped away from the bearded guy, who smiled, made a pistol out of his hand, and pointed at Ken's face. Ken nodded, and the other guy turned and walked out of the room.

Ken stood there for a minute watching the man go. Then he started back to where I was sitting.

When I swivelled round to face the bar, I saw that my drink was sitting there for me. Ken's new Martini had appeared as well.

Ken eased himself onto the stool beside me. He picked up his Martini, downed half of it, and said, 'Ahh. I needed that.'

I turned to him. 'Everything OK?'

He shrugged. 'Sure.'

'That guy you were just talking with . . .'

He waved the back of his hand at me. 'No big deal.'

'Sorry,' I said. 'None of my business.'

He grinned. 'You don't want another case, do you?'

'Massachusetts or Maryland?'

He laughed. 'You name it, pal. I got cases here, there and the Arctic Circle.'

'I assume you've got somebody handling your business,' I said. 'Someone you can trust.'

'Oh, sure.' He nodded. 'Some things, it takes more than a lawyer to fix, though.'

I looked at him. 'Are you in some kind of trouble, Ken?'

'Who, that guy?' He smiled. 'Nah. Not really. He's an old friend.' He flapped his hand. 'It's just life, you know?'

'Because if you are . . .'

He smiled. 'I know. Thanks. But really, that's not why I wanted to get together. This was just about, you know, hey, it's been, what, ten years— I got divorced ten years ago. Things were simpler back then. We had some good times, didn't we?'

'Yes, good times,' I said. 'Different times.'

'They sure were,' he said. 'Hell, we were both married, just for one thing. You haven't remarried, have you?'

'Me?' I shook my head. 'No. I've had a couple of pretty serious relationships, but I always managed to screw them up. You?'

He grinned. 'I'm having way too much fun.' He drained his Martini glass. 'Another?'

'You go ahead,' I said. 'I'm good.'

We talked about the good old days when we both were younger, raising our kids, mowing our lawns and playing golf on weekends. When Ken talked, his eyes bored into mine as if he needed desperately to be understood. He peppered me with questions—what were my sons up to, how was my law practice going, what was Gloria, my ex-wife, doing—and when I tried to answer, his eyes would shift and he'd look past my shoulder, scanning the room as if he were expecting somebody, not really listening to me.

Ken's cell phone, lying on the bar top in front of him, buzzed two or three other times while we were sitting there, and each time he picked it up, frowned at the screen and did not answer it.

We'd been there for a little more than an hour when he looked at his watch, drained his glass, took out his wallet and put some bills on the bar. 'Well,' he said, 'I gotta go.'

I reached for my wallet, but he put his hand on my arm. 'I got it,' he said. 'We'll do it again, and next time you can buy the drinks.'

'Good,' I said. 'Means there will be a next time.'

'Wish we could make an evening out of it, but I'm on a damn committee and we've got a meeting. Let's not let another ten years go by, OK?' He held out his hand.

I shook it. 'I agree,' I said. 'We should keep in touch.'

'So if I had a legal problem some time . . .?'

I nodded. 'Sure. Of course.'

'That's great.' He slapped my shoulder. 'Say hi to Gloria for me next time you see her,' he said.

'Give my best to Sharon,' I said. 'And Ken, if you want to talk, legal problems or whatever, don't hesitate to give me a call.'

He nodded. 'I might do that.'

'I mean it,' I said.

'I do too,' he said. 'I'll call you.'

TWO

To anyone who didn't know better, the four of us probably looked like some nice well-adjusted American family from the Boston suburbs, out for an authentic North End Italian dinner on this Saturday evening in April. There was the man, a tall guy, and sitting across from him his wife, still blonde and pretty, both of them fit and trim, somewhere in their forties. The college-aged son, a little rebellious with his ponytail and scruffy beard and sunburn, was clearly enjoying this get-together with his family, as was the pretty girl, small and quick, with flashing dark eyes and straight black hair, the boy's younger sister apparently, judging by the casual way they appeared to be ignoring each other.

We were sharing a platter of antipasti and a bottle of Chianti. Gloria, my ex-wife, was telling Gwen, son Billy's friend from San Francisco (not his sister, not even close), about her new photography exhibit in a Newbury Street gallery, while Billy was telling me about the good trout fishing he'd had on a little spring creek in east-central Idaho, where he was living and working these days.

Nobody had yet addressed what Billy—Gloria still called him William—had said when he told me he was coming home for a few days. He said, 'I'm bringing a friend. Her name is Gwen, and we have something to tell you. Both of you. You and Mom.'

'A friend, huh?' I asked.

'Actually, yeah,' Billy said.

'A girlfriend, you mean.'

'A friend,' he said.

'Well, it will be great to see you again, meet your friend Gwen.'

I was curious about what the two kids had to tell us. A few obvious scenarios played themselves out in my imagination.

So here we were, eating prosciutto and salami and mozzarella balls, dipping our bread in olive oil, and whatever Billy and Gwen had to tell us sat at the table like a shy elephant, impossible to ignore but pretending to be invisible.

I hadn't seen my number-one son for nearly two years—since I had ten glorious days of fly-fishing in Idaho and spent a couple of those days in his drift boat, splitting time with him at the oars. Billy was a Rocky Mountain fishing guide in the summer and a ski instructor in the winter, and I envied him. When I was his age I was ploughing through law school, hell-bent on starting my career and getting married and having a family and saving up for retirement.

Billy was hell-bent on having all the fun while he was young that I'd mostly postponed until I was middle-aged.

It had been even longer since I'd spent any time with Gloria. We did talk on the phone now and then, mainly when one of our two sons—Joey, the younger, was a prelaw sophomore at Stanford—had some kind of issue, usually involving money, that required parental consultation.

Billy had started to tell me about his five-day float trip down the Middle Fork of the Salmon River when my cell phone vibrated against my leg. It felt like an angry bumblebee in my pocket.

I fished out the phone and looked at it. *Unknown caller*, it said on the screen. I didn't recognise the number.

'Go ahead and answer it,' said Billy.

I shoved the phone back into my pocket. 'I'm having dinner with my family,' I said. 'It's Saturday night. Whatever it is, it can wait.'

'Maybe it's important,' he said. 'One of your clients. If they're calling on a Saturday night, it's probably some kind of emergency. Why don't you see if they left a message?'

I nodded and took out the phone. *Message waiting*, it said.

I accessed my voicemail. A woman's voice said, 'Brady? This is Sharon Nichols. I'm . . . it's Ken. My husband. Ex-husband. I'm at his hotel room. There's so much blood. Please. I don't know what to do. I'm frantic. I need a lawyer. Please call me.' She recited a number, the same one that appeared on my phone's screen.

It took me a minute to process what Sharon Nichols had said. Twenty-four hours earlier Ken Nichols and I had been drinking at a hotel bar, reminiscing about the days when we were golfing partners. Now his ex-wife was calling from a hotel—the same one, I assumed—talking about Ken and blood and asking for a lawyer.

I snapped my phone shut and stood up. Billy, Gwen and Gloria all looked at me. 'I'm sorry,' I said. 'This actually is an emergency. I'll be back in a minute.'

Gloria arched her eyebrows, and I could read her expression. *What the hell do you think you're doing?* it asked. *What's more important than dinner with your family?*

'I've got to answer it,' I said to her. 'I'm going outside to make the call.'

I went out to the sidewalk. The dampness from a soft April rain shower reflected the yellow streetlights and the red and green neon restaurant signs. I stood under the canvas awning and pecked out the number that Sharon Nichols had left.

She answered on the first ring. 'Brady? Is that you?'

'It's me,' I said. 'What's going on?'

'It's Ken. He's—I think he's dead. There's blood everywhere.'

'You're in his hotel room? The Beverly Suites in Natick?'

'Yes. How did you—'

'I had drinks with Ken there last night. Did you call the police?'

'No,' she said. 'I called you.'

'Hang up and call the police. Dial 911. Do it now. OK?'

She hesitated. 'But somebody killed him. Don't you see? Will you be my lawyer?'

'Sure. I'm your lawyer, and I'm telling you to get out of that room. Don't touch anything. Step out into the corridor and call the police. Then wait there for them.'

'It's kind of late for that.'

'For what?'

'For don't touch anything.'

'Whatever,' I said. 'Just get the hell out of the room. I'll be there as soon as I can. What's the room number?'

'Um, 322.'

'I'm on my way.'

'OK,' she said. 'Thank you.'

After I disconnected from Sharon Nichols, I stood on the sidewalk watching the rain drip off the awning. I was remembering when we brought Bucky, our old beagle, to Dr Nichols's veterinary hospital for the last time. Billy and Joey were kids. Bucky had been part of our family for as long as either of them could remember.

A few months earlier, Ken had told me that Bucky's tumour was inoperable. We'd nursed the old dog until he could no longer get his legs under his hind end. When I told the boys that we were going to have to put Bucky down, and I explained how Dr Nichols would do it with an injection, and how it wouldn't hurt, how Bucky would just go to sleep, they both said they wanted to be there.

So on a Saturday morning in October, Billy, Joey and I took Bucky to the vet's office. Ken and Sharon were both there, wearing white coats. I lifted Bucky onto the stainless-steel table. Sharon held him and Ken slid the needle into his foreleg, and Bucky exhaled once and it was all over.

When I looked up at Ken and Sharon, both of them had tears in their eyes. I always liked that about them.

They had two kids, a girl, Ellen, who babysat for our boys a few times, and a son Wayne, who was about Billy's age. Our kids all knew each other, though I didn't remember that they were friends.

Ken and Sharon got divorced a year or two before Gloria and I did. They sold their veterinary practice, including the animal hospital and the kennels, and I took care of the business end of it.

Ken relocated in Maryland. Sharon bought a house in Acton and brought up her kids there.

All of that happened ten or eleven years ago and, except for a few lingering tax issues related to the sale of their business, I hadn't had any further dealings with Sharon or Ken Nichols before my reunion with Ken the previous evening. Now Ken had apparently been murdered in a hotel room in Natick, and Sharon had found his body, and I was the one she called.

I went back into the restaurant and stood beside our table. 'I've got to go,' I told Gloria, Billy and Gwen. 'I'm really sorry.'

Gloria opened her mouth, then shook her head, picked up her wineglass and took a sip.

'You gotta do what you gotta do,' said Billy. 'We'll catch up later.'

'You want to tell us what it is you've got to tell us?' I asked.

'It'll wait,' he said. 'Give us an excuse to do this again.'

'And we will,' I said. To Gwen I said, 'Great to meet you.'

I turned and left the restaurant. I'd walked to the restaurant from my house on Beacon Hill. It took about twenty minutes, which was as fast as a taxi could negotiate the one-way streets, so I walked home. When I got there, I let Henry out to pee, gave him a bully stick, and told him I'd be back.

I walked down Charles Street, fetched my car from the parking garage, and pointed it at the Beverly Suites Hotel in Natick, where Sharon Nichols was waiting with the body of her ex-husband.

THE BEVERLY SUITES HOTEL was one of the countless commercial establishments that lined the Framingham and Natick stretch of Route 9. I stopped under the portico by the front entrance, got out of my car and gave my keys to an attendant. He gave me a receipt with a number on it. I slipped it into my pocket and went inside.

An electronic bulletin board in the foyer spelled out the words WELCOME, INTERNATIONAL ASSOCIATION OF VETERINARIANS. Underneath the greeting was a schedule of events. I noticed that this evening, Saturday, the annual banquet was being held in the Grand Ballroom. I guessed that the festivities had recently ended, as a number of people wearing suits and dresses were lounging on chairs in the lobby and in the bar area where I'd met Ken.

I found a bank of elevators, waited for one to open, got in and pressed the number three button. A moment later I was deposited on the third floor. A sign indicated that rooms 300–345 were to the right.

The detritus of room service littered the corridor outside some of the rooms—trays holding lipstick-stained glasses, empty wine bottles, cups and saucers, plates and balled-up cloth napkins.

When I turned the corner to where I expected to find police swarming the corridor outside room 322, I saw nobody.

The door to the room was closed. I knocked on it.

The door cracked open. Sharon Nichols looked out, then opened the door wide. 'Oh, Brady,' she said. 'I'm so glad you're here.'

I hadn't seen Sharon Nichols in over a decade. She looked pretty much as I remembered her. Blonde hair, cut a bit shorter now. Wide-set blue-green eyes. Tall and slender. An attractive woman in her late forties, although her eyes were red and swollen.

'The police haven't arrived yet?' I asked.

'I didn't call them.'

'I told you to call them.'

'Well,' she said, 'I didn't. I've been in here for most of the evening already. Another few minutes won't do any harm. Come in, Brady. You should see it.'

Sharon was wearing a pale blue jacket, an off-white silk blouse and a dark skirt that stopped a few inches above her knees. There was a reddish blotch—a dried bloodstain, it looked like—on the sleeve of her jacket.

I looked past her into the room, but I couldn't see anything.

She stepped away from the door and held it open for me. I went in, and then I saw Ken. He was sprawled across the bed, as if he'd been sitting on the side of it and had fallen backwards. He was wearing a maroon silk robe over a white T-shirt and grey suit trousers. Black socks on his feet, no shoes.

There was a big splotch of dark blood on his chest and another just under his beltline, and more blood had puddled on the bedcover. He looked smaller than he had the night before. Deflated.

I turned to Sharon. 'Did you touch anything?'

'I touched him,' she said. 'I tried to see if he was breathing. He wasn't. He was dead when I got here.'

'Come on.' I grabbed her arm and led her out to the corridor. I took my cell phone out of my pocket and showed it to her. 'I've got a lot of questions,' I said. 'I need to know everything. But first . . .'

I hit the speed-dial number for Roger Horowitz's cell phone. Horowitz was a homicide detective with the state police, one of the best. He was a crusty sonofabitch, but he was also my friend, and a solid cop, and I trusted him.

'Who's this?' he said by way of answering his phone.

'Brady Coyne,' I said. 'I've got a homicide for you.'

'Oh, goodie,' he said. 'A homicide. Just what I wanted. What more could a guy ask for on a Saturday night. Hey, Alyse, honey. Guess what? It's Coyne, and he's got a homicide for me.'

'I knew you'd be thrilled,' I said.

'Thrilled and delighted,' he said. 'Alyse and I are here on the sofa in our living room watching an old movie on TV, and I was telling her, "Honey, wouldn't it be just perfect if Brady Coyne would call with a homicide for me and drag me away from here?"'

'I'm sorry,' I said. 'It was inconsiderate of this man to get stabbed to death on a Saturday night.'

'Stabbed, huh?'

'Yes. Two stab wounds. Plenty of blood.'

'There always is,' he said. 'Where are you?'

'Beverly Suites Hotel on Route 9 in Natick. Room 322.'

'I know where that is,' he said. 'So who's the vic?'

'A veterinarian named Ken Nichols,' I said. 'Used to live in Wellesley. Ten years ago he got divorced, sold his business and moved to Baltimore. There's a vet convention here this weekend.'

'And you're there why?'

'Nichols's ex-wife called me. Sharon. She found him.'

'She's your client?'

I glanced at Sharon. She was leaning against the wall watching me. I gave her a quick nod, which I intended to be reassuring.

'Yes,' I said. 'She's my client. We used to be neighbours. Her and Ken. Our victim. I did legal work for their business back when they were together and had the animal hospital in Wellesley. I was here last night, as a matter of fact. Had drinks with Ken.'

'Drinks, huh? And now he's dead.'

'Yes.'

'The wife,' he said. 'She do it?'

'Ha,' I said.

'She called her lawyer,' he said, 'not the cops, though, huh?'

'That's right, and I called you.'

'For which,' he said, 'again, hey, thanks a lot. Makes my day. OK. Don't touch anything. We'll be there in a few minutes.' He disconnected without saying goodbye or thank you. Typical.

I snapped my phone shut. 'The police will be here,' I said to Sharon. 'So tell me. What time did you get here?'

'Nine o'clock,' she said. 'We'd planned to meet here at nine.'

'Why?'

'Why did I come here, to Ken's room?'

I nodded. 'The police will want to know.'

She looked at me. 'I was early, actually.' Her eyes looked wet. She blinked a couple of times. 'I waited in the lobby until nine o'clock. He had to go to the banquet. He was going to sneak out early.' She blew out a breath. 'It was a . . . a date. I was meeting my ex-husband. I was excited. Keyed up. Did he mention it to you last night? That we were, ah, getting together?'

I shook my head. 'No. He said nothing about it.'

I glanced at my watch. It was a little after ten thirty. Sharon had been here with Ken—Ken's dead body—for about an hour and a half. 'He doesn't look like he just came from a banquet,' I said. 'Silk robe, no jacket or tie. No shirt, even.'

She shrugged. 'I suppose he changed. He said he was going to order a bottle of champagne from room service. It was a celebration. Maybe that's how you dress for a celebration.' She cocked her head and looked at me, as if she expected me to challenge her.

'A celebration,' I said. 'Of what?'

'Finding each other again after all these years, I guess.' She shrugged. 'It was Ken's word. When we decided to get together, he said it would be a celebration. I liked that, you know?'

I looked at Sharon. I wondered if she'd killed Ken. Means, motive and opportunity. She had them all. Well, I didn't know about her motive yet, but all spouses—and especially ex-spouses—have motives for murder. That's why they make ideal suspects.

At this point, at least, Sharon was the only suspect, although I remembered the bearded guy who'd pointed his finger at Ken in the lobby last night. Also, he'd had several calls that he didn't answer but which had caused him to frown and glance round the room.

Still, Horowitz would focus on Sharon. She was the obvious suspect. Spouses kill spouses on a predictable basis.

Sharon was looking at me, and I had the feeling she knew what I was thinking. 'So what happens next?' she asked.

'It's not unlike what you see on TV,' I said. 'Lots of people. Confusion. Cops and forensics techs and maybe a county sheriff and a DA or two. They'll want to ask you a lot of questions. I'll be with you. I'll decide whether you should answer or not, and if so, which ones. You'll do what I say. OK?'

'Why wouldn't I answer their questions? Because it looks like I might have done it?'

I shrugged. 'They'll want to know why you came here tonight, how you happened to be the one who found Ken's body, and why you called your lawyer instead of the police.'

'Do you mean you want to know?' she asked.

'I need to know everything,' I said.

'Of course you do.' She looked at me and smiled. 'Ken and I might've been getting back together. He sent me a birthday card in the fall. It came out of nowhere. We hadn't talked, hadn't communicated, for years. Then I get this warm and friendly card, and he wrote something about how nice it would be to see me again. I didn't think too much about it. But then he sent a Christmas card, mentioning that he'd be coming up here for a conference in April and maybe we could get together. It made me curious. So I sent him a note saying sure, it would be nice to see him again. Then one evening he called me on the phone, and we talked for a long time, and it was as if we'd never split up. He called me again a week or so later, and it got to be that we talked on the phone two or three times a week, and pretty soon it began to feel, um, intimate. You know? I mean, here's this man I had children with, who I worked beside, who I slept with for all those years. All the things that we had going for us, they were still there. They were just dormant, and talking with Ken reawakened all those things. The good memories. Why I once loved him. It was like a courtship, all those phone calls. It was kind of . . . it was sexy.' She looked at me. Her eyes were brimming. 'I came here tonight to make love with my ex-husband in his hotel room. I felt like a teenager. I was excited. I think he was, too.' She stopped and stared. 'You believe me, don't you?'

'Sure,' I said.

'You and Gloria,' she said. 'After you got divorced, did you ever . . . ?'

'No,' I said.

'So should I tell the police what I just told you?'

I nodded. 'You should tell them the truth. You'll have to explain why you came here tonight.'

She hugged herself. 'It's sort of embarrassing.'

'Embarrassment is the least of our worries.'

She nodded.

'Whoever did this,' I said, 'Ken must have let him into his room. Him or her.'

'A woman, you think?'

I shrugged. 'Maybe.'

'Maybe that's what it was,' Sharon said. 'Maybe that's who did this. Some woman. I guess I didn't really know Ken. People change in ten years, regardless of what they might say on the telephone.'

We stood there awkwardly, waiting for the police. After a few minutes, Sharon said, 'You haven't asked me if I did it.'

'You're right,' I said. 'I haven't asked.'

She looked at me. 'Well, I didn't, you know.'

I smiled. 'Good.'

A minute later, as we stood waiting for the authorities, a man turned the corner and started down the corridor. He was wearing a black sweatshirt with a hood over his head, so I couldn't see his face, but I had the impression he was white and young—late teens, early twenties. He struck me as out of place in this fancy hotel.

He took a few steps towards Sharon and me, and then he stopped. He hesitated for a moment, and I thought he was going to speak, but then he turned and began to run in the other direction.

'Hey!' I yelled at him. 'Hey! Wait!'

He darted back down the corridor and round the corner.

I ran after him. When I turned the corner, I had the choice of an elevator, the stairwell, or a left or right onto another corridor.

I looked both ways down the corridor and saw nobody.

The numbers over the two elevators showed that one was descending from the seventh floor and one was stopped at the lobby.

When I opened the door to the stairwell, I heard footsteps below. The kid in the hoodie, I assumed, running down the stairs. Already I was panting from my sprint down the corridor. I'd never catch him.

I turned and went back to where Sharon was waiting outside Ken's room. I leaned against the wall and tried to catch my breath.

'What was that about?' she asked.

I shrugged. 'That guy panicked when he saw us standing here.'

'You think . . . ?'

'I think he was coming to Ken's room. Did you get a look at him?'

'No,' she said, shaking her head. 'You think he's the one who killed Ken?'

'Maybe,' I said.

She looked at me. 'But why?'

'Why would we think it was that man?'

'No,' she said. 'Why would he kill Ken?'

'Why would anybody?' I said.

THREE

A pair of uniformed Natick police officers arrived a few minutes later. One of them, a young blond guy, went into Ken's room. The other cop, a chunky fortyish woman named Lloyd, according to her name badge, stayed out in the corridor with Sharon and me. All she said was 'We're here to secure the scene till the staties get here.' Then she stationed herself outside the door, staring straight ahead.

The blond cop came out a minute later. Officer Lloyd arched her eyebrows at him. He shook his head. Then they both stood with us in the corridor, and nobody said anything.

Eventually Roger Horowitz and his partner, a pretty female detective named Marcia Benetti, showed up, and behind them an entourage of Massachusetts State Police officers and forensics technicians. Horowitz spoke briefly to the two Natick cops; then he and Benetti came over to where Sharon and I were standing.

He nodded at me and said, 'Hey,' and I returned his nod.

Marcia Benetti gave me a quick smile, then went over to Sharon. 'I'm Detective Benetti,' she said. 'I need your jacket.'

Sharon looked at her. 'Excuse me?'

'Your jacket,' said Benetti. 'For evidence. That appears to be a blood-stain.' She pointed at the sleeve.

Sharon slipped her jacket off and handed it to Marcia Benetti, who dropped it into a big plastic bag and carried it over to a tech.

Horowitz turned to Sharon. 'Mrs Nichols, is it?'

She nodded. 'Yes. Sharon Nichols. I kept my married name.'

'We're going to need to talk with you. I assume you'll want your lawyer'—he jerked his head at me—'with you?'

'Yes, she will,' I said.

Horowitz looked at me and gave me one of his cynical smiles. 'OK,' he said to Sharon. 'Officer Lloyd here will stay with you until we're ready.'

People kept going into and out of the hotel room. A grey-haired man, accompanied by a younger Asian man carrying a big camera bag, showed up. The medical examiner and his assistant. They talked with Horowitz, then the three of them went into Ken's room.

Horowitz then came out of the room. 'Coyne,' he said, crooking his finger at me, 'you want to come with me?'

I followed him into the hotel room. He stopped just inside the door and turned to me. 'I suppose you and your client have contaminated everything with your fingerprints and whatnot.'

I shrugged. 'Probably. Sorry.'

'Well, put your hands in your pockets. Let's try to keep the damage to a minimum.' He turned and continued into the room.

I followed him. Three young men and one woman wearing Massachusetts State Police windcheaters were conferring outside the bathroom. The ME appeared to be examining Ken's body. His assistant was taking photographs.

Horowitz went over to a closet. He opened the door and shined his flashlight inside. 'C'mere, Coyne,' he said. 'Look at this.'

I moved up beside him and looked into the closet. It was empty except for a gym bag on the floor in the corner. Horowitz knelt down beside the bag, and I looked over his shoulder.

The gym bag was unzipped. He pulled open the top and pointed his flashlight at the contents. It was full of small glass bottles. 'This bag was here. Just like this, except it was zipped up. I'm wondering if your dead buddy here might've said something about this when you saw him last night.'

I shook my head. 'What is it?'

He reached into the bag with his latex-gloved hand, took out one of the bottles and showed it to me. It contained a clear liquid. *Ketaset* was the word on the label. Obviously a brand name.

'Ketaset,' I said. 'What is this stuff?'

'Brand of ketamine,' said Horowitz. 'Common anaesthetic used in animal surgery.'

I shrugged. 'Ken Nichols was a veterinarian who performed animal surgeries, and here he is, at a convention of veterinarians.'

Horowitz smiled bleakly. 'Ketamine is also a Schedule III drug that's sold illegally and abused by humans. It's a psychedelic. What we call a dissociative. Commonly used for date-rape purposes.'

'Date rape,' I said.

'Among other things,' he said. 'Dances, concerts, parties. It loosens you up. Diminishes anxiety and stimulates your libido. It can give you an out-of-body experience. They call it K, or Special K, or Ket. A bad trip can be pretty awful. Then, as they say, it lands you in K-hole. Special K was popular back in the nineties.'

I shrugged. 'Never heard of it.'

'Well, you ain't a cop,' he said. 'Ketamine fell out of favour for a while, but it's been making a comeback.'

'And Ken, being a vet, had access to this stuff,' I said.

'And Ken,' said Horowitz, mocking my tone, 'having access to this stuff, might also have been using it. Or selling it.'

It occurred to me that Ken Nichols, expecting Sharon to show up in his hotel room, might've had a logical reason to want to give his libido a boost. 'Will it show up in the ME's tox screen?'

'We'll tell him to test for it,' Horowitz said.

'You think Ken was selling this stuff?' I asked.

'Why else bring a big bag of it with him from Baltimore?'

'Are you saying ketamine is your motive for murder?' I asked.

'I'm saying no such thing,' said Horowitz. 'We already got a perfectly fine suspect with many good motives.'

'You don't really think Sharon did this,' I said.

'Sure I do,' he said. 'She's the spouse.'

I snapped my fingers. 'I meant to tell you. After I called you, when Sharon and I were waiting for the troops to get here, this guy came round the corner, took one look at us, and turned and started running. I went after him, but I couldn't catch him.'

'You being old and out of shape.'

I nodded. 'I thought the guy was acting guilty, turning and running like that.'

'Now you tell me.'

'Sorry,' I said. 'It slipped my mind.'

'One of your animal doctor's customers, maybe,' said Horowitz, 'looking to buy himself some Special K. That what you think?'

I shrugged. 'Could be, huh?'

'Could you ID this guy?'

I shook my head. 'He was wearing a black sweatshirt with the hood over his head. He was white, male and young. Late teens, early twenties. A small guy, kind of skinny, five-eight or nine. I didn't get a look at his face. I could pick his sweatshirt out of a line-up, maybe, but not him. He could run fast, I can testify to that. Wearing baggy blue jeans and white sneakers.'

'He ran fast, and you ran slow,' Horowitz said. 'I wish you'd mentioned this earlier.'

Horowitz went over and spoke to Marcia Benetti, who was conferring with the ME beside Ken's body. When he finished, she nodded, said something to the medical examiner, and left the room.

Horowitz came back. 'We'll get some people looking,' he said, 'but I'm not holding my breath. I'd be shocked if your friend in the hoodie isn't long gone by now. Too bad.' He jerked his head towards the door. 'You got anything else I should know?'

'I told you I had a drink with Ken last night,' I said. 'While I was there, he had an encounter with a guy.'

'What kind of encounter?'

'I didn't hear what they were saying,' I said. 'I thought at the time that they must've been friends, but reading their body language, there might've been some anger going on between them. This other guy pointed his finger at Ken like his hand was a gun.'

'Could you identify this guy?'

I nodded. 'Sure. I got a good look at him. He was fiftyish, dark, neatly trimmed beard with some grey in it, big forehead, balding on top. Wearing a suit and tie. I assume he was another vet.'

'You didn't get a name, did you?'

I thought for a minute, then said, 'Clem. Ken called him Clem.'

'Clem what?'

'I don't know.'

'First name? Last name?'

I shrugged.

'We can check the registration,' he said, 'see if there's a vet named Clem in attendance. Nichols didn't say what they were angry about, huh?'

'I didn't ask, he didn't say. I'm not sure it was anger. He did seem kind of upset, though. Implied he had a lot of problems. Now that I think of it, he was pretty jumpy the whole time. His cell phone rang several times, but he only answered it that once, when the bearded guy called from the other side of the room.'

'Clem.'

I nodded.

'What'd you talk about?' asked Horowitz. 'Any hints about what was bothering him?'

'No, nothing like that. We talked about the old days. I hadn't seen him in about ten years.'

'You were with him how long?'

'Hour, maybe an hour and a half. Then he had to go to some committee meeting.'

'Did he talk about his wife?'

'His ex-wife, you mean?'

He nodded. 'Your client.'

'No,' I said.

'And if he did, you wouldn't tell me.'

I shrugged. 'She's my client.'

'Well,' Horowitz said, 'we'll check out his phone, see if we can catch up with those two you mentioned. The kid in the hoodie and Clem with the beard. You got anybody else we should check out?'

'That's all I can think of,' I said. 'Just those two. Look. What are you planning to do about my client?'

'Question her, of course. Tonight. OK?'

'It's getting late,' I said. 'She's had a traumatic experience.'

'She gonna be cooperative?'

'I don't see why not,' I said.

I went back over to Sharon.

She said, 'Is everything all right?'

'In your conversations with Ken,' I said, 'did he ever mention ketamine?'

She frowned. 'Ketamine?'

'It's a recreational drug,' I said. 'Vets use it as an anaesthetic for animal surgery.'

'I remember now,' she said. 'It's been a while since I worked in a vet's office. What about ketamine?'

I shrugged. 'There was a bag of it in his room.'

'What do they think,' she said, 'that he was selling it?'

'It kinda looks like it. Or else he was using it himself.'

She shook her head.

'Does the name Clem ring a bell?'

She frowned. 'Should it?'

'A guy Ken talked with when I was there, that's all. No reason you'd know him.'

She tilted her head. 'So now what happens?'

'They're going to question you,' I said. 'They'll want to know every-thing you can tell them about Ken. His business, his finances, his personal life. His friends and enemies. You should just answer their questions, tell them the truth. If they ask you something out of line, consult with me. I'll be there with you, and if I don't like a question, I'll tell you not to answer until we talk about it. OK?'

'I don't really know him,' she said. 'We've been apart for over ten years. Just what he might've mentioned on the telephone.'

'"I don't know",' I said, 'is a perfectly valid answer. Don't hesitate to use it.'

'They think I did it, don't they?' she said.

'They'll treat you like a suspect, sure. Don't take it personally. They consider everybody a suspect until they can eliminate them.'

'Especially the spouse. Or the ex-spouse.'

'Yes,' I said. 'Especially the spouse.'

Sharon shook her head. 'I was falling in love with him all over again,' she said. 'Why would I want to kill him?'

It was a rhetorical question, and I didn't bothering answering it.

After a while, Officer Lloyd came over. 'Mr Coyne, Mrs Nichols, would you come with me, please?'

We both stood up and followed Officer Lloyd to the elevators. We took one of them down to the first floor, where she led us to a conference room off the lobby. It was empty except for a rectangular table with a dozen leather-cushioned chairs arranged round it.

'Have a seat, please,' said Officer Lloyd. 'The detectives will be here in a minute.'

Officer Lloyd left the room, closing the door behind her.

Sharon and I sat side by side at the table. I looked at my watch. It was a few minutes before one in the morning. The door opened and Horowitz and Marcia Benetti came in. They sat across from us.

'I'm Detective Horowitz,' he said to Sharon. 'This is Detective Benetti.'

They all nodded to each other.

Horowitz looked at me. 'We're gonna be here all night. There are two hundred and seventeen veterinarians at this convention. We got to clear every one of them.' He shook his head. 'Not to mention about fifty hotel employees and all the other hotel guests.'

'Poor you,' I said.

'My sentiments exactly.' He put his forearms on the table, leaned forwards and looked at Sharon. 'We hope you can help us understand what happened here tonight,' he said. 'You won't mind answering some questions for us?'

'I don't mind,' said Sharon.

'OK, good,' said Horowitz. He jerked his head in the direction of his partner. 'We're going to record this. Save us the trouble of taking notes.' He looked at me. 'OK?'

I nodded. 'Sure.'

Benetti reached into her big shoulder bag and took out a battery-run digital recorder about the size of a television remote. She pressed a button, said, 'Just testing,' flipped another button and we heard, 'Just testing,' loud and clear. She put it in the middle of the table between us and said, 'OK. We're good to go.'

Horowitz said, 'We're here at the Beverly Suites Hotel in Natick. This is Detective Roger Horowitz. Detective Marcia Benetti is here, along with Sharon Nichols and attorney Brady Coyne. It's 12.42 a.m. on Sunday, April the 22nd.' He looked at Sharon and me. 'OK, then. Mrs Nichols. Our victim, Kenneth Nichols, he was your ex-husband, right?'

'Yes, that's right,' said Sharon.

'And you were here tonight . . . why?'

'We hadn't seen each other in a long time. It was a kind of . . . a get-together. A chance to get to know each other again.'

'Like a date.'

'Sort of, yes.'

'In his hotel room.'

Sharon nodded.

'Answer for the recorder, please,' Horowitz said.

'Yes,' she said. 'We'd planned to meet in Ken's hotel room.'

'Why in his room?'

'It was a kind of celebration. He was going to order champagne.'

'A celebration of what?' asked Horowitz.

'Of our . . . of being interested in each other again.'

Horowitz hesitated, then said, 'You were planning on, um, having sex with him? Is that what you mean?'

'I thought that might happen, yes,' said Sharon.

Horowitz leaned forwards. 'You've been divorced for how long?'

'Ten years. It'll be eleven next September.'

'Why?'

'Why what?' asked Sharon. 'Why did we get divorced?'

Horowitz nodded.

'We didn't love each other any more. We were unhappy.' She shrugged. 'No dramatic reason, if that's what you're looking for.'

'I wasn't looking for anything,' Horowitz said.

'It was mutual,' she said. 'Nobody's fault.'

'You and your husband,' he said 'Ex-husband, I mean. Did you have children?'

'Yes,' she said. 'Two. A girl and a boy. Ellen and Wayne.'

'How old?'

'Then or now?'

'Now.'

Sharon frowned for a moment, then said, 'Ellen's twenty-five. Wayne's twenty-two.'

'And where are they now?'

'Both in school,' she said. 'Ellen's getting her master's at BU. Wayne's a junior at Webster State College in New Hampshire.'

'So how did they get along with your—with their father?'

She shrugged. 'They had the normal issues. They resented him. They resented both of us. For splitting. For wrecking our family.'

'Did they keep in touch with him?'

'I don't honestly know about that,' Sharon said.

'How about you?'

'I haven't talked with Wayne for a while. Ellen and I have remained close.'

'How long is a while?'

Sharon glanced at me. 'A couple of years.'

Horowitz's eyebrow went up. 'You haven't communicated with your son for two years?'

Sharon nodded. 'Maybe a little longer than that, actually.'

'Can you tell us how to reach Wayne and Ellen?'

'You consider my children to be suspects?' Sharon asked.

'Everybody's suspects,' said Horowitz.

'I can give you their phone numbers and addresses,' she said.

'Give her something to write on,' Horowitz said to Benetti.

Benetti slid a pad of paper and a pen across the table to Sharon, who took an address book from her purse and copied some information on the pad of paper, which she then pushed back to Benetti.

'OK,' said Horowitz. 'So back to your husband—your ex-husband, I mean, Ken—he was living in Baltimore? That right?'

She nodded. 'His office was in a suburb just outside the city.'

'How would you characterise your relationship with your ex-husband for the past ten, almost eleven years?'

'We were divorced,' she said. 'We lived in different states. We had occasional long-distance telephone conversations or an exchange of emails, mostly about our children. Otherwise, until last fall, Ken and I didn't have any kind of relationship.'

'What happened last fall?' Horowitz asked.

Sharon turned and looked at me. I nodded.

'We began talking on the telephone,' she said. 'We discovered that we still liked each other. Or I should say, we liked each other all over again. We were talking about getting back together.'

'Neither of you had remarried?'

'No.'

Horowitz cleared his throat. 'In all of your telephone conversations,' he said, 'did Mr Nichols ever mention anybody he was having problems with? Any kind of enemy?'

Sharon frowned, then shrugged. 'Not that I remember.'

'What about a man named Clem?' asked Horowitz.

Sharon looked at me and shook her head. 'Like I told Brady, I don't remember Ken mentioning anybody named Clem.'

'What about the man in the hood?' Horowitz asked. 'Who you saw tonight. Did you recognise him?'

'No,' Sharon said. 'I did not.'

'Did your ex-husband ever talk about selling illegal drugs?'

Sharon turned to me, bit her lip.

I shrugged. 'Just answer his question.'

'No,' she said to Horowitz. 'He said nothing about that to me.'

'So as far as you know, he had no problems,' Horowitz said.

'Oh, he had problems,' Sharon said. 'I don't know anything about drugs, but Ken was lonely. He didn't like Baltimore. He didn't get along with his partner at the veterinary clinic. I think he was having financial problems. I don't think he was very happy.'

'Did he talk to you about his financial problems?'

Sharon shook her head. 'Not really. We didn't talk about problems. It was implied, that's all. Nothing specific.'

Marcia Benetti cleared her throat. Horowitz glanced at her, then nodded.

'So, Mrs Nichols,' said Benetti, 'what'd you do with the knife?'

Sharon frowned. 'Knife?'

'The murder weapon. How did you dispose of it?'

Sharon turned and arched her eyebrows at me.

'Don't say anything,' I said to her. I looked at Benetti. 'You want to rephrase that question?'

Horowitz had his arms crossed over his chest and a big smile on his face. Benetti glowered at me for a moment, then looked at Sharon and said, 'Mrs Nichols, did you notice a knife in the hotel room where you found your . . . Mr Nichols's body?'

'No,' said Sharon. 'I didn't see any knife.'

'It would've been a steak knife,' Benetti said, 'such as would be included in a room-service delivery along with a fork and a spoon. A serrated steak knife with a blade about five inches long.'

Sharon shook her head. 'I didn't see any kind of knife.'

'When people finish their room-service meal,' said Benetti, 'they put the tray with the dirty dishes outside their door. You could have taken a steak knife from one of those trays.'

'I guess anybody could have,' said Sharon, 'but I didn't.'

Benetti flashed a humourless smile. 'The medical examiner tells us your husband was stabbed twice with a serrated knife,' she said. 'Once in the abdomen and once under the rib cage. The wound in his chest penetrated his heart and caused him to die instantly.'

Sharon was staring at Benetti. Her eyes were brimming.

'So what about the knife?' asked Horowitz.

'My client already answered the question about the knife,' I said. 'Is there anything else? Because it's late and we are exhausted.'

'One more thing,' said Horowitz. 'Mrs Nichols, you said you came here tonight to, um, meet your husband, is that right?'

'He was my ex-husband,' Sharon said. 'We had planned to get together tonight, yes.'

'In his hotel room.'

Sharon nodded. 'That's right. I already explained that.'

'Not down in the lobby or in one of the bars. In his room.'

Sharon nodded. 'In his room, yes.'

'Why in the room?' asked Horowitz.

'I told you. We were probably going to have sex.'

'You hadn't seen each other in, what, ten years?'

'Since the divorce,' she said. 'Almost eleven years.'

'And what time did he expect you to arrive in his room?' asked Benetti. 'To have sex.'

'Nine o'clock,' said Sharon. 'We agreed to meet there at nine. There was a banquet tonight, but he planned to sneak out early.'

'To meet you. In his hotel room.'

Sharon nodded.

'To have sex.'

'Maybe.'

'So what time did you arrive here at the hotel?' asked Benetti.

'A little before eight thirty. I was early.'

'So did you go straight to the room?'

'No,' Sharon said. 'I sat in the lobby until nine o'clock. It was maybe five after nine when I got to his room.'

'Did you talk with anybody in the lobby?' asked Benetti.

Sharon shrugged. 'No. I just sat there and read a magazine.'

'Because,' said Benetti, 'it would help if you could account for your time before nine o'clock.'

'Somebody might've noticed me,' Sharon said, 'but I couldn't tell you who. I just sat there by myself reading my *Newsweek* and waiting for nine o'clock to arrive, and it seemed to take a long time. Then I went up to his room. The door was ajar, so I pushed it open and went inside, and that's when I . . .' She shrugged.

'According to the ME,' said Horowitz, 'Mr Nichols died between six thirty and eight thirty tonight. We have witnesses willing to testify that he was still at the banquet at seven fifteen, and that he was gone before eight o'clock. So we've got that hour between eight and nine, when you said you went to his room.' He looked at Sharon and pursed his lips.

'Well, I already told you, I didn't go to his room until nine,' said Sharon. 'So I guess I couldn't have done it.'

'But,' said Marcia Benetti, 'you could have gone to his room, say, at eight, and you could have stabbed him with a room-service knife, and then you could have ditched the knife and gone down to the lobby at eight thirty, then back up to the room again at nine.'

'I could have,' said Sharon, 'but—'

'Whoa.' I put my hand on Sharon's arm. 'This is getting out of line. My client is answering your questions fully and honestly. She told you where she was and what she was doing at the times you asked about.' I looked at Horowitz. 'That's enough for tonight.'

He glanced at Benetti.

'I've got one more question,' she said.

'One more question,' Horowitz said. 'OK?'

I looked at Benetti. 'Be nice.'

She smiled quickly, then turned to Sharon. 'When you went to your husband's room, you told us that you found the door ajar, isn't that right?'

'That's right,' said Sharon. 'He was my ex-husband.'

'Yes, sorry.' Benetti cleared her throat. 'So you just pushed the door open and went inside.'

'I knocked and called Ken's name first,' Sharon said. 'When he didn't answer, I pushed on it and it opened. So I went in.'

'You didn't have a key card?'

'No.'

'Mrs Nichols,' said Benetti, 'I tried to leave that door unlatched. I tried to see if I could leave it open a crack. You know what?'

Sharon shrugged.

'I couldn't do it,' said Benetti. 'That door is heavy, and the way it's hung, if you try to leave it ajar, it just swings shut and the latch engages and it automatically locks.'

Sharon shook her head. 'I'm not sure what you're getting at.'

'What I'm getting at,' said Benetti, 'is that you couldn't have found that door ajar. It had to've been locked. There were only two ways for you to get inside. You had a key card and let yourself in, or Mr Nichols let you in. Since you say you didn't have a key . . .'

'I didn't mean the door was ajar, exactly,' said Sharon. 'It was all the way shut but not latched. When I pushed on it, it swung open.'

'It wasn't ajar.'

'No. It was shut but not latched.'

'You told us it was ajar. Which was it?'

'Shut but not latched. That's what I meant to say.'

'It couldn't have been,' said Benetti.

'Well, it was,' said Sharon, 'because all I had to do was push it open. And Ken was dead when I went inside.'

'You mean,' said Benetti, 'that he was alive when you went in. But then he was dead when you left.'

Sharon turned to me.

'OK, that's it,' I said to Sharon. 'Don't say anything else.' I looked at Horowitz. 'Unless you intend to charge my client with a crime, we're done for tonight.'

He shrugged. 'We're not charging anybody with anything right now. I guess we're done anyway.' He looked at Sharon. 'We'll want to talk to you again.' He smiled. 'You've been very cooperative, and we appreciate it.'

She nodded. 'I want to cooperate. I want you to catch whoever did this to Ken.'

FOUR

We all left the conference room. Horowitz and Benetti went over to the elevators. Sharon and I headed for the front lobby. 'Did I do OK?' she asked.

'You did fine,' I said. 'You kept your cool. You didn't let yourself be bullied. You seemed entirely truthful.'

'I was entirely truthful,' she said.

I smiled. 'I didn't mean to imply otherwise.'

'I don't think they believed me, though,' she said. 'When I said why I went to Ken's room. That I thought we might have sex.'

'People who've never been divorced don't understand how complicated it can be.'

'The relationship between former spouses, you mean.'

I nodded. 'People expect us to hate each other. They seem surprised to know that we don't. That we might actually like each other. That there might still be something like love between us.'

'You and Gloria, you mean.'

I nodded. 'You and Ken.'

'You believe me, then.'

'Sure I do.'

When we stepped outside, I remembered that the police had taken Sharon's jacket. It was a chilly April evening, and a soft rain was still falling, and she was standing there in her silky blouse hugging herself. I took off my jacket and draped it over her shoulders.

She looked up at me. 'Oh. Thank you, Brady.'

I nodded. 'Do you need a ride home?'

'I've got my car,' she said.

'Did you have a valet park it?'

'No. I left it in the lot. It's right over there.' She pointed towards a sea of vehicles in a well-lit parking area. 'Why?'

'A valet might be able to corroborate the time you got here.'

'Well,' she said, 'too bad. That would help, huh?'

I shrugged. 'It would help, sure. No biggie, though.'

We were standing under the portico in front of the main hotel entrance. The misty spring rain made halos round the pathway lights.

'I don't understand about the door,' Sharon said. 'It was unlatched. I guess I said ajar, and that's not what I meant. It was closed, but I was able to push it open. So they couldn't make the door do that. I can't explain that. That's how it was. I wasn't lying.'

'There are always anomalies,' I said. 'Details that can't be explained. The police know that. When everything is orderly and logical, they begin to worry. That's a sign that something is off.'

'I can see how it looks,' she said. 'About the door. It looks like Ken had to've been alive when I got there. If the door wasn't unlatched, the only way I could've gotten in was if he let me in.'

I shrugged.

'But it was unlatched.'

I nodded.

'They were playing good cop, bad cop,' she said. 'Except the sweet-looking female was the bad cop, and the crabby man was the good one.'

'Actually,' I said, 'they're both good cops.'

'Well, Detective Benetti was pretty hostile, I thought.' She turned to me and gave me a hug. 'Thanks for being here for me.'

I patted her shoulder. 'Will you be all right?'

'Oh, sure.' She smiled. 'Of course, my ex-husband, who I was falling in love with all over again, got murdered tonight, and I was the one who found his body, and the police think I killed him. But, yes, I'm OK.' She shrugged. 'Maybe it just hasn't hit me yet.'

'Do you have somebody who can stay with you?' I asked. 'It might be better not to be alone tonight.'

'It's pretty late,' Sharon said, 'but I'll call Ellen.' She put a hand on my shoulder. 'I'm so grateful to you for being there for me. I expect we'll be seeing each other again.'

I nodded. 'I'm sure we will.'

IT TOOK A LITTLE MORE than half an hour to navigate the wet, empty city streets from the hotel on Route 9 in Natick to my parking garage on Beacon Hill in Boston, and another fifteen minutes to walk to my house halfway up Mount Vernon Street. It was three thirty in the morning when I stepped into the house.

Henry greeted me at the door with a lot of happy whining. I knew what he'd been thinking: *This time he's never coming home, and who's going to feed me?*

His entire hind end wagged when I knelt down to rub his ears and scratch his forehead. Who loves you like a dog?

I let him out into the back yard, and then I used the kitchen phone to check my voicemail. I had two messages.

The first was from Billy. 'Hey, Pop,' he said. 'Hope your lawyer thing went all right. It was too bad you had to leave. So anyway, you remember how me and Gwen wanted to talk to you and Mom? Well, I'm sorry, but we ended up telling her what we had to say. But I want to talk to you. Gwen and I do, I mean. We're going to be around for a few more days. Just let me know when's good for you. We can come to your place, have a beer, or maybe grill something. You provide the grill, me and Gwen'll bring the meat.' He paused, then said, 'Call me. You've got my cell number. Love you, man.'

The second message came at 1.14 a.m. 'Hey, Brady?' It was Alex Shaw, calling from her house in Garrison, Maine. 'Are you OK? I sorta expected to hear from you tonight. I know you were out with Billy and his lady friend and, um, Gloria, but I thought . . . Well, whatever. Look, it's around one fifteen, and I'm tucked in here for the night, all snuggly in that Red Sox T-shirt you gave me, and I'm going to read for a while and probably fall asleep after like two pages, but I wouldn't mind if you called and woke me up.' She yawned loudly. 'I hope everything's all right. Good night for now.'

I smiled. I was picturing Alex in her extra-large Red Sox T-shirt, which, of course, was her intention. When she stood up, the T-shirt moulded her body and fell to mid thigh. In bed it would ride up over her hips. She liked to lie on her side, facing away from me, and then push her butt back up against me, and she'd grab my hand and hold it against her breast . . .

Well, her message was having exactly the effect she intended.

Henry was whining at the back door. I hung up the phone and let him in. When I gave him a Milk-Bone, it reminded me that Sharon's call had taken me away from the restaurant before I'd eaten anything except a couple of olives and a hunk of Italian bread and half a glass of Chianti. I realised that I was starved.

I found a slab of leftover pork loin in my refrigerator. I sliced it, slapped Dijon mustard on four slices of bread, and made two sandwiches. I wolfed them down with a bottle of beer at the kitchen table. Henry sprawled under the table so that he'd be in a position to snag stray crumbs.

After we ate, Henry and I went upstairs. I brushed my teeth and went to bed. He curled up on the rug beside me. It was after four in the morning, but I was wide awake, with a stomach full of pork sandwich and a head full of questions. I took the phone from my bedside table, rested it on my chest, and called Alex.

She picked up the phone on the fifth ring. Her distant, muffled voice said, 'H'lo? . . . Brady? Honey? That you?'

'It's me, babe,' I said. 'I wanted to tuck you in, say good night.'

'I'm already tucked in,' she said. 'All alone in my bed. Why are you there and me here? Wanna come snuggle with me?'

'I'd love to. But not tonight, I don't think. Let's make it next weekend. Your place or mine, it doesn't matter. How's that?'

'I can't wait.' She sighed. 'You OK? Everything OK?'

'Everything's fine,' I said. 'I got called away on a case. Now here's a hug and a kiss. Go to sleep.'

She made a kissy sound. 'You too, baby. 'Night, sweetie.'

I think she was asleep before the phone disconnected.

Not me. I lay awake, with images of Ken Nichols's pale, lifeless body and questions about Sharon tumbling round in my head. Even a couple of chapters of *Moby Dick*, my never-fail soporific, failed to make my eyelids droop, and I didn't drift off to sleep until after the purple outside my window faded to silver.

Henry woke me up, whining to go out. It was quarter past nine on Sunday morning. I figured I'd had less than four hours of sleep.

I pulled on a sweatshirt and a pair of jeans, followed Henry downstairs and let him out into our walled-in patio garden. I put together a pot of coffee in my electric coffeemaker, and pretty soon the aroma filled the kitchen. I poured myself a mugful, took it out the back, and sat in one of my wooden Adirondack chairs. Henry wandered over and lay down on the brick patio beside me.

It was a warm late-April morning in Boston. The sun bathed my little back yard in its warmth, and the spring bulbs were blooming—tulips and daffodils, crocuses and hyacinths.

Evie had been in charge of the flowerbeds. She'd planted them when we first moved here, and she was the one who'd tended them. This was the garden's first spring without her.

Evie had liked gardening, and I'd liked the fact that she liked it. I used to enjoy coming home from court and finding her on her knees in our garden digging around in the earth. I'd bring out beers and urge her to take a break, and we'd sit at the picnic table, Evie in her cut-off shorts and baggy T-shirt and gardening gloves, smudges of dirt on her face, her auburn hair tucked up under one of my old Red Sox caps, and me in my pinstripe suit with my tie pulled loose.

Sometimes she'd slither onto my lap and nuzzle my throat and unbutton my shirt and get my clothes dirty, which I didn't mind at all. That's why God invented dry cleaning.

Well, Evie was gone, and she wasn't coming back. Once in a while something—like seeing the spring bulbs that she'd planted—would remind me of her, and I'd remember something specific, like how she'd stick that excellent butt of hers up in the air when she kneeled in the garden to pull weeds, or how the skin at the nape of her neck tasted when she was sweaty after gardening on a warm afternoon in July . . . and then, for a few minutes, I missed her.

But mostly I didn't think about her. She'd been gone for a long time. Almost a year.

When my mug was empty, Henry and I went inside. I fetched the *Sunday Globe* from the front stoop and took it to the kitchen. I dumped some dog food into Henry's bowl and put it down on the floor. Then I filled a bowl of my own with Cheerios.

While I ate I skimmed the paper. Ken Nichols's murder had apparently happened too late on Saturday night to make the Sunday paper. I was curious to see how the press would handle it, how Roger Horowitz would be quoted, how Sharon's role would be described, if Ken's gym bag full of ketamine would be mentioned.

IT WAS EARLY in the afternoon, and I was in my back yard sitting at the picnic table, sipping a chilled Sam Adams lager, when my cell phone vibrated in my pocket. It was Sharon Nichols.

'How are you doing today?' I asked.

'Not that great,' she said. 'I think I had some kind of delayed reaction. When I got home last night, I called Ellen, woke her up, and I started telling her how her father was dead, how he'd been . . . murdered, and suddenly I started shaking, and my throat got tight, and I was seeing all that blood, and

484 | WILLIAM G. TAPPLY

poor Ellen on the other end of the line kept saying, "Mother? Are you all right? Mother?" Anyway, she came over, and we stayed up, drinking wine and crying and reminiscing, and eventually, talking with Ellen, I started to get it together again. I'm better now. Still kinda shaky, I guess. I just woke up, can you believe it? It's after one in the afternoon.'

'This is all to be expected,' I said. 'You held it together for a long time last night. You did very well. That was pretty traumatic.'

'Yes, it was.' She was silent for a minute. 'I'm so sorry for . . . for messing up your weekend.'

'I'd say your weekend was messed up worse than mine,' I said.

'Mm.' She chuckled softly. There wasn't any humour in it. 'Well, the reason I called . . . last night you said if I needed anything?'

'Sure,' I said. 'What can I do?'

'Well,' she said, 'like I said, Ellen came over, so she knows about what happened to Ken. I haven't been able to reach Wayne yet, but I'll keep trying. It's Ken's father I'm worried about.'

'Ken's father's still alive?'

'Yes. He has outlived his only child. Isn't that sad?'

'It is,' I said. I thought of my sons, Billy and Joey. I hoped I wouldn't outlive either of them. 'So you want to tell him?'

'I think I should,' Sharon said. 'Before somebody says something or he hears it on the news.' She hesitated. 'His name is Charles Nichols. He's in an assisted living facility. It's a nice, expensive place out in Ashby. Charles is quite frail. Probably doesn't have a lot of time left. He's eighty-five or six. He's got congestive heart failure, and I'm afraid this news could, you know . . .'

'I'll go with you,' I said.

'Oh, I couldn't ask you to do that.'

'You didn't,' I said. 'It was my idea.'

She laughed softly. 'Well, I honestly don't want you to—'

'I'll go with you,' I said. 'It's what we lawyers do.'

She laughed softly. 'Somehow I doubt that.'

'It's what this lawyer does,' I said.

'Thank you, Brady. I could use some moral support. I don't know how Charles will handle it. He and Ken had their issues, and I don't think Ken visited him very often, but still, Ken was an only child, and Charles's wife is gone, so Ken was all he had left.'

'Aside from you and his grandchildren, you mean,' I said.

'Well, I'm not family. Not now anyway, not after the divorce. But still. I think I'm the one who should tell him what happened.'

'You want to do this today?'

'Yes,' she said. 'The sooner the better, don't you think?'

'I do,' I said. 'I'll pick you up in about an hour. How's that?'

'You're my hero,' she said.

When they ran their clinic and kennels in Wellesley, Ken and Sharon Nichols lived with their two kids in a gorgeous Victorian house on five or six acres off a country road. Now Sharon was in a second-floor condo in a boxy brick building on Route 2A in Acton. A different lifestyle, usually a less lavish one, was the price of freedom, and more often than not, both parties in a divorce ended up paying it.

I parked in the lot behind Sharon's building, told Henry to wait in the car, went to the back door and pressed the button beside her number. A minute later her voice came to me from a speaker beside the door. 'Brady? Is that you?'

I leaned to the speaker and said, 'I'm here.'

'I'll be right down,' she said.

She emerged from the back door about five minutes later and came over to my car. She was wearing a pair of jeans and a red and white striped, long-sleeved jersey. Her blonde hair was artfully tousled, and she'd done some spectacular tricks with make-up to hide evidence of the previous night, when she'd found the murdered body of her former husband, answered the questions of police officers, and then drunk wine and cried with her daughter.

'You look nice,' I said.

She smiled. 'Thank you.' She had the jacket I'd loaned her folded over her arm. She handed it to me. 'For this, too. Again. It was very gallant of you.'

'Gallant,' I said. 'That's me, all right.' I whistled to Henry, who came trotting over. 'This is Henry,' I said to Sharon.

'Hey, Henry,' she said. She bent over and scratched the special place on his forehead, and her ease with Henry reminded me that she used to work with Ken at their veterinary hospital.

'That's his G-spot,' I said. 'Right in the middle of his forehead.'

Sharon straightened up and smiled. 'Everybody's got one, even dogs.'

I opened the back door for Henry, and he jumped in. Then Sharon and I got in. 'Ashby,' I said. 'I assume you know how to find the place?'

'It's not that far from here,' she said. 'I feel guilty I haven't visited

Charles more often. He's been there four or five years, and I can count the times I've visited him on one hand. Good, dutiful Ellen came with me each time. Ellen still visits him once in a while. Charles never did make me feel welcome, but that's no excuse.'

'He's not your father,' I said.

'No,' she said, 'and he's never been a very loving—or lovable—father-in-law. Still, he is my children's grandfather, and he helped Ken and me out when we were getting started.'

'With money, you mean?'

'That's right,' she said. 'We couldn't have done what we did without Charles's help. Buying the house and the land, building the kennels and the hospital. We all pretended it was a loan, and maybe we would've eventually paid him back, but then we got divorced and money was an issue, and I'm sure Ken didn't give Charles a penny of what we owed him. Not that he needs it.'

The village of Ashby, Massachusetts, was a straight shot northwesterly on Route 119 from Sharon's place in Acton. Charles Nichols's assisted living place was a big, rambling two-storey redbrick structure at the end of a long country road. It sat on the edge of a meadow that sloped up to a woody hillside. A pretty little rocky stream meandered alongside the building. The stream looked like it would hold trout.

A sign directed us to the visitors' parking area, and from there another sign pointed to the entrance.

A fortyish woman sat behind a desk in the foyer. When we walked in, she looked up, smiled and said, 'May I help you?' She wore a plastic name badge over her left breast. Her name was Joan Porter. Her smile was well practised and automatic.

'We're here for Charles Nichols,' Sharon said. 'I'm his daughter-in-law.'

Joan Porter looked Sharon up and down, glanced at me, then turned back to Sharon and gave her that professional smile. 'Charles is in the day-room. Do you know where it is?'

Sharon shook her head.

'Down that corridor and round the corner on your right,' she said. 'They're watching a Red Sox game.'

'How is he?' Sharon asked.

'Charles is a lovely gentleman,' said Joan Porter, 'and he rarely complains. He's recovering from his accident.'

'Accident?' asked Sharon.

'He fell and broke his wrist a couple of weeks ago,' said Joan Porter. 'He's been having some pain, not sleeping well, and of course a man his age, he heals slowly.'

'Down this corridor, is it?' asked Sharon.

Joan Porter nodded. 'You're his daughter-in-law? Do you know about Charles's . . . condition?'

'Condition?'

'I know Charles's son has been informed,' Joan Porter said, 'and I believe Charles himself told his granddaughter. She was here a week or so ago. Neither of them has shared the news with you?'

Sharon shook her head.

Joan Porter hesitated, then said, 'Mr Nichols—Charles—he has recently been diagnosed with a brain aneurysm.'

Sharon blinked. 'Oh,' she said. 'Oh, dear. What will they . . . ?'

'There's apparently nothing they can do for him. You might want to talk with his physician, but as I understand it, a man Charles's age, with all his other infirmities . . .'

'That's why he fell, Mrs Porter?' Sharon asked. 'The brain aneurysm? He passed out or got dizzy or something?'

Joan Porter shrugged. 'That's what the doctor thinks. Charles doesn't really remember what happened. It may never happen again. There's no telling with aneurysms.'

'It could, um, burst anytime?' asked Sharon.

'As I understand it.'

'Which would kill him.'

'Oh, my, yes,' said Joan Porter.

Sharon looked at Joan Porter, then said, 'Well, thank you for telling me. Thank you for your candour.' She held out her hand.

Joan Porter took Sharon's hand in both of hers, and I read genuine kindness in the woman's eyes. 'You're one of his relatives,' she said. 'You have a right to know.'

Sharon hooked her arm through mine. We started down the wide corridor, turned a corner and came to a big open area with a giant wide-screen television showing a baseball game. A few white-haired people were sitting on the furniture, and some others were parked in wheelchairs, facing the TV, where a pitcher in a Blue Jays uniform was peering in to get the sign from his catcher, and a Red Sox runner was taking his lead from first base.

Sharon looked around for a minute. Then she said, 'There he is.'

I followed her over to a man sitting in a wheelchair. He had wispy white hair and a little white moustache. A cast covered his right arm. It hung from a sling round his neck. His lap and legs were covered with a brown blanket. He was wearing a green cardigan sweater over a white dress shirt that was buttoned to his throat.

As we approached, I heard him say, 'Try a bunt, for Christ's sake. They *never* bunt. What's wrong with a bunt now and then?' Nobody in the room was paying any attention to him. 'It's a perfect spot for a bunt. Damn prima donnas. They don't get those big contracts for laying down a bunt. Come on. Play the game right.'

SHARON WALKED UP beside Charles Nichols, put a hand on his shoulder, and said, 'Charles? Charles, it's me. It's Sharon.'

He blinked at her. Then he said, 'Oh. What are you doing here?'

'I came to visit you.' She bent down and kissed his cheek.

He neither resisted her kiss nor reciprocated it. He returned his attention to the television.

'This is my friend Brady Coyne,' Sharon said. 'Brady, Charles Nichols.'

I stepped up and held out my hand. Charles looked at it and shrugged. 'I can't shake hands.' He tapped the cast on his right arm with his left hand. 'I can't cut my food or get dressed. I can't even unzip my fly and take a leak. Whaddya think about that?'

'Is there someplace we can talk?' Sharon asked.

'Why talk?' Charles asked. 'Let's watch the ball game.'

'We've got to talk,' Sharon said. She took the handles of Charles's wheelchair, released the brakes and pushed him out of the room. I followed along behind.

'You could've waited till the end of the inning,' he grumbled.

'It's nice,' Sharon said, 'you're still so interested in baseball.'

'I'm really not. Never was.' He turned his head and looked at me. 'Baseball is boring and irrelevant. But it's what there is. As you can see, there isn't much else round here. Am I right?'

I shrugged. 'I like baseball.'

There was a balcony off the corridor on the other side of some glass doors. 'How about out here?' Sharon asked.

I opened the doors, and Sharon wheeled Charles onto the balcony, where there was a glass-topped table with an umbrella and four aluminium chairs. It overlooked the trout stream.

'This is nice,' Sharon said. 'Doesn't the sun feel good?'

'I'm chilly,' said Charles. 'It's my circulation. It's why I'm in this damn wheelchair. I can't feel my legs. They're numb, like hunks of wood. The numbness is moving up my body. They tell me when it gets to my vital organs, they'll stop working. Of course, this thing in my head will probably blow up first.'

Sharon sat in one of the chairs so that she was facing Charles. 'I'm sorry I haven't visited you more often,' she said.

He shrugged. 'I don't expect you to. Nobody visits me. Except Ellen. I don't know why she keeps coming to see me. She was here just a few days ago. She's a nice girl, Ellen is.' He narrowed his eyes at her. 'So you said you wanted to talk with me. What is it?'

Sharon looked at Charles. She reached out and gripped his left hand, the one not covered with a cast, in both of hers. 'It's Ken,' she said. 'I'm sorry . . .' Tears welled up in her eyes.

'What?' asked Charles. 'What about him?'

She cleared her throat. 'He's . . . he died, Charles. I'm sorry.'

He glared at her. 'What? What did you say?'

'Ken died last night,' she said.

Charles snatched his hand away from Sharon's grip. He put it over the lower half of his face and moved it up and down, as if he were trying to rub feeling into his cheeks. He was looking at her out of his pale, watery eyes. 'He died, you said?'

She nodded. 'Yes.'

'Last night, huh? What happened? What did my son die of? He's not that old. I'm the one who's supposed to die, not him.'

'He was murdered,' said Sharon.

'Huh? Murdered?' Charles frowned. 'Why?'

'They don't know. The police are working on it.'

Charles looked at me. 'What're you, a cop? Is that it?'

'No,' I said. 'I'm just a friend.'

'I haven't seen Ken in . . . I can't remember the last time,' he said. 'Haven't even talked to him. After a while, a person becomes an abstraction, even if he's your son. Weeks go by, Ken doesn't even pass through my mind.

I know he's got his own life, but he's my only son and my heir, and you'd think . . .' He waved his left hand in the air.

We sat there looking out at the trout stream and the woods, and nobody spoke for a while.

After a few minutes, Charles said, 'Murdered, you said? They don't know who did it, or why, is that it?' I noticed that Charles's eyes were watery.

'That's right,' said Sharon.

'Do they have a theory?'

Sharon cleared her throat. 'One of their theories is that I did it. I found his body.'

'Why would you kill Ken?'

'I wouldn't,' she said. 'I didn't.'

He wiped his hand across his eyes. 'It's a silly theory,' he said.

'Yes, it is,' she said.

'They haven't arrested you.'

'Not yet.'

'You got a lawyer, I hope.'

Sharon glanced at me. 'Yes. A good one.'

Charles turned and looked at me. 'You, huh?'

I nodded.

'Charles,' she said, 'it's possible that the police might come to talk to you. Isn't that right, Brady?'

'It's likely,' I said. 'Generally they try to talk with all of the victim's relatives and friends.'

'I didn't want you to hear about Ken that way,' Sharon said.

'I get it,' he said. 'Thank you.'

'Look,' she said, 'if there's anything you need, anytime, please just call me. Will you promise to do that?'

'I won't need anything,' he said. 'Unless you can dig up a new body for me.' He slapped the arm of his wheelchair with his functional hand. 'Let's go. Take me back to my ball game, will you?'

THE AFTERNOON SUN was low in the sky when I pulled into the lot behind Sharon's building.

'Why don't you come up, have a drink?' she asked.

'I don't think so,' I said. 'Thanks. I should get going. I don't think it's a good idea to mix pleasure with business.'

'I didn't mean anything. Sometimes a drink is just a drink.'

I shrugged.

'Are you involved with somebody, Brady?'

'I'm kind of between involvements,' I said, 'but I'm, um, working on it. How about you?'

She shook her head. 'It can be hard for a woman my age. There was a man a few years ago. It didn't turn out well.'

'What happened?'

She shrugged. 'We had fun, but I didn't love him. There was no future in it. I wasn't interested in a relationship with no future. When I told him, he wouldn't take no for an answer. He kept calling at all hours, filling up my answering machine with messages.'

'He was stalking you,' I said. 'Did you go to the police?'

'I didn't need to. Eventually he went away.'

'You were lucky,' I said. 'Stalkers don't just go away.'

Sharon smiled. 'He was, um, encouraged to go away.'

'Encouraged how?'

'Ellen was home from school—Wayne was a senior in high school—and we were eating out, my kids and I, having a nice Italian dinner. We all got along with each other back then. So we were sitting there at our table and Gary appeared. I looked up, and there he was, leaning his elbow on the bar, and when he saw me, he smiled and lifted his glass to me. I just about hit the roof. My kids, naturally, wanted to know what was going on, so I told them. Well, Wayne excused himself and went over to Gary, and I don't know what was said, but after a few minutes, Gary turned round and walked out, and Wayne came back to the table and said I wouldn't have to worry about that guy any more, and sure enough, I haven't seen or heard from him since.'

'Wayne must be a persuasive guy,' I said.

'I asked him what he said, but he wouldn't tell me.' She reached over and squeezed my arm. 'Look, Brady. I can't tell you how much I appreciate your coming with me this afternoon. I don't know as I could've managed it without you.'

'You would've done fine,' I said. 'I didn't do anything.'

'You were there for me,' she said. 'Not many lawyers would do that on a Sunday afternoon.'

'Friends would,' I said.

'Well, thanks, friend,' she said.

ON MONDAY I was in my office ploughing through a stack of paperwork that Julie, my long-suffering secretary, had dumped on me, as she did on a regular basis, when the console on my desk buzzed. 'It's Detective Horowitz,' Julie said when I picked up.

'OK,' I said. I hit the blinking light and said, 'Roger.'

'Nobody named Clem, Clement, Clementine, whatever,' he said without preamble, 'registered at the damn veterinarian convention. You sure you got that name right?'

'Yes,' I said, 'it's a lovely day, and I'm doing very well, thank you for asking. How are you?'

'Don't push me,' he growled. 'You sure that name was Clem?'

'I'm quite sure that's what Ken called the guy,' I said. 'Clem.'

'No idea, first name, last name, nickname, huh?'

'Sorry,' I said.

'Well, we're striking out on it.'

'I asked Sharon,' I said. 'It rang no bells with her.'

'Try again,' he said, and with that he disconnected.

After Horowitz hung up I called Sharon, and when her voicemail clicked in, I said, 'It's Brady. I wanted to ask you to rack your brain again, see if that name Clem means anything. If you think of anything, let me know, please. The police are pretty interested in him, and we should help them focus on suspects other than you.'

I returned to my bottomless stack of papers, and an hour or so later there came a soft one-knuckle rap on my door.

'It's unlocked,' I grumbled. 'Just come in.'

The door opened, and Julie stepped in.

'What?' I asked.

'You don't have to be crabby,' she said.

'Paperwork makes me crabby,' I said.

'You've got a visitor. A young woman.'

'Who is it?' I asked. 'What's she want?'

'She says her name is Ellen Nichols. She wouldn't tell me what she wanted. She seemed to think you'd know.'

'Oh,' I said. 'I didn't tell you about our new client.'

Julie shook her head. 'You did it again? You took on a new client without telling me?'

'She's not exactly a new client,' I said. 'She's an old client with a new problem. We used to handle the legal work for the animal hospital she and her husband ran before they divorced. About ten years ago. Her name is Sharon Nichols?' I made it a question.

Julie nodded. 'Yes, I remember them.'

'Well,' I said, 'Sharon's ex-husband, Kenneth Nichols, was murdered Saturday night, and that's their daughter out there. I'm sorry I didn't mention it before.' I stood up. 'I need to talk to her.'

Julie followed me out into our reception area. Ellen Nichols was sitting on a sofa with her chin propped up on her fists and her elbows on her knees and a pair of big round glasses perched on the end of her nose. She was a younger, darker-haired version of her mother—the same flashing eyes, generous mouth and slender body.

I started over to her, and she looked up and said, 'Mr Coyne?'

'It's Brady,' I said. 'Do you want to come into my office?'

'I know you're busy . . .'

'It's OK,' I said. 'Come on in.'

Ellen Nichols followed me into my office. She sat on the sofa by the big window that looked out on Copley Square.

I took the upholstered chair across from her.

'Do you remember me?' Ellen asked.

I shrugged. 'I did legal work for your parents.'

'My brother and I used to hang out with Billy and Joey.' She used her forefinger to push her glasses up onto the bridge of her nose. 'I've got classes later this afternoon, so I was in the neighbourhood, and I wanted to see you. If it's not convenient . . .'

'No,' I said, 'it's all right. You're at BU?'

'That's right. I'm in a master's programme. Elementary ed.'

'I'm glad you stopped in. I wanted to talk with you anyway. I'm very sorry about what happened to your father.'

'Thank you,' she said. 'I'm kind of numb about it. Actually, the reason I'm here is my mother. I'm really worried about her. I mean, is she really a suspect? Are they going to arrest her?'

'She's a suspect,' I said, 'but the fact that it's been two days and the police haven't done anything makes me believe they're not going to charge her. They don't have enough evidence for an arrest.'

'I'm worried how she's doing.' Ellen leaned forward. 'She's never been emotionally strong. She had a hard time when my dad moved out, and since then she's had one bad relationship after another. Not to mention the heartache my brother's caused her.'

'Wayne,' I said. 'Has anybody told Wayne what happened?'

'My mother said she couldn't reach him. I tried, too, but just got his voicemail. I left him a message, but he hasn't called me back.'

'If you can give me his phone number,' I said, 'I'll see what I can do. I need to talk with him anyway.'

'Sure.' Ellen fished a BlackBerry out of her purse, poked some buttons on it, then recited a cell phone number and a street address with an apartment number in Websterville, New Hampshire.

I wrote them down. 'He's going to Webster State, is that right?'

Ellen nodded. 'Neither my mother nor I have heard from him for a long time. She worries about him.'

'I can understand that,' I said.

'I'm not worried,' she said. 'That's just how Wayne is. In his own world. I love my brother, but he's awfully inconsiderate.'

'How did Wayne and your dad get along?' I asked.

'Last I knew, not so good,' she said. 'He blamed our dad for wrecking our family.'

'So he's estranged from all three of you.'

She frowned. 'Our family's kind of a mess, Mr Coyne. Even so, Wayne still deserves to know what happened.'

'Did you and your father have a good relationship?' I asked.

'I'm older than Wayne,' she said. 'I saw it differently. When my parents split, I was sad about it, but I didn't blame anybody. My dad and I kept in touch, and we got together now and then.'

'In Baltimore?'

She nodded. 'I visited him a couple of times. Sometimes he'd come to Boston on business, and we'd get together.'

'What about this past weekend?' I asked. 'He was at a conference up here. Were you going to get together with him?'

'I didn't even know about it. When my mother told me, it kind of hurt my feelings that he'd make a plan to see her, but not me.' She gave me a quick smile. 'She said they were thinking about getting back together.'

'How would you feel about that?'

'If it was true, you mean?'

'Why wouldn't it be true?'

Ellen rolled her eyes. 'I always thought they hated each other.'

'People change,' I said.

'I guess so,' she said. 'I mean, if they both felt that way, well, it would've been awesome.' She blinked, and tears welled up in her eyes. 'Anyway,' she said, 'that's never going to happen now.'

She took off her glasses and wiped her eyes on the back of her wrist. I handed her the box of tissues I keep handy for such occasions, and she took one and dabbed at her eyes with it. Then she blew her nose. She smiled at me. 'Thank you. I'm OK. Sorry.' She fitted her glasses back onto her face.

'I wanted to ask you,' I said, 'if you knew of anybody who had a problem with your dad. Did he ever mention owing money to somebody, or being threatened, or having any kind of conflict?'

'I haven't a clue,' Ellen said. 'I never had any sense of what his life was like. I never met any of his friends or business acquaintances.'

'Do you know anybody named Clem?'

She frowned. 'Clem?'

'Middle-aged man, friend of your father.'

Ellen shrugged. 'No. Sorry. Clem doesn't ring a bell.'

'Did your father ever talk to you about business problems,' I said, 'or investments he made?'

Ellen smiled. 'My dad was a vet, Mr Coyne. He liked animals. That's what he was good at. I don't think he had much interest in business. He was just a nice, uncomplicated man.'

'I expect the police will want to talk to you,' I said. 'They'll probably ask a lot of questions about your mother.'

'My mom being a prime suspect.'

'Right now she is, yes,' I said. 'So I'd like to know of anything at all that you might say to them that could incriminate her.'

Ellen shook her head. 'My mother couldn't hurt anybody, regardless of how justified she might be.'

'Do you mean she'd be justified to, um, to murder your father?'

'No, I didn't mean that,' she said. 'I only meant that my mother suffered a lot when they split. She was angry and hurt. Oh, if you ask her, she'll say it was nobody's fault—but deep down, she's always blamed him. That's all I meant.'

'She's been angry with him.'

'Oh, sure. Furious. Ever since it happened.'

'And that's what you'll tell the police.'

Ellen looked at me. 'Oh. I see. Well, what should I do?'

'It's easy,' I said. 'Just tell the truth.'

'Well, sure. Except my mother . . .'

'People who are divorced from each other do tend to be angry and blame each other. It's normal.'

'Except,' she said, 'my father got murdered.'

'He invited her to his hotel room,' I said. 'That doesn't sound like angry people to me.'

She shrugged. 'If it's true.'

'You think your mother's been lying to us?'

'Oh, no,' said Ellen. 'That's not what I meant. I'm sure she felt that way. I mean, I think she believed it. All I meant was I wonder if my father felt the same way.'

'Do you have any reason to doubt it?'

'Look, Mr Coyne, I don't want to take sides. I've always tried to show my parents that even if they didn't love each other, I loved them both, and that they could be good parents even if they weren't together. So please, don't ask me to speculate about either of them. It's hard to be objective about your parents, particularly if one of them's been murdered and the police suspect the other one of doing it. I only came here to be sure my mother was being taken care of. She has a lot of faith in you. You will take care of her, won't you?'

'Yes,' I said. 'Of course.'

'Thank you.' She stood up. 'I won't take up more of your time.'

'Why don't you leave me your phone number, in case I need to talk to you again.'

'Sure.' She told me, and I wrote it down.

'If you think of anything,' I said, 'please give me a call. Anybody you might remember your father mentioning, or any problem he might've alluded to. Anything at all. OK?' I scratched my home number on the back of one of my business cards and handed it to her. 'Call anytime, day or night.'

She took the card, glanced at it and stuck it into her purse. Then she held out her hand. 'Thanks for seeing me.'

I took her hand. 'I'm glad we talked.'

After Ellen left, Julie came in. She sat in one of the client chairs, opened her stenography notebook on her knee, and said, 'Now, you better bring me up to date on this new client of ours.'

FIVE

I'd been home from the office for about an hour. I'd hung up my tie and lawyer pinstripe and pulled on my jeans and a T-shirt, and I'd fetched myself a bottle of Samuel Adams lager, and now I was sitting out in my back yard sipping my Sam.

My cell phone, which I'd left on the picnic table, began buzzing and jumping around. I picked it up and looked at the screen. It was Horowitz. I flipped open the phone and said, 'Roger. Hey.'

'I'm parked in front of your house,' he said. 'Where are you?'

'I'm here. Out the back. You want a beer?'

'That's exactly what I want. I just went off duty. Let me in.'

'OK.' I snapped the phone shut, put it back on the table and went through the house to the front door. When I opened it, Horowitz was standing on the stoop. He was wearing his rumpled brown suit, and his red tie was pulled loose at his throat.

I held the door for him, and he pushed past me into the house.

We went out to the kitchen, where I grabbed a beer for Horowitz and a fresh one for me, and then on out into the back yard.

We each sat in an Adirondack chair. Henry came over and sniffed Horowitz's cuffs. When Horowitz ignored him, he sauntered over and sprawled on the bricks beside my chair. I reached down and scratched the scruff of his neck, which was all he wanted.

Horowitz tilted up his beer, took a long swig, and then put his bottle on the arm of his chair. 'Ahh,' he said. 'That's good. And this'—he waved his hand round my little walled-in patio garden—'this is nice. Flowers, birds, brick walls. Privacy.'

'Yep,' I nodded. 'I like it.'

'Must get a little lonely, though, huh?'

'I don't mind,' I said.

'Evie used to take care of the garden, didn't she?'

I shook my head. 'You enjoy this, don't you?'

He turned and looked at me. 'What?'

'Reminding me that Evie's gone. Rubbing it in.'

'Hey,' he said. 'You're the one who always screws up your relationships, not me. I feel sorry for you, that's all.'

'Just what I need. Your pity. I bet that's not why you're here.'

'Naw. That just occurred to me.' He took another swig of beer. 'Benetti thinks your client is good for the Nichols thing. She thinks her story about going to his hotel room is bull.' He arched his eyebrows at me.

'What do you think, Roger?' I asked.

He shook his head. 'I got doubts. But we can't eliminate her. Means, motive, opportunity. She's got 'em all.'

'You're pretty shaky on all three,' I said. 'Last I heard, you had no murder weapon. So much for means. Ken and Sharon Nichols had been talking about resuming their relationship, which hardly amounts to a motive for murder. Opportunity I might stipulate. She was there, though the times aren't right.'

'No sense of arguing about those things now,' he said. 'I wanted to ask you about when you were with our victim the night before.'

'I told you everything,' I said. 'About the bearded guy he called Clem who pointed his finger at him. The fact that Ken seemed kind of nervous. That his phone rang several times.'

'He didn't mention what he was nervous about?'

'No. He kind of hinted he was having some problems, but no specifics. You get a line on the guy with the beard?'

'Nope.'

'What about the kid in the hoodie?'

'Not yet,' he said. 'Not that I need to share with you.' He blinked at me. 'Our victim had a cell phone with him, you said.'

'Yes. You could probably get some useful numbers off it.'

'We can get his phone records, but it takes a while. Big pain in the ass. Helluva lot easier if we had his phone. Which we don't.'

'You didn't find his phone in his room?' I asked.

'Nope.' He took a swig of beer. 'Funny, don't you think?'

'The bad guy took the phone and left that satchel of ketamine?'

'No phone,' Horowitz said, 'no murder weapon. No laptop, no brief-case—but, yeah, a gym bag full of illegal drugs.'

'The killer must've taken that stuff,' I said. 'Ken had a phone, at least. Makes you wonder if the drugs had anything to do with it.'

He lifted his beer and took a long pull. He put the bottle down, wiped his mouth and looked at me. 'There was one little piece of evidence at the crime scene that you might find interesting.'

'You going to share it with me?'

'A hotel matchbook,' he said. 'One of the techs found it lying on the floor just outside the door to the murder room. It had indentations on it that exactly matched the shape of the latch on the door.'

'As if it had been wedged in there so the door wouldn't lock,' I said. 'So somebody could get in from the outside without a key.'

He nodded. 'When your client pushed on the door, it opened and the matchbook fell out.'

'She was telling the truth about that,' I said.

'Looks that way,' Horowitz said. 'But that doesn't exactly exonerate her. Her lover there, our vic, he could've jammed the latch with that matchbook so he could wait for her in his bed or something, and she could just waltz right in there with her steak knife.'

'You really think that's what happened?' I asked.

'Benetti does,' he said. 'Me, I'm trying to think about some other scenarios. The null hypothesis. Suppose the lady did not stab our vic with a steak knife in that hotel room. Suppose her story is the truth. How else could it have gone down?'

'Who put the matchbook in the latch, for example,' I said, 'if you assume it wasn't Ken?'

Horowitz looked at me and nodded. 'The killer, for example.'

'Could be, huh?' I asked.

'Why would the killer do that?'

'Because he planned to come back,' I said. 'Or he was leaving the room open for somebody else.'

'Somebody who was gonna pick up that bag of Special K.'

'Sure,' I said, 'or if he knew Sharon was expected, he could've left the door that way so she'd walk in and become a suspect.'

Horowitz grinned. 'Which she did.'

'That guy in the hoodie,' I said. 'He was heading for Ken's room. Looking to score that ketamine, maybe. The killer left the door unlatched for him. When he saw Sharon and me, he ran.'

Horowitz shrugged. 'Could be. Makes as much sense as your client doing it. Doesn't mean she didn't. Benetti might be right.'

I smiled. 'What do you want me to say? You know I can't—'

'I just wanted to relax, drink a beer, share an interesting titbit of information with you, that's all. No more shop talk, OK?'

'Sure,' I said. 'OK.'

He grinned. 'So,' he said, 'how about them Red Sox, huh?'

HOROWITZ STAYED AROUND for one more beer, and we talked baseball and city politics. After he left, Henry and I had dinner—a bowl of Alpo for him, a ham and cheese sandwich for me.

After dinner we went into my home office, where I called son Billy's cell phone. It rang just once before he said, 'Hey, Pop.'

'Hey yourself,' I said. 'I'm calling to make a date.'

We decided that Billy and Gwen would come to my place for a cookout the next evening. He and Gwen would bring rib-eyes and potatoes and salad fixin's. I'd provide beer for us guys and a good Shiraz for Gwen. If our mild late-April weather persisted, we'd cook on the gas grill and eat at the picnic table, and Billy and Gwen would tell me whatever it was that they came east to tell me.

When I hung up with my son, I realised I was smiling. I liked having him nearby. I looked forward to hanging out with him.

Julie had insisted I bring home the remainder of the paperwork that I hadn't finished during the day, and I figured I'd better get on top of it, because she'd have more for me tomorrow. I was making good headway when my phone rang.

It was Sharon Nichols. 'I hope I'm not bothering you,' she said.

'*Au contraire*,' I said. 'You're giving me a reprieve from a pile of boring deskwork. How are you doing?'

'I don't know how I'm supposed to be,' she said. 'How is one supposed to feel when her ex-husband gets murdered?'

'I guess you should just feel whatever you feel,' I said.

'And that's what I've been doing. I went to work today.'

'Where do you work?'

'I manage a shop in Concord centre. Women's apparel. It's different from being a vet's assistant. I miss the animals, but I like the people. So I worked all day, I guess I'm fine, and I'll be even finer if you can tell me they're not going to arrest me.'

'I don't know that for sure,' I said, 'but every day that goes by, the odds get better. You should just try not to think about it.'

'Easier said than done.' She was silent for a moment. Then she said, 'You met Ellen today, I understand?'

'She dropped by my office. We had a good chat. She seems like a mature young woman.'

'Can I ask you what she wanted to talk about?'

'She'll probably tell you if you ask.'

'Oh,' she said. 'I get it. It's a lawyer confidentiality thing.'

'Not really,' I said. 'It's just a human-being confidentiality thing. Ellen's not my client, so I don't have a professional obligation to her. I wouldn't tell her things you said to me, either, whether or not you were my client.'

'OK,' she said. 'That's good. I just . . .' She blew out a breath.

'What?' I asked.

'It's nothing,' she said. 'I just wondered if Ellen was blaming me. For what happened to Ken, I mean. I've always felt she blamed me for the divorce. She was always Daddy's little girl.'

'Talk to her,' I said. 'If you want, I can set you up with a good counsellor. I know a homicide counsellor. She specialises in helping the relatives and friends of people who are murdered. Her name is Tally Whyte. She works out of the medical examiner's office here in the city. If you and Ellen saw her together, you might . . .'

'Yes, hmm, maybe,' she said. 'Interesting. I'll think about it.' She hesitated. 'The other thing is, I haven't been able to get hold of Wayne. I don't quite know what to do.'

'You've tried calling him?'

'A dozen times,' she said. 'He doesn't answer. It rings five or six times, and then this recorded voice answers and invites me to leave a message. Which I have done.'

'Is it Wayne's voice?'

'The recording, you mean? No. It's the phone company. A woman's voice. She just says, "The person you are trying to reach is not available at this time. At the tone, please leave a message."'

'Is this unusual? Not being able to get hold of Wayne?'

'Truthfully,' she said, 'I don't try to get in touch with him very often any more. He never answers his phone, never returns a call. Wayne's kind of off on his own. He has been for a while. We've been shaky ever since the divorce. We've just drifted apart.' She hesitated. 'I haven't talked to him for a long time.'

'Ellen gave me his number,' I said. 'I'll try.'

'That would be great,' Sharon said, 'though I don't know what you can do that I can't do. He'll either answer or he won't.'

'Maybe he's screening his calls.'

'Because he doesn't want to talk to his mother?' she asked. 'I suppose that's possible. Well, I hope you can catch up with him.'

'I'll see what I can do. Shall I make an appointment with Tally Whyte for you?'

'Let me think about it,' she said.

After I hung up with Sharon, I tried Wayne's cell phone number. Just as Sharon had reported, a recorded voice answered after about six rings, inviting me to leave a message. I declined that invitation.

I would persist.

I finished my paperwork a little after eleven. Henry and I went out the back so he could pee and I could look at the stars. Alex loved the night sky. When she and her brother, Gus, were kids, they'd identified their own private set of constellations—Elvis and Snoopy and Marilyn Monroe. When I was with Alex after Gus was killed, she tried to teach them to me, and when she pointed them out, I could see them—Elvis's guitar, Snoopy's ears, Marilyn's bosom.

I could see nothing but a sky full of random, disconnected stars. She liked to say that it was one of the big differences between us—she saw order where I saw chaos. She said that I needed her to bring some coherence into my life, and I thought maybe she was right, although I doubted she'd ever convince me that life was orderly.

Standing out on my deck looking at the sky made me feel closer to Alex. I knew she always stepped out back behind her house up in Garrison, Maine, before bedtime to check out her constellations. She said it was almost like being kids with Gus again. I knew that she missed him all the time. She said that it helped, knowing I was looking at the same sky she was, even if I was in Boston and she was in Maine, and even if I could see only randomness.

An hour later I was lying in my bed. Henry was curled up on the rug beside me. I picked up the telephone from my bedside table, rested it on my chest, and dialled Alex's number in Maine.

It rang four or five times before she picked up. 'Hello? Wait a minute.' I heard the rustle of sheets and blankets, then Alex said, 'There. I'm all tucked in. Are you?'

'Yes. All tucked in.'

'I miss you. Why don't I come down this weekend.'

'You know how much I like to get away from the city,' I said, 'but, yes, I think it would be better if you came here.'

'Something's going on, isn't it?'

'I've got a new case that might require some attention,' I said. 'Plus, Billy's in town with his friend Gwen.'

'His girlfriend?'

'He insists on calling her his friend. Says she's not his girlfriend. Anyway, you and Billy haven't seen each other in years.'

'Not since our, um, first relationship,' Alex said. 'He was a kid back then. He must be a man now.'

'He is.'

'I like this one,' she said softly.

'This what?'

'This relationship. Our second one. Maybe we'll get it right this time.'

'I hope so,' I said. 'I bet we will.'

'Do you really hope so? Even if you still miss Evie.'

'I am still aware of Evie's absence,' I said. 'Which isn't quite the same thing.'

'You shared a house with her for all those years.'

'Those years after you,' I said. 'After you dumped me.'

Alex chuckled quietly. 'I'm not going to rise to that bait again.'

'I shared a life with Evie,' I said. 'But I'm not doing that any more. Sometimes, like when I see the daffodils blooming out the back, the bulbs she planted, I'm reminded of her, and sometimes that makes me a little sad. Then I look up at the night sky and try to find Snoopy and Elvis, and even when I can't see them, I'm reminded of you. I know you can show them to me, and that makes me happy.'

'That's nice,' she said.

'Shall I expect you at suppertime on Friday?'

'Make sure there's plenty of beer in the fridge,' she said. She was quiet for a minute. Then I heard her yawn. 'I'm pretty sleepy. Gonna shut my eyes now. G'night, honey. Sleep tight, 'kay?'

'You too, babe.'

'I didn't dump you.'

'It was my fault,' I said.

'Mmm-hmmm,' she mumbled. Then she disconnected.

I hung up the phone and put it back on the table beside my bed. I lay there for a few minutes, looking up into the darkness, and I felt happy. Then I closed my eyes and went to sleep.

I TRIED CALLING Wayne Nichols about half a dozen times on Tuesday. The first time I tried him from my office phone, I accepted the recorded message's invitation. 'Wayne,' I said, 'my name is Brady Coyne. I'm an old friend of your parents. They used to take care of my pets when I lived in Wellesley. Maybe you remember my boys, Billy and Joey. They're about your age. I have some news for you about your mother and father. It's important. Please give me a call, the sooner the better.' I left him my home, cell and office numbers.

When he didn't call me back after an hour or so, I tried again, and as the day passed I called his number several more times. Each time, the same recorded greeting answered and invited me to leave a message, which I didn't. I saw no point in repeating myself.

I didn't know how to interpret the fact that Wayne did not respond. His phone was charged up and turned on. I assumed he heard it when it rang and had been collecting his messages.

I decided that on Wednesday I'd drive up to Websterville, New Hampshire, and try to track down Wayne Nichols. He needed to know that his father had been murdered.

ON MY WAY HOME from the office that afternoon, I stopped at the spirits store on Newbury Street, where I bought two six-packs of Long Trail Double Bag Ale, a microbrew from Vermont, and a bottle of a Napa Valley Shiraz. At DeLuca's on Charles Street I picked up a wedge of brie, a hunk of cheddar and two boxes of crackers.

By six o'clock, when Billy and Gwen, each bearing a grocery bag, banged on my front door, I had the ale on ice and the wine decanted and the cheese and crackers on plates on my kitchen table.

Billy was wearing his usual outfit—jeans, flannel shirt and sandals. His long dark-blond hair was pulled back into a ponytail and tied with a length of rawhide. Gwen wore snug-fitting jeans and a scoop-neck peasant blouse. Her hair was short and straight and black. She wore it combed back, with long dangly silver earrings.

They both gave me a one-armed hug, set their bags on the floor and squatted down to rub Henry's belly. He'd rolled onto his back to make it easy for them. Then I led them through the house to the kitchen, where they stowed their provisions in the refrigerator.

Billy and I grabbed a bottle of ale, and Gwen poured herself a glass of wine, and we took the crackers and cheese and our drinks out the back and sat in the Adirondack chairs.

I held up my bottle. 'Cheers,' I said. 'Welcome to Beacon Hill.'

Billy clicked his bottle on mine. Gwen held up her wineglass.

'This is nice,' I said. 'I like having you guys around.'

'Won't be for long,' Billy said. 'We've got to head out in a few days. We've got jobs to get back to.'

'When're you leaving?'

'Sunday,' he said. 'I've got to help get the boats ready for the fishing season, and I've got a float trip next Friday.'

'Alex will be down from Maine this weekend,' I said. 'She's my, um, my new girlfriend. You met her several years ago when she was my old girl-friend. She was hoping she'd get to see you.'

'Sure,' said Billy. 'I remember Alex. We'll make it happen.'

I turned to Gwen. 'What about you? What are you going back to?'

'My publishing job in Berkeley,' she said. 'This week has been my vacation. It's my first time ever in New England.'

'So what do you think?'

She smiled. 'It's beautiful. And everywhere you go, there's all this history. Billy showed me round Boston and Lexington and Concord, and he's gonna take me down to Cape Cod tomorrow.' She turned to him and punched his arm. 'Am I right, big fella?'

'Right, kiddo,' Billy said. He gave her arm a gentle punch back, and it struck me again, as it had the other night at the restaurant, that these two treated each other more like buddies than lovers.

We were on our second bottles when Billy said, 'The other night at the restaurant? Was that Dr Nichols, the vet?'

'It was his wife who called me,' I said. 'He was murdered.'

'Murdered? Wow. Dr Nichols was the one who put down Bucky. I'll always remember that.' Billy looked up at the sky. 'They had a kid about my age.' He frowned. 'Can't think of his name.'

'Wayne,' I said.

'Right,' he said. 'Wayne. He was a strange dude.'

'How so?'

'Well, for starters, kids used to say that he tortured animals . . . and his old man a vet?'

'That's beyond strange,' Gwen said. 'That's totally sick.'

Billy looked at her and nodded. 'If it was true.' He shrugged. 'I wouldn't doubt it. I used to play with him sometimes. I guess we were ten or eleven. One time we were fooling around near some pond and Wayne caught a frog. He set it on top of a rock and stuck a firecracker in its mouth, and the dumb frog just sat there with this firecracker hanging out of its mouth like a cigar, and Wayne lit it, and . . .' Billy shook his head. 'It was pretty horrible.'

'Oh, gross,' Gwen said. 'That's evil.'

I didn't say anything more about Wayne. His mother was my client, and that gave me a certain responsibility to him, too.

So we drank wine and ale and nibbled cheese and crackers, and our conversation slid over to fishing and baseball and books, and after a while Billy and Gwen went inside to put our dinner together.

Billy grilled inch-thick rib-eyes and roasted foil-wrapped potatoes and onions on the gas grill on my back deck. Gwen tossed a big green salad and sliced a loaf of fresh-baked rosemary bread.

By the time our dinner was ready, darkness had seeped into my back yard, so we decided to eat in the kitchen. Henry stationed himself under the table—a smart move, as each of us dropped a few scraps of medium-rare rib-eye and crusts of bread onto the floor.

It wasn't until we'd moved into the living room with our mugs of after-dinner coffee that Billy looked at me and said, 'Well, we told you we had something to share with you.' He glanced at Gwen, who gave him a smile. 'Here it is. You're gonna be a grandfather.'

This was more or less what I'd expected. 'Well,' I said, 'congratulations. Both of you. Or all three of us, I guess. When . . . ?'

'October,' said Gwen. 'October fourth, says the doctor.'

'I'm not old enough to be a grandfather,' I said.

'Meaning,' said Billy, 'that I'm not old enough to be a father, huh?' He looked hard at me. No sign of a smile.

'I didn't say that. Really, I was kidding. I'm happy for you. For me, too. A lot of my friends are grandfathers. They tell me having grandkids is great fun.' I looked from Billy to Gwen, then back at Billy. 'So when are you two . . . ?'

He shook his head. 'We're not getting married.'

'We don't love each other,' said Gwen. 'Not husband-and-wife love, I mean.' She glanced at Billy.

'We're good friends,' said Billy. 'Best buddies. We don't want to wreck a nice friendship. That's what marriage does.'

I shrugged. 'Not necessarily.'

He shook his head. 'Look at you and Mom. Look at the divorces you handle. You make a living off marriages that don't work. Anyway, we've made up our minds, so don't try talking us out of it.'

'Don't worry about that,' I said. 'It's your problem. Yours and Gwen's.' I turned and gave her a smile.

'Actually,' said Billy, 'we don't have a problem.'

'Problem was a bad choice of words,' I said.

'We've both got lives,' Gwen said. 'Billy's is in Idaho. Mine's in California. My parents are nearby. They'll help with the baby.'

Billy grinned and nodded. 'We got it all worked out.'

'I'm going to raise the baby,' Gwen said. 'Billy can visit anytime he wants. He can teach him how to fly-fish and ski. You too, Mr Coyne. I want our baby to know his grandparents. You and Gloria can visit him.'

'Him?' I asked.

She smiled. 'It's a boy.'

'You should call me Brady,' I said.

'OK. Sure.'

'So that's it,' said Billy. 'We wanted you and Mom to know.'

'So you're going to keep living in Idaho,' I said, 'teaching skiing and guiding fly-fishermen?'

'It's what I do,' he said. 'It's who I am.'

'You're going to, um, support the child?'

He shrugged. 'Sure, as much as I can.'

'My job pays well,' Gwen said. 'Plus, my parents have tons of money. That's not an issue.'

'Not now it's not,' I said.

Billy looked at me. 'What're you saying?'

I shrugged. 'Just that things change. Gwen could lose her job, or she could get sick. Or Gwen might get married, and her husband might want to adopt the child. Or—'

'Wait a minute,' Billy said. 'We got this all figured out, you know? We've talked a lot about it, and we know what we want.'

I shrugged. 'I'm just thinking of the future. You never know what's going to happen. You should plan for the unexpected.'

'Why do you always complicate everything?' Billy asked.

I spread out my hands. 'I'm sorry. I'm not trying to complicate anything. It's just how I think, I guess.'

'Like a lawyer,' he said.

'In fact,' I said, 'it wouldn't do you any harm to talk to a lawyer. Both of you. A lawyer could help you anticipate issues that might come up in the future. A simple written agreement now could save you both a lot of problems and heartaches later.'

'Gwen and I trust each other,' Billy said. 'We both want the same thing. We don't need some lawyer to screw it up.'

I looked at Gwen. 'What if you get married?'

'Whoever I marry will know about our child,' she said. 'If he doesn't accept the situation, I won't marry him.'

'What if you run out of money, or the baby gets sick, or you do?'

'Look, Mr Coyne,' she said. 'Brady, I mean. Billy and I have thought a lot about this, and we're cool with it. It's going to be OK. Really. You shouldn't worry about it.'

Billy stood up. 'Come on, babe.' He held down both hands to Gwen. 'Let's get out of here. I thought he'd be happy to know about our baby. I didn't think he was going to play lawyer with us.'

Gwen allowed Billy to pull her to her feet. She looked at me. 'Everything's going to be all right, Mr Coyne,' she said. 'Please don't worry.'

'He wasn't worrying,' Billy said. 'He was trying to ruin everything. He's always picking at things, making problems where there aren't any. You were wondering why a nice couple like him and my mom got divorced? That's why, right there. Come on. Let's go.'

Gwen allowed Billy to tug her to the front door. He yanked it open, and as they walked out, she looked at me over her shoulder and mouthed the words 'I'm sorry.'

I got up. 'Wait a minute,' I said.

Billy slammed the door behind him, and they were gone.

I stood there for a minute. Then I went back to the sofa and sat down. I picked up my coffee mug and took a sip. It was cold.

'Did you see that?' I asked Henry. 'Did you see how I screwed that up?'

Henry put his chin on my leg. I patted his head. 'If I talked to you like a lawyer, butted into your personal business, questioned your judgment, would you still love me?'

Henry rolled his eyes up at me, gave his stubby little tail a couple of wags, and licked my hand.

'So why can't people be more like dogs?' I asked.

Henry shrugged.

After a few minutes I got up, went to the kitchen, cleared off the table, loaded the dishwasher. I wandered through the house straightening the furniture and banging around, cursing my stupidity.

Not that I didn't think I was right. If Billy and Gwen did what they planned to do with no written agreement, they'd be awfully lucky not to run into problems at some point.

Billy was right about one thing. It's the job of lawyers to anticipate problems and plan for them. That's why I suggest prenuptial agreements. It's one reason people don't like lawyers. We raise subjects they don't want to think about. Billy's reaction was predictable. Not many couples like to talk about problems. They believe in love for ever and ever and can't imagine anything changing.

Henry and I caught the last three innings of a Red Sox game, then I let him out the back. While I stood on the deck looking up at the stars, searching for Alex's constellations, the kitchen phone rang.

Billy, was my first thought. Calling to apologise. Maybe it was Wayne Nichols, returning my call after all. I hurried inside, picked up the phone and said, 'Brady Coyne.'

I heard a soft chuckle on the other end. 'Gloria Coyne,' she said.

Gloria. My ex-wife. Billy's mother. 'Hey,' I said. 'Hi.'

'You're all out of breath,' she said.

I sat on a kitchen chair. 'I was out the back pondering my sins.'

'Like pissing off your number-one son?'

'He went running to Mommy?'

'He and Gwen are staying here,' Gloria said. 'William came banging in like a thunderstorm a few minutes ago. I asked him what was the matter, and he said you went all lawyer on him.'

'I just talked to them as if they were sensible adults.'

'Well,' Gloria said, 'there's your mistake right there. They're scared and insecure and full of doubts and questions. The last thing they need is to be reminded of it. Especially by a parent.'

'You trying to make me feel better?'

'Why would I ever want to do that?' She chuckled. 'You screwed up, and if you were more tuned in to people's feelings, you wouldn't have done what you did. Who knows? Maybe William would've come to you for advice.'

'That'd be a first.'

Gloria laughed softly. 'Gwen's a pretty down-to-earth girl. She'll straighten him out. You were just being you. You really aren't such a terrible person.'

'Not that bad, huh?'

'William probably wouldn't agree with me right now,' Gloria said, 'but he'll come round. You've just got to be patient.'

SIX

I called my office phone on Wednesday morning while I was sipping the day's first mug of coffee out in the back yard. It was early enough that Julie wouldn't be there to answer, which was the whole point. That way, I could leave her a message without having to listen to her disapproval. 'I know I have no appointments today,' I said. 'I'm taking the day to attend to some business connected to the Nichols case. I'll check in some time in the afternoon. Take a long lunch and close up early, why don't you.'

I disconnected and blew out a breath. A day without billable hours was a lost day, as far as Julie was concerned, and I had no intention of billing Sharon for the hours it would take me to drive to Webster State College in search of her son.

Henry and I had a discussion about whether he could come along. I'm not sure I entirely convinced him that he'd be happier lounging round the back yard than spending the day cooped up in the car. I gave him a bully stick to gnaw on, though, and when I patted his head and said goodbye a little after nine, he was lying on the deck with the stick between his front paws, and he barely glanced at me.

Dogs love you, no doubt about it, but they love food best of all.

Websterville, New Hampshire, was tucked into the southwestern corner of New Hampshire near the Vermont and Massachusetts borders. The little town had just one claim to fame: it was the home of Webster State College. I'd driven through the town many times. It straddled the two-lane highway that was the most direct route from Boston to a lot of good trout fishing in southern Vermont.

It took a little over two hours to drive to Websterville, where I found Chesterfield Road. The address I had for Wayne was number 188, which turned out to be a three-storey wooden-framed building with porches spanning the front of each level.

I tucked my car into an empty space on the side of the road, turned off the ignition and took out my phone. I tried Wayne Nichols's number. It rang half a dozen times, and then the now-familiar recorded greeting came on.

I closed my phone without leaving a message, got out of my car and climbed the steps to 188 Chesterfield Road. There were three doorbells, and taped over each bell was a list of two or three names written in ink. None of the names belonged to Wayne Nichols.

I pressed the bell for apartment one and waited, and when no one came to the door, I tried apartment two. After a minute, I heard feet clomping down some inside stairs, then the inside door opened.

A young woman with tangly brown hair blinked at me through the window of the front door. I smiled at her through the glass and said, 'I'm looking for Wayne Nichols.'

She shrugged and opened the door. 'Who're you?' she asked.

'I'm a lawyer from Boston,' I said. 'My name is Brady Coyne. I have business with Wayne Nichols. I believe he lives at this address.' I fished my card out of my pocket and handed it to her.

She was standing in the half-opened doorway. She squinted at my card, then at me. 'You're a lawyer?'

'Yes, that's right. You know him?'

'Sure,' she said. 'Webster State's a small school. Everybody pretty much knows everybody. Wayne doesn't live here any more.'

'Can you tell me where he does live?'

She shook her head. 'Nope. He used to have the first floor with a couple of other degenerates. They moved out at the end of last term.'

'Do you have roommates who might help me find Wayne?'

'I have roommates,' she said, 'but I doubt they could help you. We avoided Wayne and his buddies. We travel in different circles.'

'What circles does Wayne travel in?'

'Just not mine,' she said. She glanced meaningfully at her wristwatch. 'I gotta go,' she said. 'Sorry I couldn't help you.'

I smiled at her. 'I appreciate your talking with me.'

I went out to my car, turned round and headed back the way I'd come. I passed a couple of dormitories, then came to a large building with a sign on the front that said WEBSTER STATE COLLEGE ADMINISTRATION.

I left my car in the visitors' parking lot and went into the building. A sign indicated that the registrar's office was in suite 206, so I climbed a flight of stairs, found 206 and went in. I was faced with a room-length waist-high counter with four or five people standing on the other side, not unlike bank tellers.

'How can I help you?' asked a young man on the other side of the counter. A name badge indicated that his name was Matthew Trowbridge and he was an admissions intern.

'I'm trying to catch up with one of the students,' I said. 'The address I have for him appears to be out of date.'

Matthew Trowbridge said, 'Are you on the faculty or staff here?'

'No. I'm a lawyer. I drove up from Boston today.'

'I'm not allowed to divulge personal information about our students,' he said. 'I'm sorry.'

'So who is?'

He frowned. 'Excuse me?'

'Who is allowed to divulge information?'

'I can talk to Mrs Allen, if you want,' he said. 'She's the assistant registrar.'

'Thank you,' I said.

'Who is it you're looking for?'

'His name is Wayne Nichols,' I said. 'I'm Brady Coyne.' I gave him one of my business cards.

He glanced at the card. 'Hang on.' He turned, walked down to the end of the room, opened a door and went into another room. He was back five minutes later. 'Mrs Allen can talk with you. Just go down there.' He pointed. 'It's the second door on the left.'

I followed his directions and came to a room with a plaque on the door that read CHARLOTTE ALLEN, ASSISTANT REGISTRAR.

I rapped on the door, and it opened a moment later. Standing there was a woman—middle thirties—wearing designer jeans. She had blue eyes and straw-coloured hair, and she was smiling at me as though I were just the person she'd been hoping to see.

'Mr Coyne,' she said. 'Come on in. Let's sit.'

Charlotte Allen pointed to a chair and then sat in one herself. I saw that she had my business card in her hand. 'Matthew said you were interested in Wayne Nichols,' she said.

'I need to talk with him,' I said. 'I'm hoping you can tell me where he's presently living.'

She smiled. 'I'm afraid it's not that simple, Mr Coyne. Our regulations are very clear. It's all about protecting our students' privacy. I'm really sorry. I wish I could help you out.'

'Look,' I said. 'Wayne's father was brutally murdered last Saturday night. His mother has been unable to contact her son to tell him what happened. She's asked me, as the family's lawyer, to see what I can do. I've tried calling Wayne, but he doesn't answer his phone. So I drove up here to Websterville in the hopes of tracking him down. I just came from the last address his mother has for him, and he doesn't live there any more. So now what am I supposed to do? What would *you* do, Mrs Allen, if you were in my shoes?'

'Did you say *murdered*?' she asked.

'So you can see why I need to talk to Wayne,' I said. 'We don't want him seeing it first on the news or hearing it as a rumour.'

'Of course.' Charlotte Allen cleared her throat. 'You drove up here from Boston to deliver this horrible news to Wayne Nichols?'

'The victim's son,' I said. 'Yes.'

'Let me check on something, OK? I'll be back in a minute.'

She got up and walked out of her office. She was actually gone for about ten minutes. When she came back, she sat down across from me. 'I'm sorry, Mr Coyne,' she said. 'Wayne Nichols withdrew from school before the end of the fall term. We have no information about him since then.' She held up my business card. 'If I hear anything, I'll call you.'

'That would be excellent,' I said. 'I appreciate your time.'

I walked out of Charlotte Allen's office, past the counter where I'd talked with Matthew Trowbridge, and I was halfway down the stairs when a woman's voice from behind me said, 'Hey, mister.'

I turned round, and a young woman came skipping down the steps. 'Did you say you were looking for Wayne Nichols?'

'Yes,' I said. 'Do you know him?'

514 | WILLIAM G. TAPPLY

'I overheard you up there.' She jerked her chin up to where I'd talked
with Matthew Trowbridge and Charlotte Allen. 'I'm Lila.'

She held out her hand. I took it and smiled. 'I'm Brady.'

We resumed walking down the stairs. 'Lots of people know where
Wayne Nichols lives,' Lila said. 'It's hardly a big secret.'

'I'd appreciate it if you'd tell me.' We came to the bottom of the stairs.
I opened the front door, and we both stepped outside.

She frowned. 'You're not gonna get him in trouble, are you?'

'No,' I said. 'I'm his family's lawyer. I need to talk with him.'

She looked at me for a moment. 'He's on Blaine Street. Over that way.'
She pointed down Chesterfield Road in the direction of Wayne's old apartment building. 'Go left by the church, and then Blaine Street is your, um . . .
second or third right. Wayne's place is way down the end. The house is
yellow with one of those carports.'

'You must be a friend of his,' I said.

Lila shook her head. 'I've been to a couple parties at his house is all. My
boyfriend knows him.' She looked at me. 'Look, though, seriously. I hope
you're not gonna get Wayne in trouble. My boyfriend would kill me if he
knew I was telling you this.'

'No trouble,' I said. 'Just some lawyer business.' I held my hand out.
'I appreciate your help. I didn't know what I was going to do.'

She gave my hand a quick shake.

I headed for my car, repeating her directions to Wayne Nichols's house
in my head so that I wouldn't forget them.

FIFTEEN MINUTES LATER I pulled up in front of Wayne Nichols's house in the
cul-de-sac at the end of Blaine Street. The little square of lawn in front was
overgrown with weeds. Dandelions grew from cracks in the driveway,
where an aged blue-and-rust Ford Taurus sedan was parked. The carport
was stuffed with overflowing trash barrels and cardboard boxes. The house,
a small, boxy ranch house, featured flaking yellow paint and a couple of
missing window shutters.

I sat there in my car, looking at Wayne's house, trying to detect a sign of
life inside. The place just sat there, too, still and forlorn. After a few minutes, I slid out of my car and went up to the front door. I pressed the bell and
heard the hollow *ding-dong* echo from inside.

When nobody answered, I hit the bell again and waited. Still nobody came to the door. I went round to the side door under the carport. I rapped on the window, waited, rapped again.

Maybe nobody was home, although there was that old Taurus in the driveway. I walked round to the back of the house, where there was another door. I climbed three steps onto a little concrete porch under a plastic awning, cupped my hands round my eyes, and looked in through the back door, which opened into the kitchen. Pots and pans were piled high in the sink. On a small table sat a Wheaties box, an orange juice carton, a one-gallon milk jug, and some glasses and bowls. The kitchen light was on, and I could hear the *thump-thump* of rock music coming from somewhere inside.

I banged on the frame of the storm door.

That's when I heard a car door slam from the other side of the house, and then an engine sputtered, and it roared to life, and then came the screech of rubber on tarmac.

I jumped off the back porch and ran round to the side of Wayne Nichols's house in time to see the Taurus peel round the cul-de-sac and zoom down Blaine Street in a cloud of blue exhaust.

I considered my options. I could hop into my car, and if I drove fast and guessed right at the turns, maybe I'd catch up with the Taurus. Then what? Wave for him to pull over? Sideswipe him?

Well, it didn't matter. Hamlet Coyne had once again hesitated too long and given the situation too much analysis and too little action. By now Wayne was probably several miles away.

I went over and sat on the front steps. I'd blown my chance to talk with Wayne Nichols. I'd spooked him, and he was gone. But, hey, it was a balmy afternoon, and there were worse things to do—such as shuffling papers in a law office—than sitting in the sun for a few minutes on such an April day.

Wayne Nichols, just a year or two older than my son Billy, was living here in this crappy little house on the slummy outskirts of Websterville, New Hampshire. I wondered how he made the rent. Monthly cheques from Sharon, I guessed. She probably thought she was giving her dropout son tuition and room-and-board money.

I thought about Billy and how he'd gone banging out of my house last night and was heading back to Idaho in a few days.

We'd had our rifts before. Billy was a prideful guy, but I knew he'd come round if I met him halfway. I'd call him. I'd apologise, and he'd apologise. When I got home—

I sensed motion behind me, a sudden prickly feeling on the back of my neck. Before I could react, a voice growled, 'Who are you?'

I jerked my head round and found myself looking into the bore of a square automatic pistol. Behind the pistol was a young man's face. He had black hair, cut short, with the scruff of a beard and dark, glowering eyes. Wayne Nichols, I assumed. He had evidently cut through the woods and sneaked round the side of the house.

'Brady Coyne,' I said, 'and I don't like guns poking at me.'

'What do you want?' he asked.

'If you're Wayne Nichols,' I said, 'I need to talk to you. I have news for you. Put that damn gun down, will you?'

He lowered the arm that was holding the gun. 'You left me a message the other day, right? Was that you? The lawyer?'

I nodded. 'That's right. I'm your mother's lawyer. Do you recognise me?'

He shook his head. 'No, I don't think so. Should I?'

'I used to live in Wellesley. You were friends with my son.'

Wayne Nichols frowned for a moment. Then he nodded. 'Coyne. Billy, right? He's your son?'

'That's right.'

'Billy was a cool dude. Not sure I remember you, though.'

'Look at me,' I said. 'Have you seen me recently?'

He frowned at me. 'Like when?'

'Like last Saturday night?'

'No. Where do you think I saw you last Saturday night?'

'In the Beverly Suites Hotel in Natick. On the third floor.'

He shook his head. 'I was nowhere near Natick. I've never been to that hotel. I never even heard of it before. What is this all about?'

'That's where your father was.'

Wayne frowned. 'My father? What about him?'

'That's where he was last Saturday night when he got killed.'

I watched Wayne Nichols's face. He stared at me. I couldn't read his expression. After what seemed like a long minute he blinked, and then he shook his head. 'Killed,' he said in a soft voice, making it a statement, not a question.

I nodded. 'Murdered. He was stabbed in the abdomen and in the heart. He was there for a convention of veterinarians. He was in his hotel room. Your mother found him. His body.'

Wayne looked down at his hand, as if he were surprised to see a gun in it. He stuck the handgun in the pocket of his sweatshirt, then sat on the step beside me. 'Who killed my father?' he asked.

'They don't know yet.'

'You think I did it?'

'Me?' I shook my head. 'Wouldn't matter what I thought. I'm your mother's lawyer.'

His mouth opened, then closed. 'So she did it, huh? She finally did it.'

'You think so?' I asked.

'The way he treated her all those years?' Wayne nodded. 'About time.'

'How did he treat her?'

He shrugged. 'He was always putting her down. Insulting her. I used to think, *How can she put up with that? Why doesn't she leave him? Why doesn't she kill the son of a bitch?*'

'He made you angry, then? How he treated your mother?'

'Sure. Me and my sister, we used to talk about how we wished he'd just go away.' He smiled quickly. 'Then they got divorced, and I thought after that everything would be better. But it wasn't.'

'Did you talk about murdering him?' I asked. 'You and Ellen?'

Wayne blurted out a quick laugh. 'Murder? We were kids. Who knows what we talked about. Maybe we did. The way kids do, you know. We hated him, I can tell you that.'

I wondered if abuse had actually been a factor in the Nichols divorce. If Ken had abused her—emotionally or physically or both—it could be construed as a motive for murder.

'What about you?' I asked. 'How did he treat you? You and your sister?'

Wayne shrugged. 'OK. Nothing bad. He worked a lot. Me and Ellen both helped out at the clinic, feeding the animals, cleaning the kennels, and he paid us. That's how we earned our allowances. It was just the way he treated my mother. That's what I remember.'

'So where were you last Saturday night?' I asked.

He looked at me for a second. 'You mean do I have an alibi.'

'Yes.'

'I was here. At my house. I—' Right then his head jerked up, and he looked out at the street.

A large black SUV was coming round the cul-de-sac.

'I had some people over Saturday night,' Wayne said. 'There were twenty-five or thirty people here. Of course, none of them would ever admit it.' He stood up. 'I'll be right back.'

He walked to the kerb in front of his house. He had his hand in the pocket of his sweatshirt where he'd tucked his gun.

The passenger-side window of the SUV slid down, and Wayne leaned his forearm on it and bent to talk with the driver. He kept his other hand in his pocket. I got a glimpse of the other man's face as it moved towards the window before it was hidden behind Wayne's body, enough to give me the impression that he was young, with dark hair. He appeared to be wearing a shirt and tie.

I noticed that the vehicle had Massachusetts licence plates and tinted windows. It was a Lincoln Navigator.

I took out a pen and one of my business cards from the inside pocket of my jacket and copied down the licence number of the Navigator. Detective Horowitz might be interested.

After a few minutes Wayne stepped away from the car, the tinted window slid up and the Navigator pulled away from the kerb. Wayne stood there watching it go. Then he came back and sat on the step beside me. 'So where were we?' he asked.

'You were telling me that you didn't have an alibi,' I said.

'No,' he said, 'I told you I *did* have an alibi. It's just that I'm not sure anybody will confirm it.' He looked at me and smiled. 'Do you have any idea who the guy in that Lincoln was?'

I shook my head.

'Let me put it this way,' he said. 'That kid's about my age, and he wears a suit and a tie to work, carries a briefcase, drives the company car. He was looking to do business with me.'

'Business,' I said.

'So, OK,' he said, 'I was here Saturday night, like I am most Saturday nights, and there was a bunch of people over, and they probably wouldn't ever admit it, and they'd be totally pissed if I ever gave out their names.'

'Why is that?' I asked.

'It was a college party, that's all. Use your imagination.' He shrugged. 'All I'm saying is, I'm just explaining to you that I was here, not there, and I did not murder my father.'

'What do you know about ketamine?' I asked.

Wayne cocked his head. 'Where'd that come from? Ketamine?'

'I'm inferring that there might've been drugs at your party,' I said. 'Special K is a popular drug. It's an anaesthetic commonly used in animal surgery,' I said.

'Everybody knows that,' he said. 'My father was a vet. So what? Look. I don't know anything about illegal drugs. I feel bad my old man got murdered, but I didn't do it, and I don't know who did.'

'Won't you talk to your mother?' I asked. 'She left you several messages.'

'Tell her I'm sorry,' he said. 'I'm sorry I don't want to talk to her. I'm sorry about what happened to my father, and I'm sorry that she's always been so unhappy, and I'm sorry about my screwed-up life and all the misery I've caused everybody, OK?' He stood up and faced me. 'Just go home and leave me alone, will you?'

'I'll go,' I said, 'and I won't keep bugging you—but I want you to agree that if I call, you'll either answer the phone or listen to my message, and if I ask you to call me back, you'll do it.'

'Why should I?'

I spread my hands. 'Because I don't want to have to drive for two and a half hours every time I want to talk to you.'

Wayne shrugged. 'OK. It's a deal.' He held out his hand.

I shook his hand. 'Any message for your mother?'

He shook his head. 'No, nothing. Probably best if you don't tell her you were here, huh?'

I shrugged. 'I'd like to tell her I saw you and that you're OK.'

'Really?' He smiled. 'Am I?'

SEVEN

It was four in the afternoon, and I'd crossed back into Massachusetts, heading towards Boston, when my cell phone vibrated. It was Roger Horowitz. 'You're playing hooky today,' he said.

'Sometimes my business takes me out of the office,' I said.

'Julie seemed annoyed. Don't know how she puts up with you. She said she didn't know where you were or what you were doing. So where are you now?'

'On the road. Maybe a half hour from home. Why?'

'I need you to come to my office,' he said, 'to look at something.'

'I can be there in an hour, maybe an hour and a half.'

'Good.' He hung up. No 'Goodbye', no 'Thank you', no 'Have a nice day'. That was Horowitz. Mr Charm.

I drove to my parking garage and left my car. Then I walked down Charles Street and turned up the hill on Mount Vernon to my house.

Henry was happy to see me. He whined and wagged his little stub of a tail, and I squatted down to rub his ears and tell him how much I'd missed him, and then I let him out.

I checked the kitchen phone for messages, found none, then snagged a bottle of Samuel Adams Cherry Wheat Ale from the refrigerator and a Milk-Bone from the box on the table, and joined Henry out the back. I sat in one of my Adirondack chairs and took a swig of ale. I wanted to relax for a few minutes before I trudged over to Horowitz's office.

After a while, Henry came over and plopped his chin on my leg. I scratched the secret spot on his forehead and gave him his Milk-Bone. He lay down on the patio beside me to chomp on his treat.

I fished out my cell phone and tried Billy's number.

He answered on the second ring. 'Hey, Pop,' he said.

I said, 'You're speaking to me, huh?'

He laughed quickly. 'You know I love you, man,' he said, 'but sometimes you can be a pain in the ass.'

'I apologise for that. That's why I'm calling. I was out of line the other night, trying to cram my advice down your throat.'

'Ah, your heart was probably in the right place,' he said. 'It's just, sometimes you treat me like a little kid, you know?'

'I do know,' I said, 'and sometimes the lawyer in me kicks in when I should just be the father. Anyway, I wanted you to know that I trust your judgment. It sounds like you've worked this out in a way that makes sense for you, and I wish you the best of luck and much happiness. That's why I'm calling. To say what I should've said the other night. Good luck and happiness. And to apologise.'

'I'm the one who should apologise. I said things I shouldn't've said. You know I respect the hell out of you. I hope you know.'

'Sure,' I said. 'Don't worry about it.'

'Gwen's been on my ass to call you. She says I acted like a baby. She said I was so immature that I obviously did need my father's advice, and I think she's right. So, sorry, man.'

'Look,' I said. 'I think I told you that Alex is coming down this weekend. She'd love to see you again, and meet Gwen. Can you guys come over on Saturday?'

'Sounds good,' he said. 'Hang on. Lemme check with Gwen.'

A minute later Billy came back on the phone. 'She says good. We're heading out on Sunday, you know. I'd like to see you again before we go. Alex, too. It's been a few years since you guys were together, right?'

'Seven years,' I said.

'The Evie Banyon years,' Billy said.

'Yeah, well,' I said. 'Evie's gone now.'

'And Alex is back. Cool, the way it worked out for you.'

'It's not that simple,' I said.

'I didn't mean anything,' he said. 'I liked Alex, and I liked Evie. Whatever makes you happy, man.'

'Seeing you and Gwen again will make me happy.'

After I hung up with Billy, Henry and I went inside. I gave him fresh water, then told him I had to go meet with Roger Horowitz.

Then I left the house and walked to Horowitz's office, located in the district attorney's office in Government Center on the other side of Beacon Hill. It was a fifteen-minute walk from my house.

I emptied my pockets, endured the mistrustful scrutiny of the big female guard as I passed through the metal detector, and took the elevator to the second floor. I poked my head into Horowitz's office. He was leaning back in his chair at his desk with his tie pulled loose and his fingers laced behind his neck. He was talking with Marcia Benetti, his partner, who was sitting across from him.

I rapped my knuckle on the door frame. Horowitz turned his head and looked at me. 'Oh,' he said. 'You're here. About time.'

He jerked his head at an empty chair. I went in and sat down. 'So what do you know?' I asked.

He looked at Benetti. 'Why don't you go ahead and fill him in.'

'You told him about the matchbook, right?' she asked Horowitz.

He nodded.

She opened the manila folder that was on her lap, glanced at the papers in it, then turned to me. 'The ME didn't come up with anything

522 | WILLIAM G. TAPPLY

exciting,' she said. 'TOD between seven and nine that night, just as we figured. Two stab wounds, one to the heart and one to the abdomen. Forensics found dozens of fingerprints, human hairs, fabric traces, all the stuff you'd expect from a hotel room, some of which matched up with your client, and a lot of which they couldn't match up with anybody.' She closed the folder and looked at me. 'Nothing to exonerate your client, in other words.'

'Nothing to implicate her, either,' I said.

Benetti smiled. 'Right. Nothing new to implicate her. Not yet.'

I smiled. 'What about the murder weapon?'

'It wasn't recovered,' she said. 'The ME said it was serrated, thin blade, five inches long, consistent with the hotel steak knives.'

'Of which there was an abundant supply on the room-service trays up and down the corridors,' I said. 'Killer could've grabbed one, used it on Ken Nichols, rinsed it off, and put it back on one of those trays.'

'Forensics took all the knives that were still there on the trays in the hallway for evidence, tested all of them.' She shrugged. 'None was the murder weapon. At this point, that's a dead end.'

'What about drugs?'

Benetti shook her head. 'They found nothing in his system except alcohol.'

'Did they test for ketamine?'

She nodded. 'Yes. Negative.'

I looked at Horowitz. 'You had something to show me?'

'Yeah, I do.' He took a manila folder off the top of his desk, opened it, and slid out some six-by-eight photographs. He spread them out on the desk, facing me. 'Whaddaya think?' he asked.

There were eleven photos. Each of them showed a bearded man. The subjects ranged in age from mid-thirties to about seventy. Some had dark beards, some grey. Some neatly trimmed, some bushy. Some of the men were bald; some had thick heads of hair.

None of them was the guy who'd shot Ken Nichols with his index finger the night I'd been there.

I looked up at Horowitz and shook my head. 'The guy I saw was about fifty. Dark beard with grey in it, receding hairline. Ken called him Clem. None of these guys looks like him. This all you've got?'

'What we pulled off the hotel surveillance cameras, Friday, Saturday and Sunday. When the animal doctors were there. All the bearded guys. I told you there was nobody named Clem registered.'

'Well,' I said, 'the guy I saw was there Friday night, but he's not here in your photos. He managed to avoid the cameras. Maybe he did that on purpose.'

Horowitz glanced at Benetti, then pulled open one of his desk drawers, reached in and took out a DVD. 'We got something else for you.' He pushed himself out of his chair. 'Come on.'

I followed Horowitz and Benetti down the hall to a conference room with four television sets lined up on a shelf against one wall.

Horowitz slipped the disc into one of the television sets and picked up a remote control. 'We got some stuff from two security cameras at the Beverly Suites Hotel,' he said. 'We copied the relevant parts onto this disc.'

He pressed a button on the remote, and a fuzzy black and white picture appeared. I recognised the lobby of the hotel. In the lower right corner of the screen was the date—the Saturday night four days earlier when Ken Nichols was killed. The time ticked along by the second. It showed 22:32:17 and counting.

People were moving jerkily in and out of the picture. After a minute or so Horowitz said, 'There.' He paused the picture. 'See? There, in the hoodie.'

I saw what he saw. It was a figure wearing a dark sweatshirt with the hood covering his head. He looked like he was headed for the front entrance. From the angle of the camera, his face was hidden.

I recognised him by his hoodie and his baggy jeans and his white sneakers, and by his general body shape. He was young and slender and not very tall. His movements were quick and alert, like some wild species that thought he was being stalked by a big predator.

He could have been Wayne Nichols.

He could have been a million people.

'Yes,' I said. 'That looks like him. The guy I chased down the corridor. Same size, same clothes. Did you get a shot of his face?'

'Hang on,' said Horowitz. He fast-forwarded the disc, and when he stopped it, the picture came from a different camera. It was fixed on the front of the hotel where taxis and limos were picking up and dropping off guests. The time at the bottom of the screen was 22:36:44—immediately after the previous sequence.

'There,' Horowitz said after a minute or two. 'There he is.'

The hooded figure stepped into the picture from the bottom left corner. He stood there on the sidewalk with his back to the camera. A black SUV pulled up to the kerb, and the guy in the hoodie went over, opened the door, and started to slide in.

Horowitz paused it there, with our subject bending to get in. His hood had slipped to the side, and half of his face was visible.

'I see part of his face,' I said. 'It's pretty fuzzy. Can't you enhance it or something? Somebody should be able to sharpen that image. On TV they do it all the time.'

'This ain't *CSI*,' Horowitz growled. 'Just take a look at the guy's face for me and tell me if you recognise him.'

It wasn't Wayne, I could see that. I shook my head. 'I don't recognise him. What about the driver? Did the camera get a glimpse of him?'

'Don't think so,' he said. 'Keep looking.'

He hit the play button, and on the screen the guy in the hoodie slipped into the car, which then began to pull away from the kerb. At no time did the face of the driver show itself.

'Wait,' I said. 'Pause it.'

He hit the pause button.

'Isn't that a Lincoln Navigator?'

'Yep,' said Horowitz. 'Black or dark blue, I'd say.'

'Can you read the plates on it?'

'We tried,' he said. 'Too blurry. We've got our techs working on it. We should maybe be able to get a partial read on it, at least.'

I took out my wallet and found the business card where I'd jotted down the plate number from the Lincoln Navigator in front of Wayne's house. I handed it to Horowitz. 'See if these match those.'

He took the card and frowned at it. 'What's this?'

'The plate numbers from a Navigator I saw today, looks like that one on your tape.'

'Where was this?' he asked. 'Who does the vehicle belong to?'

'Look,' I said. 'I don't want to get ahead of myself here. If this plate doesn't match that one there at the hotel, then it's irrelevant.'

'You withholding evidence, Coyne?' asked Horowitz.

'I think this would actually be called sharing evidence,' I said. 'Consistent with protecting my client's privileged status.'

'Sure,' he grumbled. 'Privileged. Of course.'

'The Beverly Suites don't have security cameras in the corridors?' I asked.
He shook his head. 'They got 'em in the elevators, but not the corridors.'
'This guy,' I said, 'when I chased him, he went down the stairs.'
'He probably came up the stairs, too,' he said, 'because we looked at the elevator tapes and couldn't find him. I'd guess he was aware of the cameras, avoiding them when he could. Those shots you just saw are all we got.'
'Trying to avoid cameras would suggest that he was up to no good.'
'Ha,' said Horowitz. 'No good, as in stabbing a veterinarian in the heart in his hotel room, you mean.'
'That would qualify as no good,' I said.

WHEN I GOT BACK from Horowitz's office, I made two fried-egg sandwiches and ate them at the kitchen table with a glass of orange juice. Under the table, Henry's tags clanged against his metal dish as he gobbled his Alpo.
After I rinsed my plate and glass and stowed them in the dishwasher, Henry and I went into my office. He curled up on his dog bed for his after-supper nap, and I called Sharon Nichols in Acton.
When she answered, I said, 'How are you?'
She hesitated, then said, 'Oh, I'm all right, I guess.'
'Tell me the truth,' I said. 'I'm your lawyer. You must always tell me the truth.'
'Well, OK. The truth? Lousy, is how I am.' She blew out a cynical laugh. 'I'm not sleeping. I lie awake. My mind whirls round. When I finally do drift off, I dream about violence and death. I wake up and can't go back to sleep. I can't control my bad thoughts. I doubt everything. The world is undependable. Bad things can happen anytime, and I lie there thinking of all the bad things, and how I can't prevent them. Do you know what I mean?'
'Yes, I understand,' I said.
'When I'm up and around,' she said, 'during the day, it's like this cloud of gloom surrounds me. I'm jumpy and irritable. Today a customer dropped her car keys on the floor, and I just about hit the ceiling.' She hesitated. 'This is to be expected, right? I mean, aren't these feelings pretty much normal for somebody who a few days ago discovered the bloody corpse of the man she was married to for many years, the man she was maybe falling in love with all over again? Not even to mention, someone who the police think did it?'
'What you're feeling might be expected,' I said, 'but it's not healthy, and

it's not normal. You need to deal with it. Do you remember I mentioned my friend the homicide counsellor to you?'

'A shrink, right?' asked Sharon.

'She's a psychologist,' I said. 'She specialises in helping the friends and relatives of homicide victims deal with their feelings. Her name is Tally Whyte, and I'd like to arrange an appointment for you with her. OK?'

'I don't feel like having to explain myself,' Sharon said.

'You wouldn't have to explain anything to Tally,' I said. 'She understands all about it. Her own father was murdered.'

Sharon was silent for a minute. Then she said, 'I don't know. It seems too hard. What I really want is not to have to think about it.'

'It's not going to go away,' I said.

'I know,' she said. 'OK. I'll try. I've got to do something.'

'I'll call Tally now,' I said. 'I'll get right back to you. OK?'

'Sure,' she said. 'OK. Thank you.'

'Before you hang up,' I said. 'I left you a voicemail yesterday asking about a man named Clem. Somebody Ken knew.'

'You asked me that before,' she said. 'It still doesn't ring any bells. I'd've called you if I'd thought of anything.'

'Could be a nickname or something.'

'I'm sorry, Brady.'

'He might be the one who killed Ken.'

'I'm drawing a blank,' she said. 'I'll keep thinking about it.'

The instant Sharon and I disconnected, I realised I'd neglected to tell her about seeing Wayne. One of my shrink friends would find some kind of vast significance in that, no doubt.

Well, I'd tell her about it when I called her back.

Over the past few years I had introduced several of my clients, people who'd brushed up against murder, to Tally Whyte, and they all told me that she'd helped them deal with their fears and guilt, their dark, oppressive thoughts and feelings. Tally had given me her home and cell numbers. I'd written them down in my old-fashioned little black address book. I tried her at home.

She picked up the phone. 'Friend or foe?' she asked.

'Friend, definitely,' I said. 'It's Brady Coyne.'

'Yep,' she said. 'My favourite lawyer. How have you been?'

'Oh, I've been fine,' I said, 'but—'

'You've got a client? Friend, relative of a homicide victim?'

'Right,' I said. 'She needs you.'

Tally was quiet for a moment. Then she said, 'The vet in the hotel?'

'That's the one,' I said. 'His ex-wife.'

'I've heard about this case. She's a suspect, isn't she?'

'Sharon is her name,' I said. 'Sharon Nichols. She found the body. They haven't eliminated her from their list of suspects.'

'Did she agree to see me?'

'Yes,' I said. 'She's not doing very well. She knows she needs help. I was thinking, if she's willing to talk to you . . .'

She hesitated, then said, 'What do you think? If she's willing to see me, it means she's innocent?'

'That occurred to me, yes.'

'It doesn't work that way, Brady,' she said. 'Anyhow, sure, I'd be happy to see her. We should do it soon. With these things, time is of the essence. How's tomorrow morning? Say around eleven?'

'Let's make it a date,' I said. 'I'll call Sharon right now, and if tomorrow at eleven won't work for her, I'll get back to you. Otherwise, I'll bring her to your office.'

'I'll be waiting in the lobby for you,' she said.

When I called Sharon back and told her I'd set up an appointment for her at eleven the next morning, she said, 'Boy, you did that fast. Before I could change my mind and chicken out, right?'

'I think it's important,' I said. 'Can you come to my office? I'll take you over there, introduce you.'

'I'll take the morning off and be at your office—when? Ten?'

'Ten or ten thirty,' I said. 'Tally's office is on Albany Street, a five-minute cab ride from Copley Square.'

'This is all way above the call of duty, Brady,' she said.

I cleared my throat. 'I saw Wayne today.'

'Really. Why didn't you tell me this when we talked before?'

'I'm sorry,' I said. 'I was focused on getting you to Tally.'

'Is he all right?'

'Yes, he's OK. I told him what happened to Ken.'

She said nothing.

'He's dropped out of school,' I said. 'He's living in a little house on the outskirts of Websterville. He seems to be . . . he's OK.' I wasn't going to tell her that Wayne fled in his car when I knocked on his door, or that when he came back, he pointed a pistol at me.

'So what's he doing?'

'For work, you mean? I don't know.'

'Back to the drugs, huh?'

'What about drugs?'

'He got busted for selling drugs when he was in high school. He was on probation for eighteen months.'

I remembered the shiny Navigator that pulled up in front of Wayne's house, and the parties at Wayne's house, and the ketamine in Ken's hotel room. Obvious connections. 'I don't know if he's into drugs or not' was what I said to Sharon.

'Did you tell him I've been trying to reach him?'

'Yes. He doesn't want to talk to you. I'm sorry.'

'No,' she said. 'I knew that. I just don't understand why.'

'I think Wayne has a lot of complicated feelings about you and Ken,' I said, 'and your divorce, and the reasons for it.'

'What reasons?' she asked.

'He thinks Ken was abusive to you.'

'Abusive?'

'Mentally,' I said. 'Emotionally.'

Sharon chuckled. 'Aren't we all?'

I thought of my marriage with Gloria. I didn't think abusiveness was a factor in our marriage, or in our divorce.

'I guess it's not uncommon,' I said, 'in failed marriages.'

'Kids misinterpret what they see and hear,' said Sharon. 'Ken and I had our problems, obviously. There was a lot of conflict and tension, no doubt about it. I mean, we did get divorced. I can see how Wayne would think that Ken was abusive to me.' She paused. 'I suppose, in a way, he was. And I was probably abusive to him, too. I mean, one of the reasons I wanted to get divorced was to separate that stuff from the kids' lives before it scarred them.' She blew out a breath. 'Sounds like we were too late. Something else to feel guilty about, huh?'

'It's something else you can talk about with Tally,' I said.

'I can't tell you how it feels,' she said, 'having a child who refuses to speak to me.'

'I can imagine,' I said. I was thinking of Billy. 'Anyway, you've got Ellen.'

'Yes,' she said. 'Thank God for Ellen. She keeps me almost sane. Well, thank you for all of this. I'll see you in the morning.'

'Get some sleep.'

'Ha,' she said.

I WAS IN BED with my tattered copy of my bedtime book, *Moby Dick*, resting on my lap. Melville, digressing again, had devoted an entire chapter to the subject of the tail of the sperm whale.

Then the phone on my bedside table rang.

I shut the book, picked up the phone and said, 'Hey.'

'Hey, yourself,' said Alex. 'Reading *Moby Dick*?'

'It's scary how you know things like that. Did you have a good day?'

'I spent all day trying to write,' said Alex.

'You saying you had a bad day at the keyboard?'

'I had a typical day,' she said. 'Maybe something salvageable came out of it. I'll have a better idea when I look at it tomorrow. How about you?'

'Billy and Gwen are coming for supper on Saturday. I hope that's OK.'

'It's great,' she said. 'It'll be nice to see Billy again. So what do you think? *Is* Gwen his girlfriend?'

'You'll see for yourself. Then you can tell me.'

I heard her yawn. 'Sleepy Alex,' she murmured. 'I just called to say good night to my honey.'

'Good night, babe. See you Friday, huh?' I asked.

'Before you know it, darlin'. Mmm. Hug and kiss, 'kay?'

EIGHT

Julie buzzed me on my office console a little before ten thirty on Thursday morning. 'Your appointment is here,' she said.

'Sharon Nichols?'

'Correct.'

'Bring her in, will you?'

She opened my office door and held it for Sharon. Sharon was wearing a narrow black skirt, with an off-white linen jacket over a tight-fitting red sweater. Some tricky make-up emphasised her big eyes and good cheek-bones and expressive mouth, although behind her eyes and round her mouth I saw sadness and fatigue.

After Julie closed the door, Sharon sat in one of my client chairs and I resumed my seat behind my desk. I looked at my watch. 'It's a fifteen-minute walk or a five-minute cab ride to Tally's office over on Albany Street. Your pick.'

'Oh, let's walk,' she said. 'It's a gorgeous day out there.'

It was an April-in-Paris morning in Boston. In the vacant lots and the little side gardens, the forsythia and honeysuckle were blooming aromatically. The new leaves on the maple trees were lime green, the size of mouse ears. The easterly breeze that came wafting in from the harbour smelled like freshly turned earth and spring rain.

Tally Whyte, as promised, was waiting for us in the lobby of the square brick building that housed the OCME, the Office of the Chief Medical Examiner for the Commonwealth of Massachusetts.

Tally was a tall, lanky gal somewhere in her thirties. She reminded me of the actress Laura Dern. She was quite pretty in an angular, interesting way, with big expressive eyes and high cheekbones and a tangle of blondish hair.

When Sharon and I walked through the front door, Tally flashed her great warm smile, came over, gave me a hug, then held out her hand to Sharon. 'I'm Tally,' she said.

Sharon took her hand. 'I'm Sharon. Sharon Nichols.'

Tally held Sharon's hand. 'My office is this way.' She tugged Sharon towards a door off the lobby in a cloud of happy chatter.

'I'll wait for you here,' I called to Sharon.

I found a sofa and a stack of magazines. I read the *Sports Illustrated* special springtime issue with the annual Major League Baseball forecast. Sharon and Tally came back into the lobby an hour later, walking slowly. Tally was tilting her head towards Sharon, talking softly to her, and Sharon was looking down at the floor, nodding at what Tally was saying.

Sharon's eyes were puffy, and I guessed she'd been crying.

Tally touched Sharon's arm. 'Next week, then?'

'Same time, same place,' Sharon said. 'I'll be here.'

'It's going to be fine,' Tally said. 'Really.'

Sharon nodded and smiled. 'I'm beginning to believe you.' She turned to me. 'She's amazing.'

'I know,' I said.

Sharon gave Tally a hug, and we walked outside. 'You know,' she said, 'I understood that I was sad and frightened, but I didn't realise how guilty I was feeling. About what happened to Ken, I mean. Tally helped me understand that I was blaming myself, as if I was the one who killed him. She got me talking, and the next thing I knew, I was telling her how it was my fault, and then I cried for a while, and pretty soon it was like I was shrugging some giant weight off my shoulders.'

'I'm glad you're feeling better,' I said.

'Tally says I should expect those awful feelings to keep coming back for a while,' she said. 'Lying awake at night, the dreams, all that. Now I've got some ways to deal with them. She gave me some tools. I'm going to keep seeing her. She's wonderful.' Sharon put her arm through mine. 'For the first time since it happened, I actually feel as if I might become normal again.'

Provided, I thought, *you don't end up going to trial for Ken's murder. That might tend to slow down your recovery.*

WE WERE SHUTTING DOWN our computers, closing the blinds, cleaning the coffee urn, when Roger Horowitz came blustering into the office. Julie smiled at him. 'You're too late,' she said. 'We just threw out the dregs of today's coffee.'

'Well, damn,' he said. 'Everyone knows Coyne's office is the place to go for coffee dregs.'

'How about a Coke?' asked Julie. 'Bottle of water?'

'I only got a minute,' he said. 'Benetti's double-parked.'

He looked at me and jerked his head at my office. I nodded, and he followed me in. 'What?' I asked.

'Your client,' he said. 'We gotta talk to her.'

'Interrogate her, you mean?'

'Call it whatever you want. Ask her a few questions, sure. Benetti was all for sending the troops to her house with sirens screaming, and hauling her in. My idea is this. Why don't we meet here in your office—your home field, you might say—tomorrow morning?'

'That's very considerate of you,' I said. 'Surprising.'

'I surprise myself sometimes,' he said. 'Can you have Mrs Nichols here at ten tomorrow morning?'

'Sure I can,' I said. 'You want to tell me what it's all about?'

'I absolutely do not,' he said.

'You come up with some new evidence on this case?'

'Don't push me, Coyne, or I'll defer to Benetti. She's ready to dust off the waterboard.'

'You better keep your partner in line,' I said. 'Whisper the word "harassment" in her ear.'

Horowitz grinned. 'We'll be here at ten.'

I held out my hand to him. 'I appreciate it,' I said. 'Whatever people say, you're not such a bad person.'

'For God's sake,' he said, 'don't tell anybody.'

SHARON SHOWED UP a little after nine thirty on Friday morning. We went into one of my conference rooms and sat side by side at the rectangular table.

She wore tailored slacks and a blouse that was buttoned to her throat. She looked tired and edgy. 'So when you called last night, you said you didn't know what was up. Can you tell me now?'

'I still don't know,' I said. 'I told you not to worry about it.'

She rolled her eyes. 'Oh, sure. You know, the things Tally and I talked about yesterday, in her office, with sunshine coming through the window, it all made sense, and I thought I was OK. But last night? Tally was right. It's not going to be easy. I stared at the ceiling for a long time, wondering what the detectives wanted to ask me.' She shook her head. 'I came up with some wild possibilities.'

'Like what?' I asked.

'Now, in the daylight, I can see that they were all stupid.'

'Nothing plausible then?'

'Well,' she said, 'if the murder weapon showing up in my kitchen dishwasher is plausible, OK, then. Or if somebody said they heard me and Ken talking or yelling or something in his hotel room that night, then, yes, my craziness was plausible.'

'Ken was dead when you got there, right?'

Sharon frowned. 'Are you questioning that?'

'If somebody could've heard you and him . . .'

'That's my point,' she said. 'They couldn't have, because he was already dead. So it's stupid of me to invent the idea that somebody heard something, then to obsess on it—but it's what I did.'

There came a discreet tap on the door, and then it opened, and Julie stepped inside. Marcia Benetti and Roger Horowitz came in right behind her. Benetti had a big leather bag slung over her shoulder. Horowitz was carrying an attaché case.

I stood up and shook hands with both of them. They nodded at Sharon, who remained seated. Julie walked out of the room.

Horowitz and Benetti sat across from Sharon and me at the conference table. Benetti took her digital recorder out of her bag and put it on the table.

Horowitz slid a manila folder out of his attaché case, put it on the table in front of him, and placed his clasped hands on top of it. 'OK,' Horowitz said. 'Let's get started.'

Marcia Benetti hit a button on the recorder, said, 'Testing,' set it on the table, and said, 'Say something, please, each of you.'

I said, 'Here we are again,' and Sharon said, 'I wonder why.'

Benetti replayed what we'd said. It sounded fine. 'OK,' she said, 'we can get started.' She cleared her throat and fixed her gaze on Sharon. 'Just so you understand, Mrs Nichols, anything you say here today can be used against you in a court of law. You have the right to refuse to answer any question. You have the right to have your attorney present. Which you do. Do you have any questions?'

'No,' said Sharon. 'I understand.'

'Attorney Coyne?'

'Are you planning to take my client into custody?' I asked.

Horowitz shook his head. 'Not at this time.'

'So why are you cautioning her?'

'We are being scrupulous about protecting her rights,' he said. 'We thought you'd appreciate it.'

'We do,' I said.

'Means she better tell the truth, though,' he said.

'We get that,' I said.

Horowitz said, 'OK, for the record, I'm Homicide Detective Roger Horowitz, Massachusetts State Police. My colleague Sergeant Marcia Benetti is here with me. We're in the office of attorney Brady L. Coyne with him and his client Sharon Nichols. It's Friday, ten oh six, April the 27th.' He slipped some papers out of the manila folder. 'What I got here,' he said, looking at Sharon but speaking for the benefit of the recorder, 'is a copy of Mrs Nichols's divorce agreement. I made copies for all of us.'

Horowitz pushed two paper-clipped stacks of paper across the table to us.

Sharon pulled one stack in front of her. I took the other one and flipped through it. There were fourteen pages. They included six exhibits, A through to F: 'Custody and parenting', 'Alimony and child support', 'Taxes', 'Division of personal and real property', 'Insurance' and 'Miscellaneous'. Standard stuff.

I looked across the table at Horowitz. 'OK,' I said.

Horowitz turned to Benetti. 'You want to take it from here?'

'I do,' she said. 'Let's look at Exhibit B, paragraph one, where it says, "The husband shall pay child support to the wife".' She looked up at us. 'Got it?'

I nodded, and then Sharon said, 'Yes.'

Benetti said, 'It goes on to say that the child support ends when the children are emancipated, and it defines that as when they've finished college or reached the age of twenty-two, whichever comes first. Is that right?' She cocked her head and looked at Sharon.

Sharon turned to me. Before Horowitz and Benetti arrived, I'd told Sharon that she should answer no questions without my assent.

'That's right,' I said to Benetti. 'It's right there in plain English, or as plain as English can be in a legal document.'

Benetti looked at me, gave me a quick smile, then turned back to Sharon. 'How old are your children, Mrs Nichols?'

Sharon looked at me.

'Go ahead,' I said.

'Wayne's twenty-two, and Ellen is twenty-five.'

'They're both in school?'

'Ellen's in graduate school,' Sharon said. 'Getting her master's at BU. Wayne was, up until . . .' She looked at me.

'Last fall,' I said. 'He dropped out.'

'So you've been getting child-support cheques every month from your ex-husband since your divorce, is that right?'

'That's right,' Sharon said. 'We renegotiated the numbers when Ellen graduated.'

'You're paying Wayne's college bills?'

'Yes,' said Sharon.

'With the child-support money your ex-husband sends you.'

'That's right.'

'Your cheques come regularly?'

Sharon shrugged. 'Pretty much. Ken missed a few payments. I called him and reminded him, and they started coming again.'

'Did the cheques stop when Wayne dropped out?'

'No,' Sharon said.

'Did you and your husband talk about it?'

I touched Sharon's arm and spoke softly into her ear, 'Tell me.'

'No,' she whispered to me. 'I didn't know he'd dropped out, and I don't think Ken did, either. If he did, we never talked about it.'

'The answer is no,' I said to Benetti. 'They did not talk about it. They didn't know their son had dropped out.'

'Now, about Ellen,' said Benetti, 'she's on her own?'

'Right,' said Sharon. 'She's taken out student loans, worked part-time. Ken and I haven't helped her since she graduated.'

'OK, Mrs Nichols,' Benetti said. 'Now I'm looking at paragraph four, same exhibit. Alimony. Your husband—your ex-husband, I should say—has been paying you alimony all these years, is that right?'

'That's right,' Sharon said.

'So every month since this agreement was approved, you've gotten cheques for alimony and child support. You've been financially dependent on him. Your ex-husband.'

'I wouldn't—'

'Don't answer that,' I said. To Benetti I said, 'The numbers are right there. You can judge them.'

'Let me put it this way,' Benetti said. 'Did what your husband pay you in alimony and child support adequately cover your children's college expenses and your own living expenses?'

Sharon looked at me, and I nodded.

'Not really,' she said. 'I've always had to work.'

'Did you ever ask him to increase his payments? Complain to him about how hard it was to make ends meet? You never told him that you were struggling, or how hard you were working?'

'You're being argumentative,' I said.

'You can't object,' said Benetti. 'This isn't a courtroom.'

'Well,' I said, 'I'm telling you, I do object.' To Sharon I said, 'Don't answer those questions.' I looked at Benetti. 'My client answered your question. She and her ex-husband did not discuss or argue about finances, and I object to your browbeating her.'

'Mr Coyne,' she said, 'this isn't a courtroom, and you can't object to something just because you don't want to hear it.'

'We don't have to sit here and pretend that this wild stuff you're throwing around should be taken seriously. You have nothing except some supposition.' I set my forearms on the table and leaned forwards. 'If this is all you've got,' I said, 'this unsubstantiated implication that my client and her ex-husband might have had a disagreement about money—which, if it did happen, which my client says didn't, would only make them just like everybody else—if that's what you've got, then we're done here.'

Benetti smiled across the table at me. 'We're not quite done yet,' she said. She looked at Sharon. 'Do you know who the beneficiary of your ex-husband's will is?'

I touched Sharon's elbow. 'Don't answer,' I said.

She looked at me. 'But I don't—'

I held up my hand, and she stopped. I looked at Benetti. 'I bet you already know the answer to your question.'

She smiled. 'In fact, I do.' She leafed through some papers and held up a thick document. 'The Last Will and Testament of Kenneth Roland Nichols.' She pushed it across the table to me.

It was nearly half an inch thick, held together by one of those big spring-loaded paper clips. I glanced through it. It had been properly signed, dated, and notarised. I pushed it back. 'It appears to be a copy of his will, all right,' I said to Benetti. 'What about it?'

'Mr Nichols had it rewritten last October,' she said. 'You can see the date.' She looked at Sharon. 'Did you know about that?'

'Stop,' I said before Sharon could say anything. 'Don't answer,' I said to her. I turned back to Benetti. 'This is relevant why?'

'Your ex-husband,' Benetti said to Sharon, 'didn't appear to have much of an estate. In fact, he owed quite a bit of money.'

'That doesn't surprise me,' Sharon said.

'Mr Nichols's father is a different story,' Benetti said. 'The elder Nichols is in poor health, and he happens to be extremely wealthy. I'm talking several millions of dollars.' She looked at me. 'Up until last October, when Mrs Nichols was the primary beneficiary of her former husband's will, she'd have been first in line for the elder Mr Nichols's estate if her husband was deceased.'

Sharon was frowning and shaking her head.

'Do you understand what I'm saying?' Benetti asked her.

'You're saying that Ken wrote me out of his will.'

'That's right.'

'So there'd be no money coming to me if he died.'

'That's right. His children are his co-beneficiaries, and they are also the contingent beneficiaries of the elder Mr Nichols's will.'

I cleared my throat. 'This is interesting,' I said, 'and we appreciate your sharing this solid evidence that since she's no longer his heir, my client would have no motive to murder her ex-husband. Or was there some other point you thought you were making?'

Benetti flipped through some documents. When she found the page she wanted, she looked up. 'Back to the divorce agreement. Let's take a look at Exhibit E. Insurance. It's on page thirteen, paragraph four.'

Sharon and I turned to page thirteen, paragraph four.

'For the record,' Benetti said, 'I will read paragraph four out loud. It says, "The husband shall maintain his current life insurance policies for the benefit of the wife and dependent children. The issue of the husband's obligation to maintain life insurance for the wife after the children's emancipation may be reviewed upon such emancipation."' Benetti looked at Sharon. 'So did he?'

Sharon frowned. 'Did who what?'

'Did your former husband maintain his life insurance?'

Sharon looked at Marcia Benetti. 'I don't know,' she said.

'You don't know? Really?'

Sharon shrugged. 'Really. I never asked Ken about his life insurance, and he never mentioned it. I assume he maintained it.'

'So you believed that he continued to invest in life insurance for which you and your children were the beneficiaries, even though he wrote you out of his will. Is that right?'

'I didn't know he'd written me out of his will,' Sharon said, 'but as far as keeping up the insurance goes, yes, I guess so. I really never thought about it. I mean, that was in our agreement so that if something happened to Ken, the kids' education would still be covered.' She turned to me. 'Isn't that right, Brady?'

'It's standard in most divorce agreements,' I said. 'A way of guaranteeing that the husband's obligations to the dependent children are fulfilled even in the event of his death.'

'So,' Benetti said to Sharon, 'as far as you know, your husband was carrying up-to-date life insurance in your name at the time of his death, is that right?'

Sharon shrugged. 'As far as I know.'

'Do you know how much coverage he had, in your name, payable to you upon his death? Money that you are now entitled to?'

'No.' Sharon shook her head. 'I have no idea.'

Benetti said, 'Your ex-husband's life insurance policies, of which there are three, are all payable to you. You are the primary beneficiary. Your children are contingent beneficiaries, meaning they'd get the money only if you were dead. Did you know that?'

'I might have,' Sharon said. 'I honestly don't remember. It's not something I've ever given much thought to.'

Benetti said, 'Does $1.9 million sound familiar, Mrs Nichols?'

Sharon said nothing. I glanced at her. She was looking down at the sheets of paper in front of her, avoiding Benetti's hard look. I read tension—or maybe it was anger—in the set of her jaw.

I cleared my throat. 'This has been a lot of fun,' I said, 'but now we really are done. On behalf of my client, I'd like to thank both of you for dropping by this morning and sharing your fascinating, and very creative, speculations about your murder investigation with us. Now, if you don't have anything new you'd like to talk about . . .'

'I'd just like a clarification,' said Marcia Benetti.

'Of course you would,' I said. 'Go ahead.'

'Mrs Nichols maintains she didn't know what Mr Nichols's life insurance was worth, correct?'

'Your recording will confirm that she said that, I believe,' I said.

'She has also told us that she and her ex-husband did not even discuss, never mind argue about, finances. She further said she didn't know that Mr Nichols had changed his will.'

'That's right.'

'Mrs Nichols,' said Benetti, looking hard at Sharon, 'you understand what you've said to us here can be used in a court of law, and that if you lied to us today, it would be tantamount to perjury.'

Sharon nodded. 'I understand that, yes.'

'I have just one more question for you, then,' Benetti said.

Sharon looked at me. I nodded.

'Mrs Nichols,' said Benetti, 'did you know that your ex-husband had requested some documents from his insurance company that would enable him to cash out his life insurance policies, and that if he had not died, he would apparently have done so?'

Sharon shook her head. 'Cash out? So he'd get the money, and I would no longer be insured? Is that what you mean?'

Benetti nodded. 'Luckily he was killed before he could complete the paperwork.'

'*Luckily?*' I said.

'I didn't know anything about this,' Sharon said.

'Please think carefully about your answer,' Benetti said.

'She said no,' I said.

'Could he do that?' Sharon asked me. 'I mean, the divorce agreement says he's supposed to maintain his life insurance.'

'The insurance company doesn't know about divorce agreements,' I said. 'They'd do it, unless your lawyer intervened.'

'How could he if we didn't know?' she asked.

'Exactly,' I said. 'So he'd do it, and he'd get the cash, and then it would be too late.' I looked at Benetti. 'Your question's been answered. My client knew nothing about this. Is there anything else?'

Benetti glanced at Horowitz. He shrugged. 'OK, then,' she said, 'we're concluding this interview now. Thanks for your cooperation.' She reached out to the recorder and snapped it off.

Horowitz slid his paper back into his manila folder and stuck the folder into his attaché case. Marcia Benetti put the recorder into her bag, and we all stood up.

Sharon and I reached across the table and shook hands with the detectives. Then I opened my office door and held it for them. I followed them out into my reception area. Sharon remained in my office.

'You'll be hearing from us,' Horowitz said.

'I hope you're pursuing some other avenues in your investigation besides this one,' I said.

'Thanks for the reminder,' he said.

'You check out that licence plate I gave you?'

'Was I supposed to submit a report to you?' he asked.

'I do have an interest in this case.'

'You take care of your client,' he said. 'We'll take care of our investigation.'

'Good deal,' I said.

After they left, I went back into my office. Sharon was standing by the window. 'So what was that all about?'

'What part of it?'

'Right there at the end,' she said, 'reminding me that what I said could be used against me, and cautioning me about lying.'

'Nothing to worry about,' I said. 'Assuming you told the truth.'

'Well, I did,' she said.

'I'm glad,' I said. 'So tell me. If the detectives look into your finances, will they find unpaid bills, maxed-out credit cards, gambling debts, anything like that?'

Sharon shrugged. 'I'm carrying a balance on two credit cards. That's about it. Why? Is that bad?'

'If you owed a lot of money,' I said, 'it would make murdering Ken for his insurance, and doing it now, before he could cash it in, a believable motive.'

'I guess it would,' she said, 'but I don't owe that much. I pay every month. I'm not behind on anything. I'm getting by.'

I nodded. 'OK. Good.'

'So now what?' she asked.

'Now,' I said, 'we go back to living our lives. Assuming they can't come up with somebody who says you were telling them about how you were going to spend his life insurance, then one of their theories was destroyed here this morning.'

'That I killed Ken for money.'

I nodded.

'I didn't, you know. I didn't kill him for money,' she said. 'I didn't kill him, period. I mean, how stupid would that be? To hang around the hotel where a hundred people could see me, and then go up to his room and kill him, and then hang around and call my lawyer, and wait there in his room for the police to show up? And do it for his life insurance? I mean, is that not the world's most obvious motive for murder? Do they think I'm completely clueless?'

'Most murderers are utterly clueless,' I said. 'In fact, the scenario you describe is quite plausible.'

'Except for the fact that I didn't do it.'

I nodded.

She started to stand up, then sat down again. 'Oh. I remembered something. You asked about a friend of Ken's named Clem, and I've been racking my brain, and I finally came up with something.'

'You remember Clem?'

'Ken had this old friend from college named Sean Clements.'

'Did Ken call him Clem?'

She shrugged. 'I'm not sure. I just flashed on his name last night. I met him a couple of times. It was a long time ago.'

'Any idea where Sean Clements is now?' I asked.

'He was teaching at BU. Or BC. History, I think.'

'When was that?'

'Back when Ken and I were still married. Are you going to tell the police about him?'

'Probably ought to make sure it's the right guy first,' I said.

She stood up. 'I've got to go. I'm supposed to be at the shop.'

'Will you be all right?'

She shrugged. 'I don't know. The fact that those detectives really seem to think I did it, that they're trying to make a case against me—I don't think it's sunk in. Like the night I found Ken's body. I thought I was fine, but pretty soon, wham, I was a basket case.'

'Call Tally,' I said.

'I already thought of that.'

NINE

I walked Sharon to the door. After she left, I went to Julie's desk. 'I'd like to talk to a man named Sean Clements,' I said. 'He might be a history professor at BU or BC.'

'Might?' Julie asked.

'That was a few years ago,' I said. 'Best I can do.'

I went into my office. My mind kept wandering back to Marcia Benetti's interrogation of Sharon. When I tried to be objective, it was hard not to take her seriously as a suspect. She had the means and the opportunity to murder Ken. She could easily have picked up a steak knife from one of the room-service trays in the corridor, and she was there in Ken's room around the time he was stabbed.

Now Horowitz and Benetti had come up with a motive. Ken's insurance money, nearly two million dollars, plus the fact that he was evidently planning to cash it in.

After fifteen or twenty minutes, my console buzzed. I picked up the phone and said, 'Yes?' and Julie said, 'I've got Professor Sean Clements of the Emerson College history faculty on line two.'

'Emerson, huh?'

'Tracked him down,' said Julie.

'You're amazing,' I said.

'And don't you forget it.'

I hit the blinking button on the phone console and said, 'Professor Clements?'

A deep voice said, 'That's right. You're an attorney?'

'I am,' I said. 'Brady Coyne is my name.'

'What does an attorney want with me?'

'I want to buy you a drink.'

'Why should I have a drink with you?' he asked. 'Am I in some kind of trouble?'

'Nothing to worry about. Meet me at Remington's at three o'clock. You know Remington's, don't you?'

'I'm not meeting some random lawyer anywhere, no matter who's buying, if I don't know what his agenda is.'

'I'm not that random,' I said. 'It's about Ken Nichols.'

'Who?'

'Ken Nichols. The vet.'

'I don't know any Ken Nichols.'

While I was talking, I googled Emerson College on my desktop computer and clicked my way to the faculty directory. I found Professor Sean Clements's name. I clicked on his name, and his picture popped up on my screen. He had a broad forehead and a neatly trimmed beard, flecked with grey. He was the guy.

'How about last Friday night. At the Beverly Suites Hotel in Natick. I saw you there. You saw me.'

'I don't like your tone, sir,' he said. 'I'm going to hang up now.'

'Fine. You don't want to talk with me, I'll just give your name to

Detective Horowitz with the state police homicide division.'

'Homicide,' said Clements softly. He blew a breath into the telephone. 'Remington's at three, you said?'

'Know where it is?'

'I do,' he said. 'OK. Three o'clock at Remington's, then.' He paused. 'You called me Clem.'

'Isn't that what people call you?'

'Not since college,' he said.

FRIDAY TURNED OUT to be another glorious April day. I walked down Boylston Street, cut across the Common and walked into Remington's about ten past three. Professor Sean Clements—he was indeed the same fiftyish man with the dark, neatly trimmed beard and the high forehead whom Ken Nichols had called Clem that night in the Beverly Suites Hotel in Natick—was sitting at a table in the corner with a glass of draft beer in front of him.

I went over and sat down across from him. He looked at me and frowned. 'I remember,' he said. 'You were with Ken at the hotel.'

'So were you. Why did you lie to me?'

'I heard what happened. I didn't want to be involved.'

A waiter came to the table. 'Can I get you something?' he asked.

I pointed at Clements's beer glass. 'One of those.'

The waiter left. I looked at Clements. 'So did you kill Nichols?'

'No,' he said. 'Of course not.'

'You were there. I saw you.'

'I was there the night before. I wasn't there on Saturday night.'

'Where were you Saturday night?'

'I was at a faculty party at the home of my department chair in Wenham,' he said. 'Not that it's any of your business.'

'Actually,' I said, 'it is my business.'

Clements shrugged. I wondered if his alibi would hold up.

'I'm going to have to give your name to the police,' I said. 'I'm sure they'll want to talk to you.'

'Must you?'

'I'm an officer of the court,' I said.

The waiter came back and put a glass of beer in front of me.

'You and Ken seemed to be having some, um, conflict,' I said to Clements.

'You made a pistol with your hand and shot him with your forefinger.'

'Yeah,' said Clements. 'Sonofabitch owed me money.'

'You shot him with your forefinger,' I said, 'and next thing you know, somebody murders him.'

'Stabbed, I heard,' said Clements. 'Not shot.'

I smiled. 'How much did he owe you?'

'Hundred thousand.'

'What was the loan for?'

'To start up an animal clinic in Maryland. This was around the time of his divorce. He tapped a lot of his friends, I understand.'

'A hundred grand is a significant amount of money,' I said.

'It is,' Clements said, 'and I wanted it back.'

'You didn't kill him, though, huh?'

'Felt like it,' he said.

'Somebody beat you to it.'

'You had to take numbers,' he said, 'get in line.' He picked up his beer and drained it. 'He claimed he was going to be coming into some money very soon, and he'd be able to clean up his debts. His father was dying. His father was rich, he said, and he, Ken, was his only heir.' He looked at me. 'Now that he's dead—Ken, I mean—will I be able to recoup my money from his father's estate?'

'You better get yourself a lawyer,' I said.

SEAN CLEMENTS and I shook hands on the sidewalk outside Remington's. I walked across the Common, and on the way, called Roger Horowitz on my cell phone. When his voicemail picked up, I said, 'The guy named Clem that I saw at the hotel, middle-aged man with the beard? He's a history professor at Emerson College name of Sean Clements. Admitted that Ken Nichols owed him money. He's got an alibi for Saturday night. Have a nice weekend.'

I picked up two takeout orders at my favourite Thai restaurant. Then I climbed the hill to my house on Mount Vernon Street. Alex's battered Subaru was parked in front of my house. She had her own key. She'd be inside waiting for me. That made me smile.

I climbed onto my front porch, unlocked the door and shouldered my way inside. I lugged my takeout bags into the kitchen and set them on the table. When I looked out through the back window, I saw Alex sprawled in an Adirondack chair, with her head slumped on her shoulder. She was wearing an orange dress hiked halfway up her thighs, as if she'd been sunning her legs. Henry lay on his side on the patio beside her. Both of them appeared to be sound asleep.

I put our dinner into the refrigerator, then went upstairs and changed into a pair of jeans and a flannel shirt.

Back downstairs, I snagged two bottles of lager from the refrigerator and took them out back. Henry lifted his head, blinked at me, and wagged his stubby tail. I gave his belly a rub, and then sat in a chair facing Alex. Her eyes opened and looked directly at me. 'Mm,' she murmured. 'You're home. Hi.'

'Hi yourself,' I said. 'Sorry if I woke you up.'

'Oh, I was sort of half awake,' she said. She sat forward and held out her arms. 'Gimme a hug.'

I got out of my chair and hugged her, and I gave her a kiss on the mouth, too, which threatened to evolve into something more before she put her hand on my chest and pulled back. 'Sweet,' she said.

I sat down again. 'How hungry are you?' I asked.

'You talkin' about food?'

I smiled. 'Not necessarily.'

'It's been a while.'

'Three weeks,' I said, 'but who's counting.'

'Three weeks is too long,' she said. 'It makes me feel . . . shy.'

'It's like we need to get to know each other again,' I said.

'You feel that way?'

'Sure,' I said. 'For me, the shy boy battles with the dirty old man. We've got all weekend. Let's just relax, go with the flow.'

'It's not that I don't want to . . .'

'I know. I brought you a beer.' I handed the bottle to her.

'Thank you.' She held up her bottle. 'Here's to our flow.'

I clicked her bottle with mine, and we both drank to our flow.

WHEN I WOKE UP on Saturday morning, Alex's side of the bed was unoccupied. The salty damp smell of fresh spring rain seeped through the open bedroom window. An April rainstorm had come and gone in the night, and it promised to turn into a nice day.

I had a shower, got dressed and stumbled downstairs. Henry was at the foot of the stairs. I rubbed his ears, and he followed me to the front door, where the thin Saturday *Globe* was on the porch.

In the kitchen, Alex was sitting at the table with her chin on her fists and a coffee mug by her elbow. She was frowning at her laptop computer, which was opened in front of her. 'I fed Henry,' she said without looking up. 'Made coffee.'

I poured myself a mugful, went over to the table, lifted the hair away from the back of her neck, and gave her a nuzzle.

'Umm,' she said. 'Nice. Cut it out.'

I sat across from her. 'You're working?' I asked.

'Sorry. Yep. Gotta.'

'Your novel?'

'Don't wanna talk about it now,' she said.

'How long?'

She turned and looked at me. Her glasses were perched down at the tip of her nose, where she wore them when she was working at her computer. Behind them, her eyes looked quite fierce. 'I'll be at it a long time if you don't leave me alone,' she said. 'OK?'

'You got it,' I said. I toasted an English muffin, poured myself a glass of orange juice, clicked my tongue at Henry and took muffin, juice, coffee and newspaper out the back.

I sat at the picnic table, ate my breakfast and read the *Globe*. After a while, Alex came out and sat across from me.

'You done?' I asked.

She said, 'I'm never done.'

'How's it going?'

She shook her head. 'I have no idea. I'm trying not to judge it. That comes later. Now it's all about getting the story out.' She looked at me. 'Sorry about last night,' she said.

'You don't need to be sorry. But you're still feeling shy, huh?'

She leaned back in her chair and looked up at the sky. 'I have trouble enough with intimacy,' she said, as if she were talking to the clouds. 'This way, the way we are, you and me, I just . . .' She shook her head.

I waited.

'We've got this whole history,' she said.

'A good history.'

She smiled. 'Mostly good.'

'Hey, it's a beautiful day. *Carpe diem*. What do you say?'

She looked at me. 'I'm just preoccupied with my novel right now.

Makes me feel moody. I'm going to go have a shower. When I'm done, I'll feel better.' She stood up, came round to my side of the table and kissed me on the side of my neck.

'Need someone to wash your back?' I asked.

She smiled at me. 'I don't think so, thank you.'

IN THE AFTERNOON Alex and Henry and I crossed the pedestrian bridge at the foot of Charles Street and walked the length of the Esplanade, from the Museum of Science to the BU Bridge. College kids from MIT and BU and Harvard were lying on blankets. They were riding bicycles and Rollerblades and skateboards, playing Frisbee and kicking soccer balls. They were doing just about everything that college kids should be doing on a fine spring day except reading textbooks and studying for exams.

We got back to the house a little before five. Billy and Gwen would arrive in an hour or so. Henry sprawled on the floor and began to snore. Alex went upstairs to change her clothes. I checked my voicemail. I had one message, from Sharon Nichols. 'There's something I need to talk to you about. Can you call me?'

I took the phone out to the patio and dialled Sharon's number.

'Thanks for getting back to me,' she said when she answered.

'What's going on?'

'Ellen came over for a visit this afternoon,' she said, 'and she reminded me of something, and it made me think . . .' Her voice trailed off. 'I'm sorry. I probably shouldn't say anything.'

'If it pertains to what happened to Ken, you should tell me.'

'I don't know if it does,' she said. 'No, that's wrong. I think it might. That's why I wanted to talk to you.'

I waited, and after a pause, Sharon said, 'There was a time back when Ken and I had the kennels when some of the animals might've had something happen to them. People told us that when they brought their pets home, their personalities had changed. They were suddenly skittish around people, acting spooky or frightened.'

'As if they'd been abused,' I said.

'Yes, exactly,' she said. 'We never figured out what happened. We had no other complaints, and the issue went away, and I hadn't thought about it for a long time.'

'So what about it now?' I asked.

'Ellen and I were talking about it today,' Sharon said. 'I don't know how it came up. We were just reminiscing, talking about her memories of growing up with animals, and how awful it was to think that something bad could happen to the animals that we cared for. Ellen said she always suspected that Wayne did something to those animals, and when she said that, I realised that somewhere inside me I had the same suspicion.'

I remembered Billy's story about how Wayne had blown a frog's head off with a firecracker. 'Suppose it *was* Wayne,' I said. 'That was a long time ago.'

'If my son was capable of that . . . do you see, Brady? Do you understand what I'm thinking?'

I hesitated. 'You're thinking that Wayne killed Ken?'

'I guess I am, yes.'

'Sharon,' I said, 'what do you want me to do with this idea?'

'I don't know,' she said. 'Nothing, I guess. I'm sorry. I just needed to get it off my chest. It's such a horrible thought. Maybe I just wanted you to tell me it's stupid.'

'If Wayne did it,' I said, 'it means you didn't. It would be good to know who did it. Even if it was your son.'

'Well, I don't know if it was Wayne,' she said, 'but I know it wasn't me. So it was somebody else. I've been trying to figure out who that could be. So, what if it was Wayne?'

'There's no evidence that Wayne was anywhere near that hotel on Saturday night,' I said. 'Nothing to connect him to what happened. Not to mention, no motive that we know of.'

'I know. You're right. Thanks for saying it. I need to think that way. About evidence. Facts, not feelings. I don't like to think that my son could've killed his own father.'

At that moment, Henry came bounding down the back steps. I looked up. Alex was on the deck with her eyebrows arched at me.

'Sharon,' I said, 'I've got to go.'

'Sure,' she said. 'Thanks for listening. I guess I just need to get better control of my thoughts.'

I put down the phone and smiled at Alex. She'd changed out of her walking clothes. Now she was wearing blue jeans and a long-sleeved striped jersey.

I gave her a wolf whistle, and she looked cross-eyed at me and put one hand behind her head and the other one on her hip and did a little pirouette on the deck.

I got up and went to her. I kissed her forehead, and she smiled and pressed the entire length of her body against me, and then she put her arms round my neck and went up on her tiptoes and lifted her face, and our mouths met, and Alex murmured, 'Mmm.'

She put her arms round my waist, and she hugged me hard against her and pushed her face into my chest.

'Wanna go upstairs?' I asked.

That, of course, was when the front doorbell rang.

BILLY AND GWEN brought three pounds of ground sirloin and two packages of bratwurst, a tub of potato salad and another of coleslaw. There were buns, jars of relish and mustard, two big tomatoes and a Bermuda onion. Billy hogged the grill, and Gwen usurped the kitchen; Henry stuck close to Billy, where the food was.

We ate on the picnic table out the back, and by the time we finished, darkness was beginning to seep into the patio. We carried the dirty dishes into the kitchen, and Billy and I told Gwen and Alex to get out of our way so we could clean up.

'You wanna wash or dry?' I asked Billy after they'd left.

'You dry,' he said. 'You know where things go.'

'Supper was great,' I said.

Billy was up to his elbows in the soapy water when he asked, 'What you were saying the other night? Got me all pissed at you?'

'I was hoping that was behind us,' I said.

'It's not about you,' he said. 'I guess both me and Gwen had already been thinking about things. You know, what if this, what if that. We didn't bring it up because we didn't want to hurt each other's feelings.' He looked at me. 'So now she says she's decided to get a lawyer when she gets home, and she says I should too.'

I didn't say anything.

'So what do you say?' he said. 'You wanna be my lawyer?'

'Me?' I shook my head. 'No. I don't want to be your lawyer. I want to be your father. It's not a good idea for a lawyer to be emotionally involved with his client. Personal things can distract a lawyer from legal things, and I happen to love you.'

'Yeah, well . . .'

'Anyway,' I said. 'You need a lawyer from Idaho, where you live. If you want, I can ask around, get some recommendations for good attorneys out there.'

The phone on the kitchen wall rang. I made no move for it.

'You wanna get that?' Billy asked.

'Let it ring,' I said. 'If it's important, they'll leave a message.'

When the phone stopped ringing, Billy said, 'I get it. There's a million lawyers. You're my only dad.'

After Billy and Gwen left, Alex and I let Henry out, and we stood there on the deck looking up at the stars.

'Thinking about Gus?' I asked her.

She put her arm round my waist and leaned her head against my shoulder. 'I think about him all the time. When I see the stars, his constellations, it makes me feel like he's up there watching over me, my big brother, protecting me like he always did.'

I hugged her against me and said nothing.

'Who called?' she asked after a minute. 'I heard the phone ring.'

'Oh, right. It did. I didn't answer it. Billy and I were talking. I'd better see if I've got a message.'

'I'm going to get ready for bed,' Alex said.

We went inside. Henry got his bedtime Milk-Bone. I picked up the phone and heard the *beep-beep* indicating I had a message.

I went to voicemail. 'Mr Coyne,' came a male voice, 'it's Wayne Nichols.' He paused, and I heard voices and music in the background. It was Saturday night, and it sounded like Wayne was hosting another party. 'I got something here I think you'll be interested in,' he said. 'So, you want to see it, come on up. You know where I live. Make it tomorrow, Sunday. Say round seven o'clock, OK? No need to call me back. I'll be here either way.'

WHEN SUNDAY MORNING dawned sunny and sweet-smelling, Alex, Henry and I piled into my car and drove out to Concord, where we rented a canoe on the Sudbury River.

Alex wore cut-off shorts, a tank top and one of my Red Sox caps with her ponytail sticking out of the back. From my seat in the stern, I enjoyed watching her paddle. Henry sat at the middle thwart, his ears cocked as we passed pairs of mallards paddling in the lily pads and a couple of great blue herons along the river bank.

The river was wide and flat, and we glided along upstream to Fairhaven

Bay. We beached the canoe, spread my army blanket on the grassy bank and had a picnic. After we ate, Henry sprawled in a patch of sunshine, and Alex and I lay back side by side on the blanket with our faces turned up to the sky and our eyes shut.

She found my hand with hers, interlaced our fingers, and held it tight against her hip. 'What's going to become of us?' she asked.

'We're going to live happily ever after,' I said.

'Ever after what?'

'After we slay the wicked stepmother,' I said, 'and escape from the castle and outwit the trolls at the bridge.'

'All that, huh?'

'Nobody ever said that happily ever after was going to be easy.'

She gave my hand a squeeze, then let it go. 'Well, I don't see why it has to be so hard,' she said.

We got back to my place on Beacon Hill a little after four. Alex went upstairs to pack. Henry and I went out the back. I thought about Wayne Nichols. He said he had something to show me. As soon as Alex left, I would drive up to Websterville to see what it was.

'And you can't come,' I said to Henry.

He was lying on the bricks with his chin on his paws and his ears perked up, watching me. It was approaching his suppertime, so nothing would escape his notice. Henry lived with the chronic fear that I'd forget to feed him. Now, when he heard my voice, he lifted his head. Had I just uttered a food word?

'Sorry,' I said to him.

He sighed. He dropped his chin to his paws and closed his eyes. He knew that 'sorry' was a bad word, an antonym of 'cookie', for example, or 'bone', or 'dinner'.

After a few minutes Alex came out. She smiled. 'All set to go.'

'What about next weekend?' I asked. 'My house or yours?'

'I don't know,' she said.

'What do you mean?'

'I don't like to interrupt my writing,' she said. 'I was in a pretty good groove for a while, and now I feel like I've lost it.'

'Henry and I can stay out from underfoot. We've done it before.'

'We can talk about it,' she said.

'What's going on, babe?'

She looked at me. 'Nothing, really. I don't mean to be grouchy. It's been a lovely weekend. I know as soon as I get into my car I'll start missing you terribly. You and dear Henry.'

'But now . . . ?'

She pushed herself to her feet. 'Now it's time to leave. I want to get home before dark. Gonna walk me out to my car?'

Her duffle and backpack were on the floor by the door. I picked them up, took them out to her Subaru and loaded them in back.

Alex was leaning against the driver's door. I went to her, and she hooked her arms round my neck. 'Thank you for putting up with me,' she said.

'Hey,' I said. 'I love you.'

She smiled. 'I know. Me too.'

'Call me when you get home?'

'Sure,' she said. 'Will you be here?'

'Actually,' I said, 'maybe not. Call my cell. I want to know you got home all right.'

'I will.' She tilted up her face and kissed me hard on the mouth. When she pulled back, I saw that her eyes were glittering.

'What's this?' I asked, touching my fingertip to her damp cheek.

She smiled. 'It feels like I've been trying to get away from trolls all my life,' she said. 'I'm ready for the happily ever after part.'

'You deserve that,' I said. 'Let's make it happen.'

AFTER ALEX LEFT, I gave Henry his supper and let him out. When he finished his business, we went inside and I gave him a bully stick. 'Guard the house,' I said. 'I'll be back, I promise.'

There were stretches of the highway from Boston to Websterville where the descending April sun hung low in the sky, dead ahead, and the glare on my windshield almost blinded me, even though I was wearing sunglasses. I strained to focus on the lines on the middle of the road so I could stay on my side and avoid a head-on.

A few minutes after seven I turned into the cul-de-sac where Wayne Nichols lived. The sun had sunk behind the house. A dim light shone through the front window, and his old Taurus sedan crouched in the cracked driveway.

I parked, went to the front door and pressed the bell. It went bong-bong inside. When Wayne didn't come to the door, I hit the bell again, and still he didn't answer.

I went round to the carport and banged on the side door, and then I tried the back door. Either Wayne wasn't home, or he'd decided he didn't want to talk with me after all.

There was another, more ominous explanation. I pulled open the storm door and tried the inside door. It was unlocked. I pushed it open, hesitated, then stepped inside. I stood in the doorway. Somewhere a clock ticked hollowly. The refrigerator motor hummed. It was grey and shadowy. Yellow light filtered in from the next room.

'Hey, Wayne,' I called. No answer.

I moved into the kitchen, and that's when the familiar harsh odour of burned gunpowder hit my nostrils.

I found Wayne in the living room. He was slouched on the sofa with his chin on his chest, his arms at his sides, and his legs stretched out in front of him. A brick-red splotch the diameter of a grapefruit stained the front of the sweatshirt he was wearing.

I went over to him and pressed two fingers against the side of his neck. I didn't expect to find any pulse, and I didn't.

When I straightened up, something rubbed against my leg. I whirled round and clenched my fists and started to drop into a defensive crouch. Then I blew out a breath and smiled.

It was a black cat with white boots and a white blaze on her chest. She was sitting there on Wayne's living room floor twitching her tail and looking up at me with her greenish yellow eyes.

I picked her up and held her against my chest. I could feel the vibrations of her purring. 'I wonder what you saw,' I said.

She was wearing a collar with a tag. The tag said *Sparky* and had a phone number.

I put Sparky on the floor, then reached into my trouser pocket, took out my cell phone and flipped it open. I hit the nine and the one. Then I stopped, snapped the phone shut and put it back into my pocket. Another few minutes wouldn't do Wayne any harm.

Sparky padded along behind me when I went to the wing on the left side of the one-storey ranch house. I took my handkerchief from my pocket and held it over my finger as I flicked on some lights. There were two small bedrooms and one bathroom. Only one of the bedrooms appeared to be used for sleeping. There was a bureau and a closet, and I prowled through them and found nothing but clothes.

The other bedroom was evidently Wayne's storage room. Some wooden chairs were stacked in a corner. Cardboard boxes sealed with packing tape were piled against one wall. I wondered what they held but decided it would be imprudent to cut them open.

In the bathroom, the medicine cabinet was empty except for a bottle of Tylenol, a tube of Crest and some hair gel. A kitty-litter box sat next to the toilet.

Sparky followed me back to the living room and the kitchen. In the living room were the sofa, where Wayne hadn't moved, a couple of mismatched easy chairs, and a flat-screen television on the wall. I found nothing of interest in the kitchen. Milk and orange juice, and a few containers of leftovers in the refrigerator.

I clicked my tongue at Sparky, and she followed me down the stairs into the basement.

A washer and dryer sat against one cement wall, and a furnace and oil tank stood next to another wall. A partition sectioned off a small office. When I flicked on the light, my finger covered with the handkerchief, I saw that it had been trashed. Papers and folders littered the office floor. The desk drawers hung open.

On the corner of the desk sat a surge suppressor with six sockets and two empty cords plugged into it. A laptop hookup and a cell phone charger, I guessed. No computer or phone, though.

So much for whatever it was that Wayne had wanted to show me. It looked like whoever shot him had got there first.

I climbed back up the cellar stairs and took one last look around. Sparky jumped onto the sofa and lay on the cushion beside Wayne, and the question occurred to me: How could somebody who'd tortured animals as a kid grow up to be a man who kept a pet?

I went outside and sat on the front steps. I took out my cell phone, dialled 911, and told the dispatcher that I'd found a dead body at a house in the cul-de-sac at the end of Blaine Street.

She asked my name and told me to wait there, don't touch anything, and somebody would be along in a few minutes.

Then I called Roger Horowitz's cell phone.

'You again,' he said when he answered. 'What is it this time?'

'Ken Nichols's son, Wayne,' I said. 'His body. It's here, at his house in Websterville, New Hampshire. Shot in the chest.'

'Websterville, huh?' he asked. 'So whaddaya want me to do?'

'I don't know,' I said. 'I figured you should know. It's unlikely that this isn't related to what happened to Ken, don't you think?'

'You call the locals?'

'They're on their way.'

'Shot in the chest? Not stabbed, huh?'

'No.'

'And you're there why?'

'He called me,' I said. 'Said he had something to show me.'

'What was it?'

'He didn't say. I don't know.'

I heard the wail of sirens in the distance, growing louder.

'The cops are on their way,' I said. 'The place has been tossed. Laptop's missing, and maybe his cell phone, too. I'm guessing they got whatever it was that Wayne was planning to show me.'

'You find any drugs? Ketamine?'

'I didn't look that hard,' I said. 'What do you want me to do?'

'Do what you're supposed to do,' he said. 'Cooperate with the authorities. Answer their questions. You don't need my guidance.'

Then he disconnected.

'You're welcome,' I said into my dead phone. I snapped it shut and shoved it into my pocket, and that's when the two black-and-white cruisers, with their sirens screaming and their blue lights flashing, came careening round the corner and slammed to a stop in front of Wayne Nichols's house.

TEN

Two uniformed officers jumped out of each vehicle. One of them stayed at the side of the road, one went round to the back of the house, and the other two approached me on the front steps. They were both male, somewhere in their forties, one black and one white. The white one said, 'You the one who called it in?'

'That's right,' I said.

'Sir,' he said, 'if you'd come with me.'

I stood up and followed him to his cruiser. He opened the back door. 'We'd like you to wait here,' he said. 'The state detectives will be here pretty soon. They'll need to talk to you.'

When I bent down to get in, he put his hand on top of my head.

He left the door open and leaned against the side of the cruiser, guarding me. After a few minutes, more vehicles appeared, and pretty soon the cul-de-sac at the end of Blaine Street looked like a multicar pile-up on the Mass Pike, with a dozen vehicles parked at odd angles, their doors hanging open, their lights flashing.

A white-haired guy in a brown suit came over and spoke to my guard. After they'd exchanged a few sentences, the white-haired guy turned and went back into the house.

When the cell phone in my pocket vibrated, I fished it out, opened it and saw that it was Alex. 'Hi, babe,' I said.

'I'm home safe and sound,' she said.

'Oh, good,' I said. 'Thanks for calling. Uneventful trip?'

'Totally uneventful. Thanks for a lovely weekend. I had fun. I know I was kind of moody. Please don't take it personally.'

'It's OK,' I said. 'You're a writer. Goes with the territory.'

'I'll make it up to you, I promise. Next weekend, right?'

'We'll be there. Me and Henry.'

There was silence for a moment. Then Alex said, 'Brady? What's going on? There are background noises. What is it?'

'I can't talk about it right now, but don't worry. I'm fine.'

'Call me when you can talk, will you?'

'I will.' I looked out of the open car door and saw the white-haired guy headed in my direction. 'I gotta go now. I'll call you.'

I shut my phone and slipped it into my trouser pocket.

The white-haired guy walked up to the open cruiser door and spoke to the uniformed officer. Then he bent down, poked his head in and said, 'Shove over, Mr Coyne.'

I slid over, and he got in beside me. He held out his hand. 'Wexler,' he said. 'Homicide, New Hampshire state cops.'

I gripped his hand. 'Coyne,' I said. 'Lawyer, Massachusetts bar.'

He smiled quickly. 'I've talked with your buddy Detective Horowitz. He filled me in.'

'I'm glad,' I said.

'So tell me what you can tell me,' he said. 'Like, for example, how come you happened to be here to find Mr Nichols's body.'

'Wayne called me,' I said, 'asked me to come up. Said he had something he wanted to show me.'

'Show you what?'

I shrugged. 'He didn't say.'

'You didn't ask?'

'I didn't talk with him,' I said. 'He left me a phone message.'

'When was that?'

'Last night. In Boston. He said he had something he thought I'd be interested in, and I should come up today around seven.'

Wexler glanced out of the window, then turned back to me and said, 'What time did you get here?'

'A little after seven.'

'And before that?'

'Before I got here? I was on the road. It takes a little over two hours to get here from my house, which is where I was before that.'

'You were in Boston,' he said. 'Alone?'

'No. My, um, girlfriend was there. And my dog.'

'This afternoon, before you were on the road? Where were you then?'

'Look,' I said. 'What time do you need my alibi for?'

He smiled. 'Between one and five this afternoon ought to take care of it, according to the ME.'

'That's easy,' I said. 'We rented a canoe in Concord—Concord, Massachusetts, that is, not your state capital. Around noon. We turned it in around four. Paid with a credit card. Talk to them.'

'What's your girlfriend's name?'

At that moment my cell phone buzzed in my trouser pocket. I decided to let it go. If it was important, they'd leave a message.

'Alexandria Shaw,' I said. 'She lives in Garrison, Maine.'

'OK, good,' he said. 'We'll check it out. So when you got here, Mr Coyne, you went right into the house?'

'I rang the bell and knocked on the doors. The back door was unlocked, so when nobody answered my knock, I went in.'

'That's when you saw the body?'

'That's right.'

'Then you called it in?'

'Not right away. I looked around first,' I said. 'After I saw that Wayne was dead, I went through the whole house.'

'What were you thinking? You're a lawyer. You know time is of the essence. You should've called it in immediately.'

'I was thinking,' I said, 'that another few minutes wouldn't make any difference to Wayne. I was thinking he'd wanted to show me something, and I wondered what it was, and I thought I might know it if I saw it. So I decided to look around.'

He shrugged. 'So did you see what you were looking for?'

I shook my head. 'I don't think so.'

'What did you touch when you were in the house?'

'The only thing I touched was some light switches,' I said. 'I used a handkerchief. Oh, and Sparky. The cat. I patted her.'

He grunted. 'You went down to the cellar?'

I nodded. 'I saw that the office down there had been tossed.'

'I bet you figure that whoever shot Nichols was looking for whatever it was he wanted to show you.'

'That occurred to me,' I said.

'Looks like they took his laptop,' said Wexler. 'We didn't find a cell phone, either. He didn't have a landline.'

Wexler leaned back against the seat and tilted up his face so that he was looking at the roof of the cruiser. 'I doubt if this has got anything to do with your case, Mr Coyne. We've had our eye on Wayne Nichols, waiting for something like this to happen.'

'Waiting for someone to shoot him?'

'Guys like him, sooner or later something happens to them.'

'Guys like him,' I said.

'Small-timers,' he said. 'You know he was into drugs? He supplied college kids. Wayne Nichols was crawling round down there at the bottom of the food chain. He owned the little corner grocery, you might say. He worked the longest hours, took the most risks, had the thinnest profit margin, and reaped the fewest rewards.'

'So you're saying that what happened to him, getting shot and killed, it was business.'

'His business,' he said. 'Retailing drugs to college kids. Weed, coke, pills, acid.'

'Ketamine?'

He looked at me. 'What do you know about ketamine?'

'Ask Horowitz,' I said.

He smiled. 'Sure. I will.'

'Whatever it was that Wayne wanted to show me,' I said. 'You think it was related to his, um, his business?'

'I don't know. What else could it be?'

'Something related to my case,' I said. 'That's what I assumed. It's the only thing that makes any sense.'

'What, then?'

'I don't know.'

Wexler shrugged. 'We're coordinating with Horowitz. Which reminds me. You are not to talk to your client until after we have.'

'That's harsh,' I said. 'You know who my client is?'

He nodded. 'Our vic's mother. Getting it from the cops is a lousy way to hear your son is dead, I know, but it can't be helped.'

'I should be with her when she hears about it, at least.'

Wexler glanced at his wristwatch. 'It's probably too late,' he said. 'When I talked to him, Horowitz said he and his partner were on their way, and that was an hour ago.' He turned so he was facing me. 'Is there anything I should know that you haven't told me?'

'I don't think so. Not that I can talk about, anyway.'

Wexler handed me a business card. 'If you think of anything.'

I stuck his card in my shirt pocket without looking at it.

'You're free to go. You're not a suspect,' Wexler said. 'I assume your alibi will check out, and Horowitz said not to waste our time with you.'

'Well,' I said, 'good. Guess I'll go home, hug my dog.'

DETECTIVE WEXLER got out of the cruiser, spoke to the officer who'd been babysitting me, and headed across the lawn to Wayne's house. I got out too. I nodded to the cop, climbed into my car, got it started and eased round the vehicles that surrounded it. Once I'd driven out of Wayne's cul-de-sac, I remembered that my cell phone had buzzed while I was talking with Wexler, so I pulled over to the side of the road, fished out my phone, and saw that I had a message.

It was from Horowitz. 'Mrs Nichols ain't home,' he said. 'I need to talk with her. Any idea how I can get hold of her?'

I rang Horowitz's number. He didn't say, 'Hello,' like a normal person.

What he said was 'Where the hell is your client, Coyne?'

'I don't know,' I said. 'I can give you her cell phone number. You're going to tell her that her son got murdered this afternoon?'

'Benetti's with me. I'm gonna make her do it.'

'You planning on treating her like a suspect?'

'I don't know,' he said. 'Should I?'

'You better not,' I said. 'Not without her lawyer present.'

'Thanks for telling me my job,' he said. 'What's her number?'

I recited Sharon's cell number to him.

He repeated it back to me, and when I said, 'That's right,' he disconnected. No 'Thank you', no 'Goodbye'. Typical.

I pulled away from the kerb and turned onto the highway heading east. I'd been driving for an hour and a half, and had just crossed into Massachusetts, when my phone vibrated. It was Sharon.

'I don't think I can do this any more,' she said when I answered. I heard the tears in her voice.

'I'm sorry' was all I could think of to say.

'You know what happened,' she said.

'I do know,' I said. 'I'm so sorry.'

'Marcia and Roger were terribly nice,' she said. 'They came to tell me personally. They just left a minute ago.'

It's 'Marcia and Roger' now, I thought. Telling a mother that her son had been murdered was a little different from interrogating her. The yin and the yang of the police officer's job.

'Are you at home?' I asked.

'I'm still here at the hospital,' she said.

'Huh?' I said. 'What hospital?'

'The Burbank Hospital in Fitchburg. Ellen and I have been here since five o'clock,' Sharon said. 'Ken's father was admitted to the ICU this afternoon. He's in a coma. They think it's his aneurysm. The facility where he's living called Ellen, and she called me, and I met her here. So we sat with Charles, and then the officers called, and they came here, and they told us about . . . about what happened to Wayne, and . . . oh, Brady. This is the worst thing.'

'Why did they call Ellen?'

Sharon hesitated. 'Well, I guess now Ken's gone, Ellen would be Charles's next of kin. He has no brothers or sisters. She's his eldest grandchild.'

'Are you going to be there for a while?' I asked.

'I guess we're going to stay here with Charles,' she said. 'He's in pretty bad shape. He might not make it through the night.'

I was heading southeast towards Boston on Route 3. 'I can be there in about an hour,' I said.

'That would be lovely,' she said. 'I'm . . . I'm touched, Brady.'

'Ellen's there with you, you said?'

'She is,' Sharon said. 'I don't know what I'd do without her.'

'She knows about Wayne, then.'

'She was here when Roger and Marcia told us. We've been crying together.'

'Where will I find you?'

'We'll be in the ICU,' she said. 'You'll have to ring the bell.'

'OK,' I said. 'I'll find you. I'm on my way.'

THE PARKING AREA at Burbank Hospital was virtually empty. It was after midnight, and visiting hours had ended a long time ago.

I followed the sign to the main entrance and went in through the glass door. I went to the elevators, where a directory indicated that the ICU was on the third floor. When I stepped out of the elevator, I found myself in an open area with closed doors on the walls. One of the doors had INTENSIVE CARE printed on it. Beside the door was a doorbell. *Ring for a nurse*, said a sign above the bell.

I rang the bell, and after a while the door opened and a grey-haired woman in a white jacket looked out at me. 'Yes?' she asked.

'You have Charles Nichols in there?'

'Yes,' she said.

'Would you mind telling Mrs Nichols that I'm here? My name is Brady Coyne.'

'All right,' she said. Then she pulled her face back, and the door shut and latched with a solid-sounding click.

A minute later the door opened again, and Sharon and Ellen came out. Both were red-eyed. Their faces looked swollen.

Sharon came over and put her arms round my waist and pressed her face against my chest. Ellen stood there hugging herself and shaking her head.

After a minute, Sharon pulled back and looked up at me. 'Come on. There's a waiting room over there. Let's go sit.'

Sharon tugged me into a little room with two sofas, three or four soft chairs and a coffee table. Sharon sat on one of the sofas and pulled on my hand to signal to sit beside her.

Ellen stood awkwardly inside the doorway. 'Why don't I go get us something to drink,' she said. 'Mr Coyne? Coffee? A Coke?'

'A Coke would be good,' I said.

'Mom?'

Sharon looked up at Ellen. 'A Diet Coke, dear. Thank you.'

After Ellen left, Sharon slouched back on the sofa. 'I thought nothing could be worse than what happened to Ken, finding his body, being accused of it—but now? Wayne? I'm numb. I mean, here we are in this hospital, and poor Charles should be getting our attention, our prayers. But my son is dead.'

'What did Horowitz tell you?'

'It was Marcia who did the talking,' Sharon said. 'She said that some-body had shot Wayne, and that you found him.' She turned her head and frowned at me. 'Why were you there, Brady?'

'Wayne called me,' I said. 'Said he had something to show me.'

'What was it?'

'He didn't say. I was going to ask you if you had any idea.'

She shook her head. 'No. Not a clue. Who'd want to kill him?'

'According to the police up there,' I said, 'Wayne was dealing drugs. He'd make a lot of enemies doing that.'

Sharon shook her head. 'I haven't seen Wayne for a long time. I can't even picture him in my head. At least with Ken, we'd been talking, and I felt like I knew him. With Wayne, I didn't even have that. I love him just as much, you know?'

'I do know,' I said. I put my arm round her shoulder.

A minute later Ellen pushed open the door and came in. She handed cans of Coke to each of us. Then she sat on the sofa with her own can. She looked at me. 'What happened to Wayne?'

'Somebody shot him. I don't know who or why.'

'You found him?'

I nodded.

'You're the only one of us who's seen him or even talked to him in a long time,' Ellen said. She looked at Sharon. 'It's been years.'

Sharon nodded. 'Since he went off to school.'

Ellen turned back to me. 'Do you think Wayne . . . ?'

'I only saw him once when he was . . . alive,' I said. 'It's not like I knew him.'

'I was thinking about what happened to Daddy,' she said.

'The New Hampshire police don't think there's any connection.'

'No connection?' asked Ellen. 'They think both of them being murdered is just a coincidence? First Daddy, then Wayne? Really?'

'Aside from the fact that they were father and son,' I said, 'there was nothing similar about their . . . about what happened.'

'But,' she said, 'I mean, they *were* father and son.'

'A father and son,' I said, 'who had been out of touch with each other—and the other members of their family—for a long time.'

Ellen nodded. 'Yeah, I guess.' She looked up at the round clock on the wall. It was after one o'clock in the morning. 'Mom,' she said, 'I've got classes tomorrow morning. I don't know—'

'Go, honey,' said Sharon. 'Go home, get some sleep. You can't do anything here. I'm so grateful you came.'

Ellen stood up. 'You'll keep me posted on Grampa?'

'Of course.' Sharon stood up, and the two women hugged.

'I'd better get going too.' I turned to Ellen. 'I'll walk down with you.'

She smiled and nodded. 'Thank you. That's nice.'

Sharon came over to me, smiled, and gave me a hug. 'You're a wonderful friend,' she said. 'I appreciate all that you do. If it wasn't for you and Ellen, I don't know what I'd do.'

'You're a tough lady,' I said. I looked at Ellen. 'Ready?'

Ellen and Sharon hugged again, and we all left the waiting room.

Sharon went over to the ICU, and Ellen and I went to the elevator. Outside the hospital, I said to Ellen, 'Where'd you park?'

She pointed to an area not far from where we were standing. There were three or four cars there. 'Mine's the old Honda.'

'I'll walk you over,' I said.

She hooked her arm through mine. 'Thank you. That's sweet.'

'How are you holding up?' I asked. 'This has to be pretty tough for you too.'

'I'm doing OK,' she said. 'I've been so focused on Mom that I guess I haven't thought much about me.'

'It's going to hit you,' I said.

'When it does, can I call you? I feel like I can talk to you.'

'Well, sure,' I said. 'You can call me if you want. Of course.'

We arrived at Ellen's car, a sand-coloured Honda Civic with missing hubcaps and a scrape along its side. A graduate student's car. She leaned back against it. 'I feel awful about Wayne,' she said. 'I was having bad thoughts about him. I even told Mom I thought Wayne could've been the one who . . .' She shook her head.

'Who killed your father?'

'Yes. And now . . .'

'You feel guilty about what you were thinking?' I said.

'Kind of.'

'It's not like you knew what was going to happen,' I said.

'I know,' she said. 'Still . . .' She dug into her pocket and pulled out a bunch of keys. She turned, unlocked her car door and slid in behind the wheel, leaving the door open. She looked up at me. 'Are you OK? You look like you've got things on your mind.'

'Actually,' I said, 'I was just thinking about Sparky.'

'Wayne's cat, you mean?' she asked.

I nodded. 'I don't know what they do with the pets of murder victims.'

'They'll probably put her in a shelter.' Ellen buckled her seat belt, turned the key in the ignition, put on the headlights. She shut the door and rolled down the window. 'Thanks for everything.'

She backed out of her parking slot and pulled away.

I watched her turn at the hospital exit. Her brake lights flashed, and then she pulled out of the parking lot onto the street.

I went over to my car, slid in and fished out my phone. I held it in my hand for several minutes, trying to figure out what the right thing was. Then I dialled Roger Horowitz's cell number. It rang several times. Then he said, 'Coyne. Do you know what time it is?'

'It's after one o'clock in the morning,' I said. 'I figured you'd be sleeping.'

He sighed. 'Not hardly. Me and Benetti are here in my office. We just got off a conference call with a New Hampshire detective named Wexler, who you met, and now we're comparing notes, trying out hypotheses and making up scenarios. So whaddaya want?'

'I just wanted to leave you a message.'

'Well,' he said, 'ain't this better? Now you get to talk to me.'

'It would be easier to leave a message,' I said. 'I'm uncomfortable with the ethics of this.'

'Spit it out, willya? Whaddaya want?'

I took a breath and blew it out. 'I want to tell you who killed Ken Nichols and his son, Wayne.'

'Really? You got it figured out, huh? Us cops, we ain't smart enough—but Mr Lawyer knows.'

'OK,' I said. 'Forget it.'

'Take it easy,' said Horowitz. 'Who is it? Who's our killer?'

'Ellen Nichols,' I said, 'and that's all I'm gonna say.'

ELEVEN

Horowitz was silent for a moment. Then he said, 'The daughter, huh?'

'I think so,' I said.

'He thinks it's the daughter,' he said, and then I heard Benetti's voice in the background, though I couldn't tell what she said.

'Benetti wants to know what makes you think it's her?' Horowitz said to me.

'Means, motive, opportunity,' I said.

'Thanks a lot. You think you could be a little more specific?'

'I thought with a little guidance, like, say, giving you the name of the bad guy, you could figure out the rest of it.'

'Why don't you come over, we can talk about it. Me and Marcia, we're here at my office. She brewed up a pot of coffee, and we got fresh dough-nuts. They're still warm. Ain't your mouth watering?'

I hesitated. 'Ellen knew about Wayne's cat. That's why I think it's her. Wayne Nichols had a cat named Sparky. She claims she hasn't seen or even talked to her brother since he went off to college, but she knew he had a cat named Sparky.'

'So how'd she know that?'

'Bingo,' I said, and with that, I snapped my phone shut. No 'Goodbye', no 'Nice talkin' to you'. Just like Horowitz.

It felt great.

I found an FM station playing smoky wee-hours-of-the-morning jazz on my car radio. The music was sexy and moody, and it made me think about Alex. Sexy, moody Alex.

I wondered what would become of us.

Traffic was light on the highway, and pretty soon I was turning off Storrow Drive onto Charles Street. I wasn't even tempted to go to Horowitz's office. Already I felt that I might've nudged my toe over the fuzzy ethical line by giving him Ellen's name.

Besides, it was way past my bedtime.

I pulled into my parking garage, nosed my car into its reserved slot, shut off the lights and the ignition, got out, locked up, and headed down the ramp for the door that opened onto Charles Street. The lights inside the garage were dim and yellow. My footsteps echoed, and somewhere in the depths of the big concrete structure water was dripping on the hood of a parked vehicle.

I was about to push open the door and step out onto Charles Street when a voice behind me said, 'Hold it there, Mr Coyne.'

It was a woman's voice, at once soft and assertive.

'Ellen?' I asked. I stopped and started to turn to look at her.

'Don't turn round,' she said. 'I'm pointing a gun at you. Back away from the door.'

'You've got a gun?' I asked. 'Ellen. What are you doing?'

'Please don't play dumb,' she said. I heard a click, the sound of a pistol's hammer being cocked. 'Step back from the door, please.'

I did what she said. 'You followed me? What do you want?'

'I want you to tell me how you figured it out.'

'Figured what out?' I asked. 'I just want to go home and go to bed. I bet you do too. You're upset. Hard to blame you. Your father getting murdered, and then your brother, your grandfather in the hospital. Let's just forget about this. Go on home.'

'You should've minded your own business,' she said.

I turned round to look at her. She really did have a gun. It was a revolver with a short barrel, and it was pointed at my midsection. I guessed it was the same weapon that had killed Wayne.

'It was the cat, huh?'

I shrugged.

'You had some kind of suspicion,' she said, 'or you wouldn't have tried to trap me like that.'

'I was just fishing,' I said. 'If you'd said 'Who's that?' when I mentioned Sparky, that would've been the end of it.'

'Now I've got to kill you, you know,' she said.

'How do you feel about that?'

'What kind of a question is that?'

'You stabbed your father,' I said. 'You shot your brother in the chest. How did it make you feel, killing people like that?'

'It didn't bother me,' she said softly.

'It's like torturing those pets in the kennel, huh?'

She shook her head. 'I'm not talking about this any more.' Ellen gestured at me with her gun. 'Move over there. Do it now.'

As I eased away from the door, I tried to figure a way out. The hammer on Ellen's pistol was cocked. All she needed to do was touch the trigger to blow a hole in me. I could make a move on her. Fake left, go right. I could drop, go into a roll, hit her at the knees. Maybe twenty years ago a sudden attack would've worked. Maybe not. Twenty years ago I was stronger and faster . . . and stupider.

I moved away from the door, keeping my eyes on the handgun. I figured as long as I kept Ellen talking, she wouldn't be shooting.

'So after you left the hospital,' I said, 'you pulled over and waited for me to go by, and then you eased in behind me, huh?'

She nodded.

'Because you made a mistake about Wayne's cat.'

'You tricked me,' she said. 'That won't happen again.'

We were standing in the entryway to the parking garage. Behind Ellen was the opening to the dimly lit first floor of the garage, where rows of cars were parked. I thought I saw the flicker of a shadow. It was quick, then it was gone. Probably my imagination.

Maybe not. Keep her talking.

'So,' I said, 'that wasn't Wayne who tortured the animals when you were growing up, right? It was you.'

She was shaking her head. 'I don't want to talk about that.'

'I already gave the police your name,' I said. 'If you kill me, it'll just be worse for you.'

'There's no proof,' she said. 'You tricked me with the cat, that's all. I can explain that.'

A shadow appeared behind her, and in the dim light I saw the shadow materialise into Marcia Benetti. She was holding her revolver in both hands beside her face, pointing up at the ceiling, and she was easing along against the wall, moving towards Ellen.

'Was it really just about the money?' I asked Ellen.

'Of course it was the money,' she said.

'Your grandfather's inheritance?'

'I've got a right to that money,' she said. 'My father didn't deserve it, and neither did my brother.'

Benetti darted out of the shadows. She slammed into Ellen, grabbing the arm that held the gun and sprawling her sideways. Ellen bounced off the wall, and when her shoulder slammed against the floor her revolver came out of her hand and skittered across the concrete, and Benetti was on top of her, rolling her onto her belly, pushing her face against the floor and twisting her arms behind her.

The door to Charles Street flew open, and Roger Horowitz burst in with his weapon in his hand. He looked at Marcia Benetti and Ellen Nichols on the floor, gave a shrug, then put his gun back into his shoulder holster. 'She's something, ain't she?' he asked.

'She just saved my life,' I said, 'if that's what you mean.'

Benetti had everything under control. Ellen was lying on her belly with her hands cuffed behind her. Marcia was kneeling beside her with her own handgun now in her hip holster.

Horowitz smiled and nodded, then turned to me. 'You OK?'

I nodded. 'Thanks for showing up.'

'Marcia's idea,' he said. 'She said we shouldn't let you off the hook. She said, let's intercept the son of a bitch, bring him in whether he wants to or not. Woulda been easier all round if you'd come to the office voluntarily, had coffee and doughnuts with us.'

I shrugged. 'You've got yourselves a real live double murder suspect. That should keep you busy for a while. I'm going home.'

I had started to push open the heavy glass door to the sidewalk when Horowitz said, 'Hold on a minute.'

I stopped and turned to look at him. 'What?'

'How'd you figure it out?'

'Ellen, you mean?'

He nodded.

'If it had been only Ken who got killed,' I said, 'or only Wayne, I probably wouldn't've. Each of them had plenty of enemies. Tonight, though, when I found Wayne murdered, I assumed it was the same killer, and that narrowed it down. I asked myself who was linked to both men, and of those people, who'd benefit from them both being dead.' I jerked my head in the direction of Ellen, who was now sitting on the floor with her back against the concrete wall. 'Ken Nichols stood to inherit several million from his father, Ellen's grandfather, who's old and in bad health. With him out of the way, the two grandchildren, Ellen and Wayne, were next in line. With Wayne gone, it'd all be Ellen's.'

'If it ain't for love,' Horowitz said, 'it's for money.'

'Just about every time,' I said.

MY ALARM WENT OFF at eight in the morning. I wasn't happy to hear it. I'd read *Moby Dick* for a while after I finally got to bed, but my adrenaline had juiced me up so high that even Melville's usually reliable prose had failed to ease me to sleep. I'd lain there thinking about what must have gone wrong with Ellen Nichols, what wires got crossed so badly that as a child she could torture pets and then, as an adult, murder her father and her brother.

I found no answers. Words like 'sociopath' and 'psychopath' were meaningless. They didn't explain anything. When I finally drifted into edgy sleep I had nightmarish dreams about blood.

I'd set my alarm so I could catch Tally Whyte before she left for her office. I called her home number. She answered with a cheerful 'Tally Whyte. Good morning.'

'Good morning yourself,' I said. 'It's Brady.'

'Uh-oh,' she said. 'What's wrong?'

'Sharon Nichols,' I said. 'She's going to need you.' I proceeded to tell her about Wayne's murder and Ellen's subsequent arrest. I left out the details of my own role in the drama.

'Ellen did it, then?' Tally asked when I finished. 'She murdered her father and her brother?'

'It looks that way,' I said.

'Wow,' Tally said. 'It's going to be tough for Sharon. She's off the hook for her ex-husband's murder, though, huh?'

'I'm sure of it,' I said.

'Well, that's something, anyway. I'll call Sharon, spend time with her today. She's going to need a lot of help with this.'

'Thanks, Tal.'

'Don't worry,' she said. 'I've done this before. I'll take care of her. Thanks for calling. You're a good man, Brady Coyne.'

I SPENT THE NEXT few days catching up with my other clients and ploughing through the never-ending reams of paperwork that Julie kept dumping into my in-tray. Sharon called me at home on Tuesday evening, just to tell me that she'd been spending a lot of time with Tally and was doing as well as could be expected.

Wednesday after work, Henry and I were sitting out on the patio. I was sipping a Sam Adams lager when my cell phone began hopping round on the arm of my chair.

It was Horowitz. 'You home?' he asked.

'I am.'

'I'm parked out the front. Got a beer for me?'

'Sure. Come on in.'

I went to the front door and let Horowitz in. He trailed me back to the kitchen, where I snagged a bottle of Sam from the refrigerator. I handed it to him, and we continued out to the back yard.

I sat in my chair, and Horowitz sat at the picnic table. He lifted his beer bottle, took a long swig, said, 'Ahh,' and plonked the half-empty bottle down on the table. 'That hits the spot,' he said.

I smiled. 'So what's up, Roger?'

He took another sip, then turned to me. 'So, about your client.'

'Sharon Nichols,' I said.

'She's no longer a suspect in the Ken Nichols murder.' He gazed up at the sky. 'Thought you should know.'

'Good. Thanks. The daughter, then, huh?'

He looked at me and nodded. 'Her fingerprints were all over the vic's hotel room, and one of the security cameras caught her leaving that same evening. That took care of opportunity, and we're already pretty solid on motive. Turns out the weapon that killed the brother was not recovered. According to ballistics, it was not the one Ellen Nichols pulled on you. When we confronted her and her lawyer with what we had, they decided they wanted to plead out.'

'You going to negotiate a plea with her?'

He shrugged. 'Leaning that way. We'd love to take her to trial, but we don't have that steak knife that killed the vet, and we haven't yet come up with the brother's murder weapon or a witness to place her in Websterville that afternoon.'

We both sipped our beers. After a minute, I said, 'So drugs had nothing to do with any of it.'

'Doesn't look like it,' he said.

'Even though Ken was probably trafficking in ketamine,' I said, 'and Wayne was selling stuff to the college kids. Right?'

'Like father, like son.' Horowitz shrugged. 'The Maryland cops had their eye on Dr Nichols, but we weren't getting very far with the ketamine piece of it from this end. We had no luck trying to ID the guy in the hoodie you saw at the hotel that night. The other guy, Clements, got a solid alibi for the night of the murder. Detective Wexler up there in New Hampshire said they've had their eye on Wayne Nichols for some time. Their dogs found his stash in his house, but there was no ketamine.' He took a swig of beer. 'Anyway, we've got a good case against the girl. Her fingerprints were on that matchbook in the hotel door.'

'She left it there after killing her father?'

He nodded. 'She knew her mother was on her way,' he said. 'She wanted to make sure she could get in.'

'So Sharon would find the body and be an instant suspect?' I asked. 'Is that what you think?'

'She's a devious one, that girl.' Horowitz shrugged.

'Any idea what Wayne wanted to show me, why he asked me to go up there?'

'We figure it this way,' he said. 'Wayne had a copy of a document about his grandfather's will. It showed that he and his sister would get the old guy's money now that their father was dead. We figure he called you to show it to you as evidence against his sister, and somehow she figured out what he was up to—maybe they talked—so she went up there and . . .'

'Killed him,' I said. 'Took the document.'

'She's a sick puppy,' Horowitz said. 'If we do end up taking it to trial, we'll call you for a witness. We have also charged Ellen Nichols with assault, among assorted other charges, for what went down with you the other night in the parking garage.'

'I don't want to be a witness,' I said.

'Yeah,' he said, 'nobody does.'

I HAD NO CLIENTS scheduled for Thursday. At noon I fished out the business card Detective Wexler had given me and tried the number. He picked up on the second ring. 'Wexler,' he growled.

'It's Brady Coyne,' I said. 'You interviewed me at the Wayne Nichols murder last Sunday.'

'Yeah, I remember,' he said. 'What've you got for me?'

'Just a question. I was wondering what happened to Sparky.'

'Huh?'

'Wayne Nichols had a cat named Sparky. Where is she?'

'Wait a minute.' I heard muffled voices, then Wexler said, 'My partner says they took that animal to the shelter in Keene. It's called the Monadnock Animal House.'

'Animal House,' I said. 'Thanks. I appreciate it.'

I called the Monadnock Animal House, and the young woman who answered recognised my description of Wayne's cat.

'Will you hold her for me?' I asked. 'I want to rescue her.'

'Sure,' she said. 'Wonderful. That's what we're for.'

So I went home and changed out of my office pinstripe, and an hour later Henry and I were heading for Keene, New Hampshire.

It cost me a hundred dollars, plus another thirty-nine ninety-five for the travel crate, to rescue Sparky. She rode in the back seat with Henry, who sniffed the crate a few times and then ignored her.

I called Sharon Nichols on my cell phone from the road. It was a little after four in the afternoon, and she was at the shop, working, which I took to be a positive sign.

'When do you get off?' I asked her.

'In an hour,' she said. 'We close at five. Why?'

'If I meet you at your house, will you have a beer for me?'

'Absolutely. It will be wonderful to see you.'

'You sound good, Sharon.'

'Tally's been amazing. I think I'm getting there.' She hesitated. 'A customer just came in. Gotta go. See you.'

I rang the bell to Sharon's condo in Acton a little after five thirty, and she buzzed me up. She was waiting with the door open when I got to her apartment. I went in and put Sparky's crate on the floor, and Sharon put both arms round my neck and hugged me tight. When she pulled back, I saw that her eyes were glittery. 'What's this?' She looked down at the crate.

I opened it up and lifted out Sparky.

She held out her arms and took the cat, which seemed to nestle against Sharon's chest. 'For me?' she asked.

'If you want her. Her name's Sparky. She was Wayne's.'

Sharon stared at me. 'Wayne had a cat?'

I smiled. 'According to the girl at the shelter, he took very good care of her. This kitty is healthy and happy. She's been well loved.'

She rubbed her cheek against the cat's fur. 'I will cherish her,' she said.

MY PHONE RANG at eleven thirty that night. It was Alex's turn to call. 'Hi, babe,' I said.

'You all tucked in?'

'I am. You?'

'Mm,' she said. 'Tomorrow at this time you'll be here tucked in with me.'

'If we can outwit the trolls,' I said.

'I'm not sure I believe in trolls,' said Alex. 'I'd rather believe in fairies.'

'I think we can have it both ways.'

'Trolls and fairies?'

'And wicked stepmothers and fairy godmothers,' I said. 'It's a more interesting world with all of them, don't you think?'

'A more complicated world, anyway.' She chuckled softly. 'I'm at a good place with my novel,' she said. 'I'm not going to think about it all weekend. I'm just going to hang out with you and Henry. Walk in the woods, paddle our kayaks, cook good food, watch some old movies and snuggle in bed. I can't wait.'

'I'm at a good place too,' I said.

william g. **tapply**

Profile

Born:
Waltham, Massachusetts.
Raised:
Lexington.
Education:
Bachelor's degree in
American studies at
Amherst College, master's
degree in Education at
Harvard.

Series characters:
Brady Coyne, Stoney
Calhoun.
Published novels:
40+.
Loved:
His family, gardening and
fly fishing.
Died:
July 28, 2009.

We feel as though we were just beginning to get to know Bill Tapply and his work when we learned that he had died at the age of sixty-nine at his home in Hancock, New Hampshire, after a two-year battle with leukaemia. But even while the cancer and its treatment took a toll on his body, his strong spirit and sharp wit remained intact throughout. And he kept writing because that's what he loved doing. As a result, three new books were published following his death in July 2009: *Outwitting Trolls* (the final Brady Coyne mystery), *The Nomination* (an action/suspense thriller), and *Every Day Was Special: A Fly Fisher's Lifelong Passion* (a collection of musings on fly fishing).

William G. Tapply was born in Waltham, Massachusetts, and grew up in nearby Lexington, where he excelled as a high-school athlete. He went on to Amherst College for a bachelor's degree in American studies and to Harvard for a masters degree in Education. Returning to Lexington in 1963, he taught social studies and worked as an administrator at Lexington High School until he began writing full-time in the late 1980s.

'He was a respected friend who contributed to the outstanding reputation that Lexington High School held,' said Pam Healey, a former Lexington High School colleague of Tapply's, quoted in the *Taunton Daily Gazette*. 'He encouraged my efforts to create an American literature course based on Walden and other environmental writing and decades later taught a similar college course.'

Tapply began publishing in the 1980s, beginning with articles that appeared in magazines like *Field & Stream* and *Sports Illustrated*. He published his first novel, *Death at Charity's Point*, in 1984. In his lifetime he completed more than forty books, among them many New England-based mystery novels.

In 1991, he met Vicki Stiefel, his second wife, at a writers' workshop. She, too, is a published author, the creator of the Tally Whyte mystery series. 'We pretty much became a pair after that,' Stiefel told the *Taunton Daily Gazette*. Each brought children to the marriage—Tapply two daughters and a son, and two sons for Stiefel—adding more joy to Tapply's life. 'Above all, Bill adored his family,' Stiefel said.

In the mid-nineties, Tapply began teaching at Clark University's English department and was the department's writer-in-residence. According to Jay Elliott, chairman of the English department, his classes always filled up fast, and he had a legitimacy that came from being a prolific, published writer. 'The students just knew they were getting the best, so they responded very well,' said Elliott.

Tapply and Stiefel moved to Hancock, New Hampshire, in 2001, settling at Chickadee Farm, where they ran a writers' workshop together. Being in a more rural environment was perfect for Tapply, who was a natural outdoorsman. 'He was happier here than, he used to tell me, any place in the world,' Stiefel said.

A look at Tapply's output as an author shows a prolific and rounded professional. There are twenty-five Brady Coyne novels, plus three Brady Coyne/J. W. Jackson tales written with Phillip R. Craig, combining the skills of these two veteran authors with their series characters working together on their cases. There are also three Stoney Calhoun mysteries, twelve nonfiction works about fishing and outdoor life, and *The Elements of Mystery Fiction*, a resource for aspiring mystery writers.

William G. Tapply created lawyer Brady Coyne for one novel only, but found he could not let him go when the novel ended. 'As much as people claim to despise attorneys, their fascination with lawyers and legal proceedings is apparently boundless,' Tapply wrote in an article. 'Contests between prosecuting attorneys and criminal defence lawyers—both actual and fictional—provide constant entertainment on television and in movies and books. Lawyers are both heroes and villains.

'It's no wonder, then, that crime fiction abounds with lawyers. Criminal lawyers, both prosecutors and defenders, make tried-and-true protagonists, both for series by writers such as Erle Stanley Gardner and for the stand-alone legal thrillers of best-selling authors like Scott Turow and John Grisham. So I made a shrewd choice when I invented my lawyer-sleuth Brady Coyne, right? He's a character designed for the long haul, a lawyer who has found himself in a position to investigate enough different crimes to keep me writing about him for over twenty-five years.'

Sadly, *Outwitting Trolls* will be Brady Coyne's last case. William G. Tapply has left behind a legacy of exceptional crime fiction and will be much missed.

COPYRIGHT AND ACKNOWLEDGMENTS

BEFORE I GO TO SLEEP: Copyright © Lola Communications 2011.
Published at £7.99 by Doubleday, an imprint of Transworld Publishers.
Condensed version © The Reader's Digest Association, Inc., 2012.

SIEGE: Copyright © Simon Kernick 2012.
Published at £12.99 by Bantam Press, an imprint of Transworld Publishers.
Condensed version © The Reader's Digest Association, Inc., 2012.

WOMEN AND CHILDREN FIRST: Copyright © Gill Paul 2012.
Published at £7.99 by Avon, a division of HarperCollins*Publishers*.
Condensed version © The Reader's Digest Association, Inc., 2012.

OUTWITTING TROLLS: Copyright © 2010 by Vicki Stiefel Tapply.
Published at $24.99 by Minotaur Books, an imprint of St Martin's Press, LLC.
Condensed version © The Reader's Digest Association, Inc., 2012.

The right to be identified as authors has been asserted by the following in accordance with sections 77 and 78 of the Copyright, Designs and Patents Act, 1988: S. J. Watson, Simon Kernick, Gill Paul, William G. Tapply.

Spine: Getty Images. Front cover (from left): © Veronique Beranger/Getty Images; (centre left): © Silas Manhood; (centre right): © Sea/Sky © Shutterstock; *Titanic*: © UPPA/Photoshot; lifeboats: © Time Life Pictures/Getty Images; (right): © istockphoto/Nick Tzolov. 6–7: illustration: Rhett Podersoo @ Advocate-Art. 160–1: images: © Getty Images: security level on 'critical' alert; bomb scare, Park Lane, London; illustration: Narrinder Singh @ velvet tamarind; 312 © Johnny Ring. 314–315: illustration: Jim Mitchell@The Organisation. 448 © courtesy of the author. 450–1: images: Getty Images: Boston skyline at dusk; illustration: David Ricketts@velvet tamarind. 574 © vicki stiefel.

Every effort has been made to find and credit the copyright holders of images in this book. We will be pleased to rectify any errors or omissions in future editions. Email us at gbeditorial@readersdigest.co.uk

Printed and bound by GGP Media GmbH, Pössneck, Germany

020-278 UP0000-1